Praise for _Isolate_

"This superior book only whets the appetite for a sequel."
—_Publishers Weekly_ (starred review)

"Delicious with intrigue and artful revelations, _Isolate_ comes at you with top-drawer world-building and compelling characters. Here we have a hot new gaslamp world fraught with political machinations that will keep you up reading into the night. Modesitt has always been great, so how does he keep getting better? Read _Isolate_ and find out."
—Peter Orullian, author of _The Unremembered_

T0002131

TOR BOOKS BY L. E. MODESITT, JR.

L.E. MODESITT JR.

ISOLATE

TOR®
fantasy

A TOM DOHERTY
ASSOCIATES BOOK
NEW YORK

This is a work of fiction. All of the characters, organizations, and events portrayed in this novel are either products of the author's imagination or are used fictitiously.

Isolate

Edited by Jen Gunnels

A Tor Book
Published by Tom Doherty Associates
120 Broadway
New York, NY 10271

www.tor-forge.com

Tor® is a registered trademark of Macmillan Publishing Group, LLC.

ISBN 978-1-250-77742-3

Our books may be purchased in bulk for promotional, educational, or business use. Please contact your local bookseller or the Macmillan Corporate and Premium Sales Department at 1-800-221-7945, extension 5442, or by email at MacmillanSpecialMarkets@macmillan.com.

First Edition: October 2021
First Mass Market Edition: June 2022

Printed in the United States of America

0 9 8 7 6 5 4 3 2 1

FOR LEANORA

MAJOR CHARACTERS

Steffan Dekkard   *Isolate, Security Aide for Councilor Axel Obreduur*

Avraal Ysella   *Empath, Security Aide for Obreduur*

Emrelda Roemnal   *District Patroller, sister of Avraal*

Markell Roemnal   *Engineer, husband of Emrelda*

Axel Obreduur   *Councilor from Oersynt (Craft), Political Leader of Craft Party*

Ingrella Obreduur   *Legalist and wife of Obreduur*

Ivann Macri   *Senior Legalist for Obreduur*

Svard Roostof   *Junior Legalist for Obreduur*

Felix Raynaad   *Commercial Aide for Obreduur*

Laureous XXIV   *Imperador of Guldor*

Johan Grieg   *Premier of Guldor, Councilor from Neewyrk (Commerce)*

Karl Bernotte   *First Marshal*

Jhared Kraffeist   *Minister of Public Resources*

Isomer Munchyn   *Minister of the Treasury*

Phillipe Sanoffre   *Minister of Health and Education*

Lukkyn Wyath   *Minister of Security*

Guilhohn Haarsfel   *Craft Party Floor Leader, Councilor from Kathaar*

Saandaar Vonauer   *Landor Party Floor Leader, Councilor from Plaatz*

Hansaal Volkaar   *Commerce Party Floor Leader, Councilor from Uldwyrk*

Kurtweil Aashtaan   *Commerce Committee Chair, Councilor from Hyarh (Commerce)*

Kaliara Bassaana   *Councilor from Caylaan (Commerce)*

Fredrich Hasheem   *Councilor from Port Reale (Craft)*

Ivaan Maendaan   *Security Committee Chair, Councilor from Endor (Commerce)*

Oskaar Ulrich   *Military Affairs Committee Chair, Councilor from Veerlyn (Commerce)*

Harleona Zerlyon   *Councilor from Ondeliew (Craft)*

ISOLATE

PROLOGUE

Dekkard followed Councilor Obreduur, one pace back. His eyes briefly took in the rain that poured down in the early evening, spilling in sheets from the tile roof gutters that barely kept the water from touching the white stone walk . . . or from dampening the councilor, Dekkard, and Ysella, who kept pace with Dekkard on the right. The greenish tinge of the clouds confirmed that they were the remnants of the waterspouts that had ripped across the ocean shallows to the southeast of Machtarn in midafternoon.

Then the councilor shuddered and went to his knees.

"Ahead to the left, twenty yards, short of the wall," snapped Ysella, her voice far colder than the lukewarm water that continued to pour down.

Dekkard drew his gladius and sprinted forward and through the downpour, half blind, because the rain, as usual with a spoutstorm, was so thick. By the time he reached a point where he could make out the chest-high marble wall that surrounded the raised topiary garden, he could see no one. He immediately sprinted back toward the covered portico where Ysella was helping Councilor Obreduur to his feet. Fearing that the assassin might have somehow circled, he still held his gladius ready in his left hand.

As he neared the two under the portico that crossed the center gardens of the square, he called out, "Did the empie head this way?"

Ysella shook her head. "There was just the one violent empblast, then nothing."

The councilor looked to her. "Was it as bad as I felt?"

Ysella hesitated for just an instant before saying, "It was meant to be a deathblast. I blocked almost all of it."

"Then I'd likely be dead if you hadn't. Let's get back

to the office." Obreduur frowned. "Did either of you mention I was going to Freust's memorial?"

"No, sir," said both security types simultaneously.

"Someone must have figured that I wanted to be there."

Dekkard could have calculated that. As a Craft councilor, and more importantly, as the political leader and strategist for the Craft Party, Obreduur needed allies from the Landors, and Freust had been well regarded by the other Landors. Freust had also held some lands north of Malek, well away from his estate near Khuld and not that far from Obreduur's district home, which might have been why he and Obreduur had become closer than was usual between Craft and Landor councilors.

But why would someone have risked a highly trained empie in a spout rain? One that had to have been illegally trained if capable of projecting the emotions of death. *Who was willing to take that chance? And why?*

"I'm fine now," snapped Obreduur. "We need to keep moving. There's no point in giving them a second chance."

As the three walked more swiftly from the Council Hall to the Council Office Building, which held the offices of the Sixty-Six, the rain continued to sheet down around the covered portico that connected the two buildings, its intensity creating a rushing susurration loud enough to drown out any sounds from more than a few yards away.

Dekkard kept his eyes open, looking for any hint of the would-be assassin, even as they reached the end of the portico, where it joined the wider roof that protected the garden courtyard entrance to the Council Office Building.

There, two guards armed with long-barreled revolvers and black truncheons stood at their posts flanking the ornate double doors—the only unlocked garden entrance after the sixth bell, the one announcing evening. To Dekkard, their pale green uniforms looked more like sun-bleached leaves in the early-evening humidity, especially in contrast to their crisp black belts and boots. Their eyes slipped past the councilor and paused as they took in Dekkard's soaked gray tunic and trousers ... and the unsheathed short-sword he still held.

"Are you all right, Councilor?"

"I'm fine, thank you." Obreduur's warm intonation definitely carried the feel of thanks. "Dekkard scared off the intruder."

But that voice is one of the reasons why he's a councilor. Not that Dekkard would likely ever be a councilor, although there was no law in Guldor forbidding an isolate from holding office. Only empaths and susceptibles were so prohibited, although isolates were regarded warily because their emotions couldn't be read by empaths.

Dekkard opened the heavy bronze door, holding it for Obreduur and Ysella, then followed them into the wide hallway inside, with its green marble floors. Once inside, he sheathed the gladius. The walls were also tiled in green marble, up to the chair rail, above which the walls were a light cream.

The hallway was only partly illuminated, with only every third bronze gas lamp lit. Later in the evening, half of those now lit would be extinguished. Obreduur led the way to the wide green marble staircase, edged with matching green marble balustrades and bright bronze bannisters, a staircase that rose to a landing halfway up to the second level, from the ends of which slightly smaller staircases extended the remainder of the way. As a councilor not in the majority party, Obreduur had offices on the second level, those of the senior Commerce Party councilors being on the ground level, and the offices of Council clericals and routine functionaries being on the third level. There was no central staircase to the third level. Strictly functional staircases at each end of the building served the clericals and functionaries.

As he followed the councilor up the stairs, Dekkard couldn't help wondering about the attack.

From the marble-railed area around the open staircase, Ysella led the way down the long corridor, roughly thirty yards, to the polished golden oak door with a bronze plaque set on the wall to the right side, two-thirds of a yard above the marble chair rail. The plaque stated simply: COUNCILOR AXEL OBREDUUR.

Ysella stepped up to the door, standing there for a long moment, then unlocked it and turned to Dekkard.

Knowing that she had sensed no one inside, Dekkard unsheathed the gladius once more, opened the door, and stepped into the large—and dark—outer anteroom, where he twisted the key on the wall lamp beside the door and pulled down on the compression lighter. The lamp flared into light, a light he utilized to confirm that the anteroom was empty. Then he walked to the side door to the staff office, opening it and finding no one there. Closing that door, he moved back to the door into the councilor's private office and opened it and then lit the wall lamp beside the window before returning to the anteroom, where Ysella and Obreduur waited.

"Thank you both," said Obreduur, before making his way into the private office and closing the door behind himself.

Once Obreduur was secure in his private office, with the door firmly shut, and the two were alone in the outer antechamber, lit by the single gas lamp, Dekkard turned to the councilor's empie and asked in a low voice, "Was that more than the usual empblast?"

Ysella nodded.

"But . . ." Dekkard shook his head. The training for an empie to learn the feelings of agonizing death well enough to project them killed most empies who underwent it—which was one reason why it was forbidden by every government in the world. *Officially, anyway.*

"She was stupid . . . or she's a fanatic—"

"A fanatic?" Dekkard wasn't that surprised that the empie had been a woman, not considering that, while empaths were rare, three out of four were women, but most women tended not to be fanatics.

"A political fanatic. What other kind is there?"

Dekkard nodded, but the question remained. *Why would anyone risk so much to target a Craft councilor, even the second-most-senior one?*

1

The giant corporacion Eastern Ironway apparently used its contacts and influence to illegally gain underpriced coal leases in the protected Eshbruk Naval Coal Reserve, according to a letter sent to the Imperador and Premier Johan Grieg. The leases were granted to Eastern Ironway by the Minister of Public Resources, Jhared Kraffeist, late last year, despite the fact that corporacions are forbidden by law to obtain coal or any other resource from such reserves . . .

. . . Eastern paid the absurdly low price of 200,000 marks, as well as a "commission" amounting to 10 percent of that sum. According to the letter, an investigation by the Justiciary Ministry found that all records of who had received the commission have vanished . . .

Obtaining those leases, also according to the letter, allowed Eastern to quickly begin mining operations and to obtain fuel for its locomotives at a far lower cost than coal obtained elsewhere . . .

Minister Kraffeist refused to comment on the allegations . . .

The signature and title on the copies of the letter distributed anonymously on Eastern Ironway stationery to newssheets all across Guldor and to all councilors were removed, but it appears to have been written by an official of Eastern Ironway privy to all the details of the leasing procedure . . .

Given the seriousness of the charges, Minister Kraffeist was summoned to the Council Hall to meet with
Premier Grieg . . .

At the request of the Imperador, the Premier has ordered the Council not to take up any legislative matters
while the Palace and Premier review the matter . . .

Gestirn, 13 Springend 1266

2

Duadi
14 Springend 1266

Dekkard woke suddenly in the darkness of his small
room above the garage, a garage housing the most
recent of the modest dark green Gresynt steamers that
were one of the hallmarks cultivated by the councilor.
Keeping with Obreduur's penchant for avoiding obvious ostentation, the garage was only large enough for
a pair of automobiles, one the larger eight-seater used
by the councilor, and a smaller six-seater driven by his
wife the legalist to and from her office and elsewhere.

Dekkard quickly rose, shaved, and took a brief lukewarm shower, then dressed in his duty security grays—a
gray military-style tunic and matching trousers, with a
black belt for his truncheon and gladius . . . and the
concealed brace of throwing knives. Out of habit, he
wound his watch, then left his room and took the rear
staircase that served the staff. Once on the main floor,
he took the back corridor to the kitchen and the small
staff room where he, Ysella, Rhosali the housemaid,
and Hyelda the cook all ate . . . or could talk or gather
in their infrequent free time.

The staff room held only Rhosali. That scarcely surprised Dekkard, since the family, except for Obreduur
himself, was not known for rising earlier than required

and since the same was true of Ysella, and sometimes even Rhosali, while Hyelda was already in the kitchen preparing breakfast, both for the four staff and for the family, those in residence at the moment, since the eldest son was in his second year at the Military Institute in Veerlyn.

Dekkard knew breakfast would be simple—café, orange juice, and heavy croissants, with a slice of quince paste, or, if Hyelda was feeling cross, tomato jelly. While waiting for Hyelda to set out the large tray from which the staff helped themselves, Dekkard poured himself a mug of café and took a sip. He was about to take a second sip when Hyelda appeared in the kitchen doorway.

"The Ritten wishes a word with you." The cook gestured.

Dekkard immediately stood, nodding to Rhosali, before leaving the staff room. From there, he walked through the dish pantry, opened the service door to the breakfast room, closing it behind him, before coming to a halt several paces from the table, where the mistress of the house presided over her end of the table. She had been a legalist long before marrying Obreduur, but he seldom mentioned her present or previous practice, and Dekkard felt he wasn't in a position to ask about specifics unless others voiced them. Just as he hadn't been about to ask why she had spent two weeks in Gaarlak, when she had no family there. But then, she had traveled to various cities in Guldor during the two years Dekkard had worked for Obreduur. Dekkard had gathered that she still did legalist work for various guilds and other clients, and that might be why the Obreduurs could live in East Quarter, given that councilors weren't paid comparatively that much.

Ritter Obreduur sat at the other end, sipping café as he read through the morning newssheet. The title, which had originally been given only to landed nobility, now also applied to councilors and their spouses, not only while they served, but thereafter, although it was not hereditary. Except for Obreduur's white linen jacket, and whatever scarf Ritten Obreduur would wear over her outerwear, the two were dressed for the day.

"You're always so formal, Dekkard, I'm sure you already know what I need."

"Lighting off your steamer, Ritten Obreduur?"

"Exactly. You can finish your breakfast first."

"I'll take care of it." Dekkard inclined his head. "Is that all?"

"That's all."

"I'll need to leave a sixth earlier, Steffan," said the councilor without looking away from the paper, a paper held in his left hand, the one with the bent and twisted little finger and the one adjoining, a legacy from his much younger days as a stevedore.

"Yes, sir." Ten minutes earlier wouldn't be too bad.

The councilor did not reply, nor look in Dekkard's direction, not that Dekkard would have expected it, and the isolate slipped out of the breakfast room and headed back to the staff room. His lighting off Ritten Obreduur's steamer would save her only a few minutes, but if that was what she wanted, he was happy to take care of it.

Ysella had arrived in the staff room in Dekkard's absence, crisp as always in her duty grays, identical to his, except that she carried only a personal-length truncheon, and she looked up from her plate as Dekkard returned. "What did she want? For you to light off her steamer?"

"Of course." Dekkard seated himself and immediately added more café to his mug and took a swallow. He noted that Hyelda had provided slightly larger slices of quince paste than usual. He appreciated that, because, as the son of Argenti parents who had fled the cold and the altitude of the Silver Heights—and the comparative lack of opportunity for artisans—he'd been raised on more substantial breakfast fare. After a little more café, he drank the small glass of orange juice in one long swallow, then split the croissant and slipped the quince paste in the middle, and began to eat it like a sandwich.

Ysella shuddered. "I still don't see how you can eat so much sweet in the morning."

Dekkard swallowed the mouthful he'd been chewing, then replied, "I've told you. Quince is bittersweet, not honey-sweet."

The empie just shook her head, as did Rhosali, who took a last swallow of café, then rose and hurried off to begin her day.

"We're leaving a sixth earlier this morning," Dekkard said. "The councilor didn't say why." He almost winced when he realized how unnecessary the second sentence had been.

"You always say something about his never explaining," replied Ysella. "By now, you should know I understand that."

"I know you understand. It's just that it feels rude to me not to say something." *And I know you can't sense what I feel.* Dekkard wondered, far from the first time, whether other isolates felt the need to explain to empath partners, given that empaths couldn't sense any emotion from isolates, while they could from normal people, and even from other empaths who weren't careful about blocking their feelings.

Ysella smiled. "Steffan . . . I know . . . but I do understand."

"Thank you."

After quickly finishing his breakfast, Dekkard rose and walked to the garage, where he opened the garage doors, then topped off the water and kerosene in both steamers before lighting off their boilers. Even with the request from Ritten Obreduur, Dekkard had the councilor's steamer under the front portico ready to go at a half before second bell, a sixth earlier than Obreduur had requested. He'd even had time to clean the few mud splatters from the glass of the front windscreen and the side windows. He rolled down the front windows on each side of the steamer a precise three digits, just enough that there would be a slight breeze in the rear on the drive to the Council Office Building.

Then he took another look at the pale green sky over the city, a sky with just a hint of haze, although that would likely thicken over the course of the day, but at least there was no sign of rain.

Ysella accompanied Obreduur down the granite steps from the small mansion that most of the Sixty-Six would have considered modest, but then circled around to the other side, because her job was to sit up front where she could sense trouble more effectively. As a security aide, while on duty she was unofficially exempted from the customary headscarf worn by either the few professional women or the wives or daughters of the upper classes, either commercial or landed.

Dekkard waited for the councilor to seat himself, then released the brakes and pressed the throttle pedal, and the Gresynt accelerated smoothly and quietly as Dekkard guided it out from under the portico and along the concrete drive leading to the gates. Once on Altarama Drive, heading west, Dekkard checked the rearview mirrors to see whether anyone was following the steamer, then looked farther ahead, but he saw only a smaller Realto steamer turning in to the drive of a mansion easily thrice the size of the councilor's dwelling. That mansion belonged to the chairman of Transoceanic Shipping, or so Ysella had told Dekkard.

Dekkard and Ysella had been especially wary ever since the attack nearly a month earlier, although there had been no other attempts and no obvious signs that Obreduur was being watched or shadowed, but all that meant was that no one had gotten close enough for Ysella to sense the range of feelings possessed by an attacker—or the total lack of emotional radiation from an isolate.

As he continued driving, Dekkard wondered who the councilor might be meeting or receiving, or what else he might be doing, because the Council was only in pro forma session pending the Imperador's decision on whether to remove Premier Grieg or to dissolve the Council . . . or possibly, to do neither in the wake of the

Kraffeist Affair and the underlying peculation, the extent of which remained to be discovered. *As if it ever will be.*

Some four blocks later, he turned off Altarama and onto Imperial Boulevard, easing the Gresynt in behind a limousine with a poorly adjusted burner, although most wouldn't have noticed the thin gray wisps of smoke. At least the smoke wasn't black and odoriferous, unlike what poured from the chimneys of the large manufactories around cities like Oersynt, Kathaar, or Uldwyrk.

Imperial Boulevard was the smooth, asphalt-paved main thoroughfare that ran north from the harbor to the Imperador's Palace, and consisted of two sets of double lanes divided by a median featuring raised marble-walled gardens flanked by soft-needled Folknor pines. Marble sidewalks not only stretched between the center gardens and the trees, but also flanked the outer sides of the roadway. By decree, later ratified into law by the Council, all structures located within a block of the boulevard had to be built of stone and roofed either with tile or slate and could not exceed five stories, although few were more than three. Dekkard had to admit, even in his more cynical moods, that Imperial Boulevard was impressive, with all the hotels and business buildings, and the view of the Palace of the Imperador was especially striking.

"Steffan," said the councilor, "we're early enough that you don't have to drop us off. Just park the steamer, and we'll walk."

"Yes, sir."

After driving a mille and a half, he turned off the boulevard onto Council Avenue, the last major cross street before the Way of Gold, which not only split around the circular Square of Heroes, but ran along the south edge of the Palace grounds. On the north side of the square was the formal entrance to the Palace. Dekkard drove another half mille, before slowing the steamer as they approached the guard post at the entrance to the covered parking area for councilors.

After visually inspecting the steamer, the emblem welded to the front bumper, and those inside, the guard, dressed in the standard pale green uniform, waved the Gresynt through the open gate. After parking the steamer, Dekkard shut off the burner, and he and Ysella escorted Obreduur from the garage across the drive to the Council Office Building and up to the office.

All councilors' offices were identical, consisting of three connected chambers: the councilor's private inner office, with a small attached bathroom containing little more than a sink, toilet, and closet; the anteroom, holding a receptionist and her desk, with chairs and a leather-upholstered backed bench for those very few waiting to see the councilor and two table desks at one end for junior assistants, usually for staffers who also provided security in some form or another; and a moderately large staff office for the councilor's senior legal or political staffers and several clerks with typewriters and their mechanical brass calculators.

Obreduur smiled warmly to the receptionist who also served as his personal secretary just before he walked past her desk and toward his office. "Good morning, Karola."

"Good morning, Councilor."

By the time her words were out, Obreduur was closing the inner office door.

"You're early," said Karola.

"He wanted to be early," replied Dekkard. "The boulevard wasn't crowded."

"I was afraid you'd be here first. They had trouble with the omnibus, something about a leak in the flash boiler. Anna and Margrit kept telling me we'd make it, but I wasn't sure."

"What about Ivann and the others?" asked Dekkard.

"All the Crafter legalists are meeting with the Craft Party's head legalist. Ivann said he didn't know what it's all about. Both Ivann and Svard went. Felix is in the office. I put the latest petitions and letters on your desk."

Dekkard nodded. "Thank you." As he walked over to

his desk, and the stack of petitions, and a handful of letters, awaiting him, he pondered the reason for the meeting of all the Crafter legalists. Had the Premier asked the Justiciary Ministry to indict someone else associated with Minister Kraffeist . . . or had Grieg asked for one or all of the indictments to be withdrawn? *But if it involved Kraffeist as Minister of Public Resources, why weren't the commercial aides like Felix invited?*

Shaking his head at what he didn't know, Dekkard sat down at his table desk and looked at the stack of paper, all presumably from the Oersynt-Malek district from which Obreduur had been elected.

Dekkard's other duties, when he was not protecting Obreduur, consisted mainly of reading petitions or correspondence dealing largely with artisan and specific craft-related matters and replying graciously to those who had simple inquiries, flagging and filing those that were insulting or threatening, while drafting a polite response saying nothing, and referring those requiring detailed expertise to Ivann Macri for his determination as to which of the three senior staffers should handle each. Ysella had similar duties for all other petitions or correspondence.

Both, but particularly Ysella, also covertly screened any visitors to the councilor.

Less than a third of a bell passed before the door began to open and Ysella said quietly to Dekkard, "An empie and isolate are coming with another person."

That person had to be a councilor. Dekkard immediately stood, the fingers of his left hand brushing the hilt of his gladius. He didn't recognize the councilor. "Welcome, sir."

"Councilor Saarh to see Councilor Obreduur," offered the security isolate, whom Dekkard vaguely recalled seeing before.

The auburn-haired councilor, who didn't appear to be more than a handful of years older than Dekkard, stepped into the office, ignoring Dekkard and looking directly at Karola.

Having already stood, she said, "He's expecting you, sir." She rapped gently on the door to the inner office. "Councilor Saarh, sir." Then she opened that door.

Saarh looked to the thin young man to his right, who nodded, indicating that he was the empie, although Dekkard would have guessed that, since the other aide in gray was more muscular and wore a sheathed gladius with a scabbard that looked considerably more worn than did Dekkard's, while the empie only wore a personal truncheon similar to the one Ysella wore.

At that moment, the inner door opened, and Obreduur stood there, smiling pleasantly. "I'm glad we have this chance to get together." He stepped back, leaving the door open.

Saarh returned the smile. "So am I."

In moments, the two councilors were alone in the inner office, the door closed.

Ysella looked to the other empie. "It's good to see you again, Micah. I didn't think you could stay away from the Council."

Micah offered a sardonic smile. "It's not as though I had much choice. Most commercial firms are leery of empies who've worked for councilors. We're not as mobile as chills are."

Especially male empaths. Dekkard knew that, but he'd never understood the reason.

Ysella half turned. "Steffan, this is Micah Eljaan."

Eljann's eyes flicked to Dekkard.

"Steffan Dekkard." Dekkard knew that the other isolate had to be at least ten years older and that he'd seen him with Councilor Freust, but he had no idea what his name was, since security staff were seldom introduced, except by other security types when councilors weren't present, and that didn't occur often, something Dekkard wouldn't have guessed before he joined Obreduur's staff.

"Have you met Malcolm? Malcolm Maarkham?" Micah nodded to the older isolate.

"We've crossed paths, but that's all."

"Barely that," affirmed Maarkham blandly. "You're from Oersynt, aren't you, before the Military Institute and security training?"

Dekkard nodded. "And you? You were with Councilor Freust for some time." That was an estimation barely more than a guess.

"Nine years. I grew up in Uldwyrk. Security training through the district patroller academy."

When no one else spoke immediately, Eljaan turned to Dekkard. "Might I ask how you came to work for Councilor Obreduur?"

"He was looking for a security aide. I was recommended by both the Institute and the Artisans Guild of Oersynt. He interviewed me and eventually hired me." What Dekkard wasn't about to mention was that Obreduur had personally observed how Dekkard had handled all the security tests and physical challenges required, known as the "chill killers."

"Artisans in your family, then?" asked Maarkham.

"Both my parents."

"That makes sense for a Craft councilor," said Eljaan cheerfully.

Dekkard caught the hint of a wince on Ysella's face, but doubted anyone else did.

"Don't let us keep you from what you have to do," said Maarkham firmly, looking at Eljaan.

"No, please don't," added Eljaan, his voice still cheerful.

"Thank you," replied Ysella quickly. "We do have petitions to go through."

"I'm glad I don't," replied Maarkham dryly, seating himself on the bench in the front of the chamber.

Eljaan sat beside him.

Dekkard reseated himself, picked up the top petition in the stack, and began to read about how the town of Elsevier had hired non-guild stonemasons to rebuild the town hall in violation of the national law that required all large construction projects to use guild workers. *Macri or Roostof have to handle this.* Dekkard suspected he knew the answer, which was that rebuilding work below a certain monetary value was exempt from that law, but Macri would definitely prefer that Dekkard not attempt a legal explanation.

Less than a sixth of a bell passed before the door to the councilor's private office opened, and Councilor Saarh emerged, smiling pleasantly, followed by Obreduur, who halted in the doorway as Saarh walked toward the outer door, where Maarkham and Eljaan stood waiting.

Eljaan opened the door. Maarkham stepped out first, followed by Saarh. The moment the outer door closed behind Eljaan, Obreduur stepped back into his inner office, closing the door.

Ysella looked to Karola. "What can you tell us about Councilor Saarh?"

"Councilor Obreduur told me that he was chosen last week as Councilor Freust's replacement by the Landor Party leadership. He's from Khuld." Karola lowered her voice. "He's married to Councilor Freust's youngest daughter. That's all I know."

"Did the councilor mention anything about Freust's death?"

"No, he didn't."

Ysella nodded. "Thank you."

Several moments later, after Obreduur summoned Karola, Dekkard looked to Ysella. "What am I missing about Freust?"

"I don't think Freust's death was . . . natural."

"Because of the timing of his death . . . or because of the emp attack on the councilor right after that?"

"Both."

"Do you know if Freust was trying to build a coalition against the Commercers? Based on the agricultural-tariff reform bill?"

"Coalitions based on a single issue don't work in the Council. Not for long, anyway. Obreduur might have been exploring a longer-term alliance with the Landors, but Freust was likely the only one who could have brokered it to his party, and one of the few Landors Craft councilors would trust." She shrugged. "Now we'll never know."

Then, as Karola stepped out of Obreduur's office, Ysella picked up a petition and began to read.

While any party could replace a councilor who died with another party member, Dekkard wondered what had determined the Landor Party to pick Saarh. Because the seat would fall to the Crafters or Commercers in the next election? Because Saarh couldn't afford to buck the Landor leadership? To pay some political debt? Or something else entirely? But then, Guldoran law didn't require a councilor to be from a district prior to an election, only that he maintain "a presence" in the district thereafter, although the majority of candidates running for a councilor's seat usually were long-term residents of the district or were from some place very close.

Shaking his head, Dekkard went back to reading and sorting petitions.

Macri and Roostof returned to the office a sixth after the third morning bell.

"How was the meeting?" asked Ysella cheerfully.

"Intriguing, but boring after the first sixth." The thin-faced and angular Macri grinned.

"Are the other parties having meetings for their legalists?" asked Dekkard.

Roostof shrugged.

"By now, Steffan," replied Macri cheerfully, "you should know that the Landor councilors don't trust legalists, especially their own, and the Commerce councilors provide extra rewards to their legalists not to talk to anyone."

Dekkard didn't try to point out that staff salaries were limited in various legal ways, because he'd already discovered that councilors had their ways of compensating staff that didn't violate the letter of the law, particularly Commerce councilors, although Landor councilors were also known for such. Most Craft councilors had more limited resources, although all councilors received stipends for housing security aides.

Dekkard spent another bell sorting through the petitions and letters, then carried a small stack to Macri and a smaller pile to Raynaad, before sitting down to handwrite drafts to more mundane petitions and letters, drafts that Margrit would type up and then Macri would review before submitting them for the councilor's signature . . . except for those on which Obreduur made corrections, but there were usually few of those. Obreduur often just added a few lines in his own hand.

Just before noon, Obreduur appeared in the front office, and both security types stood.

After escorting him to the councilors' private dining room, Dekkard and Ysella quickly ate in the staff cafeteria before escorting Obreduur back to the office.

No sooner had they returned to drafting responses than the door to the larger staff office opened and Felix Raynaad stepped out. The stocky brown-haired older economic and commercial aide looked toward the receptionist and personal secretary. "Karola, please let me know when the director of personnel from Guldoran Ironway arrives. The councilor wants me to be with him in the meeting."

"Yes, sir. I will."

Dekkard looked at the other man. "Still the yellow cedar issue, Felix?"

"What else?" Raynaad shook his head before retreating.

While Dekkard knew few of the specifics, the general problem was that the Woodcrafters Guild had filed a legal objection to Guldoran Ironway's use of yellow cedar as paneling for ironway coach cars when the ironway had shifted from black walnut earlier in the year. The guild opposed the use of yellow cedar, claiming that working with it caused consumption and breathing problems, and sometimes even incontinence, and suggested either returning to black walnut or using red cedar.

Guldoran contended that the yellow cedar was lighter, straight-grained, and stronger than the red cedar, which was not only heavier, but less regular in grain and coloration, and slightly more prone to splitting and that the red cedar was more expensive because it had to be transported by ironway some fifteen hundred milles from Jaykarh to Oersynt.

When the chimes at the top of the Council Hall tower rang out three bells, bells that had once been more necessary before the development of inexpensive spring-wound timepieces and small clocks, Dekkard looked to the main office door, but no one appeared. A sixth of a bell passed, then a third, before Raynaad peered into the front office and looked at Karola.

"No, sir, the director hasn't arrived."

At that moment, Obreduur opened his door. "He's still not here?"

"No, sir," repeated Karola.

The councilor frowned. Then he reentered his office and closed the door.

Dekkard had wondered, more than once, what Obreduur did in the office when he wasn't meeting people . . . besides reading his copy of *Rules and Procedures* or writing personal missives that he handed to Karola—and no one else—for dispatch by messenger or post. But Obreduur wrote far more than a few such missives, and they couldn't be to a mistress, not when just about the only times he was away from Dekkard and Ysella were when he was in the councilors' lobby or dining room, the main Council Hall chamber, or at home on Findi, when they had the day off.

A good sixth later, a messenger in the gold and black uniform of Guldoran Heliograph, whose solar-mirror towers conveyed messages and linked the larger cities, entered the office and handed an envelope to Karola. "For the councilor."

Karola waited only until the messenger left before standing and rapping on the door. "There's a heliogram for you, sir." Then she entered, returning to her desk almost immediately.

Within a few minutes, Obreduur walked out of his office, his jacket partly unbuttoned, and hurried into the larger staff chamber, leaving that door open, which Dekkard appreciated, because with both the door to Obreduur's private office open and the staff office door open, there was more of a breeze, although the offices weren't nearly so hot as they would be in another four weeks at the beginning of summer.

Then Obreduur walked back toward his office, leaving the staff door ajar. Abruptly, he stopped, turned, and addressed Dekkard. "Director Deron was unable to make the meeting because of an ironway problem. He'll be here tomorrow afternoon. I'd like you to join Felix at the meeting."

"Yes, sir."

"That ironway problem overloaded the heliograph system . . . everyone must have been sending messages because they couldn't get somewhere or another." Obreduur shook his head. The councilor didn't quite slam the door as he reentered his office.

"Going to meetings, now," said Ysella. "You're coming up in the world."

"I hope I do as well as you do," returned Dekkard.

"He asks for me when he wants the opinion of a working woman . . . or an empath."

Dekkard couldn't help but wonder what had been in the heliogram that had prompted Obreduur to have Dekkard join the meeting. He did know one thing—that Obreduur was far from happy. A meeting between Obreduur and an ironway director was not likely to be pleasant for Dekkard, especially if Obreduur was as unhappy as he seemed. Dekkard looked to Ysella and mouthed, "Is he as angry as I think he is?"

"More like irritated."

Even so, that meant that the drive back to Obreduur's small mansion would be very quiet.

Dekkard decided to return to drafting responses.

3

On Tridi morning, Dekkard hurried down to the staff room because he wanted to look at Hyelda's *Gestirn*. He hoped that there might be more about the Kraffeist Affair, especially after the newssheet stories on Unadi, but there had been nothing on Duadi. Unfortunately, there was still nothing in *Gestirn,* and Dekkard doubted that there would have been more in the other newssheet—*The Machtarn Tribune*—given its pro-Commercer bias.

Dekkard did see a story head that caught his eye— IMPERIAL UNIVERSITY TO CUT ADMISSIONS. Frowning, he skimmed the article, which quoted the Minister of Health as saying that providing university educations to more students than there were positions requiring such an education was a waste, and that enrollment at all government-funded universities would be capped at present levels for the foreseeable future.

While Dekkard wondered about that, and even more about why there was nothing more in the newssheets about the whole Kraffeist Affair, there was little he could do about it.

With that thought, he concentrated on his breakfast.

Obreduur was pleasant but quiet on the drive to the Council Office Building, as he usually was, but he'd been so reserved the night before, reflected Dekkard, that anyone observing from a distance, except an empie, might have thought him an off-duty isolate, although most educated isolates were in some form of midlevel security, and certainly not elected officials.

Once in the office, Dekkard began his work sorting petitions and letters, as did Ysella.

At a sixth before the third bell of the afternoon, Director Deron arrived unaccompanied, except for the usual Council Guard. He was attired in the older and more conservative style—a silvery, dark gray, formal military-style tunic with the upright collar, the kind of tunic that did not require either a formal shirt or a cravat, above black trousers and dress black boots. His smooth black hair was the only concession to modernity, cut far longer than the cropped look required of both naval and ground forces, but to Dekkard that concession seemed out of place, almost grudging, especially given Deron's military brush mustache.

"Director Deron," said Karola brightly, "let me tell the councilor that you're here." She looked to Dekkard. "Would you mind telling Sr. Raynaad that the director is here?"

Dekkard nodded, then stood and walked across the office and into the staff office. "Felix, the director is here."

In the moments it had taken Dekkard to notify Raynaad and for the two of them to return, Obreduur had opened his office door. "Welcome, Director Deron. After hearing about the ironway . . . mishap, I'm glad to see you're safely here."

"The ironway is quite safe, and I am here." Deron glanced at Dekkard, not quite askance, taking in the semi-military security grays, before returning his full attention to Obreduur.

"Sr. Dekkard has some knowledge and experience that may be useful," said Obreduur warmly, stepping back several paces and gesturing to the chairs facing his desk.

Dekkard followed Raynaad's lead and moved toward the pair of chairs set somewhat farther from the desk, but closer to the slightly open window so that the two aides would have their backs to the light. They did not seat themselves until the councilor and director began to sit down.

Obreduur smiled pleasantly, but did not speak for well over a minute. "I believe you requested this meeting."

"I did, Councilor, in hopes you might aid in resolving the situation I earlier wrote about."

"You're referring to the difficulties you face with the Woodcrafters Guild over the use of yellow cedar?"

"Precisely."

"How exactly do you think I might help . . . resolve these difficulties?" Obreduur's voice remained warm and interested, with a slight suggestion of puzzlement.

"There are certain . . . economic realities. Guldoran has to work within those realities. One of those realities is that our passengers expect a high level of quality in our facilities and carriages. Maintaining that quality is expensive, and passengers will only pay so much to travel the ironway. The yellow cedar is of better quality than the red and costs considerably less. The grain pattern of the red is also . . . seen as more common. To use a lower-quality wood at a higher price . . ." Deron shook his head dolefully.

"Your concerns are most understandable." Obreduur nodded to Raynaad. "Felix, perhaps you could address the matter in more detail."

Raynaad nodded and turned his head toward Deron. "Honored Director, I also understand that passengers can be most particular. Guldoran Ironway has the reputation for maintaining high standards, but people seem to be willing to pay for those standards. The prices of tickets in all classes have risen five percent every year for the past four years. The results of certain inquiries suggest that passenger traffic has increased enough that two extra cars have been added on most trains from Machtarn to Oersynt. Under these circumstances, can you tell the councilor exactly how the use of red cedar will impact the profit margin of passenger service, not just in general, but specifically?"

Deron's pleasant expression faded slightly. "Sr. Raynaad, you must understand that I am not empowered to reveal the specifics of the finances of Guldoran Ironway, but I would not be here if the matter were inconsequential."

"I'm not a woodcrafter," said Obreduur warmly and smoothly, "but if it's a matter of décor and style, wouldn't some other wood be equally suitable, perhaps black cherry? I understand that the presidente of Guldoran Ironway has an exquisite dining room, entirely of black cherry."

"Presidente Oliviero does have impeccable taste, but I fear black cherry is much more expensive than yellow cedar, if not quite so expensive as black walnut."

"Steffan," said Obreduur, "how do you think the Woodcrafters Guild feels about the matter?"

Dekkard had thought about how the guild members might have felt, but had not thought Obreduur would have asked his opinion. After a slight pause, he replied, "No one in the guild has contacted me, sir, but coming as I do from a family of artisans, I would judge that the woodworkers do not wish to hazard their health and shorten their lives by working with the yellow cedar. Presidente Oliviero isn't required to make such a sacrifice. Why should they?"

"That's a fair question, don't you think, Director?" asked Obreduur mildly.

"No one is forcing them to work with the yellow cedar. If they do not wish to work with it, then they can go work elsewhere." Deron shrugged. "If none of the guilders wish to work with the cedar, then we just might move carriage building to Kathaar. It's closer to the ironworks and to the yellow cedar."

"There's no Woodcrafters Guild there," said Obreduur. "That would change with a need for woodworkers, and Guldoran would have spent hundreds of thousands of marks, if not more, to move the coachbuilding facility. Then, too, the ironway would still need a guild agreement."

"You also build the military coaches in Oersynt," added Raynaad. "First Marshal Bernotte might not be exactly pleased with an inexperienced workforce and the delays. Quality would suffer."

"It might just be better to return to using black walnut for the paneling," suggested Obreduur.

"That's not possible," said Deron. "The blight has

taken too great a toll on the black walnut trees, and the timber from the infected or dead trees has ghastly yellow streaks in it."

"You seem to have quite a problem there," mused the councilor, his tone sympathetic. "The red cedar isn't of high enough quality and costs more. The yellow cedar costs less and is of higher quality, but working with it poisons the woodworkers. I wonder how many woodworkers would wish to continue for long under those circumstances."

"Your sympathy, honored Councilor, is appreciated, but it doesn't resolve the difficulty." Deron's tone was even and polite, if little more.

"Well . . . the ironway could take the high road, so to speak," said Obreduur. "You could just tell everyone that in order to maintain the historic quality of amenities and service and also to safeguard the health of the workers, the newest carriages being built by the ironway will feature cherrywood paneling, and that may entail a slight fare increase."

"Cherrywood? I don't believe that was considered."

"It's of high quality, if not as high as black walnut, and considerably less expensive than the black walnut previously used." Obreduur smiled warmly. "I believe that there is a large stand of mature cherry trees not all that far from Oersynt, certainly sufficient for the ironway's use for more years than will affect either of us or our children."

"Are you—"

"Almighty, no!" replied Obreduur. "That would be verging on conflict of interest and worse. I'm not related to the owner in any way whatsoever, but I do know that the lands might be available. I could put you in touch if Guldoran Ironway is interested. It just struck me that it might offer a solution in everyone's interest."

Deron cocked his head, frowning, before nodding. "It would be definitely worth exploring. It's not the solution that the presidente was hoping you might facilitate . . . but . . ."

"I think you'll find this solution might be far better for everyone," said Obreduur. "Far better, especially if you consider how much good will the ironway could reap from such a decision. I look forward to hearing what your presidente decides." He rose from his desk.

Dekkard and Raynaad immediately stood as well.

Deron rose also, the momentary enigmatic smile quickly vanishing from his face. "I appreciate your willingness to hear me out and your thoughtfulness in presenting a possible alternative. One way or another, I will be in touch with you." He inclined his head.

Dekkard could sense that an unspoken agreement had been reached. Also realizing that his next task was more than obvious, he moved to the door, opening it for Deron.

Director Deron turned, glancing at Felix, but not Dekkard, before he left the inner office, then the outer office, moving quickly but not hurriedly.

"I'll need a few words with both of you," said Obreduur. "Please close the door."

Dekkard did so, then turned to see what the councilor had to say, wondering whether those words would be favorable or less so. He was relieved to see Obreduur smiling.

"You both did well." He paused, then turned his eyes on Raynaad. "Give the background file on the Woodcrafters Guild to Steffan so that he can read through it." He shifted his glance back to Dekkard. "As Felix knows, nothing you hear in this office is to be discussed with anyone but those present." He held up a hand. "No. There's nothing that's either unethical or illegal. I know the Landor who has those lands and would settle for a fair price, but I don't want anyone else to find out until matters are resolved. Is that clear?"

"Yes, sir."

Obreduur smiled again. "I doubt that I had to caution you, but some things are best stated clearly. That's all for now."

Raynaad led the way out of the inner office, and Dekkard gently but firmly closed the door.

"How did the meeting go?" asked Ysella.

"How do all meetings go?" replied Raynaad gently, but sardonically. "You've been in enough of them."

Dekkard kept his smile to himself, even as he appreciated Raynaad's quickness in showing him the appropriate response. He added, "I still have a bit to learn."

"Don't we all," replied Ysella.

As Dekkard settled back at his table desk, he couldn't help but wonder why Obreduur had chosen the meeting with Guldoran Ironway to start including him in meetings. It couldn't just be because of the Woodcrafters Guild, not when the councilor dealt with a range of guilds in his legislative work. *And how does he know who has cherry orchards to sell?* Even as he thought about it, the answer was obvious, simply because Obreduur wasn't that close to that many Landors.

Was it because Obreduur had seen enough of what Dekkard had done to include him in more? Or could it just be that Raynaad had too much work?

Dekkard shrugged. He'd find out soon enough.

4

The debate and vote on an agricultural reform proposal originally scheduled for today will be postponed indefinitely, pending the Imperador's response to the recent revelations surrounding the Kraffeist Affair. As proposed by the Landor Party, the measure would address the attempt by Sargassan grain exporters to flood Guldor with inferior low-cost swampgrass rice or emmer wheat-corn, not to mention other grains . . .

The Landor floor leader stated that the proposed changes would assure that imported grains and other foodstuffs would not undercut the prevailing base prices, as reflected on the Guldoran Commodities Exchange. The legislative proposal was thought to be in response to the efforts of foreign traders to game the value-added tariff structure . . .

The Commerce Party has only said that it will consider such a proposal on the merits . . . the Craft Party has expressed its opposition to the bill on the grounds that it amounts to establishing grain price supports for the wealthiest of Landors and would increase the cost of living for all the working people of Guldor . . .

. . . with the Craft Party holding twenty-three seats in the current Council, and the Landor Party with only eighteen, the question as to whether the proposed tariff reform structure will be adopted rests with the twenty-five Councilors of the Commerce Party, which has remained uncommitted on the proposal . . .

If the Imperador should call for new elections, it is possible that the Craft Party might gain an additional seat or two, and hold a slight plurality of Council seats. For the Craft Party to form a government would require a significant number of Landor Councilors to defect from their current alliance with the Commerce Party . . .

Gestirn, 15 Springend 1266

5

On Furdi, right after Dekkard reached the office, Karola said, "The councilor is expecting visitors from Malek. Sr. Maalengad and his wife. He's the treasurer of the Metalworkers Guild there."

Dekkard glanced to Ysella, who would have to determine the feelings of the couple, but she just nodded.

Less than a sixth later by Dekkard's watch, the corridor door opened, and a Council Guard appeared. "Visitors for the councilor."

A slightly graying man in a tan suit, the lower part

of his trousers showing signs of dampness, stepped into the office, accompanied by a woman a good decade younger.

Dekkard immediately stepped forward, smiling pleasantly. "Welcome. The councilor will be with you in a moment. I hope the rain didn't inconvenience you too much . . . but we do get a bit more than in Malek."

Maalengad snorted. "A bit? It's rained more since we got here than we get in a month."

Since Dekkard could see, from Karola's movement to the door of the inner office, that Ysella had sensed the feelings of the couple and nodded to the receptionist, he turned and gestured toward Karola, who had opened the door. "The councilor is very much looking forward to seeing you."

"Unlike some of the times before," said Maalengad as he strode past Dekkard, leaving his wife to trail behind him.

As soon as Maalengad entered the inner office, Obreduur said heartily, "Fritz, it's good to see you. For your sake, I'd have wished a better day . . ."

After Karola shut the door, Dekkard turned to Ysella and said quietly, "There must have been some guild . . . disagreements."

"Is there any guild that doesn't have disagreements with someone? Including other guilds?"

Dekkard nodded.

But by early midmorning, long after Maalengad and his wife had departed, Dekkard had read through the background file on the Woodcrafters' complaint against Guldoran Ironway. The complaint was simple—the ironway had knowingly required the use of materials hazardous to the health of its employees and had made no effort to remedy the situation, thereby violating the legal requirement for a reasonably safe workplace.

The problem, as Macri had noted in a legal memorandum to Obreduur, was that the definition of a "reasonably safe workplace" had heretofore been applied to equipment, lighting, and ventilation, and not to hazards that did not apply equally to all workers . . . and not all workers reacted unfavorably to working with yellow cedar planks, although the finished wood was perfectly safe. The guild had countered by claiming that the hazard did apply to all workers, but that the time for adverse effects to appear varied with the worker, and stated that unless Guldoran changed the wood used for paneling, the guild would withdraw all artisans a month after notice.

The larger problem, Macri had also noted, was the precedent that might be created if the complaint came before the Justiciary. If the High Court ruled in favor of the guild, such a judgment could greatly expand the definition of "workplace hazards." Yet a judgment in favor of Guldoran Ironway might send a signal to various industries that workplace hazards were limited to those recognized at the time the standard was drafted and that they could subject workers to newly discovered hazards with impunity.

Dekkard could see that the second possible judgment would definitely create a great deal of unrest among the guilds. At worst, it might lead to another general work stoppage, if not on the scale of the Black Autumn riots of 1249 or the Uldwyrk Massacre. After returning the file to Raynaad, he settled back at his table desk.

By fourth bell of the morning, he had finally sorted out his share of the latest petitions and letters and could get started on drafting replies.

At that point, Karola stepped out of Obreduur's office and gestured first to Ysella and then to Dekkard. "That messenger who left a little while ago . . . the councilor has a meeting at the Machtarn Guildhall at half past first bell."

Dekkard had noted the messenger, but there were more than a score of messengers coming and going during the course of the day, and Karola could summon one by dropping the bronze indicator outside the main door, an indicator resembling a bronze flag. "We'll be ready at a third before the bell, then."

Dekkard left the office at a third after the six bells of noon in order to have time to heat the steamer's boiler—even flash boilers took a few minutes to be fully responsive—then drove the Gresynt around to the west entry to the Council Office Building. He pulled up a few minutes early, but was glad he did because he saw Ysella and Obreduur walking out toward the steamer.

The councilor said nothing until Dekkard turned the Gresynt south on Imperial Boulevard. "The Sanitation guildmeister requested the meeting. You two will be in the room as well." Then Obreduur began to read what was likely a briefing paper prepared by Macri, Roostof, or Raynaad.

Dekkard understood. They were security, nothing more. "Yes, sir."

Ysella, sitting up front beside Dekkard, smiled wryly.

Not for the first time, Dekkard was glad he wasn't an empie who had to sense every feeling in a room, although he knew that she could block feelings—just not selectively. *All or nothing.*

While he had been previously to the Machtarn Guildhall, which not only served all the guilds in the Machtarn district, but also held the Guldoran Guilds' Advisory Committee, there were a number of guildmeisters or assistants he had not encountered, the Sanitation guildmeister being one. In a way, Dekkard looked forward to those meetings because he felt, even as a security type, he learned something from each.

As he drove, his eyes never stopped moving, checking the mirrors, the intersections and cross streets, not just for careless drivers or possible accidents, but for vehicles that seemed out of place . . . or too "in place."

About three blocks before the boulevard ended at the harbor rotary, Dekkard turned right, on the Avenue of the Guilds, toward the river, the Rio Azulete. He drove for another five blocks before pulling into the covered parking and a space labeled OFFICIAL BUSINESS.

Ysella was out of the steamer first and was scanning the parking area when Dekkard opened the rear door for the councilor.

"There's no one near, except the guard at the hall door," she reported.

Dekkard's fingers brushed the grip of the black truncheon and then the hilt of the gladius as the two of them led Obreduur toward the side entrance.

"Councilor Obreduur for a meeting with the Sanitation guildmeister," Dekkard announced as they reached the guard, standing in what resembled a military sentry box.

The guard studied the three, then looked at a sheet posted on the wall. "He's in 212. First set of stairs, up one flight, third door down."

Dekkard led the way. While people were traversing the long hallway that extended from one side of the Guildhall to the other, none were close to them, and no one even gave the three a second glance.

The hallway on the second floor was quieter, and 212 turned out to be a small conference room. A sandy-haired man with a weathered but clean-shaven face stood from where he'd been seated at one side of a small circular conference table. He wore a worn dark brown jacket and trousers over a pale green shirt. A single burly younger man in faded brown coveralls and shirt stood against the dark-paneled wall behind and to one side of the guildmeister.

As he closed the door, Dekkard saw that the bodyguard carried a brace of throwing knives, similar to those Dekkard often carried, and a brown wooden truncheon.

"Welcome, Councilor. I'm glad to see you again," declared the guildmeister in a voice slightly rough but not gravelly, gesturing toward the table as if to offer a seat.

"It's always good to see you, Konrad," replied Obreduur, seating himself, and then grinned as he added humorously, "even if it's usually over some difficulty."

Dekkard and Ysella moved to stand against the wall behind Obreduur.

"Isn't that why we both have our positions?" replied Konrad. "If people didn't have problems, they wouldn't need us."

Obreduur laughed softly. "Some of them would say we caused those problems." After a pause, he went on. "Your letter was rather vague, suggesting some difficulties with Health Minister Sanoffre."

"I never put it in writing, unless necessary. The legalists can twist any written word."

"What might be those difficulties?"

"The Minister of Health says Machtarn Sanitation can't pay Guldorans more than beetles."

For an instant, Dekkard thought he'd misheard, but then realized he was talking about refugees from Atacama, because they scuttled through the desert like beetles before crossing the Rio Doro to get into Guldor.

Obreduur nodded sagely. "They have quite a few refugees in Port Reale. Are there that many here in Machtarn?"

"More every year. Who wouldn't leave there with their Presidente Supremo? It's not that the guys don't like the beetles. They work hard, but it's getting so all my shovel crews are beetles, and I need more Guldorans, because too many of the beetles never saw a steam lorry. They certainly never saw a steamloader. Most of them only talk pidgin Guld. The department chief says he can't pay Guldorans more, but they won't take a starting job at the current pay. If they don't start on the shovel crews, then they really don't understand, and they screw up pickups with the shovel crews if they don't spend at least a few months there. Also, if they start on the lorries, with the higher pay . . . well, that doesn't set well with the older fellows. The deputy assistant health director for the Machtarn district says the starting pay's got to be the same. Says he won't change the laws because I've got problems. District councilors agree."

Dekkard almost nodded at that. District councils were effectively local government, but they were designed to force compromises, and couldn't override the laws. Every district council had six members, two appointed by each political party, each serving a single staggered six-year term, with the chair of the Council shifting in rotation every two years to a councilor of another party. District councilors had to be older than fifty, unlike the councilors of the Sixty-Six, who only had to be over the voting age of twenty, although Dekkard doubted that there were more than a handful under thirty, if that.

"Why isn't the city sanitation department taking a stand?"

"They don't care much about our problems, but if the trash and waste don't get handled well, the city blames the guild, and we get fined. Maybe even cited for workplace misfeasance."

"Has that ever happened?"

"Not in Machtarn. Osterreich, he was the guildmeister in Ondeliew, he was slammed with a five-thousand-mark judgment and six months in gaol."

"Wasn't that for peculation of guild funds?" asked Obreduur.

Konrad shook his head. "The Justiciary prosecutor couldn't prove that. So he trumped up the workplace misfeasance charge. That's what the Commercers always do."

"Who sets the standards for your workers?" asked Obreduur.

"The guild, of course." Konrad's tone was cool.

"And who sets the standards for each pay grade?"

"The guild, but for government jobs, the government has to approve."

"Could you propose standards and tests for the lorry jobs that any Guldoran and the best, but only the best, beetles could pass?"

"I suppose. We do some of that now. We could add a written test. What would that do about getting me Guldorans to handle shovels first?"

"Give new hires the test first. If they pass, then tell them they'll be promoted to lorry duty after a probationary period that's long enough so that the more experienced workers won't complain too much. If men know they'll get paid more, for certain, after a time, that's almost as good as more marks in their wallet." Obreduur shrugged. "You could work out the details better."

"I'd still need government approval for changing the work standards."

"You put together a package with the changes and send it to me. Then we'll see what we can do to persuade Minister Sanoffre. If he agrees, the city will have to accept the new standards."

"That still might not solve the problem," replied Konrad.

"If the only Guldorans you can get are those who don't want to start at the bottom, even with a near guarantee of promotion, then you're better off with beetles," said Obreduur with a sadly resigned tone of voice.

"Frigging world we live in. Used to be that men were grateful for an honest job."

"Some still are."

"Not enough. Too many young fellows don't want to get their hands dirty. Think that going to a university will make them well-paid Commerce types." Konrad shook his head. "I do appreciate your help. I'll have the standards and a test to you in the next few days. Might be a week."

"I'll look forward to it." Obreduur smiled and stood.

Immediately, Ysella moved to the door and eased it slightly it open, then, after a moment, stepped into the hallway. Dekkard followed Obreduur and shut the door before moving slightly ahead of the councilor.

When Dekkard eased the Gresynt out of the parking area and back onto the Avenue of the Guilds, he noticed a small gray automobile, a Realto, waiting at the curb with two men inside. The Realto did not move into traffic until a large maroon Kharlan sedan passed, then did so, although there had been more than enough of a break in traffic for the Realto to pull out earlier.

Dekkard kept checking the mirrors, but it seemed as though the Realto had dropped back, except that when he turned onto Imperial Boulevard, he saw the Realto had been close behind the Kharlan, shielded by the larger auto. Both the Kharlan and the Realto turned north on the boulevard.

"You're checking the mirrors more than usual," murmured Ysella.

"There's a gray Realto . . . might be following us."

"Security likes gray Realtos."

Dekkard frowned. Why would Security be following a Craft councilor? Still . . . he cleared his throat.

"Not yet . . ." murmured Ysella. "See if they follow as far as Council Avenue."

Dekkard nodded. There was no sense in unnecessarily alarming Obreduur.

When he turned onto Council Avenue, Ysella turned and looked back, even as Dekkard scanned the rearview mirrors again. They exchanged quick glances, and Ysella nodded.

Dekkard cleared his throat again. "Councilor . . . it might be nothing, but there was a gray Realto with two men in it waiting outside the Guildhall. The driver let a big Kharlan get in front of him and then followed us as far as Council Avenue."

"Thank you. It might be nothing, but these days there's little that would surprise me. Please let me know if you notice anything else like that." The councilor went on, "Avraal, I take it that whoever was in the Realto was far enough back that you couldn't sense anything."

"Yes, sir."

Obreduur did not reply, except with a nod.

When Dekkard stopped at the west entrance to the Council Office Building, Obreduur said, "The work standards for the Sanitation Guild are something you two should put together for Macri's review. Once you receive the information from Guildmeister Hadenaur, of course."

By the time Dekkard had parked and shut down the Gresynt and returned to the office, it was almost third bell. He stopped by Ysella's desk and asked quietly, "What do you think our new assignment means?"

She raised her eyebrows. "What do you think?"

"That Macri and Raynaad already have too much to do." He paused. "Maybe that he wants to see what we can do. Do you have another thought?"

"Both are likely. You've worked for him long enough to know that."

Dekkard had. For all of his pleasantness and warm voice, Obreduur was quite capable of not revealing what he didn't want others to know, even to an empie as talented as Ysella. He had another question. "Why would the Security Ministry have a steamer watching the Guildhall?"

"Security has never been fond of the Guldoran Guilds' Advisory Committee."

"An advisory committee?"

"That's a misnomer, Steffan. The five advisors are all very competent former guildmeisters who effectively control the political activities of all the guilds. They also have a strong staff of legalists and even an economist or two so that, if district guilds have problems with corporacions, they can supply expertise and legal advice that the local guilds couldn't otherwise afford. And they stay in touch with Craft councilors."

For a moment, Dekkard wondered why he didn't know that. He'd heard of the committee, and he knew Obreduur had once been a guildmeister, but there was no reason why anyone would have told him about the Advisory Committee, given that he was a security aide, and his parents' guild had never needed that kind of assistance. "I'd better get back to work."

"That makes two of us."

Just before fourth bell, Dekkard, having made a dent in his response drafts, took the drafts into the staff office and placed them in the wooden box on the corner of Margrit's desk.

She looked up from the typewriter. "You took your time."

"The councilor had us occupied."

She smiled, an expression with a hint of mischief. "I like it when you get that very serious demeanor, Steffan."

Dekkard just shook his head, then smiled back and said, "And I like it when you remind me that I can get too serious. I'll have more for you tomorrow."

"We're not going anywhere. Not until after fourth bell tomorrow."

"Are you going anywhere on Findi?"

The junior clerk-typist shook her head. "I'll just enjoy the offday and come back to tease you on Unadi."

With a smile, Dekkard turned and headed back to his own desk. He spent the last twelve minutes of the day organizing the remaining responses so that he could work on them first thing on Quindi, then looked at Karola.

"A sixth after, as usual," she replied.

"Then I'll have the steamer waiting." Dekkard rose and left the office, taking the staff staircase to the main level and walking out toward the garage. He'd almost reached the Gresynt when someone called out, "Steffan!"

Dekkard turned to see that the other figure in security grays was Jaime Minz, the isolate for Councilor Ulrich and a grizzly of a man, if an incredibly cheerful one, who always had a smile on his face, unlike the incorrect image most had of isolates as stone-faced or unemotional. "Jaime . . . haven't seen you in a while."

"Since the Council's in pro forma session, the councilor did an inspection trip to the naval base at Siincleer. He wanted a better look at the *Resolute*."

Dekkard had to think for an instant. "Oh . . . the new dreadnought? What was he inspecting for?"

"Your guess is as good as mine. There's been talk about the quality of coal." Minz shrugged. "Also about the reliability of the new ship-to-ship heliograph systems . . . you know, the gaslit night heliographs?"

"There were rumors about them my last year at the Institute."

"What can you tell me about the tiff between the Woodcrafters Guild and Guldoran Ironway?"

"Workplace conditions. The councilor's trying to persuade both sides to get together."

"You can't say more?"

Dekkard grinned. "Could you?"

"Can't blame a fellow for trying. Maybe some café when things settle down?"

"That sounds good." As he walked toward the Gresynt, Dekkard worried about the not-quite-casual contact. As a Commerce councilor, Ulrich could have a number of reasons for trying to find out what was happening with the ironway, but why had Minz been so free with revealing the problems with the night heliographs? Or coal quality? Dekkard could understand the indirectness, especially given that both Minz and Dekkard were isolates, which meant that an empie couldn't gain any hint about what either felt or if either might be lying, and that also meant that Minz could deny having passed the information . . . and that Dekkard could deny having received it. But Obreduur wasn't on either the Military Affairs or Transportation Committee. So what was the purpose? Dekkard sighed. He'd have to tell Obreduur.

He did wait until he'd picked up the councilor and Ysella and pulled away from the Council Office Building. "One of Councilor Ulrich's staffers asked me what was happening between Guldoran Ironway and the woodworkers. I just told him it was about workplace conditions. He'd have to know that anyway."

"That's a good answer. What tidbit did he give you before he asked?"

"Councilor Ulrich went to Siincleer to see the *Resolute*. There are issues about coal quality and about the new ship heliographs and their night capabilities."

"Hmmm . . . interesting. Thank you." Obreduur returned to reading the sheets of paper he held.

From that interaction, Dekkard surmised his actions and words had been at least satisfactory.

Since Ritter and Ritten Obreduur had no social engagements requiring transportation or security that evening, once Dekkard parked the Gresynt in the garage, he was free until the next morning.

He ate quickly in the staff room; then he returned to his room and changed out of his duty grays and into a conservative dark blue jacket and trousers with a pale blue shirt. The duty truncheon and gladius had to stay at the house, since they were allowed only when he was in a duty status. The throwing knives were at his belt, if concealed by the jacket, because knives were considered self-defense weapons, unlike swords, firearms, or large truncheons.

He would have preferred to run wearing something like the exercise fatigues he'd worn at the Institute, but appearing like that in the area where the councilor lived would have resulted in someone messaging the local patrol station and the subsequent appearance of a patrol steamer to investigate a "suspicious person," as he'd learned the first few times he'd tried it.

So his routine was to take a long walk at a fast pace, and then return to the house and change into an old shirt and fatigue trousers and go down to the corner of the garage and go through a series of exercises and weight work, followed by practice with the throwing knives and then, after he cooled off, a warm shower, and a little time reading before he went to sleep.

He'd just come down the back stairs when he almost ran into Ysella.

"Heading out on your walk?" Her words and smile were pleasant. "Once you settle down, you won't get away with that, you know?"

"Probably not."

"Enjoy it while you can."

"I intend to." Although "enjoyment" was too strong a term, he did get a certain satisfaction out of walking, and he'd made a habit of varying his routes so that he knew most of the area within a four-mille radius of the Obreduur house.

Dekkard turned west onto the narrow sidewalk, walking along Altarama in the direction of Imperial Boulevard. He'd learned that there were more than enough people walking along the boulevard's center gardens, especially in the late afternoon and evening, that no one paid much attention to a man who didn't stand out, although the majority of walkers were young couples, those around Dekkard's age, if not younger.

When he walked past the mansion of the chairman of Transoceanic, he briefly scanned the grounds beyond the chest-high gray brick wall, taking in the gardens flanking the drive to the entry portico. By the end of Summerfirst, the mansion would be closed, and the chairman and his family would have repaired to a cooler venue, somewhere like Gilthills or a mansion above the golden beaches of Point Larmat.

As usual, he saw no one outside on their grounds for the five long blocks before he neared the white gateposts, without gates, that marked the entry to East Quarter. Beyond the gateposts rose the white marble structures that lined Imperial Boulevard.

Dekkard walked past the gatepost on his right, its white-painted bricks rising from the edge of the sidewalk. He continued alongside the building that extended some thirty yards west, to where its front stopped, and five yards of white stone sidewalk filled the space between the structure and the curb, space already holding more than just a few handfuls of people.

There he paused, looking north toward the Imperador's Palace and then south in the direction of the harbor. He decided to go south and walked to the edge of the boulevard, waiting for the young patroller on his raised stone pedestal between lanes to stop traffic.

A couple a few years younger than Dekkard stood less than a yard to his right, the younger woman wearing a fashionable net headscarf that concealed little, suggesting that the pair were unmarried, or recently married.

Then the shrill shriek of the traffic patroller's whistle signified that it was time to cross. Close to a dozen people strolled across the east side of the boulevard to the median and the narrow walled gardens it held.

Dekkard headed along the median toward the harbor, although the center gardens weren't quite so well-tended there and the stores and the buildings flanking the boulevard were less impressive. The walls retaining the center garden were built so that every few yards there was a recessed area that created a built-in stone bench. Later in the evening, the majority would be taken, especially in full summer.

Dekkard began to walk faster.

Before long, he was nearing the Circle of Commerce, at which the center gardens ended. South of Commerce Circle, the boulevard lanes rejoined each other without a median, and the traffic worsened. The circle was also best avoided later in the evening, when ladies of questionable reputation frequented the area, often accompanied or watched by their sponsors or handlers. Such women were seldom the problem, unless they were low-level empies, but sometimes their handlers could be.

Dekkard was about to turn and head back up the boulevard when, ahead, he saw an older man wearing a pale blue linen suit of a good cut and decided to follow, wondering why the other man continued toward a dubious area. As he neared the man, he saw that the fabric was shiny in places and that the man limped slightly. Then, abruptly, the man staggered, almost as if dazed, and struggled toward the nearest stone bench.

Emp attack. With that thought, Dekkard ran toward the older man, only to see another figure, that of a slender woman wearing the telltale slit skirt of those in the so-called pleasure trade, moving toward the man.

Dekkard had no idea whether she was the empie or where her handler or sponsor might be, but anyone could have been concealed behind the topiary in the center gardens.

The woman saw Dekkard and looked hard at him, a

fairly good indication that she was the empie, concentrating on projecting some strong emotion. But when he kept moving toward her, she immediately turned and hurried away.

Dekkard kept looking around, but no one else was that close. When he neared the man on the bench, the older man glared at Dekkard. "You spoiled everything."

"I just saw you stagger . . ."

The man offered a lecherous grin. "They stagger you with pleasure . . . take your marks . . . except I never have much . . . just enough that they leave me alone."

Dekkard hadn't heard of that aspect of the so-called pleasure trade, but he couldn't say he was surprised. "I was just trying to help."

"You damned chill . . . your type thinks you're so good . . . just leave me alone . . . I don't need your so-called assistance."

Dekkard immediately stepped back. "I beg your pardon. I meant no offense."

"Just go . . ." said the man. "Man's got to find pleasure where he can."

Dekkard looked at the man closely, and, for an instant, he saw, or thought he saw, a much younger and prouder face, followed by the image of the same face, as if it were composed of thousands of tiny lights. Both images vanished, and Dekkard found himself looking directly at the old man's lined and weathered face, with sad, but still angry and bloodshot, eyes.

Puzzled by the momentary images he'd seen and not wanting to intrude further, Dekkard stepped away, turned, and headed back north, glancing up at the night sky. The high haze was so thick that he could see only a few scattered stars, just the very brightest.

6

For Dekkard especially, Quindi was singularly uneventful. No information arrived from the Sanitation Guild, nor was there any additional material
involving the Woodcrafters Guild and Guldoran Ironway. The usual number of petitions and letters arrived,
and with Obreduur meeting much of the day with other
councilors, and Macri and Roostof engaged in something involving the Kraffeist matter, Dekkard and
Ysella managed to get caught up on their correspondence duties, which likely left Anna and Margrit behind
on their typing those responses for the councilor's approval and signature.

Dekkard and Ysella's last duty of the work week was
to escort the Obreduur family to Trinitarian services
on Quindi evening. Not surprisingly, a steady lukewarm
rain was dropping out of the grayish-green clouds when
Dekkard eased the Gresynt under the roof of the side
portico at a third before the sixth bell of the afternoon.
Ysella stood beside the front passenger door, while
Dekkard opened both rear doors on the side closest to
the house. Gustoff and Nellara were the first to enter, taking the middle passenger seats, followed by their parents,
who took the rear seats. Although the larger Gresynt
was rated as an eight-seater, it was only a comfortable fit
for six, and trips involving the entire family the previous
summer, before Axeli had departed for the Military Institute, had resulted in a few tense conversations among
the three siblings.

Once everyone was settled, Dekkard eased the Gresynt
out into the rain, down the drive, and out onto Altarama, going east toward the East Quarter Trinitarian
Chapel, some eight blocks east of the house and a block
south of Altarama. He wondered how long the two siblings would remain silent. Only a fraction of a sixth
passed before the silence lifted.

". . . don't see why we need to study *Idylls of the Imperador* . . . just a bunch of bad verse about Laureous the Great . . ." Nellara's voice contained more than a hint of dismissal.

". . . have to study it because each narrative poem shows the view and feeling of one of those in power around him . . ."

"Gustoff . . . stop using that condescending tone . . . I hate it . . ."

"You wanted to know . . ."

"Not that way . . ."

Dekkard smiled wryly and tried to concentrate on his driving.

Less than a sixth passed before he drove under the covered entry to the East Quarter chapel, modest in the fashion demanded by established wealth, with walls of polished gray stone set ashlar fashion. The side windows were essentially long rectangles with a triangle at top and bottom, thus making them extended hexagons composed of triangular gold-tinted individual glass panes so that when the sun did shine a golden light suffused the nave.

Ysella accompanied the family, while Dekkard continued on to the parking area. There he shut down the steamer, and, under a small umbrella, hurried back to the chapel to rejoin the family. The Obreduur family pew was toward the rear, since the councilor had only been a parishioner for a mere eleven years, and many of the worshippers were from families that had belonged to the parish for more than two generations.

Dekkard slipped into the pew at the end away from the center of the nave, still before the services began. He could hear the prelude played on the harmonium, one of the newer versions where a steam engine, similar to that of the Gresynt, but smaller, and located below the main level of the chapel, powered the wind pump that fed the organ pipes. He didn't recognize the music, but there were many pieces he didn't.

Although Dekkard had been raised as a Solidan,

which was understandable since his parents were Solidans who had left Argental to pursue artistic aspirations in Guldor, he found himself less religious than they were, or than Obreduur and his family appeared to be.

Then the music ended, and Presider Eschbach stepped forward to the center of the sanctuary, a simple raised platform with a lectern on each side. The wall behind the sanctuary was dominated by a golden-edged tapestry hung from a shimmering brass rod that extended almost the full width of the sanctuary. Against a pale green background three golden orbs formed an arc. Within the orb on the left was a silver-edged green maple leaf, while the middle and highest orb held a silver-edged ray of golden sunlight splitting a green waterspout, and the orb on the right portrayed the outline of an antique four-masted ship englobed in the reddish-gold light of sunset on a calm sea. With each season the tapestry was changed, but all that varied was the background color, which turned to a rich green for summer, a pale golden red for autumn, and an ice blue for winter.

In that moment of silence, everyone rose.

Then the presider's deep voice filled the chapel. "Let us offer thanks to the Almighty for the day that has been and for the nights and days to come, through his love, power, and mercy."

"Thanks be to the Almighty, for his love, power, and mercy."

The presider lowered his hands, and the congregation seated itself.

Then the choir, in the loft in the back and above the congregation, began the anthem.

> *"Praised be our Creator, our Definer,*
>   *and Endower,*
> *Almighty enduring truth whose love, mercy*
>   *and power . . ."*

After the far-too-long anthem, at least in Dekkard's not unbiased opinion, the presider began the Acknowledgment.

"Our days are but fleeting threads in the fabric of time, our rocks of solidity but grains of sand on the beaches of eternity, washed hither and thither by the storms of fate and chance. This we acknowledge. Our vaunted knowledge is but a single flickering candle in the darkness of the Great Night. This we acknowledge . . ."

As he soundlessly lip-synched the words of the Acknowledgment, Dekkard glanced at Nellara, who was either whispering or lip-synching herself, her face almost blank, and her thoughts certainly elsewhere. He managed not to let a smile disrupt his miming.

Following the Acknowledgment, the presider moved to the lectern on the right and began his homily.

"We all know that the Almighty is a Trinity of Love, Power, and Mercy who stands firm against doubt and evil, against the unbelievers whose facts explain only the material world on which we live, a world whose apparent solidity is but an illusion against the vastness of the universe that is the Almighty. We look at the Palace of the Imperador and feel reassured by its solidity, an existence over twenty-three imperadors since Laureous the Great . . . but nothing lasts forever . . . except the Almighty . . ."

Presider Eschbach continued in that vein for almost four sixths. Dekkard wouldn't exactly have called it inspired pontification . . . just redundant reiteration. Following the homily, the choir sang "The Golden Triad," after which the graying presider offered the closing benediction.

Dekkard forced himself to wait until the organist had played several bars of the departure music; then he hurried from the chapel through the continuing rain to get the Gresynt. Not for the first time since he'd come to Machtarn, he was thankful that the Imperial capital didn't suffer from the gray-black rains that fell around Oersynt and the more industrial cities.

When Dekkard pulled into the covered area, Gustoff opened the middle door for his sister even before Dekkard could get out. So Dekkard just opened the rear door for their parents, then closed it, and took his place behind the wheel.

No one spoke until the Gresynt was on Altarama headed back to the house.

". . . facts explain more than just our world . . ." murmured Nellara.

". . . wasn't what he meant. He was talking about what lies beyond the material," replied Gustoff.

"The whole universe is material."

"Have it your way," said Gustoff half dismissively.

"That is enough discussion of religion," said Obreduur firmly. "You both know there's no point to trying to change what people believe by arguing. That includes family. And at least use facts. They might have an effect."

Do facts ever have an impact? Dekkard wondered.

"Yes, sir," said Gustoff.

"Yes, Father," replied Nellara sweetly.

Dekkard concentrated on the road, which was necessary because the windscreen wipers weren't as effective as he would have liked in the heavy downpour.

Given the continuing intensity of the rain on Quindi evening, once Dekkard unloaded the family under the covered portico and returned the Gresynt to the garage and wiped it down, he didn't go out again.

Instead, he went to his room, and took out paper and the pen that his parents had pressed on him when he'd left home for the Military Institute. A bell later, he finished the three-page epistle to his parents, which addressed the guilt he'd been feeling because it had been two weeks since he last wrote. He sealed it, put a stamp on the envelope, and set it aside, knowing that the fastest way for them to receive it was by posting it in the box at the Council Office Building on Unadi morning.

With a smile of relief, he picked up another book he'd borrowed, with permission, from the councilor's small library—a novel entitled *The Son of Gold,* ostensibly the story of a never-acknowledged bastard son of Laureous the Great.

It should be interesting, one way or another.

7

Dekkard slept comparatively late on Findi morning, late being a little before the first bell of morning. As he sat for a moment on the edge of the bed, his bare feet on the heavily varnished white oak that floored all the staff rooms and halls, he couldn't help thinking that, at times, the week felt too long. After five workdays, Dekkard felt that the one offday sometimes wasn't enough to recover, not so much physically, but emotionally.

He didn't rush as he showered, shaved, and dressed in a more traditional fashion with a cream-colored barong over dark green trousers. He still wore black boots, since he'd never liked sandals. Then he made his way down to the staff room, where Hyelda had laid out the basics in the center of the table—café in a pot on an alcohol warmer, pitchers of orange and guava juice, a plate of croissants, and, for Dekkard, a small plate with quince paste.

Ysella was already there. She looked up from her mug of café. "The cream and green look good on you. So does the barong. Maybe that's because I usually see you in grays or trousers and jackets."

In return, Dekkard actually looked closely at her, taking in her bobbed black hair, gray eyes, and wiry figure. She was wearing a slightly daring mid-calf-length maroon skirt and matching blouse, with a pale lighter maroon jacket so filmy that it was almost translucent.

"You look very stylish. What are you doing today?" asked Dekkard.

"Since it doesn't look like rain, I'm going to visit my sister and her husband. I don't suppose you'd want to come?" Ysella's question was almost rhetorical, not surprisingly, given that she'd invited Dekkard a good half score times over the past year.

"In fact . . . I think I'd like that . . . if you don't mind?"

Her mouth half opened in surprise. Then she smiled. "I knew you'd come . . . sometime."

He poured himself a mug of café before sitting down across the table from her. "They live somewhere east of here, you said?" He took two of the croissants from the platter, and two slices of quince paste, then poured himself a glass of the guava juice, which he didn't like as much as the orange juice, but which he knew was better for him.

"A mille and a half beyond the end of the Erslaan route, but it's a pleasant walk. They'll drive us back, but since I never know when I'm leaving . . ."

"And the omnibus can be a bit . . . variable on end-day?"

"Exactly."

Dekkard sliced the first croissant almost in half, slipped the quince paste in between the halves, and took a bite.

Ysella shook her head. "You and that quince paste."

"What time were you planning on leaving?"

"Whenever is comfortable for you."

"I take it that they're not late sleepers?"

"They're not in the habit. He's an architect and engineer, and she's a Security patroller, mostly as a dispatch aide, though. For now, anyway."

For now? And working as Security patroller, even doing mostly clerical work, when her husband is a professional? Dekkard decided not to ask. "I'll be ready after breakfast. You just let me know."

"We'll leave as soon as you're ready." Ysella took a

last sip of her café and rose. "I'll meet you under the portico."

As she left the staff room, Dekkard half wondered why he'd agreed so quickly. *Are you losing your chill?* He shook his head. That just didn't happen. Besides, he'd worked with Ysella long enough to know she wouldn't have tried emping him even if he weren't an isolate.

He soon finished the second croissant and the guava juice, as well as the café. After carrying his plate and mug into the kitchen, he walked back to his room, where he picked up a few essentials, including his knives and wallet, then washed his hands and face, before heading down to the portico. As he stepped outside, he glanced up, and, as Ysella had said, the pale green sky was crystal clear, for the first time in days.

Ysella was waiting, wearing a pale maroon headscarf of the same almost translucent fabric as her jacket. She also wore gloves, which had once been expected in public of any stylish woman of taste, but was a fading custom. "You didn't take long. But then, you never do." Without another word, she turned and headed down the drive toward the pedestrian gate.

Dekkard caught up with her in three steps, although she was moving at a brisk pace, which Dekkard appreciated, given his impatience with dawdling. "The omnibus stop a block north on Imperial Boulevard?"

"Unless you know a closer one."

"That's one of the three that I know," Dekkard admitted, since he avoided the omnibus whenever possible.

"There are only four within a mille, and the fourth is only that close if you cut through the memorial columbarium behind the East Quarter chapel."

"How did you find that out?"

"Rhosali told me. It's the nearest stop on the southeast shore route."

"Have you taken it? To the shore, I mean?"

"Once. That was enough."

"I can see that. I wouldn't think that you're someone who cares much for sun and sand."

Ysella frowned.

"Or am I wrong? That was just a guess on my part."

A smile followed her frown. "No, you're not. Why did you think that?"

"You're always neat and well dressed. You're so put-together that you make duty grays look like formal-wear. Somehow ... to me, anyway ... the way you dress doesn't seem like someone who'd want to wear a soggy bathing costume that covers you from shoulder to calf where you'd swelter out of the water and itch from the salt if you went bathing."

Ysella laughed, a soft but full sound. "I wish I could say it as well as you did. And you feel the same, I take it?"

Dekkard nodded. "If I'm going to swim, I prefer clear running water that's not frigid."

"Swim? Not bathe? That comes from your parents, doesn't it?"

For a moment, Dekkard didn't understand. Then he nodded and said, "The only open water in Argental is in frigid lakes or even colder streams or rivers. You don't bathe there. You swim to keep from freezing. At least, that's what my father said. I was born here."

"You've never gone back there ... or wanted to?"

"Hardly. Here an isolate doesn't have to be a military drudge. Here I can do government security, private security, even commercial security ... or I could be an artisan or crafter."

"Commercial security?" Ysella's voice contained a hint of amusement.

"Chills are immune to certain types of persuasion, and I understand there's a great deal of temptation in certain parts of the financial world."

"Immune only to certain types?"

Dekkard could hear the continued amusement behind her words, and he replied with a smile before saying dryly, "Piles of marks and beautiful women have been known, very, very occasionally, to tempt even the most upright of chills."

"You're scarcely that," she replied.

"Exactly. Why do you think I decided against commercial security?" That wasn't the only reason, but he didn't want to mention the other one. That was the fact that an isolate could seldom ever get above mid-level administration simply because empaths couldn't sense whether they told the truth, and the corporacion and government higher-level officials liked that reassurance.

"Why did you opt for a place with a councilor?"

"Because I was told that I couldn't possibly qualify." *And stiff-necked sons of Argenti parentage hate to be told that they can't do something.*

"Who told you that? The councilor said you had the highest scores of all the available applicants."

Dekkard wasn't surprised Obreduur had shared that with Ysella, given that she had to work with whichever isolate the councilor chose. "The assistant director of training at the Institute."

"Why do you think he said that?"

"Most likely to motivate me."

"That's because you'd never make a traditional military officer."

"I understood that by the time I graduated."

Ysella nodded. "You were approached by one of the security service firms last year, weren't you?"

"How did you know that?"

"You got a letter at the office from SSA. Karola told me. They like to recruit from councilors' staffs. They pay quite a bit more than the Council does. Did you talk to them?"

"I sent a polite note back saying that I enjoyed my position."

"Did they pursue it?"

"Indirectly. Frieda Livigne—from Councilor Maendaan's committee staff—"

"I know her. How did you meet her?"

"She introduced herself. I have no idea why."

Ysella shook her head. "I do. Go ahead."

"She said that SSA paid well and promoted quickly, and that, if I ever changed my mind, to let her know."

"I take it you haven't."

Dekkard shook his head. "I'm already doing and learning more than most isolate security aides. Councilor Obreduur is different from most, from what I've seen and heard."

"Very different from most Commerce councilors. There are some other Craft councilors who allow their security detail to do more, and possibly a Landor or two."

"In any case, I never heard more."

"In another year or two, they'll try again. After three or four years, most isolates working for councilors realize they'll never go any further or make much more. For some, that's all they want, but quite a few look at the higher income, especially if they have a family to support."

"Is that true of empaths as well?"

"Not quite as much, but mostly."

Dekkard was still thinking about that when the two reached the omnibus stop. There, a half score of other passengers were already standing and waiting. Several of the women with thin faces and without headscarves looked at the two and eased away.

Dekkard hoped that the small crowd, especially on a Findi, meant that the others had been there for a time, and that he and Ysella wouldn't have to wait long. With others nearby, he didn't feel like saying much of import, and he'd never cared much for the meaningless small talk that so often passed for conversation.

In the end, they waited more than a sixth before the double-decker omnibus came to a halt, with faint wisps of gray smoke suggesting a burner not as well-adjusted as it might be. No one stepped off, and those in front of Dekkard and Ysella hurried on.

"I'll take care of the fare," declared Ysella as she led the way, dropping two half-mark coins into the box, coins that clinked slightly as they dropped. She choose a rear seat on the lower level with no one close by, seated herself, and said, "You must bring good fortune. I usually have to wait much longer."

Dekkard shook his head. "I can't say I've ever been accused of that before."

"Don't be quite so dour, Steffan. At the least you'll get a very good meal. Emrelda would have it no other way."

"I certainly didn't mean to sound dour . . . as you put it." He managed an apologetic smile.

"I shouldn't have said it that way. You're sometimes excessively serious, but not dour. What were you going to do today? Or are you coming with me because you have nothing better to do?"

Dekkard grinned. "You didn't ask me until we were on the omnibus."

"Of course."

"I read last night and wrote a letter to my parents. I usually do that on Findi. Most Findis, anyway. I'd thought about shopping, but . . ." He shrugged. "I have everything I need, and I don't see the point of buying something I don't."

"So accompanying me is just slightly better than not going shopping or reading?"

Dekkard almost missed the hint of a smile. "Much better. Why spend a sunny day reading? There aren't enough bright spring days as it is, and I realized . . ." He shrugged again, not wanting to finish the sentence.

"You realized . . . ?"

"I really wanted to come with you," he admitted. "I can't say why. I just did."

"Spontaneity doesn't come easily to you, does it?"

"You couldn't tell, could you?" he replied ruefully.

"It's not exactly a predominant characteristic of isolates."

Dekkard managed not to frown, but there was something about the way Ysella spoke . . . something . . . that he couldn't quite place. Absently, he noted that the omnibus had turned off Imperial Boulevard and was heading east on Camelia Avenue, and before long would pass on the south side of Imperial University, not only the largest university in Guldor, but certainly the most prestigious, although the Military Institute was also well-regarded, if for slightly different reasons. He still wondered about what the Public Resources minister had said, suggesting that there were too many young people going to the universities. Why did that matter so much? It wasn't as though Guldor was exactly impoverished.

"You read all the political and economic journals. Don't you find them a little . . . ponderous?"

"I skip the mathematics and the econometric models. I concentrate on the background, the assumptions, and the conclusions. I also read the critiques of previous journal articles."

"You know," mused Ysella, "I've found out more about you, as a person, in the last bell than I have in two years. Do you want to tell me why?"

"Why do you think?" he countered warily.

"The way you described me earlier says a great deal about you. So does your question. You're very cautious. You don't let people in easily. After two years, you've finally decided that you can trust me . . . at least a little."

"You've invited me . . . but never pressed," returned Dekkard. "I'd say that suggests you're cautious as well, and very polite."

Ysella laughed. "If only my parents could hear that."

"I'd be happy to tell them."

"You'd have to travel to Sudaen, then."

"That's where you're from?"

She nodded.

"But your sister lives here."

"We both left, by different means. She left first. Our brother stayed." Before Dekkard could say more, she asked, "Do you have any siblings?"

"One sister. She's an artisan, like my parents."

"You've never said anything about them."

"My father is a plaster artisan."

"Does he specialize, as in chapel work, commercial buildings, or ornate private dwellings?"

"His work is most in demand for private dwellings." Even as Dekkard replied, he had the feeling he was missing, or overlooking, something.

"Then he must be very good. What about your mother?"

"She's a portraitist, oils or pastels."

"And in demand?"

"Mainly by professional families," said Dekkard.

"That's good, and not surprising. The portraits are more often of daughters?"

"Of course. What about you? Why did you leave Sudaen?"

"That's a very long story. The short version is that Sudaen was too small for an empath who wanted to use her talent. So I begged for a training spot at the Empath Academy in Siincleer. The second year I applied they accepted me. After training, I worked a year as a parole screener at the prison there before I applied to the Council."

"That was what . . . five years ago?"

"Not quite. Obreduur wasn't pleased with the empath he had . . . he's close to being an empie himself."

"And he detected subtle persuasion?"

"I have no knowledge about that."

"That's a denial only for legalistic purposes," Dekkard said with a smile, "which I'll accept in the same terms. You've told me nothing."

"What are your most favorite foods?" asked Ysella. "Besides croissants and quince paste?"

"Crayfish bisque, cinnamon pumpkin fritters, Argenti shepherd pie, Plaatz onion soup, with a double layer of good locali cheese . . . probably a few others."

"If you like quince paste, you have to like sweets . . ."

"Aflajores and flan . . . or a good cherry pie."

The two talked food for the next half bell, until Ysella said, "Our stop is coming up."

Dekkard glanced around. While he'd noticed people leaving at various stops, until that moment he hadn't realized that they were almost the only passengers remaining on the lower level, except for an elderly couple seated near the front.

Then the omnibus slowed, and the door attendant called out, "Erslaan, last stop." Then he stepped forward and opened the door.

The elderly couple left first, then Ysella and Dekkard.

"Good day, sir, lady."

"Thank you," replied Dekkard, stepping out onto the white marble sidewalk and quickly studying the area, which looked like a miniature of the best commercial sections of Imperial Boulevard, except that the shops and other buildings were only two stories. *Definitely a stylish area.* "How far to your sister's?"

"A little more than a mille, but it will feel longer. That's why I told you a mille and a half." She pointed to the cross street some ten yards ahead. "North on Jacquez."

As the omnibus pulled away, giving Dekkard a clear view, he realized that Jacquez led uphill, and while the grade was mild, he had the feeling it continued all the way to their destination.

There was far less traffic in Erslaan, and consequently no traffic patroller, and in moments the two crossed the avenue and were walking up the sidewalk on the west side of Jacquez. A slight breeze blew in from the ocean, but didn't offer that much cooling.

"You didn't mention hill climbing," he said.

"I wouldn't have thought someone with an Argenti background would have even considered this slope a hill."

"I wasn't complaining . . . just observing," he offered in a tone of mock protest.

Ysella just shook her head.

After some six long blocks of passing more than modest well-kept one-story dwellings, all with tile roofs, they reached a set of gray gateposts on each side of

Jacquez, each post bearing a brass plaque with the name HILLSIDE.

"Your sister definitely lives in a fashionable area."

"Markell would have it no other way."

That didn't totally surprise Dekkard, although he couldn't have said why. "Is he with some big building corporacion?"

"Engaard Engineering. It's certainly not small, but it's not huge, either, from what Markell has said."

Dekkard couldn't say he'd ever heard of it.

Two blocks later, they turned west on Florinda Way, taking the sidewalk on the north side of the street.

"Her house is the third one down."

The third dwelling was more than a mere house, but less than a mansion, as were all the others Dekkard had passed in Hillside. It was also set back and on a low rise, and Dekkard followed Ysella up the score of steps that paralleled the drive leading to a covered portico on the east end of the house.

Even before Ysella reached the shade of the sheltered front entry, the door opened, and a slightly older version of Ysella appeared, although she wore a teal skirt and blouse, and had light brown hair, and stood just a touch taller than Ysella. "Is this Steffan?"

"It is. Steffan, this is my sister Emrelda. Emrelda Ysella Roemnal, if we're being proper, which is seldom."

"Come in . . . just come in. It's almost like summer out here. The back veranda is much more comfortable." Emrelda closed the front door after Dekkard stepped into the front hall, then gestured toward the rear of the dwelling.

As Dekkard followed the sisters, he took in the spacious front parlor on the right, across the center hall from the library or study. Then, on the right was another hall leading to the door serving the covered portico and the drive, while on the left was the staircase to the upper level. The dining room was next on the right opposite the kitchen, with a small separate breakfast room behind the dining room. The furniture was all in the simpler modern Imperial style.

As the three stepped out onto the roofed veranda with its polished flagstone tiles, a tall blond man rose from a white wicker chair with deep rose cushions. He wore a silver guayabera, with a narrow trim of Veerlyn blue, and offered a polite but not effusive smile.

"Markell, this is Steffan Dekkard. He's the colleague of Avraal's that we've talked about before."

Markell inclined his head. "It's good to see you. I was beginning to think you might be fictional."

"He's quite real," declared Ysella. "He's just rather retiring and cautious."

"Like someone else we know," replied Markell, gesturing to the other wicker chairs spaced roughly around a low white wicker table.

"Until she lets you know her better," added Emrelda, who remained standing as the others seated themselves. "Would you like a cold drink?" She smiled at her sister.

"Markell actually got you one of the coal-gas coolers?"

"He did."

"I thought we should try one out," said Markell. "I'm not one for freezing lager, but other foods keep better, and I wanted to see how it worked before I recommended one to any of our clients."

"It's in the rear pantry," added Emrelda.

"You can have regular lager or chilled lager," Markell offered, looking at Dekkard. "It's Kuhrs. That's the best we can get here in Machtarn, not like Nargonst or Riverfall, but you can't get either unless you go to Uldwyrk or Oersynt."

"Chilled, thank you."

"And you want the Silverhills white?" Emrelda asked Ysella.

"Please. Can I help you?"

Emrelda shook her head. "Just cool off in the shade. Markell . . . tell them about your latest project." Then she turned and headed back inside.

"We're building a new facility for the Navy outside Siincleer. It's going to be the largest such facility in Nordum, possibly in the entire world."

"What will this facility do?"

"No one is saying. One part requires thick reinforced walls. The other part has to do with lenses and mirrors. I'm just guessing, but I think they want to focus sunlight to a point hot enough and small enough to do precision cutting."

"Is that even possible?" asked Dekkard.

Markell shrugged. "It's possible to use lenses and mirrors to set wood and coal aflame, and I've seen crafters use lenses to concentrate light to burn-etch wood. Theoretically, if you built a parabolic mirror big enough and perfectly shaped and aligned you could cut through iron."

"Why hasn't anyone done it?" Ysella looked intently at her brother-under-law.

"No one has the ability to build anything that big or that accurate. Also, what would be the point? There are easier ways to cut metal."

"Then why are they going to build this facility?" asked Dekkard.

"Those questions we don't ask. Just like no one asks how your councilor voted. We just design the building to the specifications the Navy requires."

At that moment, Emrelda returned with a tray holding two beakers and two wineglasses.

"You obviously share one characteristic with Avraal," said Markell with a hint of amusement in his voice.

Ysella exchanged a quick glance with her sister, but neither spoke as Emrelda finished setting the drinks on the table in front of each of the others, then seated herself.

That left Dekkard with the need to make some response. "And what might that be?"

"You both have greater abilities than required by the standards for your positions."

"You said that so diplomatically, Markell," commented Ysella dryly. "Just like a councilor. Have you thought of offering your services to your party?"

"As I've informed you before, the Commerce Party avoids candidates who have a record of building or accomplishing things. Just as the Craft Party avoids those who think too deeply. Besides, I can't swallow all of any party's line."

"What about the Landor Party?" Dekkard asked.

"They want councilors who've never done anything and never thought about anything new or different." Markell lifted his beaker and took a small swallow of lager.

Dekkard followed his host's example, then asked, "Do you handle more of the engineering or the design work?"

"I'm an engineer working as a designer who also makes sure that the architect and the engineer both understand the other's requirements and limitations."

"Because architects want the design to be beautifully functional and the engineers want it to last forever regardless of how it looks?"

"It's more complicated than that . . ."

"No, it's not," interrupted Emrelda in an amused tone. "What's complicated is getting them to agree. And you're good at making a concept into a plan that's a working design, and also bringing everyone together."

"Then you're the project director, or something like that?" asked Dekkard.

"I don't have that title, but in practice I'm the one who keeps looking over the contractors' shoulders. Engaard Engineering is organized along projects, and each engineer in charge of a project reports directly to Halaard Engaard himself. We don't have the hierarchical structure of most corporacions. That's why we can compete with the bigger engineering corporacions like Siincleer Engineering or Haasan Design."

"Compete with?" said Emrelda. "They can't really

compete with you without losing marks, and you're among the best. That's why we can live here."

"Even if . . ." began Markell.

"We're not going there, dear," declared Emrelda firmly.

Markell smiled, an indulgent expression that suggested he'd heard those words more than once before. "Then where do you suggest we go, my lady?"

"Anywhere but there."

"What are we having for our midafternoon dinner, then?" asked Markell.

"We're having creamed noodles with lamb, as you well know, because it's one of Avraal's favorites."

"We thought about sautéed lentils and onions," said Markell.

"*You* thought about it. I thought about cold roasted pheasant."

The comments about lentils and pheasant confirmed Dekkard's previous suspicions that the sisters came from a Landor family, but most likely from one of those less wealthy. Either that, or they both were strong-willed and rebellious. *But then, Avraal is strong-willed enough that she could have come from even a wealthy Landor family.* But Dekkard wasn't about to ask that question, especially since Markell most likely did not, unless he was the youngest son of many. Instead, Dekkard looked to Markell and said, "You must have considerable aptitude in both engineering and design. Besides the obvious requirement of hard work, how did you achieve what you have?"

Markell smiled, if faintly, before replying. "Avraal said that you were perceptive. Let's just say that . . ." He paused, then went on. "Even today, for a highly talented student from a modest background to achieve notice requires skill in more than one field of study. I saw that from the beginning. Since I was more modestly talented, it took, as you observed, a great deal of effort to obtain two firsts from the Imperial College of Engineering."

Another smile followed. "Possibly not quite as much effort as for an isolate to graduate from the Military Institute as one of the Triumphing Ten."

Ysella looked to Markell questioningly.

"You didn't know that?" asked the architect, who turned his gaze back on Dekkard. "You'll pardon me for making certain inquiries, but when the sister of one's wife keeps mentioning a coworker . . ." He shrugged.

"You were naturally protective," Dekkard responded. "That's understandable. I always wanted to know about the people my sister associated with."

"Is she older or younger?" asked Emrelda.

"Older."

"You were the inquisitive younger brother, then?" said Emrelda.

"More the quiet observing type that unnerves young men, I suspect," commented Ysella.

"I'd agree with Avraal," added Markell.

Dekkard offered a sheepish grin.

"Enough of families," said Emrelda. "You two work for a councilor. What do you think about the Kraffeist Affair, Steffan?"

"The councilor hasn't ever mentioned it to me," replied Dekkard.

"Nor to me," added Ysella.

"But what do *you* think about it? Minister Kraffeist has been accused of illegally leasing part of the Naval Coal Reserve to Eastern Ironway, and now the director of logistics for Eastern has disappeared without a trace." Emrelda kept looking at Dekkard.

"There's been nothing in the newssheets about a missing director," said Ysella. "How did you find that out?"

"All the patrol stations in Guldor have been given sketches of him," replied Emrelda. "Our station got one by messenger yesterday afternoon. All it says is that Eduard Graffyn, a director at Eastern Ironway, is missing and that any information about him should be immediately dispatched to the Minister of Security . . . and that the patrol was not to mention the matter to the newssheets."

"Do you think he's the one who sent that letter to the Premier and Imperador . . . and to all the councilors and newssheets?" asked Dekkard.

"Who else could it be?" asked Markell.

"That makes the situation more serious," replied Dekkard. And Minz's mention of coal quality just might tie in to all of that, even if Dekkard had no idea how.

Markell offered a short amused laugh. "Now you're the one sounding like a councilor."

"Except he's right," said Ysella. "Even a director doesn't have unrestricted access to the level of funds supposedly paid for that commission—"

"Bribe," interjected Markell. "We might as well call it what it is."

"I don't know even as much as you apparently do, Emrelda," said Dekkard, "but it appears to me that Director Graffyn is fleeing for his life because he knows too much about what actually happened. The question isn't why he disappeared, but why he waited."

"I'd wager he didn't wait," said Markell. "He likely disappeared earlier, and since Eastern Ironway can't find him, they've dragged Security into it."

"That makes sense," said Emrelda. "That would explain why the Security Ministry is circulating sketches here in Machtarn and trying to keep it quiet. Graffyn would be in danger if he stayed near Eastern's main office in Neewyrk, and his best hope would be to get to Machtarn so that he could reveal what he knows before someone kills him."

"Unless he's already dead," pointed out Markell.

"Neither of you has heard anything?" asked Emrelda. Both Dekkard and Ysella shook their heads.

"I was so hoping you knew something else. It would have been so exciting." Emrelda sighed. "Now we'll have to talk about something much more mundane . . ."

And while the conversation for the next bell was more

mundane, ranging from the weather to the best lamb dishes besides Ysella's favorite and the local controversy about extending the omnibus route another three milles east of Erslaan, Dekkard nonetheless enjoyed it, as well as the chilled Kuhrs lager . . . and later the creamed noodles and lamb, followed by a flan vanille, and then a round of Keisyn, a clearly expensive lemon liqueur that he'd heard of but never tasted.

All too soon, it was late afternoon, and Emrelda said, "I'll drive you two all the way back to the councilor's mansion."

"You don't have to—" began Ysella.

"I want to. Besides, Markell has some work to do, and it will go faster if I'm not around. You two just go wait by the portico door. I'll meet you there with the Gresynt."

When the two reached the east side entrance to the house and stood under the extended roof waiting, Dekkard's eyes were caught by the sight of a boy hurrying out of the neighboring house. The child was not even halfway down the front steps when a woman appeared on the top step.

"Tomas! Turn around and come here."

The boy stopped as if he had run into an invisible wall, then turned and began to walk back up the steps, without hesitation.

Dekkard looked at Ysella. "Either she's a strong empie or he's a susceptible."

"He's a sussie, and she's a low-level empie."

Dekkard shook his head. The very thought of being a susceptible who could be ordered around by any empie chilled him, even though as an isolate he wasn't in the slightest susceptible.

"It could be worse," said Ysella, a trace of bleakness in her voice.

Dekkard knew that was definitely so because sussies were effectively banished from Argental and turned into near-mindless slaves in Atacama . . . and treated even worse in Sudlynd and Sargasso. Even in Guldor, where the only legal restriction on them was lack of suffrage, their lives tended to be limited economically and socially. *To say the least.*

At that moment, Emrelda guided her Gresynt up to the side entrance. The teal-colored steamer was the same model as the six-seater used by Ritten Obreduur, but it stood out with the brighter paint, whereas the darker shade of the Obreduurs' steamers made them almost indistinguishable from most other steamers, given that most Guldorans with the marks to buy and operate a steamer tended to be conservative in the colors with which they surrounded themselves.

"Are you sure this isn't an imposition?" Dekkard asked Emrelda as he opened and held the front passenger-side door for Ysella.

"Almighty, no," declared the older sister. "I don't bother Markell, and I get to spend more time with you two."

"Particularly your sister," said Dekkard as he closed the front door and opened the rear passenger door before stepping inside, seating himself, and shutting the steamer door.

"You're part of her life."

"You definitely are, Steffan," added Ysella.

Dekkard couldn't dispute that, and, as Emrelda eased the steamer down the drive, he scanned the interior of the Gresynt, quickly noting the leather upholstery and the roll-down windows that marked the vehicle in the general cost category of Obreduur's steamer, and that didn't include the teal exterior finish, which had to have been specially ordered. "I've never seen another teal steamer, especially a Gresynt."

"You likely never will," replied Ysella. "I had to persuade a few people so that Emrelda could even order it."

"After that," added Emrelda, "the Gresynt management decided it might be better to claim it was a marketing test."

Dekkard could see that.

"I asked Markell if he wanted his next steamer in

Veerlyn blue," added Emrelda. "He demurred, much as he's partial to it. He prefers more subtle statements. His gray Gresynt is practically invisible. In that way, I wouldn't be surprised if you're much the same, Steffan."

"Somewhat," said Ysella.

"I'd judge that subtlety is necessary in what Markell does."

"And it's not in what you and Avraal do?"

Both Ysella and Dekkard laughed.

Almost a third of a bell later, Emrelda stopped her steamer in front of the closed gates of the Obreduur house. She turned to look at Dekkard. "I do hope Avraal will let us see more of you."

"That's up to Steffan . . . and our duty schedule," replied Ysella.

"Thank you very much," said Dekkard, "for your hospitality, an excellent dinner, and for driving us back."

"You are cautious, but it becomes you," said Emrelda.

"He is, and it does," said Ysella. "I'll send you a message when we know more."

Dekkard opened his door and got out of the teal Gresynt. Ysella emerged before he could open her door. The two watched as the Gresynt glided away almost silently through the twilight.

As they walked toward the pedestrian gate at the side of the closed drive gates, Dekkard turned to Ysella. "You never actually said it, but you and Emrelda come from an old and established Landor family, don't you?"

"Old and established, but not that well-endowed financially," replied Ysella. "There's more than enough for our brother, but every year it costs more to maintain the lands." She paused. "You didn't ask much of Markell . . . or about him."

"He didn't volunteer enough for me to ask any more than I did." Dekkard opened the gate, then followed Ysella through and closed it behind himself.

"Still the cautious one," she replied with a smile. "I'm very glad you abandoned a little of that caution and decided to accompany me today."

"So am I. I enjoyed the day."

"So did I."

Dekkard almost said that he hoped that she'd invite him again, but didn't because that would have been presumptuous, and yet, if he wanted to pursue even just a friendly off-duty relationship, the next step was his to take. He also wondered why Ysella had continued to ask him . . . if infrequently, since she clearly hadn't hinted at anything beyond friendship. *Or is that just caution . . . or for some other reason?* "Perhaps we could do something next endday."

"Let's see what the week brings. We can talk about it later."

"Then . . . later."

"That might depend on the councilor."

"What do you know that I don't?"

"Nothing. It's just a feeling." At the side portico, she turned to him and smiled, an expression both warm and slightly enigmatic. "I'll see you in the morning."

He offered an easy, if well-practiced, grin. "That you will."

8

When Dekkard dropped off Obreduur and Ysella at the west entrance of the Council Office Building on Unadi morning, the clouds were high, thick, and gray, with no touch of green, suggesting that any immediate rain was improbable. After parking the Gresynt and entering the building, before taking the staff staircase up to the office, Dekkard detoured slightly and dropped his letter to his parents into the postbox at the end of the first level, along with a short note of appreciation and thanks to Emrelda and Markell.

By the time Dekkard reached the office, a stack of letters and petitions awaited him, and Obreduur had already left for a Waterways Committee meeting in the Council Hall, accompanied by Ysella, because, more than a few times, those attempting assassination had stolen or forged newssheet or staff credentials to gain access to the Council Hall and then entered the corridors or rooms reserved for councilors and staffers.

Dekkard settled in at his desk for a long morning. Even as he looked at the first petition, one from a steward of the Entertainment Guild in Malek about the failure of the local branch of the Corporacion Theatro to supply the proper documentation for the required monthly payments to the guild pension fund, Dekkard's thoughts drifted back to the Kraffeist Affair. Even if the patrol stations had been told not to say anything about the missing director, it couldn't be that long before something appeared in the newssheets. Dekkard was more than a little surprised that the morning edition of *Gestirn* hadn't already broken the story, but then it was more than clear that some stories or information didn't get published, likely because the Security Ministry, under Commercer control, had strongly "suggested" against it, justifying the censoring under the provisions of the Great Charter that prohibited the printing of inaccurate or inflammatory language or happenings. *Of course, that doesn't prevent the misleading use of accurate facts.*

Less than a bell later, Dekkard finished sorting through the stack of petitions and letters, handing those that obviously required legalistic or economic expertise to Macri for his delegation, and began to work on responses to those letters he would handle. Before long Obreduur and Ysella returned, but neither offered more than simple pleasantries.

Just after third bell of the afternoon, right after Macri had left the office, a messenger appeared and presented a large and thick envelope to Karola, for which she had to sign. After taking it to Obreduur, she returned and extended the envelope to Ysella. "It's from the Sanitation Guild. He said you'd know what to do with it."

Ysella looked to Dekkard. "Would you please look at it first? I'd like to finish the draft briefing paper for the talk to the women's committee of the Machtarn Textile Millworkers Guild."

"He's giving a talk to them?" Dekkard hadn't seen that anywhere on Obreduur's schedule, at least not on the one that Karola circulated to the staff.

"No, he's not. He can't accept every invitation, and he thought I'd be better for that than the legalists or Raynaad. Before long, you'll be representing him in some fashion. It sounds interesting. It's not. When any of us stand in for him, he tells the one who'll be the stand-in what he wants said, and then we have to put it in our own words, and he has to approve it."

"When are you doing that?"

"A week from Tridi, but he wants to hear what I'm going to say tomorrow morning."

"What if I rough-draft the provisions for the position descriptions, and then you change anything that I've missed or made an error on before we submit anything to Macri?"

"That would be good."

Karola walked from Ysella's table desk to Dekkard's and set the envelope down. "He wants something by the end of the day tomorrow."

Dekkard glanced at Ysella and shook his head. "I should have known." He grinned. "And don't tell me that I've been here long enough to have expected it."

Ysella was about to reply when the office door opened and Councilor Saarh appeared, followed by Eljaan and Maarkham. The two security types stopped short of Karola's desk.

Karola had barely announced Saarh when the councilor moved past her and into Obreduur's office, closing the door firmly, and leaving Eljaan and Maarkham right outside.

Dekkard glanced to Ysella and raised his eyebrows in inquiry. In return she shook her head. Then Dekkard looked at Karola, who appeared distracted, her eyes going to Eljaan and then to Ysella, and back to Eljaan, suggesting to Dekkard that emping was taking place.

Less than a sixth passed before Saarh walked out, his face impassive. None of the three said anything as they departed.

While Dekkard was definitely no empie, it wouldn't have taken one to see that Saarh was concerned about something. Dekkard looked to Ysella.

She merely mouthed the single word "Later."

He nodded and extracted the papers from the large envelope and began to read the first position description—that of an entry Sanitation shovelman. He hadn't even finished reading the first page when Macri returned.

"Did Councilor Saarh just leave?"

"He did," replied Karola.

"Then he wasn't here very long. I saw him in the corridor. He didn't look pleased."

"He looked a bit drawn when he left," Dekkard said mildly.

"That's not surprising." Macri eased closer to Dekkard's desk, glanced around, then lowered his voice. "The word is that Freust didn't die of heart failure. His heart was as tough as an ox's."

"The newssheets said . . ."

"It had to be poison. He was at his estate south of Khuld, hosting a reception. His empie was with him at the time, and another empie was within yards. Neither sensed anything resembling an empath attack."

"How do you know that?"

"I just do . . . leave it at that. If he didn't die of an emp attack and it wasn't heart failure, what else could have caused him to collapse in front of his guests? Word is that he was talking to another Landor councilor when he swallowed several times, then just went down, like he'd been needled with frog poison."

"Then why did the newssheets write that it was a heart ailment?"

"Do you really think the editors of *Gestirn* are going

to print that he might have been poisoned because he was trying to gather enough votes to get the Council to look deeper into the Kraffeist scandal? Remember . . . that was before anything came out in the newssheets and when Eastern Ironway had been able to keep it quiet. And there certainly wasn't much mention of his death, especially in the *Tribune.*" Macri paused. "Well, maybe three lines noting he died."

"But even some Commerce councilors are asking for a formal inquiry."

"Now that they don't have any choice. The last thing they want is a scandal big enough to get the Imperador to call new elections. It's meaningless battology. They won't do more because of corporacion chantage," muttered Macri, looking toward the door to Obreduur's inner office. "Think about it. I'll see you tomorrow." With that, the legalist turned and headed back toward the larger office.

After several moments, Ysella looked inquiringly at Dekkard.

"Later."

In turn, she nodded.

"Later" turned out to be well past the first bell of night on the small terrace behind the garage that was tacitly granted to the Obreduurs' staff, just after Dekkard had finished his walk and evening workout, which included practice with the throwing knives, less conventional weapons often disregarded by many. But the knives were legal, and Dekkard saw no point in not having another option.

"It's later now," said Ysella. "I heard some of what Macri said to you . . ."

"What do you think about it?"

"I told you earlier that I thought Freust's death was . . . unusual. But that suggests some of the Commercers—possibly some at Eastern Ironway—are more worried about the leasing scandal than anyone thought."

"What about Saarh? Was he as upset as I thought he was?"

"He was more agitated than he showed," replied Ysella.

"And Eljaan? He never said a word to you."

"That was because he was shielding . . . throwing up spurious feelings. Didn't you see how confused Karola was?"

Dekkard nodded.

"That was also to keep her from overhearing what Saarh was saying to Obreduur."

"Macri seems to think it has something to do with the Kraffeist Affair."

"Ivann tends to believe in the conspiracy of the moment. This time he might be right, especially if the Imperador decides to dissolve the present Council and call for new elections."

"Just because of the Kraffeist Affair?" Dekkard frowned. "Or . . . with coal prices increasing, that means gas prices are going up and everything else as well . . . and with the Minister of Public Resources giving cheap coal to Eastern Ironway . . ."

"Exactly. The Commercers don't want to lose enough seats to give the Landors more say over who the Commercers present as the next premier. The Landors might even have proposed Freust as the price of their support, especially if the Craft Party gains a few more seats."

That didn't strike Dekkard as totally improbable, given that the Commercers only held two more seats than the Crafters. But even if the Crafters gained more seats, they couldn't name the next premier, since, under the Great Charter, no party was allowed more than thirty seats out of the sixty-six, and there weren't that many Landors or Commercers who would vote for a Crafter as premier, but he only said, "But why would Saarh . . . ?"

"Landors hate owing anyone, and Saarh owes Obreduur. Have you forgotten Obreduur's patron guild? Or whose wife likely inherited cherry orchards?"

"Oh . . . Saarh ships his export wines to Sudaen on the Khulor River barges." Dekkard could see the problems

Saarh faced if he angered Obreduur. The Stevedores Guild could "accidently" misplace or drop barrels, or cases of vintages already bottled, and if Saarh went to rail transport the breakage would still be high and the costs would increase. In addition, stevedores and other guild members and friends would make a greater effort against Saarh if an election were to be called. Then, too, Ysella had essentially confirmed Dekkard's suspicion about whose cherry orchards might resolve the standoff between the Woodcrafters Guild and Guldoran Ironway . . . and net Saarh a handsome number of marks.

"But the Imperador hasn't decreed dissolution yet."

"He'd rather not. Not with the success Obreduur has had in increasing the number of Crafters in the Council. He'd prefer to work with the Commercers and not to anger the corporacions. He may not have a choice."

"What do you think will happen?" asked Dekkard.

Ysella shrugged. "I have no idea."

Neither did Dekkard. He did know that he wouldn't have wanted to be in Saarh's position.

9

As he drove Obreduur and Ysella to the Council Office Building on Duadi, Dekkard was still thinking over what he'd learned the previous day. He had no doubt that if Premier Grieg and Minister Kraffeist had been Crafters, or even Landors, the Imperador would already have dissolved the present Council.

The other thing that bothered him was how much information wasn't appearing in the newssheets, not just about Freust's death and about the Kraffeist Affair, but in other incidents he'd observed over the past year, and that censorship seemed to him to exceed the provisions of the Great Charter.

As he eased the Gresynt up to the west entrance to

the Council Office Building, he pushed that thought away, concentrating on getting the steamer as close to the doors as possible. Then, after Ysella and Obreduur were safely inside the building, he drove to the parking area, shut down the steamer, and made a quick check, especially of the fittings on the tubing from the acetylene tank to the headlamps, because those tended to loosen, despite all the advertising claims of the manufacturer.

He'd just straightened up when another figure in gray stopped a yard away. "Steffan . . . fancy seeing you here."

Dekkard immediately recognized Amelya Detauran, one of the few female isolates working as a security staffer. But then, not only was she more muscular and in better condition than many of the older male isolates, but she also worked for Kaliara Bassaana, one of the few female Commerce councilors, and a major shareholder of a number of concerns in the north of Guldor, including Jaykarh Mining & Coal.

"I thought you'd never talk to me again, except as necessary," Dekkard replied lightly, recalling all too well the not-quite-acrimonious discussion they'd had over a lunch in the staff cafeteria.

"I'd like to apologize."

"You don't have to. I was a little sharp."

"You had a right to be. I didn't." Detauran paused. "Your mother . . . I discovered . . . she's considered one of the best portraitists in Oersynt, I found out. She just did the wedding portrait for my youngest sister. Her husband insisted on the best." The older isolate offered a smile both apologetic and wry. "So I figured you just might know a little about art. Besides, life's too short."

"I'm beginning to discover that. How are things going with you and Councilor Bassaana?"

"About the same as always. I heard that you got called into a meeting about cabinetry for the ironway."

"I did. How did you find out?"

"Director Deron is a friend of the councilor's family. She asked me if I knew you."

"And you want to know . . . ?"

"Not a thing. Kaliara respects your councilor, and she's not exactly fond of Eastern Ironway."

"Because of the Kraffeist mess . . . or does it go further back?"

Detauran smiled. "Steffan . . . *everything* goes further back."

Dekkard laughed. "I'd have to agree, but you'd know better than me." He paused. "Thank you."

"The same to you. And I'd better hurry."

Dekkard gave the Gresynt a last glance, then headed for the Council Office Building, wondering about the not-so-chance encounter with Detauran. She clearly hadn't wanted anything, except to smooth things over and to let him know that Deron had told Bassaana about the problem between the Woodcrafters and Guldoran Ironway . . . and the implication that Bassaana wasn't getting involved with the Kraffeist Affair.

That was another thing he'd have to relay to Obreduur.

Once he reached his desk, he turned his attention to rewriting the position description and required qualifications for a Sanitation shovelman, as well as the requirements to be eligible for promotion. After that, he sorted his share of the letters and then began drafting responses, noting as he did that Ysella had been summoned into Obreduur's inner office, presumably to go over her talk to the women's committee of the Textile Millworkers Guild.

Ysella wasn't in with Obreduur more than two sixths, and as soon as she left the office, she walked to Dekkard's desk. "Have you finished your draft of Sanitation qualifications?"

He handed her the sheets.

She glanced at the first sheet. "In the old days, you could have been a scrivener."

"Let's hope what I've done is more than readable."

"I'm sure it will be." Ysella's tone was matter-of-fact, neither encouraging nor sardonic, and she walked back to her desk without saying more.

By noon, Dekkard had finished his drafts of responses to the latest letters and petitions. So he carried the stack into the side office and handed it to Margrit.

"You're getting faster."

"The stack was shorter today," he replied with a smile, before walking over to Roostof's corner desk.

The junior legalist looked up. "You have a question?"

"I do. On censorship. It seems to me that there's a lot that's being withheld from the newssheets. On what basis?"

"There is, and it's an extension of the section of the Great Charter that prohibits the publication of certain information, particularly the voting records of individual councilors."

Dekkard frowned. He knew, as did everyone who followed politics, that the tallies of voting on proposals were recorded, but not by the names of councilors, only by party. In fact, not even the party floor leaders knew the individual votes, because each councilor placed one of two ceramic plaques in the voting box through shielded slots. Each plaque was colored on all sides except one with the color of the party—blue for Landor, red for Crafter, and silver for Commerce—while the remaining side was either light green for approval or black for disapproval. The plaques were tallied by all three floor leaders together. The system had been designed so that enfranchised voters voted on the basis of party, as well as to discourage individual political demagoguery. The one change from the Great Charter had been the result of the Silent Revolution of 1170–71, when the definition of an enfranchised voter had been changed to include employed women, and a husband and wife, if one was employed.

"How in the world does the prohibition of printing

voting records justify not printing information about Eastern Ironway's illegal coal leases?"

Roostof grinned sardonically. "Ivann and I have raised the same question. The official answer is that revealing a specific act of a government minister subjects that minister to public pressure which is equivalent—"

"That's absurd." Dekkard managed to keep his voice down. "Newssheet reporters can report on debates on the Council floor and on the vote totals. They certainly could at least report that the Ministry of Public Resources had granted illegal coal leases."

"You think so. I think so, but right now the Commercers don't think so, and they control Security and the Ministry of Public Resources."

"Where did all of this come from?" asked Dekkard. "I mean, it's in the Great Charter, but where did it really come from?"

"Probably from the Fall of the Grand Democracy of Teknold." Roostof's voice was dry. "That's the common explanation. It's also the most convenient. And the prohibitions largely work in the original sense, as applied to councilors' votes." He offered a wry smile.

Dekkard understood why, since any newsie attributing an individual vote to a given councilor or circulating such a record in any fashion faced a possible sentence of exile to somewhere in Medarck or Sargasso, if not worse. "That doesn't explain why Laureous insisted, or why the Great Charter just states that personal and individual accountability for a vote is the first step to anarchy and civil disharmony."

"That's all you'll find anywhere. There's no record of why that provision was included in the Charter. But it was likely inspired by what purportedly happened in Teknold. I can give you the short version. The long one would take more time than the councilor would appreciate, and it wouldn't add much."

"Go on," said Dekkard cheerfully.

"Teknold was really the first world industrial power. Back then, the Teknolds had the first steam engines and distributed water power. There was a huge uproar when the army high command discovered that more than half the senators—they were the equivalent of our councilors—were taking enormous bribes from both the Illuminati Primate and from the wealthiest Landors. That led to the Coup of the Marshals, and in turn to the New Reform, which established new rules for electing senators. Any male citizen who owned property could vote. So could his wife or his widow."

"They were the first—"

"Exactly, but what happened was that, since everyone could vote, people began to vote for those senators who promised the most to the people. But the senators who did that didn't dare raise taxes or tariffs, because the workers wouldn't vote for them, and Landors would find ways to remove any Senator who wanted to increase taxes on the wealthy. Before long, the roads needed repairs, and the canals fell into disrepair. But the party leaders could do nothing because the people kept electing those who promised the most without taxing them more. It took a century, but the Empire of the Light disintegrated into warring provinces. Look at the continent of Sudlynd now. What's left of Teknold is a loose confederacy of squabbling lands, surrounding by even more fragmented countries governed by tyrants, dictators, or warlords.

"Laureous the Great didn't want that to happen. That's why the Great Charter was drafted the way it was and why councilors are prohibited from publicly discussing how they voted as individuals. Only a political party can claim credit. Or be blamed," added Roostof sardonically. "No one talks about it, but it just might be why there are only three political parties and why no party can hold an absolute majority of councilors."

"And by what legal theory does all that allow them to keep news stories from being printed?"

"No legal theory, just nearly sixty years of unbroken Commercer control of government . . . and the Security Ministry."

Dekkard couldn't argue against that. "Thank you."

"Just keep speculations about the way individual councilors vote to yourself, or at least not in public. That way, you won't have the Ministry of Security asking questions about you."

Dekkard raised his eyebrows in inquiry.

"Where do you think the custom that no one writes or talks publicly about how an individual councilor votes came from?"

Dekkard had always been told that was something that just wasn't done, and certainly his security training had emphasized that, including the fact that talking politically, especially in public, about a given councilor by name was considered impolite, if not subversive. It had just been one of those things good people didn't do. Ever. *Except behind firmly closed doors and windows.*

Roostof laughed softly. "It's become such a custom that only real troublemakers are exiled. Most people who err don't need a second warning. The only ones who do are newsies who think that people should know everything about anything, but the News Services Guild keeps most of them straight."

Dekkard could see all that, but he had to wonder why he'd had no idea about the basis for the custom. Because his parents had been immigrants? Or because no one else talked in public about how councilors might vote as individuals? Or because the newssheets couldn't print anything along those lines?

He was still mulling that over when he reached his desk and sat down. He didn't even see Ysella approaching.

"You did a good job on the Sanitation position descriptions," she said, setting several sheets on Dekkard's desk. "I've made some changes to what you wrote, mostly small additions and one clarification. If you'd read through them again and tell me what you think."

Since Ysella remained standing in front of his desk, Dekkard picked up the sheets and began to read. When he finished, he looked up. "What you did improved it. I don't have any other suggestions."

"Then we should give it to the councilor. He said he wanted it before we left today."

Dekkard looked to Karola. "Would you ask if he'll see us now about the Sanitation matter?"

"Of course." Karola rapped gently on the door, then entered the inner office, emerging almost immediately. "Go right in."

Dekkard rose, the papers in his hand, and followed Ysella into the inner office, closing the door. He offered the papers.

Obreduur took them and motioned for the two to sit down. He said nothing as he began to read. When he finished he looked up and said pleasantly, "This will do the job quite effectively. Draft a letter to Guildmeister Hadenaur telling him that we've received the materials and are working on the matter. Have Ivann go over the language to make sure all the legalities are met. After he's signed off on that, draft a letter to Minister Sanoffre enclosing the proposed changes to the job descriptions. I'd like all of that as soon as possible. Tell Ivann that as well."

"Yes, sir."

"That's all," said Obreduur.

As soon as the two were back in the outer office, Ysella looked at Dekkard. "Do you want to tell Ivann?"

"I'd be happy to." That way, Dekkard knew, Ysella wouldn't have to weather the legalist's emotional reaction to having a rush item dropped on him.

But when Dekkard approached Macri, the older man smiled wryly. "Another immediate action?"

"The councilor wants you to go over the wording in these two Sanitation job descriptions to make sure they're in accord with the law and existing regulations. He said to tell you that he wants to send them to Health and Education Minister Sanoffre as soon as possible." Dekkard handed the papers to Macri.

The legalist took them. "I can do that. Sanoffre won't be nearly that obliging, but it will keep Hadenaur from pressing the councilor."

"You've done work on behalf of the guildmeister before?"

"Yes. Not recently, though. He's easier than many." Macri paused. "I couldn't help but overhear some of what you asked Roostof. I'd emphasize that you don't want to talk about the possible votes of individual councilors except within the office or with people you can trust absolutely."

"Thank you."

"I thought you should know. Most isolates remain strictly security types. They never even deal with petitions and legislation. Councilor Obreduur's always been a bit different, but you and Ysella didn't go through the Council's professional or clerical training classes."

"What else don't I know, then?"

Macri smiled again. "You've already learned all the rest. It's mostly common sense."

As Dekkard walked back to his desk and sat down, he couldn't help frowning. At the same time, he realized that, if the newssheets never mentioned how a councilor might vote or might have voted, but only how the parties voted, most people wouldn't ask. *But some would, wouldn't they?*

Except that Dekkard had never seen a newssheet article that mentioned how a councilor voted, now that he thought about it.

Somehow, Macri finished his review, and Dekkard managed to have a letter to Minister Sanoffre typed and presented to Obreduur before the end of the day. Whether or not the councilor signed that version or had Margrit or Anna type a corrected version Dekkard didn't know . . . only that he'd done the best he could in the time allowed.

By the time Dekkard got back to the house that night and had eaten a quick dinner, he was more than ready for a walk, not just for the exercise, but also to have some time to think.

Rather than head west on Altarama, Dekkard left the pedestrian gate heading east toward the East Quarter

Trinitarian Chapel. As he walked past the neighboring mansion, a small steamer glided out of sight, heading north on the narrow cross street. In the dim light, Dekkard couldn't tell the steamer's make, but from its size and general shape, it had to be either a Realto or a Ferrum, although Dekkard would have been mildly surprised to see a Ferrum in the East Quarter area, given that Ferrums, durable as they were, offered the minimum in comfort and even less in prestige. Also, anyone who might be looking would notice how out of place a Ferrum was.

Dekkard kept walking, and before long he saw the white headlamps of an oncoming and very slow-moving steamer, as if whoever was in the vehicle was unsure of his destination or looking for something in particular. Because Dekkard was curious, and wary, given that anyone traveling Altarama after dark should have known where they were going, he watched carefully as the steamer approached—a gray Realto—but the vehicle immediately sped up as it neared, veering even closer to the sidewalk and causing Dekkard to jump back, almost against the brick wall enclosing the grounds of the house to his left. Out of caution, and possibly training, he kept moving toward the nearest tree.

With the sound of what he thought were shots, he scrambled behind the tree trunk, keeping as low as he could as two more shots rang out, seemingly aimed in his direction and sounding strangely loud in the quiet of the night.

Then, far more quickly than it had arrived, the Realto accelerated down Altarama toward Imperial Boulevard, leaving Dekkard behind the tree. He slowly stood, trying to see if the shooter had indeed departed with the steamer. After a time, satisfied that he was once more alone on the street, Dekkard inspected the tree trunk, where he found a new gouge in the smooth bark, as if a bullet had grazed the tree, but Dekkard wasn't about to search for it in the dark.

Had the shots been directed at him personally or

simply because those in the Realto had been up to something unsavory and had fired to keep him from observing more closely? Since firearms were prohibited to all except certain military units and security forces, and all but the deadliest of criminal types shied away from using them, the implications of such use in East Quarter were disturbing, to say the least.

He headed back to the house, taking a deep breath. Obreduur would have to know.

When Dekkard stepped inside, he could hear Ritten Obreduur playing the pianoforte in the music room. He walked on to find the councilor in his study.

Obreduur looked up from the papers on his desk. "Can whatever it is wait?"

"It would be best if it didn't, sir."

"Then make it quick, if you would." Obreduur did not motion for Dekkard to enter or to sit down.

Dekkard took several steps into the study, a chamber that contained only one small bookcase besides the desk and several chairs, including a comfortable-looking leather reading chair positioned so that the gas lamp in the wall sconce would provide adequate illumination. "Simply put, sir, when I left on my evening walk . . ." Dekkard went on to describe what had happened, ending with, "I thought you should know."

"You're all right, I take it?"

"Yes, sir."

"Good." The councilor frowned. "I didn't hear any shots, but Ingrella's been playing for nearly a bell, and part of that was the *Silver and Black* Overture. Did you see the shooter?"

"There were two people in the front of the Realto, but I was looking into the headlamps, I couldn't make out much more than that."

"Disturbing as this is, there's little point in reporting it to the patrol. There's no evidence, and no one was hurt, for which I'm very glad. I would appreciate it if you'd pass this on to Ysella, and no one else in the house."

"Do you think it could have been Security agents, sir?"

Obreduur frowned. "I'd say it's improbable. It could have been a case of mistaken identity on the part of private operatives."

"Private operatives?"

"Former Security agents who operate outside the law. They do exist, but at the moment, I can't see why they'd be after you." Obreduur paused and smiled wryly. "Still . . . on future walks, you might be a bit more cautious."

"I'd thought that as well, sir. That's all I had, but I thought you should know. Oh . . . and one thing more. Councilor Bassaana's isolate passed on to me that Director Deron had mentioned the Guldoran Ironway to Councilor Bassaana . . . and that Bassaana wasn't exactly fond of Eastern Ironway."

"I appreciate your informing me . . . about both. And . . . you and Ysella did a very good job on the Sanitation job descriptions. Now . . ."

"Yes, sir." Dekkard inclined his head, then turned, and headed back to the staff room.

Ysella wasn't there, and since, when he went up the rear staircase, her door was closed, he decided he'd tell her about the incident in the morning.

He'd heard rumors of private operatives, but hearing about them . . . and encountering them . . . were two different matters. But, like Obreduur, he couldn't imagine why anyone would shoot at him.

10

On Tridi morning, rather than immediately going into the staff room to eat, Dekkard waited at the bottom of the staff staircase for Ysella.

Even before she reached the last step, he said, "I need a word with you."

For a moment, Ysella frowned, then said, "What happened?"

Rather than ask how she came to that immediate conclusion, Dekkard quickly recounted what had occurred the night before, including his meeting with Obreduur, adding, "I would have told you last night, but by the time I told Obreduur, I thought you might be sleeping—"

"Or possibly in a state of less than full attire?"

Dekkard caught a glimpse of a mischievous smile, but before he could think of an appropriate reply, Ysella added in a lower voice, "Or worse?"

"I hadn't thought that, but the next time I most likely will." Dekkard didn't try to keep the amused chagrin out of his voice.

"Excellent. You're actually loosening up, Steffan."

"Thank you. How long did it take you?" he asked warmly, but cheerfully.

Ysella actually blushed and didn't quite meet his eyes for a moment before replying, "Longer than it's taken you."

Dekkard smiled, but only for a moment, before asking, "What do you make of last night?"

"Obreduur's likely right about the shooters being private operatives. Whoever sent the men in the Realto is playing for high stakes. I'd like to think that it might not involve Obreduur, but I'm afraid it must. Very few people know you take walks at night, yet it appears the shooter did."

"Could it be connected to the Kraffeist Affair . . . and the possibility that the Imperador might call new elections?"

"It might be, but it's still a huge gamble for whoever sent the shooter . . ." Ysella paused, then said, "Unless they weren't really after you, but sending a message to Obreduur."

"What message?"

"Some sort of warning . . . or for him not to press for new elections . . . although that's really up to the

Imperador. Besides, the Premier still hasn't removed Minister Kraffeist. The Imperador could just admonish Premier Grieg and insist on the removal of Kraffeist . . . or he could ask him to resign without prejudice. That would allow another Commercer to succeed him."

"In any event," said Dekkard, knowing that he needed to think over the matter more, "we'd better get breakfast."

"Which will only take you a few minutes to inhale, quince paste and all."

Dekkard shook his head, then motioned for her to lead the way into the staff room, where they joined Rhosali at the table.

Dekkard hadn't taken more than one bite of his first quince-paste-stuffed croissant when, even in the staff room, he heard the clang of the door chime and the thump of the heavy brass knocker on the front door.

"Who could it be this early in the morning?" exclaimed Rhosali as she burst from her chair and hurried toward the front door to deal with the caller.

"Calling this early is positively indecent," declared Hyelda from the kitchen.

When Rhosali did return, if not immediately, Hyelda, Ysella, and Dekkard all looked at her, but Hyelda spoke first. "Who was it this early?"

"It was a government messenger with a missive for the councilor. Wouldn't let me take it. I had to get Ritter Obreduur."

"A government messenger?" asked Hyelda. "You're sure?"

"Who else wears gray trimmed in crimson with that funny hat that points backward and forward?"

"That's not a Council messenger. That's a Palace messenger." Ysella glanced at Dekkard.

"For the Palace to send a message this early . . . it has to be important," added Dekkard. "Do you think the Imperador dissolved this Council and is calling for new elections?"

"We'll find out before long," replied Ysella. "It might be soon. So you might finish all that sour-sweet quince." The hint of a smile crossed her face.

"I'll finish it long before you can get through that third mug of café."

"Just two this morning."

Dekkard didn't gulp down the remainder of his breakfast, but he didn't dawdle, either. He left the staff room before Ysella, readied himself, and then went to get the Gresynt.

Obreduur entered the steamer without a word, but once Dekkard had the Gresynt on Altarama headed for Imperial Boulevard, he said, "You both doubtless know there was a dispatch from the Palace this morning."

"Yes, sir," replied Ysella. "Rhosali told us about the messenger."

"I'm certain she did. The Imperador has decided not to dissolve the Council. Not at present. He has dismissed Premier Grieg, and requested that the Council choose a successor. He gave no reason for his action."

"Is that usual, sir?" asked Dekkard.

"It is customary to offer perfunctory thanks or a broad reason that could mean anything. The lack of either suggests that he was not pleased with Grieg."

"Why didn't the Premier dismiss Minister Kraffeist?" asked Ysella.

"He said that there was no evidence that Kraffeist knew anything about the improper lease. That was about the worst thing he could have said. For the moment, you should keep that to yourselves."

"Yes, sir," replied Dekkard and Ysella, not quite simultaneously.

Dekkard could see why Grieg's statement had been a mistake. What he couldn't see was why Grieg hadn't understood that . . . unless . . . *Unless he wanted to be dismissed.*

Obreduur retreated into reading a sheaf of papers, most likely drafted by Macri, and Dekkard concentrated on driving, taking special care to see if anyone might be following them, but during the entire drive to the Council Office Building, he saw no sign of that.

The rest of the day was surprisingly uneventful, except for two sets of visitors, one of whom was Sr. Hoddard Caarthart, whose name Dekkard recognized because he was perhaps the most noted legalist in Oersynt, and one Althord Styphen, whose name and profession were unknown to Dekkard, but clearly not to Obreduur. Even so, Dekkard actually got to have a quick lunch in the staff dining room, where he briefly greeted Jaime Minz and had a few words with several other staffers he knew before he returned to the office so that Ysella could eat.

No one in the dining room or the office said a word about the Imperador's dismissal of the Premier, although Dekkard suspected that everyone knew and thought everyone else did—and didn't want to speculate on what might happen next. In the meantime, Dekkard did get caught up on letter and petition responses by the time he left to go to the Council covered parking.

On the drive home, Obreduur was absorbed in the contents of a large leather folder, so much so that he said nothing, even when he and Ysella stepped out of the Gresynt at the side portico of the house.

Ysella was waiting for Dekkard as he left the garage. "So far no one's saying anything."

"It's almost as if the resignation didn't happen," said Dekkard.

"No one wants to say anything until the Commercers choose someone to put up as premier. They may be having trouble finding a candidate who's willing to step into the mess."

"Why did the Imperador send a messenger to Obreduur? He's not the Craft floor leader." Dekkard paused, then asked, "Because he's the political leader? Was sending that information a way of telling the councilor that there will possibly be an election called before long?"

"That or a hint that whether he does call an election depends on what the Council does about the Kraffeist Affair," replied Ysella. "Those are my guesses."

"Does the Imperador want a real investigation . . . or a politically tactful resolution?"

"Why do you think he can't have both?" asked Ysella, in an amused tone.

"Do you really think he can?" countered Dekkard.

"Not any more than you do."

As the two walked toward the staff room, thoughts circled through Dekkard's mind.

Did the Imperador's dismissal of Premier Grieg have anything to do with the shots of the previous evening? While he didn't see the connection, he doubted that the shots were fired at random, although that possibility definitely existed. He also had the feeling that while matters might seem obvious in retrospect, they certainly weren't at the moment.

11

In a surprising move revealed yesterday morning, Imperador Laureous asked for and received the resignation of Johan Grieg, not only as Premier, but also as a Councilor. The reason for the Imperador's request was not given, but is considered likely because of Grieg's failure to remedy matters that led to the so-called Kraffeist Affair.

At present, the Commerce Party caucus has not indicated who it will put forward as a candidate to replace Sr. Grieg as premier . . .

The other development of great interest is that, because Grieg resigned at the request of the Imperador, his replacement cannot be named by the Commerce Party, but must be one of the candidates who stood against him in the last election. Based on the election results, that replacement Councilor must come from the Craft

Party. While the Commerce Party will have the same number of seats as the Craft Party, each with twenty-four, followed by the Landor Party with eighteen, it is likely that enough Landor Councilors will support the Commerce candidate . . .

Several individuals with signs appeared in the Square of Heroes in front of the gates to the Imperial Palace late yesterday afternoon, but were quickly dispersed. The reason for the public display is not known, but those believed to be behind the disruption were detained and questioned by Security patrollers before being released. Several were thought to be University students. Once the individuals left the square, several were reportedly also detained and questioned by Security patrollers. The Palace has issued no statement on the matter . . .

Gestirn, **22 Springend 1266**

12

When Dekkard eased the Gresynt away from the portico and down the drive on Furdi morning, he could see heavy greenish-gray clouds to the south, out over the ocean, but even if the clouds were moving north, rain wouldn't arrive until long after he'd reached the Council Office Building.

Halfway there, when Obreduur offered no more information on the choice of a new premier, Dekkard asked, "Sir, do you think the Commercers have decided not to put up a candidate for premier to force the Imperador to call new elections?"

Obreduur laughed, a sound harsh rather than amused. "The last thing they want right now is new elections. They're trying to decide on the best candidate to preclude elections."

"Who might that be?" asked Ysella.

"I can't say, Avraal. We'll have to see what the day brings." With that, Obreduur returned to reading the top sheet on the stack of papers he'd set on his brown leather folder.

Dekkard couldn't discern any vehicle following them, but, when he turned off Imperial Boulevard and onto Council Avenue, he did note two gray Realto steamers parked on each side of the avenue. "Sir, there are two gray Realto steamers parked at the intersection, one on each side. Each has at least two men inside."

"Thank you, Steffan. I'm not surprised. Avraal, have you felt anything?"

"Nothing out of the ordinary, sir."

"Good."

A half score of Council Guards in their pale green uniforms, far more than usual, stood at posts around the entrance to the Council Office Building when Dekkard dropped off Ysella and Obreduur, and another half score guarded the covered parking, several of whom studied Dekkard closely as he drove to Obreduur's assigned spot.

Once Dekkard entered the Council Office Building, he glanced around, hoping to see someone he knew well enough to ask if they knew anything, but he saw no one he knew, if only by name. So he took the staff staircase and made his way to the office.

"Good morning," said Karola cheerfully.

"Good morning to you," he replied with a wry grin, and then looking to Ysella, he added, "and to you once more." After those words, he went to Ysella's table desk, bent down and murmured, "Is he more concerned than usual?"

She just nodded, if barely, saying immediately, "The petitions and letters haven't arrived yet this morning."

"The Council Guards are sorting through the packages and large envelopes," explained Karola. "There was some sort of threat against the Council. No one is saying what it was or who made it."

"Could it have been made by the same group that

demonstrated outside the Palace yesterday?" asked Dekkard.

"It could be one of the radical groups like the New Meritorists," said Ysella, "or the new one, something like Foothill Freedom." She frowned. "They want independence for what used to be the old freehold of Jaykarh."

"I've never heard of either," said Dekkard, although he knew the original Meritorists had vanished decades earlier.

"Do you really think Security would allow anything in print about it?"

"Probably not," agreed Dekkard.

At that moment, the belated arrival of the morning's post deliveries put an end to speculation, and before long Dekkard was busy reading and sorting letters and petitions.

Just before the third bell of morning, a Council messenger arrived with a missive, and Karola immediately gave it to Obreduur. In moments, he stepped into the outer office and motioned to Ysella and Dekkard.

"I'll need escorts to the Council Hall. We'll need to go now."

Once the three were out in the main corridor, Obreduur said, "The Commerce floor leader will announce the Commerce candidate at fourth bell. It will be followed by debate, of the meaningless sort so dear to those who relish their title of Ritter, and a vote will be taken today . . . but it will be late. You two will return to the office—there's no sense in your waiting. Just return for me when you hear the chimes for adjournment. If I need you sooner, I'll send a messenger." Obreduur paused to allow a graying councilor and his two security aides to precede him down the steps to the main level.

Dekkard belatedly recognized Commerce Councilor Palafaux, whose primary patrons were shipyards and cargo lines, one of which was Siincleer Shipbuilding. The three followed Palafaux and his aides down the staircase and out through the east entrance and under the cov-

ered portico that ran through the Council gardens and
to the Council Hall.

Almost immediately, Dekkard's attention was caught
by the line of Council Guards—more than he'd ever
seen before—advancing beyond the central topiary garden toward a group of people in the grassy area short
of the southern hedge bounding the garden. All of the
individuals in front of the hedge wore deep blue shirts
and trousers.

True Blue . . . the color of the old-time Meritorists.

Some of the demonstrators, for that was what
Dekkard thought they must be, rested what looked to be
oblong shields on the stone walk, while the others stood
behind them holding signs. Dekkard couldn't make out
all the inscriptions on the signs, but the nearest one read,
PERSONAL ACCOUNTABILITY, NOT PARTY ACCOUNTABIL-
ITY. Another read, OPEN ALL VOTING RECORDS. A third
read, PERSONAL REPRESENTATIVES, NOT PARTY HACKS.
One near the back read, JOBS BY ABILITY, NOT PARTY.

Obreduur snorted. "They're either corporacion shills
or idiots. If every vote of every councilor is made public, it's that much easier for corporacions to buy specific
councilors or to oppose others, and it will only open the
Council to mob rule. Guldor doesn't need that."

Under the law, Dekkard knew, candidates for councilor could not use or accept funds to campaign for office. Only the three political parties could spend marks
on electioneering, and firm rules governed how parties
could spend those. Even so, there were definitely ways
around the laws. *There always are.*

Dekkard's eyes went back to the south side of the
Council grounds, where the Council Guards advanced
slowly, if inexorably, and Dekkard realized that all of
them wore some sort of body armor. About half of them
carried iron-tipped singlesticks. The other half had their
long black truncheons out. At least none had their revolvers in hand.

Obreduur began to walk even more quickly, moving

at a fast walk close to a slow run, suggesting to Dekkard that the councilor wanted to reach the Council Hall before the Council Guards reached the demonstrators. Ahead of them, Palafaux and his aides were also hurrying.

The three were well past the fountain in the middle of the grounds and were nearing the walled area short of the west entry to the Council Hall when several shots echoed through the gardens, shots that didn't sound as loud as if they had come from the revolvers of Council Guards. Obreduur broke into a run, as did Ysella and Dekkard, and in moments, all three were behind the wall leading to the entrance.

Behind them, more shots rang out, and most of those were the louder reports from the revolvers of the Council Guards. Dekkard wasn't about to look back to see what was happening. Their job was to get Obreduur safely inside the Council Hall.

Ahead of them, one of the duty guards pulled open the heavy bronze door. "Inside, Councilor!"

Once the three were inside, Obreduur immediately looked to Ysella. "Was anyone killed?"

"I couldn't say, sir. From the emotional blasts, several people had to have been wounded, but whether the wounds were fatal I couldn't tell."

"From what you felt," pursued Obreduur, continuing to walk toward the councilors' lobby, "could any of the shots have been fatal?"

"One of them certainly could have been. And the shooting was continuing."

"I hope the guards gave those ungrateful and shortsighted hotheads what they deserved."

Given Obreduur's irritated tone and disgusted expression, Dekkard decided not to mention the details of what he'd observed, not until he'd had a moment to speak with Ysella.

Obreduur stopped short of the guarded doorway into the councilors' lobby. "You should remain here until the Council Guards have cleared the grounds."

Then Obreduur walked past the guards and through the open door to the councilors' lobby. Dekkard and Ysella stepped back, then turned and crossed the hallway to the staff waiting area, which was largely filled, mostly with security aides. Ysella pointed to two chairs against the wall, well away from any others, and the two seated themselves.

"Did you read any of those signs?" asked Dekkard.

"No. You were closer." Ysella's tone wasn't quite dismissive.

"I was talking to Roostof and Macri about the prohibition on public information on how individual councilors voted the other day." Dekkard kept his voice low. "That's clearly what those signs were advocating. One of them said, 'Open All Voting Records.'"

"They're rebels who want to destroy a system that's worked well for some four hundred years. No other government in the world has lasted that long, and there's a reason for it."

"There's also a problem with their demand," Dekkard pointed out. "Voting records by councilor don't even exist."

"Of course they don't. That's the point. If they kept records, then someone would have found out years ago. You can't find out what doesn't exist."

That's also why, when new elections are called, the two most senior councilors from each party, excepting the floor leader and the deputy floor leader, cannot stand for reelection. Which meant that with the continual turnover of councilors through elections, only six people really had any idea of how the councilors in their party might have voted.

"I saw one sign that demanded jobs by ability, not party. Markell hinted at that."

"That's a real problem, especially since more university graduates aren't from Landor or Commercer families. But . . . now."

". . . isn't the time or place." Dekkard understood. "Have you heard from Emrelda?"

"I got a note from her yesterday. She said that she enjoyed meeting you. She also hoped that she and Markell would have a chance to get to know you better."

Dekkard laughed wryly. "The way you put that could be good or not so good."

"Probably both. Emrelda is very protective."

Dekkard almost said he doubted that Ysella needed much protection, except that wasn't the kind of protection the sisters were talking about. "You two have always been close, then?"

"Except for a few years when I was a brat."

"I'm afraid I was a bit like that to my sister as well. I thought I knew more than I did." Before Ysella could reply, he laughed softly and added, "I still do, unfortunately."

"You've gotten much better this past year." Ysella grinned, which surprised Dekkard.

Almost a bell passed before an officer of the Council Guards appeared and announced, "All the demonstrators have been removed. It's perfectly safe to return to the Council Office Building or to move around the Council complex."

"We should go," said Ysella, immediately standing.

Dekkard nodded. It would be several bells before a vote, and the work on his desk wouldn't get done in the Council Hall staff lobby.

13

On Quindi morning Dekkard stood in the archway between the kitchen and the staff room and riffled through the morning edition of *Gestirn* to see what the newssheet had written about the events of the previous day, since the vote had been late and Obreduur had volunteered very little, and that reluctantly.

As Dekkard read the front-page story, his eyes widened.

. . . following several bells of debate, the Council of Sixty-Six voted on a new Premier to succeed Johan Grieg, who resigned upon the request of the Imperador earlier this week. After three rounds of plaques, Oskaar Ulrich, the Councilor proposed by the Commerce Party, received thirty-four votes, the bare minimum. Of those votes, twenty-three came from Commerce Councilors, ten from Landor Councilors, and one from a Craft Councilor. The Craft vote was unexpected, since no Craft Councilor has voted for a Commerce Premier in several decades . . .

. . . is expected that the Imperador will meet with Premier-select Ulrich this afternoon to discuss matters pending before the Council . . . likely to include the so-called Kraffeist Affair . . .

Dekkard wondered not only which Commerce councilor had opposed Ulrich, but which Craft councilor had supported him . . . and why there was no story about the demonstration. Then he went through the entire newssheet once more. Finally, he found a short piece buried at the bottom of the fourteenth page, dwarfed by an advertisement for Oostermein's Sweet Oil.

A score of rowdy individuals appeared in the central gardens of the Imperial Council grounds on Furdi. Some bore signs advocating political changes in the nature of reporting voting results. When the demonstrators refused to leave the grounds, the Council Guards moved to usher them from the area. Several of the intruders illegally carried firearms and opened fire on the Guards, but the grounds were cleared shortly before noon. The extent and nature of injuries to the intruders and Council Guards is not known at this time, although early reports indicate that there was at least one fatality.

That's all? And nothing about jobs by ability and not politics? Dekkard frowned. Then he nodded. The newssheet had likely published what it thought it could, especially the fact that the demonstrators had fired first. Most interesting was the fact that *Gestirn* hadn't identified the group behind the demonstration.

Had the other daily—*The Machtarn Tribune*, often referred to as the "*Trib*" or "*Tribute*" because of its sussie-like fawning over anything Commercer—even printed anything about the Kraffeist Affair? If it had, it likely blamed everything on useless bureaucrats. Dekkard had no doubt that the *Tribune*'s article on the demonstration portrayed the demonstrators as "communalist scum" or something similar.

Another question struck him. Was personal accountability on the part of councilors for their votes that dangerous?

Certainly, Roostof, Macri, and Obreduur thought so. From the provisions of the Great Charter, Laureous the Great had definitely believed that. Yet, from what Dekkard recalled of history lessons, the Grand Democracy of Teknold had collapsed from rampant internal corruption. In the end, the poor and the workers had revolted, and the ensuing chaos had destroyed what had been the most powerful nation in the world, turning it into three separate moderate-sized states and a handful of smaller ones.

Somehow, Dekkard doubted either version. And he certainly had doubts that the prohibition on knowing how each councilor voted was all that had kept Guldor strong and prosperous for the past four centuries.

Of immediate concern to him was that the weapons of the demonstrators hadn't sounded as loud as those of the guards. That meant they had been using semi-automatic pistols. The guards outnumbered the demonstrators, but some semi-automatics had magazines that held nine or twelve cartridges, while the guard revolvers held but six. More important, the pistols could be reloaded more quickly, especially if the demonstrators carried loaded spare clips.

Beyond that was the equally disturbing question about the source of those weapons.

"You look rather preoccupied this morning."

Dekkard almost jumped as Ysella appeared at his shoulder. "I was reading about the selection of Councilor Ulrich as the new premier and this story about the demonstrators outside the Council Hall." He handed her the newssheet and pointed out the story well below the fold.

She read it and handed the newssheet back. "That's about what I would have expected."

"There's one aspect of the demonstration that *Gestirn* didn't cover. I'm fairly certain that the demonstrators used semi-automatic pistols."

Ysella frowned. "You weren't that close."

"They sound different."

"You didn't mention that to the councilor."

"You might recall that he was rather absorbed, and that he said anything that wasn't urgent could wait until this morning."

"I'd tell him once we're in the steamer. We should eat. He'll be impatient this morning."

Dekkard raised his eyebrows.

"There will be a party leadership meeting this morning, and one Craft councilor voted for Ulrich. Obreduur can't be looking forward to that."

"There's no way to tell who that was."

"Exactly," replied Ysella dryly.

Dekkard replaced the newssheet on the side table, and the two entered the staff room and immediately got their café. Hyelda had the staff platter on the table in moments, as if she knew they needed to hurry.

Dekkard looked to the cook. "Thank you, again, for letting us read your *Gestirn*. I do appreciate it."

"You're welcome, Steffan."

Neither Dekkard nor Ysella said more than pleasantries at breakfast, and he ate quickly and had the Gresynt ready at the portico early, but barely before Obreduur appeared.

Even so, Dekkard waited until he had the steamer headed west on Altarama before speaking. "Last night, sir, you said that anything that wasn't urgent could wait. I did notice something about those demonstrators. At least one of them was firing a semi-automatic pistol."

"How do you know that? You weren't that close."

"They sound different, and pistols have magazines that carry more cartridges and can be reloaded quickly. Also, so far as I know, the only forces that use semi-automatic pistols are the Naval Marines . . . and possibly Security agents or patrollers."

"Who else have you mentioned this to?"

"Just you and Avraal."

"Good. And thank you."

Dekkard *thought* he detected a slight tone of satisfaction in the councilor's voice. At least he didn't detect dissatisfaction. He glanced sideways at Ysella.

She offered the faintest of nods.

Obreduur concentrated on his papers. As on Furdi, there were more Council Guards around the Council Office Building and at the covered-parking gate.

Do they expect more demonstrators . . . or are they just being cautious?

As Dekkard walked from the Gresynt toward the west entrance, another security aide joined him—Laurenz Korriah, an imposing, if prematurely balding, figure.

"I heard that you were escorting your councilor to the Hall when the New Meritorists started shooting."

"Is that what they're called?"

"That's what the councilor said."

Dekkard nodded. Since Korriah worked for Kharl Navione, a Landor councilor who served on the Security Committee, Korriah's confirmation of the appellation of the demonstrators was doubtless correct. "What were they so upset about that they started shooting?"

Korriah laughed. "The councilor says it's about the prohibition on knowing how councilors vote. Me . . . I think it's because no one takes them seriously."

"At least one had a sign complaining that politics shouldn't determine jobs."

"Steffan . . . there are other requirements for some jobs besides academic brilliance. That's something that too many lower-class students will never understand. That's why it takes a generation or two for families to rise. Some of them get a degree and think they're immediately owed a higher-paying position. When they don't get it, they think the system's corrupt." Korriah shook his head.

"In any case," replied Dekkard, "they're in serious trouble now."

"The ones who survived," agreed Korriah. "The others don't have anything at all to worry about. Not now."

"How many guards were killed or wounded?"

"Premier-select Ulrich hasn't said."

"Hasn't . . . or won't."

"He can't keep that secret forever. Two were killed, but I didn't tell you."

"The Council Guards were wearing body armor, I thought."

"It doesn't cover your neck or face."

Then some of the demonstrators were either lucky or very good shots, but Dekkard only asked, "And the demonstrators?"

"More. How many more I don't know. For trash like that it doesn't matter."

"It might. At least one had a semi-automatic pistol, but you didn't hear it from me."

"Can I tell the councilor?"

"If you say that you overheard a conversation between several security aides and couldn't discern who said what."

"I appreciate that. Commercers don't tell the other committee members anything they can keep to themselves." Korriah paused. "Does anyone know which Crafter broke the deadlock . . . or why?"

This time Dekkard laughed, a touch of harshness in the sound. "I certainly don't." But he'd thought about it since breakfast and realized why a senior councilor who wasn't either the floor leader or the assistant floor leader might. *Because if the Imperador had to dissolve the Council and call for new elections, the two councilors in each party who were the most senior and not in leadership positions could not run for reelection.*

"But you know the possibilities," Korriah countered.

"Just as everyone does," said Dekkard easily. "And I'd wager that two of the ten Landors who voted for Ulrich were senior councilors not in the leadership or someone with a shaky seat." *Like Saarh.* But that was just a guess.

Korriah nodded. "Number-counting isn't proof, though."

"Isn't that why all votes are secret?"

"Secrecy is a knife that cuts both ways, Steffan."

"And so is openness. The question is which wound is more likely to be fatal."

Korriah offered a booming laugh. "You're quite the philosopher. That's not the best mindset for security. If you didn't think so deeply, I'd say you ought to think about becoming a legalist."

"I react as fast as anyone. The thinking comes later."

"That's fair." Korriah laughed again. "I'll see you later."

After the other had left, Dekkard frowned. Should he have told Korriah about the pistols? Then he shrugged. Sooner or later, probably sooner, Navione would find out, while the number of Council Guards killed, and the fact that quite a few more demonstrators had been fatally shot, might not emerge for some time.

He hurried across the approach drive to the Council Office Building and then inside, taking the staff staircase up to the second level and the office. Once there, he looked to Karola and asked, "Is anyone in with him?"

"No, sir."

"I need a moment."

"Just knock."

Dekkard knocked and announced himself.

"Come in, Steffan."

Dekkard had barely closed the door when Obreduur asked, "What is it?"

"I overheard an interesting conversation in the parking area. That's why I'm a little late. You might have heard this, but two Council Guards were killed by the demonstrators and quite a few more of the demonstrators were fatally shot."

"Do you believe what you 'overheard' to be accurate?" asked Obreduur evenly.

"I do."

"What did they 'overhear'?"

"Just that one of the demonstrators might have had a semi-automatic pistol. That's something that they'll know later today, in any event."

Obreduur nodded slowly. "Why were you allowed to 'overhear' all this?"

"Because someone was interested in the defecting Craft vote. Obviously, I had no idea."

"You don't?"

"Oh, I know the seniority implications, but I didn't mention them." *Korriah did.* "They apply to all three parties."

"Steffan, just how might they affect each of the parties? Your honest analysis. No political sowshit, please."

"If new elections had been required, they would have affected the Commercers the least. Even if the Craft Party gained several seats, it's likely that enough Landors would back the Commerce candidate for premier. The Landors would suffer the most. Several of their councilors would appear to have difficulty in being reelected—"

Obreduur held up a hand. "That's enough. Just keep being very careful with what you 'overhear' and allow to be 'overheard.'"

"Yes, sir."

"By the way, I just received a message from Director Deron. It appears that Guldoran Ironway will be using cherry for their carriage paneling. You were helpful in making that possible. Don't say anything yet, especially about cherry orchards. One other matter. Premier-select Ulrich has announced an investigation of the coal prices paid by the Navy, particularly the prices paid to Eastern Ironway for coal mined from the Eshbruk Naval Coal Reserve."

"Even before he meets with the Imperador," said Dekkard, realizing, if belatedly, that he'd read nothing about the missing logistics director, one Eduard Graffyn, and wondering if Ysella had mentioned that to Obreduur, since he didn't feel that was information that was his to share. "It will be interesting to see who they investigate and question."

"I thought you'd find it intriguing. That's all for now."

"Yes, sir." Dekkard inclined his head, then turned and left the inner office, closing the door quietly as he made his way to his table desk. He couldn't help but wonder if Graffyn was still even alive, but that depended on who found the fugitive first.

The rest of Quindi was like most Quindis, with no surprises, and seemingly endless drafting of responses, interspersed with escorting Obreduur to a Waterways Committee meeting and then back to the office more than a bell later. Dekkard heard nothing more about the Kraffeist Affair, the Guldoran-Woodcrafters dispute, or the Sanitation workers problem, not that he'd expected any differently.

By the time the fourth afternoon bell neared, he was more than ready for the workweek to be over, even if he wouldn't be finished until after Trinitarian services.

14

The evening was clear, and Dekkard and Ysella didn't have to deal with rain in transporting the Obreduur family to and from the East Quarter Trinitarian Chapel. Presider Eschbach's homily dealt with trust, and the fact that both families and societies required trust to function well, an observation with which Dekkard could not disagree, although it seemed to him that it was also a truth too often ignored or dismissed.

After a quick dinner, Dekkard thought about reading, then decided he really needed a walk. He was about to go upstairs to change when he saw Ysella waiting in the hallway outside, wearing a tasteful evening suit of dark lavender linen. A near-transparent headscarf of the same color was draped across her shoulders.

Dekkard was wondering how she'd managed to change so quickly, and especially to look so put-together, when she spoke.

"Would you mind if I came with you on your walk? It looks like a pleasant evening . . ."

Dekkard didn't hesitate. "I'd like that very much, but I will need to change."

"It's rather warm . . . perhaps a barong . . . ?"

"My choice there is limited."

"I'm certain you'll look good in whatever you choose."

Knowing her words were as much command as observation, Dekkard smiled wryly. "I'll be quick." Then he hurried up the stairs.

He did wash up some before donning a plain regal-blue barong over light gray trousers, exhausting the dressy but not totally formal outfits that he hadn't worn around Ysella. He eased the throwing knives into place, then made his way back down to where she waited.

She nodded. "Tasteful. I doubt you could be otherwise."

Not the way I was raised. But he only said, "Shall we go?"

The two walked to the portico, where, surprisingly, Ingrella Obreduur stood in the late twilight. "You two look very good this evening. Do enjoy yourselves."

"Thank you." Dekkard wondered if the good Ritten Obreduur knew that much about Ysella's background. While it might have pleased some women to have a Landor's daughter working for their husband, from what Dekkard had observed, it wouldn't have mattered one way or the other to Ingrella, who simply seemed to take things as they were. Or perhaps, in her time as a legalist, she had learned that ability.

Once they were walking westward on Altarama, Dekkard said, "Obreduur told me that Ulrich is opening an investigation into coal prices, especially those charged by Eastern Ironway."

"He mentioned that to me as well."

"Did you tell him that Security patrollers were looking for Director Graffyn?"

"Did you?"

"No. That was your information to provide, not mine."

"I did tell him that I'd heard it from a patroller friend. He was surprised, but whether he was surprised that I knew, surprised that I knew a patroller, or surprised that Graffyn had fled, I couldn't tell."

"There's still been no mention of even a missing director, not in the newssheets, let alone his name. Also . . . a Security bulletin wouldn't have mentioned his position, just his name, and Emrelda knew both."

"I thought you might have caught that. She and Markell have a wide range of acquaintances, Markell especially."

"She's not an empath."

"No . . . but she's close. It's difficult to deceive her. That's one reason why she's a patroller."

"What might be the others?"

"It's useful for a Security patrol station to have a few women patrollers to deal with certain situations, especially one who can usually sense who's telling the truth and who's not."

"Assaults on women, for example?"

"Household violence is a greater problem than rape or attempted rape by unrelated men."

"You don't hear much about that."

"It's much more common than you'd think. Much more."

The firmness with which Ysella said the last two words suggested to Dekkard that domestic violence wasn't just an abstract concept to her. "Sorting that out, for an empath or a near empath, has to be difficult and maybe painful, I'd think."

"It is. That's another reason why I didn't want to stay as a parole screener. You feel things lurking inside people, but it's hard to say whether they'll act on them or not. Yet you have to make a decision. I didn't like the idea of playing any part of the Trinity."

"I think I understand that." Dekkard glanced ahead, in the direction of Imperial Boulevard, but there was no one else on the walk ahead. "In what other ways does being an empath affect how you view the world, do you think?"

"That's an odd question. Why do you ask?"

"It's something I've wondered about for years."

She shook her head. "You would."

"Don't you?"

"I don't dwell on it. The world is, Steffan. It just is. Everything affects it. Doesn't the Council Hall or the Imperador's Palace look different at dawn, noon, or dusk? They're the same structures, but they look different in different light."

"I was asking how *your* being an empie affects your views."

"Views of what?" returned Ysella.

"I'm an isolate, and you're an empath. Do you and I see the same thing the same way?"

"Our eyes are similar, and we're both people. The odds are that the physical image we each see appears physically similar to each of us. Or do you mean how we perceive that image? You might as well ask if we perceive in the same way because you're a man and I'm a woman, or because you're taller and I'm shorter." She snorted.

Dekkard frowned. "What I'm trying to get at is the idea that . . . as you say, reality, or the world, it just is. Everyone calls the color of our uniforms gray. But do I see and perceive the same color gray as you do? And if I don't, what difference does it make . . . if any?"

"Well . . ." Ysella drew out the word. "My mother always insisted my father didn't see the difference between differing shades of blue and green. My brother Cliven can't see them, either. Except in pleasing a woman's sense of style, though, does that make any real difference?"

"I'm not talking about colors. I have to act based on what I see and what I've learned. You can sense what people feel."

Ysella's laugh was harsh. "That makes it harder. I can sense fear or hate or affection. In most people. Sensing fear doesn't tell me whether someone will attack or run . . . or just freeze."

"Hmmm . . . I hadn't thought of it quite that way."

"Didn't they mention that in your training?"

"Not quite like that. It was couched more like . . . 'sensing or recognizing an emotion does not by itself provide adequate information for action.' I understood that, but no one got into why. That might be because isolates are like most people in the fact that we don't sense other people's emotions. I can see why it's important for empaths to know what you just said, but I didn't think of it quite that way. Maybe because you're the one who's in charge."

"You shouldn't think of it that way. You'll be in charge somewhere . . . at some point."

"Not for a while."

"No . . . but that gives you time to learn. Don't waste it."

Dekkard had to admit that she was right. He glanced ahead, at the white brick posts that marked the western boundary of East Quarter, amazed at how quickly the time and blocks had passed. Ahead, the walks bordering the boulevard would be more crowded, because it was a Quindi evening.

He had thought to cross the eastern lanes of the boulevard so they could enjoy the gardens in the center, but Ysella said, "Let's turn north on the shop sidewalk. I know it's more crowded, but humor me, if you would."

"I'd be happy to, but why? You always have a reason," replied Dekkard.

Ysella lowered her voice. "Because I'm fairly sure someone is following us. They were on the south side of Altarama, fairly far back. If they really are tailing us, they'll have to get closer once we're in a more crowded place."

"You thought someone might be following me? Is that why—"

"Someone shot at you the other day. You're my partner. Am I not allowed to worry about you?" Ysella took his arm briefly and guided him northward past the front of a store that featured stylish leather furniture.

"That doesn't make any sense, even if the shots were a warning to Obreduur. A second warning or incident this soon wouldn't change things."

"They aren't interested in you. They're interested in the councilor's security aide."

"You're making it sound like someone wants to remove me or replace me to get closer to Obreduur."

"Can you think of a better way to find out what he's doing?" asked Ysella.

"I haven't the faintest idea what he might be doing, if anything, besides being a councilor. And who are 'they'?"

"Most people don't know what a councilor is doing, and we'll talk about who they are later. He's been preparing you, but he didn't expect matters to heat up so quickly."

Preparing me? For what? "Do I want to be prepared for . . . whatever?"

"Most likely not . . . but he needs you."

"Or someone like me."

"Steffan . . . like it or not . . . right now, there isn't anyone else like you."

The quiet certainty in Ysella's voice stunned Dekkard. He had no idea how to respond, not that wouldn't sound stupid or, alternatively, arrogant or indifferent.

"There are other talented isolates, but not ones

who come from a solid Craft background, with near-brilliant academic capabilities and a certain amount of common sense."

Dekkard smiled. "You're right. I could occasionally use more common sense."

"You also listen. By the way, the two who are trailing us are only about ten yards back. Neither is an isolate, and that's good."

"Can you tell if either is an empath?"

"The man is just muscle. The woman probably is. She's shielding her feelings somewhat."

"What do we do now?"

"We keep walking."

As Dekkard and Ysella neared the end of the block and the next cross street—as well as Julieta, a high-end women's boutique—he noticed that people were giving them more space than he usually received. Probably the work of an empath.

"We're going to stop and window-shop at Julieta, for just a moment," said Ysella cheerfully. "Then we'll go inside. They're open late on Quindi. There's also a side door, but that might not be the best option."

"Why not?"

"Because they'll still be following us, and I'd rather you didn't have to use your knives." Ysella paused in front of the window, seemingly looking at the mannequin displaying an iridescent pink summer dress. "And, before you ask, I've watched you long enough to know when you carry them."

After a long moment, Dekkard spoke, since he thought he should say something, if only for the benefit of those who were watching. "You like that dress?"

"I detest pink. I like the style, though. Let's go inside."

Dekkard moved with her, trying to keep it from being obvious that she was leading him, at the same time trying not to smile because most times the woman would be the one leading the way into a stylish women's store. A few moments later, Ysella stopped, ostensibly to look at some evening handbags finished in black and silver metallic links.

Several minutes later, she murmured to Dekkard, "They're coming in. Don't do anything until I tell you."

The man and woman who entered Julieta were moderately well-dressed, although the man, with a round face and blond hair, neither of which matched the muscular body below, wore white trousers and an unbuttoned blue linen jacket, suggesting to Dekkard the possibility of concealed weapons, while the woman was attired in shades of light gray with a translucent white headscarf, colors clearly secondary to those of her companion.

Abruptly, the woman staggered, lurching into one of the display cases featuring silk headscarves and standard scarves, any one of which likely cost more than Dekkard's weekly pay.

"Look out!" snapped Ysella. "They're thieves! Check under his jacket!"

Although Dekkard couldn't feel it, he could see that Ysella's words had been accompanied by some empforce projecting law and authority, because two guards appeared almost instantly, and as one moved toward the pair, the round-faced man started to draw a small weapon—a semi-automatic pistol, Dekkard thought. But before he could even level it, the round-faced man convulsed, and both guards immobilized him.

"We can go," murmured Ysella, leading Dekkard to the side door on the cross street. No one even looked their way.

To Dekkard's eyes, Ysella looked pale and almost shaky. Once outside, she covered her mouth and kept walking east on the cross street, if bent slightly forward.

He kept looking back, but no one followed them, and in moments, they were past another set of white-painted brick gateposts announcing the entrance to East Quarter.

Finally, Ysella straightened up.

"Are you all right?"

"I am now."

"Good. You used some sort of empblast on those two." He glanced back, but still saw no one following them.

"Nausea . . . it's effective, but it's hard on me afterward."

"Won't someone figure that out?"

Ysella smiled wanly. "They won't care. The muscle-boy was carrying a pistol, and he panicked and tried to use it. He'll be on the prison farms in less than a week. The empie will play innocent, and there's no proof that she was even involved with him. She'll claim, if it even comes up, that he pushed her into the scarf case."

"So she can try something else next time?"

"She knows that we know. They'll try something else."

"Who's 'we'? Or 'they'?"

"If the muscle-boy couldn't kill you without witnesses," Ysella said, ignoring Dekkard's questions, "the empie was going to set you up with a confrontation around witnesses. It wouldn't have mattered whether you got killed or badly injured or if you killed him. In any of those instances, Obreduur would have needed to replace you."

"But you were there. You could have pointed out what happened."

"What I might have said wouldn't matter. We're partners. The fact that we were out together while not in uniform—and that I'm a woman—would have made a justicer discount what I said."

"What if I'd gone out alone?"

"The empie would have set it up so that someone would think you hit them, and the assassin would have attacked you because you'd have been marked as the aggressor. That way, you either end up dead, disgraced, or in gaol."

"You're assuming no one would listen to me."

"The Justiciary Minister is a Commercer who's not

exactly fond of the councilor, or of isolates, and you're an isolate whose emotions cannot be sensed, unlike normal people. The justicer you would have appeared before would have shared those feelings. Witnesses would have seen you as the one in the wrong."

Dekkard felt as though he'd stepped into a maelstrom, a swirling torrent far worse than the seemingly mild political currents that had been part of his daily routine for the past two years. *But maybe you just didn't sense the depths.*

"How did you know this would happen tonight?" he finally said.

"I didn't. Not for certain, but after the other night, there was a chance they would make another move. You couldn't take a walk the last two nights. I was watching, and when I sensed two people waiting in a steamer up Altarama . . ." Ysella shrugged. "I was right."

"None of this makes sense." *Or not much.* "You never said who 'we' are. Or who 'they' are."

"We need to get back and meet with the councilor. He was worried."

Obreduur worried? That wasn't a word that came to mind when Dekkard thought about the councilor. "He knew you were coming with me?"

"Of course. After the incident the other night, he decided the shooting was deliberate and that they might try again. But that's our fault, not yours. He didn't think things wouldn't get this bad so soon." Ysella began to walk faster.

Less than a third of a bell later, the two entered the house through the west portico door. Dekkard hadn't asked any more questions, not because he didn't have more than a few, but because he suspected that Ysella would defer answering. Instead, he tried to think beyond the obvious, but he wasn't getting anywhere because he couldn't figure out why the others, presumably Commercers or their allies—or someone he didn't even know about—wanted to remove him. Or as Ysella had put it, remove Obreduur's security aide. But why? He didn't know any secrets. He wasn't from a wealthy or influential family.

Ysella led the way to Obreduur's study and closed the door.

The councilor looked up from the papers on the desk and asked Ysella, "How did it go?"

"Moderately well. You were right about it being a setup. We lured them closer and into Julieta. Their empie wasn't that good, and I staggered her. The man wasn't an isolate. The store guards took him down when he panicked and tried to shoot. In the uproar, no one really noticed us except the woman with the shooter. She'll declare she was an innocent bystander. She might get off."

"She will," said Obreduur. "That's to be expected." He turned to Dekkard. "You once told me that you believed in our government the way it has been. Do you still think that way?"

Dekkard considered the question carefully before replying. "I still believe in the way it was set up under the Great Charter. I'm not so sure that's exactly the way it works anymore."

"Not so sure?" asked Obreduur dryly.

"I'm sure it's not working the way it was set up, but I don't know how bad things really are."

"Worse than you know, but not nearly so bad as they're going to get if the Commercers aren't stopped. Some of us are trying to keep government the way it was designed. Do you think that's a worthy goal?"

"As long as trying to save Guldor doesn't destroy it. Or us."

"That's part of the problem," replied Obreduur almost sourly.

"You and Avraal keep talking about 'we.' Just who are you talking about?"

"Most of the Craft Party councilors, their supporters, and a few others who think the same way. We're opposed to the effort of the Commercers to turn Guldor into a total plutocracy. Wealth is necessary and has its place, but we don't want Guldor to go the way of Atacama or to the other extreme—like Argental. Or the Grand Democracy of Teknold, as Roostof and Macri told you. Too many of the Landors are still living in the time of Laureous the Great."

Dekkard had a more personal question. "What do you expect of me?"

"For the immediate future, much the same as you've been doing, except with a wider scope of duties. You'll still need to handle your security duties, just as Avraal does. You also need some coaching from Avraal . . . and from me . . . on presenting yourself to those audiences and personages with whom you haven't had much contact, because you'll be standing in for me as a representative of the Craft Party."

"Why me?"

"Because I can't be everywhere, and too many Crafters don't represent the party as well as they could. Too few young men from craft or artisan backgrounds with ability and intelligence understand or are interested in politics, and we need every one of you with those abilities. Also, as an isolate, you can only be convinced by yourself."

"Isolates are just as susceptible to a logical proposition as anyone."

Obreduur shook his head. "That's a rationalization. You choose whether to be convinced or not. You may choose for irrational reasons, or for love, or loyalty, or even stupidity, but the choice is yours."

Dekkard had never heard "choice" argued that way, but it made sense. He couldn't help smiling sardonically. Then he looked pointedly at Ysella.

"There's no future for women in the Landor Party," she replied. "If most Landors had their way, there'd be no future for women at all."

"What about the Commerce Party?" asked Dekkard.

"They're already destroying the land," she said bleakly.

"Can either of you tell me why the Commercers want to kill me?"

"First, because you and Avraal are good at protecting me, and some of the Commercers want to strike at me because, for the first time in centuries, the Craft Party has become a political force and potential threat to Commercer control of the Council. Second, because you and a few others could be a real danger to them. They're thinking five or ten or even twenty years out."

"How would killing me help?"

"Oh . . . that's just one way of removing you. They often buy off bright staff members who serve Landor or Craft councilors. How much did SSA offer you last year?"

"Their letter suggested I could make almost double what I was making here after five years at SSA, depending on my willingness to work."

"Legalists working for corporacions or legal consortiums can make triple what a councilor can pay," said Obreduur.

"Then how do the Commerce councilors keep good staffers?" asked Dekkard.

"They rotate staff in and out of higher-paying private jobs . . . and those high-priced legal consortiums work pro bono for Commerce councilors. The Craft Party can't match those salaries. We also don't have allies with those kinds of jobs to offer. So we have to be better at winning elections and developing talent. We're getting there. Two elections ago, there were only sixteen Craft councilors, and the Commerce Party had held thirty seats for the previous three elections. Despite their tens, if not hundreds of thousands, of marks employed indirectly in influencing elections, we've gained seats in each election, and they've lost seats. They've also lost support from a number of the Landor councilors who've discovered that recent changes in law have had adverse effects on Landors."

"They'd kill me because I might be a problem someday?"

"No. They'd prefer to buy you off, or disgrace you, or get you in trouble," said Ysella. "But since they couldn't buy you off, they tried something else. Actual killings are rare. I wouldn't be surprised if one possibility tonight was to set it up so you ended up with the pistol. A firearms charge would disqualify you from serving the Council or ever being a councilor in the future."

"Also," added Obreduur, "what do you think the story in *Gestirn* would say if you were charged with even a minor offense?"

Dekkard thought, but not for long. "It would report that one Steffan Dekkard, a security aide to Craft Party Councilor Obreduur, committed whatever offense . . ."

"And that would reflect badly on me and the party," pointed out Obreduur. "People are more inclined to remember the unfavorable when a name is linked to it. And the newssheets can mention names associated with those charged with felonies, even if they are councilors." He smiled sympathetically. "You two have had quite an evening. Steffan, you need to think matters over. If you would rather change your employment, I can put you in touch with several opportunities in Oersynt that will, frankly, pay a great deal more than the Council allows and remove you from any direct danger. If you choose to stay, you will slowly become a legalist in everything but name, and you will have a chance at an interesting and meaningful life . . . but it does involve some danger, and it will not ever make you wealthy. You don't have to choose tonight, tomorrow, or even next month. But you will have to choose, sooner or later. I won't force that choice, but events will."

"Thank you, sir. I do need to do some thinking."

"I understand." Obreduur stood.

Ysella led the way out, and the two walked without speaking to the empty staff room, where she stopped and waited to see if Dekkard had anything to say.

"It all seems so unreal," he said. "I expected to occasionally have to protect him. But this . . ." Dekkard shook his head.

"We'll still have to protect him. That threat hasn't gone away." She paused. "Why do you think we're with

him far more than most other security types are with
their councilors . . . except for the best of the Craft
councilors?"

"I thought it was possibly because he'd made enemies
as a guildmeister."

"He made a few there, but they'd scarcely be out to
get him now."

"How long have you known?"

"A little over three years."

"My predecessor? Did he really just decide to do security work in Uldwyrk?"

"He did. He's doing quite well at it, I hear. That's
where his family is, and he married a woman he knew
there. He was never that interested in politics."

"But Obreduur has to have been doing this . . ."

"He can only hire those who are available to hire,
Steffan."

Dekkard shook his head again.

"Sleep on it. I'm not going anywhere tomorrow. If
you want, we can talk some more. If you want . . ."
Ysella offered a gentle smile.

Dekkard stood there as she turned and left the staff
room. He looked down at his watch. Everything that
had happened, including the talk with Obreduur, had
taken less than two bells.

15

Dekkard woke up from a restless night early on
Findi. When he finally sat up on the edge of the
bed, his initial thoughts were almost the same as those
he'd had before he'd finally dropped off to sleep.

Why you? You're just a security aide.

Except he knew he'd been doing more than most security aides.

And you like doing that.

Enough to have to worry about what could have happened the night before?

But it didn't happen. And it hadn't happened because both Obreduur and Ysella had been looking out for him.

For their own reasons.

Yet they were looking out for him and giving him opportunities that he would never get elsewhere.

And the other side isn't exactly looking out for your welfare.

He took a deep breath, then rose and headed to shave and then take a lukewarm shower. After dressing in a plain white cotton shirt and black trousers, he headed down to the staff room.

Ysella was already there, alone, but she had only a mug of café in front of her, and she wore a simple pale green long-sleeved cotton dress.

"Good morning," offered Dekkard warmly.

She studied him carefully without speaking.

"Yes . . . I had a lot to think over," he admitted, as he poured his café and settled into the seat across the table from her.

"You must have. You didn't even look for the croissants and the quince paste." The trace of a smile vanished.

"You've also done some thinking," he said, taking in the hint of dark circles under her eyes. "Either that, or that nausea stayed with you more than you let on."

"It lasted longer than I'd anticipated." Ysella took a sip of café. "I also worried about you."

Dekkard replied quietly, "I appreciate that more than you can know. If it helps . . . I want to stay . . . and do more."

"You . . . are you sure you're doing it for the right reasons?" Her voice was almost even.

"I said I thought a lot about it. I did. It came down to one thing. They don't care. I'm just a piece in a game of crowns played to amass more fortunes and power for people who have too much already. In a different way, that was the reason my parents left Argental. The smooth running of society always came well before art, artisans, or people. For all of his reserve, the way Obreduur respects everyone on his staff shows that he cares about us. The councilor is driven, and some people may get hurt. I might be one of them. But he'll at least care to some extent."

"And me?"

"You care more than you can afford to let on." *Especially as a Landor's daughter.* "I began to understand that last endday." What Dekkard wasn't about to say was that he didn't know whether she cared because she was the type who needed to be fair and honest or because she just cared. *For now . . . does it matter?* He felt that it did, but he knew only time would determine that.

"Why last endday?"

"Your sister." He shrugged. "Don't ask me why. It's just a feeling that I got seeing the two of you together."

"You're sounding like an empath, Steffan."

"That's never going to happen. Most of the time, I'm just like all the other normal people. I just have to think about what people might be feeling."

"That may be, but you're not just . . . normal."

Not knowing how to respond to that, Dekkard finally reached for two croissants and placed them on the plate before him, followed by a healthy helping of quince paste.

"I wondered how long before you reached for that."

"What are you doing today?"

"I was thinking of trying to persuade you to go shopping."

"I'm not much of a shopper. I'd be even worse looking over your shoulder."

"I guess I wasn't clear. I'd be the one watching. You need to expand your wardrobe. If you're going to speak for the councilor, you need at least one suit that's neither flamboyant nor Landor-conservative. Another barong or two wouldn't hurt, either. You look good in them."

Dekkard was about to protest that he wasn't exactly made of marks when Ysella spoke again. "A few more clothes won't put that much of a dent in your banque balance."

"You know that, too?" Dekkard finished sandwiching a slice of the quince paste into the first croissant and took a healthy mouthful.

She shook her head. "Hardly. I do know about how much you're paid. You have no lodging expense, very little in the way of food costs, and I doubt you have to send funds to your parents." The hint of a smile crossed her lips. "You are cautious about money, though. That's good, but some investment in how you look pays off, more for men than women. Women are expected to look good. Here in Guldor, that is. Men are merely expected to look tasteful and . . . appropriate."

"But both should be dressed appropriately," replied Dekkard ironically. "For their station."

"Your station is now higher," declared Ysella. "Or it will be by tomorrow night."

"Oh?"

"You'll be promoted to an assistant economic specialist."

"And what are you, besides the senior security aide?"

"Assistant research specialist."

"We can be both?"

"The councilor can arrange and pay his staff as he pleases, just so long as his total payroll remains less than the maximum allowed."

Dekkard took swallow of café and then another bite of the croissant before speaking.

"So where do you suggest I start this shopping trip?"

"Excellencia would be a good beginning."

"Can I afford an ending if we start there?"

"It's not that expensive."

Dekkard wondered if they were even close to agreeing on what was expensive, but he merely said, "After breakfast, you lead the way."

"You'll also need a security-gray suit for when you represent the councilor away from the Council and government buildings."

Dekkard had considered that. Wearing gray wasn't actually required of isolates when not employed in physical security positions, or in their free time, but it was customary in professional positions for isolates to wear business suits in security gray while engaged in a professional setting. Not doing so was believed deceptive, which Dekkard had always thought amusing, because it wasn't considered "customary" for empaths in most non-security positions to wear gray, although many did wear simple gold lapel pins or brooches with a red starburst as a courtesy, and Dekkard had heard that the red starburst was almost a necessity at high-level business or government meetings.

After breakfast Dekkard quickly washed up and added his only other jacket—a light gray blazer—to his attire, and his knives, before heading back down to the portico, where Ysella waited, wearing an almost transparent cream jacket and headscarf over the green dress. A small green leather purse hung from a matching green shoulder strap.

"You hadn't planned to see your sister this endday?"

"I don't see her every endday, Steffan, only once or twice a month. Besides, she's working today." Ysella turned and began to walk down the drive.

Dekkard nodded as he walked beside her, although, until Ysella mentioned it, he hadn't thought about the fact that a patroller would need to work enddays. "Does the patrol know . . ."

"That she comes from a Landor background? Of course, Security eventually knows everything. But that's one reason why she got the job. You saw where they live. It's very helpful to have a woman with a cultured background in the station. Some people with massive amounts of marks can be . . ."

"Excessively convinced of their own importance?"

"You phrased that so deftly, Steffan."

"That means I was still too direct."

Ysella laughed softly.

As the two stepped through the pedestrian gate,

Dekkard glanced in both directions. He didn't see anyone. "Is there anyone lurking about?"

"In full light, you can see farther than I can sense."

The two set a pace faster than a stroll, but slower than Dekkard would have chosen on his exercise walks. Excellencia was five long blocks north of where Altarama joined Imperial Boulevard, which made for a good walk, but too short to take an omnibus, and certainly not worth hailing a steamhack on Imperial.

Excellencia's shimmering silvered widows and glowing white marble dominated the corner of Imperial Boulevard and Camelia Avenue. Like most high-end retail establishments in Machtarn, it was open on Findi, but closed on Unadi. Ysella let Dekkard lead the way inside, and he headed for that section that featured business and more formal attire.

A salesman a good ten years older than Dekkard appeared, wearing a tailored suit of silvered blue and a dark blue cravat. "Might I help you, sir?"

Dekkard smiled easily. "To start out, I need a good-quality business suit in dark security gray."

"Security gray, sir?"

"I'm an isolate taking on duties other than security."

"Oh, yes, sir. This way, sir."

At that moment, an older woman, well-dressed in the silvered blue livery of the store, eased toward the three, then moved away. Dekkard suspected she was a low-level empie who would have added her talents to support the salesman's power of persuasion, before she recognized that he was an isolate.

Ysella, standing back from the salesman, offered an amused smile.

Two bells, three emporiums, and five blocks farther north on Imperial Boulevard later, Dekkard looked at Ysella. "Two gray suits, four barongs, five shirts, four cravats, a belt, and one pair of dress boots, all of which I'll need to pick up after tailoring—except the belt, boots, and cravats. I think that's enough, and it's time to eat."

"I'd agree, but only if you accompany me to one store first."

Dekkard offered what he thought was a mournful expression. "Another store?"

"Four stores is nothing."

Dekkard had the definite impression that for Ysella, and Emrelda, four stores were only a shopping appetizer. He managed a grin. "What store?"

"Esperanza. It's only a block away. There are good restaurants in the block after that."

"Then, after we eat, we should take a steamhack back to the house."

"That's fair."

"Lead on." Dekkard shifted the shopping bag into his left hand.

Esperanza wasn't at all what Dekkard expected—a small shop, no more than five yards square, that carried only women's headscarves. He watched as Ysella picked out nearly a half score of scarves in various colors that were heavier—or more concealing—than those she'd previously worn when not in security grays.

"Those are the same color as some you already have," Dekkard said quietly. "Spares?"

She shook her head. "Mine are too transparent for speaking to certain groups. I've been meaning to do this for several weeks, but didn't get around to it." A smile followed. "But since we were only a block away . . ."

Dekkard nodded. Once she had paid for the scarves, folded them carefully, and then eased them into a thin cloth bag that she'd extracted from her purse, he asked, "Where would you suggest we eat?"

"You've never eaten anywhere near here?"

"Only at Greystone."

"We can do better than that. We'll try Estado Don Miguel. It's just a little farther."

A little farther turned out to be three long blocks. The restaurant was off the inside lobby of an imposing five-story marble structure that held the headquarters of

Nordstar, the coal-gas and natural-gas utility for most of Guldor. Nothing outside the building indicated a restaurant inside, and the warm wooden paneling and airy feel, with well-spaced tables and linen cloths and napkins, suggested that lunch would be anything but inexpensive.

The maître d'hôtel glanced past Dekkard to Ysella.

"Just the two of us, Charls. The councilor won't be here today. This is Sr. Dekkard. He's the councilor's assistant economic specialist . . . among other duties."

"A pleasure to meet you, sir." Charls inclined his head politely.

Dekkard responded in kind.

As they followed the graying maître, Ysella said, "Don't worry. The meal is on the councilor. He told me to take you here and sent a message to Charls."

"That's kind of him . . . and you." Dekkard was definitely getting the feeling that he'd be going more than a few places he hadn't even suspected existed.

"Not so much kind as practical. For lunch here during the week, you need reservations days in advance. Also, it is a treat for both of us since we don't usually have regular midday meals."

A treat . . . or compensation of sorts for the night before? Either way, it was welcome. Dekkard smiled.

Once the two were seated, Dekkard glanced around. Out of the possible fifteen tables in the restaurant, six others were taken. None of the other patrons even looked in their direction.

Ysella picked up her menu, as did Dekkard. The entrées were more limited than he would have expected, the prices in a range that matched the location and the tasteful décor. "Is there anything you'd recommend?"

"I've only been here three times. Everything I've had has been excellent."

Dekkard finally chose the breast of duck à la apricot with lemongrass rice and seasonal greens. Ysella ordered a petit filet, rare, with potatoes au gratin, and the seasonal greens, as well as a carafe of Jaykarhan Malbec.

The wine came first, and Ysella lifted her wineglass and said, "To shopping, successful or otherwise."

Dekkard raised his glass as well, then sipped the Malbec and said, "I'm no connoisseur, but I do like this."

"It's the house Malbec, and better than many of the more expensive wines."

"Your family doesn't have vineyards, do they?"

"No. The lands are too low, and the soils aren't suitable. The best vineyards are in the north."

"I still find it hard to believe . . ."

"That the daughter of a Landor is an empie security aide to a Craft councilor? Is that any less improbable than the son of noted artisans who graduated with high honors from the Military Institute is an isolate security aide to that same councilor?"

Dekkard laughed wryly. "I suppose not. Except that I don't have the talent, especially the ultrafine physical hand control, required of a great artisan."

"And I don't have the patience to watch things grow, year after year, in the same way, while nothing changes."

"Especially when you can sense what everyone feels?" Ysella nodded.

"So what happens now?" asked Dekkard.

"We talk and enjoy lunch. After that, you hail us a steamhack, and we go back to the house. Then I give you a book to read, and I write letters to my sister and brother."

"Required reading for my expanded duties?"

"Exactly."

At that moment, their respective entrées arrived.

As he ate, and talked about food and other matters neither personal nor professional, Dekkard wondered what was in the book that Ysella would give him.

16

True to her word, immediately after Ysella and Dekkard returned to the house, she went up to her room. She returned carrying an oversized book with a hand-tooled cover, which she handed to him. There was no title on the spine.

"It's a loose-leaf book," she said. "The pages are locked in place, but if you unlock the mechanism, you can add or replace pages. Please don't. There are only two copies of it, and this copy stays in the house, and in your room when you're not reading or studying it."

"What is it?"

"It's your information book. The first part is a simplified guide to the procedures of the Council. Some of that you already know. You need to learn the rest. The second part is the actual text of the Great Charter, not the summary that's available to everyone, but the original text with the few subsequent amendments. The legalists' text, if you will. The third part contains information on every current member of the Council of Sixty-Six as well information on important members of their staff. If you discover information on councilors or staffers not in the book, write it up and give it to Councilor Obreduur in an unmarked envelope."

"I'm supposed to learn all this? How soon?"

"You need to read it all in the next day or so, then start learning what you don't know. You're only to talk about what's in it to me or the councilor, or to Ivann or Svard if something you recall is pertinent to something before the Council."

Dekkard looked down at the volume that he held, neither slender nor excessively thick, but he judged that it held several hundred sheets. "I'd better get started."

"You should." Ysella smiled warmly. "I did enjoy the shopping and lunch." She paused. "I have some work to do as well. I'll see you later."

She turned and headed upstairs.

Dekkard looked down at the book, a volume that suddenly felt much heavier.

Rather than go upstairs to his room, which was often uncomfortably warm in the afternoon, he carried the book into the staff room and sat at one end of the table, where he opened the book, skimming through the first section just to get a feel for the procedures. When he got to the second section it only took a few lines to see why the version of the Great Charter most people read was the abridged and concise version.

> ... in the course of social and political affairs that both impel and constrain any political entity, particularly one as geographically and culturally diverse as the Empire of Gold, the making and enforcement of civil codes and military regulations cannot be left to the passions of a moment, or even of an age. Nor can such laws and regulations be so rigid that there is no latitude to deal with changes in the machines of men or in the threats and opportunities posed by other powers in the world ...

The rationale for the Great Charter went on for a full five pages. Dekkard had to admit that all the reasons made sense, and that Laureous the Great, or more likely his legalist advisors, had thought matters through thoroughly. *But more than five printed pages in small type before reaching the actual provisions?*

The third section began with the listing of all sixty-six Councilors, arranged by party and by seniority within that party. Next came a listing of the standing committees, followed by the responsibilities of each committee, and the current members by party. Then came the entries on each councilor, arranged by party and by seniority within the party. Unlike the first two sections, which were printed, the entries on councilors were handwritten, in various hands.

There were images in black ink of perhaps fifteen councilors, but most entries had no depictions.

Dekkard was slightly surprised that the book was already updated to reflect Oskaar Ulrich as the new premier, although the entry noted that he was actually third in seniority in the Commerce Party.

Among Ulrich's staff, Jaime Minz was listed as an isolate security aide for the Security Committee, with the notation that he also performed "other duties as necessary."

Dekkard leafed to the back of the section on Landor councilors and found the entry on Councilor Saarh.

Jareem Askal Saarh
Appointed Councilor 21 Springfirst 1266
[filling vacancy caused by the death of Councilor
    Wilhelm Kall Freust]
Committees: Agriculture, Waterways

Married Maelle Kall Freust 30 Springend 1258
Youngest daughter of Councilor Freust and Clydia
    Aash Freust [deceased]
Two children: Clydiana b. 1259
Jareld b. 1261
    Landor, Khuld—holdings comprising 5,500 hect-
    ares, 200 hectares [cherry orchards] south of Malek
    received as partial dowry. 800 hectares in vineyards,
    white commercial grapes, moderate quality, vintage
    largely exported. 4,000 hectares in melons, wheat
    corn, and maize.
Estimated annual holding revenues: M100,000
Annual Debt Service: M30,000
Annual Operating Expenses: M32,000 [est]
Holding Expenses: M30,000 [est]

Dekkard almost let out a low whistle. While Saarh also earned five thousand marks a year as a councilor, not counting a four-thousand-mark expense account, that meant his actual income after expenses amounted to thirteen thousand marks a year, and there was no way a Landor could live on that . . . unless he had significant investment income. But if Saarh had that, why was he paying debt service?

And how had Obreduur come up with the financial figures?

Dekkard kept reading.

> Voting plurality, previous election: LP 37%, CRF
> 34%, COM 29%
> Saarh is moderately good speaker, but lacks ability
> to generate confidence. Impassioned in private,
> diffident in public . . .

Then he went to look for the page on Obreduur. It only held the basics about the councilor, the names of his family, the voting percentages in the last two elections, and the fact that he'd previously been guildmeister for the Stevedores Guild and, following that, Crafters Guild coordinator for the Oersynt-Malek and Gaarlak districts.

And that his wife is a practicing legalist.

Had moving from guildmeister to a district coordinator between guilds been to reestablish Obreduur's ties to Malek and to build support for his election?

Obreduur as guildmeister of the Stevedores? That suggested a much tougher side to the councilor than Dekkard had yet seen.

He looked down at the still-open book. He had a lot to learn and not very much time in which to do it.

Do you really know what you're getting yourself into?

Dekkard shook his head, even as he realized that he didn't want to spend the rest of his life as a mere security aide . . . or even a higher-paid commercial security type.

17

When Dekkard woke on Unadi morning, it was from a sleep filled with dreams in which he had had been trying to match names and faces . . . and in which he never quite could, as if what he had learned or read about each did not quite match what he saw.

As if that's not true about most of us.

Since he was slightly later than usual getting down to breakfast and Rhosali was already talking to Ysella, Dekkard held off asking questions he had from perusing the book and merely said, "Good morning," before taking his café, croissants, and quince paste.

"Tomorrow will be tomato jelly, Steffan," said Hyelda from the door to the staff room. "We're running low on the quince."

His mouth full, Dekkard nodded.

His breakfasting time was cut even shorter because Ritten Obreduur requested him to fill up her steamer and light it off so that he had no chance to talk seriously with Ysella. Since he'd filled the steamer's tanks on Quindi, he wondered where the Ritten had been on endday that had so depleted them.

Then, on the drive to the Council Office Building, Obreduur cleared his throat meaningfully and said, "Steffan . . . Sometime this morning, I will be signing the forms to promote you to an assistant specialist. Technically, you'll be a security and assistant economic specialist. Once the forms are filed, you'll be issued a pin like the ones worn by Ivann, Svard, and Felix. Avraal already has hers. You're to keep it with you at all times, but you're not to wear it except when you're on professional duties, rather than security duties. When you leave the Council grounds to speak as an economic specialist, you'll have to change into a security-gray suit."

"Avraal had mentioned that, sir. I bought two suits

like that yesterday, but they won't be ready until Duadi evening."

"What she may not have mentioned is that you can still carry a truncheon when wearing a suit, but I'd recommend a personal length one if you're not on Council property or duties. Do you have one?"

"Yes, sir. From security training. It's a little battered, but more than adequate."

"Good." Obreduur nodded and returned to perusing his papers.

Once Dekkard reached the office, Karola already had petitions and letters on his desk. There was also no word from the office of Health and Education Minister Sanoffre, but then it had been less than a week since the proposed new job descriptions had been sent. Dekkard went to work until a third before noon.

At that point, Obreduur came out of his office and motioned to Ysella and Dekkard. "You two can escort me to the councilors' dining room and then go eat. When you finish, just wait outside the dining room. I won't be much longer than you."

Dekkard took that to mean that he and Ysella shouldn't tarry over their meal. "Yes, sir." He stood, checked his gladius and truncheon, and then led the way out into the main corridor.

When the three reached the councilors' dining room, Obreduur gestured to another councilor, and he and the other man proceeded inside.

"That's Councilor Hasheem, isn't it?" Dekkard asked Ysella.

"How did you know?"

"He's one of the few in the book where there's an image."

The two turned toward the staff cafeteria. Just as they were about to step through the archway, a blond woman in a conservative blue suit who was leaving turned toward them. "Avraal . . . I haven't seen you in weeks."

"The councilor keeps us tied down. You've met Steffan before?"

"Just for a moment."

It took several moments for Dekkard to place the aide—Shayala Raeverte, from Councilor Kuuresoh's staff—but he managed to reply. "It's good to see you again, Shayala, if only in passing."

"You're too kind." Shayala paused just slightly before asking, "Have you heard anything about Kraffeist hearings?"

"The Waterways Committee or the Workplace Administration Committee aren't exactly involved in coal leases," said Ysella dryly. "What about you?"

Raeverte shook her head. "I'm just getting the feeling something nasty is about to happen, but I couldn't say what, but the councilor's said absolutely nothing."

"Neither has ours," said Ysella.

"I'd hoped . . ." Raeverte glanced to Dekkard. "It's nice to see you again, but I need to run." Then she hurried away.

"She's gotten that feel from somewhere," said Ysella quietly, "but she doesn't want to say."

"Councilor Kuuresoh is on the Military Affairs Committee, and he's a more senior Commercer," said Dekkard. "The Navy has to be upset about paying Eastern more for coal that the ironway got cheaply and from the coal reserve. He's likely not saying, but maybe she senses something."

"That could be," replied Ysella, "but she's fishing."

"Because of Obreduur's position as Craft political leader?"

"What else?"

As the two headed toward the cafeteria serving area, Dekkard noted that the seating area wasn't nearly as crowded as usual, but then, they were early. He decided on lamb milanesia, except with a verde sauce on the side for the polenta. Ysella chose a fresh fruit salad. Since there was a corner table available, they took it.

Dekkard didn't say much until he'd eaten several bites. He'd had better lamb, but he'd also had much worse, especially at the Institute. "What do you think will happen with the Kraffeist Affair?"

"Ulrich will investigate and report the results in a way that doesn't seem like he's hiding anything, but which keeps hidden certain matters. That's what the Imperador wants."

"But if Ulrich tries to hide something," said Dekkard, "and someone can prove it, the Imperador might have to call new elections. The Commerce Party might lose more seats to the Craft Party. Isn't that a benefit?"

"It might be, but new elections would also cost senior councilors not in leadership positions in all three parties their seats. Is a new election worth it to any of them?" asked Ysella. "Beyond that, there's another reason to be considered."

Dekkard just sat there for a moment. *What other reason?*

"Think about that, Steffan. Now . . . finish your lamb. The councilor said he wouldn't be long."

Dekkard resumed eating, wondering what the other reason might be. The Landors wouldn't want new elections, because they'd lose at least one seat and possibly more. The Commerce Party wouldn't want immediate elections because the cause for those elections would have been the perceived failure of two successive premiers and that perception could cost them yet more seats. Those both made sense. But why wouldn't the Craft Party want new elections when the party kept gaining seats with each election?

Dekkard had the feeling he was missing something very obvious, but he couldn't see it. He finished the lamb and the polenta quickly, and before long he and Ysella were headed back to wait on one of the benches outside the councilors' dining room.

They hadn't even quite reached an empty bench when Ysella murmured, "Here comes Fernand Stoltz, chief legalist for the Public Resources Committee."

"It looks like you two are waiting for your councilor," said Stoltz pleasantly, clearly addressing Avraal.

"And you're doing the same, it appears," replied Dekkard cheerfully. "Or your chairman, I should say."

"You should." Stoltz's voice was neutral. "I don't believe we've met."

"You probably wouldn't remember. Steffan Dekkard. Isolate security and assistant economic specialist."

Stoltz frowned.

"He's been with the councilor several years," said Ysella. "When are you beginning the investigatory hearings on the Kraffeist Affair?"

"That's up to the chairman."

"Will the hearing deal with the differentials in coal prices?" asked Dekkard diffidently.

"That's also up to the chairman." Stoltz smiled pleasantly. "It's good to see you get out of the office every so often, Avraal. Until later." Ignoring Dekkard, he turned and walked away.

"I didn't know you'd met Fernand," said Ysella quietly.

"I hadn't. Even if we had met, he probably wouldn't have remembered. He's that type. Besides, now he'll wonder, and that's good for someone that arrogant."

Ysella couldn't quite smother a smile, although she did say, "Just remember . . . Fernand can be vindictive."

"Almost anyone who's that arrogant is vindictive, but I didn't say anything negative to him. I just asked a question, and he answered it. What was his hidden emotional reaction to my question?"

"He didn't like it."

"Does that mean that Chairman Schmidtz doesn't want to deal with that issue?"

"Would you?" Ysella turned slightly. "The councilor is heading our way."

They both stood and moved to meet Obreduur.

"Did you two have a pleasant lunch?"

"We did," replied Dekkard. "And you, sir?"

"It was . . . instructive. Did you find out anything interesting?" Obreduur looked to Ysella.

"Steffan asked the head legalist of the Public Resources Committee whether the chairman would go into prices the Navy paid for coal. He said that was up to the chairman, but he wasn't pleased."

"Excellent question, Steffan. Thank you for noting his reaction, Avraal."

The corridor and the covered portico leading from the Council Hall to the Council Office Building contained enough people that Obreduur said nothing on the way back to the office.

Dekkard went back to dealing with letters and petitions until slightly after the second bell of the afternoon, when Roostof returned from a meeting brandishing a newssheet, pointing to Ysella and then to Dekkard. "You two should see the afternoon edition of *Gestirn* now."

"Why now?" asked Dekkard.

"Because when the councilor reads it, he'll keep it, and you should see for yourselves." Roostof handed the newssheet to Dekkard, who immediately began to read.

Last week, the Ministry of Security put out a bulletin listing Eduard Graffyn as a missing person of interest. Graffyn is the Director of Logistics for Eastern Ironway, and possibly the man who knows the most about the details of the illegal leasing of the Eshbruk Coal Reserve by the Ministry of Public Resources. That bulletin went only to patrol stations and Security Ministry offices. Minister of Security Lukkyn Wyath has declined to comment on reasons behind that decision.

Premier Oskaar Ulrich, who just relieved Minister Jhared Kraffeist from his position as head of Public Resources, has indicated that the Council of Sixty-Six would be more than pleased to hear what Sr. Graffyn might be able to add to the pending investigation of the Eshbruk Coal Reserve lease to Eastern Ironway . . .

Dekkard finished the article and handed the newssheet to Ysella, then said, "Ulrich removed Minister Kraffeist? I never saw anything about that."

"Neither did anyone else," replied Roostof.

"Was there a story about his removal in any of the newssheets?"

"Not a one. But do you think the *Tribune* would print anything like that first?"

Ysella nodded, then finished reading before returning the newssheet.

"When Premier Grieg removed Schlossan as Minister of Waterways," Dekkard pointed out, "that was on the front page, and Schlossan had only disagreed with the Council over the rates charged for barge tolls."

"Barge tolls are more important than inside coal deals," said Roostof sardonically. "Every Landor and every smallholder worries about tolls. Only three iron-ways and every steamship in the Navy or the merchant shippers worry about coal prices."

"Thank you for that astute observation, Svard," said Ysella. "You'd better take that in to the councilor, just in case he doesn't already know."

Even if Obreduur knew, he'd still like to read the story, if only to see what the newssheet reported. When Roostof entered the inner office and closed the door, Dekkard looked to Ysella.

"From that story," she replied, "Ulrich knows about Director Graffyn, but he doesn't think Graffyn is going to show up. That's why he was willing to say that the Council would be pleased to hear him. The last thing the Commercers want is Graffyn to lay out ties between a Commercer minister and Eastern Ironway."

"So . . . Kraffeist insists he doesn't know how it happened; the files are missing; and so is the only man who might know everything. That means the Council won't ever hear the entire story."

"Not if Ulrich can help it," replied Ysella.

Dekkard shook his head, then forced himself back to the work at hand. A few minutes later, Roostof left Obreduur's office—without the newssheet—heading for the side office.

Half a bell later, Obreduur opened his door. "Steffan, I need a few words with you."

Dekkard immediately got up and entered the inner office, closing the door.

Obreduur stood beside the dark walnut desk. He handed Dekkard a thin folder. "I'd like you to meet with the Artisans Guild of Machtarn. The guild is considering filing a grievance against the Imperial Tariff Commission. They contend that the Commission is allowing cheaply produced works of art to be imported and tariffed as housewares, when the art is of a higher quality and is later sold at a far higher price than the import appraisal price."

Dekkard tried not to wince.

"This could harm all artisans in Guldor. Even if it does not, undertariffing imports harms the government by unlawfully reducing tariff revenues. You'll need to research this before you meet with them next week. Duadi the thirty-second, at the fourth bell of morning."

"Might I ask what you expect of me in this?"

Obreduur smiled sardonically. "To be understanding and very polite. Polite in the way that says you care, not polite in the way old Ritter families are, where their words are soothing and meaningless. To promise to look into the matter diligently and to assure them that the matter concerns me as well, which is why I've assigned the specialist with an artisan background. I can't personally look into everything. Ask Roostof to show you the section of the tariff laws dealing with that. You'll have to visit one of the Council legalists who specializes in that as well. Obviously, you'll wear one of your new security-gray suits when you meet with the Artisans Guild. You should get your specialist pin by tomorrow, Tridi at the latest."

"Is there anything else, sir?"

"Not right now. Once you've read the folder, and do your research, write up what you think about it and give it to me. After that, we'll talk."

"Yes, sir." Dekkard inclined his head, then turned and made his way out, heading directly for Roostof's desk.

When Dekkard approached, the legalist grinned. "What do you need?"

"The basic tariff law dealing with importing works of art. Also the section dealing with importing housewares."

"That sounds like an artisan petition."

"A possible grievance against the Tariff Commission. The councilor wants me to meet with them next week."

"Just don't say anything about what he'll do." After that quick bit of advice, Roostof turned to the bookshelf against the wall beside his desk. "All I have here is the basic statute. For interpretations and case law, you'll have to consult with the legalists over in the Council Hall."

"The councilor told me that, too."

After looking through several leather-bound volumes, Roostof slipped a marker into one and handed that volume to Dekkard. "We haven't done anything with tariffs in years. Read that section, and you'll know as much as I do. Best of fortune."

"Thank you," replied Dekkard wryly.

When he returned to his desk, Ysella looked up at him and the heavy leather-bound volume he carried, along with the folder.

"A problem with tariffs on works of art," Dekkard said.

"Aren't you the fortunate one," she said, her words somehow dryly sympathetic.

Dekkard sat down, putting aside the letters he had yet to deal with, and began to read. In less than a sixth of a bell, he grasped the core of the problem. The Artisans Guild of Machtarn contended that paintings and sculptures were being imported as housewares and then, once they were inside Guldor, were being sold as "fine art" at a much lower price than comparable works produced by Guldoran artists. Still frowning, he studied the statutory law on tariffs applied to imported art.

In any one year, any individual may personally carry or import up to three works of art [as defined in Section 2.a.(1)], each of such works being valued at more than a hundred marks, without paying tariffs. Those individuals importing more than three works of art annually are classified as dealers in art and must register and pay an annual fee [Section 2.b.], as well as a ten percent tariff on each work of art . . .

The "housewares" tariff section was much simpler—a straight five percent tariff on any shipment with a value of more than twenty marks, or five percent on the total of all imports of housewares off-loaded from any ship or conveyance.

After rereading the law twice, and then going back through the folder, he definitely understood Roostof's cautionary advice. Because he wanted to think the matter over, and at least sleep on it, he set aside the folder and the law book, and went back to drafting responses to letters.

18

After dinner on Unadi evening, still in his security grays, Dekkard sat reading in the staff room, where the light was better. He didn't want to think about tariffs any longer, and he'd given up concentrating on learning more about the individual councilors, and instead returned to reading various journals, beginning with an article in the Winterend issue of *Political Economics*. The title was daunting—"Climate and Iron Prices in the Black Centuries." Still, he started to read.

. . . the extreme cold of the eleventh century affected both Argental and Guldor, but in different ways. Argental suffered significant crop losses, requiring increased imports of grain and rice, resulting in higher food prices and widespread hunger, if short of actual starvation.

With the unrest of 1019, the Silver Party gained control of the Assembly, and to obtain adequate foreign exchange to subsidize bread prices, enacted the Susceptible Relocation Act, whereby susceptibles were shipped to Atacama as indentured servants . . .

That wasn't exactly the high point in Argenti history, reflected Dekkard as he continued.

. . . loss of arable land due to drought in the east of Guldor raised the price of grain and led to the Argenti Coal Embargo of 1111, and the Winter War of 1112 . . .

. . . while the Silent Revolution in Guldor in 1170–71, the result of female empath pressures on the Council, resulted in electoral changes in Guldor, the anticipatory changes were more profound in Argental, where all working individuals or property holders were granted the franchise, as well as in Atacama, where even greater restrictions were placed on empaths. While these political changes were charged and highly debated, they created minimal economic impact on Guldor and Atacama . . .

. . . purpose of this treatise is an attempt to quantify the changes in the price of coal, and thus of iron, in response to the impact of higher grain prices arising from the cold and reduced precipitation . . .

At the sight of the equations and the tables that followed, Dekkard smiled wryly and skipped to the next article, an examination of political trends in Guldoran politics over the past twenty years.

A third of a bell later, he finished it. For all the scholarly rhetoric, what the writer seemed to be saying was that despite shifting trade patterns, increased use of steam-powered equipment, wide swings in the crop production, and increasing immigrations from both Argental and particularly Atacama, the Commerce Party had retained total control of the Council of Sixty-Six.

Is that conclusion so strange that it needs a scholarly article?

As he leafed through the last pages, he came across a small sidebar article, entitled "The Great Magnetite Hoax."

The unwieldy nature of steam power and dangers of lighting homes with coal-gas, kerosene lanterns, or candles have inspired inventors to seek better forms of power and light generation . . . Magnetite Rotation, first proposed in 1171 by Elrik Moers, noted scientist at Imperial University, was a theory proposing that the barely discernible field generated by magnetite could be amplified by rapidly turning a wheel lined with magnetite close to a stationary rod of magnetite and thus create some form of magnetic "flow" . . . Multiple and continuing experiments demonstrated that while the existing field was intensified slightly, no matter how fast the wheel turned, the field around the rod never exceeded double that of the ambient unintensified field. Over a period of a decade, a great number of extensive experiments and costly devices attempted to improve upon those results. None succeeded . . .

Dekkard frowned. *Magnetic flow?* How could something you could barely measure flow?

Thinking about that, he was startled when he heard the chime of the front door, although it wasn't yet that late, just slightly after the first night bell by his watch.

Since all the other staffers had retired to their rooms, except for Rhosali, who had gone to visit a friend, Dekkard rose and headed for the front door. He'd just entered the main hallway when Obreduur appeared, still wearing his jacket and cravat.

"I'll get it, Steffan. If you'd stay down here, I might need you later."

"I'll be in the staff room, sir."

"I'd appreciate that." Obreduur continued toward the front door.

Wondering just who might be visiting so comparatively late, especially since neither of the Obreduurs had mentioned visitors, Dekkard turned and retreated slowly, trying to overhear anything that might be said.

All he heard was "Please come in."

Since he didn't want to be caught eavesdropping, he closed the door from the back hall and retreated to the staff room, where he forced his concentration back to learning more about councilors.

Slightly less than a bell passed before Obreduur appeared in the doorway to the staff room. "Steffan . . . I know it's not in your duties, but I would really appreciate your taking Sr. Muller and his assistant to wherever he directs you in Machtarn."

"I'd be happy to do that, sir." Especially since he was tired of poring over the book that was essentially a Council political reference manual . . . and he was curious about the visitors.

Dekkard closed the heavy book and set it on table.

"Take the Gresynt, and bring it up to the portico. I'll see them off there. I'll explain after you return."

Dekkard could hear what he thought was concern behind Obreduur's pleasant words, but he just nodded. "I'll be there as soon as I can."

"Excellent." Obreduur turned in the direction of his study.

Dekkard walked swiftly to his room, where he set down the book and reclaimed his truncheon. Then he headed down to the garage, where he topped off both the kerosene and water, since he had no idea how far he might be traveling—greater Machtarn extended almost fifteen milles along the coast to the east alone. After opening the garage door, he checked the Gresynt's reflectors and the gas reservoirs before lighting the headlamps and starting the steamer itself.

When he eased the Gresynt out of the garage and the short distance down the drive to the portico, he was moderately surprised that the gaslights that normally illuminated the area had been turned off and that the councilor was the one to open the rear door for the two who entered the steamer.

In the dim light, both Muller and his assistant appeared to be slender and dark-haired. Muller wore a dark summer suit, while his assistant wore what might have been security grays, and carried a short truncheon at his waist, the largest permitted for private security aides.

"Best of fortune" were the only words from Obreduur as he held the vehicle door.

"Thank you," replied Muller, although that was a guess on Dekkard's part because he couldn't see which one had spoken.

Obreduur closed the door and stepped back into the darkness that cloaked the portico.

"Where would you like to go?" asked Dekkard politely once he started the Gresynt down the drive toward Altarama.

"My assistant will tell you once we reach Imperial Boulevard," said Muller.

"Yes, sir."

Dekkard thought he heard the other passenger say, in a lighter voice barely above a whisper, ". . . strong isolate." That indicated he was also an empie. Dekkard knew that some empies were trained in weapons, but that was a rarity, given that the requirements of being an armed aide and an empath often created conflicts. But when it did occur the empie was usually male, which was another reason why such security types were rare, given the much smaller percentage of male empaths.

Neither Muller nor the empie spoke until the Gresynt neared the white brick gateposts just before Imperial Boulevard.

"Turn right on Imperial."

Dekkard turned right.

"Stay in the right lane until you pass the next cross street. Then move to the left lane."

Three blocks later, the empie said, "Turn left and follow the cross street for one block, then turn right. Go north one block and turn right again. When you reach Imperial turn south."

Dekkard understood. If any steamer followed them through that pattern, it had to be on purpose. He didn't see any headlamps that close, let alone following.

Once Dekkard had the steamer back on Imperial Boulevard, he watched as they went around the Circle of Commerce and then continued on Imperial Boulevard past the Avenue of the Guilds toward the harbor rotary.

Just short of the rotary, the empie said, "Turn right, and drive straight to the river."

After two blocks the taller merchanting and commercial structures gave way to lower warehouses, all of which were dark. Four blocks later, Dekkard slowed the steamer as they neared the river piers. The street ended in a wide cul-de-sac serving three piers. The one at the far right had what looked to be a river freighter tied up, with a single lamp at the foot of the gangway. The other two piers appeared to be empty.

"Pull up at the pier to the left."

Dekkard did so.

"If we do not come back in a few minutes, return to the house."

"After a few minutes I will."

In moments, the pair were out of the steamer and had vanished into the darkness of the unlit pier. Dekkard could see that no large or seagoing craft was tied up at the pier, but that didn't mean that a smaller boat wasn't moored out of sight . . . or that the pair might actually move to another pier after he left.

After squinting at his watch in the dimness, to make certain a good five minutes had passed, he eased the Gresynt away from the piers, not wanting to remain in the mostly dark industrial and shipping area any longer than necessary.

He couldn't help breathing a bit more easily once he was back on Imperial Boulevard heading north.

The gates to the drive were still open when he drove up to the still-unlighted portico. So he stopped the steamer and closed the gates before driving under the portico and back to the garage.

He'd just closed the garage doors and made his way into the back hallway when Obreduur appeared.

"Thank you very much, Steffan. You delivered them to where they wished to go?"

"I took them where they directed me—a river pier off the street just north of the harbor rotary."

"The older river piers. They had a small boat waiting . . . or one that would pick them up there. I'd appreciate it if you did not mention Sr. Muller's appearance here to anyone for a time. Thank you again."

"My pleasure, sir."

"Not really your pleasure, Steffan, but I do appreciate it. Good night." Obreduur turned, heading back to either his study or his bedchamber.

Dekkard walked to the staff room, where he reclaimed the book and turned off the gaslight before starting up the staff staircase to his room. He couldn't help wondering who "Muller" really was. He had a wild idea, but he couldn't figure out how that idea fit.

And that bothered him more than just a little.

19

When Dekkard woke on Duadi morning, he was still pondering the brief appearance of the mysterious Sr. Muller . . . and the fact that Obreduur had been so matter-of-fact about Muller and his empath going to a deserted river pier. But then Obreduur had been guildmeister of the stevedores and river workers.

But . . . if he knew and arranged that, why didn't Muller want to give directions until we were away from Obreduur? Or had Obreduur left the decision for Muller to make after he departed the house?

Dekkard pushed the questions away for the moment, then shaved, washed, and dressed before heading down to breakfast. As Hyelda had warned him, there was no quince paste, only tomato jelly, adequate for Dekkard's purposes, but definitely lacking the more robust taste and substance of the quince.

On the drive to the Council Office Building, Obreduur made no mention of the visitors of the previous evening, not that Dekkard expected otherwise. At that moment, and Dekkard couldn't have said why, he realized why the Craft Party wouldn't have wanted elections. *They wouldn't have changed anything.* Even if the Craft Party had gained another seat or two and held the plurality of councilors, enough of the Landor councilors would have voted for a Commerce premier to keep the Commercers in control, and the Craft Party would have lost two experienced councilors for nothing.

Dekkard still wondered about the trade-off. Wouldn't the Crafters have been better off with a few more seats in the Council?

The usual small stack of petitions and letters was waiting for Dekkard when he reached his table desk, and he immediately set to work.

Less than a bell later, a Council Guard announced a single visitor, a Sr. Jerrohm Kaas, who came and met with Obreduur for less than half a bell.

Visitors were rare, first, because appointments had to be arranged in advance; second, because most people who could benefit from seeing Obreduur were from his district, which was effectively a two-day journey by ironway; and, third, because commercial interests saw little point in trying to cultivate him. For that rarity of visitors, Dekkard was definitely glad.

A third before fourth bell, after checking with Karola to make sure Obreduur wouldn't need him until noon, Dekkard made his way to the Council Hall, where he

descended to the lower-level offices of the Council legalists.

Even before Dekkard could frame his request to the
stern-looking, dark-haired receptionist or clerk, she
spoke.

"Are you here to pick up something?"

"No, Councilor Obreduur assigned me to get background information on the law regarding import tariffs
on fine-art imports."

"You're security."

"I'm also an assistant economic specialist for the
councilor."

The clerk frowned.

"Would any security type want to know the law on
import tariffs on fine arts unless his councilor wanted
it?" Dekkard kept his tone patient and gently sardonic.

"What's your name?"

"Steffan Dekkard, Councilor Obreduur."

She opened a small book, one that Dekkard could
see was the roster of councilors and their staff members. After riffling through it quickly, and then checking Dekkard's name, she looked up. "Your passcard,
please?"

Dekkard eased it from his wallet and offered it.

After studying it, the clerk nodded, almost grudgingly.
"Let me see who would be best to advise you."

A good sixth of a bell passed before the clerk returned
and escorted Dekkard to a small corner desk in a back
room and said, "Sr. Ihler, Steffan Dekkard from Councilor Obreduur's office." Then she slipped away.

The grayed legalist smiled pleasantly and gestured for
Dekkard to take the straight-backed chair.

"Thank you for seeing me," said Dekkard. "It might
seem unlikely . . ."

"I have to admit that it's a bit odd for a security aide
to be asking about tariff laws."

"It is, but I come from an artisan background, and
there's no one else on the staff who does. My mother and
sister are both portraiture artists."

Ihler nodded. "What is the nature of the question?"

"More of a request for background, sir. Certain importers may be importing large numbers of various forms of fine art, not just a few pieces for individual collectors. These pieces of fine art are labeled as housewares, which are tariffed at less than half commercial fine art. I'm curious if there's any law or provision against misrepresentation. I couldn't find it, but I'm not a legalist."

Ihler nodded. "There are two possibilities. The first and most common charge is inadvertent misclassification, which requires paying the proper tariff and a penalty. The penalty can range from twenty percent of the legal tariff to a hundred percent, based on the volume and actual value of the art. The second and more serious charge is felonious misclassification. That would be unusual. In fact, I've never heard of a case. The penalty there could require incarceration, tripling the tariff due, and losing one's dealer import license."

Dekkard waited.

Ihler shook his head. "That, unfortunately, is the simple part. Guldor has a legal definition of fine art. It's not in the statute books, because it's based on case law, but I'll have a copy made of the pertinent language and sent to your councilor's office. Argental doesn't have a legal term for fine art, because it doesn't allow what we would call fine art. The only legally and commercially acceptable art is portraiture, because likenesses are deemed functional for purposes of records and identification. In Argental, nonfunctional art can be destroyed under the provisions of the Cultural Frivolity Act.

"Atacama allows all manner of art, but makes no distinction about the levels of art. This may be where your problem arises. Under Atacaman law, fine art is simply part and parcel of housewares. That, of course, does not excuse the importer from making the proper customs declaration . . ."

By the time Dekkard left Legalist Ihler, he just hoped he could remember everything.

When he returned to the office, Ysella looked up questioningly.

"I now know why the councilor wants me to handle as much of this as possible." Dekkard turned to Karola. "The Council legalists will be sending some legal papers here."

"I'll make sure you get them, Steffan."

"No one else will want them," replied Dekkard not quite morosely, as he returned to the more mundane, and actually more interesting, task of crafting draft replies.

Almost precisely at third bell, a Council messenger delivered a thin folder. It contained ten pages of printed case law opinions and definitions dealing with fine art. Then, just before fourth bell and the time Dekkard was about to leave to ready the Gresynt to pick up Obreduur and Ysella, another Council messenger arrived with a small box, which she delivered to Karola, who, after the messenger departed, handed it to Dekkard.

"Go ahead," said Karola. "Open it."

Dekkard did. Inside was a smaller box, the size that might hold cufflinks or a cravat pin, but inside that box was a gold-edged, square silver pin, in the center of which was a "66" on top of an ornate "C"—the same pin that Macri, Roostof, and Raynaad wore every day. Engraved on the top edge was C. OBREDUUR and on the bottom STEFFAN DEKKARD.

"Just don't lose it," said Avraal.

Dekkard just looked at it for a moment. Finally, he slipped the box into the inside pocket of his security grays. Within minutes, he was headed out the door to fetch the Gresynt.

As he walked down the staff stairs and out through the west doors of the Council Office Building, he couldn't help but smile at the thought of what the pin represented.

"Congratulations, Steffan!" called a voice.

Dekkard turned to see a blond woman standing beside a younger and very muscular isolate. It took him a moment to recognize Frieda Livigne. Wondering why she was offering congratulations, he turned and walked to join her. "Congratulations for what?"

"Your becoming an assistant specialist. Not many isolates do that. Now, it makes much more sense why you didn't want to go into commercial security."

Dekkard was more than a little puzzled. "How did you know? I just got my pin this afternoon. I haven't told anyone besides the other staffers."

"Oh, all the specialists and legalists have to be approved by the Security Committee, well, by the staff, really. I saw your name."

"Thank you. I've only really just started."

"Everyone has to start somewhere. I'm sure that you'll do a good job." Livigne smiled, an expression guardedly warm and professional. "We have to go. It's good seeing you again."

As Livigne and the isolate headed into the Council Office Building, Dekkard frowned. *Approved by the Council Security Committee?* It wasn't as though he happened to be dealing with military or security matters.

He was still thinking about it when he brought the Gresynt to a stop under the covered portico, although he also worried about the dark green clouds to the east of Machtarn, since he wanted to pick up his tailored clothes right after he delivered Obreduur to the house.

Dekkard had no more gathered up the councilor and Ysella and pulled away from the Council Office Building than Obreduur asked, "Steffan . . . how are you coming on the tariff matter for the Artisans Guild?"

"Roostof gave me the statutory language, and I met with Legalist Ihler over at the Council Hall this morning. He gave me more background on the scope of the problem, since there are conflicting legal definitions of art in different countries. He sent more material this afternoon."

"How soon can you do a summary of the problem . . . just a page or so?"

"Noon tomorrow, sir?"

"That would be fine, but I won't get to it until a little later. There's a party caucus at fifth bell, and a Workplace Administration Committee meeting at one." With that, Obreduur settled into reading the papers he'd brought with him.

After what Dekkard had read about tariffs, he was definitely beginning to see why Obreduur was reading all the time.

The trip back to the house was uneventful. Once Dekkard finished with the Gresynt, he hurried off at a quick walk toward Excellencia, glancing eastward at the slowly approaching clouds. His suits, barongs, and shirts were ready, and, once outside the store, he immediately hailed a steamhack, given that he could see the rain falling on the eastern parts of the city.

"Where to, sir?" asked the steamhacker as Dekkard closed the door.

"East Altarama Drive. Seven sixty-three."

"Seven sixty-three east Altarama Drive it is. You're a security type works there, right?"

"I work for him, there or at his office."

The hacker turned left, then left again, so that he was driving south on Imperial. "What's it like being a security type for someone that wealthy?"

Dekkard doubted that Obreduur was that wealthy, but simply said, "It's like any other security job. Most of the time it's very routine. Once in a while it's not. How long have you been a hacker?"

"Sixteen years, just like my old man."

When Dekkard didn't reply, the hacker asked, "You come from a security family?"

"Artisan family. That talent didn't find me."

"Sometimes that happens." After a time, the hacker turned left on Altarama. He didn't speak again until he pulled up in front of the house. "Nice place. Your boss ever been attacked?"

"Once." *So far.*

The hacker shook his head. "You can have it. Be two marks."

Dekkard gave the hacker two and a half.

"Thank you, sir. Good evening."

Dekkard was halfway up the drive when the first raindrops began to pelt down, but he only got a little damp before he reached the covered portico. He was about to head up to his room to hang up his new clothes when Ysella appeared, holding an envelope.

"You ran off so fast that Rhosali didn't have a chance to give you this."

"I wanted to get my suits and shirts before the rain hit . . . and the barongs you helped me pick out." Dekkard took the envelope.

She smiled. "You cut it close. I'll see you at dinner." She turned toward the staff room.

Once Dekkard hung up his shirts, suits, and barongs, he immediately opened the envelope and began to read.

Dear Steffan—

It's always good to get a letter from you. You make life in Machtarn sound so interesting, but, knowing you, you just don't mention the tedium. Every occupation has those times. You always were the restless one, and your greatest accomplishment was to surmount those times, and, for that alone, your father and I are most proud of you.

Naralta is thinking of opening her own studio. She feels that those patrons who like my work are put off by hers, and those who like her work are turned away by mine. From what I see, I fear she may not be right, but she's always wanted to be successful in her own right, and that's her choice, and she has to be the one choosing, not us . . .

Dekkard nodded as he continued to read his mother's clear and flowing script telling about her recent work and the day-to-day events in Oersynt. His eyes narrowed as he read the lines on the top of the third page.

> . . . *have you heard of the New Meritorists? A group of them assembled in Geddes Square yesterday. I couldn't understand what it was all about, except that they claimed that councilors weren't ever personally accountable for their votes. They weren't there long, though. Security patrollers showed up, along with some Army soldiers. Naralta and I hurried off as soon as I saw the patrollers. I heard shots after that. You don't ever forget that sound . . .*

You don't ever forget . . . Dekkard's parents had never said much about their departure from Argental . . . except that it had been difficult. *Difficult enough that they'd been shot at?*

> . . . *There must have been at least fifty people demonstrating. It could have been more. Some of them were students, but I don't know why they were there. The only mention in the* Gazette *was that a group of hooligans had been arrested for disturbing the peace at the square* . . .

Dekkard wondered if the demonstration in Oersynt had been at the same time as the one on the Council grounds. If so . . . that suggested a much larger and widespread organization . . . and if both groups of Meritorists were armed . . .

Dekkard finished reading the letter, then folded it and slipped it into the drawer in his nightstand table. Still thinking about his mother's words about not forgetting the sound of shots . . . and the demonstration in Oersynt, he went downstairs for dinner in the staff room, where Hyelda served a pear and cheese ravioli with veal cutlets, the same meal that was on the Obreduur dining table, which was usually, but not always, the case.

"I saw you bringing in some clothes before the rain really came down," observed Rhosali.

"Avraal persuaded me that my wardrobe needed some additions."

"You two always look so nice. When you're not in your gray uniforms no one would know you're security types."

"I hope that's a compliment," replied Dekkard.

"It is. When you two went out together the other day, folks would have thought you were swells or Landors."

"I just like to look good," replied Ysella. "Steffan looks good in anything. I have to work at it."

While Dekkard definitely disagreed, he didn't say so.

Once dinner was over and the four staffers rose, Dekkard followed Ysella into the back hall and said, "Do you have a minute?"

"I do," replied Ysella, "but if this is to be a serious discussion, it might be better to repair to the portico."

"I yield to your better judgment."

When the two stepped out of the house, still under the roof covering the portico, Dekkard realized there was another reason why she'd suggested there. The drumming of the heavy rain on the roof made successful eavesdropping unlikely.

"What's on your mind, Steffan?"

"Several things, actually. First, Frieda Livigne congratulated me on becoming a specialist. She knew because she's a staffer on the Security Committee."

Ysella frowned, but said, "That makes sense."

"It still bothers me. She also said that now it made much more sense why I'd turned down commercial security."

"Hmmm . . . you might want to mention that to the councilor. What else?"

"The New Meritorists. By the way, is that from the old Meritorists? And why did the old Meritorists choose that name?"

"The original Meritorists thought councilors should be evaluated by the merit of their votes. At least, that was what my father said. What about them?"

"The letter I just got. It was from my mother. There was a demonstration by the New Meritorists in Oersynt last week, about the same time as the one here. Security patrollers and Army troopers dispersed them, and she heard shots."

"She wasn't involved, I hope?"

"No. She and my sister left before the shooting started. They happened to be passing near the square."

"We definitely need to tell Obreduur that. Now."

With that, the two turned and made their way inside and into the main hall.

For once Obreduur wasn't in his study, but reading in the front parlor. He looked up from the journal he held. "You two look rather serious. What is it?"

Dekkard repeated what he'd told Ysella.

Obreduur nodded. "I heard about the demonstration in Oersynt yesterday. There were others across Guldor as well. Kathaar, Veerlyn, Neewyrk, and Uldwyrk. There are likely others that Security shut down and managed to cover up. You might also like to know that the demonstrators outside the Council Hall were the ones to open fire, not the Council Guards."

Ritten Obreduur, who had been reading in a green leather armchair that matched the one in which Obreduur sat, just nodded as if she'd known that all along, which she doubtless had.

"It's also not surprising that Councilor Maendaan and his staff are watching changes in the staff positions of Craft Party councilors. They hope that will give the Commerce Party some idea of what we might do. All you two can do is your best." He paused. "I do appreciate your letting me know about both events."

"Sir," ventured Dekkard, "why do you think the New Meritorist demonstrations are happening now? Times are much better than in the Black Centuries or even fifty years ago."

"For you and for me they are. For many Landors, they're not. With the growth of industries, they have to pay farmworkers more, and crop prices aren't rising that much, even with the tariffs on swampgrass rice and emmer wheat-corn from the Teknold Confederacy. You come from a family of skilled artisans, but the growth of larger workshops and steam-powered factories destroyed the skilled weavers a century ago. Those who labor in the textile mills around Veerlyn, Uldwyrk, and even Gaarlak are paid far less in real marks than the old weavers were. Steam lathes and punch-carders have replaced all but the most skilled cabinetmakers. People from those trades are angry. They need someone to blame. The Great Charter makes it difficult to blame anyone. These would-be revolutionaries and reformers claim that holding each councilor accountable for his vote will improve things. And it will, for a few years. But it will also give everyone targets at which to aim their wrath. And then we will follow Teknold down the road to anarchy. Why? Because once votes are made public, those with power and marks can target councilors who oppose them, and the temptation becomes ever greater for each councilor to give in to either marks or popularity, if not both."

"Macri and Roostof both explained that to me, but won't incarcerating or exiling or killing these demonstrators just make matters worse?"

"If that is all the government does, Steffan, you'd be right. Unfortunately, that's all that the Commercers and the Landors plan to do. Over time, that also is a path to anarchy and destruction. What we're trying to do is broaden the appeal of the Craft Party to gain enough seats to change the path of government. It takes time. It takes patience, even when people are angry."

Dekkard nodded slowly. "I see." He wasn't quite sure he did, but those words were safe enough.

"Just keep looking. Things are beginning to change."

Obreduur's smile seemed a little sad, Dekkard reflected as he and Ysella walked back to the now-empty staff room. He stopped and looked at her. "I still think shooting the New Meritorists isn't a good idea."

"What did you expect the Council Guards and Security patrollers to do? Just turn the other cheek? Or stand there patiently and get shot?"

"What if they just let them demonstrate?"

"Didn't you hear what he said? They were the ones who shot first. They invaded the Council grounds without permission."

Permission the Council would never have granted. "That raises several questions, if not more. I need to think about it."

"It's a lot to take in."

Dekkard retreated to his room. Once there, he took out the book on the Council, but his thoughts kept going back to the New Meritorists, and he put aside that book, idly picking up the Springfirst issue of *Political Economics* that he'd borrowed from Obreduur once the councilor finished reading it.

As he looked at the journal, he realized something else. In all the issues of *Political Economics* he'd perused in the time he'd spent in the Obreduur household, he'd never seen an article or commentary involving political dissent in Guldor, nor had he run across any mention of either the Meritorists or the New Meritorists, even in the *Journal of History.* It was almost as if all Guldor wanted to deny their existence, just like no one liked to mention susceptibles.

No wonder the New Meritorists shot first.

Dekkard had the sinking feeling that, no matter how long and hard he thought, he wasn't going to like where he ended up.

20

Tridi morning dawned dark. The rain that had arrived the evening before remained settled firmly over Machtarn, not a downpour or a deluge, but a steady percussion of raindrops on roofs and other surfaces more intense than merely pleasant. Knowing that traffic on Imperial Boulevard would be slow, Dekkard suggested to Obreduur that they leave earlier, to which the councilor agreed.

While fewer steamers were out, the water on the roads and the reduced visibility from the rain and windscreen wipers that weren't that effective just about doubled the travel time to the Council Office Building. But at least the rain didn't leave an ashy residue the way it almost always did in Oersynt or even sometimes in Veerlyn.

After he dropped off Obreduur and Ysella, who wore a stylish gray suit because of her meeting with the women's committee of the Textile Millworkers Guild, and secured the Gresynt in the covered parking, even with an umbrella, Dekkard got damp crossing the street to the Council Office Building.

He couldn't help thinking that with all the rain there wouldn't be any demonstrations. He also realized that he'd have to let the letters and petition responses pile up because he still had to write a short summary on how he would present the fine-art tariff problem.

As soon as he sat down he started in on writing the summary. In less than a third of a bell, he stopped and looked over what he'd written.

The problem seems to be that different countries handle art objects in a different fashion and that the customs assessors appear to be accepting the valuation of art objects according to the practices of the country in which they originated . . .

Dekkard knew he was missing or overlooking something. *What determines value?* Was it the price paid for the goods in the first country? Or the estimated price of what it would sell for in Guldor? *But how can a customs assessor determine such an estimated price?* Should he even try?

Dekkard crumpled the paper and started again.

When, just short of noon, Obreduur returned from the Craft Party caucus held in a meeting room on the first floor, Dekkard immediately got up and handed him the draft summary, or rather, the fourth draft of the fine art import problem.

"I'll have to look at this later, Steffan."

"Yes, sir, but I promised it to you by noon."

For a moment, the councilor offered an amused smile. "So you did. Thank you."

After the councilor entered the inner office, Dekkard went back Ysella's desk and handed her the keys to the Gresynt. "You'll need these."

"Thank you."

"Good fortune with the meeting." With a smile he headed back to his desk, where he went to work trying to catch up on drafting his responses.

Then at first bell, because Ysella had left to stand in for Obreduur at the meeting of the women's committee of the Textile Millworkers Guild, Dekkard escorted Obreduur to one of the committee chambers in the Council Hall for the Workplace Administration Committee meeting.

"Just get something to eat and come back here. I doubt the meeting will be more than a bell."

After that, given Obreduur's instructions, he stopped by the staff cafeteria to get a quick bite to eat, picking up a Kathaar beef empanada and café. He took an empty table for two, but before he could even start to eat, the bear-like figure of Jaime Minz appeared.

"Steffan . . . I heard you're moving up in the world."

"Who told you that? Frieda Livigne?"

Minz laughed his hearty laugh. "Who else? I'm always asking her for the latest."

"How did your councilor's inspection of the *Resolute* turn out? Did what he found out have just a little bit to do with the Imperador's request for Grieg's resignation?"

"Steffan . . . how could you possibly think such a thing? You know that so many inspections are pro forma. The Fleet Marshal makes sure the captain has everything working and spotless. Everyone is polite and helpful."

Dekkard offered an amused grin. "Since you didn't answer the question, I take it that he was really pissed at the way the Navy let itself get taken by Eastern. Especially since *Gestirn* reported that Security is looking for Eastern's missing director of logistics."

"Steffan . . . directors of logistics go missing all the time. Haven't you heard?" Minz's tone remained light and cheerful.

"Just like premiers get dismissed all the time."

"Of course, just like that . . . what else could you expect? Where's your other half? Security other half, I mean."

"Avraal? The councilor sent her on an errand. She'll be back before long."

"That's good. I wondered if you were handling security alone. Did you hear about Mathilde Thanne?"

It took Dekkard a moment to pull up the name. "You mean Councilor Mardosh's empath?"

"She's the one. She's gone missing. Just heard about it this morning. That's why I wondered about Avraal." Minz stepped back. "Anyway, it's good to hear you're both in good shape. Talk to you later."

After that brief conversation, Dekkard wasn't quite so hungry. Mardosh was one of the two Craft councilors on the Military Affairs Committee, and had been an assistant guildmeister for the Shipfitters Guild in Siincleer, the guild that built all of the Navy's warships. And Minz's quick visit hadn't been nearly as social as it sounded. First the attack on him . . . and now another Craft councilor's security empie was missing?

Something else to tell Obreduur . . . and Ysella. Definitely Ysella.

Dekkard forced himself to finish the empanada and café, then made his way back to wait outside the committee room. Several other security aides waited as well, but none he knew particularly well, and he wasn't interested in striking up a conversation just for the sake of talking to someone.

Dekkard couldn't help occasionally looking at his watch as close to a third of a bell passed. Then, out of the corner of his eye, Dekkard caught sight of a blond woman, one who seemed vaguely familiar, and when he turned to look more closely, he realized that she was Charmione Lundquist, the junior legalist for Councilor Vhiola Sandegarde, one of the handful of women councilors. That Sandegarde was a councilor was likely due to the fact that her father owned and operated Kathaar Iron & Steel.

Lundquist smiled broadly and turned toward Dekkard when she saw him looking in her direction. "Steffan . . . waiting for your councilor?"

"What else?"

"I hear you have some additional duties . . ."

How many people know . . . and how? "They're very new. How did you find out?"

"I was talking to Lionel . . . Lionel Ihler, the Council legalist, about tariffs on borax, especially since the deposits near Port Reale are playing out, and he asked me if I knew you. He thought it was . . . well, strange . . . that a security type was handling tariffs."

"I've been recently appointed to duties as an assistant economic specialist."

Lundquist offered a warm smile. "Congratulations! I always thought you could do better."

"Thank you. I hope the tariffs on borax are more straightforward than those on fine art."

She shook her head. "No tariff is simple . . . and we need the borax for both steel and glassware."

Dekkard had no idea that ironworks used borax or that glassworks needed it. "Everything is more complex when you look into it."

"How true! I do have to go, but it was good seeing you, if only for a minute."

Then she was headed down the corridor toward one of the smaller committee rooms.

Less than a sixth of a bell passed before Obreduur walked out of the committee room, followed by several other councilors. Dekkard had to hurry to join him, but he didn't say anything until they were outside and walking under the covered portico toward the Council Office Building with the rain still coming down. Only then did he relay what Minz had said.

"He actually said that?"

"In a false-humor fashion, so that if I told anyone else, he could claim he was only joking."

Obreduur's voice hardened as he said, "Avraal should have returned by now. Let her know about this and tell her that you've informed me. Both of you need to be even more careful. Once you've conveyed that to her, we'll go over your summary about the fine-art tariffs."

Once they were back in the office, and Obreduur stopped to talk to Karola, presumably about appointments or meetings, Dekkard eased over to Ysella's desk, noting again how stylish she looked in her conservative gray suit, with the silver and gold specialist pin in her left lapel.

"You look very professional. How did the meeting with the women's committee go?"

"As it should have, I thought. We'll have to see."

"Something rather odd, even ominous, happened while I was having lunch waiting for the councilor. I've told him, and we both thought you should know . . ." Dekkard relayed the conversation with Jaime Minz, finishing with, "The councilor said both of us should be more careful than ever."

"Then you'd better not be taking night walks alone."

"I haven't, not recently. You shouldn't be walking to the omnibus alone, either."

"Is that a proposition?" Ysella offered a mischievous smile.

Almost before he recognized the smile, Dekkard had been about to tell her to be serious. He didn't. "I hadn't thought of it that way. Do you think I should?" He raised his eyebrows.

"Go talk to the councilor. He's looking at you."

"Later."

"Promises, promises . . ."

Dekkard shook his head, then turned back toward Obreduur, following him into the office and closing the door.

Obreduur didn't seat himself, but picked up the summary sheet that Dekkard had written, looking at it as if to remind himself of what he previously read, then said, "Your summary suggests that valuing art-object imports at what they might bring here in Guldor is unfair. Why would you conclude that?"

"Because that's a judgment by the assessor. The only value the object has when assessed is what the importer paid for it. Whether that can accurately be determined is a separate question."

"So how would you suggest determining the tariff?"

"It's within the law to base the tariff on the purpose for which it is imported, not necessarily the purpose for which it was made in another country."

"Then you're suggesting that such objects be tariffed at the rate for art, but based on their past price?" Obreduur said carefully.

"No, sir. I'd contend that is a fair reading of the law. That may not be how customs assessors are handling it or what it should be."

Surprisingly to Dekkard, Obreduur smiled. "I'd have to agree. You can present that as a reading of the law, and then ask them if that is how they see the tariffs being applied, and if not, if they have any examples that

I can use. Then ask them what specifically they recommend."

"Is there anything else you'd like me to do?"

"Just listen. Don't commit me to anything. Don't even hint it. Just say that you understand the depth of their concerns and that you'll convey those concerns, as well as any other suggestions they may have. Ask them if there's anything else you should know . . ."

After another few minutes of suggestions, Obreduur said, "That's about all I can add. If I think of anything else, I'll let you know."

When Dekkard left the inner office, his thoughts drifted back to what Minz had said, but there wasn't much he could do at the moment.

21

Furdi morning dawned rainy once more, although the intensity was much less than on Tridi and the clouds not so dark, giving Dekkard hope that he might see sunshine by afternoon.

He had barely seated himself at the staff room table when someone rang the door chimes insistently, and Rhosali hurried off. She returned several minutes later and announced, "It was an urgent message for the councilor. The Ritter took it himself."

"Was it a Council or Imperial messenger?" asked Ysella.

"No. He was one of the private ones. He had a blue uniform with green piping."

The hint of a frown crossed Ysella's face, then vanished. "Thank you."

Dekkard looked at Ysella, but she only gave a slight nod, confirming his feeling that urgent messages arriving at breakfast were anything but good. He also knew that Obreduur would inform Ysella and him only if the message affected them. So he just took another bite of his croissant, decidedly less flavorful with the tomato jelly, followed by another swallow of café.

Then Hyelda appeared in the archway from the kitchen. "The councilor said he'd like to leave in a sixth."

"Thank you," Dekkard replied, then finished his second croissant quickly, followed by the last drops of his café.

By then Ysella had already left the staff room.

Seven minutes later, Dekkard drove the Gresynt up under the portico roof. Obreduur and Ysella were waiting, and both entered the steamer quickly.

"I apologize for having you both hurry," explained Obreduur as Dekkard started down the drive. "Premier Ulrich decided late last night that the Military Affairs Committee would hold the hearing on the Kraffeist Affair first thing this morning. Notices did not arrive at the offices of Craft councilors until after all of us had departed. Craft Floor Leader Haarsfel sent the message I received when he found out early this morning. Consequently, I need to make some changes in your duties today. Svard will be the official Craft Party observer, and, Avraal, you will be accompanying him." Obreduur paused, as if expecting a question.

Dekkard asked, "To make certain there's no hidden empath interference? Is that because she's one of the stronger empaths?"

"Exactly," replied Obreduur. "You will have to provide all my security, Steffan. Calling the hearing this way allows Ulrich and the Imperador to claim that they held a hearing open to the newssheets without giving them any time to write about it in advance or to cover it fully. Also, without advance notice, there is less likelihood of New Meritorist demonstrators, but they still might find out."

Dekkard did not point out the other obvious reason for not informing the Craft councilors in advance—that the Craft councilors on the Military Affairs Committee would have less time to prepare . . . or to be the ones informing the newssheets. "Might I ask, sir, if there was advance notice of what witnesses will be testifying?"

"The official notice only stated that First Marshal Bernotte and other Imperial functionaries were being called to testify." Obreduur's voice was seemingly unstressed, although Dekkard doubted he was that calm.

Calling the First Marshal as a witness was definitely surprising since the First Marshal, as the head of all Guldoran armed forces, was the only Guldoran minister chosen not by the Premier, but by the Imperador, although the Council could vote to remove the First Marshal, or the Fleet Marshal, also appointed by the Imperador, but not both at once. In no case could one be removed within seventy-two days of the other.

Once Dekkard had the Gresynt on Altarama headed for Imperial Boulevard, Obreduur began to write, using the case that carried his papers as a portable desk. He continued writing until Dekkard pulled up to the covered entrance to the Council Office Building. Then he said, "Avraal will have to leave for the hearing immediately. I'd appreciate it if you'd avoid delays in getting to the office."

"Yes, sir."

After Dekkard dropped the two off, he quickly drove to the covered parking, secured the Gresynt, and walked swiftly toward the west entrance.

Another figure hurried to join him—Amelya Detauran. "You're in more of a hurry than usual, Steffan."

"Some days are like that," he replied, not breaking stride, knowing that the muscular Detauran was more than capable of keeping up with him.

"For me, too." She lowered her voice. "Ulrich screwed us as well. He never let her know he was going to keep all the Kraffeist-related matters in hearings before the Military Affairs Committee. Maastach didn't tell her, either. He still hasn't."

Dekkard almost broke stride. "Just because she doesn't like Eastern Ironway?"

"I told you before. Some things go back a long ways.

We need to talk sometime. But you and your boss need to know that mine isn't that happy with all this, and she's not the only one. That's all I should say right now."

"I'll let him know . . . and thank you."

Amelya smiled. "We'll talk later. We're both in a hurry right now." With that she angled away from Dekkard as they crossed the drive in the light rain.

On his way inside and up the staff staircase, Dekkard considered what had just happened. Detauran's councilor—Kaliara Bassaana—was the second-ranking Commerce councilor on the Transportation Committee, likely to become chair after the next election, because Chairman Maastach was senior enough that he couldn't run for reelection. Yet Transportation was the oversight committee for railroads and highways, and Maastach and Ulrich had essentially bypassed Bassaana without telling her, at least partly because of her animosity toward Eastern.

Dekkard just wished he knew more, but Detauran had indicated she just might tell him . . . most likely for a future favor. *Most likely? Definitely!*

As soon as he stepped into the outer office, Karola just turned to the half-open door to the inner office and said, "Steffan's here, sir."

"Good!"

Dekkard kept moving, walked into the inner office, and closed the door.

Obreduur looked up with a slight frown.

"There's something you should know . . ." Dekkard relayed Amelya Detauran's words.

The councilor nodded. "Keeping other committees out of the investigation was always a possibility, but to strong-arm Councilor Bassaana, with her wealth and connections . . . there's something more there than the obvious."

"Doesn't that also mean that there won't be a Public Resources Committee hearing over the Kraffeist Affair?"

"What do you think, Steffan?"

Dekkard smiled wryly. "Not if Premier Ulrich can avoid it. I'd guess he'll claim that using a Naval Coal Reserve and overcharging the Navy puts the matter under the Military Affairs Committee."

Obreduur's smile was sardonic. "I wouldn't at all be surprised if Premier Ulrich will announce just that when he opens the hearing. In the meantime, we both have work to do."

"Yes, sir." Dekkard inclined his head, turned, and made his way back to his desk with the small stack of letters and petitions that awaited him. As he seated himself, he considered again the one aspect of Detauran's wording that had struck him as slightly odd. She'd said "you and your boss." Did she also know that he'd been promoted?

As Dekkard worked through the letters on his desk he did notice that, in response to the bronze messenger flag that Karola had lowered outside the corridor door, a Council messenger appeared and collected quite a few envelopes, presumably to other councilors. *About what Amelya said? Or something else about the hearings?*

Just before noon, Obreduur stepped out of his office. "Steffan, we're off."

Dekkard immediately stood. "Where to, sir?"

"The councilors' dining room. You can eat at the staff cafeteria. Councilor Ulrich is most fastidious about stopping hearings for lunch, as if he were truly a Ritter. So if you see Svard and Avraal, you might join them, but don't linger. The Waterways Committee meeting starts at first bell, and I'd like you to escort me. There will be newssheet reporters and . . . there might be others."

Dekkard understood. Obreduur worried that word about the Kraffeist hearings had leaked or been leaked for various purposes, some of which might result in intrusions of either would-be influencers or worse.

On the walk from the Council Office Building to the Council Hall, Dekkard saw more Council Guards stationed within and around the courtyard gardens, but no sign of demonstrators, possibly partly because of the rain, although it had almost stopped and was more of a light mist.

Once he saw Obreduur safely into the councilors' dining room, Dekkard walked to the staff cafeteria, looking for Ysella and Roostof. He saw neither, not until he'd gotten his meal, when Roostof called out, "Steffan! Over here."

Dekkard joined them. "How is it going?"

Roostof snorted. "Ulrich gave an opening statement saying that all aspects of the 'so-called Kraffeist Affair' will be addressed before the Military Affairs Committee. Kraffeist was the first witness. He claims he knows nothing and that the leases he signed didn't indicate they were on Naval Coal Reserve lands . . . and that he had no idea—"

"Did he say why he later said it wasn't a problem?" asked Dekkard, quickly taking a bite of his basil-lime empanada.

"Oh, yes. The same shit as before . . . that the Navy hadn't used it in a hundred years, so that it didn't seem to him to be a problem. He claims the payments were standard, and that he knew nothing of the bribe . . . I mean the commission to the nonexistent Kharhan Associates, or the disappearing director of logistics or the missing files . . ." Roostof shook his head. "Ulrich and several of the councilors said that all that seemed improbable, but they didn't press him. Ulrich did say that if proof surfaced to indicate that Kraffeist had lied or misled the committee, he would face criminal charges. Then there were four other Eastern Ironway bureaucrats who also knew nothing. The morning ended with testimony from Admiral Gorral, the head of Naval Logistics, who admitted to later discovering the price gouging by Eastern Ironway. That didn't go well, because Ulrich and the other Commercers attacked him for accepting overpriced coal. They didn't seem to care that he had no way of knowing Eastern's costs or sources. They just blamed him. This afternoon we're supposed to hear the details from Naval Supply officers." Roostof shook his head.

Dekkard swallowed a mouthful of café, then said, "It sounds like it will be a long afternoon that won't tell anyone much."

"Isn't that what Ulrich wants?" asked Roostof sardonically. "He'll have another long day of hearings tomorrow, lasting long enough so that the newsies miss their deadlines, and hope the whole thing will die down over endday, and that very few people will read the official report . . . and given that most people aren't that interested in the price of coal paid by the Navy . . . unless the Navy can't pursue Sargassan pirates because of excessive coal prices at foreign ports."

"No one's saying anything about the missing Eduard Graffyn?" asked Dekkard.

"Ulrich said that his absence was regrettable, but didn't change the nature of the offense," added Ysella. "The committee will recommend and the Justiciary will support a hefty but affordable penalty to be paid by Eastern, and life will go on . . . while certain unpleasant details vanish."

Dekkard winced, even knowing she was correct. He looked down at his empty plate. "Anything else I should tell the councilor?"

"That's pretty much it . . . so far."

"Do you know who he's lunching with?" asked Ysella. "You wouldn't be here otherwise."

"I have no idea, but he sent out a batch of messages soon after he got to the office."

"Likely an informal Craft caucus, then," she replied. "You'd better go wait for him."

"You're right." Dekkard stood, then looked to Ysella. "You haven't sensed anyone who feels out of place, have you?"

She shook her head.

"I'll see you both later. I hope it's not as late as you think."

"Optimist," replied Ysella, her voice cheerfully sarcastic.

As Dekkard hurried away from the staff cafeteria, he was careful to study those in the corridors. He'd only had to wait outside the entrance to the dining room for perhaps a sixth when Obreduur emerged, followed by several other councilors. Dekkard recognized two immediately, Harleona Zerlyon, because she was one of the few female Craft councilors, and because he knew Zerlyon's waiting empath, Chavyona Leiugan, through Ysella. The other councilor was Gerhard Safaell, and his isolate, Emile Fharkon, appeared seemingly from nowhere.

Obreduur started toward the farther committee rooms, but said nothing until they were away from the others. "Did you find them?"

"We found each other . . ." Dekkard quickly briefed Obreduur as they walked.

"That's about what we expected. Wait outside the committee rooms. I shouldn't be that long."

"That long" turned out to be almost a full bell. For a moment, Dekkard had the feeling the councilor might actually shake his head, but Obreduur merely offered a pleasant smile. "Water-shares apportionment on the Rio Doro. There were more concerns to be addressed than the chair realized. Have you seen anyone you shouldn't have?"

"Not so far, sir. I asked Avraal if she's sensed anyone who seemed out of place. She hadn't."

"Good thought, but you can't always rely on her."

"I know that, sir, but . . ."

"You like to have all the advantages you can?"

Dekkard nodded. He'd almost said that he'd use all the tools he could, except Ysella wasn't a tool, and he hadn't been able to come up with a quick change of phrase.

22

. . . Premier Oskaar Ulrich's investigation of the Kraffeist Affair began yesterday with a hearing before the Military Affairs Committee. The Premier opened the hearing by stating, "All facets of the matter will be heard before this committee and no others."

After the Premier, the committee heard from the former Minister of Public Resources, Jhared Kraffeist, who continued to insist that he had been misled and that he had signed standard lease forms that held no references to the fact that the lands leased were part of the Eshbruk Naval Coal Reserve. The original leases were presented in support of his testimony . . .

. . . subsequent witnesses included First Marshal Karl Bernotte and Admiral Gorral, who found himself criticized by the Councilors for allowing Eastern Ironway to charge excessive prices for coal mined illegally out of a Naval Coal Reserve . . .

. . . absent from the hearing was the Director of Logistics for Eastern Ironway, Eduard Graffyn, likely the only person who could explain the possible bribe paid as a "commission." Graffyn vanished weeks ago, and despite efforts by the Ministry of Security, has not been located . . .

. . . near the end of the first day of hearings, Premier Ulrich stated that, if the hearings uncovered factual evidence that any specific individual employed in any fashion by Eastern Ironway had engaged in illegal actions in obtaining the lease, the Council would request that the Justiciary Ministry seek punitive damages for violations of law and file criminal charges against those individuals . . .

Gestirn, **29 Springend 1266**

23

The first thing Dekkard did on Quindi morning was to borrow Hyelda's copy of *Gestirn*, waiting as usual on the side table for others to peruse, and read the story on the hearings. The second was to shake his head. After that, he replaced the newssheet on the side table and seated himself at the staff table. Once again, there was no quince paste, just tomato jelly.

That's annoying, but scarcely the end of the world. He smiled, then poured himself a mug of café before reaching for the jelly.

Ysella settled into the chair across from him. "What was in *Gestirn*?"

"Just what you and Roostof told me. One thing I didn't think about yesterday . . . Premier Grieg appointed Kraffeist, but even when the scandal became public, Grieg didn't remove him. Then, when the Imperador removed Grieg, and the Council chose Ulrich as his successor, there was only the smallest mention of Kraffeist's removal, and only by Ulrich, not the Imperador, as if to minimize it . . ."

"Why do you think there would be?"

The hint of the sardonic in Ysella's words made Dekkard think. "Oh . . ."

She raised her eyebrows, then took a sip of café. "Yes?"

"That way the Commercers minimize the scandal, and the Imperador isn't forced to call new elections, which he'd rather not because that could lead to an awkward political situation, especially if the Craft Party were to pick up just one or two seats."

"That would be my guess. It's only a guess, though."

"Your guesses are never just guesses," replied Dekkard dryly. "I learned that in the first month I worked for the councilor."

"That's true. I wondered why it took you so long." The hint of a mischievous smile followed her words.

"Because I'm a slow learner," he replied, deadpan.

"We'd better go," Ysella said abruptly. "He'll want to leave early again this morning."

"Do you have to accompany Roostof again today?"

"I do. It will be longer and even more boring, I suspect." Ysella stood and carried her platter to the kitchen.

Dekkard finished the last bite of his second croissant and then followed her example.

Less than a sixth of a bell later he was in the garage lighting off the Gresynt. Then, when he opened the garage door, the warm and almost steamy air oozing into the garage and the heavy haze of the pale green sky reminded him that the first day of summer was little more than a week away, although it already felt that hot and humid.

Three minutes later, he had the Gresynt under the portico, and only a few minutes after that he turned the steamer onto Altarama. By then, Obreduur was busy writing.

"Have you heard anything more about Mathilde Thanne?" Dekkard asked Ysella quietly.

"Nothing."

"How strong an empath was she?"

"Adequate but not overpowering." She paused. "Is it possible that Mathilde is just very ill, and Jaime was using her illness to get a reaction?"

"She's definitely missing," interjected Obreduur from the back. "Since Ulrich's isolate is known for subterfuge, I thought about that possibility and asked Mardosh. He wasn't happy that Ulrich knew. She went out shopping on Findi and never returned."

"Sir . . ." began Dekkard deferentially, "has this sort of thing happened before?"

"It was more common a century ago, when the Landors controlled the Council. There hasn't been an incident since before the last election . . . until now . . .

and if we count the attempts on Steffan . . . and on me and possibly on Freust, that's rather ominous. It's also why you two shouldn't be going anywhere alone for a while. Now . . . if you'd talk about something pleasant or inane, preferably quietly, I do have some missives to write."

"Yes, sir." Ysella offered an amused smile to Dekkard. In turn, he concentrated on driving.

After dropping them off and parking the Gresynt, Dekkard tried to be more aware as he made his way toward the office, although he thought it was unlikely anyone would be attacking him with Council Guards all around.

But sometimes the unlikely offers the best opportunity.

He reached the office without anyone even coming close to him, only to find that Roostof, Ysella, and Obreduur had already left for the Council Hall.

"The councilor said that you were to be outside the Waterways Committee Chamber at a third before noon," Karola informed him as he neared his desk. "There's also a letter for you from the Council Clerk on your desk. Don't let it get lost in all those other letters."

A letter from the Council Clerk? "Thank you."

Dekkard found that letter by itself and immediately opened it, then smiled. It was a standard letter informing him that his promotion to Security Specialist/Assistant Economic Specialist had been entered on the Council payroll, effective 25 Springend 1266.

He slipped the letter into his personal file, and then began to sort through the letters and petitions. Before that long, he was drafting responses. That continued until he left to meet with Obreduur in the Council Hall.

Closer to a half before noon, Dekkard stood waiting outside the Waterways Committee hearing room, his back to the wall. By the time Obreduur walked toward him, he'd been able to pick out two councilors he didn't know except by name as a result of his continued nighttime study of the volume Ysella had given him.

"Did you see anyone who you didn't think should be here?" asked Obreduur.

"Sir?"

"You were studying everyone. That's good when you're in uniform. When you're not, it's best to cultivate an expression that suggests your mind is elsewhere. You'd be amazed at what you see then. Now . . . we're headed to the councilors' dining room. You'll have almost a full bell for lunch. Don't join Avraal or Svard or sit near them. Talk to anyone who approaches you, even invite them to join you if it appears they have something in mind. But don't make any approaches to others, even by recognizing them."

"What don't you want me to say?" asked Dekkard wryly.

"Just follow the rules for normal caution. Nothing at all may occur." Obreduur shrugged. "Sometimes, silence indicates more. Meet me outside the dining room at a sixth before first bell, and we'll walk back to the office."

After making sure Obreduur was safely inside the dining room, Dekkard walked to the staff cafeteria, where he decided on a cheese-stuffed fowl breast placed carelessly on jasmine rice, along with café, then made his way to the only empty table for two. Ysella and Roostof's absence suggested that the hearing was running late, or at least to noon sharp.

Dekkard immediately addressed the fowl breast and the rice, which was at least moist and tender, and the Havarti and pepper cheese gave it a little character. When he was about halfway through he slowed down and tried to adopt a distracted look. That wasn't difficult because he was feeling somewhat distracted. After possibly a sixth of a bell, he caught a glimpse of Roostof and Ysella leaving the cafeteria serving line and making for the other end of the room.

At that moment, a balding older man with spectacles stopped at the table, and said in an apologetic tone, "Steffan . . . we only met briefly last year. In case you don't recall, I'm Avraam Pietrsyn. Councilor Hasheem's economic aide. He mentioned that you'll be dealing with economic issues. If I can ever help with forestry and anything in the entire timber industry, just drop by. I just wanted to say hello and make the offer."

"Thank you, Avraam. I appreciate it. If I need that kind of expertise, I will ask. There's a lot to learn, and I appreciate your offer."

After Pietrsyn had left, Dekkard sipped his café and let his eyes wander, noting that Frieda Livigne and another woman had taken a table equidistant from him and from Ysella. He lowered his head as if looking at his platter, then took a bite of the now-cooler rice, but could tell that the woman with Livigne had glanced in his direction. That occurred several times over the next sixth or so, but Dekkard avoided looking directly near her, even when he left the cafeteria.

Although he was only a few minutes early to meet Obreduur, he stood outside the councilors' dining room for close to a third of a bell before Obreduur appeared.

"Did anything interesting happen at lunch?" asked Obreduur cheerfully.

"Frieda Livigne and another woman in a security-gray suit with a pin—I'd guess that she's Councilor Maendaan's empie—they sat where they could watch both me and Avraal and Svard. I'd tried looking preoccupied. I had the feeling they were watching. Avraal could probably tell you more. Oh . . . and Councilor Hasheem's economic aide said hello in passing. He said that his specialty was forestry, and that if he could help me to come see him. I thanked him. He was very apologetic."

"You never know," said Obreduur as he turned toward the west doors that led to the courtyard gardens and the covered portico that would take them to the Council Office Building. "You might need his expertise sometime. Or he might need yours."

"Councilor Hasheem's on the Security Committee," replied Dekkard.

"I doubt that Chairman Maendaan is all that forthcoming to Craft councilors or their staff about more than a few Security matters. Now . . . how are you coming on preparing for the meeting with the Artisans Guild?"

While Dekkard had scarcely had time to handle everything else, let alone do more research on tariffs, he said, "I've been over the material several times, and I'll keep at it."

"It's good to know the background, Steffan, but the most important thing is to listen . . . and to let them know you're listening. Don't ever look bored, even if you've heard the same tale of woe a hundred times. It's each person's tale of woe, and they're hurting. If you look bored, it tells them that you—and I—don't care. If you don't understand anything else, learn that."

"Yes, sir."

"We'll be leaving late this afternoon. Premier Ulrich will run the hearings past the deadline for the evening editions of the newssheets."

"Will the hearings extend into next week?"

"The Premier hasn't said, but I'd be most surprised."

As the two walked out of the Council Hall and into the hot and muggy early-afternoon air that blanketed the courtyard gardens, Dekkard studied not only the shaded portico but the gardens as well, noting the greater number of Council Guards posted along the portico and wall.

"There were more guards in the gardens today," he said casually as they climbed the main staircase to the second level.

"The Premier is concerned about the New Meritorists. Apparently, you weren't the only one who noticed that they carried semi-automatic pistols with large magazines. Or perhaps what his aide 'overheard' prompted an inquiry, and he didn't like the response."

"Should I have been less overheard?"

"No. Sooner or later, it would have come out. This way he also knows that other councilors knew before he did, and that might make him less . . . impetuous."

As the two neared the office, Obreduur said evenly, "You might concentrate on those letters and petitions, since you won't have as much time next week."

"Yes, sir."

Even without Obreduur's suggestion, that would have been Dekkard's plan, even if that meant dealing with a petition about adverse work conditions created by the placement of a swine waste impoundment pond . . . and several less odious requests.

Ysella and Roostof didn't return to the office until almost fifth bell.

"That was a long hearing," observed Dekkard dryly.

"That's because Premier Ulrich wanted to finish them off this week," replied Roostof. "Supposedly so that the Council can spend the last weeks before Summerend break on supplemental appropriations."

"I thought all the appropriations were finished by last Fallend."

"That was five months ago, and priorities change," returned Roostof.

"Especially with the Security Ministry asking for more resources to deal with the New Meritorists and more military funding to patrol the Sargasso Archipelago because of the pirate attacks on Commerce merchanters," said Ysella.

"All of which is very convenient for the Commercers," said Macri from the door to the side office. "Svard . . . I need you for a few moments."

Ysella turned to Dekkard. "And how was your lunch?"

"About the same as yours. Do you know who was with Frieda Livigne?"

"She's an empath. Her name is Iferra Vonacht. She's strong and well-shielded. They were observing both of us." Ysella smiled.

"Why, do you think?"

"They're as much a part of the Security Ministry as they are committee staffers. There's almost no difference.

Councilor Obreduur has given both of us additional duties. When security aides get other duties, especially aides to a strong Craft councilor, at a time when the Commercers' margin of control of the Council is lessening . . ."

". . . they worry," finished Dekkard. "I suppose I can see that, but it seems a little excessive." Actually, to Dekkard, it seemed more than just a little excessive.

"Security Ministry types worry about anything that might change the way things are, and the way to stop change is to watch the little changes that might lead to larger changes . . . and then act before that happens."

Dekkard could see the logic of that, but her calm assessment bothered him.

"By the way," added Ysella, "you do that distracted and musing look rather well."

"Do I thank you . . . or is that the prelude to learning what else I should do?"

"No prelude this time. It looked very natural."

Dekkard grinned. "That's because it was. With everything going on, I am feeling swamped and distracted. I just let a bit of it show."

"That's the best way."

"Oh . . . Councilor Hasheem's forestry aide offered help to me. Hasheem told him I'd be doing economics as well as security. Apparently, the councilor passed that on to Hasheem when they met."

"He didn't waste any time letting other councilors know," said Ysella thoughtfully.

Dekkard had a good idea what she was thinking, because he'd thought the same thing. *Why did Obreduur pass on a change in the duties of his personal staff?* Most councilors couldn't have cared less about the duties of other councilors' staffers.

Perhaps to make Dekkard more credible? That made little sense, either. But one thing Dekkard did know was that Obreduur did nothing without a reason.

He thought about getting back to drafting more

responses, but at that moment, Obreduur stepped out of his office and said cheerfully, "It's time to close up. You've all already been here too long."

Dekkard was willing to agree with that.

24

After driving the councilor back to the house and eating a quick dinner, Dekkard and Ysella accompanied the family to services at the Trinitarian chapel. Once services were over and Dekkard had garaged the Gresynt, he began his usual nightly inspection and servicing of the steamer, only to find Ysella in the garage watching him.

"Why . . . ?"

". . . am I here? You might recall that Obreduur suggested that we not do things alone for the immediate future. Tomorrow . . . I had planned to visit Emrelda. Would you like to come?"

Dekkard's immediate reaction was to say "of course," but he hesitated. "I'd like that very much, except I wouldn't want to be an imposition . . . on you . . . or them."

"I doubt you've ever been an imposition."

Dekkard laughed. "Don't tell my sister that. She'd disagree . . . vociferously."

"I imagine she has a mind of her own."

Thinking about Naralta's determination to set up her own studio, Dekkard nodded. "And then some."

"Our sisters seem to share that characteristic." Ysella paused. "Then you'll come? I'm not imposing on your good nature?"

"I still feel like I'm imposing . . ."

"You're not. By now, you should know that I'd tell you."

"Politely, but firmly," agreed Dekkard. "What time tomorrow?"

"Third bell?"

"That sounds good."

"Then I'll see you at breakfast."

"You're not going out tonight, I hope."

"After what I said to you? Hardly. I'm behind on my letters to family, and I could use a little more sleep. What about you?"

"When I finish with the steamers, I need to exercise, here, then practice with the knives."

Ysella hesitated, then said, "Most security isolates don't carry knives. I've wondered . . ."

Dekkard smiled wryly. "You've been kind. Most security instructors think throwing knives are a waste of time or target toys. They're only really effective fairly close . . . and that's if you're very, very good and can hit the few points that will stop or slow an attacker. I think I'm better than most, but I've never had to use them for real. So . . . why do I carry them? Because they're an additional weapon. Also, they're a weapon I can practice on my own."

"That makes sense."

"I didn't answer your other question. After I practice, I need to write some letters, and then study a certain book. Someone emphasized the necessity of such study."

"I didn't say that."

"Not exactly . . . but you didn't have to utter a word."

"After working together for almost two years, I'd hope so. Good evening." With a parting cheerful smile, she turned and left the garage.

Two years. At times, it seemed like only weeks, and at other times, it felt as though he'd done nothing else for far more than a mere two years.

He returned to wiping down the larger Gresynt, his thoughts going back over the events of the past month or so . . . since the attempted emblast assassination attempt on Obreduur. The events involved members of each of the three political parties. First had come the Kraffeist Affair, involving appointees of the Commerce government. Next, if what Macri had said was correct, Freust had been poisoned, and he had been a Landor councilor, trying to expose what was behind the Kraffeist Affair. Then Obreduur had been attacked, although he hadn't seemed to be doing anything at all . . .

Seemed . . . but it's clear he's doing something, especially if "Sr. Muller" is who you think he might be. Then someone shot at you, and later two people followed you and Ysella and tried to cause trouble.

Dekkard still couldn't figure where the New Meritorists fit in, because it was clear Obreduur had no use for them, nor, apparently, did anyone in any of the political parties, nor did anyone in the Security Ministry.

And Mathilde Thanne, the security empie of a Crafter councilor, was missing and likely dead, because security empies just didn't wander off forgetfully . . . and Premier Ulrich's isolate had been the one to inform Dekkard. And all the Security Committee staff knew about Dekkard's promotion, and two of them had been studying him and Ysella during the Kraffeist hearings.

Dekkard doubted that anyone was interested in him personally, and that meant, as he'd suspected for several weeks, that it was all about Obreduur and what he was doing as political leader of the Craft Party.

So why are the Commercers so concerned when they could still control the Council, if with Landor support?

Given that he had no answer, when he finished with the steamers, he headed upstairs.

At least he could answer his mother's letter and write one to Naralta as well, since he hadn't been all that diligent in that aspect of his correspondence. Writing those missives would also keep his mind off questions he couldn't answer, and ones that he hoped that Ysella could shed some light on tomorrow—once they were somewhere secure from eavesdroppers.

25

On Findi morning Dekkard wore a plain gray shirt to breakfast, seeing no reason to risk staining the new barong he intended to don after eating for the excursion to Emrelda and Markell's house. As soon as he entered the staff room, he glanced around, but no one was there. He immediately picked up Hyelda's copy of *Gestirn* in hope of a story on the hearings.

There was, and he immediately started reading, focusing on the key details.

> Premier Ulrich confirmed that the government has filed criminal charges against Eastern Ironway, seeking more than a million marks in damages and reparations to the Imperial Navy for excessive coal purchase charges . . . Ministry of Public Resources also voided the Eshbruk Naval Coal Reserve lease on the grounds that it had been obtained through fraud . . . three legalists at the Ministry of Public Resources have been fired for failure to follow the rules of due diligence . . . Sealed charges have also been filed against Eduard Graffyn, the missing Director of Logistics at Eastern Ironway . . .
>
> Other sources indicate that, rather than face another hearing and possible disciplinary action, Admiral Gorral has taken immediate retirement . . .
> . . . Former Minister of Public Resources Kraffeist did not respond to requests for comments . . . nor did Elwood P. Drood, Presidente of Eastern Ironway . . .

"What are you looking at?" asked Ysella, coming up beside Dekkard.

"The *Gestirn* story about the hearings. It's all done. Sealed, signed, and delivered . . . except Eastern Ironway got off with a million-mark slap on the wrist, and blame for almost everything was laid on Graffyn, who's conveniently missing. There's no mention of Grieg or whoever at Eastern really profited, and no mention of the twenty-thousand-mark commission or bribe." Shaking his head, Dekkard handed the newssheet to Ysella and waited while she read it. He also noted that she was wearing a worn set of security grays.

When she finished, she looked at Dekkard. "I'm surprised they printed as much as they did. They had to have run the story by someone in the Security Ministry."

"Maybe Ulrich thought that was the minimum that would allow the whole mess to die away." Dekkard paused. "I would have thought the New Meritorists would have demonstrated more over this."

"They're more interested in what they see as true reform. To them, the Kraffeist Affair is just what happens when individual councilors aren't held responsible . . . as if the accountability they desire would make the slightest difference in the long run."

"It would have to make some difference, or Obreduur wouldn't be all that opposed to it."

"Oh . . . it would, and we can talk about it later. I need some café." She smoothed the newssheet and replaced it on the side table. Then she moved to the table, filled her mug, and sat down.

Dekkard repressed a sigh when he saw that he'd have to endure tomato jelly for yet another breakfast. He filled his mug with café and settled across from Ysella. "Did you and Emrelda have anything special planned?"

"Nothing in particular." Ysella smiled. "She did say that you were welcome any time. She likes you."

"I'm curious. Is it just my imagination, or did both of you quietly rebel against growing up in the Landor daughter mold?"

Ysella laughed softly. "You are so polite and circumspect when you ask questions about my background."

"What you're saying is that I'm not quite indirect enough, but only gently intrusive."

"I can tell you come from a family of strong women. And, yes, neither of us wanted to grow up to be intellectually bright broodmares whose every thought needed to be supportive of or subservient to a Landor male. Father just had to put all his hopes in Cliven."

"Because he's more traditional?"

"He's not only much younger, but quite stolidly conservative. He's even named after our very conservative grandfather—Cliven Mikail Ysella. Cliven's always very sweet to us, if in a disappointed way. And we're quite sweet to him and particularly to Fleur. Not that we see either of them more than a few times a year."

"Winter holiday?"

"Only if they come here or we meet elsewhere. And sometimes during the Council's Summerend recess."

At that moment, Rhosali entered the staff room, wearing a long-sleeved filmy orange shirt over bright purple trousers. Her eyes went from Dekkard to Ysella. "Gray is boring, especially on endday."

"We'll lighten up later," replied Dekkard.

"Or add some color," said Ysella.

"Don't you find it boring to wear gray every day?"

"You wear the same white apron and blue dress every day," said Dekkard.

"But blue and white aren't boring. Gray is."

"Gray is useful," replied Ysella. "It's better not to stand out in what we do." She took a small bite of her croissant.

Dekkard halved the croissant and used the knife to spread the tomato jelly, before reassembling the croissant and taking a healthy bite.

Conversation for the short remainder of breakfast was minimal.

Once Dekkard returned to his room, he donned the rich blue new barong, the one that Ysella had persuaded him wasn't excessively flamboyant, over pale gray trousers, then added the personal truncheon, not obvious under the barong, and finished readying himself before heading downstairs and out to the covered portico. He was slightly surprised that he arrived first, but he only had to wait a few minutes before she arrived, impeccably attired in a linen summer suit that was a slightly darker shade of blue than his barong, along with a matching leather handbag, matching gloves, and a near-transparent headscarf—also matching.

He had a very good idea why he'd been the first one to the portico, but only said, "Beautiful and elegant, as always."

"You've never said that before."

"I haven't? I've certainly thought it."

She paused, then studied him. "That looks even better on you than I recall. You could pass for a theatre idol."

"I doubt anyone would mistake me for Novarte or even Thaller."

"You'd be surprised."

Shocked would be more like it. But Dekkard only offered an amused smile.

"No one seems to be observing us," said Ysella. "Shall we go?"

"We shall," returned Dekkard amiably.

The two stepped out from the shade of the portico into the steamy light of the early-midmorning sun under a heavy high haze and walked down the drive to the pedestrian gate, which Dekkard opened, then closed. They walked perhaps half a block before Dekkard spoke.

"You said that, in the long run, personal accountability for votes made by councilors would make little difference."

"You never let go of things, do you?"

"Not when I need to know more. And sometimes, I'm just stubborn."

"I was paraphrasing Obreduur. Men, and women, may be restrained by laws and force, but they're governed by their self-image, their vanity, if you will. They seek more of what polishes that image. The New Meritorists think that if individual votes are made public, popular opinion will force councilors to be more accountable. It won't. It will only make them accountable to the public or whoever can buy the public's fickle feelings of the moment, rather than to their party. The vast majority of the public doesn't care about fiscal discipline or consistent policies. That majority wants either to keep what they have . . . or more . . . immediately. Those who supply more or promise that have their self-images confirmed by popular approval. Councilors will not become more responsible or better. They'll just become directly accountable to the fickleness of popular opinion."

"And what's just happened with Ulrich is better?"

"All countries have politicians who abuse power. That isn't the question. The question is what forms of government effectively restrict such abuses without unduly restricting the liberties of their people. No government is inherently good. All governments have to restrict personal freedoms to keep the majority safe, safe from everything from bad food to evil individuals. The question isn't which form of government is best. It's which form of government provides the most benefit with the least restrictions."

"You can justify any government by that standard."

"You can," replied Ysella evenly. "But why did your parents leave Argental?"

"What they could do as artists was limited."

"Why was that?"

"Originally the rationale was that art that was not utilitarian wasted scarce resources."

"And now?"

"Non-utilitarian art is frivolous and glorifies weakness."

"So Argental restricts what artists can do and exiles susceptibles because they're believed weak, instead of killing them as it used to. Guldor merely restricts knowing how individual councilors vote. Both lands have restrictions. Which set of restrictions do you prefer?"

"That's not the question." Dekkard managed to keep his voice level. "The question is how much better we can make government."

"There's a basic flaw in that statement. You're assuming that the basic structure of the Great Charter can be improved. Is that assumption valid? Optimists always assume anything can be improved, and pessimists usually believe nothing can be. Can you point out any weakness and explain what improvement is necessary and why? Specifically, is there any proof that making each councilor's vote public would improve the working of the government?"

"There's no way of proving that without trying it," replied Dekkard.

"And if we try it, and it doesn't work, the way it didn't work in Teknold, how do we return to the present system? You don't think that there weren't leaders in Teknold who didn't try? Look up Joel Janhus in the Council Library."

"You've studied all of this, haven't you?"

"How else do you think the daughter of a very conservative Landor ended up working for a progressive Crafter councilor?"

"But . . . you've just said that you don't want to change the system."

"I don't. Like Obreduur, I think we need to use the system to change the conditions. The Commercers and Landors have held power for too long. Any group that holds power for too long gets corrupt. You don't burn the house down to get rid of the rodents. You concentrate on removing the rodents. What the New Meritorists are suggesting is burning the house down, and that won't solve the problem. It just leaves you with greater problems. Now . . . enough of politics. It is a lovely day . . . if a trifle warm."

Dekkard realized that they had covered eight blocks during their discussion, except he felt more like a dull pupil who failed his recitation, and they were nearing the white brick gateposts that marked the western border of East Quarter.

When they reached the stop for the omnibus, the sidewalk fronting the various stores on Imperial Boulevard had quite a few shoppers. And, as before, the handful of others waiting for the omnibus edged slightly away from Dekkard and Ysella.

Because we're dressed a bit less casually . . . or is it because Ysella's projecting something that makes people give us some space?

Once they were on the omnibus and seated on the lower level, not close to anyone else, Dekkard said gently, "You don't like people to get too close to us, do you? People you don't know, that is."

"You noticed that?"

"I noticed it the first time, but I didn't realize that it was you."

"I don't really do it consciously."

Dekkard noted the almost apologetic tone, something he hadn't heard often from Ysella. "I imagine it's useful in escorting the councilor through crowds."

She shook her head. "It takes a moment for people to react, and he doesn't stand in one place for very long, as I'm sure you've noticed."

"Except in his personal office."

"Where he spends every minute either reading or writing."

Dekkard thought about that for several moments, then nodded. "He does send out quite a number of messages and letters."

The omnibus turned onto Camelia Avenue, but after two blocks, in the middle of the gentle curve to the south, it slowed almost to a stop before turning right.

Dekkard immediately half stood to see the reason for the change in route. For a moment, all he could see were several Security patrollers directing traffic off the avenue. But then he saw scores of students with signs and banners on the top of the wall that marked the southern end of Imperial University. He also recognized some of the slogans on the signs.

PERSONAL ACCOUNTABILITY,
NOT PARTY ACCOUNTABILITY.
OPEN ALL VOTING RECORDS.
JOBS BY ABILITY, NOT PARTY.

PERSONAL REPRESENTATIVES, NOT PARTY HACKS.
HIRE THE BEST, NOT THE BEST-CONNECTED.
ACCOUNTABLE COUNCILORS = GOOD GOVERNMENT.

There were others, but Dekkard couldn't read them. "University students . . . with signs and slogans."

Ysella rose and took a brief look before reseating herself. "No one will care, except other students. There won't even be a mention in the newssheets."

Dekkard looked around the omnibus. Of the two handfuls or so of passengers on the lower level perhaps three gave the students more than a passing glance. He saw several of the patrollers move toward the students before he lost sight of them. After traveling another four blocks, the driver turned north and after a block back onto Camelia. Dekkard stood and tried to see what was happening, but only gained an impression of students surging toward the patrollers.

He turned to Ysella. "There might be a brief mention. It looked to me like the students were rushing the patrollers."

"The newssheets won't dare to print much more than that. Security will only allow enough to claim that they weren't covering up whatever happened."

Dekkard frowned. "The Great Charter allows freedom of factual expression."

"The second half of that clause reads 'consistent with the maintenance of order.' The High Justiciary has held that so long as a factual reporting of actual events appears in print then Security is not exceeding its powers."

Dekkard had the feeling that she was right about what would appear in *Gestirn* or even *The Machtarn Tribune* . . . or other newssheets across Guldor. "Doesn't that bother you?"

"At the Council Hall demonstration, the protestors fired first. The idea was to get the Council Guards to fire back and kill and wound people so that New Meritorists could show how brutal the Council was. And if Security allowed such stories to be printed, the people who provoked the fire would be portrayed as victims. That's what they want, to show the government as unreasonably repressive. Then, the next time, they'll incite more violence, which will get more people injured or killed, some of them bystanders, and those bystanders and their friends and families will turn against the government. A totally unregulated press would just make the situation worse because sensational reports are like a drug. The more people get, the more they want. Yet they'll insist that they don't while they're rushing to buy the latest sensational story."

"You have a rather cynical view of people."

"Look at how everyone wanted to hear and read more and more about the Kraffeist Affair. Didn't you want to know more? I know I did."

Dekkard had to admit that he'd been disappointed in not knowing the entire story behind the Naval Coal Reserve leasing scandal. "Is that the same as not reporting people being shot and killed?"

"The newssheets reported that people had been shot and killed. They didn't name names because names have the power to raise emotions. They just didn't give newsprint to demagogues who want to use the press as a way to support a revolution."

"A revolution? Don't they just want a change in how votes are reported?"

"Steffan . . ." Ysella's tone held barely contained exasperation. "The voting procedures are part of the Great Charter. They were designed for a reason. That reason was to keep councilors from building personal political support, particularly support based on what they thought would appeal to people, as opposed to doing what they thought was best for everyone."

"Or for their party."

"That's fair. It's also a compromise, but at least the entire party has to take credit or blame . . . and not an individual. Do you honestly think it would be better if every councilor could campaign on the basis of promising to vote for all the popular measures and against all the unpopular ones? For all those that promised something for someone, and against all those that increased taxes and tariffs to pay for the popular promises? How long before government could not fund itself and its programs?"

Dekkard winced at that thought.

"The same thing applies to the newssheets. If they're not reined in to some extent, they'd publish anything that increased their circulation and advertising fees."

Dekkard could see that. *Just where should a government draw the line between freedom of action and expression and excessive control and repression? Can you draw such a line?*

Laureous the Great and the drafters of the Great Charter had thought so, but the Meritorists and the New Meritorists either didn't like such lines or didn't like where those lines were drawn . . . and Dekkard didn't know which. "Do the New Meritorists even have a statement of their beliefs . . . or is it all just about opening up the voting process, with no thought about where it might lead?"

"There's a statement of principles. Obreduur has a copy. He loaned it to me."

"I'd like to see that . . . if it's possible. I'd like to see how they represent themselves . . . or don't."

"You should ask Obreduur yourself. I returned it to him about three years back. When I had some of the same questions you're asking."

"Thank you. I will." Although Ysella had had questions, Dekkard sensed she wasn't entertaining them now. He wondered why, but perhaps the New Meritorists' statement of principles would shed light on that, and any questions he had could wait until he read it.

After a short silence, Ysella said pleasantly, "You never said much about your sister except that she's older than you, strong-willed, and a portraitist."

"I did get some news in my mother's last letter. Naralta has decided to move away from the studio she and Mother shared and to open her own studio. She thinks their styles are too different and that it's hurting both of them."

"I'd think the opposite, that it would give possible patrons a choice of which style they preferred."

"I'd agree with you, and so does Mother, but Naralta is going to do what she's going to do." Dekkard smiled wryly. "It seems to be a family trait."

"You were always going to be a security isolate?"

He shook his head. "I was determined I wasn't going to be a fourth- or fifth-rate artisan just because everyone else in the family was an artisan. My father wanted to know why I'd ever want to work for anyone else. I told him that everyone works for someone else in some way, and since that was so, I wanted to do something I was good at. I had no idea what I could be good at. I don't know that I'm the best security isolate, but I'm better at security than I ever would have been as an artisan."

"It's hard to know when you're young and your talents aren't what your family expects."

"I take it that there aren't any other empaths in your family?" asked Dekkard.

"Not that I know of. There was a great-aunt on my father's side who mysteriously disappeared. No one who would talk about her knew why, and any who knew why wouldn't say. I wasn't skilled enough as an empath then to ask the right questions so that their reactions would tell me what I wanted to know. By the time I was, those who might have known were dead. I have the feeling I might have liked her, but you never know. There's always so much that gets lost when people die. Do you know that much about your grandparents or their parents?"

"Not really. My father's father was a plasterer . . ." By the time Dekkard had laid out what little he knew about his family background, the omnibus attendant announced, "Erslaan. Last stop. Everyone off."

Dekkard followed Ysella off the omnibus and onto the white marble sidewalk. The two crossed the boulevard and headed north on Jacquez, leaving the stylish shopping area behind as they began the uphill walk. The little traffic on Jacquez lessened further once they passed the gray brick gateposts announcing the Hillside area. When they turned on Florinda Way, Dekkard half wondered if they'd see the susceptible boy who lived next door, but the adjoining house was shuttered, as if already closed for the summer.

Emrelda was at the door before they finished climbing the steps. This time she wore a blouse and skirt of muted rose.

"We're a little late," Ysella said. "The omnibus had to detour around a demonstration at the university, something about personal accountability."

"It can't have been much, or I'd have been asked to work today to free up others to patrol the demonstration." Emrelda looked to Dekkard. "She was a few minutes late meeting you, wasn't she?"

Dekkard grinned. "Just a few."

Emrelda turned to her sister. "You guessed wrong in what he'd wear, didn't you?"

Ysella laughed. "I had good odds."

"Steffan's not as predictable as you thought." Emrelda stepped back and motioned toward the hallway. "Come on in. Markell's on the veranda. It's already summer, no matter what the calendar says." She looked to Dekkard. "Chilled Kuhrs?"

"Please."

"Silverhills white?"

"That would be very welcome," replied Ysella.

"You two go say hello to Markell. I'll be there with your drinks shortly."

Dekkard followed Ysella out to the covered veranda, which wasn't that much cooler than the house, except for the slightest hint of a breeze. Markell immediately stood. "Welcome to the not-so-cool coolest place around the house."

"It's cooler than staying at the councilor's would have been. You have more of a breeze here." Ysella sat in the chair to the right of Markell, who reseated himself.

"How is the Navy facility in Siincleer coming?" Dekkard settled into the upholstered white wicker chair around the low table and to Markell's left.

"Two weeks further along than the last time you asked. The foundations are cured, and we're working on the structural walls."

"Do you have any better idea of what it will be?"

"Hard to say. We're just constructing the building. I supervise the subcontractors who are and then report directly to Presidente Engaard. We're still a fairly lean operation." Markell smiled wryly. "That means I keep checking on the construction manager who's on site, who in turn makes sure things happen on a day-to-day basis."

"There aren't any executives over you?" asked Dekkard. "That's . . . rather unusual."

"It is. It's also why we don't cost as much and why we've gotten contracts that used to go to Siincleer Engineering or Haasan."

"Not Siincleer Shipbuilding?"

"Siincleer Engineering is a subsidiary of Siincleer Shipbuilding. In fact, Siincleer Shipbuilding will be the one supplying the equipment that fills the structure."

"Surely you have a hint of what all that equipment will do, darling." Emrelda arrived carrying a tray that held two beakers and two wineglasses, offering Dekkard a chilled lager, Markell a warmer lager, and her sister a white wine. She set the last wineglass in front of her wicker chair, and the tray in the middle of the table before seating herself and adding, "You mentioned magnificent mirrors . . ."

"Just a guess based on what I overheard."

"What about another guess?" Emrelda bestowed a dazzling smile on her husband.

"They might be trying to use the sun to heat flash boilers."

"Why would they do that?" asked Ysella, her tone genuinely curious.

"For ships. Using the sun that way you can desalinate

ocean water. You could also generate steam to supplement the coal boilers. Ships might be able to travel farther on less coal. That would make the Navy less dependent on colliers and foreign sources of coal."

"Speaking of coal," said Dekkard as he looked to Emrelda, "did Security ever find the missing director of logistics for Eastern Ironway?"

Emrelda shook her head. "Not that I know of. There were rumors of someone who looked somewhat like him, but he vanished. That person was using the name Erich Muller . . ."

"Rumors?"

"Rumors," replied Emrelda wryly. "I'm a patroller, not a special agent, and definitely not a Tactical. Patrollers are responsible for public safety. The agents aren't in our station, and I'm just as glad. As for the Tactical Force . . . most of them . . ." She shook her head.

"I told Emrelda that was just a false lead," said Markell. "The real Graffyn is either dead or left Guldor. He knows—or knew—too much to survive and remain here."

"Why do you think that?" asked Dekkard.

"He wasn't high enough in the corporacion to have put together the lease without others. One of the others had to be near the top. So Graffyn knows who it is and could implicate him and who in government was really behind it. The Council covered it up quickly. That suggests a political tie."

Dekkard frowned. "Why in the world would Eastern risk so much for coal, even cheaper coal, if they weren't desperate? And why would any senior Commercer councilor be a part of such a scheme?"

"I'm no finance wizard," replied Markell, "but even I know Eastern's finances are dicey. Their own coalfields are playing out. Guldoran just opened a huge mine near Nullaan."

"That answers Steffan's first question," said Emrelda, "but what about the second?"

"I have no idea," replied Markell. "I'd guess that

it was done for a payoff of some sort. Possibly for a Commercer who'll have to leave office at the next elections." He shrugged. "Or maybe it was a setup to cause problems for the Commercers." Markell looked to Ysella. "Avraal, you'd know more about that than I would."

"The Landors wouldn't gain anything from that," Ysella replied. "The risk to the Crafters would be enormous if they were found to be behind it."

"All of that sounds so . . . sordid," said Emrelda. "But these days everything seems to be getting tawdry and sordid."

"It's always been tawdry and sordid," replied Markell. "You just weren't in a position where it was obvious. Now you are. Every day."

Emrelda straightened. "It may be warm, but it's too nice a day to talk about the sordid and tawdry." She looked at Dekkard. "You've done some shopping lately, haven't you?" She turned to her sister. "And you had something to do with it."

"Absolutely not," said Dekkard, managing to keep a straight face. "Being a poor and impoverished security isolate, far, far from my family, I decided to spend my massive hoard of marks on finery that is only required on the odd endday when my colleague takes pity on my hapless social state and lack of societal graces and invites me to engage in social masochism by insisting I accompany her to talk and dine with eminent architects and landed ladies—"

Emrelda began to laugh, and Markell even smiled.

"You do have a dark side," said Ysella, her tone one of amusement. "See if I—"

"Don't you dare!" said Emrelda, blotting the tears of laughter from her eyes and cheeks. "I'll invite him to bring you. That was priceless."

Dekkard caught a wink from Ysella, before she said, "I could tell a story or two."

"Go ahead," said Emrelda. "It would be more than worth it."

"That sounds like something I'd like to hear." Markell leaned forward.

"Well," began Ysella, "it all began when Landor Mheraak brought his son to the old plantation house . . . the one that burned down three years ago . . ."

"You aren't . . . ?" said Emrelda. "Not that one?"

"Yes, I am," continued Ysella. "His youngest son Dhutaar was three years older than Emrelda. This was when she was fifteen. I was ten, and Cliven wasn't quite two. When she saw their steamer pull up—they had one of the first steamers—she turned to me and said, 'I can't stand him. He makes me ill. I'd do anything not to be matched to him.' So I decided to help her out." Ysella grinned.

Emrelda shook her head.

"Go on," urged Markell.

"While the Landor was talking with Father, Emrelda was told to show Dhutaar around. I waited until they were near the stables before I woke Cliven and got him out of his trundle bed. Of course he was upset, but I wrapped him up and carried him right up to Emrelda. Then I said, 'I didn't know what to do. He wanted his mother.' Then I turned to Dhutaar and said, 'You won't tell anyone, will you?'"

Markell's eyes widened. "What did he do?"

"He fled," said Ysella dryly. "I didn't get anything to eat but porridge for a week, maybe longer. Then I had to apologize, and there were explanations and more explanations before everything was as straightened out as it could be."

"It took years for the rumors to fade," said Emrelda, "and they never did for some people. Not that I cared that much. They were all like Dhutaar. He never spoke to either of us again."

"You did say you'd do anything," said Ysella.

"That taught me to be very careful about what I asked of you."

"I've gathered that about both of you," said Markell. "I never heard that story."

"It's not one we'd ever tell around our parents—or Cliven," said Emrelda. "He's almost as conservative as Dhutaar. Now . . . I have a story about you . . ."

From that point on, the afternoon was more light-hearted, and Dekkard definitely enjoyed the conversation and the dinner—beginning with a slightly chilled cucumber soup, followed by cheese and pear ravioli, and ending with a light and fluffy glazed lemon cake.

After the midafternoon dinner, finished off with a white dessert wine, Emrelda drove Ysella and Dekkard back to East Quarter and the councilor's house. When she stopped just outside the closed gates to the drive, she said, "Thank you both so much. I had a wonderful day, and I could tell Markell did as well. Even with the Dhutaar story."

"Thank you," said Dekkard. "I enjoyed every minute."

"When will we see you two again?" asked Emrelda.

"That depends on the councilor and what the Council does before the Summerend recess," replied Ysella. "I'll let you know."

Once Emrelda had driven off and Dekkard and Ysella walked slowly up the drive, he said, "Was Dhutaar really that bad?"

"Worse. His wife hanged herself. Of course, he died shortly after that."

Despite the evening warmth, Dekkard shivered just a little. "Might I ask why you told that story?"

"You really don't need to ask, do you?"

He smiled wryly. "No. I did enjoy the day. All of it."

"So did I. You have some reading and thinking to do, I suspect."

Dekkard just nodded. He did indeed.

26

Once inside the house, Dekkard didn't go upstairs, but made his way into the main hallway, looking for Obreduur. Then he walked to the study door.

The councilor looked up from his desk. "Yes, Steffan?"

"Avraal and I had an interesting discussion, sir. She said that you had something that sets forth the principles of the New Meritorists."

"Why are you interested in their principles, Steffan?"

Although Obreduur's tone of voice was pleasant and even, Dekkard had the feeling that the councilor wasn't just idly curious.

"Because we saw another demonstration outside the Imperial University this morning, and it looked as though it might get violent."

"I understand it did. I received a message about it. Several patrollers were shot, as were several students." Obreduur looked evenly at Dekkard.

Dekkard wondered who had sent the message on an endday, but didn't ask. "I don't understand why they're doing it. I thought reading what they believe might tell me more."

"It might. It might not. Beliefs aren't rational. They're based on feelings, not thoughts. Usually, the feelings drive the reasons, not the other way around." Obreduur leaned back slightly and opened a drawer, taking out a small cloth-bound volume and placing it on the desk. "This volume stays in the house. When you're not reading it, please put it in a drawer. When you're finished with it, return it to me personally. At that time, we'll talk about your impressions of what is in the book . . . and what is not." He handed the small book to Dekkard.

"Thank you, sir."

Obreduur smiled warmly. "I think you'll find it interesting. I hope you do."

Dekkard was still thinking about the councilor's last words when he entered his chamber and lit the solitary gaslight in its brass wall fixture.

Then he took off his barong, hung it up, seated himself in the chair, and studied the outside of the book, covered in what seemed to be worn blue canvas, or something similar. There was no title on the front or on the spine. He opened the book. The first page was blank, but the second contained a title, nothing else: *MANIFESTO OF THE NEW MERITORISTS*.

Dekkard opened it to the first page and read:

Principles for a Just and Representative Government
1. All aspects of the operation and policies of government shall be open to the people, particularly the vote of each Councilor on every law or appropriation.
2. No upper or lower limits shall be placed on the number of Councilors representing any political party.
3. The number of political parties shall not be limited.
4. Any law passed by the majority of the Council cannot be overturned by the Imperador.
5. The right to a free press is affirmed, with the only limitation being that any factual inaccuracy or misrepresentation is open to legal challenge and damages or reparations.
6. All adults of sound mind are eligible to vote and to hold office, including isolates, empaths, and susceptibles, provided that none have previously committed and been convicted of a felonious offense.
7. The sole limitation on the number of terms a Councilor may serve shall be that of the electorate.

Just seven principles?
After several moments, he turned the page, headed by the first principle, and continued to read the seemingly

endless examples purporting to illustrate how the operation of government was opaque, if not totally concealed, from the public. One in particular caught his eye.

> . . . in that no legislation is presented to the people for their review before it is voted upon by the Council, the creation of such legislation allows no participation by the people and can be said to be opaque . . .

But all the new laws and provisions are reported in the newssheets and the entire text is available in every large library . . .
He kept reading.

> . . . the arcane system of secret voting whereby only the total vote by political party for or against any measure means that no Councilor can be held to task by the people for his vote . . .

Even that wasn't true, Dekkard knew, because a great many votes were strictly by party line votes. If every Crafter councilor voted for a measure, then the voters could certainly tell how a given councilor voted. And given how few defectors there were . . . except that the newssheets never printed the names of the councilors in those stories.
But the names of councilors are all public. So that meant a determined individual could certainly inform himself and his friends. They just couldn't absolutely prove in all votes whether a given councilor voted a given way, nor could they print and disseminate such information publicly because it could not meet the test of absolute proof.
What the New Meritorists wanted, it seemed to him, was for the newssheets, or someone else, to compile and print dossiers on all votes for all councilors. That would make the newssheets and such compilers the ones who

shaped public opinion, the ones who could single out individual councilors for praise or condemnation.

After two more pages, Dekkard was shaking his head. The processes for implementing laws and creating regulations weren't opaque. They were laid out in the regulatory manual that was available in every library, public or private, in Guldor. So was the process for allowing public comments . . . and councilors often weighed in on regulations as a result of letters or petitions. Dekkard had certainly seen that.

How many people understood even the intricacies of workplace rules? Or whether yellow cedar or cherry was best for paneling . . . or the health of the crafters shaping it?

By the time he had read through the entire short book, Dekkard just sat there, thinking over what he had read.

How can anyone be that simpleminded?

Let any political party have as many councilors as possible? That would remove any check on the passions of the moment and the year. Not only that, but it would remove the mechanisms for forcing compromise and co-operation.

Unlimited numbers of political parties? What could that do but create parties based on single issues or populist passions and divert energy and effort from maintaining government, defense, roads, waterways, order, and the other basic functions of government?

And the removal of the Imperador's veto? The New Meritorists would allow any law that passed by a single vote to remain law, even if it discommoded or disenfranchised forty-nine percent of the population. At present, forty-four of the Sixty-Six could override an Imperial veto, and Dekkard had seen only a single veto in two years. It wasn't as though the Imperador vetoed legislation willy-nilly.

The right of the newssheets to print anything that couldn't be refuted, except through the courts? And since only civil lawsuits could be used to check the power of the press under the New Meritorists' "principles," that meant that only those with resources could stop lies and misstatements.

Dekkard shuddered at that thought.

And empaths and susceptibles in office? The idea of an empath councilor, one who could project feelings and force or entice other councilors to follow? Or would that mean that every Council meeting would require empaths to monitor to point out undue influence? And allowing susceptibles to vote, when any empath could direct their votes?

And then, no term limits on councilors, so that the Commercers could use all their marks and influence to pack the Council? Would Guldor end up more of a plutocracy . . . until everyone else revolted?

If they even knew enough to revolt once those with all the marks controlled the newssheets, the Council . . . and everything else.

He sat there for a time, just thinking, but one of the thoughts that kept recurring was that, while the New Meritorists might be wrong about the solution, matters had to be worse than Dekkard had seen.

Why else would students and others risk being shot— even force patrollers and guards to shoot them?

Or hadn't he looked deeply enough?

27

The first thing Dekkard did on Unadi morning after dressing and heading downstairs was to find Obreduur, already in the family breakfast room with Ingrella. There, he handed the Meritorist book back.

"You read it all?"

"Yes, sir."

"What do you think . . . now?"

"We have more of a problem than I thought, and they

have an appealing solution that will only make things worse."

"That's also why you have to listen when you meet with the Artisans Guild . . . and let them know, quietly, that you listened and understood their problems . . . whatever they may be."

"I have to ask, sir . . . why me . . . and not you? You're far better at that, I'm certain."

"I learned a long time ago, Steffan, that I can't do everything. *You,* however, can learn to do what I do. In time, you might even be better . . . and then there will be two of us."

"Three. I'm sure Avraal will do as well as I do. And what about Ivann and Svard?"

"They do other things better than I can so that I can do what I do best. Now . . . I need to eat, and so do you. We'll talk more later."

"Yes, sir." Dekkard inclined his head.

"Steffan," interjected Ingrella, "since you're here, might I ask you to light off the other steamer just before you pull out?"

"I'd be happy to, Ritten." With that, Dekkard made his way back to the staff room. There, he immediately picked up the newssheet. The story about the demonstrators was on the second page below the fold, and he scanned it quickly.

. . . a student political demonstration yesterday at Imperial University resulted in injuries to more than a half score students and several Security patrollers . . . at least one fatality . . . university authorities stated that the demonstration was against university rules . . . Students carried signs advocating voting and employment "reforms" . . . When asked to disperse by Security patrollers, students attacked the patrollers. One protestor was armed and fired upon patrollers . . . additional patrollers were required to disperse the protestors and to take into custody those who assaulted patrollers . . .

Dekkard replaced the newssheet on the side table.

"Where were you?" asked Ysella quietly as Dekkard sat down. "Before you stopped to read *Gestirn*."

"Returning the book I borrowed last night."

"You read it all?"

"It wasn't that long."

"And?"

"It's either naïvely simplistic, or deliberately so."

"That's usually the case for reformers and revolutionaries." As Rhosali entered the staff room, Ysella added, "We should talk later . . . if you want to."

"I do . . . but I'd like to think a bit more."

"Do you two do anything but read and work?" asked Rhosali as she poured her café.

"We occasionally shop and go out," replied Dekkard, "sometimes together." That might have been overstating it, since they'd only been doing things together in the last month. *The last few weeks, really.*

But, thankfully, Ysella didn't correct him or qualify his words.

"That doesn't sound like much fun," opined Rhosali.

"We'll leave that to you," replied Ysella cheerfully. "Someone should have fun."

"Sometimes, I think I'm the only one. Ritter Obreduur's never upset or excited. The Ritten isn't either. Mistress Nellara is so serious, and Master Gustoff is always dour. I miss Master Axeli. He liked to have a good time."

Which was why Obreduur sent him to the Military Institute. Dekkard kept that thought to himself, and concentrated on his croissants. After several bites, he finally said to Ysella, "You might read about what happened at the university."

"I did . . . while you were returning the book. You thought the story would say more?"

Dekkard shook his head. "No. But that may cause more problems."

"Most likely."

Ysella's pleasant tone told Dekkard that she might

discuss it later, but not at breakfast. So he finished eating quickly, took his dishes into the kitchen, and then went to ready himself and the steamers.

The drive to the Council Office Building was uneventful, although the dark grayish-green clouds south of the city suggested the possibility of rain.

Dekkard was at his desk soon enough.

Ysella and Obreduur had already left the office for a meeting, and they didn't return until nearly midmorning, when Obreduur stopped beside Dekkard's desk. "I'm meeting Councilor Hasheem for lunch. The Security Committee held a short meeting this morning."

Dekkard didn't say anything, although he had an idea.

Obreduur smiled knowingly. "I'm sure it had to do with the difficulties at Imperial University. The Imperador isn't terribly fond of unpleasantnesses at universities, especially there . . ."

Because his ancestor founded it, no doubt, and it's considered one of the great universities in the world . . . and unpleasantnesses reflect badly on him and Guldor.

"You two can eat in the Council Hall and wait for me. It will be a short lunch." Then the councilor went to talk to Karola about changes to his schedule.

Ysella said to Dekkard, "That will give us a chance to talk, maybe the only chance. It's looking like a long day."

Ysella returned to her desk, and Dekkard went back to work on petitions and letters.

Obreduur, Ysella, and Dekkard left the office at a third before noon. The central staircase to the first level contained less than a score of people, and when they stepped outside, the slightly cooler but much damper air told Dekkard that it was raining even as he saw and heard the comparatively light precipitation. They walked down the center of the tile-roofed promenade to the Council Hall and reached the councilors' dining room at five minutes before the noon bell.

Once Obreduur was inside, Dekkard and Ysella

walked along one side of the moderately crowded main corridor to the staff cafeteria, picked out their meals and paid for them, and then took a wall table for two.

Dekkard took several bites of what was supposed to be a fowl piccata, lemony enough, but somehow lacking piquancy, before he said, "I was thinking of going to the Council Library and trying to find out something about Joel Janhus."

"You might find it easier if you went tomorrow," said Ysella.

For a moment, Dekkard didn't understand. Then he nodded. Wearing a gray suit with the standard staff pin, rather than duty security grays, would require fewer explanations.

"There's a reference to him in the *Annotated History of Teknold*," added Ysella. "And in other books, but I don't recall the titles."

"Do you want to tell me about him?"

"Not until you search a little." She smiled.

"Making it hard on me, then."

"No. Making so that you'll remember."

"You sound like some of the more demanding professors at the Institute."

"Weren't you there when the Imperador's eldest son was there?" asked Ysella.

"Oh . . . Landyn D'Aureous. I saw him, but never met him. He was three years ahead of me. And he went to serve in the Fleet. What else would he do?" Dekkard shook his head. "You're right, though. Maybe you should have been a professor."

"Most universities frown on empaths as professors. Besides, that would have required an advanced degree . . ."

". . . and most universities are reluctant to admit women to advanced studies."

"I could have gotten in, but at best, I would have been a token professor. It would have been almost impossible to change things. Universities are worse than government in that."

When the two finished eating, they walked back to wait across the main corridor from the dining room, back where they wouldn't interfere with councilors or staffers heading to and from committee rooms or Council messengers in green and gold hurrying by.

Less than a third of a bell later, councilors began to emerge from the dining room. Dekkard picked out Saarh, with two others, one of whom might have been Navione and another he did not recognize.

Then came Obreduur and Hasheem, still talking, and a yard or so behind them, two other councilors, one graying and much older. Abruptly, the older man staggered, then fell, while his companion stopped as if he'd been struck, as did the empie in security grays who had moved toward the older councilor, a man whose face Dekkard recognized, but whose name escaped him at that moment.

"There!" snapped Ysella, pointing to a young man in the gold and green of a Council messenger who was turning away from the dining room entrance. "Dekkard!"

The "messenger" turned, but slowly, as if hampered, which he doubtless was, by some projection of Ysella's. Those around the messenger scattered in all directions as Dekkard sprinted toward the renegade empie.

Dekkard had decided already on the truncheon, because it was safer with people in the corridors and because dead men couldn't tell anyone who sent them. The messenger looked back at Dekkard, seemingly concentrating, then realized that Dekkard was an isolate and tried to run. Dekkard was already within a yard and closing. He immediately aimed the truncheon's arc so that it struck the rear thigh nerves just above the messenger's knee.

The messenger tumbled to the ground, but twisted and tried to pull something out of a pocket. Dekkard knocked that out of his hand with a second blow from the black truncheon. A spray of red particles flew across the corridor.

Atacaman fire pepper dust.

The messenger glared at Dekkard, and he realized that the empie wasn't a young man at all, but a slightly older and muscular woman.

"Don't." Dekkard's voice was hard.

The woman in the messenger's uniform tried to use her arms to force herself to her feet.

Even as he struck her supporting arm and she collapsed to the floor, Dekkard wondered how she had managed that, given the jolts he'd applied to her nerves.

The faintest hint of the pepper mist burned his eyes, but not enough that he couldn't keep the false messenger immobilized until the two Council Guard isolates appeared and immediately bound and hooded the false messenger.

The older one turned to Dekkard. "Thank you, sir. Without you, it would have been a lot worse."

"Without me and Empath Ysella," Dekkard replied. "She blocked some of the effects."

"Convey our thanks to her as well, sir."

"I will."

Dekkard walked back toward where Obreduur and Ysella waited, but he saw that the fallen councilor was being placed on a wheeled cart. From what Dekkard could see, the councilor wasn't breathing. His empie looked stunned, an expression that suggested that the attack had been fatal. At that moment, Dekkard remembered the councilor's name—Aashtaan—

Kurtweil Aashtaan, the Commercer who was the chairman of the Commerce Committee.

Dekkard stopped short of Ysella and Obreduur.

The councilor looked at Dekkard, then Ysella. "Thank you."

"I was already shielding you," said Ysella. "The overlap partly shielded those close by. I've almost never felt a bolt of hatred as strong as hers."

"Her?" asked Obreduur.

"A woman dressed as a young male messenger," confirmed Dekkard. "I didn't realize it until after I had her down."

"That's something else the Council Guards will have to look for." Obreduur turned in the direction of the courtyard gardens and the Council Office Building. Dekkard and Ysella flanked him as he walked.

Once they were outside and away from others, Dekkard asked quietly, "The New Meritorists?"

"Most likely," replied the councilor. "The Council Guards will find out for certain. The other question is how long before the Premier lets anyone know. He'd be much happier if the assassin turned out to be merely a deranged young woman."

"Isn't that rather improbable?" asked Dekkard. "Getting the uniform right and getting into the Council Hall . . . knowing where to go . . . and when?"

Obreduur merely offered a sardonic smile.

"A deranged empie," said Ysella. "I'd rather that *Gestirn* print that she was an extremist assassin."

"That would be better," agreed Obreduur. "It's not Ulrich's way, though. Even if she is a New Meritorist, he'd never want to see that in print."

"Because he doesn't want the newssheets to mention an organized group of rebels?"

"Do you think that's a good idea?" countered Obreduur. "Recognizing that such a group exists is the first step in getting people to question why others are willing to die to oppose the Council or even individual councilors. Organized opposition suggests widespread problems."

"Problems for whom?" asked Ysella. "The Imperador, the Council, or the Commercer leadership of government?"

"That's the danger," said Obreduur. "Popular opinion could turn against any of those . . . or all three."

"Unless someone mentions one of those three," said Ysella.

"That's a gamble," said Obreduur.

"It is," agreed Ysella evenly.

"It's worth thinking about," replied the councilor.

As soon as the three walked into the office, Karola exclaimed, "You're all safe, thank the Three."

"How did you know there was a problem?" asked Obreduur.

"Druanna—from the next office. She'd gone over to the staff cafeteria. She said a renegade empie attacked some councilors and even another empie."

"The attack was on Councilor Aashtaan and his empath took part of the brunt," said Obreduur. "Steffan and Ysella captured her. The Council Guards have her in custody."

"You're all right . . . all of you?"

"We are," affirmed Obreduur.

"Who did it?" asked Macri, who had just appeared in the doorway to the side office.

"That remains to be determined. The attacker wore a Council messenger's uniform."

"It has to involve more than one person," said Macri.

"Exactly, Ivann," replied Obreduur. "At the moment, who else might be involved is unknown." With a nod, he entered his office and shut the door.

"It has to be those demonstrators," said Karola.

"It's likely," replied Macri, "but I wouldn't say anything outside the office until it's made public. If you guess before it is, and you're right, Security might find it interesting."

"They've got better things to do." Even so, Karola shook her head.

Before that long, Dekkard was back working on responses. Then, around third bell, he put those aside and began to jot down notes for his meeting the next day with the Artisans Guild.

On the way to get the Gresynt so that he could pick up Obreduur and Ysella, Dekkard saw that there were far more Council Guards everywhere, and, even with the rain still coming down, they were stopping people, most likely those staffers whose pins weren't visible or were missing, or even some who looked suspicious.

Then, once he had the Gresynt in front of the building, he had to wait almost a third before Obreduur and Ysella appeared.

As Dekkard pulled away from the Council Office Building, Obreduur said, "I'm sorry we were late, Steffan, but I had to send off messages at the last minute."

"Has Premier Ulrich announced anything?"

"Only Councilor Aashtaan's death and that the Council mourning banners will be flown for the next four days. Now . . . if you'll excuse me . . ."

"Yes, sir." Dekkard could tell, from Ysella's body posture, that she was concentrating more on everything anywhere close to the Gresynt, although she relaxed slightly while they were on Imperial Boulevard. When he turned onto Altarama, she tensed slightly, but neither she nor Dekkard discerned anyone nearby.

As Dekkard slowed the Gresynt to a stop under the portico, Obreduur cleared his throat and said, "I'd like to thank you two again. You both handled the situation magnificently, and I appreciate it very much. So will my wife and children."

"I'm just glad we could, sir," replied Dekkard.

"As am I," added Ysella.

Once he had the Gresynt in the garage, Dekkard wiped off the windscreens and checked the water and kerosene levels. The kerosene tank in the garage had just been refilled, he noted, and the water filters had been replaced.

After the initial flurry of questions from Rhosali, and a few from Hyelda, dinner in the staff room was about as usual, although Dekkard found he was hungrier than he realized, and took seconds on the cold roasted fowl.

As he stood to leave, Ysella looked to him.

"Outside?" he mouthed.

She nodded. The two of them walked to the portico, where the rain still tapped on the roof.

As they stood there, Ysella looked at Dekkard. "You're good. You're better than good."

"So are you. You made it much easier."

"How did you know about the Atacaman pepper?"

"I didn't. I just knew that whatever she had in her hand wasn't good, and I knocked it in the direction

where there were fewer people. Well . . . as best I could."
He paused. "Do you think she's the one who tried to
take out Obreduur that night?"

"I hope so," replied Ysella. "Because, if she's not . . ."
She shook her head.

Dekkard understood. "Do you think the guard empies can find out?"

"They'll find out." Ysella's tone of voice was bleak.
"Interrogation . . . that's one thing I won't do. It may be
necessary, but it's brutal. They'll find out," she repeated,
"but she may not even have a mind left when the guard
interrogators finish with her."

Dekkard had heard rumors, but nothing put quite
that starkly. After several moments, he said, "How soon
before they try again?"

"That depends on whether they change their plan of
attack and how many empaths they're willing to lose."

"You don't see them fading away?"

"Do you?"

"No, but it's more of a feeling than anything I could
support logically."

"Steffan . . . logical thought inspires people, but feelings move them. Why else do you think empaths can't
hold political offices, except as staffers?"

"Then . . . matters are going to get worse."

"Of course."

Dekkard didn't have much more to say at that
moment, and neither did Ysella.

28

Dekkard had laid out his security-gray suit with a
white shirt and a dark blue cravat the night before,
simply because he was so much in the habit of wearing
his security uniform that he wanted to make sure everything was ready on Duadi morning. He even had the

staff pin in place on the jacket lapel, but he didn't wear the jacket to breakfast, or the throwing knives, whose sheaths would be concealed under the jacket.

He took a moment before getting his café and sitting down to glance at the daily newssheet.

> . . . early Unadi afternoon, a deranged female empath disguised as a Council messenger attacked a Councilor and his aide in the Imperial Council Hall. The emp attack created a fatal heart failure for the Councilor and stunned his aide . . . an isolate and an empath who are security aides to another Councilor immediately captured and restrained the attacker . . . motive for the attack is not known . . . attacker is incarcerated and being questioned . . . the circumstances suggest the attack could not have taken place without the assistance and support of others . . . attacker obtained an official uniform and penetrated Council security measures . . .

Dekkard nodded. The "support of others" was as far as *Gestirn* would go. Those words might have been prompted by Obreduur, if indirectly, but either the source or *Gestirn* felt that linking it to the New Meritorists was politically unwise. Dekkard couldn't see who else could have been behind attacking a Commerce councilor.

But then, two months ago, you didn't even know about the New Meritorists. And he'd almost forgotten about the original Meritorists.

He'd no sooner seated himself than Ysella arrived, glanced quickly at the newssheet, and sat down across from him.

She took several sips of café before speaking. "A deranged young woman empie."

"Possibly assisted by others," replied Dekkard dryly.

Ysella just nodded.

After breakfast, Dekkard returned to his room and donned his new gray jacket and the throwing knives. He'd checked the security handbook about what weapons he could carry when not wearing a gray security uniform, and discovered that so long as he wore either security grays *or* a gray suit of the same shade of gray and a Council staff pin, he could still carry his gladius and full-sized truncheon, but only in the Council buildings. Outside of them, he could still carry the full-sized truncheon, but not the gladius, and his knives, since knives—only blade length was prescribed to differentiate them from swords—were considered self-defense weapons.

So . . . when he got in the steamer, he placed the gladius on the floor behind his seat. That way he was technically in compliance.

As soon as Obreduur entered the steamer, he said, "I've had no word on the assassin. I won't hear anything until later today . . . if then." The councilor was politely telling them not to ask.

As Dekkard headed down the drive, he saw that Ysella was especially alert, and he decided to follow her example . . . although neither discerned anyone closely following them.

When Dekkard eased the Gresynt to a stop outside the Council Office Building, there were still extra Council Guards stationed outside, as well as around the covered parking area. One of them looked at Dekkard when he got out of the Gresynt and retrieved the gladius before locking the steamer, but the guard then continued patrolling. Once inside the Council Office Building, Dekkard took the staff staircase and then hurried into the office.

Karola stared at him for a moment, then said, "You look different dressed as a professional staffer."

"Is that good or bad?" Dekkard asked in a humorous tone.

"You're . . . just different. Both of you . . . when you're not in security uniforms."

Dekkard suspected that she meant that they didn't look quite so intimidating.

Dressed as a professional staffer or not, he still faced a stack of letters, which he began to address immediately, since he only had a little more than a bell before he'd have to depart.

At a third past third bell, he stood to leave for the drive to the Machtarn Guildhall.

"Be careful," said Ysella quietly. "Especially after you've given the talk and are leaving. Most people aren't as wary after a meeting, especially if it goes well."

"Thank you. I wouldn't have thought of it that way." And he wouldn't have, not for himself, although he and Ysella had talked about that in regard to Obreduur. As he walked down the staff staircase, he just hoped that he could be a good listener and a decent stand-in.

Before getting into the Gresynt, he slipped the gladius and its scabbard off his belt and put them behind the seat again.

He didn't see any steamers following him on Council Avenue, but once he was on Imperial Boulevard heading toward the harbor, the traffic was heavy enough that any steamer could have hung back half a block and he wouldn't have seen it. He kept checking the mirrors when he turned right off the boulevard and onto the Avenue of the Guilds, toward the river, but saw nothing out of the ordinary for the five blocks that took him to the Machtarn Guildhall, where he eased the Gresynt into an "official business" space.

He moved swiftly from the steamer, locking it, and heading toward the side entrance with the sentry box and a guard. His fingers brushed the grip of his truncheon as he neared the guard.

"Assistant Economic Specialist Dekkard, representing Councilor Obreduur for a meeting with the Artisans Guild," Dekkard announced.

The guard studied Dekkard, then looked at a sheet posted on the wall. "The meeting's in 201. That's up the first set of stairs, up one flight, almost at the end of the hall."

"Thank you."

When Dekkard stepped into the building, the corridor immediately before him was empty, except for two men standing beside a small cart at the far end of the hallway. One glanced in his direction and then away. The other looked into the cart. Dekkard took the stairs, ten yards short of the workmen, up to the second level, then turned toward the west end of the building.

A man and a woman were clearly waiting for Dekkard, because both saw him and stepped forward as he neared the end of the hall.

"Sr. Dekkard?" asked the small graying woman.

Dekkard had never thought of himself as more than slightly above average in height, but for some reason he felt as though he towered over her. "That's right. I'm the assistant economic specialist to Councilor Obreduur. Since everyone else in my family is an artisan, he thought I'd be the best staff assistant to meet with you."

"That answers one of my questions," said the man, perhaps a decade older than Dekkard. "What are their arts?"

"My mother and sister are portraitists; my father is a decorative-plaster specialist."

"You didn't become an artisan, though?" pressed the man.

"I'd like to think I have the soul and the appreciation, but I definitely don't have their physical precision, and I didn't want to be a fifth-rate artisan."

"That's an honest answer. By the way, I'm Raoul Carlione."

"And I'm Verylla Wierre."

"She's the assistant guildmeister," added Carlione.

Dekkard wished Carlione had said what he was, and it was clear he was important, possibly even the guildmeister, but Obreduur had never given the names of those he'd be meeting.

"I'm very glad to meet you both. The councilor told me to place myself at your disposal and to get the full extent of the problem from you." Dekkard smiled sheepishly, and added, "Before saying much of anything."

Wierre nodded. "That sounds very much like what Konrad said about him."

Konrad? Then Dekkard remembered. Konrad Hadenaur, the Sanitation guildmeister. "He said you'd know more than I do, and that my job is to listen and to convey all that information to him so that he can address the problem."

"What do you know?" asked Carlione.

"I read your petition after the councilor did. I've checked the laws. I've met with the Council legalist in charge of tariff law. And my parents fled Argental because the laws weren't good for artisans."

"That will do for a start," said Carlione pleasantly, but not either enthusiastically or deprecatingly. He motioned to the half-open door. "This is a small meeting, just most of the senior guild members."

Since he was supposed to enter first, Dekkard did. A large circular table occupied much of the chamber, a room illuminated solely by the large north widows, although there were unlit lamps in evenly spaced wall sconces. None of the five guild members—four men and a woman—already seated around the table stood.

"Sr. Dekkard is one of Councilor Obreduur's economic specialists," said Carlione, "and the one with the most background in matters of artisans and artistry." He gestured to a vacant chair on the side of the table opposite the middle of the other five, then took the chair to the right of Dekkard, while Wierre took the seat to Dekkard's left.

"As you know from the guild petition," began Wierre, "the guild has readied a grievance against the Imperial Tariff Commission. Tariff agents are allowing cheaply produced art to be imported and tariffed as housewares, when the art is of a higher quality and is later sold at a far higher price than the import appraisal price. This is not new, but the number of instances has increased greatly in the last year."

"The guild realizes," continued Carlione, "the price of any work of fine art depends on where it is sold and the willingness of a buyer to pay, but to appraise works of fine art as housewares is absurd."

"Might I ask a question . . ." Dekkard paused, then went on. "In your petition, you did not specify what types of fine art were being classified as housewares. Is there just one category, or are the tariff agents applying the housewares tariff indiscriminately to sculptures, paintings, tapestries, jewelry, and other arts?"

"So far as we know," replied Wierre, "the housewares category has been applied only to sculptures, artistic objects, pottery and stoneware—not everyday crockery— paintings, and occasional tapestries."

"Have you been provided with any reason for this undervaluation?" asked Dekkard.

Carlione snorted. "Such objects aren't up to the standards of Guldoran artistry so they must only be housewares."

Dekkard smiled wryly. "And if you say that they are, you're denigrating the guild's standards. Is this the action of one or two inspectors or a decision by the head assessor?"

"All of the inspectors are agreeing with the idea."

Dekkard realized that he'd missed asking a key question. The guild members couldn't have been present at customs inspections and tariff assessments. "How exactly did you find out about this?"

"When the objects started appearing in art shops and galleries, and decorator supply services," replied Wierre. "It's taken several months to track all this down."

"Is it affecting all art, including very expensive and high-quality art objects?"

One of the guild members opposite Dekkard said, "That's not the problem. You don't sell truly great art objects that often. The well-crafted lamps, the decorative mirrors, the high-quality serving pieces . . . that's what keeps artisans in business on a monthly basis. These so-called houseware imports are just good enough to siphon off enough business to make it hard for solid artisans to keep going."

"Is one importer bringing them all in?" asked Dekkard.

Carlione laughed, sardonically. "For someone as

young as you are, you're rather cynical. You're on the right rails, but there are two outfits. One turns out to be a subsidiary of Guldoran Ironway. The other is called Tarn Trading. It has to be a subsidiary of some large corporacion because they're bringing in large shipments and paying the duties in a lump sum. That's what our sources know."

"Are these art objects from any one nation?"

"No, but they're all shipped on Transoceanic ships," said Wierre. "They come in large lots. That's another reason why the tariff assessors claim they're just housewares."

"Is there any way to raise the issue with the head of the tariff assessors?"

"That's another aspect of the problem," said Carlione. "If I import something, and I think the tariff was unfair, I can appeal it, even take it to the Justiciary, although that would cost more than the tariff. But there's no direct way to appeal someone else getting a lower tariff. Without specific information, we can't file a legal complaint before the Justiciary. Only a Council hearing can compel the tariff assessors to disclose those details . . ."

Dekkard kept listening, asking an occasional question, but after almost a bell, it was clear that the guild representatives were at best offering examples of the same situation. After yet another such example, he said, "I think you've made the extent of the problem very clear and the fact that it's a matter for the councilor to address."

"How do you think he might address it?" asked Carlione.

Dekkard smiled wryly. "I learned almost as soon as I went to work for him that it was unwise to speculate on how he might deal with anything. He's often been able to come up with solutions that no one else considered. You've given me additional information that will be even more helpful. I will say that matters involving ministries usually take a little time. I wish it were otherwise, as I know you do."

"You're not saying that much about what he could do," said the woman on the far side of the table. Almost testily.

"That's because he told me specifically not to speculate on what he might do," replied Dekkard. "Since I work for him, and since I've discovered he has a good reason for how and what he asks of me, I've found that it's a good idea to listen and follow his instructions."

Dekkard's reply brought the hint of a smile to Wierre's face, before she and Carlione rose. Dekkard followed their example.

"Thank you for coming, Sr. Dekkard. Please convey our appreciation to the councilor," said Carlione.

"I will certainly do so."

Carlione and Wierre escorted him out into the corridor, where Carlione said, "I didn't want to bring it up in there, but this is a sneak attack on the guild by the Commercers, and it's getting very effective. If artisans go out of business, our dues go down."

"I'll make certain he knows that."

Before Carlione could say more, Wierre put her hand on his shoulder. "Sr. Dekkard understands." She turned to Dekkard. "Thank you."

Dekkard inclined his head, then turned and walked toward the stairs.

As he neared the last steps, he glanced to where the two men had been working. Both remained near the cart. The nearer worker, who stood beside the cart next to the wall, didn't quite look at Dekkard and then turned and walked toward the door at the west end of the building. The other worker turned and seemed to inspect the wall, but Dekkard could see no sign of any work, or even fresh paint. He walked to the door out into the parking area, then stepped outside and closed the door. He stood there for a minute or so before turning back and easing the door open just wide enough to peer down the corridor.

The other worker was also gone.

Dekkard didn't much care for coincidences. He immediately hurried past the guard and toward the Gresynt, ready to use the truncheon if necessary. At first, he saw no one near the steamer. Then a figure in nondescript coveralls carrying a satchel appeared from behind several other steamers at the east end of the parking area and walked to a small steam lorry. There he set the satchel in the open bed of the lorry, not looking at Dekkard.

Dekkard judged the distance between the Gresynt and the lorry as almost twenty yards. He kept walking.

The workman didn't turn or look in Dekkard's direction until he had almost reached the Gresynt, then turned and almost stared at Dekkard.

Dekkard understood exactly what was supposed to happen, and, after considering using the knives and rejecting that option, in a single fluid motion, drew the truncheon and ran toward the empie. The "worker"/empie whirled and sprinted away. Dekkard immediately stopped and dashed back to the Gresynt, which he entered, and then lit off the burner, glancing around and hoping that no one would start shooting.

Finally, he could start the steamer moving, and he wasted no time leaving the parking area. So far as he could tell, no one followed him.

As he drove back toward the Council Office Building, he considered what had happened. From the two false workers observing him and from the empie trying to attack him, someone had known that an aide of Obreduur's would be coming. They couldn't have known who or they wouldn't have tried to kill or injure him with an empath. Since the higher-up guild members had known who he was, no one in the higher guild levels was likely the source of the information. Because Dekkard was an isolate, he also had no way of knowing how strong the empie was or what the emotion had been behind the projection.

What he didn't understand, again, was why anyone would attack a mere junior aide. Or had they thought that Obreduur himself or a senior aide might appear?

He was still pondering it all when he stepped into the office, after making his way past the additional Council Guards outside and on the lower level.

"The councilor said he wanted to talk to you immediately on your return," said Karola even before Dekkard reached his desk.

Dekkard kept walking, then knocked on the door. "Steffan, sir . . . you asked for me?"

"Come in."

Dekkard did so, closing the door.

Obreduur gestured to the chairs in front of his desk. "What happened?"

Dekkard told him, including the false workmen and the probable empie.

When Dekkard finished, Obreduur asked, "What do you make of it?"

"Someone with wealth and influence has bribed or extorted the tariff assessors. As Carlione said, it's designed to cut the incomes of artisans, in an effort to reduce the funds available to the guild and weaken it. On a practical funding level, that makes no sense, because it reduces tariff revenues to the government. It also reduces the sales-tax revenues paid by Machtarn artisans. That hurts the government doubly."

Obreduur nodded. "It does. Who would gain from that?"

"Someone importing a great amount of art objects or someone who wants to break the guilds. Either way that suggests a powerful corporacion or individual. They'd gain by weakening the Craft Party, but if it were traced back to them . . . and there were a public outcry, then the Imperador might have to dissolve the Council and call new elections, and it would cost the Commerce Party some seats."

"You're assuming there would be an outcry," pointed out Obreduur.

"If you or any councilor made the point that corporacions were undercutting Guldoran artisans and also not paying duties, while reducing the taxes paid by artisans which meant that roads or waterways don't get repaired unless taxes are raised . . . you just might get an outcry."

"If there were such an outcry and new elections, would we gain enough seats for a plurality? Would enough Landors ally themselves with the Craft Party to form a coalition government?"

"Right now, it's unlikely."

"Right now," agreed Obreduur. "How do you propose I deal with the problem?"

"As a bribery and revenue problem," replied Dekkard. "Someone is bribing tariff inspectors and assessors, and it's not only corrupt, but it's costing the government lost revenues in two ways."

Obreduur nodded again. "Draft me a letter to Treasury Minister Munchyn laying out both those points with a paragraph suggesting that failure to deal with such an instance right now might have even greater repercussions in the wake of the government's recent difficulties. Don't mention what those difficulties were. He'll understand."

"Yes, sir."

"And Steffan . . . the next time an empie attacks . . . if there is a next time, just take cover. They'll expect you to attack, and they will shoot, and no one will find the shooter."

"Why are they attacking me?" Dekkard thought he knew, but he wanted a confirmation.

"Because you work for me . . . and because you're part of the future they fear. Now . . . if you'd get to work on the letter to Munchyn . . . and another one to Guildmeister Carlione saying that I'm taking steps that I believe will be helpful in addressing the problem and that I'll keep him informed."

"Yes, sir."

"Excellent. Also, you and Ysella will have lunch with me in the councilors' dining room. That would be only fair after yesterday and today."

"Is that allowed? I've never heard . . ."

"Each councilor has ten passes a year for guests. Even the Premier only gets ten."

"I appreciate that very much, sir . . . but you don't have to. What about Ritten Obreduur?"

"Councilors' spouses are exempt, but not children." Obreduur smiled. "When the first women councilors were elected, the men-only rule had to be changed. Then, apparently a number of wives were most upset that the only women who could eat with councilors were other female councilors. So the Council exempted wives and male spouses from the limitation, not that many take advantage of the privilege. In any event, I'd rather have the lunch with you two than any corporacion type." Obreduur smiled sardonically as he added, "And any guildmeister I took would think I was just like the Commercers. We'll leave at about a third before noon. I've already told Avraal."

Once back at his desk, Dekkard had to force his mind off everything that had happened. He finally took a deep breath and began to draft the first of the letters about the tariff issue.

He finished both drafts and handed them to Margrit in less than a bell and was working on more routine correspondence when Obreduur stepped out of his office.

"Shall we go? The Premier has called the Council into session at second bell. That should provide enough time for a good meal without hurrying."

The only remaining sign of Unadi's events was the increased number of guards in the garden courtyard. The central corridor in the Council Hall was almost empty. When the three stepped inside the councilors' dining room, Obreduur handed two gold-and-black-edged cards to the host, a thin man attired in black and gold livery, who inclined his head and said, "This way, Councilor."

The large dining area held about thirty tables, half of which were tables for two, all of which were set farther from each other than in a normal restaurant. Only about a third of the tables were taken. The walls were a creamy gold-streaked polished marble, while the floor was a dark green marble, and the table linens were a light ivory. For all the outward elegance of the space, Dekkard wondered if the food would be as good as what he'd had at Don Miguel.

When they were seated at a table, Obreduur glanced around. "We're a bit early. It will be full at a sixth past noon." He did not pick up the menu as he continued. "Now . . . I'd recommend the duck cassoulet. It's what the dining room is known for, and it's also tasty and filling. If you're not fond of duck, then the three-cheese chicken is good. The only thing terrible on the menu is the ground beef and cheese sandwich. It's on the menu as the burgher's delight. I shouldn't say that since Councilor Volkaar loves it, but he prides himself on his taste." Obreduur's last few words were only slightly sardonic.

Somehow the idea of the Commercers' floor leader favoring a burgher's delight made Dekkard smile, but he just said, "The cassoulet sounds good."

In the end, Obreduur ordered a cold tomato vegetable soup and a half order of the cassoulet and Ysella the chicken, while Dekkard settled on the cassoulet.

"What do you think of the dining room?" asked Obreduur. "Honestly, now?" He turned to Ysella.

"It's clean, elegant, and somehow a little tired."

"Like a courtesan who's not middle-aged, but no longer young?" the councilor said ironically.

"More tired than that, but yes," replied Ysella evenly. "And you, Steffan?"

After a pause, Dekkard finally said, "Wearing fine jewelry that's been borrowed, I suppose."

"It's interesting that you both came up with illusions." Obreduur paused as a white-gloved server arrived with a linen-covered tray of warm bread, then withdrew. "But then, politics is a combination of bitter reality and necessary illusion."

"Isn't life, sometimes?" said Ysella.

"Sometimes," agreed Obreduur, "but not always.

Unlike politics." He looked past Ysella and said quietly. "Here comes Saandaar Vonauer. He'll make some cutting remark."

The approaching councilor wore a black suit, with a pale gray shirt and a dark silver cravat. His hair was blond streaked with silver without single misplaced strand. A strong but not overlarge straight nose was flanked by intent but watery green eyes. He stopped and looked at Obreduur. "Your security aides, I presume, Axel? Rewarding them for capturing that murderous wench? Too bad they couldn't have stopped her sooner."

"That's one way of looking at it, Saandaar. Another way might be to ask Hansaal how neither his guards nor his messenger service could discover an imposter. Or why Craft security aides had to take care of the problem." Obreduur offered the words pleasantly, following them with a cheerful smile.

"I just might. I just might." After the barest of nods, Vonauer continued toward a table where another councilor waited.

"Will he actually ask Councilor Volkaar something like that?" Dekkard had thought the Landor councilor had sounded at least half serious.

"He likely will. Since Vonauer is the Landor floor leader, Volkaar, in his capacity as Commerce floor leader, needs Landor votes, and Vonauer hates being subservient to the Commercers. So he'll find some way to needle Volkaar. He might ask him if it wasn't embarrassing that the aides of a Craft councilor had to catch the assassin. Something like that."

Dekkard nodded, realizing that Obreduur had planned for that possibility. *And for a score of others.*

A few minutes later, their meals arrived, brought by another white-gloved server, followed by another who served their cafés.

Before they could begin to eat, two other councilors approached the table. One was Hasheem, and the second one was Jorje Kastenada.

Hasheem nodded to Obreduur, then looked to Ysella and Dekkard. "I just wanted to express my appreciation for your quick action yesterday. Arthal told me that the renegade empath was the strongest he'd ever experienced."

Since the appreciation was mainly for Ysella, Dekkard inclined his head to her.

"Thank you, Councilor. We did the best we could," replied Ysella.

"You were better than that. I won't intrude further, but I had to say a few words." Hasheem smiled and nodded to Obreduur before he and Kastenada moved away.

No one else approached the table directly, and Dekkard sampled the cassoulet. It was hearty, tasty, and filling. He wouldn't have called it outstanding, but it was definitely better than the fare in the staff cafeteria.

While several other councilors nodded or offered a few pleasantries to Obreduur, the rest of the meal was pleasant and relaxed, with no talk about the Council.

29

Tridi came and went, and there were no attacks, no assassinations, no interesting problems or petitions. There was also no response from the Ministry of Health about the Sanitation Guild's jobs proposal and no word that the controversy between the Woodcrafters Guild and Guldoran Ironway had been definitively resolved. There was absolutely no mention of the Kraffeist Affair anywhere, nor any mention about demonstrations or the New Meritorists. And there was nothing about Eduard Graffyn, otherwise known as Sr. Muller, not that Dekkard would have expected that.

Dekkard still wondered about Obreduur's connection with "Muller," and exactly what the councilor had in mind. He had to be playing a longer game, but how would he be able to use Graffyn without running afoul of the law and Security? If Obreduur had received any word about the empie assassin, he'd said nothing.

Although he was wearing security grays, Dekkard put on the staff pin in midafternoon and visited the Council Library, since he hadn't been able to go there when he'd been wearing his suit. Following Ysella's recommendation, he went through the *Annotated History of Teknold* and finally found an entry on Joel Janhus.

> . . . Senator of the last Teknold Parliament who opposed the Coup of the Marshals . . . executed under martial law after publishing a broadsheet that refuted the *Principles of New Reform* . . . predicted the collapse of the Grand Democracy . . . Janhus's name is considered a scatological obscenity in much of Teknold.

Dekkard had shaken his head at that. *Reviled for accurately predicting what would happen?*

When Dekkard entered the office on a very warm, if not summer-warm, Furdi morning, he doubted that he'd find out much about any of his concerns quickly. The stack of drafts that he handed to Margrit at second bell earned him a resigned sigh from the junior typist.

"You would have to catch up in a single day."

"I'm not caught up. It will take another day or two . . . if the councilor doesn't give me another special assignment."

"I do hope so. Then Anna and I might catch up." But Margrit did smile.

Dekkard just shook his head and walked back to his desk.

Moments later, Karola said, "He needs to see you."

When Dekkard entered the inner office, Obreduur motioned to the chairs, and Dekkard seated himself, waiting.

"A little while ago, I received a message from Guildmeister Carlione. He thanked me for the rapid response.

He said that you asked good questions and showed concern and understanding. He also said you were more impressive than a number of councilors he's met."

Why would he say that? "I just followed your advice as well as I could."

"He's not easily impressed. The fact that he responded by messenger says a great deal."

"I did tell him that you acted quickly, but that didn't mean that Imperial ministries would."

"I'm sure he's well aware of that," replied Obreduur dryly, "but I'm glad you pointed that out." He paused. "I'd like you and Avraal to accompany me to meet with some guild members this evening, as specialists, not as security aides. They have some concerns, and they're reluctant to come to the Council Office Building."

Dekkard frowned. "That doesn't sound good."

"They're good people. I'd like you and Avraal to meet them. It's set for sixth bell at a bistro in the harbor district—Rabool's. There will be light fare, since we'll miss dinner. We'll stop by the house so that you and Avraal can change."

"Do you know what they want to talk about?"

Obreduur shook his head. "Only that they're worried and feel that the Council should be concerned as well . . . or at least the Craft Party councilors."

After Dekkard returned to his desk, he just looked blankly at the half-written response in front of him. He'd never expected to be promoted to professional staff, and certainly not so quickly. While he'd known that people were likely to attack or shoot at the councilor, he'd never expected to be shot at and attacked personally because he worked for Obreduur. Nor had he expected something like the New Meritorist demonstrations and violence. Those things just didn't happen in Guldor.

Dekkard frowned. While the Council had downplayed the empie assassination of Councilor Aashtaan, it was clear that personal assassinations were largely unexpected, as was the use of firearms by the New Meritorists.

Meaning that it's not just politics as usual.

He took a long slow deep breath, then picked up his pen and began to write. He finished more drafts by fourth bell, and the drive back to the house was uneventful and quiet.

Once Dekkard let off the councilor and Ysella, he turned the Gresynt and then left it under the portico roof before going up to change into his lighter-weight security-gray suit.

He was the first back at the portico. Only a few minutes later, Ysella arrived, wearing a lavender summer suit. Dekkard noticed that while her headscarf matched the suit, it wasn't the near-transparent kind she'd worn with him, but somewhat heavier, possibly one of those she'd picked up at Esperanza.

"I know," she said, "it won't be summer until Unadi, but it's hot enough to be summer."

Dekkard hadn't been about to say that, but he replied, "I doubt that anyone will fuss over your rushing summer by less than three days. They'd more likely wonder why you were wearing something heavier when it's so hot."

Ysella shook her head. "Some habits are hard to put aside."

Obreduur arrived before either could say much more, wearing a light blue linen suit, rather than the darker blues he favored as a councilor.

Dekkard opened the rear door.

"Both of you, tell me if we're being followed. It's unlikely, but I'd like to know."

Once Ysella and Obreduur were settled in the steamer and Dekkard started down the drive, the older man said, "Take Imperial Boulevard toward the harbor. When we're past the rotary, I'll tell you where to go. You won't have to worry about parking. Carlos said he'd have a man near the front door saving a place for the steamer."

That was fine with Dekkard. He had no desire to

walk far through the harbor district even in early evening, or especially after dark.

"Carlos Baartol and I go back a long ways," Obreduur continued. "Besides his Craft associations, he has contacts with Landor councilors and more than a few staffers connected to all three parties."

Rabool's turned out to be a block north of Harbor Way, the wide street that provided access to the main piers. The bistro was a yellow-brick-fronted, three-story structure with polished brass double doors lit by brass lamps. True to Carlos's word, a brawny figure wearing a maroon vest over brown trousers waved them into a space next to the sidewalk and less than five yards from the doors.

"Welcome to Rabool's," offered the greeter as he opened the rear door. "You're Sr. Baartol's party?"

"We are." Obreduur slipped a five-mark note into his hand.

"They're in the small side room, sir."

"Thank you." Obreduur led the way into the bistro.

A stocky man with slicked-back gray hair in a bright purple jacket immediately stepped forward. "Axel, it's good to see you! Not that it's been all that long."

"Longer than I'd like, Rabool. You're looking prosperous." Obreduur grinned warmly. "But you looked prosperous back when this wasn't anywhere close to what you've made it."

"I had to live up to your expectations, you glorious bastard."

"I'm afraid I've lived down to yours. You've never had a great opinion of councilors."

"Most of 'em, I still don't. That's why it's good to see you." Rabool looked at Ysella, then Dekkard. His eyes remained on Dekkard.

"The one you're looking at is Steffan. Steffan Dekkard. He's both security and an economic assistant." Obreduur inclined his head. "And Avraal Ysella, special assistant and security."

"I heard talk . . ."

"I'm even less popular with some folks than I used to be."

"Good for you." Rabool looked to Dekkard again, then to Ysella. "Keep him safe."

"They've done very well," said Obreduur. "If they hadn't, I wouldn't be here."

"Good." Rabool gestured beyond the main dining area, where only a third of the tables were occupied, to an archway on the right. "Your folks are in there."

"We appreciate it."

"Little enough after everything. Just keep doing what you're doing." Then he looked to Dekkard. "You, too."

Dekkard nodded. "We will."

Obreduur headed toward the archway.

Dekkard followed, but took in the others in the bistro, mostly hard-looking men at least fifteen years older than Dekkard himself, although there were also a few women of about the same age, but no younger women, which definitely suggested an established clientele.

As soon as Obreduur was in the smaller side room, one with just four tables, two of which had been pulled together, a dark-haired man in a black shirt and trousers stepped forward from the three men and one woman who stood there and had been talking. "Axel . . . I saw that Rabool wanted a few words."

"He deserves more than that, but . . ." Obreduur shrugged.

"We know that. So does Rabool."

Obreduur half turned. "Carlos, I brought two people I thought you should meet. Avraal, here, is my special assistant. She's also a rather strong empath, as one of your people probably noticed. Steffan is—"

". . . a totally blocked isolate," interjected the dark-haired tall and angular woman who had moved up beside Baartol.

". . . and he's also an economic specialist with an artisan background who has a few other skills," continued

Obreduur smoothly, as if he hadn't been interrupted. "Avraal, Steffan, this is Carlos Baartol." Nodding to the angular woman, he added, "And Isobel Irlende."

"I'm pleased to meet you," said Ysella.

"So am I," added Dekkard.

Baartol gestured to the joined tables. "Might as well sit. Told Rabool to bring a couple of pitchers of good lager when you got here. Be a couple of platters of assorted tapas, too."

As soon as everyone was seated, two servers appeared, one with two large pitchers of lager, and another with a tray of beakers from which he provided one to each of the seven at the combined table. Carlos and his party sat on one side, with Obreduur on the other flanked by Dekkard and Ysella.

Dekkard stood and poured lager for Obreduur, Ysella, and himself, then reseated himself.

Baartol lifted his beaker. "To a better future."

Obreduur lifted his in response. "For all you've done already."

Moments later, Baartol looked across the table at Dekkard. "Carlione said you spoke very well to his board. I heard you also scared off the freelance empie Transoceanic sent in."

"You're sure it was Transoceanic?" asked Obreduur.

The man to Baartol's right said, "You know Saul Tharsus? He's used that empie before . . . when he didn't want Commercer fingerprints lying around. Usually in claims against Transoceanic or Azulete Transport. Most times, witnesses just left town. A couple times, they vanished. Couldn't prove it, but we're not the only ones who know that."

"I thought he lost the right to appear as a legalist before the Justiciary," replied Obreduur.

Dekkard had no idea who Tharsus was, but Obreduur clearly did.

"He did," said Baartol. "He's still got an office not far from here. The other guy, his associate, Roven Kharl, handles the court stuff."

At that moment, the servers returned with platters of tapas.

Once the servers departed, Obreduur asked, "Did you have any luck in tracking down Tarn Trading?"

Dekkard tried the crispy fried aubergine with the spiced honey and thyme, and found it good, if not outstanding. The goat cheese with quince jelly was better.

"They've got an office across from the customs warehouse," replied Bartol. "Not much to go on, but the legalist on retainer is from Paarsfal and Waaghnar, one of those pretentious outfits whose priority is to use the law to protect commercial interests. Some of their clients are Guldoran Ironway, Siincleer Shipbuilding, Uldwyrk Systems . . . and, of course, Transoceanic, for matters that have political implications."

Dekkard recognized the corporacions, although all he knew of Uldwyrk was that they built steam turbines for warships and the newer freighters.

Obreduur nodded. "That suggests they're a hidden subsidiary of some well-endowed corporacion. Do you have any idea who?"

Baartol shook his head. "Could be any of those I mentioned."

"Why do you think they went after Steffan?"

"They probably thought he was Raynaad."

Obreduur pursed his lips. "Steffan's more muscular and taller . . . and much younger."

"Their hair color is about the same, and I'd wager there's not that much difference in height. Carlione also said that Steffan was in a suit and not security grays. He never told his staff who was coming, just an aide from your office."

"So one of them could have let it slip?"

"It wasn't a secret, was it?"

"I never told anyone but Steffan." Obreduur looked to Dekkard.

"The only people who knew I was going were Avraal, Roostof, and the councilor. Karola knew I was working on tariffs and so did one of the Council's staff legalists . . ." Dekkard paused as he remembered something else. "Charmione Lundquist, the junior legalist for Councilor Vhiola Sandegarde, found out from the Council legalist that I was working on fine-art tariffs."

Baartol shrugged. "That's enough people that the Commercers would know someone was coming. They wouldn't have expected a security aide like Steffan."

"Does this tie in to the disappearance of Mathilde Thanne?" asked Obreduur.

"I'd say it does," interjected Irlende. "Empaths just don't go missing."

"There's no proof," Baartol said flatly.

"There won't be," replied Irlende, her voice cold. "There wasn't any proof when Safaell's junior legalist was accidentally shot and killed as a bystander when he was leaving Haarlaan's after taking his wife to dinner. And the next Craft staffer, legalist, or supporter killed or missing won't be an empie. That would be too obvious, but it might be a key senior legalist."

Obreduur didn't look in the slightest surprised. "What do you suggest?"

"Keep doing what you're doing and have your family and staff be careful," replied Baartol. "We're doing our best to keep Security off-balance."

Obreduur offered a sardonic smile. "That's going to be harder than it sounds with the New Meritorists targeting councilors and 'renegade' Security agents targeting Craft staffers."

Why staffers and not councilors? Dekkard looked at the half-finished platters of tapas in the center of the combined table and decided he wasn't that hungry. He did take a small swallow of lager.

"The New Meritorists are going to stage more demonstrations," said Baartol. "They've been getting semiautomatic pistols from Atacaman sources, possibly even machine pistols and rifles."

"Do you have any idea when?"

Baartol shook his head. "They've reorganized into a cell system to make it harder for Security to connect people. Security only knew about the firearms because they found a shipment on an Atacaman barge that broke loose from a tow and grounded on our side of the Rio Doro."

"You're full of cheerful news, Carlos," said Obreduur.

"I have a question for you," replied Baartol. "With Aashtaan assassinated, do you have any idea who will be the next chairman of the Commerce Committee?"

"No, but it's going to be a problem. The next most senior Commercer on the committee is Vhiola Sandegarde."

"The heiress to Kathaar Iron & Steel?"

"The very same, and the next most senior is Erik Marrak."

". . . and he got on the committee because his family holds the controlling interests in Eastern Ironway and Marrak Manufacturing," said Irlende.

"But since Sandegarde has all sorts of inherited holdings beside Kathaar," added Obreduur, "and knows, literally, where a few bodies are buried, Ulrich is going to have to do some negotiating to keep the Marrak family happy. They've been pushing for him to be chair."

"Do you think the assassin knew that?" asked Baartol.

"I don't see how the assassin could have known where Aashtaan was even going to be. She just got lucky, if you want to call it that." Obreduur smiled for a moment. "But it wouldn't hurt if Security got the idea that the assassin was a New Meritorist who targeted Aashtaan. It might even be true. You have some contacts there."

"What if she denies it?"

"She can't," replied Obreduur. "She died under interrogation. They got almost nothing from her. Maendaan let that slip earlier today. You might look into Aashtaan's background, and anything you can find out about why someone might have had a grudge against him."

"We'll see what we can do. That might keep them off-balance, at least for a time." Baartol leaned back slightly. "That's all I've got. Is there anything else I should know?"

"Security . . . or some of their unofficial operatives . . . are trying to put Craft security aides into compromising positions. Isolates going out alone are vulnerable to it because they can't sense the empathic manipulation. If they react badly, they'll end up in gaol or at least being dismissed for inappropriate conduct."

"That one's new."

"It's not new," said Irlende. "It was used a lot fifteen years ago. People forget, and then it becomes useful again."

Obreduur nodded. "That's where things stand now." He pushed back his chair and rose, as did Baartol.

Dekkard and Ysella and the others also stood.

Irlende edged toward Dekkard. He smiled pleasantly and waited.

"I like what you did to Grellek—the empie who tried to mindbend you—but the next time he'll have a sniper somewhere."

"Thank you. The councilor said the same thing."

"As you have to know, he's worth heeding."

"I learned that within days of coming to work for him." Dekkard smiled ruefully.

"Good for you." With that, Irlende turned abruptly toward Baartol.

Obreduur gestured, and Dekkard understood. He led the way out of the side room, then waited just inside the polished brass doors while Obreduur exchanged more friendly banter with Rabool at one side of the main room, where most of the tables were now filled.

After several minutes, Obreduur left the proprietor, and Dekkard led the way out to the Gresynt past the doorman and bouncer, who said, "No one's touched your steamer."

Obreduur smiled and slipped him another five-mark note before letting the bouncer open the rear door.

As Dekkard eased the Gresynt away from Rabool's, Obreduur said, "I know you both have questions. Not here. Just make sure, as well as you can, that we're not being followed. I'll answer your questions when we get to the house."

Dekkard took a circuitous route back so that he ended up approaching the house slowly from the west, rather than going east on Altarama. He slowed over the last two blocks to give Ysella time to sense if anyone was lying in wait.

No one was.

Once Dekkard garaged the steamer and closed up, he made his way to Obreduur's study, where the councilor and Ysella waited.

Dekkard closed the door and seated himself in the chair beside Ysella across the desk from Obreduur.

"Questions?" asked Obreduur gently.

"Does Carlos Baartol work directly for the Guilds' Advisory Committee?" asked Dekkard.

"Why do you think that?"

"Because I don't see how he could know or find out all of what he said otherwise. If he doesn't . . ."

"He's officially a private researcher on retainer to several local guilds and to the Advisory Committee."

"And we met at Rabool's," pressed Dekkard, "because Security has a tendency to watch the Guildhall, and the Commercers get very interested if Craft councilors go there too often?"

"Partly. Also, because Rabool's is Carlos's favorite bistro, and he eats there several times a week, for lunch or for dinner. Security gave up years ago on tailing him during the late bells. Especially when several agents turned up mysteriously dead and the former Craft Party floor leader came up with a listing of all the times Security had tailed a private researcher to restaurants at night on Imperial funds. That was something that the newssheets could and did print. Baartol's empies were also watching. If Security or some Commercer private operatives had shown up, they would have had a memory overload. They'd know someone had been to meet Carlos, but not who."

"Baartol has two empies, Isobel Irlende and another?" asked Avraal.

"He may have more than that," replied Obreduur. "He also has a very good legalist—Jerrohm Kaas."

That name was vaguely familiar to Dekkard, but he couldn't say why, and he had another more personally pressing question. "Commercer private operatives? When you mentioned private operatives before, you didn't say they were Commercers."

"They aren't, not exactly. They operate for pay. Almost always, that means they're hired by Commercers or their intermediaries. As I told you before, they were most likely the ones who shot at you. I hadn't realized that my success in building the Craft Party had upset them enough to go after you, and I'm sorry about that." Obreduur paused. "You can still leave and go to Oersynt to a better-paying position. I wouldn't want you to feel coerced."

"I'm staying." Dekkard couldn't have articulated all the reasons why, only that it felt right. "But I do have one other question, sir."

"Just one?" Obreduur's voice was ironically humorous.

"To start with. Was Councilor Mardosh pushing for something about the Security Ministry that the Commercers don't like?"

"Not something. Several things. He's been forward on trying to pass legislation that prohibits tailing, surveilling, or investigating elected officials unless there is physical or other evidence that suggests beyond a reasonable doubt that there is a possibility of illegal acts. He also wants a felony charge and removal for any Security official or patroller found guilty of violating that law."

"I take it that Chairman Maendaan opposes it."

"He does, as do most Commercers. That's not surprising since Security agents have been tailing Craft political figures for years looking for any possibilities to charge them with offenses or crimes. They've seldom been able to bring an indictment, let alone convict anyone, but a charge usually destroys a Craft politician because no one prints the exonerations or the findings of innocence. The only time a Commerce or Landor politician gets charged is when all Guldor knows about it and they can't cover it up."

"You didn't seem surprised when Irlende said that the Commercers or people working for them are targeting Craft staffers and legalists," said Ysella.

"I knew that was a possibility, but I wanted to see if Carlos or Isobel brought it up."

"Why aren't they targeting Craft councilors as well as staffers?" asked Dekkard.

"It would be too obvious," said Ysella, "and very dangerous politically. Most people don't care what happens to aides. Also, it could be counterproductive. If someone removed . . . say Councilor Waarfel, then the party could pick a far better replacement, and the Commercers would be stuck with him or her at least until the next election, if not for a great deal longer."

"There's another reason for targeting aides," said Obreduur seriously. "Where do you think the Craft Party gets qualified candidates for councilor? The only three non-government occupations that provide enough training and background for those with a Craft background are either Council staff or guildmeisters or assistant guildmeisters . . . or guild legalists. And since not all guildmeisters understand or can learn politics and not all Craft staffers understand guild needs, we take the best from where we can and train them. In time, you might be one of them."

If you survive. "They're targeting me because I someday might be a Council candidate?"

Obreduur's soft laugh was sardonic. "Not just you. But you have possibilities. In time. You're intelligent. You speak well, even when you're caught off guard. You have an artisan background and that understanding. You can learn, and as an isolate, you can't be emotionally manipulated by hidden empaths. It doesn't hurt that you're good-looking. Now . . . don't get ideas. You have a great deal to learn, and you may decide politics isn't what you want."

"But green as you are," said Ysella, "you'd make a better councilor than some Landors, like Saarh, or even a few Commercers."

"Or even, unfortunately," said Obreduur, "one or two Craft councilors. But right now, I need both of you doing what you are. I'd like you to be very careful, for both my sake and yours. There are a few other things you need to know. The legalists and researchers of the Guilds' Advisory Committee have been doing some research. They've discovered that Guldoran corporacions have built and are building several massive factories in Noldar. They've reached an arrangement with the government there to employ susceptibles."

"Susceptibles? Is that legal there?" asked Ysella.

"If the government approves," replied Obreduur, "and since Guldoran Ironway and others provided healthy incentives to the Oligarch and his aides . . ."

Bribes. But Dekkard just listened.

". . . the government of Noldar, effectively the Oligarch, approved the practice. It's apparently a cooperative effort, because the Oligarch had been breeding susceptibles with the thought of using them as soldiers before he discovered that there were certain unfortunate . . . drawbacks . . ."

"Such as the need to hire empaths to keep them under control . . . and the fact that empaths couldn't easily be forced to serve as combat officers?" said Ysella dryly.

"Why didn't they think about that earlier?" asked Dekkard.

"The Oligarch doesn't like subordinates who disagree. I understand that those who agreed with the ill-starred plan are no longer . . . available, either. But . . . a surplus of susceptibles, a small army, in fact, became available, and there are certainly quite a number of low-level empies who don't mind being paid to keep workers motivated."

"Particularly in a country as poor as Noldar, I'm sure," said Ysella, acidly.

"Forced low-paid labor, in effect," said Dekkard.

"With the aim of producing goods at much lower costs to import to Guldor." Obreduur continued, "In fact, Guldoran Ironway already has a manufactory there producing textiles for the ironway, upholstery fabrics, curtain fabrics, cloth for uniforms, possibly more. Transoceanic has built several large manufactories there, and the Banque of Oersynt opened offices in Noldar, Tekkan, and Argorn over the past few months . . ."

"And the art objects being imported as housewares fit into that pattern as well?" added Dekkard. "What are you going to do?"

"Well . . ." Obreduur drew out the word. ". . . since we can't prove the bribery that's going on, we can point out that corporacions are deceiving tariff assessors and robbing the Imperial Treasury . . . and that costs all taxpayers. We can also charge them with using sussies to make cheap goods in foreign lands . . . and there may be a few other matters we can bring up, but I'll let you know about those if they pan out. Also, there's one other thing you two need to plan for."

Ysella raised her eyebrows.

"You'll both be going with me to Gaarlak, Oersynt, and Malek over Summerend recess."

"Is it going to be that dangerous?" asked Ysella. "You've not taken us both before."

"Not as dangerous as Machtarn is turning out to be, I'd say. People, especially Craft supporters, need to see you as well as me, and you won't be in security uniforms."

"Why Gaarlak?" asked Dekkard. "That's not in your district."

"No, but we'll go right through it on the way to Oersynt. It's a Landor district now—Emilio Raathan, but the next time elections are called he'll have to step down. Since I was going that way, the Advisory Committee has asked me to meet with the guilds there to see what we can do to turn out more folks who will support whoever our candidate will be. I'd like your views as well because we won't be there that long, and three pairs of eyes are better than one. I'd also like you both to think about what matters most to people, especially those things the Council ignores. We can talk about all that on the way there. We'll have more than enough time on the ironway." Obreduur yawned. "It's been a longer day than any of us planned. I'll see you in the morning."

Given that pleasant dismissal, Dekkard simply said, "Sleep well, sir." At the same time . . . there was something about Gaarlak, but he couldn't place it.

Then he and Ysella left the study. As they walked from Obreduur's study back toward their quarters, Dekkard stopped in the corridor between the kitchen and the staff room and said, "I finally managed to look up Joel Janhus."

"And?"

"Do you really think anyone who stands against the New Meritorists will be vilified through recorded history?"

"Only if the Meritorists win," replied Ysella. "Only then."

Dekkard merely nodded.

That night . . . after climbing into bed, Dekkard looked up at the ceiling in the darkness for a long time before he slept.

30

When Dekkard woke on Quindi morning, for several long moments he wondered just where he was, possibly because he'd been dreaming about trying to protect Obreduur, but found that every time he looked at the councilor, Obreduur's face changed, and, in the dream, Dekkard began to wonder who he was protecting, and if it was Obreduur at all.

Finally, he sat up. The dream made a sort of sense. It wasn't that Obreduur had really changed, but the more Dekkard learned about the councilor—and the Council of Sixty-Six—the more his own perceptions changed.

More like those perceptions have been forced to change by events.

Dekkard tried to remember what Obreduur had said about politics, then recalled—"Politics is a combination of bitter reality and necessary illusion."

In the past few weeks, he'd definitely been given a dose of bitter reality, and he'd definitely had a few illusions shredded. He'd certainly known that each of the political parties had different aims and agendas, and he'd seen early on in working for Obreduur that the Commercers were intent on using their control of government to further their ends. What he hadn't seen—or experienced—until the last few weeks was their willingness to use means outside of law and government to hold on to control.

Why hadn't he seen that earlier?

Because for the first time in years, if not decades, the Commercers fear losing power, either to the Craft Party, or even worse, to a revolt spurred by the New Meritorists?

Dekkard shook his head. The Commercers couldn't even conceive of a revolt being successful, but Dekkard wasn't so certain. Not when students and others were willing to die for what they believed in. And sooner or later, all the deaths and the repression of that news were bound to get out.

If enough New Meritorists are willing to die.

But if they were . . . and they kept getting firearms from Atacama . . . and more and more of them got killed . . . and the news got out . . .

Where does that leave you?

Dekkard shook his head again. *There's not much choice. You don't want the Commercers or the New*

Meritorists in power. The Commercers would slowly but inexorably turn Guldor into even more of a plutocracy controlled by an even stronger Ministry of Security, and the New Meritorists would turn it into an anarchistic form of mob rule, a government based on what was popular at the moment and which councilors could promise more.

He took a deep breath and stood up. It was past time to get up, shave and shower, and then face bitter reality and necessary illusion . . . and hope he could tell the difference.

31

While Dekkard began Quindi with resolution and a certain sense of dread, the day turned out to be routine, although the assistant guildmeister of the Stonemasons Guild of Gaarlak did arrive for a short morning meeting with Obreduur. One pleasant occurrence was his monthly pay slip, with the increased amount of his salary that had been deposited in the Council Banque.

Nor did Findi offer anything unforeseen or intriguing, since neither Dekkard nor Ysella was in the mood for adventure, and since Emrelda and Markell were both working. They did go out to dinner at Greystone, but split the bill, and Dekkard did agree that Estado Don Miguel was much better, but also far dearer. Ysella didn't dispute him on either point.

That routine didn't change on Unadi, even as the first day of summer, or on Duadi, or Tridi, either. Health Minister Sanoffre or his staff still hadn't replied to the proposed changes in the Sanitation Guild job descriptions, and Treasury Minister Munchyn hadn't yet replied to Obreduur's letter on undertariffing fine art, not that Dekkard would have expected a response from the Treasury so quickly. Obreduur was largely involved in dealing with the routine hearings on the midyear budget adjustments, and Premier Ulrich made no announcements or pronouncements.

When he rose on Furdi, Dekkard didn't know whether to be relieved that everything had been routinely quiet or worried that something else unanticipated would occur when and where he least expected it. When he reached the staff room, he picked up the copy of *Gestirn,* but the lead story was about Argenti anthracite-coal producers raising prices, along with speculation that more Guldoran manufacturers would switch to standard hard coal or even brown coal and how that would increase the coal fogs around industrial cities of Guldor.

The only encouraging sign was that Hyelda had replaced the tomato jelly with quince paste, and admonished Dekkard not to be excessive in its use. Hearing that, Ysella had smiled.

On the drive to work, there was no sign of anyone following them, especially in a gray Realto, and no other staffers approached Dekkard on his walk to the office, where the usual stack of petitions and letters awaited him.

Dekkard and Ysella escorted Obreduur to the Waterways Committee meeting, then went back to the office, returned at a sixth before noon and accompanied him to the councilors' dining room, after which they made their way to the staff cafeteria, where Dekkard chose beef empanadas with verde sauce.

Ysella looked at the verde sauce, shook her head, and asked, "Will you top it off with quince paste?"

He grinned. "I thought about it."

They took a table for four, since it wasn't that crowded, and since most of the tables for two were taken. Dekkard glanced around the cafeteria. "It's not as crowded as usual."

"Just wait."

As Dekkard observed over the next few minutes, she was right. He told her so.

"Thank you." She looked as if she might say more,

but then stopped as a woman headed toward them, her tray still in hand as she halted beside Ysella.

Belatedly, Dekkard recognized her as Chavyona Leiugan, the empath for Councilor Zerlyon.

"Avraal . . . I just found out that you and Steffan were the ones who caught and stopped that New Meritorist empie."

"I covered our councilor and some others. Steffan caught and restrained her."

"She slowed the attacker," said Dekkard. "Otherwise . . ." He shook his head.

"You two make a good team," replied Leiugan. "That's not always so."

"We're fortunate," said Ysella, pausing before she added, "You look like there's something on your mind, Chavyona." She gestured to the empty chair beside her. "Join us."

"Are you sure?"

"Of course," said Dekkard, even as Ysella nodded.

"Thank you so much. I don't like eating alone, and since we often have to eat quickly . . ."

"It's better to eat with other security types who understand," finished Dekkard.

Leiugan took a swallow of café, then half turned to Ysella. "You know Arthal . . . Arthal Shenke?"

"Councilor Hasheem's empath?" Ysella frowned. "Did something happen to him?"

"Not exactly. He's leaving the councilor. He's been offered a position with the Commerce Banque of Sudaen."

"Is it that surprising when a large corporacion offers more marks, especially if a staffer has a family and children?" asked Ysella evenly.

"He didn't leave for the marks. He told me that the empie who killed Councilor Aashtaan could have killed him as well, and might have without you being there. He said that he couldn't keep taking risks like that. His wife's family is from Sudaen. Don't you think the offer is a little odd?" Leiugan took a quick bite of her veal milanesia.

Ysella shook her head. "No. It fits. Corporacions like to poach empaths and isolates from Council staffs, especially from Craft staffs. We're well-trained and underpaid. It also makes matters harder for our councilors."

"Hasheem's on the Security Committee. He needs a good empath," said Leiugan. "He'll likely have to get someone right out of security training, and they'll miss things."

Dekkard understood. Even after more than two years, he was still learning.

"Councilor Hasheem could find someone stronger and better." Ysella glanced at Dekkard.

Leiugan didn't even catch the glance as she took another mouthful, then said, "Let's hope so."

"Have you or Tullyt heard anything else?"

"Not that much. The councilor isn't too happy with Chairman Palafaux. It's got to be something to do with the Working Women Guild. She used to be their legalist."

While Dekkard knew that the Working Women Guild essentially represented masseuses and those working in licensed brothels, he hadn't known that Councilor Zerlyon had been a guild legalist. "About whether the guild legalists can represent women who aren't employed by a licensed brothel?"

Both women looked at him.

"We've had some inquiries about it. I didn't handle it, because it's a legalist's issue."

Both Ysella and Leiugan kept looking at him.

"Some of the Security legalists claim that guild legalists can't represent people in a trade who aren't guild members, but there are some occupations where you can't be a guild member unless you're employed by a licensed business." Dekkard felt he wasn't explaining well enough. He paused for a moment, then said, "Artisans don't have to be licensed, but if they pay dues to the local artisans guild, they're members of the guild. Construction laborers are the same. If legal issues come up, a guild legalist can represent them. By law, sex workers can't be guild members unless they work in a licensed brothel or massage parlor. That law was enacted to make sure that sex workers complied with the health codes . . ."

"You know an awful lot about this . . ." said Ysella, with the hint of a glint in her eye.

"I didn't understand. So I asked Svard Roostof to explain it."

"So a poor girl on the street has no legal protection?" asked Ysella.

"Not really," replied Leiugan. "They're at the mercy of the local low justicer." Then she turned to Dekkard and said, "You explained that better than Morrigan did."

Dekkard guessed that Morrigan was one of Councilor Zerlyon's legalists. "I just repeated what Svard told me."

Leiugan took a last bite of her meal and stood. "I need to be going. Thank you for inviting me to join you."

"Our pleasure," said Ysella quickly. Once Leiugan was well out of earshot, she looked at Dekkard. "That business with the street women bothered you, didn't it?"

"It didn't seem fair. It also doesn't make sense. Those women are more likely to comply with the health codes if they're guild members or if the legalists can help them and talk some sense into them."

"You still surprise me at times."

"I hope so. I'd hate to be too predictable. Most isolates have that reputation."

"Just like empaths are supposed to be too emotional . . . or have no real emotions?"

"I've never thought that."

"*You* haven't."

"Before we go, I have a question. From what you've told me, there aren't that many empaths as strong as the New Meritorist assassin, are there?"

"Very few," replied Ysella, "but empaths who feel extremely strongly about something can mount a short and powerful burst. That could have been what happened with the one you restrained. She didn't feel nearly that powerful afterward."

"Will hate do that?"

"Hate . . . or love. Mothers who are empaths have been known to do almost miraculous things if they feel their children are endangered. One stopped a black jaguar with pure emotion, and nothing usually stops a big cat once they've started an attack."

"Some of the New Meritorists have been willing to get shot to make a point. That suggests strong feelings."

"That could be a real problem," agreed Ysella, pushing back her chair and standing. "We need to get back to the councilors' dining room."

As they headed to wait for Obreduur, Dekkard had the feeling that the rest of the day was going to be much like the past week had been, with no real resolutions to anything and more and more responses to draft.

He was right. For him and Ysella, the remainder of Quindi consisted of escorting Obreduur and drafting responses to letters and petitions, followed by escorting the Obreduur family to and from services at the East Quarter Trinitarian Chapel. The return from chapel was through a warm rain barely more than a drizzle, after which Dekkard donned exercise clothes and worked out, ending up by using his practice knives on the target on the garage wall. Then, as he cooled off, he retreated to his room and took refuge in finishing *The Son of Gold*.

By the time he finished the book, it was late. He turned off the light and got into bed, still thinking about the book . . . and why he found it so highly improbable, especially given the amount of overt and direct violence, because from what he'd read and seen, most violence in Guldor was far more often covert.

Except for the New Meritorists. Was it part of their strategy to force the Security Ministry into using more and more overt violence?

Dekkard had the feeling it was.

But how else can you stop the New Meritorists, when they're willing to die and use as much violence as necessary in order to get a violent reaction?

Exactly the way Security is . . . by keeping it quiet as possible.

Until they can't.

Dekkard couldn't help but wince at what would happen then.

32

Dekkard wasn't feeling that much more optimistic on Findi morning, and after he shaved and showered, he dressed in an old and rather worn set of grays. Besides Hyelda, he was the first staffer down for breakfast.

He looked at the copy of *Gestirn,* but the most interesting bit of news was that the two meisters facing off in the annual tournament to determine the best crowns player in the Imperium had tied yet another game. Not that Dekkard had ever been interested in the tactics of board games, where he had to visualize ten or twenty moves into the future. He'd often said that even thinking about that sort of mental "exercise" gave him a headache, but it was more that nothing in life could be planned out that way, and people who thought it could were invariably disappointed by the messiness in the world.

Shaking his head, Dekkard replaced the newssheet on the side table. He didn't even look at the croissants when he sat down, but just sipped his café.

"Good morning," said Ysella cheerfully as she stepped into the staff room, ignoring the newssheet and pouring her café before sitting down across from Dekkard.

"You're happy this morning."

"It's better than glumming around. It isn't raining, and it doesn't look like it's going to be as hot as it was earlier this week. We have the day off."

"Are you going to see Emrelda and Markell?"

Ysella shook her head. "They went to Hilltown, possibly for a week."

Dekkard raised his eyebrows.

"That's where he grew up. His parents died in a fire. Sometimes he needs to go there."

"She can get off for a week now?"

"She's a patrol dispatcher, remember. They still have to work during Summerend. So she only gets half her vacation then. She can take the other half whenever she wants, with the approval of the station chief patroller, of course."

Dekkard nodded and took another swallow of café.

"We need to go shopping."

"*We?* I just went shopping."

"That was three weeks ago. Besides you need two summer suits. If you don't want to die of heatstroke on our trip to Gaarlak, Oersynt, and Malek, that is."

Dekkard looked at Ysella questioningly.

"You'll need summer grays. We can't wear uniform grays unless we're on Council property or Council business. The trip to Malek doesn't qualify, and you can't carry your long truncheon unless you're in civilian grays and wearing your staff pin."

Dekkard knew that. He just hadn't thought through going to Malek in the heat of summer.

"I'll even treat you to lunch if you come with me," she added.

"You don't need to bribe me." Besides, he knew she was right, and moping around wouldn't make him feel any better. He finally picked up one croissant and put it on his plate, followed by a second, and then by a slightly smaller slice of quince paste than he usually took. "I'd like it if we went shopping." He grinned sheepishly before saying, "And I will change before we leave."

Ysella took another sip of café, then said, "You looked depressingly pensive."

"That's because I was. I don't like where either the Commercers or the New Meritorists want to take

Guldor, and I have doubts that people will back a Craft premier. For that matter, I don't see Councilor Haarsfel as the best of premiers. Either Obreduur or Hasheem would do better."

Ysella laughed softly. "Half the Craft councilors would do better than Haarsfel as premier, but he knows it, just as Volkaar knew Ulrich would be a better premier. Being premier requires a different set of skills than being a floor leader . . . or perhaps additional skills."

"Grieg wanted to be dismissed as premier, didn't he?"

A hint of surprise crossed Ysella's face. "Why do you say that?"

"Because of the reason he gave for not immediately removing Minister Kraffeist, that there was no evidence that Kraffeist knew anything about the improper coal-reserve lease. Obreduur even admitted that was the worst thing Grieg could have said, and Grieg had never said anything that naïve or stupid before."

"You never said anything about that earlier."

"It occurred to me"—*if later*—"that Grieg was literally telling the truth. He didn't say that Kraffeist was innocent. He said that there was no evidence. Grieg knew Kraffeist was guilty, but couldn't prove it, and that was his way of saying it. Admitting that openly would have meant that the leadership of the Commerce Party knew and did nothing. His statement gave the Imperador a way to dismiss him, seemingly for incompetence, although that was only implied, without anyone admitting anything. It also allowed Grieg to avoid charges against Commerce appointees or a thorough investigation. Then Ulrich's hearings shifted the blame totally on Eastern, some incompetent legalists, and the admiral in charge of logistics. Most likely the legalists had been pressured to approve the lease without any deep scrutiny, or possibly the lease they saw had a different legal description on it. Either way, legalists are more expendable than high corporacion officials or Commerce councilors. And since none of the political parties wanted new elections right now, no one pressed for a more thorough investigation." Dekkard shrugged.

"You're more cynical than your looks would indicate."

"Am I wrong?"

"I don't know anything to the contrary."

"That's a cautious reply."

"It's the only honest answer I can give. Sometimes, you think I know more than I do."

Dekkard smiled ruefully. "That's because you usually know more than I do."

"I did when you first came to work here. That's changed a lot recently." At the sound of Rhosali's steps on the stairs, Ysella added, "We should talk about that later."

Little more than a bell later, the two were walking west on Altarama two blocks east of the white brick posts that marked the western end of East Quarter. Dekkard had indeed changed into black trousers and a green barong, while Ysella wore a pale green linen dress with a matching translucent headscarf.

"Where should we go first?" he asked.

"Julieta. Sometimes they have good summerwear."

"Do you think anyone will remember us?"

"If they do, they won't say a word. We didn't do a thing." Ysella offered an innocent smile.

"You're sure no one's trailing us? I'd hate to have another incident there."

"In daylight, you can see as far as I can sense."

"Well . . . I don't think the nanny pushing the pram is following us, at least not with a sinister aim . . ."

"That's true, but she is a borderline empie. Many nannies are."

"I hadn't thought of it that way. Artisan families don't generally have nannies."

"Most Landor families don't either. It's usually mid- and upper-level Commercers."

"Why do you think it's that way?" Dekkard managed not to wince as he realized that she'd already answered the question earlier, and immediately added, "You've hinted that Landors tend to think of women more as subservient and limited to household responsibilities, but how are Commercers different?"

"They'll grudgingly admit that a few women, usually those with inherited wealth and position, can be more than decorative additions to their husband's portfolio, so to speak. Or even those who've forced themselves to be noticed by accomplishments that can't be denied. But the role most high-level Commercer women are forced into is as accomplished adjuncts to burnish their husband's accomplishments and ego, and for the wives to have the time and skills to do that, the Commercer women need nannies."

"What does Emrelda think about that? She is living to some extent in a Commercer world."

"She's never been interested in having children. That might be because she had to help raise me and did most of Cliven's care until he was old enough to go to school."

"How does being a patrol dispatcher fit in to her life?"

"Very well. She has her own income, and she could become a local or even a district administrative officer. Security likes women in those positions. They deal with details better than most men without becoming obsessed with such."

"That's also a limitation," Dekkard pointed out.

"She's not an artisan, Steffan. Neither am I."

While Ysella's voice was almost gentle, Dekkard understood. "Because art is the only field where women are allowed to compete on their abilities alone? The men still get most of the big commissions and win most of the prizes."

"But women artisans have more independence. In Guldor, anyway."

Dekkard couldn't dispute that. "Would you really have wanted to be an artisan?"

"No. I'm more interested in changing the system than fitting into it."

"Which is why you've stayed with Obreduur."

"Don't you think we're overdue for change?"

"So long as it's for the better. The Great Charter was fine, but the Commercers have found ways around its intent, and without change to restore that intent we could end up in another time like the Black Centuries."

"Steffan . . . you're actually sounding like a radical."

"I'm not that radical. The New Meritorists are idiots. Not even well-meaning idiots."

As they passed the white brick posts, Ysella said, "I'd agree, but we need to think about shopping now."

Dekkard nodded. With more people on the sidewalk flanking Imperial Boulevard, talking politics was less than wise. "Julieta first?"

"It's the closest."

Once the two reached Imperial Boulevard, they turned north. Only a few handfuls of people were walking or window-shopping, scattered along the block, but by late afternoon, the sidewalks would be far more crowded.

Ysella led the way into Julieta, and Dekkard studied the sales staff. No one stood out as familiar, but he realized that the last time they'd been there, everything had happened so quickly that he'd never looked at anyone for long.

"Might I help you?" asked an older saleswoman, her eyes on Ysella.

Dekkard smiled faintly. He might as well have not even been present as far as the saleswoman was concerned, and that was fine with him.

Three bells later, after stops at five women's shops and Excellencia, for Dekkard, the two emerged from Esperanza, with Ysella carrying a single moderately large bag, and Dekkard empty-handed since he'd have to pick up his two light gray summer suits and shirts sometime after midday on Tridi.

"Lunch won't be at Don Miguel," said Ysella.

"Not with us paying for it. Have you ever been to Octavia's?"

"I've never even heard of it," admitted Dekkard.

Ysella shook her head. "So many good places to eat, and you've never tried them."

"I never found much pleasure in eating alone, no matter how good the fare, and you're one of the few people I've enjoyed eating with."

"One of the few?"

"I occasionally ate with Amelya Detauran. Then we had some artistic differences. She apologized after she found out about my family, but we haven't been out since then."

"She's the security isolate for Kaliara Bassaana, isn't she?"

"She is. She was the one who told me that Bassaana hadn't been fond of Eastern Ironway for a long, long time."

"I don't think you mentioned that."

"I told the councilor. I probably should have told you."

"So long as he knows."

"She also told me, and I told him, that Ulrich kept Bassaana out of the loop on not letting the Transportation Committee hold hearings on the Kraffeist Affair."

"Hmmmm . . ."

From Ysella's reaction, Dekkard had a very good idea he should have shared those incidents with her.

"You did tell the councilor . . . and those incidents weren't critical . . ."

"But I should have told you as well. I'm sorry. I did tell you about Mathide Thanne, and everything else that could bear on security."

She nodded, then shook her head, even as she smiled. "I suppose I can't get too upset about your not sharing something from a girlfriend that you did tell the councilor."

"She's never been that kind of girlfriend," Dekkard protested.

"I'm glad to hear that." Ysella's smile turned mischievous. "I wasn't that upset, but you deserved a little baiting."

Dekkard was the one to shake his head. "Remind me never to keep anything from you."

"I just did."

Dekkard laughed, then asked, "Just where is Octavia's? Ten blocks north or fifteen south?"

"One block south and two blocks east. It's just far enough off Imperial that casual shoppers don't come across it, and it's not someplace that appeals to those who want to emulate the lifestyles of the rich and famous. But it's better than Greystone."

"Are you ever going to let that go?"

"Someday . . . but not yet."

Almost exactly three blocks later, they arrived at their destination.

Octavia's Bistro was located on the street-level floor of an older building constructed of alternating courses of red and black bricks, with tall and narrow windows of grayed or silvered glass and framed by the black bricks, an architectural style that Dekkard had seen occasionally in Machtarn, and always in older buildings. The front door was black, and Dekkard opened it for Ysella. Inside, the walls were light silver-gray, the floors of a similar stone, but the twenty or so tables were of what looked to be wood bleached to a pale gold, as were the chairs. About two-thirds of the tables were taken.

A hostess in gray and black stepped forward. "The two of you?"

"Yes," Ysella said immediately, "and a corner table if one's free."

"We can do that." The hostess turned and led the way to what looked to be the sole empty corner table.

Dekkard saw that the corner tables were round, while all the others were either oblong or square.

As they sat down, both with their backs to the wall and looking out over the bistro, Dekkard observed, "It's a little . . . quirky. The décor, I mean."

"The food isn't, and we're not going to talk government or politics. Food, books, and music. After we order. I'm hungrier than I thought."

A server appeared almost immediately.

Dekkard ordered the basil-cream shrimp pasta with a seasonal greens and a light chilled Kuhrs. Ysella decided on plain almond-cream pasta, also with the seasonal greens and lager.

After the server left to fetch their lagers, Ysella immediately asked, "Do you read anything besides newssheets and political and economic journals?"

"Sometimes. I just finished an actual novel—*The Son of Gold*. It's a story about a purported bastard son of Laureous the Great."

"How was it?"

"Moderately well-written, but improbable."

"Why? Laureous was quite the womanizer. He had more than one love child."

"Oh . . . that part I could believe. There was far too much overt violence. That's what I found improbable. Violence in Guldor seems to be covert—except for a recent spate of demonstrations."

"That's why the book was popular. People don't like sneaky hidden violence, especially by the hero. They also don't like their fiction to be too close to reality. That makes them uncomfortable. That's why historical romances and heroic sagas are so popular."

Their lagers arrived, and in due course, so did their entrées.

Ysella made certain that the conversation remained on books, music, and food.

When they left Octavia's more than a bell later, he realized that he'd enjoyed the lunch, and not just for the food. "We should do that more often."

"I do occasionally have good ideas."

"You do."

"Another good idea is is walking back. There's not much to carry, and the exercise won't hurt us."

"The heat might," replied Dekkard.

"It's not that hot."

"You're from Sudaen, remember? All my ancestors came from a place two thousand yards higher and a whole lot colder."

"The walk will help you work off all that flan you consumed for dessert."

Dekkard had to agree, but he just nodded . . . and smiled.

33

By the end of the workday on Duadi, Dekkard had finally caught up on his drafting of the routine replies to both letters and petitions, but the councilor still had not received any response from the Ministry of Health and Education on the Sanitation job descriptions nor from the Treasury Ministry on the matter of art-object tariffs. Dekkard could understand the delay on the part of the Treasury Ministry, but not the length of time in dealing with the job description of a Sanitation shovelman. The Health minister, or the functionaries who served him, certainly had the authority to approve or deny the proposed changes.

Tridi morning began in the same fashion as most workday mornings—until Dekkard turned onto Council Avenue heading toward the Council Office Building. The first thing he noticed was a huge plume of blackish-gray smoke billowing from a square gray building several blocks to the east of the Palace grounds.

"The Ministry of Security's burning!" Ysella turned in her seat to address Obreduur.

The councilor immediately looked up from his papers and leaned forward. "Sowshit!"

"You think it was the New Meritorists?" asked Dekkard. He doubted that it was an accident, not when Security was involved.

"They'd certainly have reason," replied Obreduur. "I don't know that they'd have the expertise and the access. Security headquarters is guarded night and day, and the building's never empty. But may the Three curse whoever did it." He shook his head.

"Who else could have done it?" asked Dekkard.

"Plenty of people have reason, and some of them might even have the expertise. Security isn't exactly beloved by those outside the law. The problem is that even those who have a reason and expertise would have difficulty gaining access."

"Except someone in Security," suggested Ysella.

"If someone inside did it," said Obreduur, "I wouldn't wager on his life expectancy." He paused. "All our speculation is just that until we know more."

Dekkard understood that as well. If Security didn't want something known, the newssheets would be limited in what they could or would be willing to print—as the news reports on the demonstrations by the New Meritorists had illustrated, especially by the fact that the name of the organization had never appeared in print. *So far, anyway.*

As he drove closer to the Council buildings, he also saw that additional Council Guards were posted at the office building entrance and at the entrance to the covered parking area. He also noticed that two armored steamers were drawn up on each side of the west entrance to the Council Office Building. "There haven't been any threats to the Sixty-Six, have there?"

"If there have been, the Premier hasn't seen fit to notify any of the Craft councilors," replied Obreduur dryly.

Even with the extra guards and the two armored steamers that bore Security markings, Dekkard had no trouble dropping off the councilor and Ysella, or in parking the Gresynt and making his way to the office.

Once he sat down at his desk, he turned to Ysella. "Is there any information about—"

"Right in front of you. I put the information sheet the Premier sent to all the councilors' offices on your desk." Ysella offered an amused smile. "Everyone else has read it. Return it to Karola after you've finished."

"Thank you." Dekkard smiled back at her, then lifted the single sheet, his eyes going to the text beneath the heading.

> . . . last night, after working bells, an undetermined malfunction in the gas lighting system serving the Ministry of Security resulted in the buildup of gas in the lower levels of the building. When the gas reached the working luminaries in the corridors outside the records storage areas, the resulting explosion caused severe structural damage and scattered fires on the lower levels. These multiple fires were fed by gas escaping at high pressure. The resulting flames were too intense to immediately quell, and the Machtarn Fire Brigade turned its efforts to keeping the blaze from spreading to the neighboring buildings . . . extent of complete damage is unknown at this time . . .

Dekkard lowered the paper as he finished. So many groups could have set the fire. The New Meritorists came first to mind, but there were certainly others who would like to have destroyed all the records stored in the chambers beneath the ministry building, and some of them could certainly have done it, thinking to put the blame on the New Meritorists. *Like Eastern Ironway.* Or some corporacion or professional Dekkard had never heard of.

The one question that came to his mind immediately was why the fire brigade hadn't turned off the main gas lines. He could see why no one could have gotten close to the building cutoff valves, but there shouldn't have been any reason why main lines couldn't have been shut off. *Or didn't anyone think of that until it was too late?*

Dekkard couldn't believe that, but decided it would be a while before he'd find out, if ever, and, in the meantime, he had responses and petitions to read and sort . . . and replies to draft.

34

The first thing Dekkard did on Furdi morning after entering the staff room was to pick up the morning edition of *Gestirn* and read the story on the Ministry of Security building fire.

SECURITY MINISTRY FIRE SABOTAGE

The explosion and fire that largely destroyed the headquarters building of the Ministry of Security and killed fifteen people, all building guards and custodial staff, were caused by deliberate sabotage of the building's gas lighting system, according to Security Minister Lukkyn Wyath.

Had the explosion occurred during working bells, the death toll could have exceeded a thousand . . . Minister Wyath would neither confirm nor deny those figures . . .

Sources from the fire brigade claimed that the reason why the fires went uncontrolled for several bells was because the control valves on the main gas pipe serving the buildings in that part of Machtarn could not be closed, either the result of poor maintenance or for some other reason . . .

Minister Wyath would also not address the extent to which the fire destroyed Ministry records, although it appears that very little stored or filed in the building survived the flames and explosion . . .

Dekkard just nodded when he read about the "malfunctioning" gas valves. *An act of arson extremely well planned.* That meant a group with expertise, resources, and contacts within the Security Ministry, although the contacts could have been low-level, since the arsonists only needed access to basement corridors and storage areas.

For all of Obreduur's words about other possible attackers, Dekkard just couldn't see why anyone else besides the New Meritorists would want to invest so much effort into destroying the building—and especially the records. Then he thought about what Baartol had said about the reorganization of the New Meritorists. The fire had destroyed a great deal of information about them, and with their new structure it would be far harder to track down individual members of the group.

He was still thinking about that when Karola handed him a large envelope, already opened, along with its contents.

"The councilor would like you to draft the transmittal to the guild and a polite reply to the minister."

Dekkard took the sheets from her, his eyes taking in the letterhead of the Ministry of Health and Education. "Did he say anything?"

"Just that you were to handle it."

"Thank you." As Karola returned to her desk, Dekkard immediately read the response, signed by the Assistant Minister of Health for Sanitation, his eyes focused on one section near the bottom of the one-page letter.

... in conclusion, the Ministry finds the proposed changes to the job position as suggested to be acceptable with a few minor changes in several phrases. Those changes are embodied in the attached revision to the original ...

Dekkard took a deep breath. Sometimes "minor" changes were anything but trivial. He dug out the file copy of the original proposal and began to compare the two documents, word by word. When he finished he could find only one change. He went through them both again, with the same result. The only change had been to clarify that the probationary period began on the first day of actual work and not the day of hire. Dekkard nodded. He could see that. Someone could be hired, but not begin work for weeks or months, and even if not paid, would serve a much shorter probationary period.

He began to draft the response to Guildmeister Hadenaur, hoping that the new description would provide some help in obtaining better shovelmen who could be promoted.

The thought crossed his mind that it was likely to be much longer before Obreduur received a response from Treasury Minister Munchyn and that the response would say little, something to the effect that the ministry was looking into the matter, because Ulrich would want to weaken the Artisans Guild as long as possible, and by stalling until just before the Summerend recess, Munchyn could prevent Obreduur from bringing it up before the Council until the Council returned to meeting the first week in Fallfirst. Dekkard also felt that Obreduur wasn't in a hurry to press the issue because, although the councilor had wanted to inform Guildmeister Carlione quickly that he was looking into the matter, since the meeting with Carlos Baartol, Obreduur had scarcely mentioned the art tariffs.

But then, it had been only two weeks since Obreduur had sent off the inquiries, so Obreduur might feel that Munchyn hadn't had enough time to reply . . . or that pressing Munchyn so soon would be useless. *Or maybe he doesn't want a quick answer so that he can attack Munchyn's delay as misfeasance in office.*

In any event, there wasn't anything Dekkard could do about the art tariffs, while he could get on with drafting a favorable transmittal letter to Guildmeister Hadenaur.

35

The rest of Furdi and all of Quindi dragged out, and everything in the Council Office Building office and at the house was routine, including the warm rain that started on Furdi afternoon and did not stop until late on Quindi night. Obreduur spent most of the days in midyear budget hearings at either the Waterways Committee or the Workplace Administration Committee, and occasionally at brief sessions of the full Council. There were two sets of visitors, one apparently a family friend of Obreduur's from Malek, and the other the legalist from the Stevedores Guild of Machtarn, who met with Macri and Obreduur. Dekkard did manage to find time to get to the Council Banque and withdraw a hundred marks, since he was down to fifteen in his wallet.

On Findi morning, Dekkard had just skimmed the newssheet and found little of interest in it, except for a short article noting that Guldoran Ironway had closed down its textile manufactory in Oersynt, idling more than four hundred workers.

Because the new plant in Noldar is now operating and can provide fabrics cheaper?

He poured his café and sat down alone at the table in the staff room.

Several minutes later, Ysella entered and poured her café. She did not look at the newssheet before she sat down across the table from him, an envelope in her hand.

"Good morning," Dekkard finally said, pleasantly.

"Oh . . . good morning." An apologetic smile appeared on her face.

"Is the letter or message that bad? Or thought-provoking?"

"It's from Emrelda. She'll be here in less than a bell."

"You didn't mention that last night. Is there a problem?"

"The message was here last night, but I wanted to think about it. Her message just said she has to drive to Point Larmat, and she asked me to go with her. Markell will meet her there. He had to go to Siincleer because of some problems at the facility his firm is building. She'd like to spend a few days with him. She wanted to know if I'd consider accompanying her there and then driving her steamer back here. She'd pick it up on Tridi. I asked Obreduur if I could park it in back, and he said yes."

Dekkard frowned. "Point Larmat is almost a hundred fifty milles. She'd be better off taking the train, and if Markell is in Siincleer . . . that's another hundred and fifty milles."

"A hundred and seventy. She's bringing him three heavy cases of expensive equipment. If they split the difference, it saves him a day in getting the equipment."

"Why didn't he take the equipment with him?"

"It might be because he took the ironway to Siincleer and didn't think he'd need it."

Dekkard frowned. *If Markell doesn't have a steamer, how did he get to Point Larmat?* He pushed away the question, since it was clear that Markell had transportation, and said, "You'd be driving back alone. It might be better if I went with you . . . if she agrees." Before Ysella could object, Dekkard added, "Yes, I know you can take care of yourself . . . and others, but it's a lot harder if you have to drive at the same time."

"Would you mind?"

"I'd mind a little. I'd mind a whole lot more if I let you drive back alone."

"Thank you for being honest about it. I'd appreciate it very much."

Another thought occurred to Dekkard. "She just thought you'd do it?"

"She said she'd do it alone and drive back, but Markell will be down there for at least another week and she has a few days left that she can use. She'll take a train back and a steamhack from the station to pick up the steamer. She said I could tell her if I could do it when she gets here." Ysella paused. "You really don't—"

"I'm doing it," replied Dekkard with a smile.

"You see me all day, every workday."

"And we're fortunate if we have a bell to talk without someone else being around."

"I can't dispute that. You're sure?"

For a moment, Dekkard wondered why Ysella kept asking that, one way or another, but then he realized. She saw her tentative request as an imposition, and unlike dealing with a normal person, where she could sense their feelings, she couldn't sense his, and she worried. "I'd much rather take a long drive with you than do anything else I might consider doing without you. I also won't have to worry about you."

"It's a very long drive."

"The drive back will be shorter."

Ysella dropped her eyes for just an instant, before saying, "Then we ought to start eating breakfast."

Dekkard agreed and reached for the croissants.

Two-thirds of a bell later, he stood in the shade of the portico, waiting for Ysella. He wore one of his new light gray summer suits, and a white shirt, but without the cravat, which was folded carefully in a jacket pocket. The jacket concealed his battered personal truncheon and his brace of knives.

Ysella appeared, in a pale maroon linen suit, with a matching headscarf, if one slightly heavier than the translucent ones she'd often worn. She also had a gray leather purse with a shoulder strap, one considerably larger than the ones she'd carried when they'd gone out together. "I'd hoped you'd wear one of those suits." Her eyes went to his neck.

"The cravat's in my jacket pocket, just in case."

"That makes sense, and so does the truncheon."

"Do you think we'll need it?"

Ysella shook her head. "But there's no reason not to be prepared."

Dekkard was about to reply when he caught sight of

Emrelda's teal-colored Gresynt coming east from Imperial Boulevard. "Here comes Emrelda."

The two walked down the drive and out through the pedestrian gate. As the steamer glided to a stop, Dekkard took in the three leather cases firmly strapped to the rear luggage rack. All three had locks and the words ENGAARD ENGINEERING branded into the smooth, golden brown leather.

Very expensive cases.

Emrelda got out of the steamer hurriedly. "Avraal . . ."

Dekkard stepped forward and smiled. "It wasn't her idea, but mine. I thought it would be better if I accompanied you two, particularly since Avraal would be alone on the return trip, and that would hamper her use of her full abilities, if she encountered difficulties."

For just a moment, Emrelda, who wore a pale green linen traveling suit, appeared startled. Then she laughed. "Markell will be surprised that I managed to get a full security team to safeguard his precious instruments." She turned to Dekkard. "I know you're a trained driver, but it's one of my pleasures. I would appreciate it if you drove back, though." She looked to her sister. "If that's acceptable to you."

"Perfectly," replied Ysella pleasantly.

Dekkard managed not to wince, but he wasn't about to get between the sisters. "If you two don't mind, I'll sit in back. That way I can stretch out my legs." He looked to Ysella. "Unless you'd rather have more space."

"If I feel cramped, I'll let you know, and we can change places." Ysella nodded to her sister. "The harbor ferry operates more often on Findi than the river ferry."

"I'd thought to take the harbor ferry."

Dekkard walked to the passenger side of the Gresynt and, while Emrelda got back into the driver's seat, he opened the front door for Ysella.

Ysella looked up at Dekkard and mouthed, "Thank you." Then she eased into the steamer.

Dekkard opened the rear door and got in, keeping a pleasant expression on his face.

Neither sister said much on the short drive to the ferry slip, located just to the east of where the Rio Azulete emptied into the harbor. Nor did either say much during the half-bell wait for the ferry. The slip attendant finally motioned for Emrelda to move forward and pay the toll, ten marks, then directed her toward the ramp. In the end, the crew directed her to the front, just behind a battered black Realto. Most of the other vehicles that drove onto the iron deck of the ferry were lorries, which wasn't surprising, given that anyone on a holiday would have left earlier. The big Voltan lorry beside the Gresynt bore an ornate presentation of the name ERISTO PRODUCE in green and silver.

"We might as well get out and stretch our legs," said Ysella. "It will take close to a bell to get to the south shore slip."

"I'll stay with the steamer," replied Emrelda.

"We'll stay close," said Ysella. "I know you worry about the cases. But we'll be better able to act if we're outside the steamer."

"Preferably standing beside the luggage rack." Dekkard got out of the Gresynt and would have opened the door for Ysella, except she had exited as quickly as he had. So he walked to the rear of the steamer, positioning himself behind the luggage rack.

Emrelda opened the driver's door, and turned in her seat, but did not leave the steamer.

"Do you have any idea what equipment is in those cases?" Dekkard murmured to Ysella. "The cases look expensive, but they're not new."

"I have no idea what might be inside, except that it has to be valuable." She lowered her voice even further. "We can speculate later. We just need to get the cases and Emrelda safely to Point Larmat and Markell."

Dekkard nodded, then glanced past her toward the wharves for the oceangoing steamships, most of which were occupied, mainly by cargo carriers. He could make out the intertwined-"T"-and-"S" logo of Transoceanic Shipping on the funnels of two ships, but didn't recognize or couldn't make out the emblems on other vessels. Even on Findi, the commerce of Guldor scarcely slowed.

A third of a bell passed before the ferry angled toward the west harbor slip. Dekkard and Ysella waited another five minutes before getting back into the Gresynt. Even so, it was another ten minutes before the bow ramp dropped, and Emrelda drove over the ramp and turned the Gresynt westward on the street leading to the southwest highway that ran all the way from Machtarn to Surpunta, passing through Point Larmat, Siincleer, and Sudaen on the way.

Dekkard hoped the next few bells were pleasantly quiet.

36

While the air was hot and muggy, the drive from Machtarn along the southwest coastal highway was relatively pleasant. Emrelda and Ysella exchanged observations on how various areas had changed since their childhood, usually not for the better, discussions sometimes expanded to answer questions from Dekkard. The road was of smooth and hard bitumen, and Emrelda kept the Gresynt at a speed of close to fifty milles per bell, providing a warm breeze inside the steamer with the windows down little more than a few digits.

By the time Dekkard could make out the lighthouse that dominated the rocky tip of land that gave the small city of Point Larmat its name, the coolness between the sisters had abated. Dekkard could hear a slight reservation on Ysella's part, which likely had always been there, but which he had not recognized earlier, possibly because of their more formal conversational style, doubtless from their familial background.

"Where are you meeting Markell?" Dekkard asked.

"At the Cleft House," replied Emrelda. "Near the beginning of the Cliff Road next to one of the overlooks.
It's popular. You two could eat there before you start
back."

"It sounds as though Markell doesn't want anyone to
know that he's bringing in special equipment." Dekkard
kept his tone casual.

"He's concerned that the building isn't being built to
specification, and that the specifications insisted on by
the Navy may not be adequate. He needs the equipment
in the cases to make certain."

"Because he doesn't dare bring up the matter without solid numbers?"

"Would you?" returned Emrelda.

"In dealing with government, you need solid numbers
or figures. Whether the minister or his bureaucrats will
do anything is another question."

"They won't do anything without hard facts," said
Emrelda, almost defensively.

"You're right," added Ysella. "Even with facts, sometimes it's hard to get them to do the right thing."

"Unless the Premier supports the matter," said
Dekkard. *Or unless the newssheets make an issue of it.*
And that, he knew, didn't happen often.

He looked out the window to his left at the marsh-
lands east of the road, and then at the dark green water
of the ocean, before looking ahead toward the buildings
that marked the northern edge of the city.

Rather than continuing on the main road, Emrelda
turned off to the left onto another well-bitumened road
that followed the contours of the point and climbed
gradually until it leveled off some thirty yards above the
rocky beaches below.

Before that long, Dekkard caught sight of what had
to be the Cleft House, a sprawling two-story yellow
brick structure perched between the edge of a cleft that
dropped almost straight down and the steep rocky de-
cline of the north edge of the point. The road curved

around the cleft and then back to a large parking area in front of the Cleft House.

Emrelda eased the Gresynt into a vacant space beside a large white Kharlan touring car.

"That's one of the corporacion steamers. Markell should be here somewhere."

Dekkard nodded. He opened the rear door and stepped out of the Gresynt. No sooner had he done so than he spotted Markell walking toward them from the covered front porch of the Cleft House. The older man wore a white linen suit, but without a cravat.

"I see someone persuaded you to accompany them," offered Markell cheerfully when he neared Dekkard.

"I volunteered."

"I appreciate your concerns," replied Markell, before turning to Emrelda and saying, "You made good time. I've been here less than a third of a bell."

"The road wasn't crowded, and I had good company."

"No one followed us," said Ysella, "but wasn't that the point?"

"It was," admitted Markell.

"What exactly is in those cases?" asked Dekkard pleasantly.

"Oh, yes. The cases. If you'd help me load them in the back of the Kharlan. It does have a capacious trunk. That will prove most useful."

"Markell . . ." offered Ysella, her voice even.

Markell stiffened momentarily, suggesting to Dekkard that Ysella had offered an empie jolt of some sort. "Ah . . . can we load the cases, and then I'll explain?"

"That would be good," said Ysella.

In minutes, Markell and Dekkard had the cases unstrapped and in the trunk of the Kharlan, along with a smaller suitcase for Emrelda that had been in front of and hidden by the larger cases. Dekkard couldn't help but notice that Markell seemed relieved once the cases were in the trunk.

"The cases?" prompted Ysella.

"They contain precise measuring equipment, for wall and material thicknesses, tolerances of machine parts, angles and arcs. Also equipment to measure hardness and other properties."

"That's all?" asked Dekkard.

"There's also a portable chemical analysis unit."

Dekkard glanced to Ysella, who gave the faintest of nods, then said, "I wish you success with whatever it is."

Markell offered a wry smile in return. "I hope I'm wrong, but I'd rather not say anything until I know more." He turned to Emrelda. "If you need to freshen up, you'd better, because we need to start back to Siincleer. I have a basket with lager and provisions in the Kharlan."

"I'll only be a few minutes," replied Emrelda, handing her keys to Dekkard before turning and walking swiftly toward the Cleft House.

"You're really worried, aren't you?" Dekkard asked Markell.

"I'm concerned. I don't know enough to be worried. That's why I wanted the equipment. A Navy engineer came to Siincleer with me. I knew weeks ago that he'd be off this endday."

"Just where in Siincleer is this facility?" asked Dekkard.

"It's not in Siincleer. It's in the sandstone hills west of the city. There's not much around it for several milles."

"So they don't want anyone close," mused Dekkard.

"But no one says why. I asked, and I was told not to ask again." Markell turned. "I need to get the steamer lit off so that we can leave as soon as Emrelda's ready." He moved toward the driver's side of the Kharlan.

Dekkard did not follow him. Neither did Ysella. Instead, they stood and waited.

Emrelda walked toward them several minutes later, making her way to her sister and taking her hands. "Thank you so much. I can't tell you what it means."

Ysella hugged her sister. "You know I'm always here."

"I know, and I'm always glad." Emrelda stepped back and turned to Dekkard. "I'm also glad that you came, and that you'll be with Avraal. I'd better hurry. I can see that Markell's getting impatient."

Ysella and Dekkard watched as the white Kharlan pulled out of the parking area heading back toward the city of Point Larmat. Once the Kharlan was out of sight, he looked to Ysella.

"Would you like to eat . . . or do you want to head back immediately?"

"We both could use a break and some refreshment."

Dekkard grinned. "That bad?"

"Not *that* bad, but sometimes Emrelda can be a bit of a strain."

"I'm no empath—"

"Thank the Three for that," interjected Ysella.

". . . but I think that at times she's more than a bit of a strain. But you never say much."

"She's my sister. I still love her. And I owe her."

Dekkard frowned. He couldn't see Ysella as owing anyone.

"I do. She and Markell persuaded the Empath Academy to take me, and they gave me the marks to live on. Father was adamantly opposed. Mother felt that was one of the things that led to his heart attack. He's never been quite the same since, and neither of us is particularly welcome at home."

"Because you wanted to use your talent? Because your sister helped you do it?"

"Landor women who are empaths are expected to use the talent to support and burnish their husbands and children. Anything else is considered dishonorable. We can talk more about it while we eat. I am hungry."

"So am I."

They walked toward the Cleft House. Dekkard doubted that the dining room would be that crowded, since it was early afternoon. He hoped it wasn't closed, but thought that unlikely in a sightseeing area. He was right, and less than five minutes later, they were seated at a table on the shaded balcony with both an ocean and a cleft view, waiting for their drinks.

Their server, a dark-eyed, dark-haired young man, returned with Dekkard's pale lager and Ysella's Silverhills white wine. "Are you ready to order?"

Dekkard nodded to Ysella.

"The summer chicken with seasonal greens."

"The veal with capers and lemon, and the greens," added Dekkard.

Once the server left, Dekkard asked, "How did Emrelda meet Markell?"

"He was the junior engineer when Engaard was rebuilding part of the harbor in Sudaen, and he knew friends of the family. They were attracted to each other. His father was a machinist who had his own shop . . . before the fire."

"And she was attracted physically and because of his ability, and he was attracted to and flattered by an attractive Landor girl?"

"Emrelda told him early that if they married she would get nothing from Father, but that she still thought she could help him."

"I imagine she has . . . and then some."

Ysella offered an amused smile. "She has, but he'll do almost anything for her. They're good together, and he's better to her than any Landor would be."

"They've been married a while, then."

"A little over ten years." After a moment, Ysella added, "And you're wondering about children."

"The thought had crossed my mind."

"If they decide to have any, there won't be many."

"Because she had to take care of you and Cliven?"

"Partly . . . and partly because she wants to decide, and Markell is totally behind her on that . . . and most matters."

"My sister could have said something like that about children, except she's not married."

"How much older than you is she?"

"Just four years."

"Just?" Ysella raised her eyebrows.

"Four years seems like an enormous gap when you're young, but it's almost nothing once you're grown."

"In some families, perhaps," replied Ysella.

"So you're regarded as past the marriageable age, and Emrelda is minimalized because she married a man who was neither wealthy nor a Landor?"

"That's about right."

Dekkard shook his head, but didn't immediately speak because the server returned with their platters.

"We'd better eat," said Ysella. "Ferry times are farther apart after the sixth afternoon bell."

Dekkard still waited until she lifted her fork before cutting into his veal and taking a bite, followed by a mouthful of seasoned rice, good, but not outstanding. "How is your chicken?"

"Tender, a little bland. The rice is better."

"That's about the same for the veal." Dekkard took several more mouthfuls. "Emrelda set it up so that there was a strong possibility that I'd want to accompany you, didn't she?"

"No." Ysella's quick smile was bitter before it faded. "She set it up so that it was almost impossible for you not to come, not if I wanted to be honest with you. If I'd even avoided you, that would have been dishonest."

Dekkard considered that for a moment. "I can see that. I wondered about the timing of the message. So what else do you think is in those cases?"

"Nothing else. Markell's very worried, but I couldn't tell why without asking some very pointed questions. I also don't know enough high science to ask the right questions."

"His company is only building the structure. That says to me that he either doesn't think that the building is being built as designed or that the design and specifications are inadequate for what the Navy has in mind. The first possibility would strike me as more worrisome for him."

"Unless he's worried about both," replied Ysella.

"Even if he does, what can he do?"

"Go to the head of the corporacion and tell him. Markell is a fairly senior engineer, but he'd need absolute proof to make such a charge."

Dekkard almost asked why anyone would knowingly underbuild the design, but instead shook his head. He knew all the possible reasons, all involved with corruption, greed, or incompetence, if not all three.

But why would Markell care so much unless . . . Unless it was his design. "Let's hope that he gets everything he needs."

"And then some," added Ysella.

The two skipped any dessert, and Ysella insisted on paying for both of them.

Dekkard didn't argue, and they left the dining room and walked swiftly back to Emrelda's Gresynt. In minutes, they were on the road. Dekkard found a service plaza on the outskirts of Point Larmat, where he topped off both the kerosene and water tanks, before turning north on the coastal highway.

37

The drive back from Point Larmat took Dekkard and Ysella almost a bell longer, because they had to wait close to a bell for the harbor ferry. They talked mainly about what growing up had been like for each of them, a conversation that, by unspoken consent, did not deal with what Markell and Emrelda might face, their work, or relations with siblings. Dekkard enjoyed learning bits about growing up in a Landor family, and, from what he could tell, she enjoyed snippets of life in an artisan family.

After they reached the Obreduur house and parked Emrelda's Gresynt out of the way, it wasn't long before both were in their separate beds.

Dekkard woke slightly earlier than usual on Unadi,

disturbed by what sounded like a steamhauler dumping a load. He heard nothing else, but he was awake, and it was close enough to his normal rising that he began his morning routine, his thoughts still occasionally drifting back to Markell and Emrelda. He looked out the window, but saw nothing amiss.

He was the first downstairs, except for Hyelda, and he eased into the kitchen. "Did you hear a loud thump this morning?"

"About a third of a bell ago?" replied the cook. "I did. Didn't hear anything else though. I didn't see anything outside." After a moment, she asked, "Since you're here, would you mind taking the croissant platter to the staff table and laying the newssheet on the side table?"

"I'd be happy to." After getting the platter, Dekkard skimmed *Gestirn,* but found nothing of great interest, until he ran across a small article buried at the bottom of the fourth page. Health and Education Minister Sanoffre had issued a regulation barring the admission of students to government-funded universities if they had a record of "public disorder" and requiring the immediate expulsion of current students with such records.

That just might push some of them into supporting the New Meritorists . . . especially expelling them for previous public disorder.

He put the newssheet on the side table, poured his café, and had just seated himself when Ysella arrived. "How are you feeling this morning?"

"I slept well, thank the Three." She frowned. "Did someone drop something heavy this morning?"

"I heard it, and so did Hyelda, but we don't know what caused it."

"Let's hope it's nothing serious."

Dekkard nodded. "There's one story in *Gestirn* that bothers me. Minister Sanoffre is banning and expelling any university students involved in public demonstrations."

Ysella poured herself a mug of café. "Any student

stupid enough to get involved doesn't deserve a university education."

"That's likely true—"

"Likely?" asked Ysella sardonically.

". . . but young people can be stupid. It's going to make some of them angry, especially the part about expelling them for previous disorderly behavior. That's punishing them for something that wasn't considered punishable when they did it." Dekkard sipped his café.

"They were part of demonstrations where prohibited firearms killed Council Guards and patrollers. You don't think they should suffer some consequences?"

"I don't have a problem with a regulation that punishes criminal behavior from the time of enactment on. I think it's bad politics to make the punishment retroactive."

"Would you have joined such demonstrations?" asked Ysella.

"Of course not. They're stupid, and they're bound to fail . . . at least until and unless they lead to a full-out rebellion."

Ysella frowned. "Do you really think that's possible?"

"Maybe not for years, but it just might happen if the Commercers and the Imperador keep doing what they're doing." Dekkard had the feeling that Ysella didn't see what he was driving at. "About a month ago, Sanoffre declared that enrollment at the universities would be capped at current levels. He said that there are far more university graduates than there are jobs requiring such skills. If enrollments remain capped, who do you think gets left out? Why do you think students are demonstrating?"

"The ones demonstrating are probably those who are less successful," she countered.

Dekkard nodded. "You're probably right. But I remember what Markell said. He had to get two degrees and excel in both to even be considered. He couldn't go with an established firm, but a much newer one. Some of his subsequent success might also be because of your sister."

"The students who are part of the New Meritorists should still know better."

"They should. But they're angry because Landor and Commercer students who aren't as good as the bright but not brilliant students from craft or artisan backgrounds are getting jobs, and they're not. Anger makes people stupid—especially young people. What makes it worse is things like the Kraffeist Affair, which show that stupid and corrupt Commercers get away with swindling thousands, if not tens of thousands, of marks, and either get off or pay damages that come from corporations and not even from their own wallets. And then the Commercers get angry and outraged when people demonstrate."

"You're sounding like you sympathize."

"I understand. To a point, I sympathize. But what they want won't solve their problems, and it will eventually destroy Guldor. That's something that Commercers and most Landors don't really understand. I don't think those types want to understand."

Ysella offered an amused smile. "You worded that carefully, Steffan."

Dekkard laughed softly. "I try."

"So what do you propose . . ." Ysella broke off her words as she heard Rhosali's footsteps. "We need to talk later."

"We do," agreed Dekkard, both realizing that she was right and glad for the break, because he had no idea what would resolve the growing gulf between Crafters, especially lower-paid laboring types, and Commercers. He took two croissants and some quince paste.

"You two sounded like you were having a spirited talk," declared Rhosali.

"We were wondering what the Council could do about the demonstrators and people who burned the Security Ministry," said Ysella.

"They could lock them up," offered Rhosali. "That's what Security usually does." She paused. "Might help for a while. That's if things get better."

"Better how?" asked Dekkard.

"My uncle and his family moved in with my parents. He was a foreman in the Guldoran Ironway textile manufactory . . . the one they closed at the end of last month. He's fifty. He knew it was coming, and he looked for other work. He couldn't find another job there, except as a laborer. They had to sell their house. What they'll do when the marks run out . . ." The housemaid shrugged, almost despairingly.

"They came here all the way from Oersynt?" Dekkard wanted to make sure that there wasn't yet another manufactory being closed.

"They didn't have anywhere else. My brother and I are out of the house." Rhosali shook her head, then poured her café and sat down beside Ysella.

"Even as an experienced foreman, he couldn't find a job in Oersynt?" asked Dekkard.

"They wanted someone younger. Maybe here in Machtarn . . ."

"Have you talked to the councilor?" asked Ysella. "He knows people who know people."

"I . . . I just . . . I couldn't . . ."

"I'll see if he has any suggestions," said Ysella.

"If you would . . . My uncle's name is Hermann Mantero."

"I'll see what I can do," replied Ysella.

"Thank you."

Neither Dekkard nor Ysella said much more as they finished their breakfasts and then left the staff room to finish preparing for the day ahead.

Dekkard had the Gresynt ready early, but waited longer for Obreduur and Ysella, who were talking even as they neared the steamer.

". . . I can do that, but it depends on him," Obreduur said to Ysella before entering the Gresynt.

"Thank you, sir." Ysella eased into the front seat.

Dekkard, suspecting the subject of the conversation, raised his eyebrows.

Ysella gave a quick discreet nod.

Dekkard repressed any expression as he eased the steamer down the drive, out through the gates, and onto Altarama heading west.

After he turned the Gresynt onto Imperial Boulevard and traveled north for a mille, he glanced to the northeast, taking in the blackened ruins of the Security Ministry. *That just might only be the beginning of what the New Meritorists could do.* He also wondered what their next target might be . . . or if the sound that had awakened him had been something they had caused.

Just before he reached Council Avenue, he could make out a barricade on the Square of Heroes, as well as Security steamers. "The Square of Heroes is closed off. There are Security forces there."

"Are there are demonstrators?" asked Obreduur.

"I can't see any," replied Ysella.

"We'll find out what it's all about before long," said the councilor.

When Dekkard turned onto Council Avenue, he could see a number of steamers, mostly Gresynts, coming from the Council Office Building, and as he drove toward the building, it was clear why. Wooden sawhorses had been placed before all the doors to the Council Office Building, and close to a score of Council Guards stood by the entrance, presumably explaining to those who drove up why the building was closed.

"The Council Office Building appears to be closed, sir." Dekkard kept the Gresynt moving around the circle toward the entrance where the guards were posted, rolling down his window as he did, then finally reaching one of the guards.

"Sir, the Council Office Building is closed because there is no water. The Premier will send messages to all councilors when the building will be reopened."

"What caused the lack of water?" asked Obreduur.

"We were not told, sir," replied the guard. "I do know that the Imperial Palace also has no water."

"We heard something like an explosion earlier this morning," interjected Dekkard. "Did that cause the outage?"

The guard looked bewildered. "I don't know, sir. The Premier will be sending messages to all councilors."

"Thank you," said Obreduur.

Dekkard rolled the window up and eased the Gresynt away from the guards.

"You might as well head back to the house, Steffan. That's where the Premier will send whatever he chooses to reveal." Obreduur didn't conceal the exasperation in his voice as he added, "This likely has something else to do with the New Meritorists—the simplistic idiots."

Dekkard wasn't so sure that the New Meritorists were as simplistic as Obreduur thought. *But maybe you're giving them too much credit.*

Once Dekkard drove through the gates to the drive and stopped the Gresynt under the portico, Obreduur said, "I'd appreciate it if you'd both remain at the house, at least until I know more."

"Yes, sir," replied Dekkard and Ysella, not quite in synchrony.

Then Obreduur and Ysella got out of the steamer, and, once they closed the doors, Dekkard drove the steamer to the garage, where he wiped it down and topped off the tanks before closing the garage doors.

Ysella was waiting in the rear hallway. "Do you want to finish our earlier conversation?"

"We have time now. We may not later. Under the portico?"

"Where else?"

As they walked outside and down the drive toward the shade of the portico roof, Ysella said, "While you were getting the steamer ready, I asked the councilor if he could do anything for Rhosali's uncle. He told me he'd write a note to Carlos Baartol about Sr. Mantero,

and to have him visit Baartol at his office late this week
or early next week."

"Do you think Baartol can help?"

"He can find him something better than a laborer's
position."

"What will you tell Rhosali?"

"Just that there's a chance Baartol can help her uncle." Ysella paused. "You were going to tell me what
you'd propose to do to deal with the New Meritorists."

"Something similar to what Obreduur has in mind.
Find a way to build enough support for the Craft Party
to select a premier and start chipping away at some
of the unseen structural inequities . . . like allowing
workers to be represented by guild legalists even when
they're unemployed . . . or possibly making all large contracts between the government and corporacions part
of the public record . . . and making the heads of corporacions personally liable for criminal and/or financial
illegalities committed by their corporacion."

"No Council will ever pass that."

Dekkard smiled. "If there are almost enough votes
to pass that, then I imagine we'd see fewer Kraffeist Affairs . . . and there might be more votes for Craft Party
councilor candidates . . ."

Ysella shook her head. "At times, you sound almost
as radical as the New Meritorists, and the next minute
you sound like Obreduur."

"I get more upset than he does about the unfair-
nesses . . . or maybe I just show it more, which isn't wise,
but I agree with his approach, or yours. I'm not in favor
of tearing down a working system for one that seems
better, but isn't. But we have to stop the present system
from being eroded any more by wealth and privilege."

"Do you think it's been eroded that much . . . or that
we expect more than people used to?"

Dekkard offered a wry laugh. "I have no idea. That's
really a guess on my part. I see Commercers using the
system to increase their power, and that things are

getting worse for many people. Is it worse now, or has it always been this way, and people are finally losing hope and getting angry? You tell me."

After a long moment, Ysella replied. "First the Landors, and then the Commercers, had too much power, but the guilds of the skilled trades kept them from the worst excesses. When steam-powered machinery began to make so many goods cheaply, the guilds lost power. The Landors did also, if more slowly. Even now, too many Landors refuse to see that the guilds would be better allies than the Commercers."

As they stood there, Dekkard saw a blue Ferrum with green stripes glide to a stop in front of the gates and a messenger hurry through the pedestrian gates and up to the front door.

"That has to be a messenger from Craft Floor Leader Haarsfel," said Ysella. "We should head back to the staff room."

"We should. In a minute. You didn't answer my question. Why now?"

"You already answered it. Because so many have lost hope."

"But how did it come to that?" Dekkard pressed.

"What do you think?"

"Because the rich are getting richer and no one else is? Because no one seems able to stop the changes?"

"That's part of it, but we need to see what the councilor has to say."

"You're probably right." Dekkard took a deep breath. He felt like he was talking and arguing in circles, even within himself.

Neither spoke as they made their way to the staff room.

Obreduur stood in the archway. "If you'd join me in the study." It wasn't a question.

Once all three were seated in the study, Obreduur looked across his desk at Dekkard and Ysella. "As you must have noticed, I just received a message from Floor Leader Haarsfel. A section of the Semille water tunnel serving the Palace and the Council was destroyed by a massive dunnite explosion. There's a huge water-filled crater there. The Premier has assured everyone that temporary repairs will be completed by tomorrow morning . . . but it will take weeks to make proper repairs. Council sessions will resume at noon tomorrow."

Dekkard frowned, wondering how anyone could place that amount of explosives under or around an underground tunnel without being noticed.

"You have a question, Steffan?"

"I thought the main tunnels were at least partly dug or tunneled through rock."

"There are a few places where the bedrock is too deep and large ceramic piping is used. One of those places is through the Hillpark Reserve. Apparently, a road-repair crew working on a drive through the park was doing more than repairing the walks and curbs." After the briefest of hesitations, Obreduur added, "That shows, again, a high level of expertise and planning. They're not just destroying things; they're sending a message that they're willing to destroy everything if the Council and the Imperador don't listen."

There's something about the two acts . . . Dekkard smiled wryly, then shook his head. It couldn't be . . .

"Steffan . . . what were you thinking?"

"Oh . . . it was just a wild thought. No one would really do it."

"Do what?" asked Ysella.

"It's stupid . . ."

Ysella gave him a hard look.

Dekkard sighed. "I was just thinking. They blew up the Security Ministry, but they also took out the lighting for that whole part of the city. Now, they've done the same thing with the water system. I was . . . it's silly . . ." When neither Obreduur nor Ysella said a word, he went on. "I was just thinking what else makes a city livable. Without sewers . . . well, everything would stink, and no one thinks about sewers . . ."

Obreduur and Ysella exchanged glances.

"I said it was stupid," said Dekkard.

"No . . . it's not stupid," replied Obreduur. "It's just the sort of thing those brilliant idiots might try. In any event, there can only be a handful of places and sewer junctions where they could create the same sort of destruction, and it shouldn't take that long for Security to investigate the possibilities. Thank you. It's a very good thought. Please stay close. I might need you two to escort me."

"Yes, sir."

The two walked back to the staff room, where Dekkard stopped and looked at Ysella. "This is going to get worse."

"They can't keep doing things like this," replied Ysella. "Security will find them, sooner or later."

"That may be," Dekkard agreed.

"And?" prompted Ysella.

"I couldn't say. I feel that we're missing something. Maybe I just don't understand. Maybe Security can round up all the New Meritorists. Maybe there aren't that many of them. That doesn't take into account the people like Rhosali's uncle. Over four hundred of them lost their jobs. How many others will lose their jobs to sussie workers in Noldar and elsewhere, or to more modern steam-powered manufactories with the new punch-card-controlled machines?"

"We can't stop progress."

"No . . . but we could manage it better. I'd like to think that, anyway." Dekkard pulled out a chair and sat down. He didn't feel like going up to his room, especially since it would be warmer than the staff room.

After a moment, Ysella seated herself across from him. "Why did you say that you'd be a third-rate artisan?"

"Fifth-rate was what I said. First, I don't have the physical skill in my hands."

"That's hard to believe. Your writing is beautiful."

"You don't know how many years it took." *And how many times my mother used a rule on the back of my head.* "It's agony for me to even try to draw a perfect circle. Or to use a wheel to throw the simplest pot or vase. But it's more than that. There's a degree of repetition involved in being an artisan."

"As opposed to being an artist?"

"There's less repetition in artistry." *And usually a lot fewer marks.*

"Steffan . . . there's repetition in everything, especially if you want to be good."

"I know that. But if you love or like doing something, the repetition doesn't bother you. Because it bothered me so much, I knew I didn't love being an artisan."

"Security is filled with repetition."

"The responses are filled with repetition. But every situation is a little different, and I learn more about people with every encounter."

"Maybe . . ." Ysella showed the slightest hint of an amused smile.

"Maybe what?"

"I need to think about it." At that moment, the door to the back hall opened, and Ysella added, "It's the councilor."

They both were standing when Obreduur reached the archway.

"I need you both. I'll tell you once we're on the way."

"Yes, sir."

Dekkard immediately headed to ready the Gresynt, leaving Ysella and Obreduur, but both were waiting under the portico by the time he arrived there with the steamer.

When they were seated with the doors closed, he asked, "Where to, sir?"

"The Ministry of Health and Education first. Sewers belong to Health. Phillipe won't do anything, but I'll still need to talk to him or his deputy before we make the second stop."

Dekkard took Altarama to Imperial Boulevard, but continued on Imperial to Heroes Square, where he took Grande Avenue, also known as the Way of Gold, east from the Imperial Palace and its grounds to the section of Machtarn that held the offices of all the ministries. The Health and Education Ministry shared a building with Workplace Administration, across the street from the Commerce building.

Dekkard pulled into the waiting space in front of the main door. The doorman started to wave him away, then looked at the Council insignia on the Gresynt and stopped gesturing.

"You'll come with me, Avraal," said Obreduur. "Some persuading might speed matters."

Dekkard remained with the steamer, half wondering and half bemused at Obreduur's certainty that Minister Sanoffre would do nothing.

Two-thirds of a bell later, Obreduur and Ysella returned.

Obreduur said nothing until he was inside the steamer. "Phillipe agreed, but prefers that I talk to Minister Wyath. So we'll go to the Justiciary building. That's where he's working now."

Dekkard eased the Gresynt away from the waiting space and continued east to the cross street, Ironton, where he turned right. A block later, he eased up in front of the gray stone structure that housed the Justiciary Ministry.

A pair of armed Security guards flanked the bronze doors at the top of the marble steps.

Once more, Ysella accompanied Obreduur, and one of the guards said something to the councilor, who replied before entering the building.

Almost a bell passed before Obreduur and Ysella returned.

Dekkard wanted to ask what had happened. Instead, he said, "Where to now, sir?"

"Back to the house. We've done what we could."

Dekkard decided to wait to see what Obreduur said, but the councilor said nothing until they were headed south on Imperial Boulevard. "Is anyone following us?"

"Not that I can tell," said Dekkard.

"Not closely enough that I can sense anyone with such feelings."

"I wasn't sure I could see Minister Wyath, but he made a few minutes available. I pointed out what you suggested. He was dubious, but he did agree that checking the few places where sewer malfunctions would have a severe impact couldn't hurt. I have the feeling he'll order his people to check just so that he and the Premier can claim they've tried to get ahead of the demonstrators."

"If Steffan's intuition is correct?" asked Ysella.

"Security will want to talk to all of us," said Obreduur dryly.

"All of us?" said Dekkard.

"They can't talk to you without my being present. No staff member can be interviewed or interrogated without the councilor being present."

Dekkard didn't recall such a provision in the Great Charter, but he wasn't about to say so.

"It is in the Great Charter, in an obscure fashion," Obreduur went on. "There's a clause that states that employees of the Council may not be interviewed or interrogated by any branch of government, including the Council, without the presence of the elected authority directly over them. That was put there to keep the Premier or the Imperador from trying to get information from staffers without the knowledge of the appropriate councilor."

"I'm not sure I want to be correct in my wild guess, then," replied Dekkard.

"There are definitely dangers to predicting correctly," agreed Obreduur. "There always have been, especially if you predict negative events."

Dekkard could see that.

38

The remainder of Unadi was quiet. There were no more messages, and Dekkard, after what Obreduur had said about the Great Charter, spent most of the rest of the day closely studying the briefing book that Ysella had given him, reading the Great Charter aloud to himself, if in a quiet voice, just so that he wouldn't miss anything.

On Duadi, after more study of the Great Charter and the rest of the briefing book, and with no instructions to the contrary, Dekkard had the Gresynt ready at a third before noon, and in moments Obreduur and Ysella appeared.

Even before Dekkard left the drive and turned onto Altarama, the councilor said, "No, I've received no messages."

When Dekkard pulled up in front of the Council Office Building, he could see that additional guards were still in place, and that they seemed to be questioning a few more people than before, although none of them stopped him, possibly because of his security grays.

So could a New Meritorist empie or isolate get into the Council Building in grays?

That was something else he probably ought to bring up as well, but surely someone had thought of it. He shook his head. It didn't appear that his last idea had worked out. He kept walking, making his way up the staff staircase to the second level and the office.

As usual, there was a stack of letters and petitions on his desk, if a short one, either because the messenger service was checking anything coming into the building more thoroughly or because fewer people were sending things, in anticipation of the upcoming Summerend recess. As he began reading the first letter, Dekkard suspected the latter more than the former.

Just before the third bell of the afternoon, a messenger

in gray walked swiftly into the office and announced, "A message for Councilor Obreduur from Security Minister Wyath. For the councilor's hand only."

Ysella immediately concentrated on the messenger, while Karola stood and knocked on the inner door. "A message for you from Security Minister Wyath, Councilor."

Less than a minute passed before the inner door opened and Obreduur stood there.

The messenger handed over the sealed envelope, along with a sheet of paper, saying, "If you'd be so kind as to sign for it, Councilor."

Obreduur signed the sheet on the corner of Karola's desk and returned it.

"Thank you, sir." The messenger turned and hurried out of the office.

Obreduur looked to Ysella.

"He was more worried about getting all of his messages delivered than anything else."

"Thank you." The councilor nodded and retreated into his office.

Less than a sixth later, Obreduur reappeared at his office door. "Avraal . . . Steffan . . ." He motioned for the two to join him.

Dekkard followed Ysella into the office. He didn't need to be told to close the door.

Obreduur said nothing until he reseated himself behind the wide goldenwood desk on which were close to a half score neatly stacked piles of papers. He picked up a single sheet of paper, looked at it for perhaps a minute before setting it down and clearing his throat.

"Steffan . . . apparently your intuition is somewhat better than Security's innumerable agents . . . and that presents a problem. We'll get into that a bit later. Security agents were too late to preclude one sewer blockage. A point where three subsidiary sewage mains joined the main sewer was plugged with underwater cement yesterday afternoon. The area includes the burned-out Security Ministry as well as the Justiciary Ministry and the Workplace Administration Ministry. Those offices and the businesses in four blocks are temporarily closed . . . and may be for more than a week because any sewage has no place else to go. Agents were more successful in dealing with the sewers serving the Palace and the Council grounds and buildings. They caught the perpetrators in the act, again using city maintenance vehicles. They appear to be New Meritorists, but interrogations are still in progress . . ."

At those words, Dekkard could see a tightening of Ysella's face, and he recalled that the empie who had attacked the councilor had quickly died under interrogation, as well as Ysella's earlier observation that interrogations by Security empaths were often brutal.

". . . and early indications suggest that finding those behind the disruptions may be difficult."

Dekkard could see that, especially since the majority of Security's records, with names and details, had gone up in flames. Even if most of the agents working on the New Meritorists were still alive, gathering them together and trying to re-create the information into usable form would take time . . . and by that time, many of the New Meritorists would have moved elsewhere or disappeared in some fashion.

"What do you think they'll do next, Steffan?"

"Something to prove they can disrupt some other necessity for governing or doing business."

"Something that will affect people?" asked Ysella.

"Anything will affect people," replied Dekkard, "but they've largely avoided killing anyone—except for Council Guards, and Security patrollers and personnel . . . and Security isn't exactly the most beloved of the Imperador's ministries." Another thought crossed his mind as well. "Also, since the newssheets can seldom mention the names of councilors, there won't be that much of an outcry over Councilor Aashtaan's assassination. I almost missed the announcement of Yordan Farris as his replacement."

"No loss," murmured Ysella.

Obreduur glanced at her for a moment.

"Sorry, sir." She didn't sound sorry.

Obreduur turned back to Dekkard as if nothing had happened and said dryly, "Security should have recruited you for a position."

"They interviewed me my last year at the Institute. I didn't pursue it, and neither did they. I think they were put off by my parents being artisans from Argental." But then, Dekkard had been put off by the arrogance of the Security official who'd interviewed him.

"That means any record they have of you was likely destroyed," said Ysella.

"That won't make any difference," Obreduur pointed out. "Too many people in Security know about you two because of the Aashtaan assassination. So is the fact that you captured the assassin without hesitation. Assistant Security Minister Johan Lorenz and an aide will be here tomorrow at the fourth bell of morning to talk to the three of us. I imagine they'll want to ask about any details you noticed about the assassin." His eyes went to Dekkard. "And why you were so accurate about the sewers."

"It just seemed to fit a pattern," Dekkard demurred.

"What do you see as the next part of this pattern?"

"Either a disruption of government or business or something that will force Security to act harshly against innocents . . . or those that most people would see as innocents. Provoking Security to act against others has been consistent from the first demonstrations, at least, those that I know about."

"You might give that some thought before we talk with the assistant minister."

Dekkard nodded. He wasn't as worried about the assistant minister as he was about whoever accompanied him. "Is there anything else we should know, sir?"

"Probably," replied Obreduur with a soft laugh. "But I don't know what it might be." He paused. "I do want all the petitions and letters answered before we leave on the trip to Gaarlak and Malek. That may be three weeks away, but you don't want to work late that last week. That's all I have." With that, Obreduur stood.

Dekkard stood and motioned for Ysella to lead the way out, then followed and closed the door. He stopped beside her table desk and murmured, "He's more worried than he's saying, isn't he?"

She smiled sardonically, answering in a low voice, "All councilors worry. And it's usually not a good idea to show it. You're mostly good about not showing it, but you need to get better."

"On the one hand, people think isolates don't feel . . ." Dekkard shook his head.

"I know that's not true, especially with you," she replied, "and because you do feel strongly, you need to be careful as you do more speaking for him . . . or for the Craft Party."

"For the party?"

"In Gaarlak, since it's not his district, anything we say will be on behalf of the party."

"So he won't just be evaluating how a future election might go . . . that's cover for getting more supporters?"

"He hasn't said . . . but why else would he be asked to spend time there? Now . . . I need to prepare for another talk for him."

"The Seamstresses Guild or . . . ?"

"The Women's Clerical Guild. And it won't be long before you get to stand in for him again." Ysella seated herself.

Dekkard got the message and returned to his desk, wondering what group he might have to address. *The Plasterers and Finish Carpenters Guild? The Commercial Security Guild?*

He shook his head and picked up his pen.

39

Dekkard didn't sleep all that well and woke up worrying on Tridi. While he certainly hadn't done anything illegal, he still worried about meeting with anyone from Security. *Could you be getting paranoid?* Except he knew that a touch of paranoia made one a better security aide. The question was how much of a touch was too much. But then, there was so much he hadn't known—*or even suspected*—about government and politics.

After taking a deep breath, he sat up on the side of the bed, then stood.

When he entered the staff room, he was surprised to see Ysella already there, but he took a quick glance at the newssheet, noting only a small story on a sewer malfunction closing a four-block area of Machtarn. He then looked at Ysella. "You didn't sleep all that well either?"

"The last thing anyone with any intelligence wants to do is to come to the attention of Security, no matter what the reason or how innocent you are."

"I had that feeling." Dekkard poured his café, and sat down across the table from her.

"That's one you can definitely trust. At least Security can't fault us for capturing and restraining that poor misguided empath. If you can avoid it without lying, don't mention anything about being an assistant economic specialist."

Dekkard could definitely understand that, but there was one problem. "The Security Committee staffers know that we do more."

"That's not likely to come up. If it does, look like you don't understand why they're asking the question. Then, if Obreduur doesn't explain, just tell them there's more work than the professional staff can do, and you help where you can when you're not escorting the councilor."

"That's certainly true." *As far as it goes.*

"What's true?" asked Rhosali as she entered the staff room.

"That the councilor's staff often has more work than they can handle," replied Ysella.

"I can believe that." Rhosali paused. "Thank you for speaking to the councilor."

"We hope it will work out," said Ysella. "Sr. Baartol knows a great many people. It might take a while."

"Good seldom happens overnight," replied Rhosali. "Only darkness."

Dekkard smiled faintly at the old folk saying, then reached for the croissants, after which he added a chunk of quince paste to his plate. Both Ysella and Dekkard ate quickly, then left the staff room.

The drive to the Council Office Building was uneventful and quiet, with Obreduur writing something in the rear seat and Ysella sensing if anyone might be following, although Dekkard certainly didn't see any steamers trailing the Gresynt. The increased number of Council Guards remained outside the building and in the covered parking area, and one even asked Dekkard for his passcard when he neared the main entrance. When Dekkard thanked him, the guard looked surprised, but didn't say anything.

Karola had an even smaller stack of letters waiting on Dekkard's desk, which was fine with him, given that the "interview" with Security would certainly take some time.

Several minutes past fourth bell, three men entered the office, all wearing jackets and trousers of a blue so dark it was almost black, the shade often called security blue, as well as white shirts and security blue ties. Dekkard assumed that the older man with blond hair streaked with white was Assistant Security Minister Johan Lorenz, and that his aide was the sharp-faced younger man, since the third man wore the security blue uniform of an agent.

"Assistant Security Minister Lorenz and Security Special Assistant Gudwaard for a meeting with the councilor and his security aides," declared the younger man almost before the security agent had closed the door.

"The councilor is expecting you," replied Karola, rising and knocking on the inner office door. "Assistant Security Minister Lorenz, sir."

Dekkard didn't hear the response, but Karola immediately opened the door and gestured to Ysella and Dekkard, who followed Lorenz and Gudwaard into the inner office. The agent did not follow. As Dekkard closed the door he noticed that another chair had been added and that the four chairs in front of Obreduur's desk had been arranged in a deeper arc than usual.

Obreduur stood and inclined his head to Lorenz. "Good morning, Minister Lorenz. Please have a seat."

"Thank you, Councilor. This is my special assistant Hans Gudwaard."

"And these are my security aides, Avraal Ysella and Steffan Dekkard." Obreduur seated himself.

Lorenz took the end chair farthest from the window, with Gudwaard next to him, while Ysella sat beside Gudwaard, leaving the chair closest to the window for Dekkard.

Once everyone was seated, Obreduur said pleasantly, "The Security Ministry requested this meeting. What would you like to know?"

"As you must know, Councilor," began Lorenz, "demonstrators have made a number of attacks . . . on the Security Ministry, in various locales across Guldor, at the Imperial University, and even upon the Council . . ."

"By demonstrators," interjected Obreduur smoothly, "I assume you're referring to the New Meritorists."

"Security would prefer not to get into names, Councilor."

"I understand that, but please don't condescend to

me. When demonstrators wave signs and placards with slogans used previously by the Meritorists, is there any doubt that these idiots are New Meritorists?"

"Those idiots, as you call them, have created a great deal of damage in some well-thought-out plans, not to mention the death of a councilor."

"They're unlikely to win, and if they did win, they'd destroy Guldor and themselves in a few years. To me, that's a form of idiocy. But that's just my view. How can we help you?"

"Sr. Gudwaard has been working on this, and Minister Wyath had thought that your security aides might be able to reveal more about the assassination of Councilor Aashtaan, since apparently no one ever interviewed them."

"That's very true," said Obreduur pleasantly. He looked to Ysella and then to Dekkard. "Is that agreeable to you?"

"It is." Dekkard nodded, knowing that was the only response.

Ysella merely nodded.

Gudwaard smiled, in a way that reminded Dekkard of a stoat, although, except for his sharp nose, the round-faced special assistant bore no particular resemblance, then focused on Ysella. "I understand that you're a talented empath. Council Guard reports suggest that you immediately pointed out the empath who attacked the councilor. Was there anything in particular that called your attention to her?"

"Yes. She fired a strong and narrow empblast, pure focused hatred. A trace of that hatred remained around her. There was also a momentary sense of triumph."

"I see. Did you notice anything physical that stood out?"

"No. She just looked like another Council messenger. She looked more boyish than most of them."

Gudwaard turned to Dekkard. "Did you see anything out of the ordinary?"

"Only that she had that focused expression that empaths have."

"I thought that she'd already killed the councilor."

"She had, but Security Aide Ysella had already pointed her out to me, and I started toward her. That was when she looked at me, as though she was trying to emp me. When she realized I was an isolate, she tried to turn and run."

"Shouldn't she have recognized your grays? You were in grays, were you not?"

"I was, but she must not have recognized them, because that's what happened." Dekkard wasn't about to suggest that Ysella had been confusing the attacker.

"What did you do then?"

Dekkard gave a complete description of his physical acts, ending with, ". . . and then two Council Guard isolates showed up and took her away."

"Did anyone question you?"

"Except for Councilor Obreduur, not until now."

"Not until now?" asked Lorenz.

"That's correct, sir."

Lorenz frowned, but nodded to Gudwaard.

"Security Aide Ysella, what exactly did you do once you sensed the empblast?"

"I did my duty. I was already shielding Councilor Obreduur and as much around him as I could. Councilor Aashtaan had already been struck, and was too far from me to do anything."

"You were already shielding the councilor? Did you have some reason for that?"

Ysella looked at Gudwaard openly. "When we're on duty, he's always shielded. No one can react fast enough to create a shield against an empblast at close range."

"You don't shield anyone else?"

"No . . . except that anyone close to the councilor might be partly shielded, depending on where an empblast comes from."

For the next third of a bell, Gudwaard kept asking

variations on his previous questions, until Lorenz said quietly, "I think that's more than sufficient." He turned to Dekkard. "Steffan, you were the one who suggested that the demons . . . the New Meritorists, that is, would strike the sewer system next. What gave you that idea?"

"It was just a thought, sir. They'd sabotaged the gas system, and then the water system . . . it just struck me that the next major system would be the sewers . . . all of them are systems that could be sabotaged without calling public attention to them. I really wasn't certain. After I said it to the councilor . . . I told him it was a wild idea . . . that it just came to me . . ."

"Have you ever talked to anyone about the gas lighting systems, or water, or sewers?"

"Not until after all these things happened . . . well, except the sewers, and I only told the councilor and Security Aide Ysella right after the councilor told us about the water sabotage."

Lorenz turned to Ysella. "Did he ever mention any of that to you previously?"

"We did talk about the gas explosion and fire after it happened, but we didn't even know about it until Steffan was driving us to the Council grounds and we saw the flames . . ."

Lorenz continued those questions for another few minutes, then abruptly turned to Dekkard. "Steffan . . . do you have any idea what these people will do next?"

"No, sir."

"None at all?"

"Only that they'll do things that make the government and Council look bad, and those things will be done by only a few people in places where no one would suspect."

Lorenz nodded, then smiled warmly, an expression that Dekkard instantly distrusted, before the assistant minister said to Obreduur, "Thank you very much for your time and cooperation, Councilor." Then he turned toward Dekkard and Ysella. "And for yours as well."

Obreduur stood. "We wish you success in your investigation and hope you're able to put a stop to such disruptions quickly."

Lorenz stood. "We will, and thank you again."

Dekkard, Ysella, and Gudwaard stood as well, and Dekkard moved to the door, which he opened, then stepped back, saying nothing as Lorenz and his assistant departed.

Once the three Security men had left the outer office, Obreduur motioned for Dekkard to shut the door, and then for Ysella and Dekkard to take their seats. After a long moment of silence, Obreduur looked to Ysella. "What did you get from them?"

"They don't like you, and there was wariness from Lorenz every time you spoke. Gudwaard worries about me. He's not quite dismissive of Steffan . . ."

"Excellent." A brief smile crossed the councilor's face. "What else?"

"They really were hoping for some insight into the New Meritorists, and Lorenz definitely understood and was concerned about Steffan's idea that the New Meritorists would continue to use comparatively few people to create disruptions. Lorenz was more focused on you, and Gudwaard on me and Steffan."

"That's not surprising." Obreduur turned to Dekkard. "You handled that very well, Steffan. Everything you said was true, and you managed not even to hint about other matters." He smiled again. "It was a performance that only Avraal and I could appreciate."

In a way that saddened Dekkard, even as he knew that Security was clearly overreaching what the framers of the Great Charter had intended.

"You're not totally pleased with that, are you?" asked Ysella.

"Am I losing my chill?" asked Dekkard.

"No. That just came from your body position and eyes," she replied.

"I'm not totally pleased," Dekkard admitted. "The Commercers are more interested in catching and killing people than in asking why the unrest is growing and what they should be doing. Unless someone . . ." He shrugged.

Obreduur and Ysella exchanged glances.

"What?" asked Dekkard.

"What do you think we're trying to do?" Obreduur's voice carried an amused tone.

Dekkard offered an embarrassed smile. "Just about what I was suggesting. It's just that the Commercers don't seem to see the need."

"They don't want to change, even as the world is." Abruptly, Obreduur picked up a sheet of paper from one of the stacks on his desk. "This is the response that came in this morning from Konrad Hadenaur. He wrote that the Sanitation bureaucrats grumbled, but accepted the new job descriptions, not that they had much choice after getting the approval from the Health and Education Ministry. Now this may not sound like much, but the result is that everyone benefits. Less talented beetles get jobs. More talented ones who can learn on the job get promoted, and the most talented ones get promoted a little faster. And now that it's been approved, sanitation guilds in other cities can benefit as well." Obreduur smiled sadly. "It's not enough. But if all councilors looked at matters that way, it could be. Instead of making things better here, the Commercers are trying to produce goods more cheaply in Noldar. What good is that if you destroy jobs here? The workers you put out of work can't buy any goods, cheaper or not. That means tax revenues go down. It also means people get angry."

"So why do they do it?" Dekkard suspected he knew the answer, but he wanted to hear what Obreduur had to say.

"Because they'll make more marks in the next few years. It's the same kind of thinking that the New Meritorists have. They both want things better immediately, and what they're doing will make everything worse in the long run."

"Can you build the Craft Party and its supporters

enough to take control of the government before all that happens?"

Obreduur didn't speak for a moment, then said, "We'll likely win more seats in the next election. I don't know whether that will be enough to take the Council. Even if we do, we'll have to accomplish reform under the terms of the Great Charter. Otherwise, we'd just be doing what you feared—destroying Guldor under the guise of saving it."

"And that makes it hard," added Ysella, "because the Commercers have already corrupted the system."

Hard? How about nearly impossible? Dekkard couldn't argue with either, not when he'd already made the same point. "So what should we do now?"

"Keep doing your job. You're already making a difference."

Dekkard didn't bother to hide his puzzlement.

Obreduur laughed. "You'll see. And if you don't by the time the Council reconvenes after recess, I'll explain. I doubt I'll have to, though. But it would be better if you see for yourself. That way, you won't wonder whether you're seeing what you're seeing or what I want you to see."

Dekkard turned to Ysella. "Did he tell you the same thing?"

"Not quite the same way, but . . . yes."

Dekkard smiled wryly. "Then I'd better get back to work."

"We all need to," replied Obreduur as he gestured toward the door.

Once Dekkard and Ysella were in the outer office, with Obreduur's door closed, Karola asked, in a low voice, "What happened in there? The assistant didn't look all that happy."

"He wasn't able to intimidate anyone," replied Ysella sardonically. "That always makes them unhappy."

Dekkard was afraid that was all too true.

40

The rest of the day at the Council Office Building was without any other singular events, for which Dekkard was thankful. He even managed to catch up on his responses.

After driving Obreduur and Ysella back to the house, Dekkard spent time going over the two steamers before wiping them down. He did notice that Emrelda's teal Gresynt was gone, and that suggested that she had returned to Machtarn without event. He stepped into the back hall from the garage to find Ysella waiting for him.

"You certainly took your time tonight."

"I hadn't really gone over the steamers in several days. So I did it now. Was there something I was supposed to do?"

"No, but I thought you might like to know that Emrelda returned safely. She left a note for both of us." Ysella handed Dekkard an envelope that she had apparently opened, although there was a sheet of folded notepaper inside. He glanced at the outside, which simply read "Avraal and Steffan," then extracted the single sheet and began to read.

> Avraal and Steffan,
>
> I returned this afternoon by train and was fortunate enough to obtain a steamhack quickly. The Gresynt was in perfect condition, and someone had topped off the tanks, for which I am most grateful. That will allow me more time to deal with other chores before I return to duty tomorrow. So thank you both for your assistance and support.
>
> Markell hasn't finished his measurements and calculations, but I have the feeling that the additional instruments will turn out to have been necessary, although he insists that thoroughness is required in all

engineering and design to assure that all standards are met.

Thank you both . . . again.

The signature was simply "Emrelda."

Dekkard refolded the single sheet and replaced it in the envelope, then handed the envelope back to Ysella. "She's worried."

Ysella nodded. "But it's her handwriting, and Rhosali said it was her."

"Rhosali's met her, then?"

"Only a few times. She doesn't forget. That's why she's the one to answer the door."

Dekkard smiled briefly. Everyone the Obreduurs hired seemed to be more than qualified for what they did. "The note's a little formal."

"That's partly her and partly because it was addressed to both of us. She wanted you to see it."

"She thinks you don't take things as seriously as she thinks you should? Or that what Markell's looking into is more serious than it seems?"

"Some of each." Ysella offered a wry smile. "She also thinks you'll take her worries seriously."

"She scarcely knows me."

"Over three enddays, she's seen more of you than most people see of acquaintances they call friends in months."

"It's more that she trusts your judgment," replied Dekkard.

"That might be part of it, but certainly not all. She thinks you're more cautious."

Dekkard choked back a laugh. Finally, he said, "I wouldn't call a man who gave up a secure position in the family plastering concern to become an armed political security aide cautious."

"You said you'd have been a fifth-rate artisan."

"I would have been, but I was good at cleaning up and routine work, and that's always necessary. And it's much safer than what we're doing now."

"Isn't that what Obreduur wants—to clean up and repair politics?"

"So you're saying that I've traded a safe job of one kind of cleanup for another that involves a more dangerous type of cleanup?"

"Haven't you? Haven't we?" Ysella was smiling sardonically as she finished.

"When you put it that way . . . yes. But I'd still rather do it than clean up plasterwork. What about you?"

"You don't even need to ask, Steffan."

"What do we do about Emrelda and Markell?"

"Not much. Not at the moment. Markell's in Siincleer, and Emrelda's in Machtarn, and they're both doing their jobs. We can worry, but nothing's happened, and it may not."

"You're not as sure about that as you sound," suggested Dekkard.

"I worry . . . but we don't know enough to know what to worry about."

Dekkard had to agree. "So . . . we might as well get on with things and hope dinner isn't spinach milanesia."

Ysella winced, then smiled. "Have you ever had it?"

"Twice. I'd prefer not to try it a third time."

Ysella shook her head. "I'll see you at dinner." She turned and headed for the stairs.

After several moments, Dekkard took the stairs as well, still wondering what Markell was discovering.

41

On Furdi, Obreduur directed Dekkard to help Raynaad with some correspondence because Dekkard had actually caught up on his work while the economic assistant had fallen behind as a result of his duties in recording committee discussions where Obreduur had wanted a verbatim transcript.

For all of Dekkard and Ysella's worries, when Dekkard asked her if she'd heard anything from Emrelda after they got back to the house on Furdi night, Ysella's answer was simple.

"She hasn't sent a message, and she would have if there was trouble."

Quindi turned out like Furdi in terms of work, with Dekkard splitting his time between his own letters and the simpler ones that Raynaad had given him. But by the end of the workday, he finished both sets of responses. Even after he got the Gresynt and picked up Obreduur and Ysella, the councilor didn't say anything until Dekkard had been driving south on Imperial Boulevard for several minutes.

"There's been no word either from the Premier or from Security. Hasheem hasn't heard anything, either, and there aren't any meetings by the Commercers on the Security Committee." After a moment, Obreduur asked, "What do you make of that, Steffan?"

"The New Meritorists are working out another way to show the government's lack of control or incompetence. I have no idea what that might be, but it will be obvious in hindsight."

"Why do you say that?"

"That way, they can get people to say that it was obvious . . . and ask themselves why the government didn't do something to stop it."

"Do you really think they're thinking that far ahead?" asked Ysella.

"So far, only a handful of them have been caught, and none of those detained knew anything beyond what they did," replied Obreduur. "If they had known, Wyath wouldn't have sent Lorenz. I admit that's more based on feel than knowledge."

"Would Minister Wyath tell anyone? Would Premier Ulrich or Chairman Maendaan even know?" asked Ysella.

"Minister Wyath would be a fool to hide anything like that from Ulrich, but it's possible Ulrich could be keeping it to himself. If he keeps it to himself for long, that will erode confidence in him, and they don't have that many Landor votes to spare at the moment."

"I have another question, sir," said Dekkard. "It's been almost a month since Kraffeist's resignation, but there's been nothing said about appointing a new Minister of Public Resources."

"Steffan . . . would you want to be minister there right now? Until it's clearer who did what or that the matter is settled, I doubt anyone truly qualified would be interested. Ulrich is acting as he thinks prudent—not to move quickly and let the bureaucrats quietly run matters."

"As he thinks is prudent?" asked Ysella.

"He thinks the matter will go away. He's certainly done his best to set it up that way."

"You have some doubts?" asked Dekkard.

"Until matters are resolved, nothing is settled. Sometimes, not even then. In politics, apparent settlements can sometimes be illusions. As can quarrels."

"Thank you," replied Dekkard, checking the mirrors, and then concentrating on the late-afternoon traffic on Imperial Boulevard.

Neither Ysella nor Obreduur said anything more, and after dropping them off under the shade of the portico, he drove the Gresynt into the garage. He was still wiping down the Gresynt when Ysella joined him.

"What happened? A message from your sister?"

"What else?" She offered a smile that conveyed bitter amusement. "For someone who conveys the outward impression of an impervious isolate, you see more than some empaths. Her note basically says she needs to see us both and that she'll pick us up at third bell tomorrow morning." She extended a single sheet of notepaper. "You should read it yourself."

Dekkard took the note and began to read.

I just wanted to thank you and Steffan again for helping us out last endday, and for taking care of the Gresynt.

Since we had such a wonderful time together in Point Larmat, I thought I could pick you both up tomorrow morning at third bell and bring you here for the day, since I'll be alone, and I do so enjoy your company and thoughtful insight.

Until tomorrow.

The signature was simply "Emrelda."

Dekkard looked to Ysella as he returned the note. "The way it's written, she's worried about someone else reading it. It's about Markell, and whatever it is, it's not good."

"No, it's not," replied Ysella.

"I worry. She's really not offering a choice and insisting on picking us both up."

"So do I. She wants your judgment as well as mine."

"She doesn't need mine. You've got more experience in political matters than I do."

"What about your judgment on the use of weapons? Or Navy matters. You know more about than that I do."

"Only from the Institute."

"That's four years more training in that than I have," Ysella pointed out. "It is a Navy facility that he's working on."

"And something that I know nothing about."

The two just looked at each other. Then Ysella smiled wryly. "What if she's just lonely, and we're making something out of nothing?"

"Then we'll look very foolish . . . if only to ourselves," replied Dekkard. But he hoped Ysella was right.

"We might as well go to the staff room and wait until it's time to go to services," Ysella said. "I just hope Presider Eschbach doesn't give another homily on yet another facet of trust."

After two years of listening to the august presider, so did Dekkard.

42

Both Ysella and Dekkard were waiting in the shade of the portico well before third bell on Findi morning, one of the warmest of summer so far, and one that promised to get even warmer, if the thick green high haze was any indication.

"I still hope we misread her note." Ysella glanced from the empty street to Dekkard.

"So do I," replied Dekkard. "Do you think we're reading too much into what she wrote?"

"I hope so, but the note's not like her. She's not . . . It just feels wrong."

Dekkard didn't know Emrelda well enough to comment, but Ysella usually had a solid feel for matters. But then, he'd thought he'd known his own sister and been surprised at times.

"There's her Gresynt," declared Ysella, immediately starting down the drive.

Dekkard followed. They reached the curb just as the steamer glided to a stop.

Emrelda immediately opened the door and got out. "I'm so glad to see the two of you." She was pale, and there were dark circles under her eyes.

"What happened?" asked Ysella gently.

Emrelda handed the keys to Dekkard. "You drive. We need to get back to the house, just in case. I'll tell you both on the way."

"In case of what?" asked Ysella. "Something with Markell?"

"He's missing. I'll tell you on the way. I'll sit in back with you."

Dekkard looked to Ysella, who nodded. "Then we'd better get moving."

He opened the driver's door and slid into the seat, then closed the door. In a few moments the sisters were seated. "Is there anyone looking for us?" he asked Ysella.

"Not that I can sense."

Dekkard immediately made a U-turn and headed toward Imperial Boulevard.

"Now . . . what happened?" asked Ysella, gently but firmly.

"Markell sent me a message yesterday, to the patrol station. What he wrote was stated cautiously, in generalities, about his measurements being a significant variance from the anticipated. He also wrote that the specifications being used by his construction manager were unfamiliar, and that the optimal possibilities had been foreclosed . . . and he would let me know as soon as he could."

Dekkard swallowed. He almost couldn't imagine such a blatant effort to cut costs by reducing safety margins, but after all he'd seen recently . . . that was all too possible. Except that the construction manager was employed by Engaard Engineering . . . and if the manager was using different specifications, either he'd been bribed or Markell had been bypassed in some fashion.

Except that Markell had said that he reported directly to Halaard Engaard.

Emrelda paused, as if she had had to catch her breath . . . or regain her composure.

"Had you two talked about this before you left Siincleer?" asked Ysella.

"We did. He was worried, if something went wrong, he'd be the one blamed. That's not the worst of it. Just before I left to pick you up, I got a heliogram saying that Markell had disappeared, and that Security patrollers in Siincleer were looking for him."

"Who sent the message?" asked Dekkard.

"It was signed by Halaard Engaard himself. He said he was on his way to Siincleer and would be in touch when he knew more."

"If the head of the corporacion is going there to

investigate . . ." Dekkard began, then broke off as he braked to avoid hitting a gray Ferrum that darted out of a side street, then slowed down as it came to Imperial Boulevard. Fortunately, the Ferrum crossed the boulevard and turned south around the garden median, while Dekkard turned north.

"You were saying?" prompted Ysella.

"It's good that Engaard is investigating personally." That wasn't exactly what Dekkard had been about say before being interrupted.

"Markell said that Halaard always backed his people."

"Then he may be able to discover what Markell found out," said Ysella. "You said he was an excellent engineer."

"Wouldn't most people familiar with Engaard know that?" asked Dekkard.

"Only people within Engaard Engineering, or a few competitors. Halaard started with Haasan years ago before going out on this own," replied Emrelda. "Markell went with him because he'd never get far at Haasan Design or Siincleer Engineering, if they'd even considered him. Siincleer wouldn't even consider Halaard when he started."

"I just hope Halaard Engaard is very careful," said Dekkard. "*Very* careful."

"You think he's walking into a trap, don't you?" said Ysella.

"I don't see that it could be anything else."

"Can't you warn him?" asked Emrelda.

"How?" asked Ysella. "If he's driving, there's no way to reach him, and we don't even know where to send a message to Siincleer. The same's true if he took the ironway. There won't be anyone at Engaard headquarters on endday."

"But . . ." Dekkard broke off his words.

"But what?"

"Then how did Engaard himself find out this morning?" asked Dekkard.

"The Security patrollers contacted him. He's always the emergency contact. He insisted on that. Construction projects have to list emergency contacts with the nearest patrol station."

"If the specifications being used are wrong," said Dekkard, "then the construction manager in Siincleer is involved."

"Why would the construction manager sabotage his own project?" asked Emrelda.

"Who else?" asked Dekkard. "It can't be Halaard Engaard. Why would he do something that could destroy everything he's built? Even if he wanted to blame Markell, that wouldn't work, because too many people know that the engineer in charge reports directly to him."

"But why?" asked Emrelda again.

"Either for a load of marks or because he was blackmailed in some fashion," replied Ysella. "The next question is why someone would risk bribing or blackmailing."

"For marks and control," said Dekkard. "It's almost certainly someone at Siincleer Engineering, but it will have been done through several intermediaries, and I doubt we'd be able to trace them. Engaard underbid them, I'd wager. Markell didn't quite say that—"

"That's right," declared Emrelda. "Markell said that Halaard was so pleased to have gotten the bid away from both Haasan and Siincleer Engineering . . ." Emrelda's voice trailed off. "They wouldn't . . . they wouldn't . . . just for a single bid?"

Not for a single bid. But Dekkard let Ysella speak to her sister, especially since he needed to turn onto Camelia Avenue.

"We don't know if Markell is missing," said Ysella, "or if he's trying to stay out of sight until Engaard gets to Siincleer so that Markell can tell him what's happened."

That's very unlikely . . . but still possible. Dekkard

concentrated on driving, especially since he was nearing Imperial University, where there might be another demonstration.

"You haven't said anything, Steffan," said Emrelda.

"Avraal's laid out the possibilities. We don't know which is more possible. The one thing that is likely is that Siincleer Engineering is behind it. What Engaard has been doing has cut into their business, and the big corporacions don't like competition, especially from smaller competitors who are more effective or those that threaten their control of an area."

"It doesn't make sense," said Emrelda. "Engaard Engineering isn't that big."

"It isn't that big . . . yet," replied Ysella. "It's already big enough to take large contracts and do them better."

"It's also more vulnerable now than it would be later," pointed out Dekkard.

"That's despicable!" said Emrelda.

"Some Commercers are. We've seen that before," said Ysella.

"Can Councilor Obreduur help?"

"No one we know could get to Siincleer and do much today," said Ysella, "except possibly Halaard Engaard himself, and he's already on his way. We'll let the councilor know. Sometimes he can help—"

"I know. He can't help now. No one can. I hate feeling helpless," snapped Emrelda.

Dekkard kept driving, not knowing what he could say that would make Emrelda feel better without being transparently false or inane.

"We're here," said Ysella gently. "We'll do what we can."

"I know." Emrelda sighed. "I just want to get to the house in case there's a message."

"They have to try again," said Ysella, "and leave a note saying when. But you're right. It would be better if you're there."

"Much better."

When Dekkard finally eased the teal Gresynt up the

drive at Emrelda's house he didn't see a messenger flag, but he let Emrelda and Ysella out so they could check while he turned the steamer and backed it into the garage. Then he shut down the steamer and checked the tanks before closing the garage door. When he entered the house through the portico door and glanced to Ysella, she shook her head.

"Did Markell leave any notes or any information?" Dekkard asked Emrelda.

"No. He sometimes brought papers and renderings here to study, but he never left anything here. That was something Sr. Engaard insisted on. No company papers were to be left unattended at homes or anywhere except at headquarters."

Dekkard couldn't help but feel that Engaard's tight controls and lean and direct management style were working against the corporacion and especially against Markell. *You never thought that sometimes bureaucracy could be a benefit.*

For the rest of the day, Dekkard did whatever he could, while being as quietly cheerful as possible and joining in the conversation where appropriate. He did volunteer to wash and dry the dishes from the afternoon meal, and the sisters gladly let him do that, although Dekkard had the feeling that Emrelda was slightly surprised at the offer.

By sixth bell on Findi afternoon, it was more than clear that Emrelda wasn't going to receive any messages until Unadi, since the commercial heliographs shut down at sunset, and so did their delivery messengers.

"You should come back to Obreduur's with us," said Ysella.

Emrelda shook her head. "I'll drive you back. I need to be here. Besides, I'm on duty tomorrow. That's just as well. I'd just sit and worry."

"Are you sure?"

"I'm sure."

Dekkard glanced at Ysella, who nodded.

None of the three spoke much on the return drive,

and Dekkard sat in back, happy to leave the disjunct bits of conversation to the two sisters, as he tried to figure out what he and Ysella might be able to do . . . and feeling rather helpless because he didn't see much that they could, at least not with what they knew—and didn't know.

When Emrelda stopped the Gresynt before the pedestrian gate, Ysella turned to her. "Are you sure—"

"There's nothing you can do. All we can do is wait. You know how I feel about waiting." Emrelda's voice contained both iron and despair.

"Promise to let us know if there's anything . . ."

"I promise."

"And if you learn anything," added Dekkard.

"I'll let you know as soon as I can."

After Emrelda's teal Gresynt disappeared on its way toward Imperial Boulevard, Ysella turned to Dekkard. "What do you think? Honestly?"

"I'm afraid Markell's dead, and I think it's likely that Halaard Engaard is . . . or will be very soon. The irregularities that Markell discovered will be uncovered, and the blame will be laid upon him." He paused and looked at her. "What do you think?"

"I *hope* it's better. I fear it won't be." Ysella shook her head.

"When do we tell Obreduur?"

"Now. He'll sense something's wrong, and he might come to the wrong conclusion."

The two walked toward the pedestrian gate, through it, up the drive, and into the house.

Obreduur, unsurprisingly, was in his study. He looked at Ysella and then Dekkard. "Neither one of you looks pleased. Is it a disaster or a difficulty?"

"A difficulty that has the possibility of being at least a personal disaster," replied Dekkard. "I think Avraal should tell you."

"My sister's husband is missing after discovering certain problems with a naval construction project . . ." Ysella outlined the situation, ending with, "We're not asking you to do anything. Right now, I don't know anything you could do, but I might need some time off if this goes badly."

Obreduur nodded slowly. "You can certainly have all the time you need. Would you mind if I told Carlos Baartol? He might have some ideas . . . or know someone who does."

"Anything that you think would be helpful," replied Ysella.

"I'm not certain how much immediate help he could provide, but it can't hurt. He also might be able to find information that might be useful."

"So long as it won't hurt Markell," said Ysella.

"I'll make that very clear to him."

"Thank you, sir," replied Ysella.

"Is there anything else you can think of?" asked Obreduur, looking from Ysella to Dekkard, then back to the empath.

"Not at the moment," said Ysella.

Dekkard shook his head.

"Then I'll see you in the morning." Obreduur paused, then added, "I'd like to say something reassuring, but this kind of event often doesn't turn out well. We can only hope that Sr. Engaard is careful and resourceful."

Ysella frowned. "You said 'this kind of event.' That suggests you're aware of others."

"I've heard rumors and secondhand reports of such. They're almost always hushed up because there's never any hard evidence, and without it, nothing ever comes of it. That's why, if you or your sister come across anything like that, you shouldn't let anyone know and you should bring it to me . . . or to someone who has proven that you could safely entrust your life to."

Dekkard almost shivered at the cold feel of truth in Obreduur's words.

Ysella nodded, then said, "Thank you again."

Neither she nor Dekkard spoke until they were alone in the staff room.

"This is even worse than I thought," she said quietly.

Dekkard nodded.

"You don't look that surprised."

"I've been concerned ever since we helped Emrelda take those instruments to Markell. I wish we'd known what Markell told Emrelda sooner."

"I thought the same thing."

Dekkard shook his head. "I doubt that I'd have believed all this a year ago, even five months ago, and I don't think most people in Guldor still would." *Just like they don't understand why the Great Charter was set up as it was or how the Commercers are undermining it.* "The New Meritorists see it, but their solution is even worse than the problem."

"Don't say that too publicly."

"I know. But I don't have to like the fact that even saying that the New Meritorists understand a problem is regarded as treasonous. Or that the Commercers don't understand that their actions are why support for the New Meritorists will only grow."

"I need to think," Ysella said. "I'll see you in the morning."

"Until tomorrow, then."

Dekkard waited until she reached the top of the back staircase before he headed up to his own room.

43

Dekkard woke early on Unadi morning. The first thing he did after dressing and hurrying down to the staff room was to immediately read through *Gestirn*, looking for a story about Engaard Engineering and a missing engineer. There was nothing. The only story of interest was the one about the sewage backup in the eastern part of the administrative center of Machtarn.

Not even a hint about the New Meritorists. Dekkard had to wonder whether they'd have to storm the Imperial Palace with signs proclaiming who they were before the newssheets would name them. *Just how long can Security keep them effectively unknown and anonymous?*

He looked up to see Ysella staring at him. "There's nothing in the newssheet."

"There won't be—if there's anything—until the afternoon edition."

"The only thing about the sewage backup is that it was caused by illegal dumping of industrial underwater cement."

"Did you expect anything else?" Ysella's tone was more sardonic than he'd heard before.

"Not really." He offered the newssheet, but she shook her head, and moved to pour her café before sitting down. He replaced the newssheet on the side table, then poured his own café and sat across from her.

Neither spoke much at breakfast, nor on the drive to the Council Office Building. Obreduur didn't offer any conversation, either. As Dekkard pulled up in front of the building, it seemed to him that there were somewhat fewer Council Guards. There was still an extra guard patrolling the covered parking, but the man gave Dekkard a quick look and continued his rounds.

When Dekkard reached the office, there was a small stack of petitions and letters waiting for him, and Ysella was already sorting through her stack. Dekkard settled down to work, but, before long, he couldn't help noticing the flurry of Council messengers, far more than usual.

Sometime after fourth bell, Obreduur opened his office door and said, "Avraal, Steffan, I'll be having lunch with Councilors Mardosh and Hasheem. You can eat at the staff cafeteria and then wait outside the councilors' dining room before escorting me to the floor."

"Yes, sir."

Once Obreduur closed his door, Dekkard looked to Ysella, who looked back and nodded.

Dekkard doubted it was coincidence that the three councilors were meeting, since Hasheem was on the

Security Committee and Mardosh was on Military Affairs and his district encompassed Siincleer. Whether the meeting would help Markell was another question. That the three were meeting suggested that Obreduur felt the matter was more than the disappearance of a young senior engineer.

Since worrying wasn't going to help Markell, Ysella, or Emrelda, Dekkard forced himself back to the necessary but tedious task of drafting replies, until Obreduur stepped out of the inner office at a third before noon, when he and Ysella then escorted the councilor from the office and out into the summer heat of Machtarn, a heat slightly lessened by the fine spray from the courtyard fountains and the shadow cast by the covered portico that led to the Council Hall.

The heat reminded Dekkard that he and Ysella were going to have hotter times to come, since the occasional sea winds kept the capital cooler in summer than the inland areas where they were headed. Both of them kept their eyes and senses moving as they entered the moderately crowded main corridor of the Council Hall until Obreduur entered the councilors' dining room, where Hasheem stood waiting just inside the entry.

"It's going to be crowded at the staff cafeteria," said Dekkard.

"We'll find a place somewhere," replied Ysella.

The two had about reached the archway into the staff cafeteria when a tall ursine figure moved toward them.

"Here comes Jaime Minz," murmured Ysella, "and it looks like he's pleased to see us, but not in the nicest of ways."

"Avraal . . . Steffan . . . imagine seeing you two here, but where else would I see you? You're both so dedicated to your duties."

"We don't see you that often," replied Dekkard pleasantly. "It appears that you're even busier now that your councilor is Premier."

"Not too busy to have a word with fellow security

professionals. Not at all. Even when it gets busy . . . or even a bit . . . rancid."

"Rancid?" asked Ysella, apparently guilelessly.

"You know, the difficulty with the sewers? Very rancid. Disgusting, really. Can you imagine anyone blocking the sewers and thinking it would reflect badly on the Council?"

"It would seem odd," said Dekkard agreeably.

"But then, I'm sure you both know that, seeing as your councilor has worked on Sanitation matters before, and even made some recommendations to Minister Sanoffre . . . oh, and Minister Wyath." Minz smiled cheerfully.

"The councilor offered a suggestion to deal with Sanitation workers in Machtarn," said Dekkard. "He said that Minister Sanoffre was most helpful, but then, everyone will benefit from the results, even if it had nothing to do with sewers."

"Oh . . . don't be so modest. Everyone knows you both do more than security, even if security is just another form of cleaning up."

Ysella smiled brightly. "You would certainly know, especially given all your experiences with the Premier. Far more experience than either of us would claim."

"I knew you'd understand." Minz smiled broadly. "If I don't see you before recess, enjoy the hinterlands." He nodded pleasantly and then moved on.

Ysella waited a moment, then said, "I'm just as glad I can't sense what lies beneath that superficial cheer and good-naturedness. I suspect it's very deep and dark."

"Most likely," agreed Dekkard. "It also sounds like Ulrich asked all the ministries what Obreduur has brought before them lately. Or do they report that to the Premier already?"

"They have for years, particularly about Craft and Landor councilors."

Two years earlier, even a year earlier, that might have surprised Dekkard. "We'd better get something to eat and look for a table. You lead the way."

Dekkard settled for a pork empanada along with cumin-pepper rice and white beans, while Ysella took a green salad topped with grilled chicken and a vinaigrette dressing.

As he'd predicted, there seemed to be no free tables in the cafeteria, and he just followed Ysella.

Then a dark-haired woman in security grays gestured from ahead of them. "Avraal, Steffan . . . you can sit with us."

Dekkard recognized her immediately—Sumra Velle, the empath for Councilor Safaell. Sitting with her was Emile Fharkon, Safaell's isolate.

When they neared the table, Ysella said, "Thank you so much. We expected crowded, but not this crowded."

"Premier Ulrich will address the Council. Some think he might say something about the explosions and the sewer mess," said Fharkon. "If he does, it won't be much. It never is."

"Has anything from that come before the Justiciary Committee?" asked Ysella.

Velle shook her head. "Not that the councilor has said. Explosions may be crimes, but the committee doesn't get oversight until after a conviction—that's if Security doesn't object." She paused, then asked, "You heard about Arthal, I take it?"

"That he was offered a position in Sudaen, at the Commerce Banque there?"

"He's already gone. Poor Erleen. Doing Councilor Hasheem's security by herself right now . . . with the demonstrations and that New Meritorist empie assassinating Councilor Aashtaan. How did you two take her down?"

"I didn't," said Ysella. "Steffan did."

"After Avraal slowed her down," added Dekkard.

"I wouldn't have wanted to be there," said Velle. "Arthal said she was the strongest empath he'd ever faced."

"Part of that was hatred-fired," replied Ysella. "The New Meritorists recruited someone who had a deep-seated hatred of the Council."

"Even so . . ." mused Fharkon.

"How long can Security keep their name from coming up?" asked Dekkard casually.

"Just about forever," replied Fharkon sardonically.

"As long as they can threaten the journalists, anyway," said Velle. "Or find and burn the New Meritorists' broadsheets . . . and seize unlicensed printing presses."

"There are still typewriters," said Ysella.

"Without a fast way to make copies, that's a lot of work for typewriters or pens," Velle pointed out.

"You have a point, Sumra," said Dekkard, "but I still wonder."

Fharkon laughed. "You're always wondering, Steffan, but wonder doesn't go far against Security."

Not right now . . . but how long can it continue? Rather than say that, Dekkard took another bite of the empanada, which was adequate and tasty, followed by a mouthful of rice, which was spicier than he liked and dry, leading to a swallow of café.

Before long, the four finished eating and left the cafeteria to go their separate ways.

Dekkard and Ysella took their position outside the councilors' dining room and were soon joined by Hasheem's isolate—Erleen Orlov—a modestly muscled woman who was only a few digits shorter than Dekkard and who moved like a panther.

"Are you going to get a partner any time soon?" asked Ysella.

"We're interviewing, but it doesn't look promising. Good empaths can do better outside government . . . and it's usually less dangerous. That's what they think, anyway. That's because no journalist ever writes about how many empies die in commercial work."

"And the councilor needs a very good empath," replied Ysella.

"More than that," answered Orlov, before gesturing. "Here they come."

The three moved forward into their duties.

In less than a sixth, Ysella and Dekkard had escorted Obreduur to the Council floor, where he had told them to return at a third past third bell unless he sent a messenger.

As they walked across the courtyard back toward the Council Office Building, Dekkard asked, "Do you think there will be anything in the afternoon edition of *Gestirn*?"

"I'm not hopeful, but we should look."

So, before they headed up the stairs to the second level, Dekkard stopped at the newssheet kiosk and bought a copy of the afternoon edition, then offered it to Ysella.

"No. You read it."

Dekkard did, quickly. "There's no mention of anything in Siincleer, no mention of Navy construction, and no mention of any engineering or any missing person."

"You can give the newssheet to Roostof when we get to the office."

Dekkard nodded.

At a third past three, Dekkard and Ysella were waiting outside the entrance to the Council Hall, but Obreduur didn't come out until just before fourth bell. He was shaking his head.

Neither Ysella nor Dekkard said anything until they were in the courtyard and not that close to others.

"Can you tell us what happened?" Dekkard finally asked.

"Almost nothing. Premier Ulrich spoke for over a bell. He reported in mind-numbing detail on the damage created by the Security Ministry fire, the exploded water lines, and the blocked sewers. He didn't say anything about who was behind it except that they were members of a secretive group that clearly wants to disrupt the government and social order of Guldor. When councilors asked questions, he replied in generalities, or said that Security was following up. He also said that the government would be introducing a supplemental authorization to pay for the repairs and damages. The rest was about necessary changes to the floor schedule and committee hearings." Obreduur shook his head again.

After several moments, he added, "Hasheem and Mardosh will also be looking into the possibilities of something being amiss with the naval construction in Siincleer. Mardosh has heard some disturbing rumors from the Shipfitters Guild there. Again, so far it's all rumor."

"Thank you, sir," said Ysella quietly.

"We'll do what we can."

Shortly after they returned to the office, Obreduur declared it was time to leave. Dekkard was more than willing, especially since he'd managed to finish his drafts and turn them over to Margrit for typing. He also knew that Ysella wanted to get back to the house to see if there were any messages from Emrelda.

The drive back to the house was especially quiet. After Dekkard dropped off Obreduur and Ysella at the portico, he didn't know whether to hope there was a message from Emrelda . . . or not. When he finished with the steamer and left the garage, he went looking for Ysella. He found her in the late-day shade of the portico.

Even before he could ask, she said, "There's nothing from Emrelda. Nothing."

"That means it will be tomorrow morning at the earliest before we hear anything."

"The heliograph is open for another two bells."

"That's true," Dekkard agreed, although he thought it unlikely that they'd find out anything before Duadi morning. *But you could be wrong. You have been wrong before.*

But no messages arrived by the time Dekkard climbed the stairs the last time, after exercising and practicing, and headed for bed.

44

While Dekkard didn't sleep all that well on Unadi night and woke early on Duadi, by the time he shaved, washed, and dressed—and made his way downstairs—early as it was, Ysella was already seated at the table and staring at the empty mug of café in front of her. The morning edition of *Gestirn* lay on the table beside her.

Without looking directly at Dekkard, she said, "The bottom of page two."

Dekkard immediately picked up the newssheet and began to read.

> . . . Halaard Engaard, Presidente of Engaard Engineering, died of an apparent heart attack just after inspecting a significant construction project in Siincleer late on Unadi afternoon. The project had been contracted to his corporacion by the Imperial Navy. The founder of the rapidly rising and creative engineering firm was reportedly traveling to the port city to look into the progress of construction and the disappearance of a senior engineer tasked with overseeing the project . . .

> Sources have reported that Engaard was also looking into irregularities in the construction . . . With Engaard's death and the disappearance of the engineer, Naval Procurement authorities are rumored to be looking into alternatives for remediation and continued construction of the project . . .

Dekkard quickly went through the rest of the newssheet. He found nothing else that might bear on Markell's disappearance or Engaard Engineering. He set the newssheet down.

"Emrelda's already on her way to Siincleer," said Ysella. "She left a note in the message basket here, sometime before dawn. She said that we could do more here than going with her. She also wrote that she doubted she'd find anything, but that she had to go because she just had to . . . and that if she didn't, she'd always worry that she could have done something . . ."

"I can understand that. Have you brought the article to Obreduur's attention?"

"I just got back from talking to him. He's always up early."

Dekkard knew that. He also knew that the councilor worked late, and at times he wondered if Obreduur even slept. "I'm sorry. Is there anything I can do?"

"Not any more than you are. We won't hear more from Emrelda until tomorrow sometime . . . if then."

"Do you think she'll find out anything?"

"If there's anything to find, she will. Knowing her, she'll have a letter from her Security chief and she'll show up in uniform."

For some reason, for all that Ysella had mentioned it, Dekkard hadn't really thought of Emrelda as a Security patroller type, possibly because she'd never said much about it. "She can discover more than we could."

"She could also get herself killed."

She may not care at this point. But what Dekkard said was "Toughs hired by corporacions wouldn't want to kill a Security patroller. On top of a missing engineer and a problematic heart attack, a murdered Security patroller looking into her husband's disappearance would be bound to get into the hands of reporters, and enough rank-and-file Security types would be willing to let that story see print. Even Siincleer Engineering wouldn't want that story."

"So all the evidence will vanish . . . if it hasn't already."

"They'll try. But I doubt anyone in the Siincleer organizations ever knew that Emrelda worked for Security. I don't see her mentioning that socially, especially because of Markell."

"You're right. She once said that people would get the wrong idea."

"That *might* mean that there are a few loose ends."

"We can always hope." Ysella's tone of voice was anything but hopeful.

Dekkard refilled Ysella's mug and then poured himself café. Only then did he sit down across from her. "Sometimes, it hurts to hope, but in the end, it hurts more not to."

"I'm not in the mood for philosophy, Steffan."

"Neither am I. If you give up hope, you're also giving up on that person." He took a sip of café and waited.

"You scarcely know Markell."

"I know Emrelda better, and she's the one you're really concerned about . . . and I worry about what concerns you. And that's not just because we're partners."

Ysella looked up. "Are you trying to make me feel better?"

"I'd like to, but that wasn't why I said that. I have a sister, remember? I care about her, and, even from hundreds of milles away, I worry about her. If she were in danger because she loved someone enough to risk her life . . ." Dekkard paused. "I think I understand, at least a little. That would be true even if we weren't partners. But we are, and I'm an isolate, and that means, sometimes, I have to tell you what I feel." *And hope you listen and really hear.*

After a long moment, Ysella said, "Thank you." She frowned momentarily. "You've always trusted me . . . without being able to sense my emotions directly."

"That's because you're not only good at what you do, but you've always been honest."

"Mostly." Ysella dropped her eyes for a moment.

Neither spoke.

The one who broke the silence was Hyelda, who appeared in the archway from the kitchen. "Ritter Obreduur wants to leave a sixth earlier than usual."

Dekkard turned. "Thank you, Hyelda."

"Don't look so serious, you two," returned the cook. "You're still young." Shaking her head, she headed back into the kitchen.

"We probably ought to eat." Dekkard looked directly into Ysella's gray eyes. "At least something." He managed a smile. "If not quince paste."

A hint of a smile was her response, although it vanished so quickly that Dekkard barely saw it. "I suppose you're right."

"About that, anyway." Dekkard reached for a croissant, then took a second, along with a slice of the quince paste.

"You two are here early," declared Rhosali as she entered the staff room.

"The councilor wants to leave earlier this morning," replied Dekkard, not about to go into the real reason they had both come down early. "What are you and Hyelda going to do when everyone else leaves in Summerend?"

Rhosali grimaced as she sat down with her café. "That's when we do all the deep cleaning. No one else is around to mess it up." She smiled mischievously after the last words.

"We're not that bad," Dekkard mock-protested.

"Wasn't saying it was you and Avraal."

"And after that? It doesn't take a month, does it?"

"Then I'll sleep late for a week or two."

Before long, Dekkard and Ysella had finished with their breakfast, and Dekkard headed up the back steps to finish getting ready. After that, he hurried down to the garage and had the Gresynt waiting under the portico even before Ysella and Obreduur appeared.

Once the two were inside the steamer, even before Dekkard started down the drive, Obreduur said, "Councilor Hasheem and Councilor Mardosh will be helping me look into what happened to your sister's husband and to Sr. Engaard, and what other corporacions might be involved. I didn't mention her or the relationship, only that the disappearance of a senior engineer and the strange death of Sr. Engaard was most disturbing. Carlos Baartol is also following up with his contacts and several guilds."

Even before Obreduur finished, Dekkard realized that the councilor wasn't offering any hope about Markell.

"I appreciate that, sir," replied Ysella.

"There is a slight possibility that Sr. Roemnal may be found. Even if matters don't turn out optimally, what we learn should prove useful in reining in the increasing abuses of power by corporacions."

"If someone doesn't," replied Ysella evenly, "in the end the New Meritorists may destroy Guldor."

"That's what many of us fear," said Obreduur.

When neither Ysella nor Dekkard spoke, the councilor began writing.

Dekkard noted Ysella's tenseness and murmured, "Is there anyone nearby I'm not seeing?"

She shook her head before answering quietly, "Not so far, but I worry."

Understanding her concern, Dekkard paid even more attention to other steamers on the drive, especially when he turned onto Council Avenue.

As Dekkard eased the steamer to a stop at the entrance to the Council Office Building, he had the feeling that the day wasn't going to bring any answers, whether about Markell, Emrelda, the Commercers, or the New Meritorists.

45

As Dekkard had suspected, nothing beyond the normal routine occurred at the Council Office Building for the rest of Duadi, at least not for him or Ysella. Even the rain that poured down around midmorning was neither a drizzle nor a downpour. It was also a touch ashy, because the wind was out of the northwest and carried soot from inland manufactories.

On the drive back to the house, all that Obreduur said was "It will be days before I find out anything. Sometimes, waiting is the hardest part."

Until you actually receive the bad news you feared was always coming. Dekkard kept that thought to himself.

"Do you think anyone will find anything?" asked Ysella.

"I'd judge that there will be suggestive traces, but whether there will be more than that . . ."

Ysella nodded, but did not say more.

Once Dekkard garaged the steamer, he had to take a little more time wiping it down to remove the residue from the rain and then topping off the water and kerosene tanks. After that, he went to look for Ysella, but she wasn't in the staff room. As he was about to go to the back veranda, Rhosali appeared.

"Steffan, you got a package this afternoon. I put it on the side table in your room."

"Thank you." *A package?* His parents usually didn't send packages, but he couldn't think of anyone else. "Was there any return address on it?"

"Some place in Sudaen, I think."

"I appreciate your taking care of it." Dekkard managed a smile. Then, because it was so unusual, he immediately headed up to his room.

The package was on the side table and was the size of a stationery box, give or take a few digits, and wrapped in brown paper, secured with heavy brown paper tape. He immediately read the addresses, both written in impeccable script in black ink. The return address was:

M&ER
PR 3, Stop 51
Sudaen

The addressee was:

> *Sr. Steffan Dekkard*
> *763 Altarama Drive*
> *East Quarter*
> *Machtarn*

M&ER? For a moment, the initials didn't make sense. Then they did. He immediately left his room, closing the door behind him and walking down the short hall to Ysella's chamber, where he rapped gently on the door.

"Who is it?"

"It's Steffan. There's a package you need to see. Right now."

"I'll be there in a moment."

It seemed like several minutes before Ysella appeared. Dekkard noted a slight redness in her eyes, but wasn't about to say anything.

"You said there was a package?"

"It's in my room."

She frowned.

"You need to see it just the way I did. Rhosali said it was delivered to the house this afternoon. She put it on the table."

"Why are you being so mysterious? Who's it from?"

"I'm not. I didn't even want to touch it. You'll see why." Dekkard turned and walked toward his room.

After a moment, Ysella followed.

Dekkard opened his door and stepped back. "It's on the table. Take a good look at it."

He watched as she walked to the table and bent over. Her mouth opened, then closed. She looked at Dekkard. "This isn't some horrible joke, I hope."

"If it is, it isn't my doing. I'm just guessing, but is the return address that of your parents?"

"Theirs and Cliven's."

"Do you see why I wanted you to see it before I even touched it? Do you think we ought to open it with Obreduur present?"

"That would be a good idea. Since it's addressed to you, you carry it." As Ysella moved away from the table, she added, "You do keep your room very neat. That's not a surprise, but . . ."

"But?" asked Dekkard with a smile, picking up the package, which was heavier than it had looked.

"It's nice to have positive suspicions confirmed."

The two caught up with Obreduur as he looked about ready to go upstairs.

"What is it?"

"We don't know," replied Dekkard. "It could be very important, and that's why we didn't want to open it without you present. It's a package, addressed to me here, with the initials of Markell and Emrelda above her parents' address. The Imperial postal stamp is from Siincleer, and it's dated last Quindi."

Obreduur did not quite sigh. "Let's go to the study."

Once there, Dekkard set the package on the table, then took out one of his throwing knives and carefully slit the brown wrapping paper and the paper tape on one side with the sharpened tip of the knife, then eased out a silver and gold cardboard box, one designed to hold fifty sheets of Magnificat stationery, according to the legend on the top. Dekkard lifted the top and set it to the side. Inside was a letter, on top of folded sheets of thin paper.

Dekkard lifted the letter and read it.

17 Summerfirst 1266

Dear Steffan and Avraal—

I'm sending this to Steffan by Imperial Post while I have the time, and I don't think anyone here knows his connection to me or to you.

I've enclosed a copy of the main specs for the building as finalized by Engaard Engineering and accepted by the Engineering Division of the Naval Ministry and also a working copy of the specs being used by the construction manager. You can see that while every page of our specs identifies it as an accepted document, the working document is in a different style and the specifications differ significantly.

I'm supposed to meet with Halaard when he gets here on Unadi, but I thought it best to send copies just in case. I'm probably being slightly paranoid, but it can't hurt in case Siincleer Engineering and its parent corporacion are even less scrupled than they've so far proved to be.

The signature was that of Markell, and scripted below was the phrase "Tell Emrelda not to worry."

Dekkard handed the letter to Ysella, who held it so that she and Obreduur could read it.

After several moments, Ysella gently replaced the letter on top of the plans.

Dekkard swallowed, then said, "He actually named Siincleer Engineering."

"He did," agreed Obreduur. "Unfortunately, that doesn't prove they're behind it. They could even claim the working prints were forged. But the original specifications will be on file with the Naval Ministry, and I don't think they'll dispute that."

"What do we do now?" asked Ysella.

"Nothing, except let your sister know when she returns," replied Obreduur. "We need to see how the Navy and Siincleer handle the matter."

"This confirms that they were behind it," said Ysella.

"To us, to Emrelda, but not to anyone else," said Obreduur. "At best, the letter and the plans confirm that someone tried to sabotage the building. The letter strongly suggests that it wasn't Markell, because he was the designer and engineer and had everything to lose, and because he disappeared after posting this."

"So what do you suggest we do, besides wait?" asked Ysella.

"Don't you think we should wait until we hear from your sister?" asked Obreduur. "I assume she planned to appear in full uniform to talk to the Security patrollers in Siincleer. What she discovers or does not should inform what we do next."

"Can we do anything else?"

"I'll let Hasheem and Mardosh know we have proof that someone subverted the engineer by getting the construction manager to use altered plans and specifications." After a long pause, Obreduur looked to Dekkard. "Since it was sent to you, what do you plan to do with it?"

"Find someplace where it will be safe."

Obreduur turned to Ysella. "Your thoughts?"

"Do you have a safe? Neither of us does, and I don't trust banque safety vaults."

"I do have a sufficiently large safe. Bring the package and its wrapping and follow me . . ."

Dekkard put the top back on the stationery box, then eased the wrapping back over it and lifted the package.

As soon as Dekkard finished, Obreduur turned and led the way from the study out to the kitchen then down a narrow staircase to the basement, a basement whose walls, Dekkard knew, had been constructed of underwater concrete, a necessity in the porous damp soils of Machtarn.

Beside the provisions pantry door was a second door, which Obreduur opened, revealing a set of shelves containing large spice jars. The councilor did something and the spice shelves swung to the side, revealing a solid safe as tall as Obreduur.

Dekkard stopped and waited, as did Ysella.

After opening the safe, Obreduur took the box and the wrapping and eased them onto a lower shelf. Then he closed and locked the safe, after which he swung the spice shelves back into place and closed the closet door. "That should keep it secure until we decide how to use it."

"Do you have any idea . . . ?" asked Ysella.

"Only in a general way. If we can link this to Ulrich and the Commerce Party as another example of what happened in the Kraffeist Affair . . . and several smaller scandals that were covered up . . . it might help discredit the Commercers. We'll have to see what develops in the next week or so . . . and what Baartol, Hasheem, and Mardosh have come up with. And your sister, of course." After a pause, he added, "It won't be quick. Nothing effective ever is. It only seems that way because very few see all the preparation that goes into what appears to be a quick resolution. For those involved, it often seems agonizingly slow." He gestured toward the stairs up to the kitchen.

Dekkard led the way.

Once the three were back in the study, Obreduur said to Ysella, "I hope you will keep me informed of any developments involving your sister or her husband, and anyone who contacts you."

"We will," replied Ysella.

Dekkard just nodded.

Then he and Ysella left the study.

Once they were alone in the back hall, he asked quietly, "The portico?"

She just nodded.

Once they reached the portico, Dekkard turned to her. "What do you think? Honestly?"

"Obreduur doesn't think Markell's still alive. He thinks that Markell's disappearance and what's behind it can help change things, but he's not certain. He certainly doesn't want to cover it up." She paused, then said, "I never knew about the safe. I supposed he had one, but I never knew."

"His way of showing more trust in us, then?"

"Something like that. He's very sorry about Markell. Both the package and Markell's disappearance were surprises to him. He's much more worried about the Commercers than he was even a week ago."

"That could be because of the blatant nature of Siincleer Shipbuilding's attempt to destroy Engaard and his corporacion."

"It might be, but there's something more."

"Do you have any idea?"

Ysella shook her head.

"Then it has to be something he heard from Hasheem or Mardosh."

"Or something small he noticed that's indicative of something much larger. You two are alike in that."

That surprised Dekkard, since he'd never thought of comparing himself to Obreduur.

"Well . . . you are. So perhaps you should think about small things that mean more than they seem on the surface."

"I'll see what I can do," replied Dekkard dryly.

Ysella reached out and touched his shoulder momentarily. "I wasn't being critical. You can be so much more, Steffan."

The gentleness in her voice melted away anything he might have said. "I'm sorry. I didn't mean it the way it sounded. I just never thought . . ." He shook his head.

"You should. Why do you think Obreduur pushes you and gives you opportunities? He wouldn't if you weren't able." She looked toward the house. "We can't do anything more right now, can we?"

"Not that I can think of. We might be able to persuade Hyelda to find some lager and wine, though."

Ysella forced a smile. "Let's do that."

46

Lager, followed by a dinner of shrimp basil pasta, and chilled sliced fruit, left Dekkard in a more relaxed mood, enough that he read an issue of Obreduur's *History* magazine, which included an article on Joel Janhus, or rather his impact on the government of Argorn in the 1100s, when one Baron Luunh ridiculed anyone who contradicted him by calling them Janhusans. In one way, Dekkard found it hard to believe, because Janhus had been correct, and so had Luunh's critics. Yet anyone tarred with Janhus's name was unpatriotic.

Are all societies like that, where an accurate prophet of a coming unpleasant and unpopular truth is reviled down through history?

Even with that question in his mind, he slept decently and felt rested when he woke on Tridi. He still couldn't help but think there was more than the obvious message conveyed by historical perception of Joel Janhus. *Is what they all believe an illusion . . . or is history the illusion? Or are they both illusions?*

The New Meritorists weren't an illusion. But were they a real broad-based movement . . . or only the illusion of such a movement? *Are you seeing an illusion of something that isn't, or does Security have its own illusion, one that portrays a broader movement as the work of a handful of malcontents?*

Still, any group that could create simultaneous demonstrations in a half score cities, recruit empies and others willing to die to make their point, and that had the expertise to destroy the Security Ministry building and cut off water supplies and sewer trunk lines wasn't an illusion. All that suggested to Dekkard that, before long, the New Meritorists would try something else. With all those thoughts racing through his head, he washed and shaved, then dressed, and headed downstairs.

Since he was there before Ysella or Rhosali, he looked through *Gestirn,* but there was nothing mentioning Markell or Engaard, nor any demonstrations or the sewer mess. Dekkard shook his head, set down the newssheet, then poured his café and sat down, wondering if Emrelda had discovered anything and hoping she was safe . . . and would stay so, as much for Ysella's sake as for Emrelda's.

"You look pensive," said Ysella when she arrived a few minutes later.

"I am. Aren't you?"

"How could I not be? But we can't do anything right now." She poured her café and seated herself.

"Except our jobs," replied Dekkard.

"You'd rather do something else, Steffan?"

"No. I just wish . . ." He shook his head.

"Steffan . . . I can't read your mind or emotions. Just what do you wish?"

"That we could do more."

"So do I. We can't. All we can do is get better at what we do. You can do that by taking advantage of the opportunities Obreduur is giving you."

"So can you," he pointed out.

"Not so much as you can. I'm an empath, remember? The Great Charter forbids certain things to us."

Not that many. But saying that would only have been callous. "You wouldn't abuse your abilities." He took a bite of his quince-filled croissant.

"I might not, but how many empies have you seen who do?"

"Who do what?" asked Rhosali, almost bouncing into the staff room.

"We were talking about people who abuse their power," said Dekkard.

"Like too many Commercers?" replied Rhosali with an amused tone.

Ysella smiled briefly, then turned her attention to the single croissant that was her breakfast.

Before long, Dekkard was back in his room, arming himself with truncheon, gladius, and throwing knives. He also made sure he was wearing his staff pin on his grays, just in case he had to do any research. He still recalled the puzzled and slightly condescending attitude of the Council legalists' receptionist.

Then he went to get the Gresynt ready. While the sky was a hazy greenish gray, as it usually was when the wind blew from the north or east, he doubted that it would rain, but he had the steamer under the portico a good five minutes before Obreduur and Ysella arrived.

Once he dropped Obreduur and Ysella off, he didn't waste any time in parking the Gresynt. He checked it over before straightening up as he saw a Council Guard walking toward him, with another some fifteen yards away, but not moving. He wondered at the pair of guards, given that there were only a few additional guards outside the Council Office Building.

"Just a moment, sir. I need to see your passcard." The nearer Council Guard moved smoothly toward Dekkard.

Dekkard's eyes flicked to the black leather holster and immediately back to the face of the man who had to be an imposter. "Of course."

The false guard's hand darted toward the butt of the gun in the holster, but he never completed the draw because Dekkard's throwing knife went through his throat, and an instant later, Dekkard's truncheon slammed across his temple.

At that instant, and only for an instant, Dekkard saw an older and more tired face, yet it was somehow the same man, before it transformed back into the face of the dying man, but thousands of tiny lights comprised that face. Then the light image vanished, and the attacker pitched forward onto the asphalt at Dekkard's feet.

Dekkard froze for an instant before he looked around for the other figure in the greens of a guard, but the second man abruptly turned and started to run. Dekkard let him, instead yelling out "Guards! Guards!" before quickly returning his truncheon to his belt.

He stood very still, his hands open and visible for several minutes as he tried to determine what the face image in tiny, indeed infinitesimal, lights meant, and why he'd seen the same kind of image twice. He called again for guards and waited until two apparently genuine Council Guards approached.

"What is it?"

"The man on the asphalt . . . he's an imposter. He tried to kill me. There was another one, but he ran off."

"Who are you?" demanded the taller guard, his pistol still pointed at Dekkard.

"Steffan Dekkard, security aide and assistant economic specialist to Councilor Obreduur."

The guard's eyes took in the staff pin. While he lowered his pistol, he didn't holster it. "What happened here?"

"I dropped off the councilor and Security Aide Ysella at the main entrance. Then I drove here and parked. I'd just left the steamer . . ." Dekkard went on to describe what had happened.

When he finished, the shorter guard asked, "Why did you think he was an imposter?"

"I couldn't see the end of the barrel of his gun. Guard revolvers are long and the barrel protrudes. And he reached for the gun when I looked at his holster."

"He's not moving," said the taller guard.

"He's dead. I used a throwing knife on his throat and crushed his temple with my truncheon. The other imposter fled before I could do anything."

"Turn him over." The taller guard gestured to the other.

The shorter guard turned the corpse faceup, and a small semi-automatic pistol slipped from the dead man's hand. The throwing knife was still in place, if flattened to the side. There was blood everywhere.

"Never saw him before," said the shorter one.

"That's not any gun we use. Go get the guard captain. We'll wait here." The taller guard holstered his revolver and turned back to Dekkard. "I've got lots more questions. There's no point in asking them because the captain will want to know the same things." He paused. "I've seen you around."

"I've been with the councilor for two years. I've never had anything like this happen."

"Beats me," said the guard. "No offense, but why would anyone attack a security aide. It's dangerous . . . and . . . well . . ."

"It's not as though I'm a councilor or even a senior legalist," finished Dekkard.

Almost a sixth passed before the shorter guard returned with an older blond guard officer.

"This is Guard Captain Trujillo," said the returning guard.

"Steffan Dekkard, security aide and assistant economic specialist to Councilor Obreduur."

Trujillo nodded and continued to look at the dead man for several moments before he said, "Might I see your passcard?"

Dekkard handed it over, trying not to appear irritated.

Trujillo looked at the passcard and frowned, clearly thinking. Then he nodded again. "Dekkard? You were the one who caught that empie who killed the councilor, weren't you?"

"I was, Guard Captain."

Trujillo turned to the shorter guard. "Paarken . . . go on up to the councilor's office. Councilor Obreduur. Tell them what happened, and that it will be a bit before we finish going through the routine with his security aide." He returned Dekkard's passcard, not saying anything until Paarken was on his way toward the entrance to the Council Office Building. "Now . . . tell me what happened."

Dekkard repeated what had occurred.

When he finished, Trujillo asked, "Where did the other imposter go?"

"He ran to the northwest corner of the parking portico and then climbed the west wall. I couldn't see him after that."

Trujillo looked to the other guard. "Get Meurys, and the two of you go see what traces they left. Gather any evidence you find, if there is any."

Once the taller guard had left, Trujillo looked down at the body. "You're obviously good with a knife, even as close as you were."

"I practice most nights."

"Have you ever seen this man before?"

"Not that I'm aware. I certainly don't recognize him."

"We'll check him over once the cleanup team arrives. Unless I'm mistaken, there won't be anything that would identify him or who hired him—except for the pistol."

"The pistol?" asked Dekkard, although he had a good idea exactly what the guard captain meant.

"Certain groups favor certain weapons."

"That's a semi-automatic," said Dekkard. "That's how I knew he wasn't a guard."

Trujillo frowned. "Oh?"

"You all carry longer-barreled revolvers. I couldn't see the barrel protruding from his holster."

"You noticed that?"

"We're trained to notice everything, Captain."

"Why do you think the other man ran instead of attacking?"

"I have no idea," replied Dekkard honestly. "Maybe he was only a lookout. Maybe he left when he saw me take down the first man with a knife . . ."

The questions went on for more than two-thirds of a bell, by which time the cleanup guards arrived with a cart and examined and searched the dead man. As Trujillo had suspected, there was no evidence of any sort, except the gun. In the end, the guards wiped off Dekkard's throwing knife and returned it.

Once the other guards carted off the body, Dekkard asked, "You said the gun was evidence of a sort?"

"You brought down the renegade empie. She was associated with the demonstrators who carried the same kind of weapons."

Dekkard couldn't help but note the circumlocution, but did not remark on it.

"The only thing that makes sense is that they found out who you were and targeted you. You must be on their hit list."

"My name was never mentioned in the newssheets or elsewhere," Dekkard pointed out.

"Any group that can sneak a messenger into the Council Hall can discover who the isolate and empie were that subdued and captured her."

"Did you ever find out much about who sent her?"

"She fought the interrogation empaths so much that

the conflict shredded her mind. She died almost immediately."

"That's unfortunate." Dekkard thought that a less violent form of interrogation might have revealed much more, but there was little point in saying that, either.

"Very much so. A gentler approach would have provided more information, if indirectly. I was not consulted." Trujillo smiled. "I'll deny that, but you already understand as much."

"Just as you're required not to ever name the group behind the demonstrators and the so-called renegade empie?"

"Of course." Trujillo glanced toward the Council Office Building and then to the darkening clouds to the northeast. "I'll walk across the street with you. We'll let your councilor know if we discover more. I don't think we will, but you never know."

After leaving Trujillo, Dekkard headed up the staff staircase, still going over what had happened.

As soon as he entered the office, Karola gestured toward the door to the inner office, and Ysella rose from her desk.

Dekkard smiled raggedly. "I wouldn't have thought otherwise."

He and Ysella walked into Obreduur's office, and she closed the door.

Obreduur remained seated behind his desk and gestured to the chairs. "You need to sit down. Tell us what happened. All of it, and take your time."

"It all started a few moments after I closed up the Gresynt . . ." Dekkard then related the entire episode, including all the questions and statements from Guard Captain Trujillo. When he finished, he just waited.

"That's quite a morning for you," said Obreduur. "Who do you think is behind it?"

"Despite Captain Trujillo's words and apparent beliefs, I doubt that it's the New Meritorists. I suspect they don't even know who I am. Nor do they care that much. I think someone else is behind it, someone who wants me out of the way, for whatever reason, and wants to pin the blame on the New Meritorists. Why they're after me, I don't know, because I'm not anyone of import. I don't see how it can be because of Emrelda and Markell, either."

"You're not quite as insignificant as you profess, Steffan," returned Obreduur. "And if we and you can avoid or forestall further attempts on your life, you may well be even less so in times to come. You're also correct about Markell, but it's clear that Markell's efforts have uncovered another insidious effort on the part of key Commercers."

"What? That they want to control all military engineering projects?"

"Can you imagine a better way to make the Navy, in particular, beholden to them, especially if there are no other engineering corporacions capable of handling such projects? Then the Council will have to pay whatever they charge."

"Can't the Council look into those situations?" asked Dekkard.

"In theory," said Obreduur sardonically.

Dekkard understood—not unless the Premier and the party in power were so inclined. But since Obreduur hadn't answered his main question, he asked again, "Why me?"

"Because you're getting more and more capable, and because you and Avraal are extraordinarily good at protecting me."

"And because," added Ysella, "he's the only reason why the Craft Party has gained seats in the Council, and the Commercers know it and fear him."

"You're not even floor leader," said Dekkard quietly.

"My strongest skills don't lie in parliamentary maneuvering," replied Obreduur. "Haarsfel is much better at that than I'll ever be."

"So long as he stays alive," added Ysella, looking at Dekkard. "That means we both have to stay alive."

"Avraal is perhaps overreaching—"

"No, I'm not . . . sir."

Obreduur offered what Dekkard could only interpret as an embarrassed smile, then said, "In any event, you're safe. That brings up another possibility. If someone associated indirectly with the Commercers is behind the attack, in the next few days you may be offered, seemingly out of concern, a lucrative and safer position with a well-established corporacion."

"After attacking me? Why?"

"Because they really don't care whether you're dead or whether you move on and aren't protecting the councilor," replied Ysella, almost tartly.

"They'll use nettles or niceties, whatever works," added Obreduur. "If this happens, whatever your decision is, I'd like to ask that you tell them something to the effect that you hadn't thought about it earlier, but that recent events have made you think the matter over, and that you'd like a few days to consider it."

"That makes sense." Dekkard nodded, then said, "There's one other thing. Even if the Commercers are behind it, they've effectively shifted the blame to the New Meritorists."

"That may be for the best. Letting them know what we've learned won't serve us well right now." Obreduur smiled again, this time pleasantly. "Is there anything else I should know?"

"I've told you everything about this that I can recall, sir."

"Then we all need to get back to work."

Dekkard and Ysella stood, then turned and left the office.

Once the door was closed, Karola looked to Dekkard. "Are you all right, Steffan?"

"Outside of the surprise that anyone would attack a mere security aide, I am." He smiled. "But thank you. I appreciate the thought very much."

"I don't understand all of this," replied Karola. "It's like everything changed. People are shooting at the guards and councilors, and empies are attacking coun-

cilors and trying to shoot aides, and aides are missing."
She shook her head.

"It's a different time," said Dekkard. "We're just living at one of the few times when it happens that way." *But maybe all times are like this, except no one recognizes it.*

He walked back to his desk and the small stack of waiting letters and petitions.

47

The Tridi afternoon editions of *Gestirn* and *The Machtarn Tribune* had no stories about Markell or Engaard, and there were no announcements from Premier Ulrich.

Then, just after Dekkard and Ysella returned to the house that afternoon and he'd finished with the Gresynt, when he entered the staff area from the garage Ysella informed him that there was no message or letter from Emrelda, finishing by saying, ". . . means that she's all right."

"Because the murder or disappearance of a Security dispatcher looking for her missing husband wouldn't be a story that Security would suppress or that the newssheets could resist printing?" asked Dekkard.

Ysella nodded. "She also may not learn much . . . but . . ."

"Learning too much might be dangerous for her?"

"I worry about that."

"Exposing what powerful people don't want known is always dangerous," Dekkard said.

"All we can do is our best . . . and wait."

"I think we've said that before," said Dekkard.

"Right now . . . we'll just have to hope. I'll see you at dinner." She turned and headed for the back staircase.

Dekkard returned to the garage to practice with the throwing knives . . . and then sharpen them . . . and his gladius. He couldn't help feeling that he might need both in the days ahead.

A little over two bells later, Dekkard and Ysella had just seated themselves for dinner at the staff table when Hyelda entered to join them and said, "Ritter Obreduur said that he'd like a word with you two later this evening. He'll let you know."

Dekkard and Ysella exchanged glances.

"Most likely—" began Dekkard.

"More than likely," interrupted Ysella, "but we'll have to see."

Rhosali shook her head. "You two are so secretive. No one's ever going to ask us"—she nodded to Hyelda—"about what you said."

"Who'd believe us, if they did?" added the cook.

"They'd be smart to believe you over some of the councilors," said Dekkard cheerfully.

"That won't ever happen," replied Hyelda.

Dekkard looked down at his platter—cold sesame noodles with chicken and cucumbers, garnished with toasted almonds—then smiled. "This looks good."

"Ritten Obreduur requested it."

"I'm glad she did," added Ysella.

Dekkard took a sip of the pale lager, then began to eat. Across from him, so did Ysella.

After dinner, Dekkard and Ysella walked down the drive to the portico.

"You know I don't like waiting, Steffan," she said quietly.

"I know." Dekkard debated about telling her the way he'd seen the attacker's face as the man was dying, then decided against it. The last thing Ysella needed to worry about was whether her partner was beginning to lose his mind. But it still bothered him.

"You look worried," she said.

"I am. The Commercers and Security are underestimating the New Meritorists, and I'm not sure that many of the Crafter or Landor councilors understand how much the Commercers are subverting the Great

Charter. Obreduur's working on it, and Hasheem seems to understand, but does Haarsfel?"

"Not fully, I think," admitted Ysella, "but there's only so much Obreduur can do."

"Even if the Crafters could win enough seats to reach thirty, would even four Landors support a Craft premier?"

"At the moment, I have my doubts. It's also unlikely that enough Landors will stop backing the Commerce Party to require new elections. The Imperador certainly won't call new elections unless something major and unforeseen occurs, and it's almost two years before the limitation clause would require it."

"So we just keep working."

"Unless you can find a way to totally discredit the Commercers," replied Ysella.

"The New Meritorists are more likely to do that."

Ysella shook her head. "That will give the Commercers a mandate to use more force."

"Until they do and massacre a lot of innocents," suggested Dekkard.

"I have my doubts about people being that intelligent."

"Do you think Emrelda will discover anything?"

"She'll discover something. It's more likely to be circumstantial, and not enough to prove anything conclusively. The corporacions are too clever for that."

Dekkard had the same feeling.

Less than a bell later, Obreduur summoned them to his study, then waited until they were seated before speaking. "I've received some information from Carlos Baartol. He said that if I could get ahold of the altered building plans, or at least a sheet, that would tell something about who provided them. Apparently, most of the major engineering concerns have their own specifications for planning paper. It wouldn't be conclusive, but it might help."

"You'd like to take a sheet of the altered plans and see if he can determine where it came from?" asked Ysella.

"Only if you approve." Obreduur looked from Ysella to Dekkard.

Dekkard turned to Ysella. "I think it's worth a try, but it's your decision."

"Just a single sheet," declared Ysella, "and the one that has the least revealing information on it."

"I'd already thought of that. I can't send it to him until tomorrow morning."

"That delay won't hurt Emrelda." Ysella's voice was flat. "Is there anything else?"

"Councilor Hasheem mentioned the financial destruction of a machine works that developed a better punch-card lathe. Guldoran Ironway now owns the rights to and the equipment of that firm. By itself . . ." Obreduur shrugged.

"But if you can find more examples?" asked Dekkard.

"It will help in dealing with the Commercers."

But not with finding out about Markell.

"Thank you," said Ysella.

"I wish I could offer more, Avraal," said Obreduur kindly.

"You're doing what you can. No one can ask more."

"Carlos also sent me some information about Councilor Aashtaan. For now, it should stay between the three of us." Obreduur paused.

"Yes, sir," replied Dekkard.

Ysella nodded.

"Aashtaan had a series of . . . shall we call them . . . liaisons . . . with a young woman. She disappeared without a trace. The empath who killed him was her sister."

"Then the New Meritorists weren't involved at all?" asked Dekkard.

Obreduur shook his head. "Not initially. She apparently sought them out."

"That explains why she could kill him," said Ysella. "She truly hated the bastard. It's not exactly without precedent. What do you think was behind the Silent Revolution?"

All Dekkard really knew about the Silent Revolution

was that, after a series of senior councilors had died "mysteriously" over the course of a year and a half, the Council had voted to change the suffrage requirements to include women working outside the home and the wives of working men, as well as all adults over fifty who had worked and paid taxes for more than thirty years. The laws governing household violence had also been revised and strengthened, and any prohibition on women entering any organization or guild had been declared void. While it was known that women empaths had been behind the deaths, little more had ever been made public, at least not anywhere that Dekkard knew.

"This is somewhat different," said Obreduur mildly.

"That's why it's so dangerous," replied Ysella. "The Silent Revolution didn't change the basis of the Great Charter. Using unhappy women empaths to attack . . ." She shook her head.

"That's another reason why we need to stop the New Meritorists," suggested Dekkard.

"I'd agree," replied Obreduur. "I'd be happy to see any solid suggestions."

While Obreduur's voice was mild, even Dekkard had the feeling the councilor was displeased. *As if he's trying everything he thinks is workable . . . and you just say it has to be sooner, without any plan.*

"I don't have any new suggestions, sir. It's just that the situation is more urgent than I realized."

"I'd also agree with that, Steffan." Obreduur's tone of voice was warmer. "We can talk about it later." He stood.

So did Dekkard and Ysella, and the two walked from the study, down the hall, and through the kitchen to the staff room.

"Would you like to talk some more?" asked Dekkard.

"You're kind, Steffan, but I need to think. I'll see you in the morning."

"In the morning, then." He let Ysella leave the staff room first, then waited until she was up the staircase before following her.

48

F urdi morning brought no messages from Emrelda, not by the time Dekkard drove the Gresynt out from under the portico, heading for Altarama Drive. Ysella, understandably, remained tense, although neither she nor Dekkard saw or sensed anyone following them. After Dekkard dropped off Obreduur and Ysella, he was more cautious than usual when he parked the steamer and then walked across the street, but no one even came close to him.

Only a few petitions and letters awaited him, at a glance less than ten, and he settled behind his desk and began to read. As the morning progressed, and he made his way through the letters, he did notice a flurry of messengers.

Slightly after midmorning, Obreduur opened his door and looked in Ysella's direction. "I'll be meeting for lunch with Hasheem and Floor Leader Haarsfel. So you two can escort me there, eat at the cafeteria, and then meet me to escort me to the Waterways Committee meeting."

Obreduur returned to his inner office. At a third before noon, he reappeared, and Dekkard and Ysella immediately escorted him from the office and down the main center staircase, keeping to one side to allow the messengers the other.

As they stepped out of the Council Office Building and into the damp and oppressive summer heat, Ysella said quietly, "Someone's tracking us. They're far enough back that I can't identify them."

"Is there a sense of danger?"

"Not now," murmured Ysella.

Dekkard looked around, but while there were scattered staffers on the walkway, and several councilors with security aides, none were close enough to identify. When they entered the Council Hall, the main corridor contained more people, from guards and messengers to a few councilors and more than a few staffers.

"Are they still following?" asked Obreduur.

"If they are," replied Ysella, "right now they're too far away for me to sense them. We'll stay close until you're well inside the dining room."

"I'd appreciate that."

Once Obreduur had entered the comparative sanctuary of the dining area, Dekkard turned to Ysella. "What do you sense?"

"Just emotional chaos. Nothing focused."

"Then we should go eat."

She nodded, and the two headed for the staff cafeteria. As they neared the entrance, a tall brawny figure turned and smiled—Jaime Minz, Dekkard realized, along with a shorter but muscular woman, although she was anything but short, except in comparison to Minz, because she was only a few digits shorter than Dekkard and carried herself more like an isolate than the empath she most certainly was.

"Steffan!" declared Minz heartily. "It's good to see that you're still around."

"So far," replied Dekkard.

"That's good to hear. Have you met my other security half, Cherlyssa Maergan?"

"I'm pleased to meet you," said Dekkard.

"We've met," said Ysella a trace too politely.

"We have," replied Maergan in a similar tone.

"Does the Premier have any surprises for the Council?" asked Dekkard. "More than the usual, I mean."

"I'd be the last to know," said Minz cheerfully. "I doubt it. Surprises reflect bad politics and worse government. It's so much better to do things so quietly that no one notices . . . or cares."

Dekkard nodded. "There's something to be said for that." *Especially for those who are devious and underhanded.*

"It's good to see you both," said Minz. "If I don't see you before recess, do enjoy it."

"We'll definitely try," returned Dekkard.

"So should you, Jaime," added Ysella.

"I'm always trying," replied Minz. "You should know that, Avraal." With a broad smile, he turned, and he and Maergan continued along the main corridor toward the floor and the committee rooms.

As soon as Minz and Maergan were out of earshot, Ysella said quietly, "Obreduur couldn't have handled it any better. I'm also fairly sure that Maergan was the one tracking us. Or me and Obreduur, because she couldn't track you. She doesn't much care if we know."

"Neither does Minz. Seemed as if it was all to deliver that pleasantry. Or message."

Ysella paused, then said in an even lower voice, "Have you done something I don't know about? It sounds like more than a few people don't want you around."

Dekkard shook his head. "You know everything I've done. Getting rid of me is just a step toward getting rid of Obreduur. He was right about that."

"He needs to know about this, but not until he returns to the office."

Dekkard nodded.

Ysella led the way to the cafeteria line, where she chose what looked to be a casserole of rice, mushrooms, and chicken. After looking at the spiced ribs and the pasta salad, Dekkard followed her example. Since all the tables for two were taken, they settled at a four-top.

Both ate several mouthfuls before Ysella said quietly, "Laurenz Korriah is heading toward us, along with Shaundara Keppel."

"Would you mind if we join you?" asked the balding burly Korriah, looking to Ysella.

"Please do. I haven't seen either of you in months. How are things with you?"

Korriah and Keppel slid into seats across from each other, and Korriah said, "I was actually wondering about Steffan. I heard someone impersonating a Council Guard attacked him the other day."

"Did that come up with the Security Committee staff?" asked Dekkard.

"How else would we know? Are you all right?"

Korriah sounded truly concerned, Dekkard had to admit, and the other isolate had always been straight with him. "I'm fine. There were two, and the second one got away."

"And the first one?"

"He had a semi-automatic pistol. I didn't have time to try for a capture. He's dead. No identification."

Korriah shook his head. "Was he looking for you?"

"All he did was ask for my passcard. He didn't look quite right, and he went for his gun. I was faster. The other one sprinted off when I yelled for the Council Guards."

"Semi-automatic pistol? Like certain demonstrators."

"And others," added Ysella.

Keppel lifted her eyebrows and looked at Ysella.

"Sometimes, it's easier to see what people put in front of you."

Korriah nodded slowly. "That's a good point."

"Very good," added Keppel. "Especially now."

Korriah turned back to Dekkard. "Do you know why someone might be after you?"

"No more than all the other security aides working for Craft councilors."

"Strange how Commerce councilors get killed or into trouble," said Keppel, "but how it's always security aides for Craft councilors."

"That might be because Commerce councilors don't have security aides who are as good," replied Ysella in a voice cheerfully sarcastic.

Korriah grinned. "I like that. It might even be true. What about Landors?"

"Landors must have good security aides, but it doesn't matter as much because no one wants to antagonize either their councilors or aides," said Ysella.

"For now, anyway," added Dekkard.

Korriah turned back to Dekkard. "When do you think that will change?"

"I have no idea. I only know that things always change. You've got more experience than I do. When do you think they will?"

Korriah shrugged. "I don't have any better idea than you. Except that if the demonstrations get worse, some folks might get nastier."

"Security, you mean?" suggested Ysella.

"Don't you think so?"

"They've been quietly strong, even brutal, already," said Dekkard.

"It could get worse," said Keppel.

Korriah glanced at her, not quite disapprovingly.

"Minister Wyath believes in strict adherence to the law," continued Keppel. "So does Premier Ulrich."

"I've heard that Ulrich believes in more than that," said Dekkard. That wasn't quite true; it was more that Minz's behavior implied that.

Korriah glanced around, then lowered his voice. "That's true, but it's not wise to say it in public."

Dekkard smiled warmly. "I appreciate the caution, but you and Shaundara aren't public."

"Thank you. How is that rice mess the rest of you are eating?"

"Less liable to burn out our guts than those ribs," replied Dekkard. "I don't have your porcelain-lined stomach."

"Neither do I," added Keppel.

From there the conversation was about food.

After finishing their meal, Dekkard and Ysella made their way back to the councilors' dining room. They waited less than a sixth before Obreduur walked swiftly out and toward them. "Excellent lunch. I'll tell you about it later."

As they headed toward the committee room, Ysella said quietly, "Sir, when we're back in the office, we also need a few minutes to tell you about an interesting encounter."

"I'm not sure we need any more of those," murmured Obreduur. "Just wait for me outside the committee room. This will be a short meeting."

Dekkard had his doubts, but this time Obreduur was right, and he rejoined them in less than two-thirds of a bell—one of the shortest committee sessions Dekkard could recall.

Once they reached the office, Dekkard let Obreduur and Ysella precede him into the councilor's private chamber. He followed and closed the door.

"You tell me about your encounter first," said Obreduur, settling behind his desk and gesturing to the chairs.

After both staffers were seated, Dekkard nodded to Ysella.

"Someone was tracking us," began Ysella. "I'm fairly certain it was Cherlyssa Maergan. She's Premier Ulrich's empath. She and his isolate Jaime Minz just *happened* to run into us . . ." She described the brief encounter, relating Minz's words verbatim.

"He actually said that? That it was good to see that you're still around?"

"He did," confirmed Dekkard.

"That's more than a little disturbing."

"What, if anything, should we do?" asked Dekkard.

"Be very careful . . . and survive. Outlasting the bastards is often the optimal survival strategy. Revenge for the sake of revenge is a fool's game."

"Just . . . survive?"

"Steffan . . . in the end, survivors write the laws, and write the histories. They're also still around to seek and wield power. If you don't survive, you can't do even a Three's curse on anything." After a moment, Obreduur said, "Now, let me tell you about my meeting with Floor Leader Haarsfel and Councilor Hasheem. Haarsfel said that Security Minister Wyath believes the New Meritorists are planning demonstrations during the Summerend recess. Ulrich told Haarsfel that if any councilor knows anything about even the possibility of such an event, failure to report it would be considered treason."

"Why would he say that?" asked Ysella. "Councilors can't be tried by the Justiciary for anything except high crimes. Only the Council can discipline its members."

"That just might be why he used the word 'considered.'" Obreduur turned to Dekkard. "You've done better than the rest of us in predicting what they might do. What do you think?"

"I'd have to agree with Minister Wyath. I'd already thought that they might try something during Summerend. The Council is scattered, and a Council response would take more time if necessary. But what exactly they might be planning . . . I have no idea."

"If you do come up with some ideas, please let me know immediately. If there's nothing more . . . ?"

Dekkard and Ysella exchanged glances. Then she said, "No, sir."

They both stood and made their way out of the inner office. Once outside, with the door closed, Dekkard accompanied Ysella to her desk, where he said quietly, "Things keep getting worse, faster than he expected."

"But not faster than you expected?" she replied, equally quietly.

"Faster than I thought at first. Too much is evident, and when that much is evident, there's even more we don't see, because so much is done quietly."

"That's a good point. Why didn't you bring it up with him?"

Dekkard offered an abashed grin, not quite meeting her eyes. "Because I didn't think of it until now."

"I'll tell him about your insight on the way to the steamer. Now . . . I don't know about you, but I have a few things to draft."

"So do I." Dekkard returned to his desk and picked up a pen.

At a third before fourth bell, Dekkard finished up the last of the draft replies he'd been working on, a response to an inquiry about whether waterway fees would be increased, and headed from the office down the staff stairs on his way to get the steamer. He was almost to the main doors to the west when a blond woman with a pleasant smile gestured to him.

Dekkard immediately recognized Frieda Livigne and smiled in return, then stopped and waited for her. "Good afternoon, Frieda."

"The same to you, Steffan. I'm glad I ran into you."

Although Dekkard doubted that the meeting was exactly by chance, he replied, "Oh? Why might that be?"

"Because you and Ysella know a number of the Crafter security teams. I recently got word that Gresynt, Limited, is looking for someone to be assistant director of security for their Oersynt facilities. They'd prefer someone with security and political experience, as well as a craft and artisan background. I know that you said you weren't interested some time ago, but I thought you might be able to let others know."

"I did." He paused. "Times change . . . or maybe we all do over time."

Livigne frowned. "You'd be interested?"

"I don't know. I never wanted to be just a security aide for the rest of my life. I think you know that. But . . . with everything that's happened recently, I've been thinking."

Livigne put her hand to her mouth, in apparent surprise, but a gesture that looked almost practiced to Dekkard. "Oh! I'm so stupid. You were the one that was attacked yesterday."

"It's strange," replied Dekkard. "In one way, it seems like it just happened, and in another, it feels like weeks ago." He shook his head.

"In something like the Gresynt position, you wouldn't be just a security aide. There'd be very little of that, just escorting corporacion higher-ups on occasional facility tours. Most of the job is involved with keeping facilities safe from intrusion and in complying with security rules. Do you think you'd be interested?"

"I don't know," Dekkard repeated. "I want to wait

until the Summerend recess when I have time to think it over."

"If you're thinking of moving on, don't wait too long," replied Livigne. "The really good opportunities aren't open forever."

"You're probably right," said Dekkard, "but I don't like making major changes on impulse."

She smiled again, knowingly. "Most good security types don't. That's why they're good at it. Whether you're interested or not, I'd appreciate it if you'd tell Ysella and pass it on."

"I can do that. Thank you for letting me know." Dekkard inclined his head and then made his way out of the building and across the street to the covered parking, his eyes scanning the parked steamers.

Even with the delay occasioned by his brief meeting with Livigne, he had to wait outside the building, noticing that the Council still was maintaining a greater number of guards around the entrance. He also saw darker clouds building up to the south, suggesting a heavy rain or even waterspouts in the ocean south of the city. Almost a sixth passed before Obreduur and Ysella entered the Gresynt.

As Dekkard guided the steamer out and onto Council Avenue, Obreduur said, "Avraal relayed your astute observation about the subterranean nature of occurrences in Guldor, but do you think it's as applicable to the New Meritorists?"

Dekkard considered Obreduur's question for several moments before replying. "I think they've gone to more public actions simply because less public ones get hushed up. But it took a lot of effort to organize the demonstrations and the explosions, fire, sewer blockage, and none of that was visible until the events themselves."

Obreduur fingered his chin. "Have you thought more about what they might do?"

"I have, but I don't have any more or better ideas, except that, whatever it is, it will result in people getting killed, probably innocents shot by patrollers and Security, or military units."

"Why do you think that?" asked Obreduur.

"There was little public reaction to the destruction of the ministry building, the water-main destruction, or the sewer blockage. Those acts didn't generate public outrage. I don't think they were aimed at that, but at government and the Council. But by minimizing and effectively hiding the name of the New Meritorists, Security and the Council have kept people from associating them with destructive acts. So . . . what happens if there are wide-scale and disruptive demonstrations, and a few New Meritorists shoot at government forces . . . and the return fire kills lots of innocents? I could be wrong, but I think many people will believe the government overreacted."

Obreduur said nothing for a time. "You're saying that the Security fire, the water-main destruction, and the sewer blockage were all designed to make the Imperador, Security, and the Council angry without upsetting most people."

"I'd say that they had two purposes. The first I said before. That was to show that they could strike and disrupt things without being anticipated. The second is what I just suggested."

Obreduur shook his head. "That makes sense, but did they actually think it out or stumble into it?"

"I have no idea. It just makes sense to me." *Just like whatever they do next will make sense . . . after they've done it.*

"Most people aren't that logical."

"You did call them brilliant idiots, as I recall."

"They might just be academics, except I'm certain that Security has infiltrated every university in Guldor. So, if they are, they're keeping their academic duties and their political activism so separate that Security hasn't been able to connect them. I find that unlikely."

"So do I, sir, but I'm not exactly an expert on universities." Dekkard did have his own idea, but he wanted to run it by Ysella before telling Obreduur. "Oh . . .

there's something else. You said that someone might hint at or offer a better job outside the Council. You were right . . ." Dekkard quickly related his encounter with Frieda Livigne.

After Dekkard finished, the councilor replied, "They didn't waste much time. Your saying that you needed Summerend recess to think it over was a good reply."

"She may think that I'm still saying no, but more politely."

"You didn't say no this time," pointed out Ysella. "That should tell her that you're reconsidering."

"Or that I'm not quite as naïve as I used to be."

"We'll just have to see," said Obreduur. "Remember, you can leave at any time, and I'll give you the highest recommendation."

"That's kind of you, but I don't have any intentions to leave." *Not after seeing what goes on in the large corporacions.*

"I have to say I appreciate that," replied Obreduur. "Now . . . if you'll excuse me . . ." He returned to writing.

After dropping off the councilor and Ysella under the portico, Dekkard garaged the Gresynt and began his routine chores with the steamers.

Ysella eased inside the garage as Dekkard was doing the last polishing of the windscreen. Cloth in hand, he looked up.

"Just finish up. Then we'll talk."

Several minutes later, he walked over to her, noticing that she held an envelope and a sheet of stationery. "A letter from Emrelda?"

She handed the letter to him. "You can read it. I'd like your thoughts."

He immediately began to read the missive, addressed this time just to Avraal.

I told you it would be difficult to find hard evidence. That has proved to be true. No one can recall seeing Markell after Quindi evening, the seventeenth, but he was not in his room on the morning of the eighteenth, and nothing appeared to be missing except Markell and what he was wearing, including his wallet and engineering timepiece.

. . . the Siincleer Security patrollers have been incredibly nice and helpful. They're not exactly on the best of terms with the guards at the various facilities owned and operated by Siincleer Shipbuilding. I've gotten the impression from them that SS has ties with less than reputable professionals both in Siincleer and Machtarn, but the station head of the west post— that's the closest to the facility Markell designed and engineered—has hinted, very indirectly, the investigations into those ties never get anywhere. That may be the most I discover, just like what happened that one time with Seek and Find when we were so much younger . . .

Dekkard pointed to the last line he'd read. "That means something else, doesn't it?"

Ysella smiled. "I've always said you were good. It does. It means she has something, but doesn't know what it means or where it leads."

"And she doesn't trust anyone there enough to let them know what she's discovered."

Ysella nodded.

Dekkard returned to the letter.

. . . so unless I find out more, I'll be driving back on Quindi, and I'll be working the next weeks straight through, including enddays, to make it up to those who covered for me while I've been in Siincleer. If the timing works out, I'll stop by on my way home. Otherwise, we can get together as we can on Findi.

The signature was simply "Emrelda."

Dekkard handed the single sheet back to Ysella. "Your thoughts?"

"She's found more than she's saying. She's upset

and doesn't want to show it, and she's fairly certain Markell's dead. That's why it's so . . . unemotional."

"That's how I read it."

"The conditioned Landor response?" he asked gently. "Or just the way you both handle really bad news?"

"Both, I think. Father's never liked it when we showed emotion. He'd just say that he couldn't talk to us when we were 'like that.' Mother said any emotion except quiet happiness should stay behind closed doors." Ysella swallowed, then said, "I don't want to talk any more about Emrelda and Markell. Not now. We'll talk about it after we see what she's discovered and if it fits with what Markell sent you."

"Us. He just addressed it to me."

"That's because he saw immediately what you really are." She shook her head slowly. "You'd be totally wasted if you spent the rest of your life just in security, even in a position like the one Frieda Livigne dangled in front of you."

"I don't know that. I do know I'd be bored out of my mind."

"We can't have that." Ysella forced a smile.

Dekkard wanted to hold her, just put his arms around her. He didn't, knowing that would be an intrusion, and instead said, "I think you need a glass of wine and some quiet time. I'll keep you company . . . quietly."

"Thank you." Her words were low.

49

The rain that Dekkard had predicted arrived sometime during the night and was still beating down heavily when he woke on Quindi to a dismal gray-green dawn. When he got to breakfast, *Gestirn* held no news about Markell or about the Council. Ysella arrived for her café and breakfast looking drawn, and the quince paste was gone, again replaced by tomato jelly. The drive to the Council Office Building was slow through the pelting rain, and even with the protection of an umbrella, Dekkard's trousers got more than a little damp below the knees from the brief dash from the covered parking to the roofed entrance to the building. Part of the dampness was because he held the umbrella high enough to look in all directions.

The rain offered little respite from the heat, so that even the inside main corridor of the Council Office Building felt like the anteroom to a steam bath. The staff stairs weren't any better, Dekkard reflected, as he made his way up them.

The rain was the most interesting part of a long workday. There were no committee meetings and no Council sessions, and no conferences with Obreduur . . . and not even any visitors, not that there were ever many. Dekkard spent the day drafting responses. While he worried about Ysella and Emrelda, there was little he could do about either, and by the time fourth bell neared he was definitely glad to leave his desk and fetch the Gresynt. The rain had finally slowed to a drizzle, which meant that it was warmer and the air was stickier, but that he didn't get as wet.

On the drive back to the house, Obreduur said nothing. After dropping Obreduur and Ysella off under the portico, Dekkard garaged the Gresynt, but didn't wipe it down, since it was still drizzling, and he and Ysella would be escorting the family to services at the East Quarter Trinitarian Chapel in little more than a bell.

Ysella met him as he was leaving the garage. "Emrelda was here much earlier. She left a note." As she finished speaking, she handed Dekkard a single sheet of paper.

He read it quickly.

Avraal—
    I didn't sleep very well last night. So I got up well before dawn and started driving. I got here at a third

past first bell. There was no point in waiting until fifth bell for you and Steffan.

I'll pick you both up at third bell tomorrow morning, and then we can discuss matters.

The hurried signature was that of Emrelda.

"What now?" asked Dekkard as he returned the brief note to Ysella. "Go find Obreduur and tell him immediately?"

"Not at the moment. I was going to tell him as soon as I read this, but he had just marched Nellara into his study and closed the door. Whatever it is, I wouldn't want to be in her shoes at this moment, and I don't think it's a good idea to interrupt. Not when a bell won't make any difference. I can always tell him before he gets into the steamer for services."

"I think you're right." He paused. "Do you have any idea what Nellara did?"

"No, but Ritten Obreduur usually deals with problems with their children. Very impartially, but that's not surprising, given her background. If he's involved . . ."

"Was it that way in your family?"

"Yes, thank the Three. I never wanted to end up in my father's study." Ysella offered a wry smile. "Mother often used that as a threat, and it was a real threat. What about you?"

"My mother took care of it all. I think she was afraid my father would be too lenient, but while he might have been, he wasn't ever about to change or soften one of her decisions or punishments."

"That explains a few things." For an instant, the hint of a mischievous smile appeared. "Maybe by tomorrow morning Obreduur will have something to say. We need to tell him that Emrelda's back, though, and she also needs to see and read Markell's letter to you."

"To us," Dekkard corrected gently.

"You can be stubborn."

"Aren't all isolates?"

"I thought you were different," she replied in a tone that was clearly one of mock disappointment.

"I am," he answered cheerfully. "I'm nice about it."

Ysella shook her head, then laughed softly. "I'll see you later."

For the next bell or so, Dekkard read an earlier issue of *History* that he'd somehow missed. He finished reading with enough time to have the Gresynt under the shelter of the portico a sixth before sixth bell. Moments after he pulled up, Obreduur and his wife, as well as Gustoff and Nellara and Ysella, appeared. Nellara was noticeably subdued.

When Ysella slipped into the front seat beside him, she nodded and murmured, "He wants to talk when we get back, before dinner."

Dekkard eased the Gresynt down the drive and out onto Altarama, heading east. Eight blocks and one turn later, he pulled up under the covered entry to the East Quarter Trinitarian Chapel. During the entire time, neither Gustoff nor Nellara said a word, a silence almost unprecedented in all the times Dekkard had ferried the family to services. He wondered what she'd done that had so displeased Obreduur, but doubted he'd ever know . . . and he certainly wasn't going to ask.

After dropping everyone off, he parked the steamer and then hurried into the chapel, where he managed to get to his seat at the end of the Obreduur family pew as the opening hymn began. The best that he could have said about the service was that it was relatively brief and that Presider Eschbach did not deal with yet another aspect of trust, but had moved on to the basics of belief, dwelling primarily upon the sin of believing in order to gain material success.

At the beginning of the recessional, Dekkard slipped out of the pew to retrieve the Gresynt and subsequently Ysella and the family. Nellara remained stone-silent on the drive back to the house, while Obreduur and Ingrella conversed quietly in the rear seat, and Gustoff looked in every direction but that of his sister.

After letting everyone off under the portico, Dekkard garaged the Gresynt, then did his cleanup and maintenance chores before closing up. When he came out of the garage, Ysella immediately appeared.

"He wants to see us now."

Dekkard followed her to Obreduur's study, then closed the door in response to the councilor's gesture for him to do so.

"I'm sorry for the delay, sir, but I had to finish with the steamers."

"That's scarcely a problem, Steffan. That's another thing I admire about both you and Avraal. Even when you're given more challenging and interesting work, you don't neglect the necessary routine tasks. That's a rare trait, especially these days. Now . . ." He paused for a moment before going on. "About your sister's missing husband . . . While we were at services, a messenger dropped off a message and a package from Carlos Baartol. I don't think you'll be surprised. The paper used for the unidentified plans is identical to that used by Siincleer Engineering. No other engineering firm uses it, and each engineering firm has its own plan-drafting paper, something that they agreed on years ago so that they could find out if engineers were stealing plans from other firms." Obreduur smiled sardonically. "Or perhaps so they'd know from whom plans were stolen."

"They could claim that the paper was stolen," said Ysella. "Or that the construction manager was trying to shift the blame elsewhere."

"They could, but it's a weak defense, especially if your sister has discovered something else."

"She hinted that she had, but we have no idea what."

"Then the four of us should meet as soon as your sister arrives tomorrow morning. That should work out since Ingrella and I had not planned to go out until tomorrow afternoon."

"Yes, sir." Dekkard saw no need to say more.

Ysella merely nodded.

"Have as pleasant an evening as you can."

Dekkard inclined his head, then turned and opened the study door, letting Ysella leave first. Neither spoke until they were alone in the staff room.

"One of the Siincleer corporacions was behind it all," said Dekkard, "but there won't be enough to prove who did it . . . and in the end business will go on as usual. Unless . . ."

"Unless what?"

"Unless Obreduur and the others . . . and the three of us . . . can find enough examples tied to the Commerce Party."

"The newssheets won't print it, and unless they do, no one will believe it. Most people won't even if *Gestirn* and the other newssheets do print stories."

"Not if we can convince people that they're lying."

Ysella laughed bitterly. "How will we do that?"

"I don't know . . . but we need to find a way." At the sound of Rhosali's footsteps, Dekkard halted and turned.

So did Ysella.

Rhosali hurried into the staff room and threw her arms around Ysella. "Thank you! Thank you so much!"

"For—" Ysella broke off. "Did your uncle get a job?"

Rhosali smiled broadly. "He did. Sr. Baartol found him a foreman's position at a small machine-tool manufactory. Well . . . an assistant foreman's position, but he will be a foreman in a year if he does well. He's already on the payroll, and he starts on Unadi."

"Is he pleased with it?" asked Dekkard.

"He is. He won't make quite as much for a while, but it's so much better than anything he could find."

Dekkard nodded. He had a feeling that Rhosali's uncle had just become another part of Baartol's information network. *Just out of gratitude.* He smiled slightly. *Are you any different?*

Rhosali looked back to Ysella. "You two were busy, but I wanted to tell you. Thank you." Then she turned and headed into the kitchen to help Hyelda.

"That's good, anyway," said Dekkard.

Ysella nodded.

Dekkard wished that he could say the same about Markell and poor Emrelda. Instead, he said, "Did you know that the structure of Argenti society actually came from early Jaykarh? I was just reading that in one of the issues of *History*." He smiled at her puzzled expression. "I was just trying to distract you until dinner's ready."

She shook her head ruefully, then said, "I appreciate the effort. Since I'll worry if I'm not distracted, why don't you tell me how Jaykarh shaped Argenti culture?"

"I thought you'd never ask."

50

After dinner on Quindi, Dekkard spent almost a bell writing to his parents, a missive that mentioned his promotion, but none of the more exciting events in his life, except that Machtarn had also seen demonstrations at the Council and at Imperial University. He also told them that he'd be coming to Oersynt in Summerend as a security aide. He thought about reading when he finished the letter, but decided he was too sleepy and went to bed.

When he woke on Findi the sun was already up, and the day promised to be clear, hot, and muggy. Knowing that Emrelda would be at the house by third bell, he immediately got up, washed, shaved, and dressed, then headed downstairs. He checked the morning edition of *Gestirn*. In the only news of the Council, the Premier assured the Imperador that the supplemental funding would be available before Summerend recess. There was nothing about demonstrators, missing engineers, or Siincleer corporacions.

Dekkard poured his café and sat down, hoping Ysella had gotten a decent night's sleep. He took several sips before reaching for the croissants and, reluctantly, the tomato jelly. He had just spooned some of the jelly into his split croissant when Ysella arrived, wearing a rose blouse, and a skirt of a darker rose. Dekkard had no doubt that a suit jacket left in her room matched the mid-calf skirt.

"I hope you got some sleep."

"More than on Furdi night." She took a slow sip of café. "You look good in that green barong, but then you look good in everything."

"I have to, if I'm with you." He smiled warmly.

"Emrelda would laugh at that."

"Why? Because she remembers when you were rebellious and wore mismatched clothing on purpose?"

Ysella's eyes narrowed. "Who told you that?"

Dekkard laughed gently. "No one. It was a guess. Anyone as stylish as you rebelled in one way or another. I just thought that would be your way."

"Steffan . . . if I find out that Emrelda told you . . ." Her voice was somewhere between amused and menacing.

"You can ask her. You might also think about eating. It could be a long morning."

Ysella slowly reached for a croissant.

"How about some tomato jelly?" asked Dekkard.

"That's even worse than quince paste."

"I think so, too."

"Then why do you eat it?"

Dekkard shrugged. "It's better than no paste or jelly."

Ysella looked at the tomato jelly, then at Dekkard and, without a word, took a healthy bite out of the croissant.

Dekkard took an enormous bite out of his tomato-jelly-filled croissant, chewed and swallowed it, and then smiled broadly. "Not bad."

Ysella shook her head slowly, but Dekkard thought he saw a hint of amusement in her eyes. As he took a second and far more modest bite of the croissant, he hoped so.

Well before third bell, Dekkard and Ysella were standing in the shade of the portico, looking out at Altarama Drive and waiting. Dekkard had already opened the gates.

As soon as he saw the teal Gresynt, Dekkard hurried down to the gates and motioned for Emrelda to drive in. Instead of coming up the drive, she stopped short of the gates. Dekkard gestured again for her to drive to the portico, then turned and walked alongside the Gresynt as she slowly drove up and into the shade of the portico.

Emrelda got out of the steamer. "I thought we were going to my house."

"There's something you need to see first, and Councilor Obreduur wants to meet with the three of us," said Ysella.

Dekkard looked at Ysella. "I believe you had a question for your sister."

For an instant, the younger sister looked surprised. Then she shook her head and asked, "Did you *EVER* tell Steffan about how I dressed?"

Emrelda looked totally puzzled. "Why would I? You always dress so well."

"When we were younger, I meant."

"For the Three's sake, no. Outside of that afternoon at our house, I've never said a word to him about . . ." Then she laughed. "You mean about how you deliberately mismatched—"

"Did . . . you . . . tell . . . him . . . that?"

"No. I haven't thought about that in years."

Ysella turned to Dekkard. "You are scary, sometimes." Then she turned to Emrelda. "He guessed that—right out of the green sky."

"Right out of the green?"

"Not exactly," protested Dekkard. "She's always so matched and stylish that I just guessed that any rebellion would be within the rules, just to make it hard on everyone."

Emrelda nodded, then asked, "What is it that I need to see, and why does the councilor need to talk to me?"

"You'll see," said Dekkard. "He's waiting in his study."

"Have you found out anything about Markell?" demanded Emrelda.

"Nothing recent, unless it's something the councilor knows and hasn't told us," replied Dekkard, knowing that his words, while technically correct, were misleading, but he didn't want to say more until they were in the study.

"You're not telling me something," said Emrelda, almost angrily.

"That's right. Rather, there's something you need to see, and, no, it's not any personal item of Markell's." Dekkard gestured toward the portico entry door. "This way."

In moments, Ysella led her sister into the study.

Obreduur stood immediately and inclined his head to Emrelda. "I'm sorry to meet you this way. However, there are some things you should know and see." He gestured toward the three chairs.

While Dekkard closed the study door, Ysella guided her sister into the center chair, then took the chair to her left.

After everyone was seated, Obreduur eased the package Dekkard had received across the desk to where Emrelda could see the address on the outside of the wrapping resting on the box.

She stiffened and paled slightly as she read it. "That's Markell's handwriting, but why to Steffan?"

"The letter explaining it is in the box with some papers," said Dekkard. "I was as stunned to receive it as you are now. It arrived here late on Duadi, and we had no way to reach you. It's been kept in a safe since then."

Emrelda's hand was steady as she lifted the wrapping off the stationery box, but she frowned as she saw the box. "There was a stack of stationery, without a box, in his suitcase, but why . . ." She opened the box and saw the letter.

"Do you want me to read it?" asked Ysella gently.

Emrelda gave a curt shake of her head as she took the letter. Her hands were shaking as she finished reading and replaced the letter on top of the set of plans. Her eyes glistened.

Ysella handed her sister a handkerchief.

"I'm sorry," said Dekkard as gently as he could. He'd worried about Markell's last lines at the bottom. "I couldn't see any easier way."

"No . . . it's better . . . I saw for myself." Emrelda blotted her eyes, then said, her voice icy, "Those bastards. Those absolute bastards." After several moments, she said, "There must be more, or we all wouldn't be here."

"Councilor Obreduur has some contacts," said Dekkard. "We gave a sheet of the working plans to them. They discovered that the plan paper is only used by Siincleer Engineering. For us, that's conclusive."

"But not for a Security patroller or agent," replied Emrelda.

"Some other councilors have found two instances where similar apparent mishaps and accidental deaths destroyed growing organizations competing with larger corporacions," said Obreduur quietly. "Again, it's not proof, but the similarities are disturbing."

Emrelda looked at Obreduur. "What else do we need? What else can we do?"

"You suggested you had something," said Ysella gently.

"It's not as much as you have, and that's not enough to prove anything."

"If we get enough pieces . . ." suggested Dekkard.

Emrelda straightened herself in the chair. "The nearest Security patrol station assigned me a local patroller to help me. He was there as much to see that nothing happened to me and that the area chief wasn't surprised if I turned up something. It was all political. The area chief wants to stop the quiet strong-arming by Siincleer

Shipbuilding, but he can't investigate too much without things happening, either to him or his family ... or his better patrollers. But if a patroller from Machtarn who's looking for her vanished husband turns up with some answers ... well, if something happens to her, then he's got some leverage. I wish I'd found more, but it was all what wasn't there."

"What wasn't there?" asked Dekkard.

"Too much," replied Emrelda. "Both the security guard and the night clerk at the small hotel where Markell and the on-site project manager and a few others from Engaard Engineering were staying don't remember anything from the night that Markell disappeared. The local patrollers even brought in an empath to check that, but the two were telling the truth."

"Then a high-level empath or possibly two overloaded their short-term memories with conflicting feelings," said Ysella.

"That's not quite in the report," said Emrelda. "It just says that it was verified that neither man could remember events between the fourth and fifth bells of night."

"What else wasn't there?" asked Obreduur.

"The on-site project manager is also missing. That didn't make the newssheets, because he didn't disappear until the afternoon just before I arrived. Well ... no one could find him on Duadi, and no one bothered to look because he was very agitated after he'd gotten word his wife was deathly ill. She lives on the south side of Siincleer. When they went there on Furdi, she was fine, and denied sending any messages. They didn't find any trace of him until late on Furdi. What they found was his jacket in a dinghy borrowed from one of the piers that had grounded on the rocky beach five milles southwest of Siincleer."

"All of this reeks of empaths," said Ysella. "Halaard Engaard's death was no natural heart attack, but brought on by projections of strong emotions. Markell was abducted with the aid of empaths, and the one man who was directing the flawed construction has vanished or is dead, most likely because he was lured away by a forged message or someone who convinced him emotionally that his wife was dying."

"Everyone will blame it on Markell," said Emrelda. "He did the engineering design. They'll say that Engaard's death was due to his shock at discovering the bad design, and that the on-site project manager discovered he'd be found out because he colluded with Markell."

"That doesn't make logical sense," said Ysella, "but with all three missing or dead, who's going to question it except us?"

"Markell's not merely missing," said Emrelda bleakly. "He'd never vanish. And he'd never agree to anything corrupt."

No one said anything for several moments.

Finally, Ysella turned to her sister. "It may be that all we can do is bring this to light and, if we're fortunate and able, try to punish those responsible and keep them from doing it again."

"That's a start." The cold steel in Emrelda's voice sent a shiver down Dekkard's spine.

"Are you sure?" asked Obreduur quietly.

"I'll do whatever it takes. Where do we start?"

"We've already begun," replied Obreduur. "Do you know the name of the on-site project manager?"

"Pietr Vonholm. I don't know much more than that."

"I'll have an operative look into certain aspects of his financial or work-history matters. In the meantime, you need to keep doing your job and keep your eyes and ears open. For now, I think we need to keep the letter and the plans locked away."

"For now," agreed Emrelda.

Dekkard could tell she wanted that last letter from Markell, and he couldn't blame her, but he also knew she was more likely to have it in the end if it stayed in Obreduur's safe.

"I'd also suggest sending letters to the patroller who assisted you and to that patrol chief, thanking them and asking, should they run across anything else, that they keep you informed," said Obreduur, "because you've since uncovered more information."

"Do you think that will do much good?"

"I don't know, but I've found that if you don't remind people they forget too quickly. The reference to more information might stir things up, and I'll see about having someone in Siincleer keep an eye out for any reaction."

Emrelda took a deep breath. "I don't want to sound pushy . . . but is that all?"

"No. There are several other angles I'm pursuing, but they'll take a little more time. I can plant some information with the newssheets to see who gets the building contract and what their ties might be, and also see if political contacts are involved." Obreduur paused, then asked, "Do you have any recommendations on what else I might do?"

"You said this sort of thing happened before," returned Emrelda. "Could you find out if the small organizations were led by outsiders, ambitious people outside the Commercer network, so to speak?"

"Was Halaard Engaard a comparative newcomer?" asked Dekkard.

"His father was a smallholder near Khuld. Not a Landor and not from Commerce marks."

Obreduur nodded. "That might be very useful. Is there anything else?"

"Are there any Security records on missing people? Records that would show how many engineers, troublesome legalists, guild staffers just vanished?"

Obreduur laughed bitterly and sardonically. "If there were any such records, they were destroyed when the fire gutted Security Ministry headquarters."

Dekkard grinned. "What if that was the reason the fire was set? What if outsiders didn't set it?"

"Are you suggesting that I propose that?" Obreduur's tone was curious.

"No . . . but it might be interesting if speculations along those lines appeared. That just might force

Minister Wyath to make public more information about who did set the fires. Or he might refuse to divulge more, in which case a councilor might honestly ask why he refuses to make the information public . . . and what other information is being withheld . . . and why?" Dekkard paused. "It might even be possible to raise the question of what Security knew about the Kraffeist Affair."

Obreduur nodded again. "That has possibilities." He turned to Emrelda. "If you come up with any other information or suggestions, you can let me know or tell Avraal."

"Thank you. I appreciate your looking into this." Emrelda rose before Obreduur did.

"I will keep you informed," replied Obreduur, "largely through Avraal."

Ysella led the way from the study back out to the portico, where the three stood in the shade beside Emrelda's teal Gresynt. "Would you still like us to come over today?"

"I'd like that very much." Emrelda handed her keys to Dekkard. "If you wouldn't mind?"

"If that is truly your wish."

Emrelda just nodded.

Dekkard opened the rear door. After both were inside, he got in the driver's seat and lit off the steamer, then backed carefully down the drive.

He did not use the mirrors to look into the back seat on the drive to Emrelda's house. The quiet sobbing and murmured words between the sisters told him more than enough. When they turned north on Jacquez, the sobbing died away, and when he pulled off Florinda Way and into the drive, Emrelda said firmly, "Just leave it under the portico. I'll drive you back later."

Dekkard did as he was told, but did get out of the Gresynt fast enough to open the rear door and hand the keys back to Emrelda. "It's a good steamer to drive."

"I've enjoyed it."

"I can see why."

"Do we need to go shopping?" asked Ysella.

"I did that yesterday afternoon. I had to do *something*. I just couldn't sit or pace around thinking. I thought the two of us could fix a veal dish for an early-afternoon dinner."

Dekkard nodded. The rest of the day was going to be very quiet and very domestic, and no one was going to talk about anything upsetting.

51

As Dekkard had predicted, Findi ended up as quiet, sad, and bittersweet, if more bitter than sweet. He did enjoy the excellent veal Kathaar that Emrelda and Ysella fixed, especially with the cremini risotto and the green beans amandine. He endeavored to be quietly cheerful and did his best to support the conversation, rather than direct it.

When it was time to leave, Emrelda said, "You could just take the other steamer."

Dekkard noticed that it was "the other steamer," rather than "Markell's steamer."

"That's sweet of you," replied Ysella, "but there's nowhere to garage it at the Obreduurs' house, and the weather could harm it."

"I didn't think about that," said Emrelda. "But if you want to use it on enddays . . . it really should be driven."

And she doesn't want to drive it.

"We'll keep that in mind," said Ysella. "Now . . . you're sure about tomorrow?"

"I need to go back to work. When I'm there I can keep my eyes open for the sorts of things I didn't ever think would happen to us." Emrelda's voice turned harder. "You don't think it can until it does."

Unless you've seen it happen more than once. But Dekkard just nodded.

"We could take the omnibus," offered Ysella. "You're tired."

"Steffan can drive us over. I can certainly manage driving back. Then I might even sleep."

Ysella gave the smallest of winces. "You're sure?"

"I am." Emrelda handed her keys to Dekkard. "There's no point in talking about it. You'll just get back to the Obreduurs later and get less sleep."

"Then we should go," agreed Ysella.

Dekkard understood. She didn't want Emrelda driving back in full darkness. So he led the way to the teal Gresynt. He was also doubly careful in backing down the narrower drive.

Ysella and Emrelda talked quietly in back while Dekkard chauffeured them to the Obreduurs' driveway gates. There he got out and opened the rear door. As soon as Emrelda stepped out, Dekkard returned her keys.

Surprisingly to Dekkard, Emrelda hugged him, then murmured, "Thank you so much."

Ysella got a longer hug before Emrelda got into her Gresynt and gave a brief wave, before pulling away from the drive.

Dekkard and Ysella watched, but as soon as Emrelda was out of sight, he turned to Ysella. "She's stubborn, but she hurts a lot."

"She never looked at anyone else. Neither did he. Have you thought of anything else we could do?"

"Outside of kidnapping the head of Siincleer Engineering and interrogating him? And a few others. Not a thing. What about you?"

"I said I'd never do interrogations. I might make an exception here . . . if I get the chance." Ysella's voice was cold in the same fashion as Emrelda's had been. "I almost agree with the New Meritorists . . . except doing it their way would give the Commercers more power in the long run."

A thought occurred to Dekkard, but he frowned, wondering if he should bring it up.

"What is it?" asked Ysella.

"I was just remembering. That night after Councilor Freust's memorial when the empie assassin targeted—"

"What about it?"

"You said she was stupid. Was that because you thought she'd undo all the reforms created after the Silent Revolution?"

"Not exactly. I could see it if she'd targeted someone like Ulrich or some of the hidebound Landors, but Obreduur isn't like them."

"Maybe that's exactly why he was targeted," suggested Dekkard.

"Oh . . . they're afraid he might get enough reform to cut support for a total revolution?"

"It makes sense to me, either way. The Commercers don't want any change, and the New Meritorists want total change. Neither has much use for anything else. That's why we need to get the Commercers out of power soon . . . or it won't make any difference," said Dekkard bleakly. "I knew there were problems, but not that they were like this. Did you?"

"That the Commercers were into disappearing people? I didn't know they'd stooped that low. I've known that political rivals had unexplained difficulties, but those were short of murder or vanishing. Councilor Freust's death was the first I saw as a possible political removal."

"It also explains why the logistics director of Eastern Ironway is missing. He was either disappeared or fled in fear that he would be."

"Do you think he's still alive?" asked Ysella.

"There's a good possibility, since they sent descriptions to all Security stations."

"You really do keep confidences, don't you?"

Dekkard frowned. "What do you mean?"

"Obreduur told me that you drove 'Sr. Muller' to the docks."

"He told me not to say anything. Usually, he tells me if he's told you."

"I admire that in you. In fact, there's a lot in you I admire."

"I admire pretty much everything in you," Dekkard admitted. "I can't imagine partnering with anyone else." *In anything.* But he wasn't ready to say that. Not yet.

"I feel the same." Abruptly, Ysella looked toward the house. "We should head in."

"I suppose so," said Dekkard. "Tomorrow could bring anything."

"Or nothing but the routine," she replied dryly.

They turned and walked through the pedestrian gate and up the drive.

52

Unadi, Duadi, and Tridi dragged out for Dekkard and Ysella. Obreduur was involved in Craft Party caucuses and floor debates over the supplemental funding, although he had assured both of his security aides that he'd had no word back on his inquiries about Markell and Siincleer Shipbuilding.

When Dekkard scanned the morning edition of *Gestirn* on Furdi and found stories on flooding along the Rio Doro, more piracy by Sargassan brigands—involving, of course, vessels owned by Transoceanic Shipping—and unseasonably warm temperatures in Surpunta, he didn't know what to think, because it had been days, if not longer, since the newssheet had run a story on the Council, on demonstrators, on any aspect of coal or natural resources, or anything at all happening in Siincleer . . . and there certainly hadn't been any mention of the New Meritorists.

Why are you so surprised? he asked himself. *Until the last few months nothing like any of those appeared in the newssheets.* At the same time, he had the feeling that more was happening than most people were seeing, including the newssheets and the Council.

But since he just might be very much mistaken, he

said nothing about his feelings at breakfast or while he drove Obreduur and Ysella to the Council Office Building. After he dropped them off and parked the Gresynt, warily watching the area all around him, he noted that the number of Council Guards was less than it had been recently, as if Premier Ulrich had decided that there was no additional risk to councilors and staff.

Except to one particular staffer.

He climbed the staff stairway and was walking along the corridor toward the office when he saw coming toward him Stavros Rhennus, the isolate for Councilor Mardosh.

"Stavros . . . I haven't seen you in weeks. Both Avraal and I were shocked when we heard about Mathilde's disappearance. How are you doing?"

Rhennus barked a bitter laugh. "It's a bitch doing security without a partner. I may not have one for quite a while, either. Word gets around."

"About Mathilde, you mean? Occasionally, that happens. Security isn't without risks. We all know that."

"It gets harder to find good empaths when corporacions are paying considerably more. Marks matter."

"Unless other things matter more," Dekkard replied.

"That's not always enough . . . especially when you add in the danger." After the briefest pause, Rhennus moved closer and lowered his voice. "I heard that your councilor is looking into some military contracting problems in Siincleer."

"There have been some very odd occurrences there."

"There have always been odd occurrences there. They usually involve Siincleer Shipbuilding. If he goes down there, you and Avraal need to be doubly careful. Especially now."

"Do you know why?"

"Only that strange things happened to some important people, and that a certain engineering firm isn't pleased that people are nosing around. Keep that tight. I'm not supposed to know. I just happened to overhear it . . .

and after Mathilde, I don't want anyone else I know not to be wary."

"Thank you. I will keep that tight. Can we help you in any way?"

"Not right now, but if I need anything . . ."

"Just let me know."

As he left Rhennus and covered the last few yards to the office door, Dekkard couldn't say he was surprised. While it was a confirmation of sorts, it certainly didn't qualify as legal proof.

When he stepped into the office, Ysella was already drafting a response, and only a handful of letters sat waiting on his desk. By midmorning, he'd finished his drafts and given them to Margrit to be typed up.

"Are you caught up at the moment?" Macri asked Dekkard.

"For now."

"Good. Here are some letters you should be able to handle. The councilor wants to answer them even though they come from out of district. Give the drafts back to me, rather than Margrit."

Dekkard took them with a smile. His smile turned wry when he returned to his desk and read the first one, which was from the junior legalist with the Working Women Guild in Gaarlak, who wanted Obreduur's support for legislation to allow women of the streets to be represented by legalists from the nearest Working Women Guild.

From Gaarlak? Where Obreduur was visiting in less than two weeks?

He couldn't help but nod. Since the incumbent Landor councilor couldn't run for reelection in the next election, whenever that happened to be, Obreduur wanted to curry favor with both the ladies of the brothels and their less fortunate compatriots on the streets—and, even more important, with the women legalists who represented both.

The remaining letters, also from Gaarlak, were on issues Dekkard knew well enough to draft, so that Macri would, hopefully, only have to make minor corrections. At least he wasn't doing make-work, but he questioned if even dozens of letters to people there would make any difference—since it was still unlikely that elections would be called any time soon.

53

Slightly after third bell on Quindi afternoon, Obreduur summoned Dekkard and Ysella. Once they were seated in his office, with the door firmly closed, he cleared his throat.

"Carlos Baartol sent me information about Pietr Vonholm."

For a moment, Dekkard couldn't place the name, but Ysella immediately said, "The Engaard on-site project manager who disappeared."

"Apparently, he didn't disappear. Not totally. Yesterday, his wife took a Transoceanic steamship—the type that carries passengers as well as cargo—bound for Noldar. The circumstances of her departure suggest she has no plans to return. Noldar is also where, incidentally, Siincleer Engineering is building another textile manufactory for—"

"Guldoran Ironway?" asked Dekkard.

Obreduur nodded.

"Why would they do it that way?" asked Ysella. "Why not just send Vonholm to Noldar?"

"That would leave tracks," replied Obreduur. "I suspect that his 'bonus,' if you could call it that, was enough for him to live very well in Noldar, even without a job. There won't be any trace of him that we can use, except circumstantially, and, even if we could find him, as Ingrella has pointed out, we certainly can't compel someone in Noldar to come to Guldor, especially without the assistance of the Minister of the Justiciary and the threat of naval action. That resolves several problems for Siincleer Engineering. While denying everything, the corporacion lets it be known quietly that it rewards dubious deeds handsomely, while removing two witnesses from Guldoran justice."

"Is Security following up on the matter?" asked Ysella.

"They have noted that Carissa Vonholm has left Guldor, but there is no evidence about Pietr Vonholm. If such evidence is found, they will pursue the matter."

"They're sticklers for the law when they don't want to do anything," said Ysella bitterly.

"Their elective application of the law is another example of corruption," added Dekkard.

"Or their self-preservation," said Obreduur. "Emrelda said that one patroller station chief would have liked to do more. If he'd stopped Vonholm's wife from leaving Guldor, a woman who did nothing wrong, how long before the Commercers would have had the newssheets on him for persecuting a woman whose husband vanished and is presumed dead? How long would he last as a station chief?"

After a moment, Ysella asked, "Did Baartol come up with anything else?"

"Not so far. I'll let you know."

"There's another thing," said Dekkard. "If Guldoran Ironway is building another textile manufactory in Noldar, are they planning to close one here? Or will they produce textiles there more cheaply and drive out a smaller or more costly manufactory here in Guldor?"

"The new manufactory is designed to sell textiles more cheaply in Noldar. Their previous textile manufactory in Noldar doesn't produce textiles for sale. It produces semi-finished cloth for use in products manufactured here in Guldor."

"Meaning that tariffs are much lower."

Obreduur nodded.

"In the meantime," said Dekkard, "could we add Carissa Vonholm's departure to the circumstantial evidence, possibly for trial in the newssheets? At the appropriate time, of course."

"What are you suggesting, Steffan?" asked Obreduur, his tone implying he knew the answer.

"Compiling event after event with all these suspicious items, including, of course, the Kraffeist Affair, perhaps even typesetting a sheet on each event so that when the time comes, the whole country can be flooded with them. Then, if the newssheets don't follow up, some councilors might bring up the matter before the Council. If that gets hushed up, print up sheets on that." Dekkard shrugged. "There is the danger that the New Meritorists might take that information and create even larger demonstrations. An adroit councilor might be able to suggest that if the Council didn't do something, then that would prove that the entire Council was owned by the Commercers. But you might find a better way. Those were just my thoughts."

"If you weren't so devoted to restoring the Great Charter to its original intent, Steffan," said Obreduur, "you could be very dangerous. Perhaps you, Ysella, and Emrelda might consider drafting such a dossier or sheet on the destruction of Engaard Engineering by Siincleer Shipbuilding to remove competition to Siincleer Engineering. Every fact must be accurate, but you can pose leading questions."

"How soon would you like a draft?" asked Dekkard.

"It would be useful to have a draft a few days before we leave for Gaarlak . . . if you're interested."

"We're interested," declared Ysella without even looking at Dekkard.

Dekkard hid an amused smile and nodded.

"Good," replied Obreduur. "I'll look forward to seeing what you present. Now . . . I do have a few other matters to deal with before we finish here for the week."

Dekkard and Ysella both immediately stood and made their way from the office. Once they were outside, Dekkard said, "We should get together with Emrelda tomorrow."

"She has to work until third afternoon bell, to make up the time she took off."

That had slipped Dekkard's mind until Ysella had mentioned it. "We could meet her there after three."

"I'll send her a message. If she can't do that, she can send a message to the house. We can talk more later."

"Later" turned out to be a while in coming. After driving back to the house, escorting the family to services at the Trinitarian chapel, and eating dinner, the two walked out to the portico.

Once there, Ysella turned to Dekkard. "A message arrived while we were at services. Meeting at three at Emrelda's is fine with her. What else did you want to talk about?"

"You said we were interested without even looking in my direction. Was that 'we' because you knew Emrelda would be interested or were you speaking for me as well?"

"Steffan . . . you don't have to—"

"I agree, and you know it." He smiled. "I did want to give you a little trouble about it."

For a moment, she was silent. Finally, she said, "That's fair. I'm sorry."

"How do you think Obreduur plans to use what he's compiling?" asked Dekkard, not wanting to dwell on her assumption of his agreement.

"You seemed to know that already."

Dekkard shook his head. "That was a guess, but as I see it, right now very few people would even care. We could flood Guldor with detailed broadsheets, and they'd end up largely as grease paper. The only time they'll be useful is after something larger gets people riled up."

"You think he hasn't thought about that?" Ysella replied.

"I'm sure he has. But the only things I can think of are some sort of economic collapse that is clearly caused by the Commercers or widespread riots by the New Meritorists. The riots would strengthen the Commercers, especially if Minister Wyath puts them down quickly without too many deaths." *But then, given the New Meritorists, that might be difficult.*

"More than a few of them have been willing to die for their principles," said Ysella, "but how many of them are like that? For that matter, how many New Meritorists are there?"

"Thousands of dedicated believers, and maybe tens of thousands who like their ideas."

"Security can deal with a few thousand spread across Guldor. Tens of thousands might change things, but we want reform, not destruction."

"I wonder where that line is," replied Dekkard. "Commercers would say that what we want would destroy Guldor. We think they've at least partly destroyed the Great Charter."

"I'd rather live under the Commercers, bad as it's getting, than under the New Meritorists. Wouldn't you?"

"That's a terrible choice, but I'd agree. Not at all happily, however."

"We're not going to solve that dilemma tonight. We'll also have a long day tomorrow, since we'll have to work on drafting what Obreduur wants so that Emrelda can add or change things once she gets home, but that won't be until after third bell." Ysella paused, then added, "She will have changes. More than a few."

That did not surprise Dekkard.

54

By third bell Findi morning, the staff quarters of the Obreduur house were quiet, since Hyelda and Rhosali had the day off after breakfast, and both had already left. Dekkard and Ysella sat on opposite sides of the table, each with a pen and paper.

"Why don't you start with the background on Engaard Engineering?" said Dekkard.

Ysella frowned. "I think we each should write up the entire story as we know it, and then the questions. That way, we're less likely to leave out anything."

"So we both put in everything we know . . . and then edit it down."

Ysella shook her head. "We both put in everything we know. Then we argue over whose words or presentation of each fact or event is better and decide how to combine them. We don't edit anything out until Emrelda reads it and makes changes and additions." She smiled slightly. "Then you draft all the leading questions, and we suggest any changes."

"Why do you want me to do the questions?"

"You have a more doubtful outlook on the current governance of Guldor than either of us. Your words will appeal more to men. That's important because men, for all their protests to the contrary, tend to be more emotional about politics. A strong emotional reaction is exactly what we'll need."

"None of that is exactly a compliment," replied Dekkard.

"It wasn't meant to be," returned Ysella sweetly.

Dekkard just shook his head. Then he picked up his pen.

Just before noon, Dekkard finished his draft, or rather the cleaned-up version. "How are you doing?"

"Probably another third of a bell, maybe two," replied Ysella. "Why don't you think of some provocative leading questions?"

"I thought you wanted me to wait on that."

"You might as well start now."

Dekkard managed three leading questions in the next third of a bell, discovering that formulating questions that did what they wanted sounded far easier than it turned out to be.

"Why don't you let me read what you've done so far?" he asked.

Wordlessly, Ysella handed him five sheets of paper, then returned to writing.

Dekkard began to read. After the first sheet, he could see that her account of the background was far better than his, not surprisingly, although she had left out one fact.

A few minutes later, she handed him two more sheets. "Let me read yours."

Dekkard passed over his four sheets. "What I've read of yours so far is better."

"I probably know more of the details."

I did mention that. But he kept that thought to himself as he kept reading. When he finished, he waited until Ysella looked up.

"You write well," she said, "but I already knew that."

"You have more details and facts, except you left one out. Emrelda said that Halaard Engaard was never considered by Siincleer Engineering when he first became an engineer. That allows a leading question about Siincleer's hiring practices."

"I did say you're better with the questions. Also, there are several sections on your fourth page that you do better, and I like your wording better in some places earlier."

After another two bells, Dekkard had written out a seven-page document that combined their efforts, and the two had to hurry to get to the omnibus, Dekkard wearing his green barong and black trousers, Ysella in a dusky-rose linen suit, with another almost transparent headscarf. Dekkard carried the draft inside a leather folder as they walked down the drive.

Dekkard glanced both ways after they went through the pedestrian gate, but saw no one and no steamers except a dark blue Kharlan heading east. Ysella had an intent expression on her face for several moments, before she relaxed.

"Obreduur definitely wanted our draft before Summerend recess," said Dekkard. "Do you think he wants to show it to someone here before we leave or someone in Oersynt?"

"Possibly both places, even in Gaarlak. He is in touch

with a number of people whose judgment he respects. We'll meet some of them."

"So that they'll know us if we have to stand in for Obreduur?"

"Partly, but also because you need to make a good impression and meet influential Craft people. When we make a good impression, it strengthens the party . . . and Obreduur."

The omnibus stop on Imperial Boulevard was crowded and so was the omnibus, although the numbers on the lower level slowly dwindled once the conveyance was headed east on Camelia Avenue. For that reason, neither said much until they reached Erslaan.

Even before they crossed the avenue and started walking up Jacquez, Dekkard had his handkerchief out and was blotting his forehead. "It's hot."

"It will be hotter in Gaarlak," she replied cheerfully. "And we'll be wearing suits."

Dekkard winced. "You're wearing one now, and you look so cool compared to me."

"You'll get used to it."

Dekkard definitely had his doubts.

The two reached Emrelda's house slightly before three and took refuge in the shade of the drive portico.

"How do you think Emrelda's doing?" asked Dekkard.

"She's devastated, but she won't show it."

"Is that a family trait?"

"Only on Mother's side," replied Ysella dryly.

Dekkard was about to ask which side their brother Cliven favored when he saw the teal Gresynt. "Here comes Emrelda."

In moments, Emrelda had parked the steamer under the portico and had emerged in a dark security-blue patroller's uniform, with a black full-length truncheon at her side.

Dekkard had to admit that she looked very professional. Although he'd never thought of her otherwise, the uniform added a greater impression of power and gravitas.

Emrelda spoiled some of that by hugging Ysella and even Dekkard. "I'm so glad to see you both. I'm sorry—"

"You don't have to be sorry," interjected Dekkard. "We're the ones imposing on you. You had to work."

Emrelda looked to Ysella with an amused smile. "Did he come this way, or have you had to train him?"

"I haven't done a thing," replied Ysella.

"I just watched her," said Dekkard, grinning and then saying, "and I have an older sister."

Emrelda smiled, but the expression quickly faded. "We need to go inside and then onto the veranda. Well . . . you go out on the veranda, Steffan. I need to change out of this uniform and have a few words of woman talk."

"Can I get you both some wine and take it out on the veranda?" asked Dekkard.

"If you would, that would be lovely. You know where the lager is."

Dekkard didn't dawdle in getting the wine— Silverhills—and the Kuhrs lager, but he didn't rush. Even so, he sat alone in one of the white wicker chairs, with the leather folder on the low table, for a good third before Ysella and Emrelda reappeared.

"Thank you, Steffan." Emrelda settled into a chair across the low table from him.

"It was the least I could do." He looked at the leather folder, then to Ysella.

"I already told her about the idea."

"It's not enough," said Emrelda. "But nothing would be enough. It's better than anything else."

"We're just starting," said Ysella, lifting her wineglass and taking a sip.

"You're both kind to come." Emrelda took a swallow from her glass. "How will this . . . summary, broadsheet . . . do any good?"

"I have no idea," replied Dekkard. "Obreduur believes it will make a difference. So far, he's usually been right. He's also been trustworthy."

Emrelda took another swallow of the Silverhills. "I'll read what you've written."

Dekkard leaned forward and opened the leather folder, handing the sheets across the table to Emrelda. Then he leaned back and took a swallow of Kuhrs.

Emrelda looked at the first sheet and turned to her sister. "You didn't do the writing, I can tell."

"Steffan has a much better hand."

"I can see that."

Dekkard took another swallow and waited, watching while Emrelda read.

When she finished, she lowered the papers, but did not relinquish them. She seemed to think for several minutes before she spoke. "It's not bad. There are a few facts that aren't quite right, and the timing is off in places. There's also more about Halaard that you wouldn't know. When he started at Haasan Design, he had to work for no pay for two months until he could prove that he was a good engineer. That was the only way he could get into the field back then. He loved to tell that story, especially to any junior engineer who mentioned anything about pay."

"I doubt he ever told it to Markell," said Ysella.

"No, but Markell . . ." Emrelda swallowed, then continued, "Markell enjoyed telling me about it when Halaard told the story to someone."

"Was all that why Engaard was so successful?" asked Dekkard. "Because he hired engineers and others based on ability and not family background?"

"That was one of the reasons. I doubt it was the only one."

"We should work that in somehow," suggested Dekkard.

Another bell passed before the three agreed on additions, deletions, and changes, at which point Ysella turned to Dekkard. "If you wouldn't mind writing out a fair draft . . . then we'll fix something to eat. It might be easier writing that on the dining room table. Just take one end, and I'll set up places at the other end."

"I can do that." Dekkard understood. Ysella didn't want him invading Markell's study.

Dekkard finished the redraft a good third before Ysella and Emrelda served dinner—a cucumber and tomato salad with a red pepper and onion omelet, along with cheese skillet biscuits. At dinner, no one talked about the draft, nor about Markell. Dekkard asked about Emrelda's duties and day, and she replied in detail, clearly glad to talk about something else.

After the three cleaned up, Emrelda insisted on driving Dekkard and Ysella back to the house.

Once the teal Gresynt disappeared into the dusk, Ysella turned to Dekkard. "Thank you for understanding."

"I just thought she didn't want to talk about Markell. Everyone handles grief a different way. You don't think there's any chance Markell's alive somewhere, do you?"

"I'd like to think that, especially for Emrelda . . . but no . . . I don't. And she doesn't, either. While we were fixing dinner, she said she had an awful feeling on the Quindi night he disappeared."

"That was before she knew anything," Dekkard said.

"It was. That was why she was so upset that Findi morning."

"She didn't mention that feeling before."

"I wondered about that." Ysella started walking up the drive as she went on, "Emrelda doesn't trust feelings as much as I do. She and Markell both liked facts and figures more."

Dekkard kept pace with her, thinking, *Which was why Markell wanted to verify numbers and measurements before he said anything.* Dekkard could understand that, but he also felt that sometimes waiting to act until getting absolute factual confirmation was the most reckless decision of all. "Don't you think we should wait a day or so and then reread the draft—just

404 | L. E. MODESITT, JR.

in case we think of something else—before giving it to Obreduur?"

"Two days might be better," suggested Ysella.

The two walked quietly the rest of the way up to the portico and then inside the quiet house. At the bottom of the stairs to the staff bedrooms above the garage, Ysella turned to Dekkard. "Thank you . . . again. You've been very supportive, especially to Emrelda. I appreciate that."

That's because of you. "I've tried to do the best I can. I'm just following your example."

"That's kind of you, but I'm not always the best example. I'll see you in the morning."

"In the morning." Dekkard watched as she climbed the steps, following only after she reached the upper level.

Much later, Dekkard sat on his bed, thinking. The Great Charter worked. At least, it had worked for longer than any other government in history. So why were the Commercers trying to change it one way and the New Meritorists the other way? While one could claim that the Commercers were motivated by greed for marks and power, there had to be more than that, didn't there?

Except the motivation isn't all that different. Both wanted to force society to recognize or at least acknowledge that certain individuals mattered more than others. Amassing marks and power was the Commercers' way of demonstrating individual worth, while making individual politicians visible and responsible was the New Meritorists' methodology of affirming each individual's worth.

Everyone wants to be considered of worth. But how does the Great Charter fit into that?

Was it that the Great Charter, as it originally operated, separated politics and governance from wealth and acclaim? *Until the Commercers ousted the Landors from power and began to use government to enhance their power?* Why had that happened? Because industrialization allowed for the creation of more wealth, and that surplus of wealth was far more mobile and not tied to the land?

Dekkard rubbed his forehead. He needed to think about that more. *A great deal more.*

55

Dekkard woke later on Unadi morning and had to hurry down to breakfast, where he found Ysella was already sipping her café. He glanced at the side table, then at her. "Is there anything interesting in *Gestirn*?"

"Only that all the universities in Guldor will have to admit fewer students this year because the Council didn't increase funding and the universities don't have enough marks to repair the damages caused by the demonstrations unless they cut enrollment."

"The demonstrations were on the streets, not in the buildings." He poured his café, then sat down across the table from her.

"It makes a good excuse."

"Did the newssheets point that out? Did anyone from any university?"

"Did the sun rise in the west this morning?" she returned sardonically.

Dekkard offered a wry smile, then took his two croissants. He frowned as he looked at the greenish-brown slices where the quince paste usually was.

"Yes, it's guava paste." She grinned. "You should like it. It's almost as sicky-sweet as the quince."

"But it doesn't have the same tanginess." At least tomato jelly had tanginess.

"You mean it's actually too sweet for you?"

"I'll make do." Dekkard offered a mock-mournful expression.

"You poor fellow."

"I don't notice you taking any. But then, in the morning, sweetness . . ." Dekkard let the words dangle.

Ysella reached for the plain croissant, then took a single deliberate bite, after which she said, "I don't require excessive sweetness. Unlike some people."

"I don't either," declared Rhosali as she entered the staff room.

Seeing as he was definitely outnumbered, Dekkard asked, "How is your uncle doing?"

The maid smiled. "He says he has much to learn, but that it's also no different."

"In what way?"

"The Commercers in charge have rules that make no sense, and the foreman has to find ways to get things done by the rules when there are better ways."

"Does he like the job?" pressed Dekkard.

"Oh, yes. The manufactory is cleaner, and the air is better. Machtarn doesn't have the black fogs. He hardly coughs at all now." Rhosali poured her café and sat down beside Ysella.

"That's good," replied Dekkard.

"That was why Mother came here. She could hardly breathe without coughing growing up. That's what she said, anyway. Uncle Hermann says it wasn't that bad, but he admits he isn't coughing as much." Rhosali looked at the greenish-brown paste slices and smiled. "Guava! That's so much better than quince or tomato jelly." She immediately took two slices.

Ysella looked from Rhosali to Dekkard and shook her head.

Dekkard tried not to smile.

For the rest of breakfast, and during the drive to work, Dekkard's thoughts kept coming back to the question he continued to ponder—just what could shake people's confidence in the Commercers? *Would anything at present?*

Once he was at his desk, he concentrated on the letters that Karola had left him. Over the time he worked on those, several messengers came and went.

Obreduur appeared just before noon. "You can escort me to the dining room and then get yourselves something to eat. I'm lunching with Councilor Waarfel. After that, you can take me to the floor for debate on the funding bill. It will probably last until fifth bell, but I'd appreciate your returning about a sixth before that. If debate ends earlier, I'll send a messenger."

Dekkard and Ysella immediately stood, Dekkard so quickly that his gladius hit his chair.

Obreduur hadn't met with Waarfel in some time, as Dekkard recalled. Could it be because Waarfel was from Aloor, one of the districts adjoining Siincleer? Or because Waarfel was on the Public Resources Committee, the committee that should have held hearings on the Kraffeist Affair?

Obreduur said nothing as the three headed down the open central staircase to the main level. Once they were outside and walking along the covered walkway, Dekkard heard chants, possibly just on the other side of the south wall of the Council Square.

"More university funds! More university funds!"

"Reveal the votes! Open votes . . ."

"Personal responsibility! Personal accountability!"

Dekkard glanced toward the wall, but unlike before, no one had climbed it, even though the lowest part of the wall was less than two yards high, but just from the chants, he had no trouble determining who was demonstrating.

Obreduur lengthened his stride, and Dekkard kept glancing toward the wall, but the chants grew fainter, as if the Council Guards were pushing the chanters back. Dekkard waited for shots, but while the chanting continued, he heard no shots.

"The guards are advancing," said Ysella, "and the demonstrators are retreating."

"Good," replied Obreduur. "We don't need any more guards shot."

By the time the three reached the entrance to the

Council Hall, the chants were still fainter, and no shots had been fired.

"Go get something to eat," said Obreduur. "I'll see you here at a sixth before first bell."

Once Obreduur was inside the dining room, Dekkard looked to Ysella. "Should we find out what happened with the demonstrators?"

"They were already dispersing, and I didn't sense that anyone was hurt. I'd rather eat."

Since Dekkard had never known her senses to be wrong, he just said, "Lead the way."

When they reached the cafeteria, Dekkard could see that plenty of tables were empty, although by a third past noon, that would change. Dekkard decided on olive, beef, and raisin empanadas with a cucumber salad, while Ysella picked a milanesia of some kind, with a green salad, and, after paying, led the way to a four-top. "We'll see if anyone wants to join us."

"Are you looking for someone in particular?"

"More like any number of people." Ysella took a sip of café, then some of her milanesia.

Dekkard glanced at the suddenly lengthening food line, looking for more familiar faces, catching sight of Frieda Livigne with another woman he didn't recognize, and farther back, Councilor Saarh's security aides, Micah Eljaan and Malcolm Maarkham.

"Not Micah and Malcolm," said Ysella quietly.

Dekkard glanced back to the line, seeing Amelya Detauran and Elyssa Kaan. "What about Amelya Detauran and Elyssa?"

"If they come our way."

Dekkard didn't even have to raise a hand, because, after she paid the cashier, Detauran led Kaan straight toward Dekkard.

"Steffan, Avraal . . . could we join you?"

Ysella smiled warmly. "Of course."

Amelya seated herself beside Ysella, the more slender and shorter Elyssa beside Dekkard.

"I promised Steffan I'd explain about the Kraffeist mess, almost a month ago," said Amelya, "but we've never crossed paths."

"We were both in a hurry then," added Dekkard.

"You both know," continued Amelya, her voice lower, "that the Kraffeist Affair should have involved two committees—the Public Resources Committee and the Transportation Committee. The coal overcharges by Eastern Ironway were separate from the coal leases and the misuse of the Eshbruk Naval Coal Reserve, but they both should have come before the Transportation Committee. It didn't happen that way. It didn't because, when the next elections are called, Maastach can't run again, and Ulrich told him that if Councilor Bassaana brought up everything she had on Eastern Ironway, it could cause such a turmoil that the Imperador might have to call new elections. Maastach didn't tell her anything until it was already a done deal."

For a moment, Dekkard didn't connect the pieces, but only for a moment. "And your councilor's in line to be the next chair of the Transportation Committee." *If the Commercer-Landor coalition remains in power.* "And neither Ulrich nor Maastach let her know?"

"They still won't talk about it. They claim involving her would have been a conflict of interest because she has a large share of Jaykarh Mining & Coal."

"They never consider that when the councilor's a man," said Ysella.

"They won't admit that, either," agreed Amelya. "I just thought you should know."

"We appreciate it," said Dekkard warmly. "That clears up part of the mystery." *And opens other questions.*

"Did you see what happened with the demonstration a little while ago?" asked Ysella.

"Not all that much," replied Elyssa. "There weren't many demonstrators. Less than fifty. They yelled and waved signs. When the Council Guards ordered them to disperse and fired a warning shot, they backed up. They kept yelling, but they broke up. Then they scattered. The Guards might have caught three or four."

"That won't do much," said Amelya in a disgusted tone. "The ones they catch and detain never know anything. The plotters behind the demonstrations stay out of sight."

"Those behind burning down the Ministry of Security building planned that well," said Ysella. "Do you think Minister Wyath will ever catch them?"

"He's in no hurry," said Elyssa. "With people's attention on the demonstrations, Ulrich doesn't have to answer for the Kraffeist Affair, or the excessive rail rates Eastern Ironway charges northeastern mining companies, or the way that all the big engineering firms drive out competitors and keep the costs of building or rebuilding anything high."

At the last item, Dekkard managed not to show surprise. "Isn't that playing with fire?"

"The demonstrators aren't that much of a problem," replied Elyssa. "Besides, it's hard to pick them out unless you catch them in the act."

"If there were any way, though," added Amelya, "Ulrich would already be using it. He hates the New—I mean, the demonstrators. He likes peaceful streets and law and order."

"Provided the order benefits the Commercers who back him," countered Elyssa.

"There is that," said Amelya quietly. "We'd better finish eating and go wait for her."

"We're in the same situation," admitted Dekkard, although he was still thinking about Amelya's comment about Ulrich, his hatred of the New Meritorists and there being no way to identify them.

A few minutes later, the four all left the table, but Amelya and Elyssa moved away quickly, as if worried they might be late.

"You've made quite an impression on Amelya," said Ysella, smiling.

"I like her. She's always struck me as a very honest and good person," replied Dekkard. "Unlike someone like Frieda Livigne or that legalist Stoltz . . . or a few others."

"She more than likes you, I suspect."

"I don't like her *that* much," said Dekkard quietly.

"Then you're handling the situation as you should," said Ysella.

Dekkard heard a hint of satisfaction in those words, but decided a comment would be unwise. *Most unwise.*

"There's one thing about the demonstration. They knew what was in the legislation, even before it was presented on the floor."

"Of course. *Gestirn* wouldn't have printed what it did otherwise," replied Ysella.

"There weren't very many, and none of them shot at the Council Guards." The fact that the New Meritorists hadn't used weapons this time intrigued Dekkard. Did the comparatively more peaceful demonstration merely represent a change in tactics or did it reflect a new strategy? Or just a desire not to get shot?

Once they reached the councilors' dining room, they still had to wait almost a third before Obreduur appeared, although he smiled as he approached. "I'm sorry. It took a little longer. I wanted to see if he could tell me anything he knew about the Siincleer corporacions that wasn't common knowledge. He knew a few things, but I suspect that, were either of you councilors, you'd have known more. Still . . . it was pleasant."

In minutes, they were at the lobby to the Council Hall, and Obreduur hurried inside.

"Almost four bells to finish up letters and petitions," said Dekkard, turning to head back to the Council Office Building.

"More like three with the walking back and forth," corrected Ysella.

"I was being optimistic. I am occasionally."

"Just occasionally?" Ysella offered an amused smile.

"Maybe a little more than occasionally."

As they walked, Dekkard's thoughts went back to

the New Meritorists and what Amelya had said about Premier Ulrich. *Does he hate them enough to do something stupid . . . or is that just a political position?*

He nodded. There might be one way to find out . . . and put some pressure on the Commercers. He also had to tell Obreduur the additional details about what Maastach and Ulrich had done to Councilor Bassaana.

56

Despite the New Meritorist protests and demonstration, late on Unadi afternoon the supplemental funding legislation passed the Council with a cap on university funding and an enrollment limit for new admissions or readmissions. The story in *Gestirn* mentioned both the cap and the prohibition, but nothing about the New Meritorist demonstrators.

Duadi and Tridi were slow and routine, since the Council was in pro forma session until officially adjourning for the Summerend recess on Quindi. On Duadi, Ysella wore her gray suit, and took the Gresynt to her talk to the Women's Clerical Guild. After reporting to Obreduur, she told Dekkard that it was low-key, but that the women received her well.

Dekkard kept looking for Jaime Minz, because he wanted a "casual" encounter, except on his terms. Finally, on Furdi morning, just after he'd crossed the street from the covered parking, he saw Minz's tall burly form and angled his steps to almost bump into the tall isolate.

"Jaime! I haven't seen you in days. I didn't think I'd see you until after recess."

For a moment, Minz looked almost annoyed, before smiling broadly. "I thought the same, but you can never tell. Life has its surprises, as you've found out. I hear your councilor is visiting Gaarlak, as well as his own district."

Dekkard doubted that Obreduur had told Ulrich his

plans for the recess, but merely said, "Does Security check bookings on Guldoran Ironway, or does the ironway just report to him?"

"My, you're suspicious, Steffan."

"The councilor has some political obligations to the Craft Party, just as the Premier has political obligations to the Commerce Party. They both know there will be elections at some point in the next two years."

"Elections won't change anything, Steffan. You know that."

"The New Meritorists might have something to say about that."

"That handful of superannuated students and disgruntled academics? Hardly."

"They did a pretty thorough destruction of the Security Ministry building. That suggests more than academics. They have enough followers to create demonstrations all across Guldor."

"If necessary, Security can track them down, but I doubt it will be necessary."

"How? From the demonstrators I've seen, they look like anyone else. Or will Security just assume that everyone who reads their manifesto or principles is a Meritorist?"

"You sound like you've read it."

"If there is such a thing, I wouldn't even know where to find a copy, but all serious would-be revolutionaries have a set of principles or something of the sort. Even so, that doesn't mean whoever has a copy is a New Meritorist."

"I'd say it was a good indication."

"Even if it were, how would you find out who had a copy? Or who printed it?"

"They couldn't be that stupid."

Dekkard shrugged. "We're not in the age of scriveners. If there is a book, someone printed it."

For just an instant, Minz's face appeared different, as if Dekkard had given him an insight. Then he said, "There's probably no book."

Dekkard shrugged. "Have it your way. That's what I

heard. Is the Premier going to spend some of the Summerend recess in Veerlyn?"

"He hasn't said."

Dekkard laughed. "He plans everything out. Don't tell me you don't know. If he's going to stay close to the Imperador and Minister Wyath, it doesn't bother me."

"Steffan . . ." Minz shook his head, then said cheerfully, "Don't let your modest promotion go to your head. Security involves more than either of us knows."

"I'm sure it involves more than I know. But you know a great deal more than you're saying."

"Not that much more."

"As you've pointed out, there's a lot I don't know." Dekkard grinned. "But do you really want to wager you don't know more about Security than you're saying?"

"You know security aides shouldn't wager," declared Minz heartily. "I need to be going. Enjoy your time in Gaarlak, Oersynt, and Malek."

"If we go there, I will," returned Dekkard as warmly as he could, just remaining where he stood for several moments as Minz walked away.

He thought Minz had taken the idea, but if he had . . . Dekkard couldn't help but wince. *Do you really want that to happen?* Except he knew that not only Minz and Ulrich, but even Obreduur, were underestimating the anger behind the New Meritorists.

He was only a few minutes later than usual when he entered the office. Neither Karola nor Ysella looked up as he settled behind his desk and looked at the seven letters waiting.

By midmorning, he'd turned his drafts over to Margrit.

As he walked back to his desk, Karola said, "Steffan, the councilor wants to see you."

"Did he say why?"

Karola shook her head.

When he entered the inner office, Dekkard still worried about what Obreduur wanted, but the older man just smiled and gestured for Dekkard to take a chair. Dekkard did . . . and waited.

"Steffan . . . you're caught up on your work, aren't you?"

"Yes, sir."

"Good. I'd like you to write a speech. A very specific speech. One that explains in simple, but not simplistic, terms why voting for the Craft Party is in the best interests of crafters and artisans, and also in the best interests of all people. Especially those who want Guldor to continue as a land where a laborer's children can become crafters and artisans, and where their children can become professionals and magnates of commerce."

"Are you expecting the Imperador to call elections?"

Obreduur shook his head. "I hope to the Three not. That wouldn't be in our interests at the moment."

"If I might ask . . . then . . . ?"

"Because I want you to come up with phrasing and words from your heart as well as from your mind. It might take a while. So it's a good idea to start now."

"A speech for you from my heart?"

Obreduur actually grinned. Dekkard had seen him smile often, but never grin. "No. It's your speech. After recess, possibly even during our tour, you may have to represent me. For anyone to speak from someone else's heart never works as well as from one's own heart. You need to have ideas and phrases that you're comfortable with locked into your very being, and they have to be honest words and feelings. Otherwise, the people you're talking to will sense that something's not right." Obreduur paused. "A few councilors have the gift of believing that whatever they say at the moment is true. They're the most dangerous because the only truth they know is deception. That's why you need to write out what you can say to anyone and feel comfortable with. You also need to phrase it in a way that attacks no one or their beliefs. That's going to be harder than you think. That's why you need to start working on it now." He paused again. "Have I made myself clear?"

"Yes, sir. You said not to attack anyone or their beliefs. Does that mean ever?"

Obreduur shook his head. "You never begin by attacking. You always begin by saying what the Craft Party and you stand for and why those stands are good. We'll talk about attacks later. First, you have to give people a reason to vote for the Craft Party. So start there."

Dekkard wasn't totally satisfied with those answers, but he could see that Obreduur was serious about beginning with the positive. "Then I will, sir."

"Try to enjoy it." Obreduur smiled. "On your way out, have Karola come in. I have some messages for her to dispatch."

Dekkard walked back out and conveyed the message to Karola, then to his desk, sat down, and just looked at the blank sheet of paper he'd taken out without even thinking about it.

Why did he believe that the Craft Party was the best choice for artisans and crafters, indeed for everyone . . . and not just because the Commercers and Landors were worse?

It took him a bell to come up with a very short list:

1. The Craft Party stood for fair pay and good jobs.
2. It fought for the rights and safety of workers at all levels.
3. It supported and pressed for access to education and jobs to be based on ability and skills, not on wealth or parental economic or social position.
4. It stood for the Great Charter as drafted and originally implemented.

Everything else he'd come up with was essentially negative. The party opposed preferential tax treatment for corporacions. It opposed tariffs on agricultural imports, because that raised the cost of food for workers. It opposed differential treatment of workers and the poor by Security forces. It opposed excessive restrictions on the newssheets . . . and so on.

After looking at his list, Dekkard shook his head. Those basics looked so simplistic when put down in ink on a sheet of paper, and every party could come up with such a list. So what made the Craft Party different? Because its councilors worked and fought every day? Didn't all councilors . . . or their staffs?

Dekkard looked down at the list again. He didn't get any more ideas. Finally, he started thinking about a second list, on why he was a Crafter. Was it just because he believed in the value of all work, from the menial to high art and professional expertise, and that he didn't see that respect in the other two parties? Or because the Craft Party best supported that ideal? Or because he respected its councilors and staffers? Or simply because it was a family tradition?

By noon, he wasn't that much farther along, but the lack of progress reminded him of something else. He turned and looked to Ysella. "We need to agree on a final version of that draft Obreduur asked for."

Ysella looked up, momentarily puzzled.

"The engineering one," he prompted, not wanting to say aloud that it was about Siincleer Shipbuilding and Engaard Engineering.

"You're right. Later today."

Dekkard nodded in return and went back to pondering his party and principles paper. By the end of the workday, he'd drafted and destroyed more than a few sheets of paper.

He and Ysella also received copies of their itinerary for the recess tour of Gaarlak, Oersynt, and Malek, a tour that would take most of the month and not return them to Machtarn until the thirty-second of Summerend.

As he drove Obreduur and Ysella back to the house, dropped them off under the portico, and garaged the Gresynt, he wondered why he was having such difficulty with a simple speech.

When he left the garage, Ysella was waiting. "We can go over the Siincleer paper before dinner."

"That would be good."

"You're upset. What did he ask? You were fine until you came out of his office."

"He has me working on a speech on why people should support the Craft Party . . . and it has to be—"

"From your heart," interjected Ysella, smiling. "It's harder than you thought, isn't it?"

"Then he asked the same of you?"

"Over a year ago, when it became clear that you were the right security aide for him."

What does my being the right security aide have to do with Ysella writing a speech?

At Dekkard's obvious expression of puzzlement, she replied, "Before that I had to spend more time getting you used to being as effective as possible for Obreduur, and if you hadn't worked out, I would have had to do it again with another isolate."

"You weren't sure about me for a year?"

"I didn't say that," she replied calmly. "We both knew you were an outstanding security aide. That was only half the question. The other half was whether what you believed wasn't in conflict with what he believes. We also needed to see if there was any conflict between how you acted and what you said. That took longer because you're so reserved."

"More like cautious," said Dekkard.

"I'd agree," replied Ysella, "but at first it was hard to tell." She paused for a moment, then went on, "Why don't we go over the engineering paper now? Then we can talk about the speech after dinner. We'll have more than a bell before Rhosali sets the staff table."

"We should be able to finish by then . . . unless you have major changes."

"I don't. Just some wording suggestions."

Only a few minutes passed before the two were in the staff room. They made very few changes, and Dekkard wrote out two fair copies before surrendering the table to Rhosali and Hyelda.

Then they entered the family's side of the house, where Obreduur was actually in the sitting room reading. He looked up, almost as if he'd been expecting them. "Yes?"

Dekkard handed one of the copies to the councilor. "The paper on the Siincleer corporacions."

Obreduur read possibly the first two lines, and then handed it back. "If you wouldn't mind leaving it on my desk. Thank you both."

After that, despite the early-evening heat, while he waited for dinner, Dekkard went out into the side garden, composed entirely of herbs and vegetables cultivated by Hyelda, to be alone and think.

He still didn't understand why Obreduur, and even Ysella, had invested so much time and effort in training him. He was an isolate, and while there weren't any restrictions in the Great Charter set forward on isolates, unlike those on susceptibles, who could not hold public office or vote, or empaths, who could not hold any elective office, Dekkard didn't know of any isolates who rose much above the position of chief security officer in corporacions, or, occasionally, chief of a Security or patrol station.

When dinner came, he tried to put those thoughts aside, but, afterward, when he and Ysella walked down the drive to the portico, they flooded back.

"Are you still concerned about writing that speech?"

"I am, but that's not all. I'm sorry. It doesn't make sense. Why invest in a security aide? I'm not a legalist. I'm not from wealth or power—"

"That's exactly why," she said calmly as she stopped under the portico. "You have an Institute education. You're intelligent. You speak well. You believe in what he and the Craft Party are trying to do. You work hard and learn quickly. You don't put on airs just because you're a Council staffer. And you're honest. Do you know how few young men, especially young men from a Craft background, have those skills? Very few, the Three know."

"What does he expect of me?"

"I don't want to guess. I do know that, one way or

another, he thinks you have the chance of a bright future if you just keep working at it. I also know it won't be easy. You've already seen the reaction of people like Frieda Livigne and Fernand Stoltz."

"And Jaime Minz."

There were several moments of silence before she said quietly, "Do you want to talk about the speech itself? It might help for you to just talk."

"When I think about what I believe . . . it's so simple. It sounds like a slogan. We're for good and meaningful jobs for people, and we want fair wages for those people. Doesn't every councilor or candidate for the Council say something like that? We're for worker rights and safety . . ." Dekkard shrugged, almost helplessly.

"Others say it. That's true," agreed Ysella. "What did we do with the Sanitation jobs? Or last year, with the workers in the ceramic pipeworks plant? We didn't just talk, did we?"

"So . . . the Craft Party doesn't just speak the words people want to hear. Others will claim the same."

"What would you say to someone who says all politicians are the same?"

"That they have to look beyond the words and claims . . ." Even as he talked and got a better feel for what he might say, Dekkard understood that he had even more to learn.

57

Once he stepped into the office on Quindi morning, Dekkard immediately went to work drafting replies for the eight letters that Karola had laid on his desk. When he finished those, he returned to working on the "Craft" speech.

Just before the first bell of the afternoon, Dekkard and Ysella escorted Obreduur to the Council Hall for what would be Premier Ulrich's Summerend address, traditionally little more than a brief speech filled with platitudes, regardless of who was Premier.

Once Obreduur left them and they eased back to the far side of the corridor to allow access to the Hall by other councilors, perhaps two out of three with security escorts, Dekkard said, "How much do you think Ulrich will say?"

"As little as he can."

Dekkard nodded. "Have you heard any more from Emrelda?"

"Only a brief note. She's fine, and she doesn't have any more information."

"Are you going to see her tomorrow?"

"I'd thought I would."

"Is this a sisters' day, or would you like company?"

"I like the order in which you phrased that. Since she's picking me up, I'll ask her if she'd like the three of us to go out to dinner. Then I can tell you . . . if that's acceptable."

"More than acceptable. I'll be here. All I'll be doing is writing a letter, working on that speech, and trying to figure out what to pack."

"On that speech . . . don't be so logical. Write down what you feel, whether it seems logical or not. After you've written what you feel strongly about, then make it logical."

Dekkard smiled ruefully. "I'll try that. What I'm doing isn't working all that well."

Little more than a third of a bell later, the Council was officially recessed. In moments, councilors began to leave the Hall and come out into the corridor. Dekkard kept watching, but he saw no sign of Obreduur. Finally, Obreduur appeared, walking with the Craft floor leader, Guilhohn Haarsfel, and Councilor Hasheem.

Haarsfel nodded to something Obreduur said, as did Hasheem, if after a moment.

Then Hasheem was joined by Erleen Orlov, who, as his isolate, was still handling security alone. Haarsfel, interestingly enough, appeared to have no security aides, at least not meeting him.

Obreduur motioned to Ysella and Dekkard, and they flanked him as he strode down the corridor toward the courtyard and the covered walkway to the Council Office Building. He did not speak until they were outside and no one else was that close.

"He spoke a little longer than usual. He didn't say much besides the normal platitudes, that Guldor remained economically and militarily strong, that trade talks with Argental would prove fruitful, and repairs to the Security building were well underway. He also said that some minor demonstrations were a nuisance rather than a real danger and that the small size of the latest demonstration showed that whatever group was behind it was losing support."

"He's never mentioned dissidents before," said Ysella. "Is the Council reconvening earlier than usual?"

"No. We go back in session at the usual date, Unadi, One Fallfirst."

"No mention of the Kraffeist Affair?" asked Dekkard.

Obreduur smiled sardonically. "Steffan, that's buried."

"I forgot," Dekkard declared dryly.

"By the way, you two did a very good job on the engineering paper, as you've called it. It could prove very useful at the right time."

"When will that be?" asked Dekkard, suspecting that Ysella wanted to know.

"That depends on what happens for the rest of the year," replied Obreduur. "How are you coming on that speech, Steffan?"

"I'm working on it, sir."

"Let me see what you have at the end of the day."

"Yes, sir." Dekkard kept his voice pleasant, although the last thing he wanted was for the councilor to see what he had written.

"Good."

When the three reached the office, once Obreduur

closed his door, Dekkard ducked out and headed to the Council Banque, where he withdrew far more marks than he was usually comfortable carrying and then arranged for a more than modest letter of credit. That way he wouldn't have to return to the banque and would have a backup if he needed marks in Oersynt.

When he returned, he immediately got out the speech and read over the first lines. He shook his head and started again. After almost a bell he read what he'd written.

When I first tried to explain why you should vote for the Craft Party, I tried to explain with numbers. Then I tried laws and the Great Charter. But none of that satisfied me, and if it didn't satisfy me, it surely wouldn't satisfy you. Why I believe in the Craft Party is simple. It's the only party that is concerned with people, people like you and me. I don't come from marks and other wealth . . .

When he finished reading it, Dekkard didn't quite shake his head. It was better than what he'd tried before . . . but it definitely needed work . . . and possibly some additions, if he could figure out what they might be.

Just before fourth bell, Obreduur stepped out of his office and walked over to Dekkard.

Dekkard, who was looking at what he'd written and feeling a mixture of frustration and despair, looked up. "Yes, sir."

"How are you coming? Are you happy with what you wrote?"

"What I wrote is how I feel, but it could be better."

Almost gently, Obreduur asked, "Are you happy with it?"

"No, sir."

Obreduur nodded. "Keep working on it until you are." Then he turned and walked into the staff office.

Dekkard looked over at Ysella, who showed a bemused smile. He wanted to snap that it wasn't all that amusing, but decided against it, instead asking quietly, "Is it that amusing?"

"You're hoping one of us will help you out, but you're the only one who can do that."

While Dekkard knew she was right, it didn't help any.

58

The rest of Quindi passed slowly for Dekkard, filled with driving, first back to the house, then escorting the family to and from services at the East Quarter chapel, followed by the usual later dinner, after which he spent another bell struggling with his speech before going to bed.

Surprisingly, he slept late on Findi morning, and found an envelope from Ysella in the breakfast room. The note inside was simple.

> Steffan—
> I didn't want to wake you. We'll have dinner at Estado Don Miguel. We'll pick you up at a third before six.

The signature was a single ornate "A."

Dekkard read the note a second time, then replaced it in the envelope. Dinner at Estado Don Miguel definitely meant wearing a suit. He poured his café, took the last two croissants . . . and looked at the guava paste, before reluctantly adding two slices to his plate.

After breakfast and washing up, he settled in the empty staff room and wrote a letter to his mother, letting her know more about the new duties involved with his recent promotion and also when he'd be in Oersynt, while cautioning her that he didn't know how much free time he might have, since Summerend recess wasn't a vacation for him, but a working trip.

Once he sealed the letter and readied it to post, he took a deep breath.

Time to work on the Three-cursed speech.

A second thought occurred to him. *You need to think about what you'll take on the trip.*

He shook his head, knowing that would just be procrastination. Instead, he looked at the latest draft of the speech. After rereading the first lines, he realized that no one cared about him, only how what the Craft Party did would affect them.

He took out a fresh sheet of paper, but sat there thinking for some time before he began to write. More than a bell passed before he had what might be the beginning of a beginning. He read it slowly.

Let me start by asking you all a basic question. Do we really need politics and political parties? Why? When you think about it, all life is a balance between what each of us thinks is best for us personally and what is best for our community as a whole. Experience has taught us that we need rules. Those rules should protect each of us from the worst people and impulses in our community, but also protect the community from attack . . .

After rereading what he'd managed to put down, the next question was what he should say next . . . or should what he said next depend on the group and the situation?

He took another deep breath. He'd listened to Obreduur speak more than a few times, but what he'd written didn't sound like the councilor. *But he said to write it from your heart and not his.*

After writing for a time, he gathered the papers together and took them upstairs to his room. There, he went through his limited wardrobe to see what would be best to pack for the upcoming trip.

At fifth bell he quickly began to restore order to his room and small closet, before washing up and readying himself for dinner. Well before the time Ysella had asked him to be ready, he came down the staff stairs wearing a gray suit, a white shirt, and a blue cravat with narrow, diagonal gray stripes. He did put his silver staff pin on his lapel, although he hoped it wouldn't be necessary. He also carried his knives and his personal-length truncheon.

Almost to the minute promised in Ysella's note, Emrelda's teal Gresynt pulled up on Altarama opposite the pedestrian gate. Even before he entered the steamer, Dekkard was glad he had worn the suit, given that both sisters were in similar semi-formal dinner dresses, with the near-transparent headscarves they both preferred. Emrelda was in deep green, Ysella in red.

As he climbed into the rear seat, Emrelda turned to her sister. "You're right. He could pass for a theatre idol."

Dekkard winced, but said to Ysella, "Did you tell her to say that?"

"She didn't," replied Emrelda with a mischievous grin. "She did say she thought you were that handsome, but not to tell you."

Dekkard wasn't totally surprised to see Ysella blush slightly.

"That's just payback for the story about Haarlakt," added Emrelda, easing the Gresynt into a U-turn and heading back down Altarama toward Imperial Boulevard.

"You already had your payback with the story about Tammal," mock-protested Ysella.

"What did you do today, Steffan?" asked Emrelda, not looking in her sister's direction.

"First, I read a note directing me where to be," replied Dekkard, trying to replicate the officious tone of a certain legalist. "Then I ate breakfast, suffering horribly through the guava paste necessary to impart some sweetness and taste to my croissants. After that, I labored over a dull speech, endeavoring to put some life into it. Following that drudgery, I searched through my sparse wardrobe to determine what I should pack for the forthcoming trek through the wilds of Gaarlak, Oersynt, and Malek. In the end, declaring everything but the contents of the note in vain, I dressed for dinner."

Ysella tried not to laugh . . . but failed. Then she shook her head. "You sound so much like Fernand Stoltz."

"That's because I was trying to."

"Whoever Fernand is, after that I don't think I'd want to meet him," declared Emrelda.

"He wouldn't want to meet you," replied Ysella, "especially if you were in uniform. He doesn't like to recognize any authority except himself."

"Can you imitate anyone else?" asked Emrelda.

"I really couldn't even imitate Fernand," demurred Dekkard. "It's more my feel of what he's like."

"It's an excellent feel," said Ysella.

Dekkard wouldn't have known, but he trusted Ysella's judgment.

Emrelda found a parking space less than a block from the five-story building, and the three walked to the nearest entrance, the one above which, five stories up, was the silver and black metal plaque that bore the name NORDSTAR.

"Has either of you been inside the Nordstar offices?" asked Emrelda.

"We're security aides for a Crafter," said Ysella. "Unless we went with the councilor, the only aide to be allowed in there would be Ivann Macri, and only if it involved a technical legal matter."

"That's too bad. I always wondered if the offices were as pretentious as the building."

"Do you even have to wonder?" asked Ysella.

Emrelda laughed softly.

Once they entered Estado Don Miguel, Emrelda stepped forward and declared, "Party of three—Roemnal."

The maître d'hôtel—who wasn't the same one as

when Ysella had taken Dekkard to the restaurant before—nodded and said, "Of course, Ritten Roemnal." Before he led them to a table set for three, his eyes lingered on Dekkard for just an instant.

That surprised Dekkard, but he had to assume that had something to do with Obreduur, and he said nothing until they were seated and momentarily alone. "Ritten Roemnal?"

Both sisters smiled.

Then Ysella said, "We're paying for it, but Obreduur arranged it. He just said it was a small thing, and that Emrelda deserved it."

Dekkard thought for a moment, then said cautiously, "Does your father hold the title of Ritter?"

The two exchanged glances, almost guiltily.

Then Ysella said, "The title, and most of the original lands, but the marks from the lands barely support Father and Cliven."

You knew they were Landors, but from the ancient landed nobility? That also explained the maître d'hôtel's glance at Dekkard, most likely assessing him as their security aide.

"It's only a courtesy title for daughters," added Emrelda. "Obreduur was stretching matters."

"Which he loves to do when he can secretly poke fun at Landors and Commercers," added Ysella.

"I haven't seen him do that often." While Dekkard had heard certain veiled statements and asides the councilor had made, he really hadn't thought that much of it at those times, possibly because he agreed with Obreduur.

Trying to gather his thoughts, Dekkard let his eyes roam around the restaurant, noting that the tables already occupied held well-dressed men and women, early as it was, and that none of the conversations were what he would have called boisterous. He glanced down at the starched and spotless white linens and napkins.

He managed an amused smile when he looked up. "You two never cease to surprise me."

"Aren't women supposed to do that . . . occasionally, anyway?" asked Emrelda.

"I don't know whether you're supposed to, but you certainly do," replied Dekkard dryly.

Ysella smiled warmly. "Now that we've surprised you, we all should enjoy dinner."

Dekkard knew she meant it . . . and that there would be no more surprises . . . for the evening, at least.

59

The pleasure of the dinner at Estado Don Miguel was short-lived, because the next morning, the first day of Summerend, Dekkard began packing for Duadi's departure. He'd largely finished when Ritten Obreduur enlisted his strong back to carry the heavier suitcases down to the side hall leading to the portico. Not long after he finished carting those, Obreduur asked him into the study, where he read the latest draft of Dekkard's speech.

The councilor's comments were direct. "Your introduction is adequate. Possibly better, depending on how you deliver it. You've provided a general reason for them to support you and the party, but you've given no specifics. No gut reasons they can latch on to."

"Sir . . . I'm not the councilor. I hesitated to give specific legislation in your name." Part of that was because Dekkard couldn't recall a specific measure presented by Obreduur.

Obreduur smiled. "That doesn't mean you can't take a stand on a specific issue. If you're going to speak for me, I'll have to read what you'd say, of course. You haven't heard me be too detailed. Detailed legislative measures presented to the public always get a councilor in trouble. You need to mention a specific point without technical details."

"Like saying all large military procurements need to be made public?"

"That's general enough, but most people don't care about naval procurements."

"That basic foods shouldn't face high tariffs?"

Obreduur shook his head. "First, most people don't understand tariffs. Second, if you lower tariffs on swampgrass rice, for example, some farmworkers will lose their jobs."

"What about establishing a minimum wage for all full-time workers?"

"Then manufactories will just hire part-time workers."

Dekkard began to wonder if Obreduur was toying with him, but he said, "What about saying near-starvation wages are unacceptable for the work that Guldoran workers provide?"

"That's better. Especially since some textile manufactories still pay near-starvation wages."

"What about requiring healthy workplaces?"

"That would work as well."

"What if someone asks how exactly we'll provide that?"

"Ask them, what is their biggest concern in where they work? If it's a newsie, tell them that, beyond basic safety rules, standards have to be developed on an industry-by-industry basis by both guilds and manufactories, because the guilds know what's safe and what's not and the manufactories have to pay for the changes."

"Being specific without being too detailed, then?" asked Dekkard dryly.

"There's no point in being too detailed. The Council will change what anyone proposes to some extent. If I give any specific number, then I'll be held to it, even when I can't do anything about it. That's true of any councilor, not just me." He offered an amused smile. "Now . . . if you can get a guildmeister or a corporacion functionary to come up with a number, you can say that they recommended that number . . . and then we're not tied to it. Or if it's a bad number, you can say that it's too high or too low, and that gives us room to maneuver."

All that made sense to Dekkard. He just hadn't thought of it in quite that way.

"That's enough for now," said Obreduur. "I need to get back to packing and writing some last-moment messages, but see if you can come up with a nonspecific specific that's not general and will appeal to both Craft voters and others. You're on the right rails. Just keep at it."

Dekkard walked from the study, thinking. *He wants you to be able to make speeches for him. On this trip? What is it about Gaarlak?*

When he stepped into the staff room, he was so preoccupied that he almost ran into Ysella, who carried a small and narrow cloth-wrapped package. "I'm sorry."

"That's all right. I was looking for you anyway." She handed him the package. "These are for you. You need to bring them with you on the trip."

"I do?"

"They're formal cravats. I've noticed that cravats tend to suffer when there are receptions and dinners, and you won't have time to buy more."

"How much do I owe you?"

"Steffan, they're not that expensive, and you've been really sweet with Emrelda. They're a present, but please pack them." Before Dekkard could object, she went on, "You were just talking to Obreduur, weren't you?"

"I was . . . about my speech." Before she could say anything, he went on. "There's something different about this trip, isn't there? Not just about Gaarlak, either."

"That would be my guess. He hasn't said anything to me . . . except that it's important, and that I could be helpful with women's guilds there."

"Working Women Guild and who else?"

"Why did you guess the Working Women Guild?"

The guild serving the women in brothels and massage parlors had just come to mind, but Dekkard wasn't about to say it was a guess. "It seems to me that only the Craft Party is willing to deal with them and their problems."

"That's half of it. But the other half is that as working women they're entitled to vote . . . and they haven't voted as much as they could. Except in a few places, like Ondeliew."

"And that's how Harleona Zerlyon was elected?"

"The women made the difference. It was actually Ritten Obreduur's idea."

That did surprise Dekkard. "No one ever mentions Ritten Obreduur in a political context, only as a legalist."

"She was trained as a legalist, and worked for the Hotel and Food Service Guild of Malek. She met the councilor through the guilds. After they'd been married several years, she and her friends persuaded him to run for the Council. She worked to get the guilds where women were strong behind him. Before the last election, back in 1261, the councilor from Ondeliew tried to pass legislation that would have classed women who worked in the brothels as part-time workers, which would have meant they would have lost the right to vote. Ingrella went to Ondeliew to help Harleona Zerlyon get elected."

Dekkard managed to keep his jaw in place, realizing finally what had been nagging him about Gaarlak. "Something more is definitely happening. Remember that Ritten Obreduur spent some of the spring in Gaarlak. She was gone almost a month."

"I knew she'd gone, but Obreduur mentioned she was consulting with guild legalists."

"If we're going, for the first time, and Ritten Obreduur spent a month there, and all three of us are speaking, there's definitely more happening than we've been told."

"Or perhaps the councilor is planning in case more does happen," suggested Ysella.

"Something will happen during Summerend recess," said Dekkard, "something planned by the New Meritorists. What that might be, I don't know. I just feel it will."

After a moment, he added, "I need to see if Ritten Obreduur needs anything else hoisted or carried."

"Gustoff should be doing that."

"Axeli didn't when he was here last year. So why do you expect Gustoff to carry anything this year?"

"Oh . . . I could hope . . ."

Then they both laughed.

60

On Duadi, everyone was up early, because the Oersynt Express left Imperial Station precisely at two thirds after the first bell. While the Obreduurs visited family in Malek every Summerend, usually the visit lasted four weeks, not counting the two-day trip each way by express train. On the way, Obreduur stopped and spent several days in Oersynt on political and guild matters, while the family continued on to Malek. According to the itinerary, though, this time the entire family would stop in Gaarlak for three days, and then in Oersynt for another four.

After breakfast, Dekkard helped load all the luggage into the two large Kharlan limousines in the drive. The limousines pulled away from the house well before first bell, with Ysella and the family, except for Axeli, who was serving as a temporary midshipman on a Guldoran cruiser, in the first Kharlan and Dekkard and the bulk of the luggage in the second.

Imperial Station was a half mille west of Imperial Boulevard on Council Avenue, and both Kharlans arrived together just before first bell, moving into the unloading zone reserved for councilors, ministers, and deputy and assistant ministers. Despite frequent scrubbing, the tall golden-white marble columns were slightly tinged with soot, but the windows sparkled in the early-morning sun. When Dekkard got out of the

Kharlan, he could see the heat haze spreading over the city, although the Imperador's Palace shone golden white to the northeast of the station.

In another fifteen minutes, with the aid of three porters and their carts, the entire party was on board the Oersynt Express, in three first-class compartments. Dekkard just hoped that Nellara and Gustoff remained civil in the compartment they shared. For the moment, the door of the compartment Dekkard and Ysella would share remained open so that she could more easily sense anyone of a dubious nature.

Dekkard stood inside the open door and surveyed the compartment, since his ironway travels had afforded him only the dubious comfort of standard carriage seats, while the dark blue velvet seat on which Ysella sat, half-turned from the large window, promised greater ease and far greater legroom, not to mention privacy. The paneling was the older black walnut, rather than yellow cedar, although not many carriages had been finished with the cedar, which pleased Dekkard, while the floor was carpeted in gray with a design of intertwined gold and blue spirals.

"I didn't see anyone following us. Did you sense anything unusual?" he finally asked.

"Not so far. Except that Nellara's anything but pleased."

"Because of Gustoff?"

"More because she doesn't want to leave Machtarn and her friends. She's at that age where family is a bother."

"Is that more of a problem with girls? I don't recall feeling that way."

Ysella just looked at Dekkard. Finally, she shook her head. "You just ignored family and did as you wanted. You probably stayed close to family rules, unlike most young men. Girls don't have that freedom. Especially girls from well-off or powerful families . . . or long-established Landor clans. So friends, or those whom they convince themselves are friends, mean more. That's because parents never understand." The sarcasm of the last sentence wasn't lost on Dekkard.

The first-class steward, wearing a deep blue uniform trimmed with silver piping, strode down the center corridor, saying, "The express will be leaving in half a third, half a third."

Dekkard waited until the steward passed, then said, "I didn't dare break the rules. If my mother's words didn't blister me, my father would have made sure I never thought about breaking them again."

"I thought you said your father was the lenient one."

"He was—until my mother laid down the law. If she said I'd disobeyed her, my father would have made certain I couldn't sit down for a week."

"Did that ever happen?"

"Only once. I was thirteen and made a condescendingly flippant comment about how she couldn't possibly understand what I felt."

"Only a problem with girls?" asked Ysella gently.

"I never thought they were a bother . . . only that they didn't understand. Since I never had many friends, I didn't miss being away from them. But I never said anything about them not understanding again. That one time Father had me against the wall in a moment. He's broader than I am, and he's almost fifty. I still remember standing to eat because I couldn't sit down."

"Your mother's the reason they left Argental, isn't she?"

"They never spoke of it." Dekkard paused. "I always had the impression that leaving wasn't easy, but the only specific I ever heard—saw, really—was what she wrote in a letter a month or so ago. The one where she mentioned the demonstration in Oersynt. She wrote that she heard the shots, and her exact words were 'you don't ever forget that sound.' So it was obviously much harder than I'd thought, but I never thought it was easy."

"How did they feel about your attending the Institute?"

"After it was clear I was an isolate and that I'd never

be a good artisan, they were for it. Being an isolate meant I had one of the important talents for security. My father felt people should follow their talents and love what they did. Loving what they did came first, but he also said people who loved what they didn't have the talent for were fools."

"He sounds like a very practical man. Did they ever talk about Argental?"

"They'd occasionally describe Cimaguile, or how cold the winters were, especially if any of us complained about being cold. Father used to say, 'You don't know what cold is.' My mother gave a knowing smile when he said that, because that was always what he said."

"Parents often have a habit of repeating themselves," said Ysella.

"What phrases did your parents repeat?"

"'The melon stays close to the vine.' That was one of my father's that I particularly disliked. The one that Emrelda detested was the one he threw at her when she married Markell—'Early ripe, early rotten.'"

"That's terrible."

"Mother's sayings were like platitudes. 'There's never an ill wind that doesn't blow some good.' Another was 'Small potatoes are sweeter.' None of us are much for sayings. Then that might be because none of us have children."

At that moment, there was a slight jolt, and the carriage began to move, slowly at first. Within a sixth, the train was moving close to thirty milles a bell as it turned northeast. To his left, Dekkard could see only the top of the Imperial Palace above the low buildings flanking the three parallel sets of rails that stretched ahead through the level and fertile lands and woods separating Machtarn and Gaarlak.

He just hoped that Nellara would settle down so that her emotions didn't grate on Ysella and that he and Ysella could get some enjoyment out of the trip.

61

While the first-class carriage and the dining carriage of the Oersynt Express were elegant and comfortable, and Dekkard and Ysella had time to talk and read, the scenery on the way to Gaarlak was pleasantly repetitious, with the low hills north of Machtarn giving way to fields of all sorts, and then more fields, interspersed with small forests better termed woodlots, in turn giving way to more fields, occasionally spiced by a pond or small lake, or a stream . . . for the entire ten bells it took to reach Gaarlak. Even the dinner in the dining carriage was pleasant, although Dekkard's cumin-roasted game hen verged on the bland. When the express neared Gaarlak, the fields were a sea of blue flax flowers, not surprising, given that Gaarlak was the center of Guldoran linen and linseed oil production.

From what Dekkard could see from the carriage window as the Oersynt Express pulled into Gaarlak, the city was perhaps a tenth the size of Machtarn, with the ironway station near the center, and there was even less haze than in Machtarn. Two steamhacks conveyed the Obreduur party to the Ritter's Inn, a modest four-story red brick structure in the upper side of the center city. Farther to the east lay the mills powered by the waters of the Lakaan River where they left the higher ground that sloped into the fertile lowlands.

Dekkard was sweating when they reached the inn, because Gaarlak was warmer than Machtarn, and the air was damper. The Obreduur family took the Knight's Suite, while Dekkard and Ysella had separate rooms, on each side of the suite. Even though Dekkard hadn't exerted himself that much, he discovered that he was more tired than he realized, and he found himself dozing off while trying to read a sequel to *The Son of Gold,* entitled *The Scarlet Daughter,* which he had borrowed from the Obreduurs' library. The novels might have reflected Ingrella Obreduur's tastes more than her husband's, but he had no way of knowing that.

When he woke on Tridi morning, Dekkard felt sticky, but shaving and a shower helped, and he was ready well before Obreduur's breakfast meeting with the Gaarlak guildmeisters and others in the inn's private dining room. He wore one of his light gray summer suits with the long truncheon and his staff pin, which was definitely bending the rules, and his concealed throwing knives. Ysella was ready as well, also wearing a gray suit and a small gray purse with narrow straps. They waited for Obreduur outside the door of the second-floor suite.

When the Obreduurs appeared, the Ritten's presence was a momentary surprise, but it made sense, given that she was a legalist and already involved in guild affairs. The councilor wore a white linen suit, while his wife also wore a linen suit, except hers was pale green.

Obreduur gestured to Dekkard, who led the way to the wide staircase connecting the first two levels. The third and fourth stories were accessed by narrower staircases, in the style of structures built from the mid-1100s until just before the turn of the century, but the heavy maroon carpeting on the steps was nearly new, and the brass lighting fixtures on the wall glistened from a recent polishing. From the staircase, Dekkard led the way across the smooth dark gray slate floor past the small restaurant, seemingly only a third full, toward the private dining room.

A short and wiry man with thinning brown hair and a high forehead stood outside the open door.

"That's Jens Seigryn," said Obreduur quietly. "He's the Craft Party coordinator for the Gaarlak district."

As the four neared, Seigryn stepped forward and said, "Axel! Welcome to Gaarlak . . . and to you, too, Ingrella."

"It's good to see you again, Jens," declared Obreduur warmly.

Ingrella smiled and inclined her head.

"I'd like you to meet two of my assistants," said the councilor. "The tall young man is Steffan Dekkard. He handles economic, tariff, and other trade matters—"

"And security, I'd wager," replied Seigryn.

"—and this is Avraal Ysella, who handles agriculture and women's guild matters . . . and security."

Seigryn grinned, looking at Dekkard and then Ysella. "He'll never change. He wants anyone who works for him to handle at least two jobs. That because he's usually doing three or four, and he thinks that's normal."

Obreduur said cheerfully, "I'm not that bad. Most of the time, anyway."

Ingrella looked to Seigryn and said dryly, "He still has certain illusions."

Dekkard had to struggle to keep from grinning.

"It's good he has you, Ingrella," replied Seigryn. "Before we go in, I thought I'd better tell you who's here. I couldn't get everyone, but I did get most of them, except for Yorik Haansel of the Stonemasons Guild. There's Arleena Desenns, guildmeister of the Weavers Guild . . ." His eyes went to Dekkard with the words of explanation, and Dekkard understood that they were for him and Ysella. ". . . Gretna Haarl, assistant guildmeister of the Textile Millworkers, Haasan Decaro, guildmeister of the Machineworkers, Jon Eliver, deputy guildmeister of the Farmworkers, and Johan Lamarr, guildmeister of the Crafters. I'd have preferred Kharl Maatsuyt, the Textile Millworkers guildmeister, instead of Gretna Haarl. Gretna can be . . . difficult."

"You did the best you could," replied Obreduur.

Dekkard concentrated on the names, trying to remember them all and suspecting that he'd have even more names to know, or at least recognize, by the time they left Gaarlak.

"What can I say about your aides?" asked Seigryn.

"You know about Avraal. Steffan comes from a solid artisan family, was a top-ten graduate of the Institute, and deals with trade and other issues affecting crafters and artisans."

"You got a Triumphing Ten, Axel?" Seigryn looked to Dekkard. "Why did you ever agree to work for him?"

Dekkard smiled sheepishly. "I liked what I saw."

"Good choice." Seigryn turned to Obreduur. "I'll lead the way in. You and Ingrella come in last. There are place cards for each of you. I had trouble getting a big enough circular table, but that's what you wanted."

Place cards? That meant that Seigryn had known who he and Ysella were, but wanted to see how Obreduur presented them and how he and Ysella reacted. *Welcome to the meet and greet side of politics.*

Seigryn turned and walked toward the open door.

Dekkard gestured for Ysella to walk beside him. She shook her head and murmured, "We're not married. So I'm less important here where it's traditional. I need to go first."

Since it wasn't his place to argue, he just smiled wryly and nodded, then followed her.

The private dining room was simply an oblong chamber some eight yards long and six wide. Below the chair rail, the walls were of darkened oak paneling, while the plaster walls above were a pale cream, as was the ceiling. The maroon carpeting was the same as that on the main stairs, and the crown molding was painted to match the carpet.

Five people stood to one side of the table, set with silver cutlery and a plain white linen cloth, two women and three men. Once everyone was inside, Seigryn closed the chamber door and said, "All of you know Councilor Obreduur, and we're glad that you kindly agreed to meet with him. Besides the councilor, and his wife Ingrella, the noted legalist who has been assisting craft guilds here, and all over Guldor, are two of his assistants. Avraal Ysella is experienced in land-management issues and has worked with guilds on workplace problems. Steffan Dekkard comes from a long line of artisans, but is also experienced in security matters and artisan issues dealing with tariffs, trade, and workplace conditions."

After the briefest pause, Seigryn went on. "As you've

noticed from the place cards, we've spaced out the councilor, his wife the legalist, and the aides among you, but feel free to move to discuss whatever you have in mind as the breakfast progresses. If you'd find your seats . . . we'll have the blessing." Seigryn nodded to Obreduur. "Councilor . . ."

Although Dekkard knew that the Trinitarian faith was stronger in smaller cities, and especially in rural communities, and that a blessing before a meal was usual, he'd been in Machtarn long enough that the request almost surprised him.

The councilor bowed his head slightly, and intoned, "Almighty and Trinity of Love, Power, and Mercy, we thank you for the solidity you bring to this world, for the order of time and of the material. We also ask that you grant us the wisdom to understand that the world is filled with illusion, that all material goods are fleeting vanities, and that the greatest vanity of all is to seek power for its own sake, rather than to share it in doing good. We humbly ask you to bless the companionship of this gathering and for the food we will partake, in the name of the Three in One."

"The Three in One," murmured those around the table, including Dekkard.

Before they all took their seats, Dekkard glanced around, noting the handsome black-haired man seated between Obreduur and his wife, and asked Seigryn, whose place at the table was to Dekkard's right, who the man between the Obreduurs was.

"Haasan Decaro."

"The Machineworkers guildmeister?"

"And the man who wants to and might be the next Craft candidate for councilor from Gaarlak. That is, unless Johan Lamarr decides to run. He could gather more party support, but he's said nothing."

That made sense to Dekkard, given that there were usually more Crafters Guild members than members of specialized guilds. "Thank you."

Dekkard found himself seated not only with Seigryn

on his left, but with Johan Lamarr on his right. No sooner had they been seated, and a server began to pour café, than Lamarr said, "Jens said you came from a long line of artisans. How did you end up in politics?"

"My father is a plaster artisan, and so was his father. My mother is a portraitist, as is my older sister. It became clear at an early age that the talent didn't lie in my hands. So, when a chance to go to the Institute arose, I took it—"

"You won one of the regional grant positions?"

Dekkard hadn't ever liked mentioning that, but he wasn't about to lie. "I was fortunate enough to gain a position."

"How did you do at the Institute?" pressed Lamarr.

"Well enough that the councilor interviewed me."

"Steffan is being unduly modest," interjected Seigryn. "He was one of the Triumphing Ten in his graduating class and was the top of his security training after graduation."

"But you do more than security, obviously," said Lamarr. "What sort of issues have you worked on?"

"The most recent issues involving crafters were the dispute between the Woodcrafters of Oersynt and Guldoran Ironway and tariffs on imported artworks."

"I heard that the Guldoran Ironway dispute was settled. How did the Woodcrafters fare?"

"They were opposed to using yellow cedar because it was unhealthy. The councilor worked out a compromise that led to Guldoran using cherry for carriage paneling."

"What about the tariffs?"

"We're still working on that." Before Lamarr could raise another question, Dekkard asked, "What is the matter of most concern to crafters and artisans here in Gaarlak, one that the Council could address or that it has failed to address?"

"You didn't say how you were working on the tariffs," said Lamarr.

"No, I didn't," returned Dekkard amiably. "The

councilor has made it clear that we say nothing in detail until we have resolved any matter or we have been unable to resolve the issue. This came up less than a month ago, and since it involves both law and workplace discretion, it will take a little longer."

"In short," said Seigryn in a light tone, "he's not about to promise anything until it's settled. He never has."

"In the meantime," added Dekkard, "knowing about other concerns might help the councilor."

"How?" asked Lamarr. "Gaarlak's not in his district."

"If we know that an issue affects other districts as well, it's easier to get the ministry involved to address it, or to get other councilors to get involved, if not both. The fine-art tariff practices, for example, could affect artisans not only in Malek, but in Machtarn, Siincleer, Ondeliew, Uldwyrk, Port Reale, and Neewyrk. Possibly even Gaarlak."

"How might that be?"

"If tariffs on imported artistic items, such as porcelain, metalwork, and the like, are too low, then people will buy the cheaper imports. That means artisans everywhere are affected. If they're too high, then there's a greater profit in smuggling, and that hurts both government and artisans. That's why I asked you about possible problems. It's helpful for us to know those things. The councilor himself has pointed out more than once that because he's only one person we need to find out as much as we can as well and let him know."

Lamarr's laugh was sardonic. "I've never even seen any of Councilor Raathan's aides. For that matter, I've never met him. We asked several years ago, but he never answered repeated requests."

"The guild had a problem, and no one even contacted you?"

"That's not unheard of here," said Seigryn dryly.

"What was the problem?" asked Dekkard.

"The way the Undstyn Pottery manufactory glazed their earthenware. The older method used a cupric frit, which gave the fired work a greenish tinge, but they started to add lead to the frit to make the glaze shinier. They claim that the firing process sealed the lead away. Maybe it did, but the glaziers were getting sick. They still are. The only people who will work as glaziers are those who have no other way of living . . . or who don't know any better."

"What happened?"

"The guild petitioned for a return to non-lead frits. The district council ordered a hearing before the local workplace administrator. He issued a finding that the manufactory just had to improve the lead-handling processes. We appealed. The Justiciary declared that the guild could not require a corporacion to change an entire manufacturing process because workers failed to follow proper procedures."

"So they changed some procedures, but there's still too much lead in the workplace, and it takes longer for workers to get sick, and the corporacion claims it's the workers' own fault?" asked Dekkard.

"That's about it," replied Lamarr. "Lead gets everywhere. If you're handling it at all, you can't get rid of it. Leastwise, not with the equipment we have."

"I hadn't heard about that. In a way, though, it's very much like the problem with the woodcrafters at Guldoran Ironway. That's why I'd also wager that there are similar problems with work safety standards in other kinds of manufactories."

"The Council should do more."

While Dekkard agreed, he only said, "It's something I'll definitely mention to the councilor. Is there anything else the councilor should know?"

"The gross-receipts tax needs revising. Corporacions get to deduct what they pay workers as a cost. Small crafters can't deduct the costs of family members who work for them. Doesn't seem fair when you think about it . . ."

Dekkard kept listening for the next bell, seldom needing even to prompt Lamarr. He did manage to eat two croissants, with some sort of apricot preserves, which were better than guava slices, but inferior, in his opinion, to quince paste. He also drank three mugs of café.

At close to the third morning bell, Seigryn stood up and said, "I did promise all of you that we wouldn't push you beyond third bell, and there's about a sixth before that happens."

Rather than sitting down, Seigryn stepped away from the table, and Lamarr again turned to Dekkard. "You're Steffan Dekkard . . . did I get that right?"

"That's right. I have to say I've appreciated what you had to say, and I definitely learned things we don't hear in Machtarn."

"It was good talking to you, Steffan. I'd hope that you might get to Gaarlak occasionally, because I'll never get Councilor Raathan's ear. Leastwise, you listen."

"If you think we can help, write the councilor. I can't promise what he'll do, but he does listen, and he tries to help. I can say absolutely that he'll read what you write and respond."

"You're cautious, aren't you?" For the first time, Lamarr smiled, an amused expression.

Dekkard managed a grin in return. "I learned early what I can promise from him . . . and what he has to decide. I can suggest, but he decides."

Lamarr pushed back his chair, but did not rise. "Does he take your suggestions?"

"Sometimes. Many times, he has a better idea, and I try to learn from that."

Lamarr nodded, then stood, as did several others.

Dekkard quickly got to his feet.

"A pleasure meeting you, Steffan. Enjoy Gaarlak, as you can."

"Thank you." Dekkard nodded in return, then turned toward Ysella, who stood talking to the comparatively light-skinned Jon Eliver, whose complexion was even lighter than Dekkard's, although that was to be expected for a farmworker, even a farmworker deputy guildmeister. Dekkard, and indeed most people hailing from Argental, was slightly lighter-skinned than the average

Guldoran, except for agricultural workers and, of course, beetles, both of which groups had skin and complexions even lighter in shade, possibly because lighter skin shades reflected more sunlight and thus tended to be better suited to outdoor work and activities.

"If you would pardon me . . ."

Dekkard turned to find Gretna Haarl, the assistant guildmeister of the Textile Millworkers, standing there. He smiled at the almost frail-looking woman, who had to be a good fifteen years older than he was. "Is there anything I can help you with . . . or you would like to know?"

"Why did you let Avraal Ysella precede you? She's senior to you, isn't she?"

"She is indeed. When she ordered me to follow, I obeyed."

Haarl paused for a moment. "You're serious, aren't you?"

"This is the first trip like this that I've made with the councilor. I have a good idea of what I don't know, and Avraal knows much more than I do about meetings."

"Why didn't you insist?"

"Because I trust her judgment. She's told me when she thinks I'm wrong or when I need to look further." *And she's saved my career and possibly my life.*

"How will things get better if women always have to defer to younger men?"

"She doesn't defer to me, but she is polite when she thinks I'm wrong. You'd have to ask her for her answer, but mine is that nothing will change until the Craft Party controls government, and if deferring slightly to patriarchal feelings in Gaarlak or anywhere else helps elect more councilors for the Craft Party, then a little deferral might just be worth it." Dekkard saw Ysella watching, but not moving toward them, and her body posture told him he was definitely on his own.

"Women have deferred for centuries. Where has that gotten us?" Haarl's voice was low and even, but cold.

"I never said all deferral was good. I said that if a small deferral to expected custom helped the greater cause, it might be worth it."

"Small deferrals add up."

"They do, but I suggested I should precede her, and she was the one to decide the order. It wouldn't have happened that way if she hadn't insisted."

Haarl abruptly motioned to Ysella. "Avraal. If you'd join us." Her words weren't a request.

Ysella smiled pleasantly as she stepped forward, but before she could speak, Haarl did. "Steffan said you told him to follow you, even though you're senior."

"I've been with the councilor longer, but we both have the same job description. I've been led to believe that both Guildmeister Decaro and Guildmeister Lamarr are rather traditional in their outlook—"

"Compared to what they are, you're being complimentary." Despite the venom in her words, Haarl kept her voice low.

"That may be," agreed Ysella pleasantly, "but I preferred not to start out by putting Steffan in a junior position or by giving them offense even before we met."

"You would put political positioning first?"

"Being political when it doesn't cost much generally gets better results," said Ysella, her tone polite and pleasant.

Dekkard noticed Jens Seigryn easing toward them, while Obreduur talked with Lamarr and Eliver, and Ingrella was conversing with Arleena Desenns of the Weavers Guild.

"If we don't change things at the bottom, nothing changes at the top," countered Haarl.

"The Silent Revolution changed a great deal from the top," Ysella pointed out, "even if it took pressure from women empaths."

"They didn't push far enough or hard enough," returned Haarl, turning abruptly to Seigryn and saying,

"Not a word from you, Jens." Then she strode from the small dining room.

"Might I ask . . . ?" said Seigryn.

"I chose to go first into the dining room," said Ysella. "Assistant Guildmeister Haarl took offense at that choice because I've been with the councilor longer, although we have the same job description."

Seigryn nodded slowly. "Gretna feels very strongly about certain matters, even when not emphasizing them is to the party's benefit. I'll talk to her and to Guildmeister Maatsuyt about the situation." Then he smiled. "From what I saw and heard you both did well in answering questions and representing the councilor."

After Haarl's almost murmured but intense outburst, Dekkard had his doubts. He also had a question. "What does Lamarr do, besides being guildmeister? Or what did he do? He seems knowledgeable about a great deal."

"He and his family are clock- and watchmakers."

Dekkard immediately felt incredibly stupid. "I never connected him . . . Lamarr & Sons?" The Lamarr watches weren't flashy, but were considered one of the more reliable timepieces, and in fact, that was what Dekkard's father had.

"The same. He's very modest." Seigryn smiled. "And don't worry about Gretna. We'll take care of it. Guildmeister Maatsuyt understands about her."

"Has there been a problem with women feeling put down?" asked Dekkard.

For a moment, Seigryn didn't meet Dekkard's eyes. Then he said, "There has been. All the guilds here in Gaarlak have been working to change that. Gretna wants change overnight, even in the next bell. That's not possible."

"That was why she was appointed assistant guildmeister?" asked Ysella.

"One reason," admitted Seigryn.

Ysella just nodded.

"Things have been difficult, then?" asked Dekkard,

thinking about Haarl's placement at the table, between Seigryn and Ingrella Obreduur. "And you hoped that Ingrella Obreduur, as a legalist, might be able to mention legal and practical reasons for proceeding with care?"

"That was my hope." Seigryn shook his head. "Gretna wasn't pleased with what Ingrella told her, although Ritten Obreduur was exceedingly courteous and patient."

"Does she have a large following within the guild?" asked Dekkard.

"Not an excessively large one, but a significant and devoted group of women." Seigryn paused, as if he was considering what to say or how to phrase it, before going on. "Some of them have very strong views."

Dekkard had a sudden thought. "Perhaps about making councilors personally accountable for the improvement of women's positions in society?"

"I'm sure that few of them would go that far," replied Seigryn.

"That's very good," said Ysella. "Thank you so much for setting this up so that we had a chance to hear what they all had to say. I'm certain it took a great deal of work on your part."

"I'd like to add my thanks," said Dekkard. "I especially appreciated hearing what Guildmeister Lamarr had to say."

At that point, Obreduur finished his conversations with Lamarr and Eliver, who left the room separately, and moved toward Dekkard, Ysella, and Seigryn. "Is everything set for what's next on the agenda, Jens?"

"It is. The Kharlan steamer is waiting outside for a brief tour of the city, with a few stops along the way."

"Excellent." Obreduur looked to his wife. "Shall we go?"

Ingrella nodded.

Dekkard let the others move on, hoping that Ysella would stay back with him, which she did. Then he asked quietly, "Was the assistant guildmeister as angry as she seemed?"

"Most likely. I couldn't tell, though. She's also an isolate."

"And she's not in security of some sort? Most isolates are . . . unless they're artisans."

"She may not even know she's an isolate. Or didn't until there was no point in training her. She's not built for physical security, and the other jobs in security require an education. How did you find out you were an isolate?"

"The same way almost all children do. In school. I was tested by a visiting empath."

Ysella offered an amused smile. "That doesn't happen in most schools until children are around ten. Farmworker children don't usually stay in school that long. Neither do the children of most millworkers, especially the girls. At ten or eleven, they're taking care of younger children so that their mothers can work."

"Naralta took care of me some, but she still finished an education." Dekkard saw that Obreduur, Ingrella, and Seigryn were heading for the front entrance of the Ritter's Inn.

"You come from a family of educated artisans. Many people don't."

"And, among other things, that's where the . . ." Dekkard paused for a moment, realizing that they were in a very public place, although the inn's lobby contained only a handful of people, before he continued with slightly different wording than he'd first thought, "the unnamed demonstrators get their empaths."

"Most, I'd judge," replied Ysella, before smiling wryly. "Although there might be a few disaffected Landor women." She slipped a translucent gray headscarf from the small purse she carried and eased it into place. Then, as she and Dekkard neared the front doors of the inn, she added, "We can talk later about that."

"We should." Ahead of them, Dekkard noticed that Ingrella Obreduur had also donned a headscarf matching her ensemble.

Outside, Seigryn was opening the doors of the large open and older Kharlan touring steamer that stood waiting. Dekkard had a feeling that the "brief" tour would be anything but.

62

The "brief" tour of Gaarlak not only lasted the remainder of the morning but stretched into mid-afternoon. Dekkard was glad the touring steamer had three rows of wide seats, with the driver and Seigryn up front, Gustoff, Ysella, and Dekkard in the middle, and the Obreduurs and Nellara in the rear seats.

Dekkard saw the center square, which held an imposing marble statue of Laureous the Great, not surprisingly, since most cities in southern Guldor had similar monuments; the banking quarter, where the façades of the three- and four-story buildings looked worn and grimy; the slate-roofed Grand Trinitarian Chapel, constructed of granite transported some distance and dating back five hundred years; the grand houses of the North Quarter, although some of those had seen better days; the textile mills along the Lakaan River, most moderately well-kept but definitely aging; seemingly endless streets of tiny brick houses, their slate roofs a patchwork of various shades of gray; and, of course, more than a few milles of flax fields about ready to be harvested.

The steamers on the streets were generally older and in poorer condition than those in Machtarn, even than those in the Machtarn harbor district or in the poorer river districts. And, outside of Gaarlak proper, he also saw wagons still pulled by horses on dirt side roads.

The stops between sights began at a modest house west of the North Quarter, converted to offices holding several legalists. There, while Nellara and Gustoff waited with the driver, Dekkard and Ysella were introduced to a graying woman, one Namoor Desharra, who looked barely younger than Obreduur.

"Namoor is the Craft Party legalist for Gaarlak," explained Seigryn. "She helps Craft Party members with legal problems that the guild legalists either can't or won't do."

Dekkard glanced to Ritten Obreduur.

She smiled and said, "Yes, Steffan, Namoor and I go back a long time, and she's one of the reasons why I was in Gaarlak earlier this year."

"She's been of great assistance," added the graying Desharra. "Her legal reputation doesn't hurt, either."

Dekkard winced inside. He'd obviously missed something, except . . . *How would you know? Obreduur never talks about her professional life.* Because he regarded it as a conflict . . . or it just never came up? And if Obreduur never mentioned it . . . how could Dekkard comment or ask leading questions?

Deciding not to be that deferential, Dekkard asked, "In what legalist issues has Ritten Obreduur's expertise proved most valuable?"

With an amused smile, Desharra replied, "In all of them, but, most recently, in the appeal against Gaarlak Mills' practice of classifying women supervisors as 'work coordinators' and men with the same job as assistant foremen or foremen. That allowed mills to pay women less. Now, regardless of gender, men or women are classified as line supervisors or section supervisors, and paid equally as such. The High Justiciary just affirmed that in Summerfirst."

And Gretna Haarl wasn't satisfied with what Ingrella said . . . and has done? "That sounds like you established a precedent with Gaarlak Mills."

"It's going to take a while," replied Ingrella. "We'll have to file a petition for compliance corporacion by corporacion for a time. At some point, hopefully, the Council will pass a bill mandating it just to save corporacions the marks required to fight the petitions. If not, we'll plod along. It's a practice that's still widespread. Even after seventy years, some people don't like to recognize that some things have changed."

Dekkard noticed Ysella's almost imperceptible nod.

"I shouldn't keep you," said Desharra. "You have others to meet, but it's always good to see Ingrella, and I enjoyed meeting you young people. Ingrella's told me so much about you."

Before anyone else could speak, Dekkard did. "Thank you for seeing us. I can't tell you how much I appreciated your explanation of the Gaarlak Mills situation."

"I thought you might," returned Desharra. "Ingrella tends to be far too modest."

"Modesty tends to work better," replied Ingrella. "We're interested in improving conditions for women, not in gaining notoriety or making marks."

Work better? Because male Commercers don't see legal action coming until it hits them?

Ysella just said, "Thank you," but did so warmly.

Then Seigryn escorted them back out to the Kharlan, and the tour continued.

The second stop was at a small and neat, but clearly older, red brick house in the area between the grander houses and the rows of tiny, cot-like dwellings.

This time Obreduur spoke as the Kharlan came to a halt. "Julian Baurett is a stipended patroller who was the head of the local Patrollers Benevolent Society. He's also a friend."

Dekkard nodded, because the local Benevolent Societies were the closest thing to a guild for patrollers, given the specific prohibition on a guild for Imperial Security patrollers or agents.

"I'll stay with the steamer, and tell your children some tall tales about you," said Seigryn. "It's likely to be a little cramped in there anyway."

"We won't be too long," returned Obreduur, leading

the way to the narrow front porch, where he rapped on the door, then called out, "Do you still brew that fermented swill you call sparkling wine?"

"Come on in, you worthless politician," came the reply from within.

Obreduur opened the door and motioned the others to enter the small front sitting room, then followed and closed the door.

The white-haired man who rose from the armchair in the front parlor was straight and trim, although Dekkard could see that he once had been an even more imposing figure. "Axel, it's good of you to come see an old has-been."

"Julian . . . you're anything but a has-been." Obreduur half turned so that he could take in Ysella and Dekkard as well as the former patroller. "I can't tell you how helpful Julian was when I happened to be saddled with coordinating guild actions in Oersynt, Malek, and here."

"You give me too much credit, Axel. Way too much. Sit down, if you would." Baurett gestured to the chairs and to the settee.

After noticing the wince as the older man lowered himself back into his chair, Dekkard took one of the straight-backed wooden chairs, leaving the worn cream and maroon settee and the remaining armchair for others.

"Not worth a Three's curse these days," grumbled Baurett. "Almighty knows I haven't been worth that for years."

"You were saying that when you were picking up drunken millmen one-handed," replied Obreduur.

"Back then I was just talking. Now it's true." Baurett paused. "What can I tell you? Thoughtful as you've always been, Axel, you're not here just to cheer me up."

"Besides hearing what you know, I wanted you to meet Ingrella, because you never did, and my two aides, Avraal Ysella and Steffan Dekkard."

Baurett looked at Ingrella and smiled. "I can see why

he didn't want me looking at you. Back then, he might not have been able to keep you."

Ingrella smiled back. "He might not have been able to, but I would have been."

Baurett laughed, lightly slapped his knee, then looked at Ysella. "Empath . . . and a lot tougher than you look." He turned to Dekkard. "You look like a pretty boy. You're anything but. Good thing you work for Axel." After a moment, he cleared his throat, once, and then again. "You've got good instincts, Axel. Gaarlak could go up like linseed in a cotton bale."

"Go on," said Obreduur.

"Decaro's pushing the mill owners too hard. Their margins aren't what they used to be. So they're squeezing the farmworkers to keep production costs down. Desenns has managed to keep things even, but that firewitch Haarl is turning too many of the guild women against Maatsuyt, and he's not seeing it. Lamarr's kept the Crafters Guild out of it . . . so far."

Dekkard could see why Obreduur had wanted to see Baurett, even as he wondered how a stipended former patroller knew all that, but he wasn't about to ask. Not immediately, anyway.

"And your boys are having to break up more fights?" asked Obreduur.

"Some of them are Decaro's boys now. They like the way he talks tough about the mill owners. And you're right. There are always fights now, usually on Quindi night. Thing is, there's more household violence, especially among the foremen, except they're called supervisors now. Name doesn't change anything."

"Why?" asked Obreduur patiently.

"That new gadget . . . cotton engine, they call it. Gets the seeds out of the cotton faster. Cotton from Surpunta and the southwest is getting a lot cheaper. Margins on linen are down. The old Phanx mill closed down last year . . ."

For all of Obreduur's talk about it being a short visit, the four listened to Baurett for nearly a bell. When they finally stood to leave, Baurett said, "Hope that helps." He smiled. "It's good to feel useful again—even if you are a worthless politician, Axel."

"It's good to see you again, Julian, even if you can't make wine worth swill."

As Obreduur headed to the door, Baurett gestured. "Keep him safe, pretty boy."

"That's why I'm here." Dekkard didn't know what else to say.

"And don't let him believe Decaro. Now . . . get out there and keep him safe."

Dekkard nodded, then moved toward the door. As the last one out, he also closed it quietly but firmly.

When Dekkard neared the Kharlan, Obreduur asked quietly, "What did he say to you?"

"To keep you safe and not to let you believe Decaro."

"They've never seen eye-to-eye," replied Obreduur, "but Julian's right about that."

After driving past the Grand Trinitarian Chapel, Seigryn had the Kharlan stop at a cobbler's shop, emphasized by the boot affixed to the sign over the door that said COBBLER.

Obreduur looked to Ysella and said, "Who's inside?"

"Just one person."

"Then we'll make this quick. Steffan, you come with me."

Ysella glanced to Dekkard, and he understood. He immediately left the steamer and led the way into the shop, not that he could go very far because there was a counter set little more than a yard back from the door.

"Be with you in a moment!" The call came from the rear of the shop where a woman was doing something to a boot on a last.

More than a minute passed before the cobbler hurried up to the counter. She looked first at Dekkard, clearly puzzled, then at Obreduur. After a moment, her eyes widened.

"I never did pick up my work boots, Myshella," said Obreduur quietly. "You know why."

Color seemed to drain from the cobbler's face.

Dekkard's hand went to his truncheon.

Obreduur smiled warmly. "You didn't have much choice." Then he laid a twenty-mark note on the counter. "I don't need the boots now, but I'll still pay for them."

"You don't have to . . ." The woman's words were low.

"No. I have to. I don't like not paying debts . . . regardless." Without taking his eyes off the cobbler, Obreduur added, "This is one of my aides, Steffan Dekkard. Steffan, this is Myshella Degriff, the best bootmaker in Gaarlak."

"I'm pleased to meet you," Dekkard replied. "If the councilor says you're good, you're very good."

Degriff swallowed. "Thank you."

"By the way, Myshella," said Obreduur casually, "it was Haasan, wasn't it?"

The bootmaker swallowed again.

Haasan? Haasan Decaro? Dekkard managed not to react.

"I thought so. He told me it was Reinguld." Obreduur shook his head. "Poor Olof was never that crafty." Then he stepped back.

"I'll follow you, sir." Dekkard was ready to move at the slightest provocation.

The cobbler's eyes went to Dekkard as Obreduur said, "Thank you, Steffan," and stepped from the shop.

Noticing that the twenty-mark note was still on the counter, Dekkard said, "It might be best if you took that and went back to that boot you were working on." After a pause, he added, quietly, almost gently, "Just do it."

The woman took the note and backed away from the counter, still looking at Dekkard as she retreated.

Keeping an eye on her, Dekkard said cheerfully, "Good day!" then left the shop, hurrying to catch up with Obreduur.

Obreduur stood beside the Kharlan, watching Dekkard. "What did you say to her?"

"I just told her to take her payment and suggested she get back to work." Dekkard said quietly, "Haasan? Haasan Decaro? The guildmeister?" He wondered at the oddity that Haasan Design and Haasan Decaro, while certainly not connected, both seemed to have a shady side.

Obreduur just nodded, then said, "We'd better get on with the tour." He returned to his seat in the third row, beside Ingrella, and Dekkard took his seat beside Ysella.

"You'll tell me later," she murmured, her words clearly not a question.

"I will." Dekkard could definitely tell her what had happened, but he wondered if she could shed any more light on the matter and why Obreduur had wanted him to be the one guarding him, rather than Ysella—unless he knew that Myshella was an isolate. "Is the cobbler an isolate?" he asked as the Kharlan pulled away from the shop.

Ysella nodded.

That answered one of his questions.

From then on, the "sightseeing" was simply riding around Gaarlak, occasionally stopping so that Obreduur could pass a few words with an old acquaintance, or in some cases, fail to pass those words when the former acquaintance was elsewhere. Dekkard tried to remember the names and wished he'd brought a notepad and a pencil.

When they returned to the Ritter's Inn, just before the fifth bell of the afternoon, Seigryn said, "Another Kharlan will be here at six to take you to the residence of Regional Justicer Chaelynt for the reception and dinner."

The itinerary Dekkard had received had only mentioned "reception and dinner," and he had wondered if the details had been late to be arranged or if Obreduur had kept them to himself. After the encounter with the cobbler, Dekkard definitely suspected the latter, but he said little until he and Ysella had escorted the Obreduur family into their suite.

"We need to talk," he said. "My room or yours?"

"Yours."

The two walked to Dekkard's room, and he unlocked the door to the modest chamber with the one double bed, the small washroom with toilet and shower, a wardrobe, a writing table, and a single chair.

"Do you want the chair or the bed?"

"Neither, but I'll sit on the bed."

Dekkard moved the chair and sat so that he was facing her. "Why didn't anyone tell me about how accomplished Ingrella Obreduur is?"

"You never asked," replied Ysella. "You knew she was a legalist. You could have asked what kind . . . or the kind of cases she handled."

"Being that blunt . . . it's hard for me. I need a fact or two."

"Sometimes . . ." Ysella shook her head. "What happened in the cobbler's shop?"

Dekkard related the sequence of events, including Obreduur's response to the question about Haasan Decaro.

"That had to be back when Obreduur was the regional coordinator for the guilds," said Ysella. "I wonder why Decaro was after him . . . and why Obreduur said nothing."

"It's hard to prove an attempted murder when the attempt was never made and where there's no evidence," replied Dekkard. "Obreduur likely let on that he believed Decaro's lie." He paused. "There's one other thing I found out. Jens Seigryn said that Decaro was pushing to be the next Craft candidate for councilor from Gaarlak. Do you know anything more?"

She shook her head.

"Baurett told me not to let Obreduur believe Decaro."

"You didn't mention that."

"I was going to. He said that as I was leaving. I was the last one, remember?"

"So why would Baurett think Obreduur would believe Decaro?"

"The message wasn't for the councilor," suggested Dekkard. "It was for us, or for me, because you can sense duplicity." After a moment, he added, "If the councilor knew that, years ago, Decaro set him up for something, why would he ask for Decaro to be included in the meeting . . . unless he didn't want to let Decaro know that he knew. But then why would Obreduur do what he did with the cobbler?"

"Maybe it was a quiet and untraceable way to send a message to Decaro not to run."

"No one could tell whether she's telling the truth with that message because she's an isolate."

"And so are you, and Decaro knows that."

Dekkard shook his head. "All that had to be planned out well in advance."

"Doesn't he always plan in advance?" Ysella stood. "Speaking of planning in advance, we need to freshen up for the reception and dinner."

"All I have is gray suits."

"They'll be fine. Just wear a solid black or dark gray cravat. One of the ones I gave you."

Dekkard laughed softly. "Obreduur isn't the only one who plans well in advance."

"Don't tell me you haven't planned," she replied with a smile. "Now I need to go change. Women shouldn't wear suits to receptions, unless they're supposed to be obvious as security."

Dekkard walked to the door and opened it, then walked with her to her door, waiting until she was safely inside before returning to his own room. Once there, he took off his jacket and carefully brushed it, as well as his trousers, before washing up and changing his cravat to the dark gray silk one that Ysella had given him. He also switched truncheons, to the shorter one that fit under his jacket, and removed the staff pin from his jacket.

Just before it was time to escort the Obreduurs, Dekkard knocked on Ysella's door. "Are you about ready?"

"Just a moment."

It was more than a moment, but only several minutes before Ysella appeared, in a stylish dress of a shade darker than imperial blue but lighter than security blue, accentuated by a brilliant gray short jacket and a filmy gray headscarf.

For a long moment, Dekkard just looked.

Ysella finally said, "That was the loveliest nonverbal comment I've ever had."

"I'm sorry. You just look stunning."

Neither said much more as they waited and then escorted the older couple down to the main level of the Ritter's Inn.

The black Kharlan limousine that picked up Obreduur and his wife, and Dekkard and Ysella, was polished and spotless, but definitely several years old. Once the Kharlan was moving, Dekkard turned and asked, "What do we need to know about Justicer Chaelynt and those he's invited?"

Obreduur nodded to his wife.

"Wynan is young for a regional justicer," Ingrella began. "That is, only a few years younger than we are. He's from a Landor background, but the youngest of a number of sons. So he decided on a career as a legalist. After about ten years of practice in Uldwyrk, he became known as a very effective litigator. When a Landor slot for a regional justicer opened four years ago, he was close to a unanimous choice because of his integrity, because he was thought to be as impartial as could be expected, and because his knowledge and understanding of the law is quite comprehensive . . ."

All that made sense to Dekkard, because with the Great Charter's requirement that a third of all justicers, both on the regional and the High Justiciary level, had to be presented to the Council from each political party, comparative impartiality was in everyone's interest.

"... He is personally a little reserved, but he does like to host gatherings, with a variety of guests. The only rule, if unspoken, is that practical politics and pending legal issues are not to be discussed. Legal and political theory can be and usually are. As for who will be there ... that is always up to Wynan and Vivienne."

After a little more than a third of a bell, the limousine slipped through the open gates of a dwelling on the north side of the North Quarter on a smooth bitumened drive up to a two-story brick mansion perhaps twice the size of the Obreduur dwelling in Machtarn, stopping under the covered front portico. Seeing no doorman, Dekkard immediately got out and opened both doors.

A serving maid in green and black livery did open the front door and escorted them to the covered east veranda, where already a score of people had gathered. As Dekkard led the four onto the veranda, a man in a white linen suit with a broad and warm, but slightly shy, smile moved quickly toward them.

"Ingrella, Axel, I'm so glad you're both here." Then he turned to Ysella and Dekkard. "These must be your aides."

"Avraal Ysella and Steffan Dekkard," said Ingrella.

"Dekkard ... you wouldn't be the Dekkard who won the Institute Martial Arts trophy ... six years ago? I'm just guessing, but you look to be about the right age."

Dekkard had the feeling he was blushing, but he replied, "If it was six years ago, then yes. Might I ask ... ?"

"An older partner in the legalist firm to which I belonged asked me to accompany him to the finals. I couldn't very well refuse. His son was one of the finalists. You bested him rather effectively. It was a bright spot on that trip." Chaelynt offered an embarrassed smile.

"I don't believe you mentioned that in your credentials file," said Obreduur with dry amusement.

"The credentials meister suggested that including it was redundant," replied Dekkard sardonically.

"Redundant or not," replied Chaelynt, "I'm indebted to you. That episode was one of those that inclined me toward a justiciary career." He gestured. "The sideboards have wine or lager. Please enjoy yourselves. I hope you don't mind if I spend a few moments reminiscing with Ingrella, Axel."

"Not in the slightest," said Obreduur heartily. "A good lager sounds very welcome."

The three moved slowly toward the sideboard on the north edge of the veranda.

"You've never said anything about that," murmured Ysella.

"It was a long time ago. I always disliked it when I heard older men boast of their schoolyard successes. I said I'd never do that."

"You still surprise me, Steffan," declared Obreduur.

Both Obreduur and Dekkard decided on Laencar, a local pale lager, while Ysella had a white wine whose name Dekkard didn't catch, then they moved out of the late-afternoon sun into the fully shaded part of the veranda. Dekkard sipped the Laencar, then decided it was as good as, if slightly different from, Kuhrs, and it was also not cool, but cold, which he appreciated.

"How's the wine?" he asked Ysella.

"Good. I still think I prefer Silverhills." She glanced around, trying to sense any possible hostility.

A tall and broad man a good decade older than Obreduur approached. "Councilor, Wynan pointed you out to me. Orvul Scarsenn."

"Of Lakaan Mills?" asked Obreduur.

"The very same."

"It's good to meet you at last. I've heard a great deal about you over the years. Might I introduce you to my aides, Avraal Ysella and Steffan Dekkard."

Scarsenn smiled. "Dekkard. Wynan said you were one reason he became a justicer."

"Just one of many, I suspect," replied Dekkard.

"Would you enlighten me?"

"I'm afraid I can't, sir. I'm pleased he's so complimentary, but that story is strictly his."

"Well, since you won't I'll have to ask the lady"—Scarsenn turned his attention to Ysella—"how the councilor ever persuaded someone so beautiful to work for him."

"He asked me, and I've always liked doing security work."

"And she's very good at it," added Obreduur. "Tell me. Do you think cotton is going to overtake linen any time soon?"

"Oh . . . well, it's bound to happen, but not quickly. Cotton's more durable, and the cotton engine reduces the time it takes to deseed the lint by a factor of forty, maybe fifty, but it takes a lot of labor to grow the cotton, and you can't use steam tractors, not so far anyway . . ."

Dekkard and Ysella eased away from the councilor and mill owner.

"Did he feel as obnoxious as he sounded?" asked Dekkard, keeping his voice low.

"Worse." Ysella took a healthy swallow of her wine, then studied the two nearest couples, shifting her focus to a man standing alone, who was joined shortly by a woman most likely not his wife, with whom she exchanged a few words before she moved on.

At that moment, Ingrella appeared, escorting, if not almost dragging, a woman in a pale green dress with a filmy white jacket. "Ysella, Steffan, since Axel's tied up with Orvul Scarsenn, I wanted Martenya to meet you two. Martenya, here are the two I've been talking about."

Dekkard wished he knew why Ingrella wanted them to meet the woman, but he only said, "I'm pleased to meet you."

"As am I," added Ysella.

"Is it really true that you two were the ones who

stopped and captured that empie assassin who killed Councilor Aashtaan?"

Ysella nodded to Dekkard.

"It would be more accurate to say that Avraal blunted the empie's attack and saved two councilors and then slowed the attacker enough that I could catch and restrain her."

"He not only did that, but he also stopped her from poisoning a good score of people with Atacaman fire pepper dust," added Ysella.

"Where exactly in the Council Hall did this happen?" asked Martenya.

"Just outside the councilors' dining room . . ."

For almost a third of a bell, Dekkard and Ysella answered the woman's questions, until Obreduur freed himself from Scarsenn, and she turned her attention on the councilor.

Dekkard and Ysella eased back, and Dekkard asked Ingrella, "Might I ask who—"

The first response to his question was an impish smile. "Martenya Oguire is the owner and publisher of the *Gaarlak Times*. She wanted a word with Axel, but I pointed out that combining just meeting him with his two aides who were heroes would make a better story, since the full story was never printed in *Gestirn*. She agreed."

Dekkard took a healthy swallow of his remaining lager. He was about to head back to the sideboard when a thin man about Ingrella's age approached.

"Ritten Obreduur? I'm Maximus Heinel."

"Gabrel Heinel's father? How is he?"

"Doing very well, thank you . . ."

Dekkard and Ysella moved away, and Dekkard could see that a few more people had arrived so that there were perhaps fifteen couples.

A few minutes later, Ingrella disengaged herself and Obreduur moved toward the three, accompanied by a white-haired man in a pale lavender linen suit, a dark lavender shirt, and a cravat lighter than the shirt and darker than the suit.

"Ingrella, dear, might I present Emilio Raathan, the noted councilor from Gaarlak?"

"I'm scarcely noted, Axel," protested Raathan, "but I did want to see if perhaps you and Ingrella, and your aides, could join Patriana and me for light midday refreshments tomorrow, say around first bell."

Obreduur looked to his wife, who immediately replied, "That would be so lovely, Emilio, but we wouldn't want to put you out or disrupt any plans you might have made."

"Oh, no, it would be our pleasure. It truly would be."

"Then we will be there," replied Ingrella.

"We will see you at first bell." Raathan extended a card. "Here is our address. Patriana will be so pleased." Then he inclined his head, smiled warmly, and turned away.

"Interesting," said Ingrella. "From that, one would think that you were close friends."

"When we're barely acquaintances, you mean?" replied Obreduur.

Ingrella offered an enigmatic smile.

Dekkard turned to Ysella. "He seemed genuine. Was he?"

"Mostly. There weren't disturbing undercurrents."

Dekkard nodded. That didn't mean they wouldn't have to be alert. "I imagine the food will be good."

"It will be very good," said Obreduur. "Emilio is said to be a gourmet."

Within moments, a series of chimes echoed across the veranda, rung by a tall woman in a shimmering and almost slinky white dress that particularly suited her. Since she stood beside Justicer Chaelynt, she had to be his wife.

The justicer's voice was strong as he declared, "Vivienne has informed me that dinner will be served at the tables on the west veranda in exactly one sixth. So if you would make your way there and find your place card . . ."

Dekkard and Ysella trailed the Obreduurs as they made their way through the veranda doors and along the corridor to the central hallway and then to the west veranda. The corridor was decorated with paintings of landscapes, none of which Dekkard recognized, flanked by green velvet hangings and against an off-white wall.

"Very modest," murmured Ysella. "Still, even a regional justicer couldn't afford this, and since he has a reputation for impartiality and integrity, his wife must have brought some wealth to the marriage. She is rather striking."

"She is," Dekkard replied politely, thinking that he found Ysella more striking. "They're an imposing couple."

"I wonder what their children are like," mused Ysella.

"Children? How do you know they have any?"

"Because I saw one of them peering down the center hall steps when we came in."

Dekkard hadn't noticed that at all. "How old?"

"She looked to be about ten. She was composed. Not at all excited, and very serious."

When they stepped out onto the veranda, Dekkard immediately saw two long tables, covered in dark green linen, with places set.

"Let's see where the Obreduurs are seated. They won't be together, and neither will we."

Dekkard and Ysella followed and observed, discovering that the Obreduurs were seated at the same table and that Ysella had been positioned at the second table, but where she could observe Obreduur easily. Dekkard was at the second table, near the end, where he could move easily . . . if necessary.

In the end, Dekkard found himself between two women, Amarra Hyelsted and Rachyla Haelkoch, both of whom he seated. Then he sat down.

"You must be one of Councilor Obreduur's aides," said Amarra Hyelsted.

"I am, but why do you say that?"

The older black-haired and narrow-faced woman offered an amused smile. "Because I know most of the others and because you're too young and handsome to be anything else. What sort of an aide are you?"

"I'm an assistant economic aide and a security specialist."

"My . . . an economist with weapons. How good are you?"

The younger Rachyla Haelkoch, younger meaning that the darker-skinned blonde was only about a decade older than Dekkard, said, "Justicer Chaelynt said he was one of the best. He saw him in action years ago."

"How interesting," said Hyelsted blandly. "Wynan knows so many unusual people . . . from his . . . profession. It's very nice to meet you, Steffan." She smiled politely and turned to talk to the man to her left.

"I think it's more than interesting," declared Rachyla Haelkoch, adding under her breath, "Don't mind Amarra. She prefers to talk upward . . . as if it made any difference. If you wouldn't mind, could you tell me how you ended up working for the councilor?"

Dekkard had no doubts about whom he'd be conversing most with over dinner.

63

On Furdi, since the Obreduurs had breakfast delivered to their suite, Dekkard and Ysella met in the restaurant of the Ritter's Inn to eat and to discuss what they'd learned the night before. According to Obreduur's instructions, Dekkard wore black slacks and a green barong, which meant he definitely had to carry the much shorter personal truncheon, but the brace of throwing knives was still practical. Ysella wore a cream summer jacket and skirt with a maroon blouse. Her headscarf, loosely around her neck, was a near-transparent cream.

Neither said much until after their first mug of café.

"What did you think of Chaelynt?" Dekkard finally asked.

"He's all that Ingrella said . . . and that's rare among Landors."

"It's even rarer among Commercers, I suspect. What about Scarsenn?"

"I told you last night. There's nothing to add."

Dekkard nodded. "After we eat, we need to see if that newssheet owner actually ran a story."

"I already picked up a copy," said Ysella. "Two, actually. I thought you might like one to give to your parents." She handed a newssheet across the table. "It starts on the front page."

"Is it good or bad?"

"You tell me."

Dekkard began to read. The small headline read COUNCILOR AND HEROIC AIDES IN GAARLAK. He winced and continued.

A midweek reception with dinner is rare enough in Gaarlak, but more so in Summerend . . . and even more so when among the invitees are the noted Crafter Councilor, Axel Obreduur, his equally noted wife, Ritten Ingrella Obreduur, the legalist whose efforts resulted in obtaining equal pay for women supervisors in Gaarlak Mills, and the Councilor's two aides—Avraal Ysella and Steffan Dekkard—whose efforts captured the killer of Councilor Aashtaan and protected a number of Councilors . . .

Dekkard skipped over the account of the attack and concentrated on the part dealing with Obreduur.

. . . when asked why he was visiting Gaarlak when his own district was Malek, the Councilor said that he and his family were spending only a few days in Gaarlak to visit old friends, pointing out that earlier in life he'd been the guild coordinator for an area that included both Malek and Gaarlak and that Ritten Obreduur and Regional Justicer Chaelynt had been professional associates. In commenting on the Kraffeist Affair, Councilor Obreduur said that the matter was "totally unacceptable" and "amounted to the theft of public resources." He also said that the ruling Commerce Party had failed to dig deeply enough into the scandal . . .

When he finished, Dekkard looked at Ysella. "There's as much in the story about us as the councilor."

"Why wouldn't there be? People like to read about assassinations and violence more than about what politicians think."

Dekkard had to agree with that. He started to hand the newssheet back.

"Keep it. That's your copy. I bought the last two. The desk clerk said that for some reason the newssheets were selling out early this morning."

"Did the clerk say anything to you?"

Ysella smiled. "Not a word. I don't look like a hero."

Dekkard shook his head, then took a bite of the croissant he'd ordered—stuffed with quince paste. "What about your dinner companions?"

"One was the head legalist for Gaarlak Mills, and I asked him about the supervisory rule. He said he was glad that Ingrella and Namoor Desharra had won. He meant it. So I asked why. He said that most of the women supervisors had less trouble and fewer slowdowns on their lines, and he'd never thought it was fair they weren't paid as much, but he'd never been able to do much. He was polite, even if his feelings of attraction were a little much."

The legalist's emotional pressure on Ysella irritated Dekkard, but he knew it had bothered her even more. "What about your other companion?"

"He was a much older Landor with estates to the west. Very nice. He treated me like a favorite granddaughter. He did say he was disappointed that Councilor Raathan didn't seem willing to stand up to the Commercers the way the Craft councilors did. What about your companions?"

"One older Landor snob who was rather condescending and only gave me a few perfunctory words and one charming wife of the district manager of Guldoran Ironway. She wanted to know about being an aide to a councilor, but we finally talked about the ironways. She professed not to know much, but I think she knew more than Deron—"

"Deron?"

"Oh . . . you weren't there. The Guldoran Ironway director who visited Obreduur. Anyway, she told me about scheduling and shunting problems, and others. Interesting, but not political. Except there was one thing . . . something to the effect that the special supplemental ironway funding wouldn't be as large this year, and that would cause maintenance delays in the Gaarlak area. I was under the impression that the maintenance funding for all ironways had to be in one package. I never saw a special ironway supplemental. It could be it has another name, but I'd at least like to ask Obreduur about it." Dekkard shrugged. "So . . . nothing really exciting or interesting."

"We've got another two thirds before we meet Obreduur. Since he's on the Waterways Committee, it's obvious why we're visiting the Upper Gaarlak Locks, but do you know why we're visiting Gaarlak Cabinetry?"

"It's on the way to the locks, and it must be owned by someone Obreduur knows."

"Brilliant deduction, Steffan."

"Offer me a better explanation."

"There's some political advantage involved."

"That's even more brilliant," he said cheerfully, before finishing off his second croissant.

Ysella offered him a mock glare in return.

A sixth later, the two returned briefly to their rooms, where Dekkard tucked the morning edition of the *Gaarlak Times* into his suitcase, and then waited for a bit before leaving his room.

Ysella joined him immediately outside the suite entrance.

Obreduur left the suite alone, wearing an off-white linen summer suit without a cravat.

"Ritten Obreduur?" asked Dekkard.

"She'll be spending time with Gustoff and Nellara. They'll do some shopping. There are several nice emporiums nearby, as well as a bookstore. More books might help, since they're not invited to the luncheon or tonight's guild leadership dinner. Shall we go?"

The touring Kharlan was waiting outside, with Jens Seigryn and the driver. Obreduur took the rear seat, and Ysella and Dekkard the middle one.

Once the Kharlan pulled away from the Ritter's Inn, Obreduur said, "I saw the newssheet story. It portrayed you two as quite the heroes. That wasn't widely recognized in Machtarn for reasons we all know. That publicity here in Gaarlak can't hurt. Did you find out anything else?"

Dekkard nodded to Ysella, and when she finished, he added his bits, then waited.

"Avraal . . . that's very interesting about the legalist's views. It might help a little if the Imperador calls elections sometime in the next year." The councilor turned to Dekkard. "When we get back to Machtarn, you and Ivann need to track down that so-called supplemental. If it's hidden that way, especially if it has favorable terms for Guldoran Ironway and not for Eastern or Southwestern, that might prove very valuable."

Once past the square and the Grand Trinitarian Chapel, the driver continued eastward until he reached River Avenue, where he turned left. The avenue took them past three successive mills, all three of which had signboards identifying them as Gaarlak Mills. Ahead,

Dekkard saw a closed and dilapidated structure on the far side of the stone-channeled river.

Less than a mille later, the driver pulled into a brick-paved parking area in front of a well-kept single-story red brick building some twenty-five yards long and perhaps ten wide.

"Why don't you both come with me?"

The words weren't really a question, and he and Ysella immediately got out of the big open Kharlan.

Obreduur gestured toward the building. "Years ago, I spent time with Hrald when I came through Gaarlak. He was the local woodworkers' steward. There weren't enough woodworkers here for a guild, so they were part of the Woodcrafters Guild in Oersynt. He's still with the guild, but he didn't like the politics and stepped down. He follows what goes on very closely."

Ysella and Dekkard followed Obreduur to the small door to the left of the loading dock. A small sign was affixed on the outside brick wall.

GAARLAK CABINETRY:
Hrald Iglis, Owner

Obreduur opened the door and looked to Ysella.

"Four people. One in the room behind the foyer."

"That would be Hrald. We'll see if I'm still welcome." Obreduur stepped into the small front room, bisected by a wooden counter of what looked to be black walnut, and well-constructed with clean lines. The left end stopped a yard short of the wall. The chair-rail design was similar to old Imperial, but less ornate, and topped black-walnut wainscoting. The crown moldings were in the same style.

Dekkard nodded.

"What do you think?" asked Obreduur.

"It's very good."

"Hrald!" called the councilor. "Are you hiding somewhere?"

Almost a minute passed before a stocky, but somehow angular, man with short-cut and thinning gray hair stepped into the front room. "Can't mistake your voice anywhere, Axel. I saw the newssheet story this morning. Wondered if you'd be by."

"I've always stopped by when I've been in Gaarlak. You weren't always here, but I stopped. Why wouldn't I now?"

"You never know," said Iglis.

Dekkard thought he caught a glimpse of a twinkle in the older man's eye.

"By the way"—Obreduur motioned in Avraal's direction—"Avraal Ysella and Steffan Dekkard. My aides. Steffan comes from an artisan family, and he was admiring your work."

Sensing he needed to say something, Dekkard added, "I like the way you simplified the old Imperial design of the chair rail. You kept the feel of the Imperial without the . . . ornate . . ."

"Frippery," finished Iglis. "Where'd you learn that?"

"My father's a decorative-plaster artisan. He made me learn all the styles. Unfortunately, even he conceded that I didn't have the touch, and that getting a formal education was the best I could hope for."

"Something to be said for that," replied the cabinetmaker with a small smile.

"You'd know," said Obreduur. "You make the best cabinets and paneling in this part of the country, possibly in all Guldor. I'm sorry I never could buy any. I thought I'd have the chance. You know that the Advisory Committee was going to send me here—except . . . that business with Lewes."

Iglis nodded slowly. "It was bound to happen with Marjoy. She never cared about his being councilor. She sure didn't take to what he did. Worked out for you, though."

"It wasn't anything I'd considered. You know that. I'd even looked at that house on Parmeter Court. Some things don't go the way we plan . . . or even the way the

Advisory Committee plans." Obreduur shook his head. "I heard that Haasan Decaro said he'll run in the next elections . . . whenever they're called."

"I heard. That . . ." Iglis glanced to Ysella.

Ysella grinned. "Whatever you'd say, I've heard worse."

"No need to say it then." Iglis turned his eyes back on Obreduur. "What does the Advisory Committee think?"

"They don't know yet."

"What does the Gaarlak Craft Party think?"

"No one's saying. Is there a better candidate? Besides Johan Lamarr? Jens says Lamarr's inclined not to run, but won't say other until elections are called." Obreduur looked directly at Iglis.

"I haven't changed my mind. Besides, it's still a Landor district."

"Raathan can't run again, and he hasn't kept in touch. A strong local Crafter . . ."

"Axel . . . no." After a brief hesitation, Iglis asked, "What's Raathan saying?"

"I have no idea. He's asked us to his estate for midday refreshments. He may want to know who the Craft Party candidate could be."

"Will you tell him?"

"What do you think?"

Iglis offered a sarcastic laugh. "Don't tell him anything. He never tells anyone anything. So why give him what he won't give." He looked at Dekkard. "Where are you from?"

"Oersynt."

"Too bad. Good-looking young fellow like you with experience in Machtarn and an artisan background might do well here."

Obreduur laughed good-naturedly. "I've told Steffan there's a future, but he needs a bit more experience. And Oersynt and Malek are both in my district. I'm not quite ready to step down." He looked back at the cabinetmaker.

Iglis shook his head. "I told you. I can't even think of that, Axel."

"I thought that would be what you'd say, but I had to ask. How's Kassy?"

"Mean as ever, but I wouldn't have it any other way . . ."

Dekkard listened as the conversation turned to personal generalities.

Perhaps a sixth later, Obreduur said, "Now I have to do some official inspecting. The Upper Locks. I'm on the Waterways Committee."

"Aren't you the fortunate one." Iglis paused, then said, "I'm sorry to disappoint you . . . but that's one thing Kassy just might kill me for doing. She hated it when I was just steward."

"I understand. Believe me, I do. I hope it won't be too long before I'm back this way, but it doesn't happen often."

"You're welcome, whenever it is."

Moments later, the three were walking back to the Kharlan.

As they took the seats, Jens Seigryn looked to Obreduur.

The councilor shook his head.

"Too bad, but it was worth a try."

Dekkard had the feeling that Seigryn wasn't that upset.

"Might as well get on to the Upper Locks then," said Obreduur.

The driver eased the touring steamer back onto the avenue, still heading northeast, paralleling the Lakaan River.

A third of a bell later, they reached the Upper Locks, and the driver eased the Kharlan parallel to the lower lock.

"They're twin locks, one for southbound boats, one for northbound," said Obreduur. "There's another set of locks about a third of a mille farther north."

Dekkard studied the nearer lock, roughly fifty yards

long, and holding two canal boats, tied together, end-to-end. He also saw a tug hauling two canal boats linked together. Another set of linked boats was about forty yards downstream, connected to the first set of boats by a hawser.

Dekkard didn't know much about the locks, except what he'd read. The Upper Gaarlak Locks had been far more important during the earlier years, when the most economical way of moving freight had been by river and canal, because they had added another hundred milles to the navigable length of the Lakaan River, and they were still used because the freight costs were much lower than those charged by Guldoran Ironway.

Dekkard and Ysella followed Obreduur as he walked to the nearer lock, where he stopped and surveyed the lock gates.

"The seals are still tight and there's no sign of water coming under the gates," said Obreduur.

All in all, the councilor spent less than a bell inspecting all four locks as they operated before walking back to the Kharlan.

Once they were headed back toward Gaarlak, Dekkard asked, "Will you need a written report on the locks?"

Obreduur shook his head. "I'll send a note to the Minister of Waterways saying that I observed the locks and that they appeared to be functioning, although the bottom seal on the upper eastern lock may need repair soon. I'll also send a copy to the committee chairman."

"So that you're on record as undertaking duties related to your duties in the Council?"

"That . . . and also letting the Waterways minister know that I actually look at the waterways, and not just in my district." Obreduur leaned back in his seat, giving the impression that he did not wish to be disturbed.

Dekkard turned to Ysella, saying in a low voice, "Are you sure what I'm wearing is appropriate for midday refreshments at a Landor's estate?"

"It's not only appropriate, but likely what Raathan will be wearing."

Slightly before midday the touring steamer returned to the Ritter's Inn.

"The limousine will be here in a few minutes," Seigryn said. "You should leave the inn before a third past the bell. I'll be back after fifth bell to give you anything else I've learned about those who will be at the dinner tonight."

"I appreciate that, Jens. I did my best with Hrald. He can't be forced to do anything."

Seigryn laughed. "Everyone knows that. Still, your presence here will help, and we all appreciate your coming to Gaarlak."

"Except for Haasan."

"That was to be expected. I'll see you this evening."

After Seigryn and the touring Kharlan left, Obreduur turned to Ysella and Dekkard. "I need to wash up a bit. We can talk on the way up . . . if you have any questions."

Since Dekkard had no questions, he just kept pace with the councilor.

As they started up the wide stairs to the second level, Obreduur turned to Dekkard. "What do you think of Gaarlak?"

"It seems pleasant enough. It does seem like it's . . . possibly excessively . . . traditional."

Obreduur chuckled. "That's one way of putting it, but you should have been here twenty years ago. The guilds were dispirited, and several of the mills were ready to close."

"What did you do to change that?"

"You give me far too much credit, Steffan. I just listened to good suggestions, added a very few of my own, and the leadership of the guilds went to the mills with them. It eventually worked out. You need to listen to almost everyone, and then choose the best suggestions."

"Often everyone has a different idea of what's best. How did you determine that?"

"Corporacions and their managers think about immediate profits, and workers think about immediate pay. You have to look further. Getting paid more today is a fool's game, if you don't have a job next year. If higher profits today mean that you don't improve and maintain your mill, you'll have unhappy workers because more will get hurt, and your operating costs will increase each year. You can't tell anyone that. You have to ask gentle but firm questions. Sometimes, you can't save people from themselves. I made that case to Charls Hareem back then. He rejected it. He was the owner of the Phanx mill."

"The one that closed?"

"It took eight years, but in the end, he lost everything. He could have sold it to Gaarlak Mills and come out ahead. Or he could have improved the mill. He did neither." Obreduur stopped in front of the door to his suite. "I'll see you both shortly."

Dekkard returned to his room, brushed off his trousers and boots, and washed up, wondering about the references to Lewes and Marjoy. When he left his room, a bit early, he found Ysella already out in the corridor. "I have a question—"

"About Lewes? He was Obreduur's predecessor as councilor. A year after he was elected, his wife shot him and then herself. The party picked Obreduur as his successor. He won the seat on his own in the next election."

"So Obreduur has only stood for election once."

Ysella nodded.

Meaning that he won't have to stand down for at least another two elections.

Dekkard was still pondering that when the suite door opened. Obreduur had not changed, and Ingrella wore an ensemble very close to that of Ysella, except her summer suit was pale blue with a slightly darker blue blouse.

The black Kharlan limousine was waiting outside. The driver asked, "The estate of Councilor Raathan?"

"That's correct," replied Dekkard.

The driver turned west coming out of the inn's drive and continued west for several blocks before turning northwest on a boulevard without a name, at least one that Dekkard could discern. Before too long they reached the edge of Gaarlak, and the avenue turned into a narrower bitumen road that made a wide sweeping turn around a marsh before turning north.

Another mille passed before the driver slowed the Kharlan and then turned left between two red brick posts that might once have held gates onto a bitumened lane, flanked by a chest-high and well-trimmed boxwood hedge. A half mille from the road, the lane began to rise gently through the blue-flowered fields to a low ridge on which sat a long two-story mansion surrounded by gardens set amid a well-groomed lawn.

"Positively modest . . . for a holder," said Ingrella dryly. "That suggests his lands are extensive."

Recalling that the book on councilors he'd been studying had only said that Raathan's total assets were unknown, Dekkard asked the driver, "Do you know how extensive Councilor Raathan's lands might be?"

"I've heard that he's one of the wealthiest in these parts, sir. That's all I know."

Extensive enough that no one can really determine how well-off he is. "Thank you."

The drive did not lead to the center of the mansion, but to a covered portico at the south end, where the driver eased the Kharlan to a stop.

Waiting by the door was a man wearing a silver-trimmed blue barong over white linen trousers. He stepped forward and opened the rear door of the limousine. "We've haven't met, Ritter Obreduur, Ritten. I'm Georg Raathan. Father asked me to meet you and show you to the east veranda. He and Mother are fussing over some last-minute details."

"Thank you," replied Obreduur. "My aides here are Avraal Ysella and Steffan Dekkard."

Georg, who looked to be about ten years older than Dekkard, inclined his head. "I'm pleased to meet you both." After the briefest hesitation, he asked Ysella, "Your family wouldn't be from Sudaen, would it?"

"It would," replied Ysella lightly, "but don't hold me against them."

Georg smiled in return. "Just so long as you don't hold me against my parents."

"Then we're agreed," replied Ysella.

Georg opened the single door, heavy golden oak, and gestured for everyone to enter. Then he led them down the beige-tiled hallway, past a receiving parlor on the left, opposite an office of some sort. Beyond that were a library on the left and a closed door on the right. The next door on the right opened into a music room, containing a harpsichord, rather than the newer pianoforte.

When Georg reached the center hallway he turned to the right, leading them past a salon on the south side and a formal dining room on the north, and out through an open door onto the east veranda. Emilio Raathan and his wife turned immediately, as did the younger red-headed woman to whom they had been talking.

"Welcome to Plainfields," said Raathan. "My great-grandfather named it that. He said the lands were plain fields, and nothing more, and he didn't want anyone in the family to put on airs. Just take a seat. Georg and Katryna will take care of the beverages."

"What can I get you?" asked Georg cheerfully.

"A cool pale lager," replied Obreduur.

"A full red wine, or as close to it as possible," said Ingrella.

In the end, drinks in hand, the eight sat in cream-painted wicker chairs upholstered in dusky rose around a low table with a shimmering black lacquer top.

"It's very kind of you to ask us," offered Obreduur.

"And us," added Dekkard.

"I wouldn't not have asked you two. In the first place, it made Axel's acceptance more likely, and in the second, I thought Georg and Katryna would appreciate having company closer to their own age. It's not as though they get to see that many, since they're responsible for all the lands most of the time, and since holdings around Gaarlak are spread out."

The last words could have meant anything, but Dekkard suspected Raathan didn't want to be outnumbered as well as wanted to introduce Georg to Obreduur . . . and possibly he also meant there weren't many Landor holdings anywhere nearby.

"Nonetheless," replied Obreduur, "it's very kind of you, and we appreciate it."

"I must say," added Patriana, looking to Ysella, "Emilio never mentioned that you two were the ones who stopped that New Meritorist empath. How did you manage that?"

Raathan looked sideways at his wife.

"Emilio, don't give me that look. You all may have to pretend that they don't exist when you're at the Council, but I don't have to in my own house." Patriana returned her eyes to Ysella.

Dekkard managed to smother a smile.

Ysella didn't bother, then recounted what had happened.

"Does anyone know why an empath would work with people like that?" asked Katryna.

"She had a grudge against Councilor Aashtaan," replied Obreduur smoothly, but quickly, "and the New Meritorists were quick to exploit it."

Raathan raised his eyebrows. "Oh? You're hiding something, Axel."

"It's not exactly a secret that Aashtaan had liaisons with young women not his wife," replied Obreduur. "It's also been rumored that at least one of them vanished."

"You think that the empie was related?" asked Katryna.

Obreduur glanced to Ysella.

"The empath who attacked Councilor Aashtaan was focused on him," Ysella replied. "She dressed as a Council messenger, and she could have been in the Council Hall for days."

"But . . . Ulrich suggested . . ." said Raathan.

"She couldn't have gotten as far as she did without help," Obreduur pointed out. "That's the real danger with the New Meritorists. If Ulrich and the Commercers keep abusing their power and position, and the Council doesn't rein in those abuses, more people with grudges and grievances will turn to the New Meritorists."

"I've said that all along," murmured Patriana.

"Yes, you have, my dear," said Raathan, "but until there are elections . . ."

"I do hope they come soon," added Patriana. "Then you won't have to deal with such people like Ulrich. He's so . . . commercial."

"Councilor Obreduur," asked Georg, "do you think that the Imperador will call for elections any time soon?"

Obreduur laughed wryly. "I can't claim to know what's on the Imperador's mind, but unless something unforeseen occurs, I would doubt it."

"How likely is something like that to happen?" pressed Georg.

"I'm not about to try to foresee the unforeseen," returned Obreduur. "Who could have foreseen the Kraffeist Affair?"

"Or Eastern Ironway being so incredibly greedy . . . or stupid," added Raathan, turning to Dekkard and asking, "What do you think, Steffan?"

"I'd agree with Councilor Obreduur about the difficulty of foreseeing the unforeseen. I also think that sometimes we don't see things coming because they've never happened before and because we never thought about it. I certainly never thought about demonstrators with firearms shooting at Council Guards, or burning down Security headquarters."

"We can't have that sort of chaos and disorder. Not if Guldor is going to remain prosperous," asserted Georg. "Security has to do more to keep people in line."

Dekkard decided to be more vocal than he might have been in such a gathering. "Keeping people in line will just make matters worse if other things don't change.

The Commerce Party leadership doesn't seem to realize that happy people don't participate in demonstrations, yet there are more demonstrations."

"Why are people so unhappy?" asked Katryna. "We're not at war. There haven't been any famines. Life is better than ever."

Raathan laughed. "You might be better at explaining that than I am, Axel."

"It might be better if I did," said Ingrella. "I see the people who are unhappy a bit more than he does now." She turned to Katryna. "For us, life is better. The manufactories produce better cloth at lower prices, and that means clothing is more varied and less expensive. The same is true for other goods. We don't always see that what makes life more comfortable for us makes it less so for others. Steam tractors and threshers mean that holders need fewer farmworkers than years ago or that they can manage more cropland with fewer workers. What happens to those workers? They go to the cities. If they're fortunate, they work in the mills. If not, they struggle as messengers or day laborers or pieceworkers. Or they go hungry. For poor but attractive women, there are the brothels. None of this is unknown. What is new is that there are more poor and more without work than ever. At the same time, industry and steam power have created more very wealthy people than ever, and those without see this."

"Then they should work harder," declared Katryna.

"You can't work harder if there isn't a job for you . . . or if you haven't been able to learn the skills for the available jobs," pointed out Obreduur. "We are, however, not going to resolve these problems this afternoon, although the Council will face them, I fear, for years to come." He lifted his glass of lager. "May we all enjoy the afternoon."

"To the afternoon," added Dekkard and Ysella.

Raathan offered an amused smile as he lifted his wineglass and sipped the hearty red, then said, "How did you ever end up making Malek your home, Axel?"

Obreduur smiled in return. "I didn't, properly speaking. My work with the guilds brought me there, and I ended up having heated words with a young but distinguished legalist over the legal interpretation of work rules. We compromised on the legalities, but I surrendered totally and agreed to her terms otherwise before she would assent to my proposal of marriage. So our family in Malek is her family. It couldn't be otherwise, because my mother died young, and my father was killed in a dock accident in Machtarn when I was in my early twenties."

"Romantic, but sad," said Patriana.

With that exchange, Dekkard knew the rest of the afternoon would be filled with pleasantries and, hopefully, with excellent light fare.

64

As Dekkard had anticipated, the remainder of the afternoon at Plainfields was pleasant and uneventful. He definitely enjoyed the fare—especially the cool, thick, and spicy tomato soup with the fresh garlic croutons and the sugared lime shortbread squares that followed.

Once they were in the limousine headed back into Gaarlak proper, Ingrella turned to her husband. "Did that go as you'd hoped?"

"We'll have to see. I worry a bit about Katryna."

"Don't," replied Ingrella. "I saw Patriana's reaction to her statement that the poor should work harder."

"Is it just my impression," asked Dekkard, "that Councilor Raathan is a bit disillusioned about being a councilor? His wife certainly appears that way."

"Any councilor who isn't at least slightly disillusioned is either a fool or an idiot," replied Obreduur. "Raathan is neither."

"Or a megalomaniac," added Ingrella sardonically, "which Ulrich is."

"There is that possibility," Obreduur agreed cheerfully.

Just before the limousine pulled into the Ritter's Inn, Obreduur said, "Both of you, dress grays, and please wear your Council staff pins tonight." Then he addressed Dekkard. "And your Council truncheon." After a pause, he said, "Tonight, I'm going to say just a few words. Then I'm going to ask you to say a few more about why Gaarlak needs a Craft councilor."

"Me?" blurted Dekkard.

"You. You come from a long line of crafters. I don't. I come from the rivers. Why do you think I had you working on all those versions of speeches?" Before Dekkard could say more, Obreduur concluded, "Not another word. We'll see you both just before sixth bell."

After Dekkard and Ysella escorted the Obreduurs to their suite, Ysella turned to Dekkard. "He's worried. That may be why he wants you to speak. That way he can study everyone."

"But . . . me? Did he say anything to you about this?"

She shook her head. "Just keep it short and heartfelt."

Dekkard returned to his room, washed up, and changed into a gray suit, deciding on the black cravat that Ysella had given him, and carefully adjusting his Council staff pin. Then he paced around his room trying out possible variations on what he'd written. Finally, at a third before sixth bell he was out in the corridor.

A few minutes later, Ysella joined him, wearing a light summer suit of a gray identical to his.

"Just let me know if you sense anything antagonistic and who might be feeling that way . . . if you can."

"If I can. As you know, it's difficult when there are a lot of people close together."

Dekkard smiled at the mild rebuke in the words "as you know," then asked, "Did you get a chance to be close to Haasan Decaro the other morning?"

"He avoided me."

"He avoided us both. No one else did, although I never talked to Arleena Desenns."

"I did. She seemed pleasant enough . . . very concerned about how the punch-card looms were reducing the number of women weavers, though."

"What sense did you get from Eliver?"

"Practical and cynical. He felt straightforward. He doesn't care much for Decaro." Ysella grinned as she added, "You didn't ask me about Gretna Haarl."

"Should I have asked?"

"No. I don't think she tends to physical violence, but you can't tell with isolates. I'd guess she wouldn't hesitate a moment to scheme if she thought it to her benefit."

Neither spoke for several minutes.

Then Ysella said, "Just keep it short and from your heart."

"That's hard. I have a wordy heart."

She only shook her head.

Then the Obreduurs appeared. He wore a black suit with a red cravat—an unofficial symbol of a councilor—while she wore a deep blue gown with a white jacket. Obreduur just nodded, and Dekkard and Ysella led the way down the stairs to the main floor of the inn.

Jens Seigryn was waiting for them at the bottom of the stairs, wearing a dark blue suit, but not of security blue, with a bright blue cravat. "You all look very official."

"I believe that's the purpose," said Obreduur in a warm but ironic tone.

"Everyone's here but Haasan. He'll make an appearance now that you've entered."

"Haasan will be Haasan," returned Obreduur mildly.

As they passed the door to the restaurant, Dekkard could hear a raspy voice accompanied by a mandolin.

*"There's folks who live both high and grand
And those who've lost their life and land.
If life is but illusion, so be it
It's real enough the way I see it . . ."*

If life is but illusion . . . it's real enough the way I see it. Not for the first time, Dekkard wondered how much of life was illusion, but he forced his thoughts back to the dinner ahead.

When the five entered the banquet hall, Dekkard quickly scanned those inside, estimating that there were slightly over fifty people, roughly equal numbers of men and women, given that spouses had been invited, gathered in small groups generally close to the two sideboards where servers in maroon and black livery provided either wine, lager, or ale. He immediately picked out those who had been at the breakfast meeting, although Jon Eliver was the only one who looked in Dekkard's direction. He smiled pleasantly. Gretna Haarl looked quickly at Dekkard and Ysella, but her gaze definitely didn't linger on either.

Arleena Desenns was the first to approach the Obreduurs, inclining her head and saying, "It's so thoughtful for you to arrange such a dinner."

"We don't get here often," replied Obreduur. "It's been a few years, and after the business meeting, we thought we should have a more enjoyable evening."

The next to approach was an older man, and Seigryn murmured to Dekkard and Ysella, "Kharl Maatsuyt, Textile Millworkers."

"Councilor." Maatsuyt inclined his head, then continued, "I regret that I missed yesterday's breakfast, but I had previously scheduled a meeting with the managing director of Gaarlak Mills."

"I trust that your meeting was productive," replied Obreduur.

"We'll have to see." Maatsuyt's smile was pleasant. "It would help if we had a Craft councilor from Gaarlak."

"I heard that Haasan was thinking about running in the next election."

"That would be an improvement," replied Maatsuyt. "Is there any way I might help?"

"I do appreciate the offer. I won't keep you any longer." Maatsuyt's second smile was warmer. "I see a few others wanting a word with you."

A very fair-skinned man in a dark brown suit neared.

"Alastan Cleese, guildmeister of the Farmworkers," murmured Seigryn.

After Cleese came Johan Lamarr, the Crafters guildmeister, with Decaro still not having appeared. Then came a short but burly man not quite bursting out of a dark blue suit.

"Yorik Haansel," said Seigryn quietly.

Belatedly, Dekkard recognized the burly guildmeister of the Stonemasons, who had visited Obreduur in Machtarn.

"Yorik," said Obreduur warmly, "it's not often I get to see you twice in the same season."

"Sometimes, it happens," rumbled the stonemason.

The two chatted for almost five minutes by Dekkard's watch, and he wondered just how long Obreduur would wait before the Machineworkers guildmeister deigned to appear, but, finally Decaro appeared, clad in a stylish dark green suit, his shimmering black hair combed back. He immediately made his way to Obreduur, where he offered the barest inclination of his head before saying warmly, "Councilor . . . and Ritten Obreduur, we meet again, twice in two days."

"Sometimes it happens that way, Haasan," replied Obreduur. "I understand you're considering running for councilor. The Machineworkers will lose a very strong guildmeister."

"But Gaarlak will gain more power in the Council."

"If you win, that it will," agreed Obreduur. "Now that you're here, we should take care of the brief formalities so that everyone can enjoy themselves." He nodded to Seigryn.

The guild coordinator must have signaled someone, because a set of chimes rang out.

After the various conversations died away, Seigryn

spoke. "This is meant to be just an enjoyable evening. I've persuaded Guildmeister Decaro to offer the blessing, and after that Councilor Obreduur will say a few words."

"A very few," interjected Obreduur strongly but warmly, before nodding to Decaro.

Decaro stepped slightly away from Obreduur. He did not speak immediately but let the silence draw out before finally beginning. "Almighty and Trinity of Love, Power, and Mercy, we thank you for fruitful days and for the success and growth of the guilds of Gaarlak. We also acknowledge your support and guidance for those who lead us and pray that you will continue to bless and guide them in the future. Tonight, we thank you for this opportunity to share food and fellowship in this gathering of your faithful, in the name of the Three in One."

"The Three in One," came the murmured response.

Obreduur stepped forward. "Most of you know me as a councilor . . . and as a Crafter guildmeister and politician. But I'm not a crafter. I'm from the rivers. We all know that Gaarlak will have a new councilor when elections are next held, and that councilor should come from crafters. That's why I'm going to ask Steffan here, who comes from a very long line of crafters and artisans, to tell you why."

The silence that followed was half respect for Obreduur and half stunned astonishment, Dekkard thought.

All he could do was his best. "It's true. My family has been crafters and artisans for generations, and I appreciate that dedication and skill enormously, largely because those talents skipped me. The best I can do is work for the councilor to support crafters and artisans. Today, all the Commercer councilors do is work to increase the power of corporacions, but the strength, the real strength, of Guldor lies not in banques, not in Security patrollers, and not even in a massive and mighty Navy, but in the hands and skills of its people. People like every one of you, people who make the tools and goods that make life better. People who create unique woodwork, portraits, the very linens that we wear and appreciate. No one more than a Crafter councilor could appreciate and support that." Dekkard paused. "And since the councilor told me to be brief . . . do everything you can to find and support the best Craft candidate possible . . . and, of course, enjoy the dinner."

The applause was modest and polite. Dekkard was not quite shaking as he inadvertently stepped back.

"Good for a first time," said Obreduur. "And very effective."

Effective? Then Dekkard realized exactly what Obreduur had done. He'd avoided supporting Decaro without seeming to do so. "Won't that make Decaro angry?" he asked quietly.

"Anything other than my full support would make him unhappy, but he can't be publicly unhappy. You said to find and support the best Craft candidate possible. Besides, he couldn't expect me to support him, and enough people know it that they'll find what we did a polite way of dealing with a difficult situation. Still . . . he might not see it that way. So keep your eyes open . . . and go find your seats. Ysella will be at my table."

"Good."

"Enjoy yourself, Steffan . . . as much as you can."

Dekkard found himself seated at table with Arleena Desenns at his right; Charlana Boetcher, an assistant guildmeister for the Crafters Guild, at his left; and Myram Plassar, the regional steward for the Working Women Guild, across from him, with Thor Boetcher and Hans Desenns flanking her.

Dekkard actually got to take a sip of his cool but not chilled lager, after introductions were completed and before the questions began.

"Do you often speak for the councilor?" asked Guildmeister Desenns.

"I do speak for him occasionally," replied Dekkard, "but not usually when he's present. He felt that I could speak more to crafters and artisans."

"Were you ever actually an artisan?" asked Plassar, a vaguely amused tone in her voice.

"I was an apprentice decorative plasterer for five years to my father. By then, he realized I had a great appreciation and understanding of the craft, but not the physical skills to be really good at it."

"So you actually did get your hands dirty," said Charlana Boetcher.

"Very dirty. I was very good at cleaning up . . . and prep work."

"Isn't that what you do now?" asked Thor Boetcher.

"Isn't that a good part of anything?" Dekkard replied amiably.

"Sometimes, it's most of everything," suggested Plassar sardonically.

Charlana Boetcher couldn't quite conceal a wince.

"I saw the article in the *Times,*" said Hans Desenns. "That seemed . . . a bit . . . overdramatic. Did it really happen that way?"

"Generally. The article didn't mention that the attack also injured another councilor and another staffer. The staffer would have died without Avraal's shielding him."

"Do councilors really need two security aides?" pressed Hans Desenns.

"For the most part, only if they're Craft councilors. I've been involved in four attacks this year. The attack on Councilor Aashtaan is the only one on a Commercer councilor."

"Isn't that because Councilor Obreduur is the political leader of the Craft Party and because he's been very successful at increasing the number of Craft councilors?" asked Plassar.

"It just might have something to do with it," replied Dekkard, following his words with another small swallow of lager. "He works extremely hard."

At that moment, attendants appeared at the table and supplied each diner with the single entrée—veal milanesia with risotto and green beans amandine—as well as a salad of mixed greens.

As soon as everyone was served and the ladies on each side of him lifted their forks, Dekkard did so as well, hoping to get in some nourishment before the questions resumed.

He was pleasantly surprised to discover that the scattered questions that followed were more about Machtarn and the Council and about how he became an aide than the pointed ones that had preceded the arrival of dinner. Dessert was flan accompanied by petite alfajores.

As the dinner finally ended, and Dekkard stood, Myram Plassar moved around the table and said, "You handle yourself very well, may I call you, Steffan?"

"You may."

"I presume you understand why the councilor asked you to speak."

"I do, although it wasn't until the arrival of Guildmeister Decaro that I realized why."

"Do you think the councilor's decision to have you speak was wise?"

"I've questioned his decisions in the past. So far, he's turned out to have a much better record than I would have. In this case, I wouldn't question him."

"Might I ask what you think of Haasan Decaro?"

Dekkard smiled wryly. "Anything I might say would be based on hearsay because he's avoided speaking to me, and only said pleasantries to the councilor, at least in my presence."

Plassar offered another pleasantly amused smile. "You do speak well. In conversation and to a group. I hope we'll see more of you."

"Right now . . . that's not exactly in my hands."

"Keep it in mind, when it is." After a parting smile, she turned and headed toward the door.

Dekkard glanced around, looking for Haasan Decaro, but decided that Decaro must have left already. *As soon as he could without being obvious.* So Dekkard moved toward Obreduur, flanked by Ysella and Ingrella, and talking to Guildmeister Maatsuyt. Jens Seigryn stood several paces behind the group. Even before he reached the group, all the other guild attendees departed, leaving the banquet room empty except for the servers, who began cleaning up, and those around Obreduur.

". . . thank you again for coming, and for hosting this dinner." Maatsuyt turned to Dekkard. "That was a very encouraging short speech . . . and well thought out. Who wrote it?"

"It wasn't written out, Guildmeister. The councilor told me to speak from my heart. That's what I did."

"Then you have not only a good heart, but a very well organized one as well. Thank you all." And with that Maatsuyt turned and strode briskly from the banquet chamber.

"We should have an aperitif in the suite," said Obreduur. "Would you like to join us, Jens?"

"I think I'll pass. It's been a long day. I'll see you all off in the morning."

"Then try to get a good night's sleep," returned Obreduur.

The Obreduurs, Ysella, and Dekkard walked past the now-shuttered inn restaurant and up the maroon-carpeted wide stairs to the second level. As they turned down the side hallway toward the Knight's Suite, a man in the maroon and black livery of the inn appeared, carrying a tray with covered dishes on it.

"He's an isolate," murmured Ysella.

Even before her words, Dekkard saw a shift in the way the apparent server carried the tray, and realizing he was too far away to use the truncheon, drew and threw the first knife. The attacker dodged just as he fired the pistol. That shot went wide, but the attacker tilted the tray, spilling the dishes, then grabbed the edge of the tray with one hand, using it as a shield against Dekkard's remaining throwing knife.

Shifting his aim to avoid the shield-like tray, Dekkard threw the second knife into the man's exposed thigh, immediately charging as the knife left his fingers and bringing up the truncheon.

The attacker winced but swung the tray and turned

the pistol back in the direction of Obreduur—but not quite fast enough before Dekkard struck with the truncheon in the only place he could reach that would stop the false server—in his temple. The crunch of bone suggested he'd been more than successful.

Instantly, Dekkard saw the attacker's face illuminated as if from within, then replaced as an image of thousands of tiny lights, yet somehow recognizable as a man's visage, before Dekkard once more beheld the stunned yet frozen expression of the attacker, as the pistol dropped to the carpet.

"He's dead," snapped Ysella.

"Then he has to die another way. Leave the pistol and tray and dishes where they are." After recovering both knives, Dekkard immediately lifted the body and heaved it over the balcony railing so that it fell and then hit the slate floor below with a dull *thud*. Then he hurried down the steps, Ysella right behind him.

The desk clerk was already in the lobby, moving toward the body.

"That man!" Dekkard pointed to the heap on the slate floor beside the staircase. "He tried to attack the councilor. He fired at him and then tried to flee, but he jumped over the railing before we could restrain him."

"He tried to shoot . . . the councilor?"

"Didn't you hear the shots? You can see the pistol and the dishes upstairs. We didn't touch them." Dekkard walked over to where the man lay, face against the slate. He reached out, but did not quite touch the body before straightening and saying, "He's dead. I'd hoped we could find out who sent him."

"You'd better summon Security patrollers," said Ysella.

Obreduur and Ingrella returned to their rooms, while Dekkard and Ysella waited with the desk clerk, and the evening manager scurried around trying to find out how and where the dead man had come from.

As he waited Dekkard couldn't help but wonder at the point-light-illuminated image he'd seen. *Did you really see those lights? Is your mind playing tricks on you?* Finally, he said quietly to Ysella, "Did you see anything odd about the attacker?"

"I didn't see anything odd," she replied. "It was strange that he attacked without saying anything at all. He didn't even make any sounds when he was trying to shoot the councilor."

Dekkard decided to save his questions about the point-lights for later.

Two Security patrollers arrived within a sixth of a bell. They immediately asked for Dekkard's story. He told them.

Then they asked Ysella, "Is that what happened?"

"That's what I saw."

"You're an empath, aren't you? Why didn't you sense something?"

"I did. I sensed that he was an isolate. That was why I warned Steffan."

"You two stay here."

For more than a third of a bell, the two investigated the upper corridor and talked to the night manager and the desk clerk. Then they returned.

"Most of what you say checks out. The dishes are all clean. So is the tray. There's no trace of food. But there's a knife wound in his thigh."

"I told you. When he first approached, he was too far away to use my truncheon. So I threw a knife to distract him. That's when he used the tray as a shield, but he still had the pistol. His leg was the only target. I'd hoped that would distract him. There's nowhere on the front of the leg that would be fatal. But he dropped the gun, and when I rushed him with the truncheon he scrambled over the railing and dropped or fell."

The two left Dekkard and Ysella and went up the stairs to talk to the Obreduurs.

More time passed before they returned with Obreduur.

The two patrollers looked at Dekkard, then Ysella, then Obreduur. Then they looked at each other.

Finally, the shorter one said to the taller one, "The dead man stole a tray, stole a uniform, stole the dishes, and shot at a councilor. Everyone agrees on that. There's a set of clothes in the staff room with no identification and nothing on him. He sneaked in with everything going on with the banquet. No one in the inn knows who he is. The pistol is Atacaman. Whoever was behind it didn't want any ties. The councilor's aide tried not to use excessive force against a firearm."

The taller patroller looked to Obreduur. "Will you be around, Ritter?"

"I'd planned to leave for Oersynt tomorrow morning." Obreduur smiled wearily. "It's not as though you can't find me or Sr. Dekkard if you need more information."

"True enough," replied the taller man.

The other patroller said to his partner, "You know we're not going to find anything else."

The first one shook his head. "You've been through enough, Councilor. We'll take care of the rest of this. Have a safe trip."

"Thank you," replied Obreduur. "I'm sorry that we couldn't provide more information, but it was all quite a shock."

The three slowly walked up the stairs and then to the sitting room of the suite, where Ingrella, Gustoff, and Nellara sat waiting.

"They say that there's nothing else we can do," said Obreduur.

"They won't make us stay?" asked Nellara.

"Your mother was quietly very convincing when she talked to the patrollers," said Obreduur. "They also don't want to detain a councilor who's been the target of an assassin. They'd prefer we be somewhere else before whoever was behind it attacks again." He took a deep breath. "I think we all need that aperitif."

65

After sipping a Silverhills fine brandy, and following a brief discussion of who might have been behind the assassination attempt, and a consensus that it could have equally been Commercer private operatives, covert Security agents, someone hired by Haasan Decaro, or one of the aforementioned trying to remove Dekkard and/or Ysella, Dekkard and Ysella left the suite.

Outside in the corridor, Dekkard said, "We need to talk. At least, I do. My room or yours?"

"Yours is neater. Right now, anyway."

As the two neared the door to his room, she said, "There's no one inside . . . or nearby."

"You really think they were after one of us?"

"It's a real possibility."

Dekkard unlocked and opened the door. After they entered and he closed and locked the door, he walked to the wall sconce and used the compression lighter. This time, Ysella settled herself into the single chair, and Dekkard sat on the edge of the bed.

"The attacker was an isolate," he said. "That suggests it's someone who knows about you, but not very well."

"Decaro fits that profile, but only if Obreduur was the actual target. If you or I were the target, it makes no difference because the odds were that either of us or the attacker would be dead. If you hadn't thought quickly tonight, you'd have been placed in a very difficult position, just because you'd be involved in a lot of questioning or even a trial over the question of whether you needed to actually kill the attacker. You'd be acquitted, but it would be messy and time-consuming . . . and Obreduur wouldn't be as well protected."

"The attempt in Julieta did come to mind," he said. "Or rather your analysis of it. I also have to admit that there have been rather more than a few attempts at removing me, in one way or another. One might be co-incidence, but three?"

"Five," corrected Ysella. "The nighttime shots at you. The incident at Julieta. The empath attack at the Machtarn Guildhall. The two false Council Guards at the covered parking . . . and this one."

"Four," said Dekkard. "The Guildhall incident was aimed at Raynaad."

"You're right about that, but that confirms that someone is targeting both Obreduur and his staff. Or that one group is after Obreduur and another after staffers."

"Why? Just because he's been effective in increasing the number of Craft councilors?"

"Just?" Ysella's voice oozed heavy sardonicism. "By the time the next elections are called, he might well have gained enough votes in borderline districts for the Craft Party to take the maximum number of Council seats, and he just might have enough backing among Landors and one or two Commercers to take control of the Council. Do you honestly think that Ulrich or his corporacion backers wouldn't consider any possible measures to stop Obreduur, legal or not? Why do you think Ingrella is constantly in contact with Craft legalists all over Guldor? Her success in legalistic efforts to strengthen the guilds might also be why the latest efforts against Obreduur himself have been anything but legal."

"Do you honestly think any Commerce councilor might vote for him as premier?" asked Dekkard, his voice skeptical.

"It's a secret vote. There are a few who might do it to remove Ulrich. Then, later they might force a vote of no confidence and require a vote on a new leadership . . . or even new elections."

That Dekkard could definitely see, but he had another question. Although he suspected he already knew the answer, he wanted to know what Ysella thought. "Why aren't they targeting other Craft councilors and staff?"

"Steffan . . . are you deliberately being dense? How

many other Craft staffers have been bought off, intimidated, or disappeared in just the past few months? Also, the last thing that the Commercers want is more competent Craft councilors. If a councilor dies in office, in any way, the party gets to pick his successor. Take a councilor like Waarfel, or especially Nortak. The last thing Ulrich would want would be to give Obreduur the chance to replace Nortak, with say, Svard, who comes from near there."

Roostof as a councilor made sense, as did the Commercers not wanting anything like that. "So what do we do now?"

"We keep doing what we've been doing. And you'd better keep thinking about what you're going to say, because I'd wager we're both going to be speaking more. Especially you."

"You know more than I do."

"Not that much more. Not any longer. I'm amazed at how fast you learn and can use that knowledge. So is Obreduur."

"He doesn't say much about it."

"That's not his style. His form of praise is giving you more to do."

Dekkard offered a mock groan that wasn't totally feigned.

"Don't groan. Neither of us does as much as either of the Obreduurs."

While Dekkard had known that about the councilor for years, he hadn't realized it also applied to his wife the legalist until the last few days. Late as it was, however, he did have one more question. "Did you see or sense anything strange about the attacker right after I hit him?"

"No, except I felt him die." She paused. "You asked that before. Why?"

"What does it feel like . . . when you sense someone dying?"

Ysella frowned.

"Please . . ."

"There's a sparkle of tiny invisible lights—that's the only way I can describe it, at least that's the way I feel it . . . and then there's nothing . . . just nothing. Why?"

"Because . . ." He shook his head.

"Steffan," she said gently.

"I think I saw something like that. For just an instant, his face was a pattern of tiny lights . . . and then they were gone." He swallowed. "The same thing happened with the false Council Guard I had to kill. I thought . . . I just wondered . . ."

". . . if you were losing your mind?"

Dekkard nodded.

"You don't feel anything? You just see the lights?"

"And only for an instant."

"That's odd. I wonder if other isolates would see that."

"I don't know." Dekkard wasn't certain whether he should feel relieved . . . or even more worried . . . or if it was just a part of being an isolate that seldom came up. *After all, it's not as though isolates kill many people or are around when they die . . . or maybe it's only when people die suddenly.* But why had he seen it with the old man? Or had he been close to dying?

The two just sat there for a long moment.

Then, inadvertently, he found himself yawning.

"It's way too late," said Ysella, rising from the chair. "We need to get some sleep."

"You're right. I'll walk you to your door." Dekkard stood.

"Steffan . . . it's only twenty yards."

"It was much less than that, earlier tonight," he said quietly.

Abruptly, she nodded. "You're right."

When they reached the door, she said, "There's no one outside."

"Good." Dekkard unlocked and opened the door, leaving it closed but not locked as he walked Ysella to her room.

"There's also no one inside."

"Leave the door open. I'll wait until you light the lamp."

She nodded, then unlocked the door and entered.

Dekkard waited until she had the lamp lit and returned to the door. "Good night. Lock the door, and I'll leave." He stepped back and waited for the lock to click into place before he walked back to his room.

66

Quindi morning, both Dekkard and Ysella were up early and ate a quick breakfast in the inn restaurant. After that, Dekkard largely managed baggage, while Ysella kept her eyes and senses alert for any possible intrusion or attack, either at the Ritter's Inn or at the ironway station in Gaarlak. Obreduur met briefly with Jens Seigryn, but the councilor said nothing to either Ysella or Dekkard about the short meeting. By a third before second bell, the Obreduur family and Ysella and Dekkard were in their compartments on the Kathaar Express, and at precisely second bell the express began to move away from the station as it began the six-bell trip to Oersynt.

Once the express was moving northwest through the blue-flowered flax fields, Dekkard turned to Ysella. "Are you ready for a repeat of Gaarlak . . . without the excitement?"

"I'd be fine with pleasant boring dinners, meetings, and rallies."

Dekkard winced. He hadn't exactly forgotten the political rallies; he'd just tried not to dwell on them.

"Remember," said Ysella mischievously, "we'll have to come back to Oersynt again in three weeks and do it all over."

"I so appreciate the reminder," he replied, picking up *The Scarlet Daughter*. "Boring is acceptable, even twice, but now, I'm not going to think about it. I'm just going to read."

"How is it?"

"The history is plausible. The politics and economics are anything but. The social infighting is believable enough that the author likely had some experience. It's pleasantly enjoyable."

"Unlike those political and economic journals you usually read."

"It is Summerend," he replied amiably.

Ysella just shook her head, then leaned sideways against a pillow and closed her eyes.

Less than half a bell later, when he read the same page three times and didn't remember a word, Dekkard followed her example. He hadn't realized how tired he was.

Some five bells later, after two long naps and a decent but not outstanding meal in the dining carriage with Ysella, Dekkard watched as the express started over the massive bridge that crossed the Rio Mal into the Oersynt river district. Less than a half mille southwest and downstream, the Mal flowed into the Rio Azulete. Upstream of the junction, along the eastern shore of the Azulete and on the western edge of Oersynt, between the ironway right-of-way and the river, various mills stretched for milles.

From the express carriage window, even in late mid-afternoon, Dekkard could easily make out the smoky pall that filled the river valley as far as he could see. The ground on which Oersynt was built gradually rose over some ten milles to the north and east into rolling hills, hills that held the summer residences of the city's more affluent families. While Dekkard had often been in some of those residences when his father had done work there, his parents lived south of the more affluent areas, but in a modest section of Oersynt away from the mills and the crowded warrens that housed millworkers and those even less fortunate.

He had no idea exactly how the late-afternoon meeting with the various district Craft Party officials might develop, since he had met none of them previously, or what he might learn there or at the dinner that would follow . . . but he was certain he'd learn.

The next bell was simply tiring, because the Guldoran Ironway station in Oersynt was crowded, as were the narrow streets around it, and Dekkard had to keep track of all the luggage—until it was all stacked in the lobby of the Hotel Cosmopolitano. Then Dekkard watched carefully as hotel valets carried it all up to the Obreduurs' second-floor suite.

Once the luggage had been delivered to the proper rooms, Dekkard washed up and changed from the bar-ong and trousers he'd worn into one of his gray summer suits in preparation for the meeting.

When Obreduur left his suite, he was accompanied by Ingrella, but then, Dekkard reflected, that made even more sense because she'd been a power in her own right in Oersynt even before she'd met and married him. *Even if you didn't know it.*

Ysella and Dekkard escorted the Obreduurs down the long and high staircase from the second level to the lobby and then down a side corridor to a small meeting room.

Outside the door stood a square-faced black-haired man close to Obreduur's age, who immediately offered a broad smile and stepped forward. "It's good to see you, Councilor."

"Axel, please." Obreduur gestured. "You know In-grella, but not my aides, Avraal Ysella and Steffan Dekkard. This is Jareld Herrardo. He's the Advisory Committee's liaison to the district Craft Party."

"I'm happy to meet you, and very happy you kept the councilor safe." At Obreduur's inquisitive expression, Herrardo added, "Jens Seigryn sent me a heliogram about the attempt on you last night."

Obreduur frowned.

"I know," replied Herrardo. "Security likely found out before I did, but Jens must have thought they'd find out before long anyway."

"Did he give any details?" asked Obreduur.

"None. He just wrote that your security thwarted an attack on you."

"Good," replied Obreduur. "It was more than an attack. He was disguised as an inn server and had a pistol."

Herrardo winced.

"Did you tell anyone?"

"No, but there was an article this afternoon in the *Press*."

"Is everyone here?" asked Ingrella.

"Yes, Ritten. Chairman Foerrster, Vice-Chair Koerr, Treasurer Martaan, and Ryanna Wreaslaan. She's the new guild liaison. Martaan's a little weak, but he said he wouldn't miss the meeting. He's recovering from a bout of lung fever."

Dekkard noted that Ingrella nodded at the last name.

"We might as well go on in," said Obreduur cheerfully.

Once again, the rectangular room held a large round table, and the four Craft Party officials stood at one side. All four turned as Obreduur led the way.

"Good afternoon, everyone," declared Obreduur firmly and cheerfully. "The sooner we start, the sooner we finish, and the sooner we all get to eat. Before we sit down, though . . . all of you know Ingrella, but you don't know Avraal Ysella and Steffan Dekkard. They do double duty, both as security and as specialists in various areas. Steffan's family are artisans in Oersynt, but he was a top Institute graduate several years ago, and Avraal deals with land and women's guild issues." Obreduur gestured to the table.

The four Craft Party officials seated themselves on one side, facing Obreduur and Ingrella in the center of the other side, with Dekkard beside Ingrella, and Ysella beside the councilor. Herrardo took a chair and sat against the wall.

"There was a report in the afternoon editions of the newssheets," began the older man, Foerrster, Dekkard assumed, "about some . . . difficulty in Gaarlak."

"There was an attack by a single individual, dressed in the inn's livery. He had a pistol concealed by a tray. Steffan and Avraal thwarted the attack, and the attacker died when he tried to escape and fell from the balcony onto the slate floor of the lobby. He hit headfirst. Security investigated, but he had no identification, and the pistol was from Atacama."

"Rather convenient," commented the man Dekkard thought was Martaan, given his pallor and hoarse voice.

"If the Imperador announces elections," said Koerr, "we could see more of those."

"That's always possible," agreed Obreduur. "We have to be prepared. Just have your people look for strange servers." He paused just briefly, then said, "The New Meritorists had a demonstration here a month or so ago. Have they done anything else?"

Foerrster glanced to Ryanna Wreaslaan.

"Last week there was a small fire in a Security station near the Guldoran Ironway western switching station. One Security patroller died, according to *The Oersynt Press*. One other individual died as well, but his body was too badly burned to be identified immediately. A single room in the basement level was damaged."

"What didn't the newssheets report?" asked Ingrella.

"That room was a filing room. Word is that several other Security agents were shot. Security didn't capture anyone."

Dekkard managed not to frown. Why would the Meritorists even bother with a Security patrol station?

"Did anyone on the district council say anything?" asked Obreduur.

"Chairman Vandenburg offered a brief statement that said nothing," replied Wreaslaan, "except that no vital services—gas, water, and sewage—had been affected."

"Are there any signs that the New Meritorists might do something else or stage another demonstration?" asked Obreduur.

"There weren't any signs the last two times," replied Wreaslaan. "I doubt there will be any the next time."

"Is there anything else unusual that I should know?" Obreduur glanced from face to face.

No one answered.

Obreduur smiled. "Then let's go over what you planned for us to do for the next three days . . ."

For almost a bell, the meeting covered the dinner to come, the places and people the Obreduurs would visit on Findi, Unadi, and Duadi, the guild afternoon dinner on Findi, the tour of Guldoran Ironway's new switching yard and roundhouse on Unadi morning, the legalists' reception and refreshments on Unadi evening, and the dinner for Craft Party volunteers and supporters on Duadi evening.

After the official meeting concluded, Leon Foerrster led the way to a private dining room for dinner. Dekkard ended up, once more, recounting how he'd come to work for the councilor, what his family did, and what working for a councilor involved. From what he could tell, Ysella went through a similar semi-interrogation.

By the time he got to bed, he was asleep almost instantly.

67

Dekkard and Ysella had breakfast together on Findi, both wearing less formal garb, as per Obreduur's instructions, which for Dekkard turned out to be a blue barong and gray trousers. Ysella wore a blue linen suit, with a less transparent headscarf loosely around her neck. They met the Obreduurs outside their suite at a sixth before third bell. Obreduur wore the off-white linen suit without a cravat, while Ingrella again wore light blue.

Ingrella immediately spoke. "Steffan . . . I assume you'd like to see your family."

"If it's possible," replied Dekkard cautiously. "I don't like the idea of leaving the councilor unprotected."

"After the guild function this afternoon, we'll be spending the rest of the afternoon and early evening at my cousin Clarissa's home, from about fourth bell to around second bell. Gustoff and Nellara are there now. We know that doesn't give you that much time, but her house is on Quadrangle Court, just off Fifth Boulevard. That should take less than a sixth by steamhack to your parents' house. It's on Perimeter Lane, isn't it?"

"It is." It didn't particularly surprise Dekkard that Ingrella knew, since Obreduur had doubtless investigated him thoroughly before hiring him.

"Will you be needing me?" asked Ysella.

"No. You'd both be free."

Dekkard looked to Ysella. "Would you like to meet the family . . . or whoever's there?"

"If it wouldn't be a problem."

"You're never a problem," Dekkard replied instantly.

Ysella laughed. "Wait until I tell Emrelda that."

Dekkard looked to Ingrella. "Do we have a moment so that I can send a messenger?"

"Axel's schedule this morning is flexible enough to deal with a few minutes."

Once the four were all down the staircase and in the hotel lobby, Dekkard immediately hurried to the message clerk at the hotel desk, where he filled out the message blank, gave the address, and paid the fee—a mark and a half, much higher than it would have been if he'd contacted a service directly, but that would have taken more time . . . and his knowledge of Oersynt messenger services was out-of-date.

Then he hurried back to where the Obreduurs and Ysella waited, just inside the hotel door. He looked to Ysella, then grinned. "You're committed."

Ysella smiled sweetly. "Of course I am. I do hope your sister will be there."

"I doubt that she'd miss the chance," replied Dekkard wryly.

At that moment, Jareld Herrardo arrived at the wheel of a Gresynt similar to the one Dekkard usually drove, except that the steamer was dark blue, not dark green. Dekkard led the way out of the hotel, opening the rear doors for the Obreduurs and Ysella. Dekkard had no idea where they'd be going, since the itinerary merely said, "Local visits."

Once everyone was inside, Obreduur asked, "Where are we headed first, Jareld?"

"I thought we'd stop by Carla's before she opens. She's always been a strong supporter."

"And after that?"

"We're stopping at Syntaar Field. There's a game between Oersynt and Aloor. Then we'll go to the Guildhall for the reception." Herrardo pulled away from the hotel and turned onto Copper Avenue heading west toward Central Square, then turned right on Second Street.

"There's someone following us," said Ysella. "Three steamers back."

"Is it a dark blue Realto?" asked Herrardo.

Dekkard turned and studied the steamers behind them. "It's dark blue and looks like a Realto, but I can't tell for sure."

"It's likely a Security steamer, then. Here in Oersynt they like dark blue, and one followed me to the Cosmopolitano. It's likely the same one."

"How many are in the Realto?" asked Obreduur.

"Just one," replied Ysella. "There's no one else near focused on us."

That suggested to Dekkard that Security was more interested in surveillance than something more sinister. *So far, at least.*

About a half mille later, Herrardo turned left on Ragona, before pulling up in front of a modest three-story brick building with the name "Carla's Place" in brass cursive letters, outlined in red, above the door. Moments later, the blue Realto drove by and kept going.

"He'll be back later," said Ysella.

"Later is fine," said Obreduur.

Although the tavern was located only three blocks west of Geddes Square, Dekkard didn't remember it, possibly because it was on the west side of the square, as well as more than three milles from where he'd grown up, and because no one in his family frequented taverns.

Dekkard was out of the Gresynt first, checking the sidewalk, but only a handful of passersby were near the tavern, and the Obreduurs and Ysella quickly joined him.

Obreduur led the way inside the tavern, where a stout red-haired woman immediately appeared and threw her arms around him. "Axel! I was afraid you wouldn't come by."

"I'm here, Carla. You had to know I'd be here. Besides, if I'd thought of not coming, Herrardo would have insisted. But he didn't have to."

Ingrella turned to the older graying man standing several steps back, who offered an amused smile. "How are you, Isaak?"

"Good enough that I don't need a legalist, Ritten."

"That's good for both of us."

Isaak laughed, briefly.

Dekkard glanced to Ysella, who just nodded, even as she concentrated.

Over the next third of a bell, Obreduur and Ingrella had a few words with each person in the tavern, including the dishwashers. Then, after a few last words with Carla and Isaak, Obreduur nodded to Dekkard and Ysella, who led the way out of the tavern and out into the faint acrid haze that clung to the city, a haze that Dekkard couldn't say he'd missed in Machtarn.

Even before Ysella could say anything, Dekkard spotted the blue Realto parked near the end of the block and asked her, "Is there still just one Security agent in the Realto?"

"So far."

Once everyone was in the steamer, Herrardo waited for a break in the intermittent traffic, then kept the Gresynt on Ragona, heading west toward Syntaar Field. The blue Realto followed.

"We should get there about two thirds before the game starts," announced Herrardo. "That will give you time to talk to people. Arturo is already there with the banner."

"Arturo Degarcion?" asked Ingrella.

"The same. He volunteered."

Ingrella smiled. "He always volunteers."

"Provided we invite him to whatever function follows," replied Herrardo.

To Dekkard, the objective of webball seemed to be to use a staff topped with a leather mesh basket to bash players on the opposing team . . . and occasionally to fling the purposely unbalanced hard leather ball into one of the net goals. Nonetheless, there were definitely tens of thousands of Guldorans who cheered either university or city teams at the games played almost invariably on Findi mornings from early Springfirst to Fallend.

Syntaar Field consisted of a playing field and a stadium, such as it was, of two curved concrete and stone stands. Tiered benches seated about ten thousand on each side. The field proper was mostly covered in meshgrass, and the sharp edges of the tough grass blades resulted in slashes of unprotected skin for the unfortunate players who went down.

The parking area south of the field was more than two-thirds full, but the parking monitors waved Herrardo through to a space holding a small RESERVED sign with Obreduur's name on cardboard.

"The same arrangement as last year?" asked Obreduur as Herrardo eased the Gresynt to a stop before the sign.

"The new manager of the Mechs is fine with it, so long as we fold the banner when the game starts. If people want to talk longer, that's all right, so long as the banner's not up."

"Good."

Dekkard hurried out and opened both rear doors, then glanced toward the weathered stone and concrete of the west half of the stadium, which seemingly hadn't changed from when he'd first seen it as a boy, when friends had taken the family to a game. Dekkard hadn't cared for webball then, and his opinion hadn't changed over the years.

Herrardo hurried ahead of the other four to the booth by the gate, where he purchased five admission tickets—two marks each with seating on a first-come, first-seated basis.

Just inside the gate, against the concrete wall that formed the back of the stadium, a lanky middle-aged man in the brown shirt and trousers of a machinist stood beside a banner attached at each end to sturdy poles more than two yards long. The oblong banner was simple enough, dark green block letters on a white background:

MEET COUNCILOR AXEL OBREDUUR
CRAFT PARTY COUNCILOR FROM OERSYNT & MALEK

Several men stood waiting, talking with Arturo Degarcion, who said, "Everything's set, Councilor."

Obreduur immediately moved forward to the group of waiting men, turning to face them.

Dekkard and Ysella stood a step back on the councilor's left, while Ingrella stood beside him on the right.

A man in faded blue shirt and trousers and a worn brown leather belt and sandals immediately stepped up. Ysella gave the faintest nod, and Dekkard shifted his eyes to the beginning of a short line that was beginning to form.

"I always wanted to meet you, Councilor. My brother's a stevedore on the old river docks. When you were the guild coordinator, you got everyone back to work with a raise after that trouble with Malek Barges."

"I'm just glad I could help," replied Obreduur. "What about you? What do you do?"

"I'm with the Painters Guild, working right now for Central Homes . . ."

After a minute or so the painter moved on, and an older white-haired man stepped up. "Don't have much to say. Just wanted to meet you. Good to put a face with the name. Hope you can do more to keep those Commercer bastards in line."

"Most of them aren't bastards," replied Obreduur with a smile. "They're just badly misguided. They think marks are more important than people."

Dekkard understood the feeling, even as he wondered just how many marks were "enough." *But then, he has to get them to feel what he's about, and he doesn't have time to explain about how high-paid corporacion legalists can change a seemingly simple law.*

More and more people began to stream through the admission gate, and while only a small percentage stopped to see or talk to the councilor, the line to meet him was growing.

A boy stopped to one side and looked up at Dekkard and pointed to Obreduur. "Is he really important? Like the Imperador?"

Dekkard was at a momentary loss for words, but finally managed to say, "What he does and how he does it is important, just like the Imperador. He's one of the Sixty-Six who make the laws and rules."

"That means he's important."

"For what he does and how he does it, not just for being a councilor."

"Guerdyn . . . stop bothering the man," said a woman who looked to be younger than Dekkard, but who appeared to be the boy's mother.

"He's not a bother," replied Dekkard. "He asked a very good question."

"You work for the councilor?" asked the woman.

"We do. Is there anything we can do for you?"

She smiled. "You just did." She looked to the boy. "Tell the man 'thank you,' Guerdyn."

"Thank you, sir."

"You're more than welcome, Guerdyn."

As soon as the boy and his mother moved on, Dekkard shifted his attention to those in line.

"That was a good answer," murmured Ysella.

"Thank you," he returned quietly, wondering just how he'd managed it.

A minute or two later, a stocky man in in white barong with green trim strode by, talking to another man attired in a similar fashion, except the second man's barong was violet with silver trim. "Crafter politicians . . . never give a thought to who pays them."

Dekkard couldn't help thinking that Commercers seldom wanted to pay what the job was worth and felt that they were doing crafters a favor with whatever they paid. He kept smiling pleasantly.

Even more people were streaming past, and Dekkard had all he could do to study those who neared the councilor, and he couldn't help but wonder at how all the emotions rushing past were affecting Ysella, although it was likely easier because they weren't directed at her.

Then, after a time, a bell pealed, and the number of people entering the stadium began to drop off, and those who did enter hurried quickly, presumably to find seats.

Arturo reappeared from somewhere, and he and Herrardo began to roll up the banner, while Obreduur talked to those remaining. Almost a third of a bell passed, while the crowd in the seats behind them shouted—and occasionally groaned—at what happened on the field.

When no one remained to talk to Obreduur, Dekkard asked Ysella, "How are you doing?"

"A bit of a headache, but it will pass."

"Until we get to the reception," he murmured wryly.

Obreduur turned to Arturo. "Thank you for helping with the meeting."

"It was my pleasure, Councilor."

"And we'll see you at the reception?"

"Wouldn't miss it for the world, but I'd better take care of the banner now." With that Arturo hurried off, the poles over his shoulder.

Herrardo led the way back to the admission gate.

As they stepped out through the gate, a group of

boys in clothes that were not rags but that had definitely seen better days approached, then stopped. One of the smaller boys said politely, "Sirs and lady, would you be finished with your tickets?"

Herrardo grinned, then said, "You five," pointing out the five shortest of the group. "One at a time." Then he gave each a ticket and watched while that boy went through the gate. "That's all we have."

The remaining three boys retreated glumly.

"Imps," declared Herrardo, "but I used to do the same. I was always the smallest. Almost never got a ticket."

Within a few minutes, everyone was back in the steamer. Dekkard was just happy to sit down in the Gresynt, hot as it was from being in the sun, but once the steamer was moving, the breeze from the slightly opened windows made the inside at least bearable as Herrardo turned south toward the Oersynt Guildhall.

A sixth later, Herrardo eased the Gresynt into the "official business" section of the parking area behind the three-story yellow brick building that was the Oersynt Guildhall. "We'll go in the back way to the kitchen," he declared. "That way, you four can get something to drink before the reception starts."

"And Axel can thank all the volunteers in person," said Ingrella before turning to him and adding, "but not until you drink some lager or water and get a bite to eat."

"If we don't have to wait too long for the food," replied Obreduur.

Since the kitchen was at the rear of the main hall, the walk from the Gresynt was short, and Herrardo escorted the four to a small table set up in the corner of the kitchen. Almost immediately, one volunteer server brought four lagers to the table while two others brought plates for the Obreduurs, and for Dekkard and Ysella. Herrardo stood nearby, eating from a plate he held.

Dekkard looked at Ingrella.

"We need to eat now. We won't get a chance later. He'll talk to as many people as he can during the reception—that lasts a bell—and he'll visit every table and talk while they're eating."

"And you'll be visiting as many as you can in a different order?" asked Dekkard.

"Naturally. With both of us separate, it makes a stronger impression."

Dekkard hadn't thought of it that way, but it definitely made sense.

"The dinner's officially over at second bell," added Ingrella, "but it will be close to another bell before we're done. Axel doesn't like to give the impression of hurrying off."

That also made sense. Dekkard looked down at the plate, which held what looked like fowl milanesia, with golden rice and raisins, along with thin slices of toasted parmesan bread, and green beans with mushroom and shallots. He only waited until Ysella and Ingrella lifted their forks before immediately trying the rice, which tasted better than it looked. The milanesia had more cheese than it needed, and the fact that the cheese almost burned his mouth led to a quick gulp of lager. His next bite was smaller . . . and with less cheese. "How many people will be at the reception and dinner?"

"Usually, it's around three hundred, not counting the volunteers," Obreduur replied, "but there are more this year, especially from the Woodcrafters Guild, apparently."

"Might that just be because of a certain agreement?" asked Dekkard.

Obreduur offered an amused smile. "Who can tell? I doubt it hurt, though." He returned to eating, but only ate about half of what was on his plate before taking a last swallow of lager and standing, "I'm going to talk to some of the people here in the kitchen while you finish up."

Dekkard quickly finished his plate and stood, following behind Obreduur as he moved from person to person, exchanging warm comments or pleasantries.

". . . so glad that you're here to help with the function . . ."

". . . very much enjoyed the chicken milanesia . . . Was that your recipe?"

". . . unique touch to the golden rice . . ."

". . . still working at Guldoran Ironway . . ."

". . . glad you're here . . . give my best to Berthold . . ."

By the time Obreduur returned to the table, and took a last swallow of lager, the others had finished eating and were standing, waiting. He offered a smile and said, "We'll have a little time to talk to the volunteers in the hall before they open the doors."

As the councilor stepped away, Ingrella said quietly to Dekkard and Ysella, "You don't have to stay too close until people start entering."

Dekkard nodded, then moved after Obreduur as he left the kitchen.

The main hall was square, extending from one side of the building to the other, with dark wood paneling below the chair rail, and plaster walls above that had been painted a blue-tinted off-white. The numerous wide windows on the east and west sides were open, and the faintest hint of a breeze came from the east. All the tables were covered in white linen cloths, and set with ten places, four at each side and one at each end. There was no head table, and from what he could tell there were six rows, each row six tables deep, with three additional tables set closer to the kitchen and spaced between the two large double doors. Three sideboards were set up between the windows, with lager and wine at each and a server to dispense the beverages.

Obreduur headed for the nearest sideboard on the west side, and Dekkard followed, glancing at the nearest table as he passed, noting that each setting had place card with a name.

Ysella hurried up beside Dekkard. "This is well-organized."

"Isn't everything?" he replied quietly. "He was the guild coordinator here for years, and he likes to train people to think and be organized."

Ysella laughed softly, as she and Dekkard stopped well short of where Obreduur talked with a bearded man in a white jacket with blue piping and a military collar, the same jacket as worn by the other attendants.

". . . and the lager?"

". . . Riverfall . . . it's like Kuhrs . . . but with a little more bite . . . personally. I'd prefer it . . ."

Dekkard kept from smiling, although he knew Obreduur well knew the difference between the two lagers.

". . . guild are you with? I have to confess I don't recognize you."

The server smiled. "You wouldn't, Councilor. This is my first reception. I was laid off from the Guldoran Ironway textile mill. I just got a job with Centralan Machine last month."

". . . you ever run across a Hermann Mantero?"

The server frowned, then smiled. "He was a line foreman, wasn't he?"

"He was . . . he's now working as an assistant foreman in Machtarn . . ."

Dekkard wasn't surprised at all that Obreduur never mentioned or even hinted that he'd been instrumental in finding Rhosali's uncle a new position.

After a few more words, Obreduur moved on to the next sideboard.

Somehow, in the third of a bell before the doors opened and people began to flood in, Obreduur managed to spend a few minutes with each of the sideboard attendants, somehow touching a chord with each, and yet leaving without seeming rushed or rude.

Then, for the next three bells, he managed to do something similar with everyone else.

By the time the Obreduurs, Ysella, Dekkard, and Herrardo all left the Guildhall at just after third bell, Dekkard was tired . . . and all he'd been doing had been watching, but neither he nor Ysella had seen or sensed a single hostile sign, not totally surprising, given that the dinner had been a guild function and that Obreduur was clearly liked and respected.

But still . . . you never know . . . and sometimes when you think it's the safest . . . Dekkard shook his head.

Once everyone was in the Gresynt, Ingrella said, "Four fifty-seven Quadrangle Court, south on Quadrangle off Fifth Boulevard."

Herrardo turned and grinned. "I remember, Ritten."

"Legalists never assume anything," added Obreduur dryly.

"And aren't you glad I don't," she replied sweetly.

Obreduur winced, just slightly. "I am, indeed."

Dekkard managed not to grin. Then he took a deep breath and leaned back in his seat.

"I hope that's to recover," said Ysella, "and not in anticipation of seeing your family."

"Actually," said Dekkard, totally honestly, "I hadn't even thought about that until you mentioned it. I don't see how you can look so composed after being surrounded by so many people for so long."

"That's because I'm not surrounded by a host of strangers right now, and it's a relief."

"Good." Dekkard closed his eyes.

It only seemed like moments later when the Gresynt came to a stop. Dekkard couldn't help yawning.

"You did need that nap," observed Ysella.

Dekkard checked his watch. He'd slept a sixth and not even known it. Then he hurried to open the rear doors before looking up the short drive to the two-story brick dwelling that stood perhaps a yard higher than the street and looked to be perhaps two-thirds the size of the Obreduurs' house . . . and slightly more worn.

As he stood there, Ingrella eased out of the Gresynt and then walked to the front of the steamer, where she said to Herrardo, "You're headed back to your house for a while, aren't you?"

"Yes, Ritten."

"Could you drop Steffan and Avraal off at his parents' house on the way? It's eight-nine-one Perimeter Lane, I think."

"Easily," replied Herrardo. "That's only about five blocks out of the way. If they're coming back here, I could pick them up on the way back, too."

"That would be wonderful. Thank you so much."

Dekkard turned to Ingrella and said quietly, "Thank you."

She smiled. "You're welcome, but that makes it easier on everyone."

She'd no more than finished her words than two girls hurried down the drive toward the Gresynt.

"She's here!" called out the shorter one, although both were older than children and younger than women.

"Why don't you three go," said Ingrella. "We'll introduce you to everyone when you come back."

Since Ingrella's words weren't really a question, Dekkard and Ysella got back into the Gresynt, where he looked at her, questioningly.

"There's no one around showing anything but happiness or resignation," Ysella replied.

Dekkard had to be content with that.

"Now . . ." began Ysella, "how about telling me more about your family?"

"You know that they came from Cimaguile before I was born, and that I only have one sister." Dekkard grinned. "What else do you need to know?"

"Do you want me to have Herrardo stop and let me out?" Ysella smiled sweetly.

"Well . . . if you put it that way . . . My mother and Naralta are almost as tall as I am. My father's shorter, but broader—"

"Stop. I don't even know your parents' names."

"Raymon and Liliana, but my mother's always gone by Lila. Naralta's always been Naralta, except for when I called her 'Alta' because she was so much taller than I was at the time. I never did that again."

"I think I just might like her."

"The house is modest . . . about half the size of Ingrella's cousin's place, and what was once a study off the front hall is Mother's studio. She has a few portraits on display at WestArt so that people who don't know her can get an idea of how she paints. There's nothing in the house that reflects Argental, and neither of my parents like to talk about Argental. They will talk about their childhood, but only about a few family members. They were both single children, and their parents died not long before they decided to leave Cimaguile . . ." Dekkard continued to offer what he could.

"We're on Perimeter Lane," said Herrardo from the front a sixth later.

"It's another three blocks, on the left side," replied Dekkard. "Red brick, with white trim, just like most of the houses in the neighborhood." He watched Ysella as she looked at the modest dwellings that they passed, all neatly kept with small front yards of meshgrass, rather than the greener leafgrass that comprised the larger front lawns of the houses in East Quarter or in the Hillside area where Emrelda lived.

"The house just after the one with blue-gray trim," said Dekkard.

Herrardo made a U-turn in the lane empty of traffic at that moment and brought the steamer to a halt right in front of the house. "I'll be back here for you two at a third before second bell."

"We'll be ready," promised Ysella.

"Thank you so much, Jareld," said Dekkard as he opened the door and then held it for Ysella.

She had just stepped out of the Gresynt, and Dekkard had closed the rear door, when the front door opened and a tall sandy-haired woman in blue trousers and a white shirt stepped out onto the narrow covered front porch.

"That's Naralta," murmured Dekkard before calling out more loudly as he and Ysella walked toward the porch, "We're here, just about when I said we'd be."

"I'd be shocked if you weren't," returned Naralta, turning to Ysella and saying, "I'm Naralta, as if Steffan hasn't already told you."

"And I'm Avraal, as if he didn't put that in the message he sent."

"Please come in. Mother and Father are on the back porch, where it's cooler."

As they entered the small front hall, little more than three yards square, Dekkard glanced toward his mother's studio, but the door was closed, and he smiled.

"You know better than that, Steffan," said Naralta, amusedly. "She let me in only after I promised never to say anything or look long at an unfinished portrait."

The front parlor, opposite the studio, was neat and immaculate, the age-darkened oak furniture recently polished. Dekkard did note that the settee and matching armchairs had been reupholstered in deep green velvet, but they'd needed it long before he'd left the house.

Naralta led the way down the narrow center hallway, past the staircase to the upper level, and then past the small dining room on one side and the modest kitchen on the other side, out through the open door to the covered rear porch overlooking the extensive vegetable garden that filled the area behind the house, bordered by a waist-high brick wall that Dekkard remembered helping his father build. The dark green wicker chairs with matching upholstered cushions looked the same, except that the wicker had to have been repainted because the chairs appeared almost new.

Dekkard's mother immediately stood, a woman almost as tall as her daughter, her sandy hair shot with silver, while Dekkard's father, his thick short hair almost totally silver, stepped forward.

"I'd like all of you to meet my security partner, Avraal Ysella. She's saved my life a time or two."

"And he's saved mine at least twice," replied Ysella.

"You're an empath . . . aren't you?" asked Naralta.

Ysella nodded. "I am."

"Then . . . you know . . ."

"I do now. Steffan never told me you're an isolate."

"We've always thought that it was best they kept that to themselves," explained Liliana. "Socially. Not professionally."

Ysella smiled. "My family feels . . . much the same way."

Raymon nodded, then looked to Naralta.

"Oh . . . what would you like to drink, Avraal?" asked Dekkard's sister.

"If you have a white wine, I'd like that. If not, lager is fine."

"We have Silverhills white or Northcoast."

"I'd like to try the Northcoast. I've heard about it, but never tasted it."

"I prefer it to the Silverhills," admitted Naralta, looking next to her brother. "And you get chilled Riverfall . . . unless you've changed."

"Not in that regard."

In minutes, Naralta returned with beakers of lager for Dekkard and both parents, and wine for her and Ysella.

"What exactly do you two do on a trip like this?" asked Naralta.

Dekkard and Ysella looked at each other. He nodded to her.

"We're there to make sure that nothing happens to the councilor. He's effectively the one who's led the resurgence of the Craft Party, and that's created enemies."

"More than a few, I'd wager," said Raymon. "Has . . . anything happened . . . on this trip?"

"He was attacked the other night in Gaarlak. The attacker was an isolate with a pistol wearing the inn's livery," said Ysella. "Without Steffan's response and quick thinking, it could have been fatal."

"Without Avraal's early warning, I couldn't have acted fast enough," Dekkard added. "That's why there are two of us."

"Have there been other attacks?" asked Naralta.

"I wrote about the empath who attacked and killed a councilor," replied Dekkard.

Liliana shook her head. "You'd be much safer here in Oersynt."

"You know I'd be a very poor artisan. I'm much better at this. Also, since I got promoted to an assistant economic specialist, it's gotten more interesting. I've even had to deal with problems involving artisans . . ." Dekkard went on to explain about the fine-art tariff problem and about the Woodcrafters Guild's problems with Guldoran Ironway. ". . . you can see that all you taught me has been helpful . . . if not quite in the way you thought."

"That's good to hear," replied Raymon with an amused smile.

Naralta looked to Ysella. "How did you come to work for a councilor?"

"I wanted to use my abilities for more than a husband and children. My father was violently opposed to that. So . . . I left and went where I could get training . . ." Ysella gave a condensed version of what she'd told Dekkard. ". . . and after all that, I applied for the position with Councilor Obreduur. That was five years ago." She smiled. "Steffan's told me how artistic you all are, but was there a reason why you came to Oersynt?" She looked at Raymon.

"I only knew we had no future in Argental. Lila especially." Raymon shrugged.

"Steffan said that it was hard leaving Argental."

"That is in the past," said Liliana. "It's better left there."

"Why Oersynt, then," prompted Ysella.

Raymon shrugged again, then said, "We knew we had to live in a city large enough to support artisans. It also had to be a place where things were changing. Oersynt seemed best."

"Changing?" asked Ysella.

"Cities that haven't changed are set in their ways. People know which artisans they like. It's hard for new artisans to find work. When we came here thirty years ago, Oersynt was changing and growing with the steam-powered mills. The old artisans couldn't handle all the business. So no one minded too much if other artisans came."

"You thought that out when you were young?" Ysella smiled warmly. "I'm a bit older than you were when you came here, and I never would have realized that."

Raymon smiled sheepishly. "I didn't either. Lila did. She was right."

"She usually is," added Naralta. "She was the one who insisted that Steffan compete for a position at the Military Institute."

"Steffan has the spirit of an artist and the hands and mind of a warrior," said Liliana. "Art cannot be conquered. It must be lived."

"Speaking of living art," said Dekkard, turning to Naralta, "you wrote about possibly setting up a separate studio . . ."

Naralta laughed. "I decided against it. Right after Mother suggested that two possible clients would be happier with me. She was right, and they were happier. Then, last week, I returned the favor."

"How would you describe the difference in the way you two paint?" asked Ysella.

Mother and daughter exchanged glances. Then Liliana nodded to Naralta.

"In basic technique, there's not that much difference. I'd say it's almost a feeling. I'm a little brighter. She's . . . deeper. Maybe I'll be able to do that later . . ."

"You're closer than you think, dear," replied Liliana.

"Not yet."

After several minutes' more conversation about art, Dekkard said, "You wrote me about a demonstration by the New Meritorists. Has anything more like that happened?"

Liliana smiled. "You see? Ten minutes about art, and he wants to know about politics."

"I know," replied Dekkard, "I'm hopeless."

"No, you're not," replied his mother. "You're interested in what you do, and that's good." Her smile vanished. "There have been no more demonstrations, but there have been flyers and broadsheets. Security takes them down, but they reappear. Always about the need for a change in government, the need to make councilors personally responsible." She shook her head. "That is the first step toward worshipping people instead of the Almighty."

While that was the first time Dekkard had ever heard his mother say anything like that, he couldn't say he disagreed. "How do you think people feel about what they're doing?"

Liliana shrugged. "I think it's foolishness."

"Foolishness, indeed," added Raymon.

"Some of those younger don't feel that way," said Naralta. "They say that good jobs and decent wages are harder to get, and that the Commercers won't ever change, and the Crafters aren't strong enough to take power."

"We're gaining seats with every election," Dekkard said mildly.

"They'd say that nothing's changed, and it's getting harder for working people," countered Naralta.

"It's also getting harder for small businesses who are competing against large Commerce corporacions," added Dekkard, thinking of Markell and Halaard Engaard.

"I saw that earlier this year with one of the local plaster-supply places," said Raymon. "It was forced out of business. The Imperador doesn't seem to care, though."

"Neither do most of the Commercer councilors," replied Dekkard.

The various threads of conversation continued through light refreshments of assorted empanadas made by Naralta and shortbreads from Liliana until Dekkard checked his watch and realized how late it was. "We need to get ready to go. Herrardo will be here any moment."

"It seems like you just got here," said Naralta, almost plaintively.

"Will you be back in Oersynt any time soon?" asked Liliana.

"In about two weeks, for the Summerend Festival and some appearances," said Ysella. "We don't know the daily schedule yet."

"You'll let us know?" asked Raymon.

"I will," promised Dekkard, rising from the comfortable wicker chair.

Everyone else stood. Dekkard offered his mother a full warm hug, and then his sister, but only shook hands with his father, knowing hugs made the family patriarch uncomfortable.

Naralta leaned close to Ysella and murmured something that Dekkard didn't catch and wasn't supposed to, but since Ysella smiled, it couldn't be too bad. *You hope.* With sisters, Dekkard had observed, there were always surprises.

By the time they all made their way to the front porch, Herrardo was easing the Gresynt to a stop, and Dekkard and Ysella hurried down the walk to the steamer, where Dekkard opened the rear door, and they both settled into seats.

"Did you have a good time?" asked Herrardo.

"We did," answered Ysella cheerfully.

Dekkard suspected she'd thoroughly enjoyed herself. "It was good to see everyone. It's been a long time."

"It won't be that long before we pick up the Obreduurs. We'll be full-on crowded on the way back."

"One of us can sit up front," said Dekkard.

"That might be better."

"You," Dekkard suggested to Ysella.

She grinned. "I won't complain."

Several minutes passed before Ysella said quietly to Dekkard, "Your mother's very perceptive. That comment about you having the spirit of an artist but the hands and mind of a warrior . . . did she ever tell you that?"

"Only the first half. She said that I had the spirit of an artist, but not the skills to be good or happy at it."

"That's probably true, but I think what she said this evening was more accurate. You are an intelligent, sensitive, and perceptive man, but a warrior all the same. It's a good thing you've worked for Obreduur, though."

"Though?"

"I think he's taught us both the limits and the use of power. With the wrong councilor, you could have turned out more like Jaime Minz."

Dekkard shuddered at that thought. "What about you?"

"Like Frieda Livigne."

That was even more frightening to Dekkard. "You couldn't—"

"Trust me, Steffan. I was so angry when I started with Obreduur that I really could have. You can ask Emrelda."

"When you say I can ask your sister, it means I don't need to," he replied, pausing before adding, with a smile, "unless you make it a habit."

She just shook her head.

68

On Unadi, Dekkard and Ysella once more met for breakfast in the hotel restaurant. The two aides were dressed slightly more casually, with Dekkard in a green barong, and Ysella in the cream linen suit.

"What did you think about the family?" Dekkard asked, holding his mug of café and waiting on Ysella's reply . . . and his order of croissants with quince paste.

"I like them. Your mother's very perceptive, and so is your sister. They worry about you."

"I know . . . but you can see why I couldn't stay in Oersynt."

"I knew that before I met them. You're meant for what you're learning to do."

"You mean more than security, I take it?" Dekkard

paused as the waiter appeared with his croissants and maize flatbread with thin cheese slices for Ysella.

"You have little left to learn about security, except what time and experience can teach. You have a talent for seeing possibilities. You immediately recognized where the New Meritorists might strike again."

Dekkard had his doubts. "That was a fortunate guess. I have a great deal to learn."

"We all do, but it was more than a fortunate guess."

"Can you tell me what Naralta whispered to you?" Dekkard grinned, winningly, he hoped.

"That's between us . . . for now, anyway."

"When it's not . . . ?"

"I'll tell you."

Dekkard shook his head, then halved one of the croissants and placed a quince slice in the middle before taking a healthy bite. He also realized that he'd never had a chance to give his parents the newssheet from Gaarlak. *You should get another chance in the next month.*

The two ate quickly, then left the restaurant and returned to the Obreduurs' suite, from which they escorted the councilor down to the lobby. Obreduur wore a crisp off-white linen suit, most likely the same one he'd worn the previous day, except spot-cleaned and freshly pressed. When everyone was in the Gresynt, Herrardo turned east on Copper Avenue.

For a moment, Dekkard was confused, because he recalled that all of the Guldoran Ironway facilities were on the west side of Oersynt along the Rio Azulete, but then he remembered that the itinerary had listed the new switching yard and roundhouse. After little more than two blocks, Herrardo turned south on Fifth Boulevard, heading toward the Rio Mal. Then at the rounded edge of the bluff that sloped down to the river, where the boulevard had ended, there was a gate. At the top of each red brick gatepost was the emblem of Guldoran Ironway—the simplified image of a steam locomotive with the initials "GI" just below the locomotive's headlamp.

Herrardo slowed to a stop at the gatehouse, rolling down the window and saying, "Councilor Obreduur for a meeting."

"He's expected. Go to the bottom of the drive and turn left. Then go to the operations building. That's the building with the tower on the south side. Park in front of the building."

As Herrardo eased the Gresynt through the gate and down the drive, Dekkard took in what lay below, through a haze that looked thicker than what always lay over Oersynt.

The ironway yard paralleled the river, if well above flood level. Farther to the northeast were three long loading tracks all linked to switches connected to the two main parallel tracks that stretched northeast to Malek and southwest to the junction with the lines to Machtarn and Kathaar. West of the loading lines was the roundhouse, and between the loading lines and the main lines was the new operations building with two towers rising above the rest of the structure. One of the towers held a huge four-faced full-day clock, with all eighteen bells shown in thirds. Dekkard could make out the lamps placed to illuminate the clock face at night. The top level of the second tower was windowed on all sides, with signal semaphores above it and heliographs on the east and west ends.

While the bricks of all the buildings were barely smudged, and the windows shined and clean, Dekkard wondered how long that would last with the smoke from all the locomotives. By the time Herrardo had parked the Gresynt in front of the operations building three men stood waiting outside the doors, all of them wearing black suits and white shirts, if with various colored ties.

"The one in the center is Thorrsyn Torvald," said Obreduur. "He's the director of operations for the entire Guldoran Ironway system."

Dekkard quickly got out of the Gresynt and opened the rear door for Obreduur.

"Councilor, welcome to our new operations and switching yard," declared the handsome smiling man in the center. "We're so glad you could come."

"Thorrsyn . . . how could I not come?" replied Obreduur. "Especially when so many of my constituents will welcome the upgraded service these improvements will doubtless create."

"We wanted you to see it in person. The new roundhouse and switching yard, and the state-of-the-art operations center, have already improved operations on the Rio Mal lines and the lines to Port Reale without adversely impacting traffic on the major through lines between Machtarn and Kathaar. The night heliographs even allow us to use fewer signalers . . ."

"They're acetylene-powered, aren't they?" asked Obreduur.

"They are, but they're much more powerful than steamer headlamps." Torvald gestured.

"Arken Janes, here, is the East Oersynt operations manager, and Sandaar Treyaal is the freight manager."

"In turn," said Obreduur, "my aides, Avraal Ysella, who deals with agricultural logistics and employment issues, and Steffan Dekkard, who deals with ironway and tariff matters."

"Pleased to meet you both," replied Torvald. "Now . . . let's head up to the operations control center."

Dekkard glanced to Ysella, who offered the slightest of nods, as they brought up the rear, just behind Treyaal, the freight manager, who looked distinctly uncomfortable in his black suit.

The narrow staircase to the top of the operations tower was already warm and would be stifling by midday. Dekkard blotted his forehead surreptitiously just before he stepped out of the staircase and into the single large room that was the top floor of the tower.

In the center of the room was a model. As Dekkard eased forward, he could see that it was a miniature of all the rail lines in the area around Oersynt.

Then Arkan Janes cleared his throat and said, "This

model shows all the lines in fifty milles around Oersynt."
He nodded to the wiry older man beside the model, who
moved a miniature freight train along the tiny track from
Malek. "Korry gets regular heliograph reports and up-
dates the positions, sometimes minute by minute."

"Very impressive," said Obreduur, studying the
model, and then moving forward, where he glanced out
through the glass windows of the operations tower.

"We're certain that ironway freight users will be
pleased with the improvements."

"I imagine the service is already better, but it must
have cost a half million marks or more."

"The savings and increased earnings from higher
freight loadings will pay for it in less than five years,"
returned Torvald.

"That profitable?" returned Obreduur. "You do have
an eye for the bottom line."

"Without profits nothing can continue."

Obreduur smiled. "And, as I've told you before, without good workers, there are no profits."

"We agree on that, Councilor." Torvald paused. "Do
you have any questions?"

"How long does it take you to get a heliograph signal from fifty milles out to the operations center here?"

"If it's not raining, about a sixth of a bell."

"That's faster than Guldoran Heliograph."

"We're sending simpler messages with short codes for
frequently used complex terms."

"That makes sense."

After a silence, Ysella asked, "Don't you worry about
the river flooding the yard?"

"That's not a problem. The lowest point here is
fifteen yards above the average high-water mark. The
marshes on the other side of the river are much lower,
and there's only cropland south of Point of the Rivers
on the Rio Azulete."

*So the growers or landholders are the ones who get
flooded.* But Dekkard only nodded.

Following the tour of the operations tower came one

of the roundhouse, which happened to be not in use at that moment, and less than a sixth later, Obreduur, Dekkard, and Ysella were in the Gresynt headed back up the drive to the gate.

Dekkard couldn't help but wonder at the purpose of the invitation, unless people had been complaining about ironway service. "You didn't mention freight rates, sir."

"There wouldn't be much point, except to antagonize Torvald. He knows that I think their rates are too high, and what I think, so long as the Craft Party doesn't control the Council, doesn't matter." He paused. "Now . . . we're going to visit small shops in the millinery district. Steffan, you don't have to say much. Just smile and be charming to the women."

For the next three bells that was what Dekkard did, as Obreduur, Ysella, and Dekkard walked a good three milles through the side streets and lanes of the lower west side of Oersynt, the center of headscarf- and hat-making in Guldor. Dekkard understood exactly why the councilor was doing it—because working women voted at far higher rates than working men and they were concentrated in an area comparatively easy to cover by foot.

After a brief lunch at an establishment too modest to be termed even a bistro, the three undertook another three bells of walking and talking, and mostly smiling for Dekkard, after which Herrardo arrived and drove them back to the Cosmopolitano to rest and dress for the more formal reception and dinner for the prominent legalists of Oersynt, an appearance no doubt arranged by Ingrella.

A black Gresynt limousine conveyed the Obreduurs, Ysella, and Dekkard to the Oersynt Lawn Club, a drive of nearly two-thirds of a bell out Fifth Boulevard, then northwest on a divided tree-lined avenue into low hills festooned with mansions and grounds that made the Obreduurs' dwelling in East Quarter look like a small cottage in comparison. Growing up, Dekkard had heard all the explanations of why it wasn't the Lawn Bowling Club, but still felt none of them made sense. What did make sense was that only well-off legalists could turn a simple game into the requirement for an expensive private club devoted to lawn bowling and lawn racquet courts . . . and three exclusive private restaurants—a men's bistro-tavern, a women's tearoom/bistro, and a larger formal restaurant—as well as a large private reception and dining area for special functions hosted by members.

The entrance drive went through two modest gray stone gates, one of which bore a bronze plaque with the words LAWN CLUB, then wound around a small lake with a stone-columned circular building in the middle. Beyond the lake was a tall boxwood hedge, through an opening of which the drive passed, revealing a score of lawn racquet courts on one side and at least that many lawn bowling courts on the other side. On the top of a low rise whose slope was covered with a well-tended lawn not quite overwhelmed by various gardens tastefully punctuated with winding stone paths was a sprawling stone structure that covered several hectares.

The limousine carried them to the third entrance. "The function entrance, sirs and ladies," said the blue-liveried driver.

"Thank you," replied Obreduur, as Dekkard opened the rear door for him. The councilor wore a white dinner jacket with black trousers and shimmering white shirt and black cravat. Ingrella wore a deep purple, nearly formfitting long gown, with an almost transparent light purple half jacket, while Ysella wore the same blue dress and ensemble she'd worn to the justicer's reception in Gaarlak, and Dekkard a gray suit with a black cravat.

Dekkard and Ysella followed the Obreduurs along the fountain-lined stone walk that led to the entrance where a massive bronze door was opened by an attendant in livery of rich brown with yellow-gold piping.

Once inside, Dekkard immediately heard music,

strings and clavichord, being played as background and coming from the large chamber beyond an archway directly ahead.

An older white-haired man appeared, smiling as he approached the Obreduurs. "Ingrella . . . Councilor, it's so good to see you both."

"It's good to see you, Jakob," Ingrella replied, half turning and adding, "Avraal Ysella, of the Sudaen Ysellas, and Steffan Dekkard, both aides to the councilor." She gestured slightly to the older man. "Jakob Dehahn, High Justicer Emeritus, and still an excellent legalist."

"I'm pleased to meet you both," replied Dehahn in a sprightly but slightly raspy voice, "and you're far too kind, Ingrella."

"I'm only giving you your due, Jakob."

"If she gives you your due," said Obreduur wryly, "we both know you deserve it."

"Come on in . . . we have quite an assortment of fine lagers . . . Riverfall, Kuhrs, and even Karonin . . . and the same for the wines . . ."

As the five entered the large chamber, set up with sideboards and servers and small tall tables without chairs on one side and a score or so of as-yet-unused tables for dining on the other side, Dekkard studied those already there. With men in white dinner jackets and women in near-formal gowns of every color and shade but similar to the one Ingrella wore, Dekkard, in his gray summer suit, felt very much the security aide, unlike Ysella in her fashionable blue.

As Ingrella and Dehahn chatted and walked toward the nearest wine sideboard, Obreduur turned and said quietly, "You don't have to stay too close, but I'd feel better if you weren't too far away."

Dekkard raised his eyebrows as if to question.

"A white dinner jacket doesn't guarantee anything but marks. Some of those here didn't get where they are by obeying all the laws." Obreduur smiled and returned his attention to Ingrella and Dehahn.

Dekkard moved closed to Ysella and murmured, "You'll have to tell me who to watch."

"Just look out for anyone who's more interested in people other than those immediately around them . . . or someone with a pipe or something like it. Sometimes, they're altered so they can be used as short-range blowpipes with tiny frog-poison darts."

"Ivann said he thought that Freust was killed that way."

"It's actually more likely at something like this where everyone is above suspicion."

"Theoretically above suspicion, you mean?"

"It's not theoretical. You'd have to catch anyone here with a bloody knife or a smoking pistol in their hands before anyone would admit to believing they'd do something so crass as murdering someone in person. Let's circle around, but keep an eye on Obreduur. If anyone is likely to try something, it won't be until this part of the room is more crowded. We might as well get something to drink. You can always spill it strategically."

Dekkard fingered his truncheon, more effective in a crowd, then walked to a sideboard, where he ordered Karonin, simply because he'd never had it and had often heard of it.

He took the fluted beaker and eased back toward the sideboard where Ysella was getting a glass of a dark red wine. He continued to survey the gathering, noting that while those present ranged from what he thought were the mid-thirties to white-haired, he and Ysella were by far the youngest present—except for several young women presumably married to much older men.

Just as he reached Ysella and lifted his beaker with a smile, a middle-aged man and his wife moved to join them.

"You two must be Councilor Obreduur's aides."

Brilliant conclusion. I'm the only one in gray, and Ysella is with me. "How could you tell?" asked Dekkard pleasantly, careful to keep the sarcasm out of his voice.

"Because you're both younger than most here, and you keep studying the room. By the way, I'm Maxim Defaarest, and this is my wife Maerthe."

"Steffan Dekkard and Avraal Ysella," Dekkard replied.

"And you're in security . . . or some form of it?" asked Ysella in a cheerfully guileless voice.

"Of course. It takes one to recognize one. I handle the legal branch of Oersynt Security."

"Some of the staff in livery are yours?" asked Dekkard.

"Now . . . this is purely a social occasion for us," replied Defaarest.

"Of course," replied Ysella. "I shouldn't have thought of it any other way." She glanced at his wineglass. "I see you're having Laanar red. It's quite full-bodied. Personally, I like a red with body, but one not so overpowering, and with a hint of cherry, perhaps Gilthills dark."

Defaarest inclined his head and smiled warmly. "We won't keep you. Enjoy the reception and dinner."

"A pleasure to meet you, Maerthe . . . Maxim," Dekkard said warmly in return.

With the slightest of nods, Defaarest turned, and he and his wife edged away.

"I detest nouveau snobs," murmured Ysella, "and thank you for asking that question about staff. From his reaction, he has people in place here."

"That could be very good . . . or very bad."

"Assume the latter."

"I already had," replied Dekkard dryly, half turning and scanning the room again.

One of the younger men, a decade older than Dekkard, approached and said to Ysella, "I couldn't help overhearing your name, and I have to ask if you're related to Nathanyal Ysella."

"I am. How do you know him?"

"I don't. My father does . . . or did. He inherited a small parcel of land adjoining Ritter Ysella's lands, and sold it to him."

"Then you must be from the Yerkes family."

"Emile Yerkes. My father was Ephraim."

"I'm Avraal Ysella, Nathanyal's daughter."

"How is . . . I mean . . ."

"He's still alive and contrary as ever. My brother Cliven handles matters pertaining to the lands."

Yerkes nodded. "We don't have any holdings near there any longer. We never did have many. I assume you must be associated in some fashion with the councilor because I know almost everyone here . . . by either name or sight . . ." Yerkes paused. "But I could be mistaken."

"You're not," replied Ysella very warmly. "Steffan and I are two of his aides. You're a legalist, then?"

Yerkes laughed. "In a fashion. I'm a district justicer. I've always been impressed with the professional accomplishments of Ritten Obreduur, but I've never actually met her."

"Then let us introduce you," said Ysella.

In moments, the three neared Ingrella, who turned at their approach.

"Ritten," began Ysella, "District Justicer Yerkes is an admirer of yours, but he's never met you. We thought it was time to remedy that."

"It's quite an honor to meet you," said Yerkes, inclining his head deeply.

"You flatter me," said Ingrella, "and I'm not too proud to say that I appreciate your words."

Dekkard and Ysella eased away.

"He's a little awkward," she said quietly, "but very honest feeling, and his father was as well. Unlike that Defaarest toad, who fits so well with Security."

As Dekkard looked past the nearer sideboard, he saw a server collecting spent glasses and putting them on a tray held up by a portable stand. *Something . . .*

"That server with the tray, this direction from the sideboard," he said quietly.

"He's concentrating too hard on the glasses, as if he's trying not to feel anything, but he's worried."

"I need to get closer." Dekkard walked swiftly, but not hurriedly, toward the server. As he neared the man, he saw him slide a long paper straw from his tunic and turn toward the sideboard where Obreduur stood talking to another man whom Dekkard didn't recognize, not that he'd recognized anyone so far. Obreduur's back was to Dekkard and the server, who was bending over the tray, seemingly arranging the glasses.

Dekkard kept moving, but tried not to look in the direction of the server until the last moment when the man straightened and lifted the straw to his lips. By then Dekkard had his truncheon in hand and held low, and as the server looked toward Obreduur, just before he finished turning, Dekkard took two quick steps and thrust the truncheon just under the server's slightly raised arm with all the force he could.

The server convulsed in reaction to the impact on his nerves. Then his eyes went wide, and he grasped at his chest. His body began to convulse. Moments later, a tiny cascade of point-lights appeared in place of his face, then vanished, and he started to fall forward.

He's dead? That fast? Dekkard glanced around, but since no one was looking in his direction, he simply grasped the man one-handed and lowered him to the floor, then straightened, replaced the truncheon, and took two steps and several more, but still no one seemed to notice. So he just walked away and circled back to Ysella.

"What did you do?" she murmured. "He's dead."

"I put a truncheon in his side just as he was getting ready to blow something through a long paper straw. Should we say anything?"

She shook her head. "Unless someone says anything about you, leave it a mystery. Just don't look back. I projected a little distraction, and no one seems to have noticed."

"I wondered about that."

"We should find our table for dinner." She took his hand and moved toward the tables, as many others were doing, although Dekkard hadn't seen or heard any overt sign that dinner was being served.

Dekkard was amazed at her calmness. "Just like that?"

"He was an assassin. You dealt with him well enough that his handler will wonder whether it was an accident or whether we stopped him . . . and how. Even if he's working for Oersynt Security and Defaarest, no one will say anything." As they neared the table area, she murmured, "There's a little emotional kerfuffle around where that server went down. From one reaction, I get the feeling that he was another infiltrator who shouldn't have been here."

"Interesting." Dekkard kept looking for place cards, and finally found that he and Ysella were seated at a side table, but one next to the one where the Obreduurs were seated. He also noted that while couples were seated at the same table, they were not seated together, but without knowing social and economic status, Dekkard had no idea whether the seating had been done by precedence, or merely to facilitate conversation. At least, the Defaarests weren't at the table, and he would be able to see Ysella in case she sensed something out of the ordinary.

Dekkard found himself seated between one Malendya Haaland and Bernyce Pentico, both of whom kept asking him questions about how the Council "worked in practice" and what he did for the councilor. Both of whom seemed vaguely disappointed when he explained how a councilor's office actually functioned. He did not bring up the matter of the empath assassin, and neither did they. Ysella was alert for the entire dinner, Dekkard could see, but never gave him any indication that any action on his part was necessary.

The dinner itself consisted of four courses beginning with freshwater crayfish stuffed with chilies, followed by a mixed green salad, a main course of coriander and oregano brined pork loin slices with a cool cucumber cream sauce and corn and pepper suffused rice, and with caramelized flan for dessert.

Even so, pleasant and superficial as the conversation was, Dekkard was more than grateful when the dinner was over, and he and Ysella joined the Obreduurs to leave the event.

"We need to talk once we're alone and back to the hotel," Dekkard said quietly to Obreduur as they walked to the waiting black Gresynt limousine.

"I'll be interested to hear what you have to say," replied Obreduur.

Interested . . . or surprised . . . or even appalled.

Once the four were in the limousine headed back to the Hotel Cosmopolitano, Ysella turned to Dekkard and asked, "What did you think of the food?"

"In my humble opinion," replied Dekkard dryly, "slightly better than the councilors' dining room and not nearly so good as Don Miguel's . . . or anything that your sister has cooked."

"I'd agree," replied Ysella.

"So would I," added Ingrella, "but you're being charitable to the councilors' dining room."

"Ingrella isn't fond of the councilors' dining room," added Obreduur, "although she will admit that the duck cassoulet is better than decent."

None of the four said more than pleasantries until after they arrived at the Hotel Cosmopolitano and had walked up to the Obreduurs' suite, where Obreduur paused, then looked to Ingrella. "You'd best make sure Gustoff and Nellara are in their beds with the doors closed."

"Is this something I should hear?" asked Ingrella.

"Yes," replied Dekkard, knowing that Obreduur would tell his wife anyway.

"We'll just wait for you in the sitting room," said Obreduur, unlocking and opening the suite door, then gesturing for his wife to enter first.

Led by Obreduur, Dekkard and Ysella followed. Dekkard was last and closed the suite door quietly but firmly, then joined Ysella and Obreduur in the sitting room, lit dimly by a single wall lamp. Obreduur had taken one side of the settee, and Ysella a straight-backed chair. Dekkard took the other straight-backed chair.

Within minutes, Ingrella returned and sat down beside her husband. "They're sleeping . . . or feigning it, but their doors are closed."

"So what is it that we need to know?"

"I don't know if you noticed that a server collapsed during the reception," said Dekkard. "He was likely to have been found to have died of a heart attack. He was aiming at you and attempting to use a paper blowpipe. I interrupted him. His eyes went wide, and he died. Thanks to Avraal, no one seemed to notice until later. Also, Oersynt Security had men in the room."

"I have doubts that they were there as part of security arrangements," added Ysella, "but whether they were involved with the attempted assassination, there was no feasible way to tell."

"His eyes went wide, and he died?" Obreduur raised his eyebrows.

"I used a truncheon on certain nerves," replied Dekkard. "He must have inhaled. I'm assuming it was a frog-poison dart, but I didn't see any point in lingering, since no one noticed."

Obreduur's laugh was low and slightly bitter. "Someone will have noticed that he wasn't effective, and that you two were present. But I presume you left no marks on him?"

"If he'd lived, there might have been a slight bruise."

"With no overt marks, and a blowpipe lying around, and with quite a number of prominent individuals at the reception, the only result is that the next time, if there is a next time, they'll try something more direct."

"It's likely the same method someone used on Councilor Freust," Ysella pointed out.

"That's why there will be no mention of the blowpipe and only that a server suffered a heart attack at the dinner," said Ingrella. "The dead man will be a server even if he wasn't one."

"Is there anything else?" asked Obreduur.

"No, sir," replied Dekkard.

"Then we all need to get some sleep. There's nothing more we can do, and tomorrow will be a very long day."

Dekkard and Ysella immediately stood. Dekkard inclined his head, and in moments, he and Ysella were out in the hallway. Behind them, Dekkard could hear the click as Obreduur locked the door.

"What do you think?" Dekkard asked Ysella as he walked her to her door.

"He was definitely aiming at Obreduur. A private operative, hired indirectly by Security or by Commerce interests. Impossible to trace." She unlocked the door and stepped inside, but did not close it, instead turning to Dekkard. "Did I ever tell you that you're very, very good?"

He smiled. "Once, I believe."

"Good night, Steffan." She closed the door.

Dekkard turned and walked back to his own room.

69

After breakfast on Duadi, and absolutely no mention of the legalists' reception and dinner in *The Oersynt Press,* Ysella and Dekkard accompanied Obreduur on a long morning of visits, arranged by Herrardo, of modest shops owned and operated by crafters and artisans. After a brief midday meal, the afternoon was filled with more of the same. The dinner for Craft Party volunteers and supporters was a lower-key artisan and crafter version of the legalists' dinner, except without anything resembling excitement, for which Dekkard was exceedingly grateful.

Tridi morning, everyone rose early to catch the ironway, and Dekkard decided he didn't know when he'd
have a chance to personally present the edition of the
Gaarlak Times to his parents. So he dashed off a brief
note and sent it and the newssheet to his parents by
messenger. Then he managed the luggage and transition
back to the ironway station where they would catch
the Veerlyn Express, which only made two stops, first at
Malek, and then at Suvion. The express left precisely
at the first morning bell. Since the trip to Malek would
take just over two bells, the Obreduur entourage was
seated in the parlor carriage, which contained more than
a few Commerce types who clearly weren't headed for
Veerlyn, given that they were in suits and carried little
or no luggage. Most of them weren't that much older
than Dekkard.

As the express left the Oersynt station, one man rose
and walked to where Dekkard and Ysella were seated.
He was even taller than Dekkard, if more slender, wearing a light blue summer suit, and his golden-blond hair
was slicked back. He smiled warmly and said, "It appears you two are headed to Malek." But his eyes were
clearly on Ysella as he went on. "Your suit is the same
shade as mine, and so is your headscarf, what color
there is."

"That's all true," replied Ysella politely. "Why are you
going to Malek?"

"Business. Why else would one go in Summerend?
What about you?"

"Business."

"You don't look like the business type." The smile
widened. "For whom do you work? For yourself, perhaps?"

"Oh, no, we work for the Sixty-Six. We . . . look into
things." Ysella smiled sweetly, adjusting her jacket so
that the Council staff pin was clearly visible. "What sort
of business are you in?"

"Ah . . . industrial sales. Reciprocating pumps." His
smile faded. "I wish you well in Malek."

"I hope your sales calls are successful," replied Ysella politely.

"Thank you." The salesman eased away and returned to his seat.

Dekkard looked at Ysella. "You were exceedingly polite."

"There wasn't any reason not to be. It would only have called attention to us. He's feeling very embarrassed . . . and more than a little worried. I didn't even use a touch of emping."

"Good," said Dekkard, quietly, but firmly.

"You were good, too," she murmured. "You let me take care of it."

"I was very close to not . . . if he'd even reached out to touch you . . . I know you can take care of yourself in a situation like that . . . but . . ." He shook his head.

"Steffan . . . your restraint . . . and your feelings . . . mean . . . I can't tell you how much I appreciate both."

"The restraint was the hard part."

"Thank you." Her eyes dropped for an instant.

What Dekkard didn't mention was the fact that he was also angry that the salesman had acted as though Dekkard hadn't even been there. Had he thought Dekkard didn't matter? Or had he thought at all? Or had he been so entranced by Ysella's appearance that he'd seen nothing at all besides her? Dekkard smiled wryly . . . but he still would have liked to have taken the boor down a peg or two.

Except that could have led to trouble. Had it been another setup? He shook his head. *Not when Ysella had been able to sense the man. But what if an isolate did the same thing?*

"You're very quiet, Steffan," Ysella said quietly.

"I was just thinking."

"About what?"

He debated avoiding a direct answer, then decided against it. "I care for you, and because I do, I realized that, if I weren't careful, something like what just happened could be used against me . . . against you and Obreduur. And yet . . . not reacting . . ."

"It could be . . . but you're aware of that now. And you told me how you felt. I know what you could have done to him. He wouldn't have had a chance."

That would have been even worse. "Sometimes . . . feelings . . ."

She reached out and touched the back of his hand. Gently . . . and only for a moment. "I understand." She smiled. "After we get to the house at Malek, we'll have a few days off. We both need it."

When the express slowed and came to a stop at the ironway station in Malek, the salesman in blue was the first one waiting by the carriage door . . . and he was gone as soon as the door opened.

Dekkard worked at getting two steamhacks to carry everyone and all the baggage, then sat with most of the luggage in the second steamhack, which followed the first to Jasmine Street. There, both pulled up in front of a two-story yellow brick house with a weathered gray slate roof, a structure somewhat smaller than the dwelling in East Quarter, but with far smaller grounds, since the space between houses amounted to only about four yards.

Once all the luggage was out of the steamhacks and they departed, Obreduur announced to Dekkard and Ysella, "Findi will be a very busy day, but until then, we all have today and the next two days without any party or Council duties, but, in view of what has occurred, I'm afraid I will need you both whenever we leave the house. That won't be often, and I'll give you notice. Tonight is largely family, and you two are family. We will be going to Ingrella's cousin Tybor's house for refreshments and dinner . . . but that's a very short drive." Obreduur gestured to the house. "There are two rooms available. One is Axeli's former bedroom, and the other is a smaller room over the garage."

"I'll take the smaller one," Dekkard said immediately.

"That will also put Ysella closer to you and Ritten Obreduur. Her close presence is more valuable at night."

Obreduur nodded. "There's a bathroom with a shower on the hall between the two rooms. You two will share that, and, starting tomorrow, we'll have a day maid who can take care of the house and laundry. Also, Tybor's wife stocked the kitchen. There's bread and some sliced meats in the cooler if you feel hungry."

"Thank you," replied both Dekkard and Ysella, not quite simultaneously. Sharing with one other person, rather than three others, was a definite improvement, and Dekkard's comparatively sparse wardrobe definitely needed laundering and cleaning. Having something to eat later didn't sound bad, either.

"Now I'll leave you and see what Ingrella has for me." With a smile Obreduur walked toward the front door.

While Gustoff and Nellara had already carried their luggage up to their rooms, Dekkard still had to deal with the remaining suitcases—and one trunk.

"I can help," said Ysella.

"I'd appreciate that, but you just take the smaller and lighter cases."

"I can do that."

Sometime while Dekkard was organizing and hauling luggage to various rooms, he noticed a dark blue, but somewhat older Gresynt parked in the narrow drive, and, when he later reached the front hall, Obreduur handed him a set of keys.

"Those are for the Gresynt out in front. We've leased it for the month."

"Is the garage empty?"

"It is. It might be a little dusty, but don't worry about that now."

All that meant was that, sooner or later, Dekkard would have to sweep it out, but he merely said, "Thank you," and pocketed the keys.

After he'd unpacked the best he could, Dekkard put on his dirtiest trousers and shirt and swept out the garage and gave it a rough cleaning. In the process, he found leaning in the corner of the garage a battered target, one that hadn't been used recently, with a small wooden box that held practice knives, knives that had been sharpened, and which showed no sign of rust. He wondered which of his predecessors had used it, since he doubted that Obreduur had. *But Axeli might have.* And the practice knives were of very good quality.

Next he checked over the rented Gresynt, a three-seater, before garaging it. Then, and only then, did he shower. Because the house was still warm, he saved the cleanest barong for the evening. Wearing a plain shirt, he found a shady corner of the rear covered porch and settled down in a wicker chair to read *The Scarlet Daughter.*

Before long, Ysella appeared, carrying a lapdesk, borrowed from somewhere in the house. After moving another wicker chair into the shade beside Dekkard, she said, "Would you mind if I sat here? I promised Emrelda I'd write. I'll be good quiet company."

"I'd like that."

"Good."

Neither said much for a good bell.

Then Ysella folded the letter into an envelope and slipped away, leaving the letter and lapdesk on her chair. She returned in less than a third with a single platter, which she handed to Dekkard. "One is for you, one for me. I'll be right back."

Dekkard looked at the two sandwiches, which looked to be ham and cheese on dark bread, each neatly cut into two triangles, and decided to wait for her, but it was only a moment or two before she returned with two beakers, one of which she handed to him.

"It's Riverfall, and it's cold."

"Thank you. You didn't have to . . ."

"You can return the favor . . . sometime." She set the lapdesk and letter on the tile floor of the porch, then seated herself.

He extended the platter to her, and she took the

nearest half sandwich. He let the platter rest on his legs and took a half sandwich himself. After a bite, he said, "This is good. I didn't realize that I was hungry."

"I thought you might be."

"You were right. You usually are." Dekkard paused. "The house doesn't look like it's been empty for months." He took several bites of the sandwich, then a swallow of lager.

"It hasn't been. Ingrella's great-aunt and her husband live here and take care of it except when the Obreduurs come. They stay with her daughter when the family's here. The house is Ingrella's. It was her mother's. She was also a legalist, one of the first notable woman legalists."

Somehow that didn't come as a surprise to Dekkard. He finished the first half of the sandwich and started on the second.

"How is the novel?" asked Ysella.

Dekkard had to swallow before answering. "It's light, somewhat enjoyable . . . and not necessarily true to the political situation at the time, I suspect."

"Suspect?"

"I haven't read much history about the early years of the Imperium."

"All I've seen you read has been Obreduur's scholarly journals."

"I won't be reading those any time soon." Dekkard looked down, realizing he'd finished off the sandwich, and took a healthy swallow of Riverfall.

"There's a whole shelf of history books in the study."

"I didn't see those." Dekkard hadn't actually looked, not that he'd even thought about it.

"Well, there was, when I came here three years ago, but nothing seems to have changed."

At that moment, Nellara marched out onto the porch and toward the north end away from Ysella and Dekkard. She stood there, her arms crossed, looking across the meshgrass to the low brick wall that marked the rear of the property.

Dekkard and Ysella watched silently.

Gustoff followed her out and said, "We could play triple-trey or twenty-square."

"We always do that," Nellara replied sulkily.

"Suit yourself," said her brother cheerfully. "You said there was nothing to do. I offered something."

"I meant nothing new to do. Something besides reading a new book that's old. That's what everyone else is doing."

Dekkard looked to Ysella and raised his eyebrows.

She offered an amused smile in return.

"So what would you like to do that's new?" asked Gustoff.

"I don't know. There's nothing new around here to do."

Dekkard grinned, then said, "Nellara . . . if I come up with something new that you've never done . . . will you stop complaining?"

Nellara froze. "Sir . . . I didn't see you."

Gustoff was trying not to grin . . . and failing.

"When I was cleaning the garage, I found something interesting, and I'd wager it's something neither of you has done. If you go to the Institute, though, Gustoff, you will at some time. You never will, Nellara."

Nellara said nothing.

"You were the one complaining that there was nothing new to do." Gustoff's voice verged on taunting.

"What do you have in mind?" murmured Ysella.

"Knife-throwing lessons," Dekkard murmured in return.

"Can I come too?"

"If you want. Certainly."

"All right," said Nellara reluctantly. "What is it?"

"Knife-throwing lessons," replied Dekkard, standing as he spoke.

"You really would?" asked Gustoff.

"You'll have to learn sooner or later, and it might just be a useful skill for you, Nellara."

Nellara frowned for a moment, then smiled abruptly. "I think I'd like that."

"Then meet me in the garage in a few minutes. I'll need to move the steamer out and set up the target."

From the porch Dekkard had to go up to his room for the keys and then to the garage. He moved the dark blue Gresynt and was setting up the heavy wood target when Ysella, Nellara, and Gustoff arrived. He finished with that and then took the wooden box and opened it, showing the knives racked within. "Gustoff . . . do you know if these belong to Axeli?"

"No, sir, I don't."

"If they do, I trust he won't mind our using them." Dekkard took out one of the knives, and set the box down. "Always handle a knife carefully, especially throwing knives. You can see that it has no hilt or guard and that it's double-edged, and that both blades are sharp near the tip. A throwing knife is a weapon. Technically, it's a short- to mid-range standoff weapon. It's designed to wound or kill someone before they get too close to you."

He balanced the knife on the edge of his index finger. "You need to find the balance point on a knife first, because that determines your grip . . ."

From there he went over the basics before showing each of them the basic overhand throwing grip and release. "You'll start with that, Nellara, but you'll need to learn a sidearm grip and release as well. Or maybe an underhand cast."

Nellara offered a puzzled expression.

"Not all women's clothes are free enough to let you throw overhand."

Ysella nodded at that.

From there, Dekkard helped each to determine the position of the knife in their hand and the placement of their index finger. Then he demonstrated, with the knife not quite in the center of the target. *A little sloppy, there.*

Then, one at a time, each took a turn. Not surprisingly, not a single knife stuck.

Almost a bell later, Dekkard said, "That's enough for today. You've all got the idea." That was true, since, by then, each of the three had had a few semi-successful throws.

Nellara and Gustoff left immediately, Gustoff saying, ". . . a lot harder than he makes it look . . ."

"It is very much harder than you make it look," added Ysella.

"I had to practice more than most in security training. I suspect I still do."

"You were irked that one of your throws wasn't perfect, weren't you?"

"I was. Anything less than perfect aim could be disaster." He took a deep breath. "I need to put everything away."

"Then I'll see you in a few minutes . . . but thank you. I'm going to like this . . . very much."

"I hope so. I wouldn't want you to detest it."

She smiled, then turned.

Dekkard sharpened and cleaned the knives, then boxed them and replaced the target in the corner before garaging the steamer.

Just as Dekkard left the garage, Ingrella appeared. "Steffan . . . ?"

"Yes, Ritten?" he replied, warily.

She smiled. "I'm not displeased. Axel is a little startled, but I think working on perfecting her knife-throwing skill will be excellent for Nellara. I only ask one thing—that when the novelty wears off, you require her to continue until she is at least competent with a throwing knife. If she complains, just tell her that her parents agree with you."

"I'll also tell her it's a skill that's as dangerous to the thrower until it's mastered. Not in practice, of course, but elsewhere."

"Like many skills," returned Ingrella. "And thank you." She turned and headed in the direction of the study.

After a moment, Dekkard walked back to the rear porch to recover *The Scarlet Daughter* and possibly to sit down for a few moments.

Ysella looked up from where she sat. "Thank you. I did enjoy that. You're going to continue, I hope?"

Dekkard grinned. "I don't have any choice. First, after everything that's happened, I can't afford to get the slightest bit rusty. And second . . ."

"And second?"

"Ingrella met me and told me to work with Nellara until she was competent, no matter what. It was a gentle command to require her to finish what she started."

"It also won't hurt for her to be able to defend herself."

"That's going to take a while." *And it may not be easy on either of us.* "How did she feel afterward?"

"A bit pleased, a bit disappointed, and definitely a little frustrated. She needs someone besides her parents or instructors requiring accomplishment."

"And I'm the fortunate one."

"It was your idea," Ysella replied with a smile that was definitely mischievous. "We'd better get ready to leave for the family get-together."

Dekkard picked up *The Scarlet Daughter.* "I'll have to see if any of Ingrella's histories cover this period."

"I'd be surprised if at least one didn't."

Dekkard wasn't about to contest that. He smiled as he headed for his temporary quarters.

Just before fourth bell of the afternoon, after asking Ingrella for directions to her cousin's house, he eased the older Gresynt out of the garage and turned it so that it was ready to leave.

Ysella immediately joined him, wearing her blue linen suit.

Dekkard looked down at his rich blue barong and then at her. "Why am I not surprised?" Then he grinned.

She shook her head.

The next to arrive and enter the blue Gresynt were Nellara and Gustoff.

"Sir," said Nellara as soon as she seated herself in one of the middle row of seats, "when can we practice with the knives again?"

"Tomorrow," replied Dekkard. "You'll need to work on them almost every day, even when we get back to Machtarn. A few weeks here won't be enough. It takes time and practice to be good . . . and to stay good."

"He practices almost every night," added Ysella.

As soon as Axel and Ingrella Obreduur were seated, Dekkard eased the steamer away from the summer house. Tybor's house was a short drive, about six blocks, but slightly uphill. The house itself was the same size and looked similar to the Obreduur dwelling on Jasmine Street, but was obviously newer, with darker slate shingles and a "crisper" feel, but the front lawn was still meshgrass. Dekkard parked in the drive, at Ingrella's urging, although he was blocking a green Realto right in front of the single garage door.

No sooner was the Gresynt parked and everyone out of it than a short and wiry graying man in a black barong and gray trousers appeared on the front porch. "Everyone's in back. Just come in and go to the rear veranda."

"That's Tybor," Ingrella said quietly. "Tybor and Auralya only have one child. That's Nancya. She's about Gustoff's age."

"Thank you," replied Dekkard as he and Ysella followed the Obreduurs to the steps to the porch and into the house.

70

The dinner at Tybor and Auralya's house on Tridi evening was indeed low-key, featuring empanadas and three different salads, lubricated with ample beakers of Riverfall and glasses of Northcoast wine.

About all Dekkard learned was that Tybor was a legalist specializing in property law, and that Auralya taught mathematics and basic science at the Malek School for Girls, from which Nancya would graduate at the end of the coming school year.

On Furdi morning, Dekkard slept later, as did everyone, and woke to the smell of baking. When he washed, shaved, and dressed, and made his way down to the breakfast room, both Obreduurs were there, but no one else.

"Any chair," said Ingrella. "Elgara will have eggs Malek ready in a few moments."

"Thank you." Dekkard poured a mug of café and sat across the table from the two.

"Did you sleep well?" asked Ingrella.

"Better than in a quite a while," Dekkard replied. "How about the two of you?"

"Much better," admitted Obreduur. "Since we're definitely not going anywhere today, what do you have in mind for the day?"

"I've been reading the novel I borrowed from your library in Machtarn—*The Scarlet Daughter*—and it's raised some questions in my mind about the early history of the Imperium. Avraal said you had a shelf of histories . . ."

The councilor smiled broadly but said nothing.

"I know just the one for you. I'll show you after breakfast . . . and here comes Elgara with the eggs." Ingrella paused until the cook entered the breakfast room, then said, "Elgara, this is Steffan. He's one of the councilor's aides."

"I'm pleased to meet you, Elgara."

"Pleased to meet you, sir." After setting the platter on the table, she turned to Ingrella and asked, "How long might it be before the dream children appear?"

"Very shortly," said Obreduur, "one way or another."

"Then I'll start the next batch." With that, the cook returned to the kitchen.

Dekkard waited for the Obreduurs to serve themselves,

then took two of the eggs Malek, which turned out to be a cooked egg enclosed by a thin sweet cinnamon pastry crust glazed with honey. Tasty as the two eggs were, he couldn't help but wonder how the cook had managed it without overcooking the egg or undercooking the crust. That wonder didn't stop him from enjoying them.

Just as he finished the last of his eggs, Ysella appeared, wearing what appeared to be old security-uniform trousers and a plain white shirt, as casual as Dekkard had ever seen her, except in a robe leaving the bathroom, but she made that simple outfit look stylish. In fact, he thought, she even looked stylish in a bathrobe.

"I'm sorry I'm a little late." She sat down beside Dekkard.

"The eggs are still warm," said Ingrella. "Please help yourself."

Ysella only took one, then looked at Dekkard. "Why don't you take the last one?"

"Are you sure?"

"I'm very sure."

Dekkard looked to the Obreduurs. Both shook their heads. So Dekkard enjoyed the last egg on the platter.

After breakfast, Ingrella and Dekkard went into the study, where she handed him a modest-looking leather-bound tome. "It's not the most comprehensive, and it's over fifty years old, but it's by far the best. It has all the important names as well as an excellent description of how the first Councils and the Imperador worked matters out. It also has fairly complete, if concise, biographies of the first few generations of Imperial families, those family members who were important for some reason or another."

"Thank you."

"And, Steffan, please be careful with it. There are very few copies of it available."

"I will, Ritten."

Pondering over why Ingrella would insist on his reading a particularly rare history and why there were so few copies available, Dekkard made his way to the rear porch and settled into the old wicker chair, where he opened the small tome to the frontispiece, which proclaimed:

EMPIRE OF GOLD:
The First Imperadors

The date at the bottom of the page was Fallfirst 1207. He turned to the first page of text and began. He read some twenty pages before pausing. He had to admit that the writer presented the summary of the unification of the five kingdoms far more succinctly and clearly than any previous texts he could recall. He was about to resume reading when Ysella appeared, again with the lapdesk. "More letters?"

"I really do owe one to Mother and Cliven. After I finish, do you think we could borrow the Gresynt and post it?"

"We can ask. I doubt it will be a problem."

"I see you found a history."

"Ingrella suggested it."

"Then it's one of the best." She looked at the tome. "I don't think I read that one."

"It's about the early Imperadors. But I'm still on Laureous the Great. I wanted to find out how much of the novel might be remotely real or at least realistic."

Ysella smiled. "Let me know what you find out." With that she settled into the other chair, adjusted the lapdesk and paper, and then took her fountain pen and began to write.

Dekkard returned his attention to the history.

He read for another two-thirds of a bell before he reached a section entitled "The Forgotten Son," which, as he read it, turned out to be about the illegitimate son of Laureous. As he suspected after the four short paragraphs that summarized the man's comparatively short and obscure life, which did, in fact, end in the same mysterious sailing "accident" as in the novel, the writer of the novel had done a great deal of embellishment on the facts, except for the ending.

Several pages later, he came across what he'd been looking for—"The Scarlet Daughter."

This time, however, as he read, he got the immediate feeling that the novelist had understated just how "scarlet" Delehya, the Imperador's youngest daughter, had been, since at the age of fifteen, she'd seduced the Admiral of the Fleet, then forged a warrant from the Treasury for ten thousand marks in order to set up a small banque in Enke, to which an assistant minister of finance, in response to her considerable charms, also diverted an unknown amount of funds. Just before those schemes were discovered, Delehya seduced and subsequently married the then Landor premier Iustaan Detruro, who had been recently widowed. Detruro immediately pushed through legislation to formalize the Banque of Enke as a regional banque. When this was revealed, Laureous, infirm as he had become, dissolved the Council and called for new elections. The new premier worked out a compromise between Laureous and the Council, using Delehya's behavior as a wedge, with the threat of revealing the full extent of her embezzlements and the threat of even further revelations about the Imperial family, to further limit the powers of the Imperador and lay out the Great Charter in close to its current form.

The next words caused Dekkard's mouth to drop open. He read them twice.

> . . . ironically enough, the Landor premier of the Sixty-Six who put an end to the "Scarlet Daughter Scandal," as it later became known, was Dominic Mikail Ysella, the grandson of the last ruler of Aloor before it was conquered by Laureous . . .

No wonder this history is rare . . . and also why Ingrella wanted you to read it. Dekkard looked to Ysella. "You need to read this."

"Now?"

"Now."

Ysella capped her fountain pen, then took the history tome from Dekkard.

He pointed. "Starting right here." He watched as she read and as her eyes widened.

Then she lowered the book so that it rested on the lapdesk. She looked straight at Dekkard. "I never knew this. Father said we had a long and distinguished lineage and that his father had said we were related to one of the old rulers before Laureous the Great. He also said that one of his forebears had been involved in a rather shady political issue that was best left unmentioned, but he wouldn't say more. I've never seen this."

"Ingrella was quietly insistent that I read this particular history, and she asked me to be careful with it because it was rare. It was published in 1207."

"Rare?" Ysella snorted. "That might be the only copy. I wouldn't be surprised if the Imperial family bought and destroyed all the copies they could find . . . extraordinarily quietly, of course, figuring that very few people besides scholars would read it. And anyone who made a big fuss about it . . . they just might have had trouble. Sixty years ago, that would have been easier."

"Ingrella must think you know . . ."

"Or she wanted you to let me know," returned Ysella. "She just used your interest to let us both know."

"You're definitely descended from royalty," he said with a smile, "but I think I knew that already . . . in a way."

"From almost anyone but you, that wouldn't be a compliment." She handed the history back to Dekkard.

"When you finish the letter I'll see about taking the Gresynt to a post drop."

"I'd appreciate that."

Dekkard looked blankly at the page before him, realizing that Ingrella's introduction of Ysella at the legalists' dinner in Oersynt hadn't been just a pleasantry.

He smiled ruefully, then decided to keep reading. *Who knows what else you might find out?*

71

As Obreduur predicted, life was very quiet for the remainder of Furdi and all of Quindi, with the only thing that was "interesting," according to Nellara, being her sessions practicing with throwing knives. While she had no innate skill at it, from what Dekkard saw, her determination and willingness to take instruction more than compensated for any lack of natural talent.

Dekkard did see that several envelopes arrived by messenger bearing the Council seal, presumably reports from Macri, and he also noted that Obreduur sent at least one reply.

By Quindi evening Dekkard had finished *Empire of Gold: The First Imperadors*. He asked Ingrella if there was a successor volume, since the title suggested there might be.

"Three's, no. The author died shortly after the book was published. Heart failure." Her last two words were sardonic.

Halfway surprising was that the family did not attend services on Quindi evening, and Dekkard did not ask why. He went back to finishing *The Scarlet Daughter*, just to see where else the novel and the history diverged.

Findi morning, everyone rose early, because the Obreduurs had a full day of visits and events, beginning with a breakfast meeting with the Pipefitters Guild, open free of charge to any pipefitter who belonged to the guild . . . and his spouse. Because Obreduur wanted to spend the time talking to people, he, Ingrella, Dekkard, and Ysella ate before they left the house. Obreduur showed Dekkard where another banner was stored, similar to the one used in Oersynt, except with poles that screwed together, and Dekkard packed it in the blue Gresynt. Then he drove the other three to the breakfast, where he and Ysella, in gray suits again, stayed close to the councilor.

After not quite two bells at the breakfast, Dekkard drove the other three to Malek Field, where Obreduur stood under the banner that Dekkard and Ysella assembled and set up. Until the webball game between Malek and Chuive began, Obreduur met and talked with anyone who stopped. As soon as the game began, Dekkard and Ysella took down the banner while Obreduur talked to the last spectators who wished to meet him.

From the webball game, Dekkard drove everyone to North Park, a tree-filled expanse of actual bladed grass with scores of picnic tables, where Obreduur made the rounds, sometimes being rebuffed, but seldom, possibly because Ysella was projecting a certain amount of friendliness, which was far more feasible in dealing with families than amid crowds and people moving swiftly, as they did at Malek Field.

After covering North Park, the four returned briefly to the house for lager, wine, and sandwiches. Less than a full bell later, they sallied forth to the Women's Clerical Guild Summerend Social, held in the assembly hall attached to the Trinitarian Riverside Chapel. Both the chapel and the assembly hall looked to have seen better days, but that was to be expected, Dekkard thought, given their proximity to the river mills, which included a massive flour mill, a furniture works that made oak and pine household furnishings, and several others.

Following the social, everyone returned to the house for dinner.

Unadi morning began in a similar fashion, except the breakfast meeting was with the leadership of the Malek Textile Millworkers Guild, and the next two bells were spent visiting crafters' shops in the southwest part of Malek, and the afternoon was devoted to seeing a number of acquaintances of both Ingrella and the councilor who were active, or had been, in various guild, civic, or business activities.

That pattern continued for the next two weeks, with variations on whom Obreduur or both Obreduurs met and under what circumstances, but by Furdi evening, the twenty-second of Summerend, Dekkard was definitely feeling overwhelmed by meeting people, and he very much enjoyed the break afforded by the knife-throwing lessons and practices every evening, especially since Nellara and Gustoff continued to improve and Ysella was now working on learning how to change her grip and release instantly, depending on the distance to the target, as well as throwing either overhand or sidearm.

On Furdi evening, after putting away the target, cleaning the knives, and garaging the Gresynt, Dekkard and Ysella retreated to the two chairs on what had become their corner of the porch and where various bugs, including mosquitoes, weren't quite so prevalent. Over the past weeks, Dekkard had also learned that such pests seemed to avoid Ysella, which was another advantage of being with her . . . not that there was anyone else with whom he preferred keeping company.

"Nellara is very determined, at least with throwing knives," he said.

"She feels it's a way to gain a power that's uniquely hers in a very powerful family, and she'll keep at it long after Gustoff. He just wants not to be disgraced at the Institute."

"If he keeps it up over the next year, he'll be better than most new midshipmen." Dekkard paused. "You're thinking of something else, aren't you?"

"I worry about what might happen in Oersynt. Especially at the Summerend Festival," she said quietly.

"I've thought about that," replied Dekkard. "Most cities in Guldor have some sort of large public event in the last week or two of Summerend. But the New Meritorists have been extremely careful in not harming anyone not in Security or government, and most of the public events are local, but they usually have councilors of the Sixty-Six or district councilors speaking, if briefly, or sometimes government ministers."

"You know what you're suggesting."

"I do. It's possible that there will be attacks on Security or government ministers or councilors at those events. The problem is that I can't figure out how that will further their ends, and they've been consistent in avoiding anything that would turn working people against them. Yet I have the feeling that something is about to happen."

Ysella nodded. "So all we can do is to be aware of the possibility?"

"And tell the Obreduurs," Dekkard added, thinking that it might also be a good idea to carry a spare throwing knife in a boot sheath, just in case.

Ysella nodded, then asked, "What did you think of *The Scarlet Daughter*? You never said."

"The book or the real Delehya?"

"Both."

"The author was far kinder to Laureous the Great and his family than they deserved, but then, if they hadn't gone to excesses, your ancestor wouldn't have been able to make the changes to the Great Charter that have enabled Guldor to survive." *So far.*

"Don't you think excesses often lead to change for the better?"

"They usually lead to change. It's not always for the better. In Teknold, it certainly wasn't, and it won't be here if either the Commercers or the New Meritorists have their way."

"Do you think Obreduur and the Craft Party can change things?"

"If they can win thirty seats in the next election, if they can get at least four Landor or Commercer councilors to support them, and if they can push through changes to undo the worst of what the Commercers have already done and make a few positive changes. That's four enormous 'if's. The odds are against us."

"I like the way you said that."

"Said what?"

"Us." She leaned over and kissed his cheek, then stood. "I don't know about you, but I'm tired, and tomorrow and Findi are going to be long."

Stunned by the kiss, brief as it was, Dekkard remained

seated for a moment before he stood. He didn't quite know what to say, but finally said, "We'll just have to find a way to manage. You're good at that."

"We're better together."

"I'm slow, but that's something I've learned." He smiled and followed her into the house.

72

Quindi morning meant a very early breakfast for the councilor, Ingrella, Ysella, and Dekkard, especially since Dekkard woke early, still thinking about the Oersynt festival. He decided to borrow a knife from the set in the garage to add to the spare he'd already brought and that would go in his boot sheath. The second spare would go in his suitcase. After getting the knife, he finishing dressing in one of his summer gray suits, since Obreduur's appearance at the festival opening was an official event.

Once dressed, he headed down to breakfast, which, early as it was, meant that Gustoff and Nellara weren't present. That allowed Dekkard and Ysella to voice their concerns about the next three days in Oersynt.

When they finished, Obreduur said, "If you hadn't brought it up, I would have. On Tridi I received a detailed letter from Carlos Baartol. The New Meritorists are planning something. Exactly what, he has been unable to determine. He also discovered something else disturbing."

Dekkard frowned.

"Apparently, Security has been visiting all the book printers in Machtarn, and elsewhere. Especially small printers. What do you make of that?"

Dekkard wasn't totally surprised, but he was disturbed that Security hadn't tried that earlier, because it likely meant his suggestion to Minz might have been the cause. "It sounds like they found a copy of the New Meritorist principles and are trying to track down who wrote it or who arranged for it to be printed . . . and possibly who has copies. They're trying to use the book as a way to track down suspected New Meritorists."

"That agrees with what Carlos, Ingrella, and I think. If the New Meritorists do create demonstrations or other actions during the last two weeks of summer, Security will likely start arresting and detaining anyone with a connection to the book."

At Ysella's concerned expression, Obreduur shook his head. "There's nothing to worry about there. My copy came through Carlos. The question is, however, what should we do?" His eyes came to rest on Dekkard.

"It might be an opportune time to make public all the material on Commercer misbehavior and illegal actions. You'd have to do it through the Council in open session. Even then, the newssheets might not print much of it."

"No . . . but we could, and once it was on the street, Security couldn't hush it up, not completely, especially where there's known factual evidence." Obreduur shrugged. "Then again . . . nothing may occur. Or Security may preclude any acts or demonstrations so effectively that most people won't even know they occurred."

"If . . . if the New Meritorists do something, sir," replied Dekkard, "I doubt that Security can keep it hidden."

"Your instincts have been unusually accurate, Steffan, and Carlos is seldom wrong. But we will see." Obreduur picked up his mug of café, as if making a toast, then drank, a gesture that there was nothing more to be said, and that it was time for everyone to finish eating.

Within a few minutes, Auralya arrived to spend the next three days with Nellara and Gustoff, along with Tybor, who would drive the four to the station.

With lightly packed cases, the four travelers arrived at the Malek ironway station at two thirds before the first bell. Less than a third passed before the Veerlyn-Oersynt Express pulled into the station. Once again, the four sat in the parlor car, but less than a handful of other travelers joined them, since few would be heading to Oersynt on commercial matters just before endday, particularly the one that began the Oersynt Summerend Festival.

Just after third bell, the four left the Oersynt station, once more driven by Herrardo to the Hotel Cosmopolitano, where they left their luggage. They continued to Central Square, or rather to a parking area more than two blocks from the square, since the streets leading to the square were blocked off and filled with booths selling almost anything, whether lager or lemon-orangeade, hand foods of all sorts, as evidenced from the odors of various grilled meats, and, of course, gold and black paper streamers and crowns.

The five left the Gresynt and walked along the Avenue of Victory toward the square where Obreduur would speak, along with the head of the district council, as part of the official opening of the three-day festival. Dekkard had forgotten, or perhaps had not wanted to remember, what the square was like during the festival, with temporary booths scattered everywhere, especially on the side streets, because booths weren't allowed on the square proper. While there were already scores of people in sight on just the avenue, Dekkard knew there would be far more by the time Obreduur spoke.

There were only a few tent booths ahead. That wasn't surprising. The Avenue of Victory wasn't a shopping street. That was clear enough as they walked past the closed bronze doors of the Banque of Oersynt, followed by the Brokerage Mercantile, and Fischer & Caltarro, all of which employed well-paid security specialists. Dekkard shook his head.

"What was that for?" asked Ysella.

"I was thinking that I could have been a commercial security specialist."

"Not for long, you couldn't."

Knowing she was correct, Dekkard laughed softly. "Besides, I wouldn't have met you."

"Is that good?" she asked, with a hint of teasing in her voice.

"Very good." Dekkard couldn't help but think of the unexpected kiss of the night before. At the same time, he worried. Security was one kind of partnership. Romance . . . or more . . . was another. And Council regulations forbid married security partners or physical attachments.

"The best-smoked meat in Oersynt!" called a man from a tent booth just ahead. "On fresh-baked flatbread and sweet loaves!"

Dekkard looked past the vendor to the building on the other side of the street, a structure without any name over the entrance. Somehow, it looked familiar, and he felt that he should know it. After a moment, he remembered. *Of course.* "Jareld . . . is that building there still the regional Security headquarters?"

"Yes, sir. Unless they've moved since last week," responded Herrardo cheerfully.

"Thank you." Dekkard turned to Ysella. "Can you sense if there are people inside?"

"Not behind all that brick."

"I didn't think so, but I wondered. There shouldn't be anyone there. Today's a holiday, and patrollers don't operate out of regional headquarters."

"And if anyone is there . . . that might suggest what?" she replied.

"I couldn't say, except I'd worry."

"Get your smoked meats before they're all gone," called the vendor as the five walked past him toward the square, less than a block away.

In the block just off Central Square, Dekkard saw two bistros. The one on the left bore the name Gordiano. On the right was Blackberry's, which had been there for as long as Dekkard could remember, and all the outdoor tables under the narrow brown-and-gold-striped awning already appeared to be taken. Dekkard thought that he smelled fresh-baked blueberry pie, one of the bistro's signature desserts, but that might have been wistful thinking.

"We're to meet District Councilor Vandenburg on the far side of the square," said Herrardo. "Right in front of the Fairwind Hotel. That's the closest shaded place to the platform where the two of you will speak."

"The same as last year?" asked Obreduur.

"Just the same. I hope the band is better."

From the sounds that Dekkard could make out drifting from the square, the band sounded in tune, but the tempo seemed to drag. *Or maybe that's the way what they're playing is written.*

As they walked past the railing separating the tables of Blueberry's from passersby, Dekkard studied those seated there, but no one seemed much interested in the five, except one bearded man who said to the others at his table, "Stuffed suits . . . idiots in this heat . . . be blathering to announce some meaningless crap. Rather hear the band."

Dekkard had to admit it was already hot, and it was only midmorning, but after a bell or so, Obreduur was scheduled for a reception and cool refreshments with the district council in the Fairwind. After that, Herrardo would drive them to picnics and gatherings around Oersynt until dinner, when the Obreduurs would dine with the district commerce board members and their spouses . . . and Dekkard and Ysella would watch.

"Do you feel anything?" he asked Ysella.

"Nothing near, and there are too many people in the square."

When they reached the edge of Central Square, Herrardo turned to the right, following the arc of the pavement as Copper Avenue made its elongated oval around the half hectare of the central area, graced with the near-obligatory fountain and statue of Laureous the Great upon a charger that more resembled a draft horse.

Dekkard suspected that most of the people thronging

the square weren't there for the ceremony or the speakers, but for the prizes and vouchers for free or reduced-price food or goods that would be released from the bags suspended from poles around the square. Growing up, he'd only come to the opening ceremony once, because his parents had thought that he and Naralta should know what it was . . . *and possibly how hot and uncomfortable.*

The evening activities he'd enjoyed in the year or two before he left Oersynt had been far more pleasant and definitely cooler, especially in the last year when he'd gone with Aethena, even though he'd never heard from her once he entered the Institute, and his letters had gone unanswered.

As they neared the Fairwind Hotel, Dekkard saw an area under the awning cordoned off with green velvet ropes attached to brass stands. Only a few men stood there, presumably from the district council, one of whom was doubtless Arturo Vandenburg.

Herrardo looked back and said, "The roped-off area is where you can wait."

A stocky man in a dark blue suit with a brilliant blue cravat turned as Herrardo led the four into the reserved area and said, "Axel, welcome to the seasonal heat of the festival. You, as well, Ingrella."

Ingrella nodded her head politely.

"Arturo," said Obreduur in a hearty voice, "it's good to see you're in good health."

"I look better than I feel, Axel. Days like this, I'd almost rather be in Argental. It never gets this hot there."

"It never even gets warm," added the shorter man to his left.

"You didn't have security aides last year," said Vandenburg. "Is that because . . . someone . . . is going after councilors?"

"You don't have to worry, Arturo," replied Obreduur. "They're only going after those of us in the Sixty-Six."

"So far."

"Arturo, my aides, Steffan Dekkard and Avraal Ysella."

"Dekkard . . . any relation to the portraitist?"

"My mother and sister are both portraitists."

"Your mother's been gifted by the Three."

"She's worked hard to perfect that gift, Councilor."

Vandenburg laughed. "You even talk like her. Tall like her, too. Same color hair. Give her my best."

"I'll do that, Councilor," Dekkard replied pleasantly.

Vandenburg turned back to Obreduur. "You speak first. Then I declare the festival open. What are you going to say? The usual platitudes?"

Obreduur shook his head and said genially, "I thought I'd try some new ones. I don't intend to speak for very long. Most of those in the square are only waiting for the prizes."

The shorter man, also in a dark blue suit with a brilliant blue cravat, spoke. "There are quite a few more people in the square this year. The opening-day prizes must be better."

"Armando," replied Vandenburg, "they're not any different." He turned to Obreduur. "I don't believe you've met Armando Garcia. He's the Landor replacement district councilor for Jorge Sammons."

"I'm pleased to meet you," said Obreduur.

Dekkard eased away from the hotel and toward the square, where he could get a better look. The fountain and statue of Laureous were in the middle of the oval, opposite the main entry to the Fairwind Hotel, while the temporary wooden speaking platform was some five yards from the east end of the oval. Dekkard began to study the crowd, his eyes going from one person to another. There had to be well over a thousand people in the square, although it could have held twice that, and there were more men than women, but not noticeably so, but there was something about the crowd that bothered him, and he couldn't place it.

Finally, he turned to Ysella.

Before he could say a word, she said, "There are hints of something. People anticipating, but it doesn't feel like anticipating prizes and it doesn't feel like violence. That sort of anger or outrage isn't there . . . or not enough for me to sense."

"Could you sense if there are some feeling that way?"

"Not unless there were a lot or they're close to me."

"We'd better . . ." Dekkard nodded toward Obreduur, and the two eased closer to the councilor.

Obreduur half turned as they closed the distance, then took several steps away from the district councilors, followed by Ingrella.

"What is it?" asked Obreduur.

"There's a different feel about the crowd," said Ysella, "but it's not anger . . . more like anticipation . . . but not the kind for prizes."

"Do you think it could get violent?"

"It doesn't feel that way, but there are a lot of people out there."

"Are there children?"

That question Dekkard understood. "Not many in the center of the square, just a few, mostly older, but there wouldn't be. There are quite a few younger ones with their families on the outer sidewalks. We'll follow you to the speaking platform, but stay below in back."

"You'll let me know if it changes?"

"Yes, sir," said Ysella.

Obreduur nodded, then eased back to the district councilors.

"If there's *anything* . . ." said Ingrella quietly, but firmly.

Dekkard nodded.

Ingrella joined her husband and the handful of district councilors.

Almost another third of a bell passed before Vandenburg turned to Obreduur and said, "It's time to start making our way to the platform."

Herrardo moved closer to Ingrella, and Dekkard led the way through the sparser crowd milling around on the pavement of Copper Avenue, while Ysella followed directly behind. When the four reached the area behind the speaking platform, they joined four trumpeters in dark blue livery, who stood flanking the wooden steps up to the platform.

The group waited until several minutes before fourth bell, as shown by the hands on the clock tower north of the square. Then the trumpeters started up the rear wooden steps to the platform. When they got there, two posted themselves at one end, and two at the other. Next Vandenburg and Obreduur climbed up, and Dekkard and Ysella moved to the base of the stairs.

Four chimes from the clock tower rang out in succession. After a moment of silence, the trumpeters began a fanfare.

When the lengthy fanfare ended, Obreduur stepped forward. The square quieted to scattered murmurings, but the councilor waited for perhaps a minute before beginning.

"Welcome to the Summerend Festival of Oersynt. As the councilor of the Sixty-Six for Oersynt, I'm supposed to say something either witty or humorous . . . and if I can't do either . . . at least I should be brief. Since it's hot and since you're more interested in fun, food, drink, and prizes, I'll choose brevity. Welcome to the festival!" With that, Obreduur stepped back to a short but enthusiastic round of applause.

District Councilor Vandenburg stepped forward and declared in a surprisingly booming voice, "Following Councilor Obreduur's example of brevity, I hereby declare that the Summerend Festival of Oersynt has begun."

Within instants of Vandenburg's last word, the trumpeters played another loud and almost blaring fanfare. As they did, the attendants at the base of the poles pulled their cords, and hot air rushed up the tubes in the poles to the paper globes opened as well by the cord pulls, and papers and small prizes spewed across Central Square. While the crowd in the center of the square, or most of it, scrambled for prizes, paper vouchers and a scattering of one- and two-mark notes, Obreduur started down the wooden steps, followed by Vandenburg.

At the moment, a chant began, seemingly coming from everywhere around the square.

"PEOPLE, NOT PARTIES! PEOPLE, NOT PARTIES . . ."

Dekkard immediately glanced around. In the square, and along Copper Avenue, protestors unrolled banners and flourished signs, even as the chant continued.

Dekkard took quick inventory of the signs, his eyes going from one to another.

VOTE PEOPLE, NOT PARTY!
NO MORE FACELESS COUNCILS
PEOPLE! NOT PARTIES!
DOWN WITH FACELESSNESS!

There were others, too many to remember, but Dekkard saw that some were professionally printed and some hand-lettered, if almost elegantly. He immediately moved to Obreduur. "We need to get you out of here."

"PEOPLE, NOT PARTIES! PEOPLE, NOT PARTIES . . ."

"To the hotel! There are Security patrollers there," declared Vandenburg.

Dekkard had his doubts, but he looked to Ysella.

"There's no anger or hate in that direction. But there's anger growing in the middle of the square."

"WE WANT PEOPLE, NOT PARTIES! WE WANT PEOPLE, NOT PARTIES . . ."

As the two pushed through the crowd, Dekkard used his truncheon to move people out of the way, while Vandenburg and Ysella hurried to keep up.

By the time the four reached the shade of the hotel awning, the hotel doormen and two Security patrollers had cleared the area, except for the other district councilors, Ingrella, and Herrardo. The chanting continued, not necessarily louder, but certainly not weaker. Dekkard holstered the truncheon.

"Do you think we should go to the steamer?" asked Herrardo.

"No," declared Dekkard and Ysella almost simultaneously.

"Not now," added Ingrella.

Dekkard studied the center of the square again, which held far fewer people. Most of those remaining were either chanting or parading with signs, if not both, possibly because the prize-grabbing types had gathered up what loot they could and then fled.

WHUUUMMP!!!

The sound was so loud and intense that Dekkard froze for an instant. During that instant the pavement beneath his feet vibrated. He looked toward the Avenue of Victory, expecting to see smoke and dust. He did, and then there was another rumble, and even more dust.

"That was the regional Security headquarters," he said to a clearly startled Obreduur. "And I'd wager the same thing will be happening in cities across Guldor."

Ingrella nodded, even as she looked from the square toward the hotel.

Herrardo's mouth hung open.

"We should go inside." Ingrella gestured toward the hotel doors, just as a doorman stepped out under the awning.

"How could this happen?" demanded Vandenburg. "How?"

"They have to have been planning it for months, if not years," said Dekkard.

"To your left!" hissed Ysella.

Dekkard whirled, drawing a throwing knife as a man in a Security patroller uniform raised a pistol, clearly turning toward Obreduur and the district councilors. Dekkard threw the knife before the patroller could fire, and then moved toward the man while drawing the second knife. The first knife angled into the right side of the patroller's chest, enough to cause the man to fumble the revolver to the ground. Then several shots rang out, and the patroller dropped to the pavement.

Dekkard immediately turned back toward Obreduur and Ysella, only to see that she'd pushed the councilor down, and that one of the attendants in hotel livery had shot Vandenburg and was turning toward Ysella.

Dekkard's second knife went straight into the attendant's neck.

As the man dropped his pistol and reached futilely for the blade, Dekkard took three quick steps and yanked Ysella to her feet, then Obreduur. "Inside!" By then he had the truncheon out again, despite the brief flash of lights as his eyes passed over the attacker, but there was no one standing between them and the door, which Ingrella held open. The four dashed into the lobby past two clearly bewildered doormen and back into the side hall by the restaurant.

"Are you all right?" Dekkard asked Ysella, even while he kept his eyes on the door, while holstering his truncheon and then reaching down to get the spare knife from his boot sheath.

"I'm fine."

"You, sir?" Dekkard slipped the spare knife into the waist sheath.

"My knees will be sore for a while. That's all."

Dekkard's eyes turned to Ingrella. "You were right. We should have moved into the hotel immediately."

"She usually is," added Obreduur, looking at Dekkard. "I still can't believe that they attacked Arturo." He looked to Ysella. "How is he?"

"He's dead, sir. I'm sorry."

"You did what you could," said Ingrella. "Both of you."

Obreduur looked to Dekkard. "You suggested that the New Meritorists tried to keep violence against people down."

"They did. They're unhappy with Security and the Council. I'd wager that similar events happened in larger cities in Guldor today, and that the vast majority of deaths were either Security types, more likely agents than patrollers, and councilors and district councilors." As Dekkard spoke, he watched the front doors, where several Security patrollers had appeared.

"That certainly follows," said Ingrella.

Moments later, Herrardo hurried inside, looking one way and the other.

"Back here, Jareld," called Obreduur.

The political coordinator hurried toward them. "Are you all right, Councilor?"

"Outside of a few bruises."

"And you, Avraal? I thought that man was going to kill you."

"I'm fine."

Herrardo looked to Dekkard. "I don't know how you managed that."

"Good training and luck," replied Dekkard. *As well as fear and anger.* "What's going on out in the square?"

"The demonstrators have all run off. They left their signs and banners everywhere. The rest of the crowd scattered. There are Security steamers on Victory Avenue and in front of the hotel."

"Did you see any other weapons besides the two pistols?" asked Dekkard.

Herrardo frowned, then said, "I don't know. I wasn't thinking about weapons. I just saw that patroller aiming at the councilor, and your knife stopping him, and another patroller shooting the first one. Then, the doorman shot District Councilor Vandenburg, and you stopped him with another knife. After that, there were more shots, and everyone started screaming and yelling and running away. The patrollers asked me a few questions and told me to come inside here and wait. You're all supposed to wait also."

"Right now, where would we go?" asked Obreduur dryly. "Were any other district councilors hurt?"

"No one else seemed to be."

"It could be worse," mused Obreduur.

"It could be much worse elsewhere, Axel," said Ingrella. "We need to gather the children and get back to Machtarn as quickly as possible."

"Why don't you and Jareld take the steamer and drive to Malek, pick up the children and whatever all of us have left there, and drive back here. We'll find a way to get on an express tomorrow back to Machtarn. I know it's a three-bell drive each way, possibly longer, but the ironway would take more time, given the schedules."

"We can do that."

"Shouldn't we go with you to the steamer?" asked Dekkard.

"I'll go," said Ysella. "You stay here with the councilor. Security will want to talk to you, and they won't be pleased if you vanish." She turned to Obreduur. "Is that acceptable?"

"It's the best we can do under the circumstances," replied Obreduur. "Go out the side door."

In moments, Dekkard and Obreduur remained alone in the back of the hotel lobby.

"Did you think something like this would happen?" asked Obreduur.

"I thought the New Meritorists would do something. I also thought that they hadn't recruited enough supporters for something like this."

"What made you think that?"

"Little things. Like capping enrollment in the universities, requiring expulsions of students who demonstrated, the closure of the Guldoran Ironway textile mill, everything connected with the deaths of Halaard Engaard and Markell, an old man letting himself be empstunned and robbed because he didn't have any other pleasures left, the cover-up involved with the Kraffeist Affair, even the attitude of Guldoran Ironway about using yellow cedar, cheating on art tariffs to weaken the Machtarn Artisans Guild . . . probably a few others I can't recall."

"Some of those aren't that little, but I see your point," replied Obreduur, his voice both sardonic and wry.

"Also the fact that the New Meritorists behind everything were able to avoid getting caught, and only lower-level volunteers were captured . . . and that so many were willing to risk falling into Security's hands."

Obreduur nodded. "What would you do in my position?"

Dekkard looked squarely at Obreduur. "Unless I'm very much mistaken, and I could be, I'd do what you would do, and that's do everything possible to force new elections and discredit the Commercers in every way possible. Isn't that why Ingrella wants you back in Machtarn as soon as possible? Hasn't she been working with legalists to point out the decay and misuse of the legal structure by the Commercers so that the legalists, at the least, won't violently oppose the possibility of a Crafter government?"

"You haven't shared that with Avraal, I take it."

"Some, but not all. I didn't think about Ingrella and the legalists until recently. And for some of that I had no real evidence."

Obreduur shook his head ruefully. "You're incredibly good as a security aide, and yet . . . Why do you think I've been pushing you to do more?"

"Jens Seigryn said it was because you needed everyone to do more, including yourself. You also wanted me to see more . . . once you found out that we have similar views."

"That's true enough." Obreduur looked toward the door. "We'll have to talk more later."

Dekkard looked across the hotel lobby.

A Security patroller walked through one of the hotel doors and asked one of the doormen standing there something. The doorman gestured in the direction of Obreduur, and the patroller walked toward the two. As the patroller neared, Dekkard could see that he was older and wore the insignia of a lieutenant. He also carried something wrapped in cloth.

"Councilor Obreduur?"

"Yes?"

"I understand you were attacked by two different men. One posed as a Security patroller, and the other as a hotel doorman. Is that correct?"

"It is, Lieutenant. My aide here wounded the false patroller and then stopped the false doorman."

"That's what everyone who was there said. I just wanted to make certain neither of you were injured, especially after District Councilor Vandenburg's death."

"I'm fine, thanks to my aides."

"Did you know either of the attackers?"

"Lieutenant, I barely had a chance to look at either of them. I don't think I'd ever seen either before. They weren't friends or anyone I'd recognize immediately . . ."

For a good third of a bell, the lieutenant asked questions of both Dekkard and Obreduur, politely and patiently, including questions about where Herrardo and Ingrella had gone, although he didn't press too hard on their absence, especially when Obreduur pointed out that Ysella was protecting his wife. The lieutnant's tone suggested he had to ask questions to which he already knew the answers. Finally, he looked to Obreduur. "That's what I thought, but I had to make sure."

"Will you need anything else from either of us?" asked Obreduur.

"No, sir. You were clearly a target." Then the lieutenant turned to Dekkard. "As far as Security is concerned, you wounded someone attacking the councilor. He was one of those frigging New Meritorists, and that allowed us to shoot him before he shot any of the councilors. No one knows who the false doorman was, and we'll never know." He handed the cloth-wrapped object to Dekkard. "It's much simpler this way. Thank you."

Dekkard took the object. The cloth was wrapped around his knives. "Thank you, Lieutenant."

"My pleasure, sir. You kept things from being much worse." Then the officer turned back to Obreduur. "There's an unmarked patrol steamer outside the side door. The driver will take you both back to the Cosmopolitano." He inclined his head politely. "If you'll excuse me now, there's still a great deal to handle on the square . . . and on Victory Avenue."

"Thank you very much, Lieutenant," said Obreduur. "I very much appreciate what you and your patrollers have done."

"We do the best we can, sir. I appreciate your understanding."

As the lieutenant walked back to the front door, Dekkard couldn't help thinking about the slightest emphasis the officer had placed on the words "patrol steamer."

"Is it a trap, do you think?" asked Obreduur, almost casually.

"I don't think so, not the way he said it was a patrol steamer . . . and with the slight resignation in the way he mentioned Victory Avenue." Dekkard paused. "I could be wrong. You've spent more years reading people than I have."

"If you're wrong, then we both are. Let's get out of here before anyone changes their mind. That's definitely what the lieutenant wants."

Dekkard unwrapped the knives. They were spotlessly clean without a hint of dampness, although there was a slight odor of kerosene on the cloth. *Probably the only cleaner they could find quickly.* He swiftly replaced one knife in the waist sheath and the second in the boot sheath, then unholstered the truncheon and led the way to the side door.

Just as promised, a blue Realto steamer waited at the curb. No one else was close by.

Dekkard took a hard look at the young uniformed patroller behind the wheel, before opening the rear door, then closing it behind Obreduur and opening the front door to sit beside the driver, who swallowed. Dekkard wondered what the lieutenant had told the patroller, but it might also have been that he still held the truncheon.

"The Hotel Cosmopolitano, sirs?"

"That's right, Officer," said Dekkard politely. "No excessive speed is necessary."

"Yes, sir."

The young patroller drove swiftly but carefully, avoiding Victory Avenue, and in roughly a sixth of a bell, stopped in front of the Hotel Cosmopolitano. "Sirs . . ."

"Thank you very much," said Dekkard as he eased out of the steamer, still holding the truncheon and watching the patroller as he opened the rear door. Only after Obreduur was out did Dekkard close both doors.

Once the patrol steamer moved away from the hotel, Obreduur smiled at Dekkard. "You know you scared the shit out of him?"

"That was the general idea, but I was very polite." Dekkard holstered the truncheon.

"You were. Let's go to the restaurant and have a lager and something to eat."

As they walked to into the hotel, another thought crossed Dekkard's mind. He'd seen the flash of tiny lights when the doorman died, but nothing when the false patroller had. *Or were you so concerned that you ignored it? Or was it because you weren't the one who killed him?*

He wondered if he'd ever know.

The restaurant was almost empty, possibly because it was only a third past fifth bell and most midday customers hadn't arrived, and also because far fewer would frequent the hotel restaurant on the first day of Summerend Festival.

The two sat down at a corner table. After their lagers were delivered and their orders taken, Obreduur lifted his beaker. "To surviving the bastards."

"To surviving."

"What did you think about the lieutenant patroller?" asked Obreduur.

"He wanted us out of there, and he wanted us gone safely. I don't think he likes Security agents, but he knew more than he should. He knew where we were staying. Of course, he might have asked Jareld, but would he have done that in a quick questioning?"

"I usually stay there." Again, Obreduur's tone was casual.

"But he didn't even ask if you were staying there, as

usual. Also, a patroller shot the false patroller, and that happened almost instantly."

"You noticed that."

"After the fact. I was too busy dealing with the other one at the time. What do you think?"

"You first, Steffan."

Dekkard took a second swallow of Riverfall before answering. "I think the false doorman was a New Meritorist planted to kill District Councilor Vandenburg. He's a Commercer, isn't he?"

"No . . . he was a Landor, but in outlook he might as well have been a Commercer."

"Then he probably did something that injured someone very close to the doorman, and the Meritorists used an empath to instill cold determination in the false doorman to kill Vandenburg . . . and then any other councilor close by. Avraal didn't sense him because he stepped outside just after the demonstrators started chanting and Security headquarters exploded. That also showed that someone knew you'd have an empath. They also might have picked Vandenburg because the hatred wouldn't have been focused on you."

Obreduur took a small swallow from his beaker. "What else?"

"I think the false patroller was a freelance special operative planted to kill you, and someone in Security killed him because I only wounded him and they were afraid Avraal might get some revealing information from him. That's really a guess . . . because there's nothing to support it except the speed with which he was killed."

"The lieutenant didn't want to explain to his superiors about you, either," said Obreduur.

"If he's like some patrollers, he doesn't like the higher-ups in Security . . . or Security agents."

Obreduur nodded, but only looked toward the server who approached with their food, a lamb cassoulet for Dekkard and a chorizo sandwich for Obreduur, with a fresh fruit salad.

Once the server left, Obreduur said, "That's likely,

even if we can't prove it. I also think the lieutenant wants it all to go away, because he can't bring out what he suspects. If you hadn't stopped that patroller, he would have vanished, and my death would have been attributed to the false doorman and the New Meritorists." Obreduur smiled. "Needless to say, I'm very grateful to you and Avraal."

"What happens now?" asked Dekkard.

"Do you mean what do I intend to do now? As Ingrella said, we need to get back to Machtarn. So, as soon as we finish eating, we're going to the ironway station. If that doesn't work, we'll go to Guldoran Ironway headquarters, but that may not be necessary."

Dekkard had the feeling that, one way or another, they'd all be on an express headed to Machtarn on Findi. He also needed to send a message to his parents.

73

By first bell on Findi morning, Dekkard and Ysella— and the four Obreduurs—were all in private compartments on the Machtarn Express. Obreduur hadn't even had to leave the station on Quindi. Once the arrangements had been made, Dekkard had sent a message to his family telling them he was headed back to Machtarn because of what had happened at the opening of the Summerend Festival.

Ingrella, Herrardo, Gustoff, Nellara, and Ysella hadn't gotten back to Oersynt until the second bell of night on Quindi, but Ingrella and Ysella had also brought all the clothing that Dekkard and Ysella had left in the house in Malek. Dekkard was most grateful, since it was a significant fraction of his total wardrobe, unlike Ysella, who he suspected might scarcely have noticed the loss. Ysella had also brought the box of practice knives, pointing out that they weren't doing anyone any good being unused in Malek. The other fact of note was that none of the Security patrollers had questioned Herrardo about where Obreduur was staying in Oersynt.

As the express pulled out of the Oersynt station, Dekkard sat beside Ysella rereading the news story that had been in *The Oersynt Press*, a story that he'd barely had time to glance at, since the morning edition had just hit the streets when they had arrived at the station.

NEW MERITORISTS ATTACK GULDOR
Yesterday, the subversive group termed the New Meritorists staged demonstrations in more than twelve cities and a handful of towns. In Oersynt and other cities, explosions destroyed the regional Security headquarters. It is estimated that more than a hundred Security personnel and others died as a result. Those cities included Oersynt, Eshbruk, Endor, Neewyrk, Ondeliew, Siincleer, and Kathaar . . .

Not Machtarn? But since the story had other news from Machtarn, it was likely that there had been no demonstrations there. But had there been demonstrations in smaller cities like Gaarlak or Suvion?

. . . In six cities, District Councilors were attacked, three of whom died, including District Council head Arturo Vandenburg of Oersynt. Four Councilors of the Council of Sixty-Six were attacked, three fatally. Most noted of those killed was Ivaan Maendaan, of Endor, Chairman of the Council's Security Committee. The other two Councilors who died were Antony Devoule of Chuive and Demarais Haaltf of Eshbruk . . .

Dekkard could see why the New Meritorists had targeted Maendaan, but not the other two, since Devoule was an almost unheard-of Landor and Haaltf a Commercer placeholder. He looked to Ysella. "Do you have any thoughts on why the New Meritorists would have

targeted Devoule or Haaltf? They're not exactly well-
known."

"Maybe to make the point that councilors are
faceless?"

"That's true enough, but . . . that's awfully intellectual
for a supposedly popular uprising."

"You said that they were intelligent, and the councilor
called them brilliant idiots."

"Good point." Dekkard went back to reading.

. . . Premier Ulrich has called the Sixty-Six back into
session on Duadi, saying that was "the soonest feasible date for all Councilors to be able to return to
Machtarn."

. . . none of those who attacked councilors appear to
have survived . . .

*None? Because Security immediately shot them or
they died being interrogated or they suicided or were
killed by other New Meritorists so that they couldn't reveal anything? Or some of each?* Regardless . . . any of
those were chilling.

. . . Minister of Security Lukkyn Wyath declared that Security was already detaining and questioning all known
members of the shadowy organization . . .

Dekkard winced at that, wondering if his suggestion
to Minz had spurred that . . . or if Security had already
been tracking down existing suspects as well as those
who printed and received the New Meritorist book.

When he finished the article, he looked to Ysella.
"Would you like another look at this?"

She shook her head. "I read it when you were dealing with the baggage. Once was enough."

"What do you think?"

"You were right. There are more unhappy people
than Obreduur and I thought."

"I never said that."

Ysella smiled. "You didn't have to. The questions you asked and your physical reactions to what the councilor said or proposed indicated you thought they were a bigger problem than we did. He'll probably ask you for suggestions in dealing with them."

"Ingrella will have better suggestions than I do."

"Possibly, but the more good ideas he has, the more effective he can be."

"So long as Ulrich is the Premier and the Commercers control the ministries," said Dekkard, "matters will get worse."

"Why do you think so?"

"Because they think in terms of controlling people. That only works if most people accept things as they are . . . or if the government is willing and able to apply massive force against them . . . and the people know the government *will*. The numbers of demonstrators show that those who are dissatisfied aren't a tiny minority—"

"Do you think there are that many?"

Ysella looked up at Obreduur standing in the open compartment door.

The councilor stepped into the compartment and closed the door. He nodded to Dekkard. "Go ahead, Steffan."

Dekkard moistened his lips, then said, "The *Press* reported at least twelve cities had demonstrations. There were possibly five hundred demonstrators just in Oersynt. That's people who were willing to risk detention, interrogation, and possibly death. How many others are there that believe the same thing, but aren't quite that strong in their belief, and how many more will turn against the government after the Commercers crack down on the New Meritorists? Five times the number in the square? Ten times? Multiply that by twelve cities as well. Also, if the government cracks down hard, that will cut two ways. It will please those with wealth and power, but it's likely to create more support for the demonstrators from those who've lost jobs to the new mills and to new machines like the punch-card looms.

They're the ones who don't see government doing that much for them. Many will be shocked by the use of force because the government has minimized reports of how it used force before."

"That's true," agreed Obreduur. "Do you really think the New Meritorists will gain that much support? Even if they have a few hundred thousand followers, that's less than half the population of just Oersynt . . . let alone of Guldor."

"It's not just the numbers," Dekkard pointed out. "It's also who's among those numbers. We don't know how many regional Security headquarters buildings were destroyed, but I'd wager it's more than ten. Any organization that can destroy that many buildings across Guldor almost simultaneously without being detected is going to be a problem . . . and not a little one. They have people with technical expertise and enough knowledge of Security to have avoided being caught." Dekkard paused. "They've targeted agents and their supervisors and records, and not day-to-day street patrollers. These people aren't thugs or common criminals."

"They're highly skilled political terrorists, you're saying." Obreduur looked to Dekkard.

"I don't know what they are, but the Council and the Security Ministry are underestimating them."

"You've made that point before," said Obreduur. "What do you suggest we do?"

"Do whatever's necessary to discredit the Commercers and keep doing it."

"Keep doing it?" asked Ysella.

"As the councilor has pointed out before, even thirty Craft seats won't be enough to form a government . . . unless people are convinced that the Commercers have made such a mess of governing that a significant number of councilors don't want to be tied to the current government . . . or even to the Commerce Party. In my opinion, a quick push for new elections will just result in cosmetic change, with them still in charge. The only hope we have is to keep enough unfavorable information flowing so that if the Imperador calls for new elections it will seem like they're trying to keep it from coming out."

"In short, keep them busy trying to put out fires, and create the impression of unending incompetence and corruption?" asked Obreduur dryly.

"Impression?" asked Dekkard sardonically.

"Most people think they're competent," replied Obreduur. "Self-centered and greedy, but competent."

"How competent is a government that allows its regional Security headquarters to be blown up? Or refuses to collect proper tariffs to impoverish starving artisans? Or allows corporacions favorable tariffs for their foreign manufactories so that they can close those in Guldor and throw workers on the streets? Or looks the other way when the key personnel of small corporacions vanish or are killed when they underbid larger concerns? Or when corporacions use influence to plunder a Naval Coal Reserve and none of the senior officials are given more than a slap on the wrist?" Dekkard paused, then added, "That's just what I've seen in the last year. I'm sure there's more."

"The newssheets might not print any of that," Obreduur pointed out.

"The Security buildings have been destroyed. The ministry headquarters was gutted. It's fair to ask why. And if handbills start showing up asking why Security was pressuring the newssheets not to ask why they can't find the perpetrators, and why it's more important to keep it out of the news than to find who's behind it . . . ?"

"That's a dangerous approach," Obreduur said. "You'd need a number of councilors willing to speak up. Would you . . . if you were a councilor?"

"If we want to restore the Great Charter, I don't see any choice, because if the Commercers stay in power, they'll use the New Meritorists as an excuse to consolidate and increase their power over everything. This might be the only choice—"

Obreduur laughed. "You outlined the case for why

a councilor should speak up, but you didn't answer the question. If you were a councilor, knowing it might cost you your life . . ."

"I've already made that choice in a way."

For a moment, Obreduur frowned. Then he nodded. "I hadn't thought of it that way, but you have . . . and you've acted on that decision."

"So have you, sir."

Obreduur shook his head. "Not as openly as you and Avraal have." He paused. "You know . . . and I hate to say this . . . but in a way the New Meritorists have a point. Not enough councilors have been willing to stand up openly for what they believe in. That's something we'll have to change, without changing the Great Charter."

"That won't be easy," said Ysella. "Especially with Ulrich's control of Security."

"What about introducing legislation to split Security into two separate ministries?" suggested Dekkard. "A Ministry of Public Safety and a Ministry of National Information?"

"National Information?" Ysella raised her eyebrows.

"A polite way of saying that they gather information on everyone and police the newssheets," returned Dekkard. "Even debate over such a bill might be useful. You already have the votes necessary to force a floor debate, and the Great Charter doesn't specify ministries by name. And the newssheets might actually find it interesting."

"Security might shut them down," pointed out Ysella.

"More information for broadsheets," replied Dekkard.

"At times, Steffan," said Obreduur, "your proposed tactics seem more like those of the New Meritorists."

Dekkard shook his head. "You use the broadsheet to point out that Security won't allow the newssheets to print what the Council is debating. Then when someone gets detained, or a story gets pulled by Security, Ingrella and the legalists file a motion with the High Justiciary pointing out that Security is censoring public debate and that the Great Charter specifies that all matters debated by the Sixty-Six must be a matter of public record. Since Security is forbidding the release of that information, it's acting against the Great Charter, and the broadsheet publishers are acting in accord with the Charter."

"You have some intriguing ideas," replied Obreduur. "I'll consult my legalist. In the meantime, get some rest. I have the feeling we won't get much in the next few weeks." He opened the door and moved toward his own compartment.

"Did you mean to unsettle him?" asked Ysella. "What you proposed . . ." She shook her head.

"Are you hinting that I'm not that different from the New Meritorists? The only thing we share is the feeling that things aren't right. But the Craft Party won't be successful unless it reaches the people in the middle. That's people like Halaard Engaard . . . or poor Markell. The Commercers believe everything they do is in accord with the Holy Three. It's their divine mandate to control everything, and they can't be convinced otherwise. The workers and crafters already support the Craft Party. Those in the middle have to be shown what evil the Commercers have done and are doing. If you and the councilor have a better way of doing that . . ." Dekkard shrugged, a gesture of helplessness, frustration, and a bit of anger. "I know I'm just a security aide who's learned a bit, and that little bit makes me dangerous to myself and everyone else, but just getting four more Craft seats in the next election won't do it. If we don't make certain that everyone knows the current mess has been caused by the Commercers, the Craft Party could even lose seats, because, when the Commercers crack down on the New Meritorists, it will seem like they're doing something, even if it's putting more chains on everyone except the wealthiest Commercers." Dekkard stopped, offering an embarrassed smile.

"Obreduur knows that," replied Ysella, "but he could never afford to say it that bluntly, without losing as many people as he gained. Great conviction expressed passionately in support of a political view scares people . . . especially those people in the middle that you mention."

Dekkard opened his mouth, then thought better of it and considered Ysella's words for a time before finally replying. "That makes sense. I don't like it, though. How . . ."

"How much you say and how you say it depends on whom you're saying it to . . . and where you're saying it."

Dekkard shook his head. "It's a good thing I'm not a councilor."

"Do you want to be one?" Her tone was curious, not sardonic.

"I never thought about it. As an isolate . . ."

"As an isolate you can be a councilor. There have been a few. Just not in the last century. I'm the one who can't be."

"I understand the reason, but you're not like that."

"The Great Charter's based on the common good, not on the behavior of the best."

"If it is . . ."

"Why are the Commercers effectively ruling for their good and not everyone else's?" asked Ysella sardonically.

"That's a good way of putting it."

"Thank you." She paused. "If you don't mind, I'm going to try to sleep a little. Last night . . . I had trouble."

"I'll be quiet." That wouldn't be hard for Dekkard. He needed to think.

74

By the time Dekkard and Ysella were back in Machtarn at the Obreduur house, and they'd taken care of everything that was necessary so that they could go back to work at the Council Office Building on

Unadi, it was late, partly because the Machtarn Express had been delayed by rerouting near Gaarlak, due to track damage from excessive rain, rain that had never reached Oersynt or Malek. By then, neither wanted to do much more than to get some sleep.

Even so, Dekkard woke up early on Unadi and was the first down to breakfast, except for Hyelda, of course, who immediately asked, "Is it true what *Gestirn* said? Did someone try to kill the councilor?"

"Yes, someone did," lied Dekkard, since there had actually been three, but it was best that the other two attempts remain publicly unnoticed.

"What did the councilor do to deserve that?"

"I don't know for certain. Dead would-be assassins usually can't tell you why," said Dekkard dryly. "I'd guess that they were hired because he's been effective in strengthening the Craft Party. There's no possible way to prove that, though."

Hyelda shook her head. "Even the Three don't seem to know where this poor world's going."

Dekkard wasn't about to disagree. Instead, he picked up the morning edition of *Gestirn*. "Let's see what's in the newssheet."

"Not much." Hyelda snorted and stepped back into the kitchen.

Dekkard poured himself a mug of café and quickly scanned the newssheet. The story on the demonstrations included others he hadn't known, in Uldwyrk and Surpunta, and the destruction of regional Security headquarters in those three cities as well. The last paragraph added that a number of the buildings had been destroyed by dunnite explosions.

He replaced the newssheet on the side table and was still thinking when Ysella arrived.

"Any more news about the demonstrations?"

"More cities and three more regional Security headquarters damaged or destroyed, some confirmed to be from dunnite explosions. I'd wager they all were."

"Dunnite? They use that for naval shells, don't they?"

"Also for commercial blasting. It's fairly safe, essentially inert until detonated. They could have placed those charges a year ago, or longer. They probably did, in fact. That way, they could create the impression of a far larger movement than really exists."

"Planted the way that they did when they destroyed the water tunnel?"

"Most likely. Street repairs, sewer inspections or repair. Especially sewer repairs. No one really wants to inspect sewer repairs."

"Do you think there will be more explosions?" asked Ysella.

"There might be, but if there are, the dunnite's already in place. For now, Security will be watching for something like that, and the New Meritorists have to know it." Dekkard smiled as he saw the quince paste and immediately took two slices for his morning croissants. "Also, there aren't that many regional Security headquarters left, although most people wouldn't know." He frowned. "Even with controlled demolition techniques, at a guess, that amounts to probably five tonnes of dunnite. My question is where they got so much dunnite without Security knowing about it. Only mining corporacions . . ."

". . . or ironways with mines," added Ysella. "You need to mention that to Obreduur on the drive this morning."

"I will." *And if I don't, you'll remind me.*

"What else might they have planned?" she asked.

Dekkard shrugged as he took several bites of his croissant, then finally said, "Something vulnerable, and something that only hurts or kills people in Security or councilors. And not Security patrollers, just Security bureaucrats and agents. That's mostly the way they've been attacking."

"They have to have sources inside Security," added Ysella. "More than one or two."

"But they could be clerks."

"They most likely are. No one pays much attention to women." Ysella's tone was sardonically bitter.

The two only talked about the New Meritorists for a few minutes more, until Rhosali appeared. Then they finished eating. After that, Dekkard readied himself and the Gresynt.

Once Dekkard had the dark green steamer on Imperial Boulevard, he said, "Sir . . . there's something about those explosions. They were apparently all accomplished with dunnite, and it took quite a few tonnes. So how did the New Meritorists get their hands on so much? It's supposedly restricted to the Navy and Army . . . and licensed corporacions . . ."

"That's a very good question, Steffan. Why don't you write me up something about that today? It could be useful when the Council goes back in session tomorrow. Don't ask anyone outside the office for information, either."

"Yes, sir."

The first thing Dekkard noticed when he neared the Council Office Building was a far greater number of Council Guards, both around the entrance as well as at the entrance to the covered parking, where he had to stop and show his Council passcard, despite the Council staff pin he wore on his security grays. He was stopped again at the building entrance and had to produce the passcard once more. He also saw the guards inspecting cases and boxes.

The main hallway in the Council Office Building wasn't as crowded as it usually was in the morning, because the Council wouldn't be in session until Duadi and some councilors and staffers hadn't yet returned from their districts or vacations. But when Dekkard reached the office he found a stack of letters and petitions on his desk.

"Welcome back," said Karola cheerfully.

"Thank you. It's a bit earlier than anyone planned."

"Especially the councilor," returned Karola. "He asked for Ivann as soon as he walked through the door."

"That's not surprising. Has anything happened here?"

Karola shook her head. "You and Avraal were where things happened."

"We did have an interesting three weeks." He glanced to Ysella, who was sorting through a stack of letters and petitions. "And now we're back to correspondence and petitions."

"For the moment," murmured Ysella.

Dekkard settled behind his desk and eased the pile to one side. Writing about the dunnite issue for Obreduur was more important than the correspondence. He paused, recalling he also had to ask Macri about the hidden supplemental funding for Guldoran Ironway.

First things first.

After less than a bell he had a very rough draft, but he needed more on one aspect of the law. So he made his way to Macri's desk, since the senior legalist had finally finished meeting with Obreduur.

Macri looked up. "You need something for him, I take it."

Dekkard nodded. "Two things. The first is the legal restrictions, if any, on who can manufacture, store, and use dunnite. I know it's the basis for munitions, but not small arms, because cordite is used in bullets."

Macri frowned.

"At a rough estimate, it took several tonnes of dunnite to damage as many as fifteen regional Security headquarters buildings. Where did the New Meritorists get it? Could they just go to Northwest Industrial Chemical and buy five tonnes?"

Macri smiled. "You're likely right, but Svard knows more about that than I do."

"Thank you." Dekkard heard a groan from Roostof. Then he walked to Roostof's desk. "You heard the question?"

"I'd have to go to the regulations library and have someone dig out the requirements—"

"The councilor says we can't do that. Not right now. What can you tell me?"

"This is from memory . . ."

Dekkard nodded.

"Any single purchase of more than a decem of dunnite has to be recorded and turned in to Security within a week."

"Just ten pounds' worth?"

"Just ten. Any single purchase of ten decems has to be reported the next workday. Also, you have to have a license from Security to purchase or store more than five decems at a time. Failure to have a license the first time is a fine of ten thousand marks. A second violation means five to ten years' incarceration, in addition to a twenty-thousand-mark fine."

"Then they either got it through an industrial front corporacion or stole it."

"That would be my guess," returned the legalist. "I'd be willing to bet that they stole it from either Northwest Industrial Chemical or Suvion Industries. But it wouldn't have seemed to be a theft. They likely used a Navy supply lorry, or a lorry marked perfectly as one, with a legal-looking manifest. Maybe they even caused the breakdown of a real lorry and then made the pickup of a shipment destined for the naval munitions factory in Siincleer. That's how I'd do it."

Dekkard nodded. "I'd wager they did it over a year ago."

"So everyone would lose track of it."

"And because it took a lot of time and effort to transport that all over Guldor and get it placed."

"That wouldn't be as hard as it sounds. It just looks like some sort of yellowish powder, like the color of yellow brick."

"Turn it into false bricks, and you could carry it anywhere," mused Dekkard.

"If you didn't get it too hot."

"I imagine they were careful." Dekkard paused. "You're sure about the regulations."

"The basics, but there's a lot more paperwork involved, especially for the manufactory."

"What you gave me will do for now. Thank you."

Roostof paused. "You and Avraal had a few problems, didn't you?"

"Did the councilor send a report to Ivann?"

Roostof nodded. "That's all he said."

"There were two attempts on him, one in Gaarlak, and one in Oersynt at the Summerend Festival." Dekkard decided not to mention the server at the legalists' reception.

"Did they catch them?"

"In a way. They're both dead. One fell off a balcony trying to escape, and a patroller shot the other one after I wounded him."

Roostof smiled ironically. "That's not the whole story."

"That's what's in the Security reports," replied Dekkard blandly. "That's the way it is."

"Then that's the way it will be." Roostof shook his head. "Better you than me."

"Thank you for the information. I need to finish writing it up for the councilor."

Dekkard returned to Macri's desk.

The senior legalist looked up with a tired expression. "What's the second thing?"

"A hidden use of supplemental funding . . ." Dekkard went on to explain what he'd found out from his dinner conversation with the wife of Guldoran Ironway's district manager and the so-called special supplemental funding for the ironway. ". . . and Obreduur said I should let you know about it because, if it's so, then the Council is giving special treatment to Guldoran, and not to Eastern or Southwestern . . . and that might be very useful to know right now."

Macri frowned. "It might be hard to find out." He took a deep breath. "I'll see what I can do."

"Thank you." Dekkard walked back to his desk just as a Council messenger left the office, no doubt with a number of missives from Obreduur. Dekkard sat down and continued work on the dunnite paper, after which he returned it to Roostof for him to review before giving it to Margrit.

Once that was done, he went to work on the letters and petitions, beginning with one asking why Obreduur had been in Gaarlak when it wasn't even in his district. Dekkard decided to tell the truth, if gently—that Obreduur had two jobs, one as a councilor for his district and one as the political leader of the Craft party, which meant that, when the local Craft Party requested his presence, it was his duty to work that request in, if possible, and that he'd done so at a time that did not impinge on his duties as a councilor.

By the end of the workday, Dekkard was caught up with the letters and petitions and, unsurprisingly, he'd also caught only glimpses of a very busy Obreduur, who had sent out a storm of messages, and received almost as many, and met with three other councilors who had come to the office—Hasheem, Mardosh, and Wersh, the latter a former Lumber guildmeister from Jaykarh.

Once Dekkard picked up Obreduur and Ysella, and they were headed back to the house, Obreduur said, "That was just the right touch on that letter asking why I was in Gaarlak. I only changed a few words. Also, the dunnite report might prove useful."

"I checked on the law with Roostof. He said that was as specific as he could get without getting a search of the regulatory library."

"We'll just have to see what happens."

"Ivann's looking into the special ironway funding," Dekkard added.

"Good." After a moment, Obreduur added, "Both of you, get a good night's sleep. Tomorrow could be longer and busier."

Dekkard didn't have any doubts about that.

"Are you practicing tonight?" asked Ysella quietly.

"I think it would be good for both of us . . . and Nellara, as well."

"Especially Nellara," added Obreduur from the rear seat.

Ysella smiled.

75

In some ways, when he woke up on Duadi morning, Dekkard wondered if he'd even left Machtarn because so much had happened in Gaarlak and Oersynt that seemed so unreal, except the "unreal" events, especially the assassination attempts, had just been a continuation of what had been happening before he'd left. The other thought that crossed his mind was that he'd carried a gladius for two years and never used it, while the knives had been far more useful. It was almost as though the gladius was as much ceremonial as functional.

Dekkard shaved, washed, and dressed quickly, then headed downstairs, where he poured his café, then scanned *Gestirn,* in which there was a story about the Council returning for an early session to deal with the New Meritorist "problem." The past two days were the first times Dekkard could recall the newssheet identifying the group. There was also a story about a legal petition by the son of the owner of a small manufactory claiming that his expulsion from Imperial University was unjust because he had merely watched the demonstration and that others who watched had not been expelled and because the penalty had been imposed after the fact.

What wasn't in the story, Dekkard suspected, was that the other bystanders came from more prominent families. *Aren't you jumping to conclusions?* That was possible, but Dekkard would have wagered his premature conclusion was correct. The fact that there weren't any other stories about the New Meritorists suggested Security was once more leaning on the newssheets.

He'd just gotten his croissants and seated himself when Ysella appeared.

She looked to the newssheet on the table and then to Dekkard.

Dekkard told her.

"Then nothing's changed much." She poured her café and sat across from him. "Do you think that Ulrich can damp everything down and hold on to the government?"

"He'll try . . . and he'll succeed if enough people don't put the pieces together . . ." Dekkard paused. "But there is one other thing."

"What?"

"Security has lost most of its records. That's going to limit who they can round up." He cut the croissants and put a slice of quince in the middle of each.

"The Justiciary still has its records."

"Only on a case-by-case basis. Then there's the Imperador to consider. If the Commercers are shown publicly to be corrupt . . . and he doesn't call for new elections . . ."

"He becomes part of the corruption," concluded Ysella. "We should mention that to Obreduur on the way to work."

"He's likely thought of that." Dekkard took a bite of his quince-filled croissant.

"We shouldn't assume that. He's handling a lot right now."

"Who's handling a lot?" asked Rhosali as she entered the staff room.

"The councilor," replied Dekkard. "With all that happened with the New Meritorists."

"Can't say I blame them." Rhosali poured her café and sat beside Ysella. "Every time you turn around, some Commercer gets away with something they'd gaol me for. That Eastern Ironway scandal . . . someone steals twenty thousand marks from the government . . . and no one gets locked up . . ."

"That was just the bribe," said Dekkard dryly. "They got coal on the cheap and then overpriced it and sold it to the Navy."

"See what I mean?" replied Rhosali. "The minister resigned, and nothing happened. Nothing ever does to the folks at the top. You two risk your lives . . . and no one much cares, except the councilor, and he can't do much with the Commercers in power." She shook her head. "More folks than you think understand why those Meritorists are angry."

"Like your uncle?" asked Dekkard.

"That's right. He worked for the ironway for more than twenty years. They might as well left him on the street."

Hyelda appeared in the archway to the kitchen. "The councilor asked me to tell you that he wants to leave in a third, sooner if you can manage it."

"We'll manage it," replied Dekkard, then took another sizable bite of croissant.

A few minutes shy of a third later Dekkard eased the Gresynt away from the portico and down the drive. As soon as he headed west on Altarama, he said, "Sir . . . there's one thing . . . You may have considered it, but I thought I'd pass it on . . . and that's the possible impact of all this on the Imperador . . ." Dekkard summarized the earlier discussion, then waited.

"That's a good thought. Those of us in the party leadership discussed that before the recess. Do you think matters have changed that much?"

"No, sir," replied Dekkard, "except in one way. You couldn't get the word out as widely before now, and with Security more disorganized and people likely to be a bit more receptive . . . spreading the examples of that corruption might be easier."

"We'll consider that. Thank you both."

From Obreduur's tone, Dekkard couldn't tell anything except that he didn't want to talk.

None of the three said anything more on the way to the Council Office Building, somewhat more guarded than on Unadi. Once again, after dropping off Ysella and Obreduur and then parking the Gresynt, Dekkard had to show his passcard twice before he entered the building.

By the time Dekkard reached the office, Obreduur was behind closed doors, and a small stack of petitions and letters waited on Dekkard's desk. He sat down and began to read. One of the letters was even about the New Meritorists, demanding that Obreduur and the Council do something immediately. Not surprisingly, it was from one Khermit Franklyn, one of the two Commerce district councilors for the Oersynt district. The others were routine, among them one dealing with the diversion of revenues supposed to go to the Actors Guild of Oersynt and another with the inequality of transit fees for the locks on the Lakaan River.

As Dekkard began to draft his first response, a Council messenger appeared and delivered several missives to Karola, picking up several for dispatch. Dekkard had just about finished his last draft when Obreduur appeared in the inner office doorway.

"The Council session begins at noon, but I want to be on the floor early. We'll leave in a sixth. The session will last a bell, possibly two. You can take a leisurely break to eat, but then wait for me by the councilors' entrance."

"Yes, sir," replied the two.

Dekkard finished the last draft and handed it to Margrit with minutes to spare before Obreduur stepped out of the inner office.

Both Ysella and Dekkard were especially alert on the walk to the Council Hall. When Obreduur stepped through the guarded door into the councilors' lobby, Dekkard almost felt like heaving a sigh of relief. Instead, he looked at Ysella. "So far, so good."

"For another two bells. Let's go eat. I didn't eat much breakfast."

Dekkard refrained from commenting that she seldom did, instead turning and letting her set the pace toward the staff cafeteria.

There, Ysella actually selected empanadas and golden rice, and Dekkard followed her example. After they paid, Ysella motioned to a four-top. "We'll see if anyone interesting wants to join us."

Dekkard immediately took a bite of one of the empanadas, and then a sip of café. He looked up and saw Jaime Minz peer into the cafeteria, but he didn't enter. Several bites later, from the other direction, a pair approached, Laurenz Korriah with Shaundara Keppel. Keppel took a table for two, and Korriah set his tray there, but then walked over to Dekkard. "I read that there was some trouble in Oersynt. How's your boss?"

"He's fine," replied Dekkard. "The New Meritorists shot a district councilor and tried for Councilor Obreduur. We managed." Hoping Ysella wouldn't say too much more, he asked, "What about Councilor Navione?"

"Seibryg's too small for them to bother." Korriah paused. "Well . . . there were a handful of demonstrators, but his personal guards suggested they move on. They did."

"You mean *you* suggested they move on," said Dekkard with a smile, imagining just how intimidating the big isolate could be.

"Shaundara and I might have had a little to do with it. Nothing happened. That's what counts." Korriah smiled warmly. "Just wanted to see how you two were doing . . . and your councilor." With a nod, he turned and walked back to his partner.

"He actually sounded concerned," said Ysella. "But he knows more. He would, since Navione's on the Security Committee."

Dekkard had taken another mouthful, this time of rice, when Ysella gestured. He turned his head as Amelya Detauran and Elyssa Kaan neared the table.

"May we join you?" asked Detauran, looking to Ysella.

Dekkard managed not to offer the amused smile he felt.

"Of course," replied Ysella, gesturing to the open chair beside her.

Elyssa Kaan took the place beside Dekkard.

For several minutes, no one spoke as they ate.

"The newssheets said there were attacks on councilors in Oersynt . . ." offered Detauran almost tentatively, again looking to Ysella.

"There were. They attacked Councilor Obreduur and District Councilor Vandenburg. Steffan took care of both . . ." Ysella looked to Dekkard.

"I wounded the man attacking Councilor Obreduur, and a patroller killed him. The other attacker shot Councilor Vandenburg while I was dealing with the first attacker, but Avraal dropped the councilor out of the line of fire, and I managed to kill the second attacker before he turned his gun on Obreduur."

"You two are good," said Detauran.

"We're at our best together," returned Dekkard.

"Did anything happen in Caylaan?" asked Ysella before anyone else could say anything.

"There was a small demonstration. They scattered when the patrollers opened fire. Two men were killed, and one woman was wounded," replied Kaan.

"That wasn't in the newssheets," said Dekkard.

"There were several smaller cities where demonstrations weren't reported," said Detauran. "Maybe more than that. Security's trying to keep the numbers down."

"Who's heading the Security Committee?" asked Dekkard. "I read that Councilor Maendaan was killed, and the next ranking councilor is Ulrich . . . and he's the Premier."

"Right now, the Premier is handling that, according to Councilor Bassaana," said Kaan. "There's talk . . ." She shrugged.

"Talk?" questioned Dekkard. "Perhaps transferring Marrak from Commerce and making him chair? Why him?"

Detauran smiled sardonically. "You know that as well as anyone. Anyway . . . nothing's been announced. I have a question. The New Meritorists attacked four councilors. Two were Commerce, one a Landor, and one a Crafter. Why those?"

"It's just a guess," replied Dekkard, "but the New

Meritorists don't like Security, and they don't like the Council much. Maendaan was head of the Security Committee, and then one from each party. Most likely they picked the three whose appearances made them most vulnerable."

"It makes sense . . . but . . ."

"If you have a better idea," replied Dekkard, "I'd love to hear it."

"Councilor Obreduur is the political leader of the Craft Party, and Councilor Maendaan headed the Security Committee. That makes them more prominent," suggested Detauran.

"That's true," agreed Dekkard, "but neither Haaltf nor Devoule were particularly noted."

"You do have a way with words, Steffan. Not particularly noted? How about embarrassments to the Council? Maybe those behind the assassinations picked either councilors they saw as threats or those whom few would miss?"

"That makes sense, too." *Especially since Security is most likely among the assassins.*

"You don't think it was random, just whoever they could get?" asked Kaan.

"Aashtaan's death wasn't random," replied Dekkard. "Neither were all the attacks on Security buildings, or on water and sewage systems."

"Aashtaan's death? What do you mean?" asked Detauran.

"It's likely that the empath who killed him went to the New Meritorists and offered to kill him if they'd help her. Aashtaan was a womanizer. He was seeing her sister. Then that sister vanished. Shortly after that the empath sister appears in the Council Hall as a messenger—"

"I knew it had to be something like that!" interrupted Kaan. "I couldn't figure out how an empath could kill someone that way and then be caught without creating more emotional damage." She turned to Ysella. "So there was only one really strong emotional blast?"

Ysella nodded.

"That's not widely known." Dekkard wondered if he'd made a mistake in revealing what he had.

"It will stay that way," said Detauran.

"You can tell your councilor."

"Thank you. Kaliara might enjoy it. She never cared for Aashtaan."

Dekkard nodded.

Detauran took a last swallow of her café, then stood. "We need to go."

Once the other two left, Dekkard looked to Ysella. "Your thoughts?"

"Telling them about Aashtaan was a good thing. I'm certain Ulrich already knew what you told them, and Bassaana might be quietly helpful . . . in the future."

Dekkard hoped so.

"We'd better finish and go wait," suggested Ysella.

Dekkard took a last swallow of café. "I'm finished."

"I don't eat as fast as you do. Almost no one does."

A few minutes later, Ysella said, "I've had enough."

Dekkard glanced at her plate. "We have time. You can finish."

Ysella smiled sweetly, and said, "I've had enough."

Dekkard winced. "I'm sorry."

Her smile turned mischievous. "I really did have enough. Those empanadas are heavy."

The two stood and headed for the main corridor, more crowded than before.

Dekkard noticed that Ysella had an expression between intent and distracted. "Is there something wrong?"

"I don't think so, but there are more feelings of agitation. They're not as strong as when the empie attacked or when the Council Guards were shooting at the New Meritorists, but they're more widely dispersed."

"People are worried, then."

"Aren't you . . . a little?"

"Of course, but I'd wager I'm not worried about what they are," replied Dekkard.

"That's not a wager I'd take, not as well as I know you."

Dekkard nodded, but he couldn't help wondering how well they did know each other. When they reached the area across from the councilors' lobby where staff waited, most of the space on the staff benches was taken. They took a position against the wall. A good sixth passed, and still no members left. Then two others in security grays approached them. Dekkard immediately recognized Chavyona Leiugan, Councilor Harleona Zerlyon's empath, and, after a moment, the stocky isolate Tullyt Kamryn.

"They're still talking, then?" asked Leiugan.

"No one's come out," said Ysella.

"Is your councilor all right? The newssheets in Ondeliew said there were deaths in Oersynt. Since we didn't hear anything . . . well . . . we would have heard if he'd been killed."

"He wasn't wounded, either," replied Ysella. "He has some bruises on his knees and legs, but they did kill the head of the district council. Steffan took care of the assassin."

"Only because of Avraal," insisted Dekkard.

Leiugan whistled softly. "It was that close?"

Ysella nodded. "What happened in Ondeliew?"

"It started peacefully. Just those New Meritorists with signs and placards, but when the regional Security headquarters building exploded—half of it, really—then the patrollers started shooting . . . mostly in the air. The demonstrators scattered. It would have been fine, except a bunch of Security agents—not patrollers—shot down some women running away. From somewhere, snipers took out the entire squad of agents. Then more agents started shooting anyone who looked like a demonstrator. More of the agents got shot. I wouldn't be surprised if some were shot by patrollers. Almost a hundred people died. The councilor sent a report to Minister Wyath yesterday. She told him that until his agents shot six women in the back not a single person had been hurt. There were broadsheets out everywhere on Unadi describing the murder of the women. One was a grandmother. Three of them had children at home . . ."

"None of that was in *Gestirn*," said Ysella. "That's not surprising, and it certainly won't be in the *Tribune* . . . unless the women are called useless communalist scum."

"I wouldn't be surprised if, by the end of the week, those broadsheets will be in every city in Guldor," said Dekkard. "Minister Wyath will claim the New Meritorists started it, and that rioters and lawbreakers deserve what they get."

"The regional director of Security already said that," added Tullyt Kamryn.

"Oh . . . and she sent a copy of that letter to your councilor," added Leiugan. "And to all the woman councilors."

"Good," said both Ysella and Dekkard.

"It looks like they're done," said Kamryn. "Some of the councilors are coming out."

"Thank you for letting us know, Chavyona," said Ysella.

"I thought you should. Sometimes, things don't get where they should soon enough."

While councilors continued to walk out from the councilors' lobby, not including the Premier, since his floor office could be accessed directly from the floor and also had a private door off the main corridor, Obreduur was one of the last to leave. He and Hasheem were still talking as Dekkard, Ysella, and Hasheem's isolate, Erleen Orlov, joined them. Both Dekkard and Ysella kept scanning the main corridor, but it was comparatively empty, since most councilors and their security aides had already left for the Council Office Building.

"Have you had a chance to read the message from Councilor Zerlyon, sir?" asked Dekkard once the three were outside on the covered walkway.

"I did. Why do you ask?"

"We were talking to her security aides while we waited for you. They said that Security agents, not patrollers, started the violence by shooting unarmed women in the back."

"Her message mentioned that."

Dekkard said nothing more, since it was clear that Obreduur didn't wish to say anything . . . about anything.

Just before they reached the door to the office, the councilor finally spoke. "I'll tell you about the session on the way home. In the meantime, I'd like each of you to write up what steps or statements you think I should take in the next week . . . and why. Have them ready no later than first thing tomorrow morning. Handwritten please, and don't have them typed up. Don't talk to each other about this. I've also asked Ivann, Svard, and Felix. I want your individual ideas. Is that clear?"

"Yes, sir."

By a third before fourth bell, Dekkard had his recommendations ready. He read through them a last time.

After reading through the six reccomendations, he stood and walked to the door of the inner office, knocking and saying, "Steffan, sir. I have the recommendations you asked for."

"Come on in."

Dekkard opened the door and entered, closing it behind him. Then he walked to the desk and handed the two sheets to the councilor. "Before we start, sir, we overheard the possibility that Councilor Marrak will be considered for the chairmanship of Security."

"He's not that senior, but with Ulrich the ranking Commercer . . . we'll have to see." Then, Obreduur began to read. He said nothing. Finally, he looked up and offered a weary smile, then said, "You're suggesting I take on the Commercers head-on."

"I can't think of another way, sir. You're more skilled at this than I am. I'm sure you could approach the issues more effectively, but I do see those as the issues where the Commercers are most vulnerable."

Obreduur laughed wryly. "You're right. They're vulnerable. But there are two other questions. Are they vulnerable enough? And . . . do enough people really care?"

"Most people don't, I'd say, sir. But isn't it part of the job of a councilor to inform people and get them to care?"

"I'd agree with that but how? Thank you for being so quick and concise."

"Are you leaving at the regular time, sir?"

"I'll be later. Karola or I will let you know." Obreduur paused. "Thank you . . . again."

Dekkard inclined his head, then turned and left the inner office, glad that he hadn't upset the councilor, but wondering what else they could do to make more people understand.

In the end, it was well past fourth bell before Dekkard left to get the Gresynt, and almost a third before fifth bell when Ysella and Obreduur got into the steamer.

"What did Premier Ulrich say?" asked Ysella several minutes later.

"As little as he could," replied Obreduur. "He said that fifteen regional Security headquarters had been damaged or largely destroyed, and that there were New Meritorist demonstrations in nineteen cities and eleven towns. He also said that Security was busy tracking down the perpetrators. In short, they've caught almost no one of import."

"Did anyone question where the explosives came from?" asked Dekkard.

"Someone did. Councilor Bassaana. She wanted to know if the explosives used were dunnite, as reported by the newssheets, and if so, how the New Meritorists managed to get hold of that much without Security even knowing it was missing. She also asked whether it was necessary for Security agents to shoot unarmed women in the back." Obreduur paused, then added, "Premier Ulrich wasn't pleased at the questions. He didn't answer either. He immediately said that Security was tracking down members of the New Meritorists through their publications, and that they would have answers soon. Saandaar Vonauer then asked if Security intended to interrogate Guldorans on the basis of what they read. At that point, Ulrich said that was all the information that Security had and that a supplemental appropriation would be necessary to rebuild and repair all the damage to public structures. He talked for almost a bell about the need for more funding. The two points made by Councilor Bassaana still might make it into the newssheets. I think she knows more than she's revealed. In her own right, she has a large minority interest in Northwest Industrial Chemical."

So she'd be concerned personally as well. Dekkard nodded.

"Northwest and Suvion Industries supply all the naval munitions works," said Ysella. "I found that out from Markell when he worked on a project for Suvion."

"The regional Security headquarters in Siincleer was one of those damaged," said Dekkard. "According to Markell and Emrelda, the Security agents there were pressuring the patrollers. Is there any way we can tie Markell's disappearance and Engaard's death to that . . . possibly pointing out that matters there were more than a little strange?"

"I've already asked Carlos if he can add more. He was working on a report that a Commercer public prosecutor there was closing cases for lack of evidence when he was the one who'd ordered the evidence moved to filing rooms where it was inadvertently discarded."

"Emrelda might be able to provide the name of that patroller area chief who hinted about that," said Ysella.

"If she could, that would be helpful," replied Obreduur.

"I'll send her a message," Ysella promised.

Obreduur returned to writing.

After several minutes, Dekkard quietly asked Ysella, "Did you ever get any letters back from Emrelda?"

"Just the one a week ago. I send her a message yesterday, but I haven't heard back."

"I'll wager there's a message waiting for you at the house."

"I hope so. I worry about her."

As Dekkard left the garage after tending to the steamers—and noting that Ingrella's was still warm—Ysella was waiting for him in the hall, message in hand.

"She had to work the evening shift yesterday. So she didn't get my message until this morning. She was worried about me . . . you, too . . . because the newssheets often don't mention what happens to aides."

"Only in Gaarlak . . . and well after the fact," said Dekkard wryly.

"She wants us to come over on Findi."

"I'd like that . . . if you would. I mean . . . you haven't really seen her in a month. I wouldn't . . ."

"Steffan . . . that's sweet of you, but I'd really like you to come."

Dekkard couldn't help but smile broadly. "Then I will. I just never would want to come between you two."

"You won't . . . and you had me with the smile."

"But . . . you'd better tell her . . . that unsettled as things are . . . Obreduur might need us."

"I'd already thought of that, but I'd be very surprised if he'd need us this Findi. Next Findi might be different."

"You think things are going to get worse?

"Don't you?"

He nodded, then said, "One way or another."

Because the three arrived home later, Dekkard postponed knife-throwing practice until after the evening meal. After two throws, Nellara complained that the dimmer light in the garage in Machtarn made it hard to judge distance.

Dekkard just said, "There won't be very good light when you'll need to use a knife."

"Like at the Ritter's Inn," said Ysella.

"Sir . . . ah . . ." began Gustoff, "how many men have you killed?"

"More than one," replied Dekkard, after a long pause. "And that's one too many. Some security aides never kill anyone in years."

"But . . . why . . . you, I mean, sir."

"I can't give you a good answer. Partly because we guard your father, and he may be the most important councilor in Guldor in the weeks ahead. He's working to return the Empire to what the Great Charter meant it to be. The Commercers and some Landors don't want that."

"Could he be premier?" asked Nellara.

"The next elections could still be two years away," said Ysella. "The Imperador hasn't shown any sign of asking Premier Ulrich to step down or of calling for elections. Even if the Craft Party wins thirty seats, that may not be enough for the party to name the next premier."

"We think he would make a good premier," added Dekkard, "but the best-qualified councilors don't always become premier."

"Some who get elected to the Council aren't that good, either," said Gustoff.

"That's also true," said Ysella.

"And it's time to get back to practicing before it gets too late," declared Dekkard.

For the next two-thirds of a bell, Dekkard's attention was on knife technique. Then he called an end to practice.

"Do you have another waist sheath?" asked Ysella. "One that I could borrow?"

Dekkard couldn't help frowning. Nothing forbade an empath security aide from carrying weapons. Some did, but he'd never thought of Ysella that way. Then he smiled. *You should have.* "I only have a spare single knife sheath, but you're welcome to it."

"Could I get one?" asked Nellara.

"If your mother agrees, then I'll get you one, but once

I do, you can only use it for practice until you're much better and until your parents agree you can carry a knife." Dekkard turned to Ysella. "I'll see about a pair of matched knives and sheath for you as well. Better yet, we should see about them together."

"I'd appreciate it."

"Now . . . we need to put away the target and clean and sharpen the knives." Dekkard looked to Gustoff and Nellara.

"Yes, sir."

As soon as the chores were done, the two young people hurried off.

"They're good children," said Dekkard. "Much better than I was at their ages."

"I doubt that. Especially since I've met your parents and sister."

"Will I ever meet your parents?"

"At some point, I imagine, but it's not going to be soon. Remember, I'm not welcome there, and they've shown no sign of wanting to come here."

"That's sad . . . unfortunate."

Ysella nodded, then said, "You finished your statement for Obreduur this afternoon, didn't you?"

"I did."

She smiled wryly. "I didn't. I was worried about Emrelda. Now I need to do it."

"Then I'd better let you get to it."

"I'll see you in the morning, Steffan." She took his right hand with her free left hand and squeezed it gently. "Thank you." Then she turned and headed for the staircase.

Dekkard just stood there for a moment. He'd wanted to put his arms around her, but that would have been an imposition. *And an incredible complication.*

He swallowed and walked toward the staff room.

76

Dekkard woke up on Tridi morning, knowing that he'd dreamt about Ysella, but found himself unable to remember any of the details, except a feeling of urgency. He couldn't even remember the reason for urgency. He was still pondering that when he stepped into the staff room and saw that she was already there.

"You're early this morning," Dekkard said cheerfully.

"I've been up for a while. I was too tired to finish my recommendations last night. So I got up early."

"Are you satisfied with them? I'm not asking for details," he added quickly as he poured his café, then added two croissants and two slices of quince paste to his plate before sitting down.

"Not really. I have the feeling I've missed something."

"I can see that. I felt the same way."

"But you still handed yours in."

"I also had the feeling that I wasn't going to think of anything more or better. And if I did, I could write up another page this morning." He offered a pseudo-mournful smile. "I didn't." He took a sip of café. "With all five of us coming up with our own ideas, maybe that will be enough. Did you read *Gestirn*?"

"I did. There's nothing much except what Obreduur said would be . . . but he was right. They printed Councilor Bassaana's questions and the fact that Ulrich didn't answer them."

"I imagine the New Meritorists will spread that . . . if the newssheets elsewhere in Guldor don't. Shooting unarmed women in the back . . . that plays right into the New Meritorists' strategy . . . and the dunnite also weakens Security."

Ysella shook her head. "That will make some of the Security agents angry."

"If they show it, it will make matters worse."

"Not if they crack down hard enough to stop any

more demonstrations. That's what most Landors and Commercers want."

"Sometimes getting what you want is the worst thing possible, especially if people get hurt." Dekkard finished off the first quince-filled croissant.

Ysella took a sip of café. "Do you think anything will happen today?"

"I'd be surprised. Everyone's preparing for Findi. If not this Findi, then next Findi."

She nodded. "More like next Findi . . . but things are more unsettled than I expected. You were closer to seeing what happened."

"Closer, but I underestimated how many followers the New Meritorists have. Then . . . maybe they don't have that many, but there are a lot of dissatisfied people, and the Meritorists are the only group able and willing to act."

"That could be."

Dekkard agreed, but concentrated on finishing breakfast, although he did look at Ysella more than a few times, thinking, as he often did, how she made anything she wore look stylish.

After breakfast, he finished preparing for the day and had the Gresynt ready a few minutes early and watched as Obreduur and Ysella entered the steamer. Obreduur carried his case and several sheets of paper, most likely Ysella's recommendations, Dekkard suspected.

The drive to the Council Office Building was quiet. The increased number of Council Guards on duty appeared to be the same as on Duadi, and they continued to check passcards.

When Dekkard reached the office, he found a somewhat larger pile of letters and petitions on his desk. He looked to Karola.

She smiled. "The councilor said to give you all the ones about what he was doing over Summerend. Avraal got all the ones about Ritten Obreduur."

"People are complaining about her?"

"Some are; some want to know why she hasn't been allowed to do more," replied Ysella.

"More of the first than the second, I'd wager."

"Not as many more as I thought," replied Ysella.

Does that reflect how people think . . . or that those who want a stronger role for women are more likely to write? Dekkard hoped it was the former, but feared it was the latter.

The remainder of the day was long and quiet, except for the constant flow of messages in and out of the office, but Dekkard did manage to get through all the petitions and letters before he left to get the Gresynt. When he entered the parking area, he did notice that the Council Guards were actively patrolling the parked steamers.

Because of the earlier incident you had? Or because now they think it might happen to Commercer aides or something might involve Commercer steamers? Dekkard snorted to himself as he unlocked the Gresynt and got in.

Obreduur and Ysella arrived outside the Council Office Building moments after Dekkard pulled up. The councilor said nothing until Dekkard had turned the steamer south on Imperial Boulevard.

"Premier Ulrich announced that the remainder of the week will be devoted to hearings on Security matters and hearings to determine the necessary scope of supplemental funding. That will include potential new revenue sources. The Council sessions next week will be on the enabling legislation and funding."

"Who are they going to tax?" asked Dekkard.

"Newssheets and printers, among others," replied Obreduur. "The Premier apparently feels both have contributed to the current unrest."

"Did he say that?" asked Ysella.

"No. He let it be known indirectly. That way he can have Security shut down any newssheet that suggests he's behind it."

"Can't they print that it's under consideration?" Dekkard thought he knew the answer.

"Not unless they want to risk being shuttered. There

was nothing said on the floor about it, but I'm certain *Gestirn* and *The Machtarn Tribune* will get the message, one way or other."

"And Security will be watching all the printers to see if any are producing broadsheets," suggested Dekkard.

"They've been doing that all week. They seem to think that strategy is working. That's what Councilor Marrak said in the councilors' lobby."

"Is he the new head of the Security Committee?"

"It hasn't been announced, but it appears so." Obreduur paused. "Do you think Security will be able to stop the broadsheets?"

"If the New Meritorists were able to place tons of dunnite inside Security buildings, I don't see Security being able to stop them from printing broadsheets. Security had no idea about all the signs and placards that appeared during the Summerend demonstrations."

"That's been my feeling as well. It's going to lead to more unrest and trouble."

"Is there anything we need to know about?" asked Dekkard.

Obreduur shook his head. "No. Not yet, anyway. It's too early to make a political move. Right now, it won't have any effect, and it will be lost or smothered if there's more unrest."

Sitting beside Dekkard, Ysella nodded.

77

On Furdi morning, *Gestirn* quoted Ulrich saying that the repair of the damage caused by the New Meritorists required funding for "enhanced security measures" supported by "targeted revenue enhancements." Ulrich also called the demonstrators "criminals trying to destroy the long-standing Guldoran tradition of civil order."

Dekkard shook his head as he replaced the newssheet on the side table. He poured his café, took two croissants off the serving platter with two slices of quince paste, and sat down to sip his café while waiting for Ysella. He didn't wait long.

When she entered the staff room, rather than talk about the news, he said, "You did well with the knives last night. Do you think we could shop for knives for you before we go to Emrelda's on Findi?"

She stopped, clearly surprised, then smiled. "You do know how to surprise a woman. If we start early, she might not even know."

"You'd tell her. Besides, we'll have to take a steamhack. Garlaand's is a good three milles from here, and you'll want to try several different varieties. You might do even better with one that has a narrower blade."

"Provided the councilor doesn't need us on Findi." Ysella looked toward the newssheet.

"There's nothing there," Dekkard replied to the unspoken question, "except Ulrich fulminating against the New Meritorists and insisting on more taxes to pay for the damage to Security buildings. The story doesn't mention any of those who might be taxed."

"That's no surprise. This way he can keep everything quiet until no one can do much to stop him." Ysella poured her café, then sat down.

"That will just make the Meritorists angrier."

"Which will justify his taking stronger measures." She paused, then said, "As for Findi, right after breakfast, I'll write a quick note to Emrelda and have Rhosali send it off with any other messages."

After breakfast, while Ysella wrote to her sister, Dekkard readied the Gresynt. The drive to the Council Office Building was uneventful . . . as was the morning, until slightly after fourth bell, when a messenger arrived with a cardboard tube and presented it to Karola. "A Council missive."

"In a tube?"

"They said it was a proclamation."

Karola signed for it, then opened the tube and extracted the proclamation. Without a word, she turned and carried it into Obreduur's office.

A few minutes later, Karola stepped out of the inner office, followed by Obreduur.

"Have everyone join us," Obreduur said quietly.

When everyone was gathered around Karola's desk, Obreduur laid the "proclamation" on the desk, a proclamation that turned out to be a broadsheet.

"You all need to read this," said the councilor.

Dekkard's eyes widened at the very first words he read.

Government Corruption

Corporacions steal from the public lands, then overcharge the Navy.

No one goes to gaol; no one is punished; but everyone else pays.

Five Hundred Deaths Every Year!

Security detains more than five hundred people every year who either die under questioning or in custody or simply vanish. This doesn't include the nearly one hundred shot or killed for peacefully protesting during Summerend.

Security Censorship!

Anything the Commercer Premier doesn't want printed never gets in the newssheets. More than 5,000 stories set to be printed by *Gestirn* were either heavily edited or deleted by Security censors over the past two years.

Privilege and More Privilege

The government now restricts university enrollments to the well-off, cutting funding even for the brightest students from working and craft families.

Join the New Meritorists for Better Government!

"I imagine there are other versions," said Obreduur mildly. "The fact that the New Meritorists could get this to the office shows they're far more entrenched than Security knows."

Or far more clever. Dekkard did not voice that thought, deciding to listen, instead.

"How could they do this?" asked Raynaad.

"It wouldn't be that hard," said Anna, surprisingly to Dekkard. "Message tubes all look alike. The Council seal is everywhere. Anyone could copy that. You can open them, and if the broadsheet is slipped in with the print side out you can't see what's on it. Put a note on top of the basket with the tubes signed by the Premier's office that says 'Send one to every councilor.' We get one or two of those every week. Usually it's the legislative calendar or a notice to be posted. Nothing that's all that urgent."

"Very effective," said Obreduur. "Council Security will become even more intrusive. Right now, it would be wise to be careful in any private messages you dispatch from here."

Measured as Obreduur's voice sounded, Dekkard doubted he was that calm.

"Are those numbers correct?" asked Margrit after a moment.

"For the most part," replied Obreduur, "I imagine they are. Some might be out of context. The deaths in custody, especially. There are roughly forty cities of some size and several thousand towns and villages. That works out to a little more than one death or disappearance a month in each city. Some of those deaths are not the fault of Security. Now it may be that the Meritorists are only listing the questionable deaths. But the other charges and figures suggest an even greater range of problems for Guldor."

"So it was sent to every councilor to prove they could send them?" asked Roostof.

"Also to let councilors know what's already on the

streets." Macri's voice turned sardonic as he added, "They're hair-splitting over the term 'peaceful protests.' The protests were peaceful, but there had to be Security personnel, perhaps hundreds, killed in all those buildings destroyed by explosives."

"Can you blame them?" asked Karola. "The Premier is always hair-splitting." She swallowed, then turned to Obreduur. "I'm sorry, sir."

"That's all right. In here, you can say that. It is the truth. I wouldn't do it elsewhere in the building or near Security. Agents are going to be . . . sensitive . . . for quite some time."

Especially where Craft councilors and staffers are concerned, thought Dekkard.

"The Premier is likely to call a brief Council session." Obreduur looked to Dekkard and Ysella, standing side by side. "I might need you two on short notice. In the meantime, all of you, just go back to work." Obreduur turned and headed back into his office.

"I wouldn't want to be in charge of the messenger service right now," said Roostof.

"You think not, Svard?" said Macri with dry humor.

Dekkard returned to letters and petitions. Just before noon another messenger arrived. That one Karola took to Obreduur. Then she returned to the front office and said, "The Premier is calling the Council into session at first bell. The councilor will need both of you, and you'll have to wait for him outside the councilors' lobby."

Obreduur came out of the inner office more than a third before first bell. "It's better to be there early."

On the way to the Council Hall, Dekkard saw several other councilors with aides, but none were particularly close, not until they reached the entrance to the councilors' lobby, where there were now two Council Guards posted and where he saw Laurenz Korriah and Shaundara Keppel watching closely as Councilor Navione stepped into the lobby. Neither moved as Dekkard and Ysella made sure no one was targeting Obreduur.

Once Obreduur was out of sight, Dekkard turned toward Korriah. "Did your office get—"

". . . one of those New Meritorist propaganda sheets? Didn't everyone?"

"We thought so."

"They're frigging idiots," said Korriah. "Frigging idiots. All this will do is get Ulrich and Wyath even madder and ready to kill more of them."

"And a lot of innocents with them," said Dekkard. "That could be what they want."

"That's sowshit. More dead workers and students won't change anything."

"You might be right, but I'd wager that they think it will."

"How do you know that?"

"I don't *know* anything," replied Dekkard, "but they've planned everything incredibly well. They're misguided, but they're not stupid."

"That's sick . . . getting Security to shoot people to get more people upset so more will get shot?"

"It's happened before. Just not in Guldor."

Korriah shook his head, then motioned to the waiting area. "We might as well get seats while there are still some."

The older isolate was absolutely correct, because in minutes the corridor was filled with councilors and aides, and both Keppel and Ysella were concentrating to see if they sensed anything untoward. But, by the time first bell rang, nothing happened, and only staffers remained in the corridor, sitting and standing around the waiting area.

The session was short, and, when it was over, Obreduur was again one of the later councilors to leave the floor, talking with both Hasheem and Jorje Kastenada, the other Craft councilor besides Hasheem on the Security Committee. The conversation ended before any of the three councilors were close to their aides.

"Councilor Hasheem will be walking back with us," Obreduur said.

Dekkard saw an expression that might have been relief on the face of Hasheem's isolate, Erleen Orlov, there as sole security for the councilor, apparently since Hasheem had still been unable to replace Arthal Shenke.

As the five crossed the garden courtyard, the air was as damp and hot as at full summer, and Dekkard was sweating heavily when they reached the Council Office Building, even though they'd walked in the shade of the covered portico. Once they reached the second floor, Hasheem and Orlov continued down the corridor while Dekkard, Ysella, and Obreduur entered his office.

"Karola, would you ask Ivann, Svard, and Felix to join us in my office." Obreduur smiled warmly if briefly.

Obreduur did not sit down but walked to the window and looked out until the other three had entered. Then he turned and began to speak. "The Premier was upset. It wouldn't be an exaggeration to say that he was coldly furious that the New Meritorists compromised the Council message system. The message supervisor and assistant supervisors have all been replaced, temporarily, by message specialists from the Security Ministry. All four were interrogated. One did not survive, regretfully, although Security found him innocent. So were the others, but, according to Ulrich, poor security and sloppiness allowed the infiltration, and that is why the three survivors were dismissed with loss of any possible retirement stipends.

"Any Council staffer meeting with New Meritorists without the explicit written consent of the Premier will be tried by the Council on charges of treason ... and likely found immediately guilty," added Obreduur sardonically. "The Security Ministry has granted its agents the unrestricted right to use lethal force against any New Meritorist who attempts to escape custody or who refuses to obey Security orders."

"How is anyone supposed to know who's a New Meritorist?" asked Roostof.

"Right now," replied Obreduur, "a Meritorist is anyone Security says it is."

Macri gave a low whistle. "That requires Council consent."

"Ulrich called for a vote. He got exactly thirty-four. I doubt that most of the Landors or Craft councilors were pleased. But I wanted all of you to know that even saying a few words to a New Meritorist could be dangerous, and would cost you your positions . . . if not your life."

"Am I missing something," asked Macri, "or does this suggest that the Imperador is not pleased?"

"He didn't mention the Imperador, but that's the conclusion I'd draw." Obreduur cleared his throat. "Ivann, if you'd relay that to Anna and Margrit, and I'll tell Karola." After a pause, he added, "That's all that happened, but I wanted to let you all know immediately."

"Thank you, sir," Dekkard said, with the others adding their voices almost immediately.

Then the five left the inner office quietly, and Obreduur beckoned for Karola.

Dekkard turned to Ysella. "This is going to get worse than I thought. Ulrich is scared of the Imperador calling new elections, and scared people are dangerous."

"Why is he that scared?"

"I don't know exactly, but Obreduur said he only could manage thirty-four votes. That's not exactly a position of strength. The Commercers are short one vote, since they haven't chosen a replacement for Maendaan, but his replacement would only haven given them thirty-five. Why else would he react that way? He doesn't need to threaten to shoot staffers to prove he's the Premier."

"There's something else there," said Ysella.

Dekkard smiled ironically. "Maybe he's afraid the Kraffeist Affair might reappear . . . or there's something else we don't know. Obreduur's right, though. We all need to be careful."

Since there wasn't anything else they could immediately do besides worry, both of them went back to work, although Dekkard wondered if the Commercer hold on the Council was that fragile, or whether Ulrich's anger was because he didn't want to be dismissed as premier. He also wondered how Macri was doing on tracking down the hidden subsidy to Guldoran Ironway.

When Dekkard picked up Obreduur and Ysella after work, she was carrying not only the small gray purse she used when in grays, but also a leather portfolio that looked full of something. He gestured to it.

Ysella murmured, "Later."

Once he finished with the steamers—and again Ingrella's was warm, as if she'd come home only shortly before the others—Dekkard looked for Ysella and found her in the shade of the drive portico. "You were carrying a portfolio I never saw before."

"It's one of Obreduur's. It had messages in it. Ingrella will send them from her office in the morning."

"I'd wager at least one is to Carlos Baartol."

"I didn't look. But do you blame him after what Ulrich said? By the way, Rhosali says there's a letter for you from Oersynt." She grinned.

"The way you're grinning, it's from Naralta."

"The sender's address just says Dekkard."

"You're likely right."

"Go read the letter. We can talk after dinner."

With that humorous dismissal Dekkard went to get the letter, which he took up to his room, warm as it was, before opening.

Steffan—

We were all relieved to hear that you survived the uprising in Oersynt and that you returned safely to Machtarn. Both Mother and Father were glad to spend time with you and your security partner. They had obviously hoped to see you again, but it certainly wasn't your doing that the New Meritorists decided to stage demonstrations all across Guldor . . .

No, it wasn't. Dekkard shook his head at the thought, then kept reading.

By the way, they were both impressed by the newssheet article. You didn't tell the whole story in your letters. That also reinforces what I saw of Avraal. In my opinion, she's an incredible woman, and if you feel the way about her as I suspect you do, you'll regret it for the rest of your life if you don't court her and tell her how you feel. She's more reserved than you are, and that's saying a lot. She'll only give hints, if that. I can see that she thinks highly of you . . .

Dekkard paused. Naralta wasn't saying that Avraal would agree to marry him, only that she was worth the effort and then some.

. . . and I sense that you worry that her rejecting you might jeopardize an amazing working partnership. Don't worry about that. You two respect each other too much. You both deserve more than that, and it's worth the risk. Not that I'm the one who should tell either of you about risk. Besides, you're used to a slightly older woman speaking her mind . . .

He winced slightly at that, but also smiled and went on to read the remainder of the letter, mostly about what had happened in Oersynt after the demonstration. He did linger over a few sentences.

. . . newssheets didn't express much sadness about District Councilor Vandenburg's death. They observed that he was a Landor with the ethics of a Commercer and financial sense of a child . . .

That's bitter . . . but accurate if it made it into the newssheets.

He put Naralta's letter with the others from his family. Since they were all fine and knew that he was, he could write on Quindi evening. Besides, he wanted to think over what Naralta had written about Avraal.

78

Dekkard was still thinking about Naralta's letter when he came down to breakfast on Quindi, but he immediately scanned the copy of *Gestirn* on the side table.

The lead story was predictably about the emergency legislation allowing preemptive use of lethal force against identified New Meritorists or anyone acting in an aggressive way that might result in violent civil disorder; death or injury to patrollers, Security agents, or innocent bystanders, or significant damage to public or private property. The story was strictly factual, including the closeness of the vote, but there was no mention of the broadsheets sent to councilors, and there was a large white space at the bottom, with a single sentence in the middle.

> As required by the Ministry of Security, this story has been edited and a portion removed.

Dekkard had never seen anything like that. He also suspected it might be the last time. Other than that one story, there was nothing else about government or the New Meritorists, although there was a small story about the Fleet Marshal dispatching another flotilla to Sudlynd to deal with pirates preying on Guldoran ships involved in trade with Noldar, and with other countries in the Teknold Confederacy. *A confederacy largely in name only.*

Dekkard replaced the newssheet, poured his café, obtained his croissants and quince paste from the serving platter, and sat down. He'd taken perhaps two sips of café when Ysella arrived.

"You might take a glance at the front page."

"Oh? Why?"

"You'll see."

Ysella immediately picked up the newssheet. After reading it, she set it back on the table. "What do you think Security objected to? Do you think Security will shut down *Gestirn*?"

"No, but I do think we won't see a statement like that again. Security will make that happen . . . possibly claiming that the newssheet risks being found as an accomplice of some sort to the New Meritorists. As for what Wyath's minions felt was objectionable . . . it could have been anything. A comment on the broadsheets that were distributed to the Council and what was in them . . . or a statement about Security shooting unarmed women in the back . . ."

"That hasn't showed up in the newssheets, either. It might have if they'd shot unarmed boys." Ysella's tone was faintly ironic as she poured her café and then sat down.

"No . . . it wouldn't. Security wouldn't want something published that upset Commercers."

"Of course . . . how thoughtless of me. But enough of Security. How is your family? You never said anything last night." She took a sip of café.

"Everyone's fine. They all enjoyed meeting you, especially Naralta. You definitely impressed her."

"She impressed me. Actually, your whole family did. I'd still like to hear the story of how your parents left Argental."

"So would I," replied Dekkard. "It must have been incredibly difficult, but all either will say is that it's better left in the past. The only hint I ever got was in that letter I mentioned to you where my mother wrote that she could never forget the sound of shots."

"That could be why she has mixed feelings about you being in security."

"I do know that they were relieved I didn't go into the Army or Navy."

"You'd have been wasted there. You also would have lost your mind. Just as you would if you'd gone into commercial security or remained as strictly a security aide. That was a gamble on Obreduur's part, but at the least we knew he'd be well-protected for a few years."

"We? You told him that. How did you know? You never even met me."

"A brilliant, driven young man from an artisan background who excelled in everything against some of the best and most talented young men in Guldor?" She laughed softly.

"You're making me into something—"

"I'm not. No false modesty, Steffan. It doesn't become you. At least, you're not inclined to arrogance."

For a moment Dekkard was silent. "You wouldn't do well with an arrogant partner."

"I've done it before. I didn't like it, but arrogant competence is preferable to modest incompetence."

"He was barely competent," declared Rhosali as she entered the staff room.

"Better than that," said Ysella.

"Not much," returned Rhosali.

"In any case," said Dekkard, "you and the councilor survived, and I'll try to avoid either arrogance or false modesty." He took a healthy bite out of his first croissant, followed by café.

The remainder of breakfast was quiet, as was the drive to the Council Office Building, which remained surrounded by guards. Once more, Dekkard had to show his passcard, first to get into the covered parking, despite the councilor's emblem on the Gresynt, and then to enter the building. When he entered the office, even before reaching his desk, he asked, "Does anyone know whether the Premier has called for a Council session?"

"Not so far," replied Karola. "You might even be able to finish that stack on your desk."

Dekkard looked at the envelopes. There had to be thirty, far more than what he'd had to deal with recently.

Ysella looked up from her desk. "I'd wager most of yours are from Commerce sympathizers who think the Premier is being too soft on the New Meritorists."

"That would make sense," replied Dekkard. "Not that many workers and crafters write the Council, and those who might sympathize aren't about to put their thoughts in words."

"Especially with Security looking over everyone's shoulders," said Karola.

Dekkard sat down and began to read. Almost a bell passed before he had the letters sorted into two piles. The larger pile was what Ysella had predicted, but there were five letters that said, effectively, that while the writers didn't agree with the tactics used by the demonstrators they did feel that times were getting worse for most people and only better for the wealthy—and that they hoped Obreduur would do something for most of the people and not just those well-off.

Dekkard drafted two responses, one for those who wanted Security to hammer the New Meritorists and one for the few who wanted Obreduur to help more than the wealthy. The draft for those who wanted a crackdown said that the councilor favored law and order, and that those who used violence shouldn't be allowed to get away with it, but that innocents who demonstrated without violence or weapons should be allowed that right within the law. The second draft said that and added that the demonstrations were the unfortunate result of the Council's failure to address the problems created by recent and rapid industrialization, a solution to which Obreduur and the Craft Party had been pressing for, while the Commercers had ignored that problem.

Then he took them to Margrit and had her type up each for Macri's review and Obreduur's because there wasn't much sense in drafting replies until he knew what wording was acceptable to the councilor. He'd just returned to his desk when Roostof also returned to the office from wherever he'd been, holding the midday edition of *Gestirn*.

"That broadsheet we saw yesterday? Well, the New Meritorists have flooded the city with copies, and

Gestirn actually wrote about them." Roostof shook his head. "They didn't say what was in the newssheet, because that would amount to spreading the demonstrators' propaganda—yes, that's in the story—but they did say that the inflammatory broadsheets were widely distributed in every quarter of the city . . . and at least in some other large cities. They also quoted the Premier as saying that the demonstrators were scum trying to destroy the greatness of Guldor from within and that the government would take all steps necessary to exterminate them."

"Exterminate them?" asked Karola.

"Those were his words. I don't think *Gestirn* would dare print them if they weren't."

Dekkard winced. *Ulrich must honestly think he can get away with a massacre . . . or that his words will stop the New Meritorists.* While the Premier *might* cause a massacre and still hold on to his government, Dekkard had no doubt that words from Ulrich wouldn't stop the demonstrations and broadsheets.

"Why would he say something like that?" asked Karola.

"Because he thinks that will have some effect," said Ysella. "When it doesn't, he can say that they were warned, and it was their own fault so many were killed."

Dekkard could definitely see that.

"I need to give this to the councilor," said Roostof.

Karola just nodded.

Roostof knocked, then entered the inner office. In only a few minutes, he came out without the newssheet. "He didn't look surprised. Not happy, but not surprised."

The rest of the day was routine, and Macri or Obreduur, or both, made small changes to the two drafts Dekkard had submitted, and Dekkard drafted personal openings to each of the letters dealing with the New Meritorists, and then turned them over to Margrit just before third bell. "Do what you can, and leave what you can't for Unadi."

"Why do so many people want others killed because they're unhappy with government."

Dekkard said gently, "They're more than just unhappy. You don't blow up fifteen Security buildings because you're unhappy. I'd say that they're furious because no one is listening. Or the Commercers aren't."

"Can the councilor do anything?"

"Not unless the Imperador calls for elections. Even if all that happened, the New Meritorists still won't be satisfied." *And if Obreduur did become premier, the Commercers and most of the Landors would be furious with what would be necessary to fix all the problems. And if he didn't deal with them . . .* He managed not to shake his head.

"You're worried, aren't you?"

"Anyone who's not worried doesn't understand how bad things could get."

"Everyone here is so quiet about it. I thought I was the only one."

Dekkard smiled wryly. "You're not. There's just not much point in talking about it. We're all working to find a way to head off the worst." *And most of the Commercers and Landors don't seem to see it . . . or they see it and refuse to admit it.*

"Thank you, sir." Margrit offered a tentative smile.

"Start with the smaller group of letters. Those writers seem to understand the problem."

"Yes, sir."

Dekkard turned to Macri. "Are you having any success with that ironway supplemental?"

"There's definitely something. It's entitled Miscellaneous Reallocations of Surplus Funds. The floor draft isn't finished, but I should have a copy first thing on Unadi." Macri smiled. "I'll be interested to see what's in it."

"So will I. Thank you."

Macri shook his head. "You're the one who found out about it. But I do want to know how they drafted it so that it's gone unnoticed."

"I wondered about that. You and Svard usually catch that sort of sleight of hand."

"Not always, unfortunately." Macri glanced at the papers on his desk.

Dekkard got the hint. "Later." Then he turned and headed back to his desk, where he resumed drafting, starting on the handful of letters dealing with other matters. *We're facing a revolt . . . and you're drafting letters?* He almost laughed at the absurdity of it all.

Yet, when the workday ended, and Dekkard had finished his drafts, if at the last moment, and headed out to get the Gresynt, nothing in the corridors of the Council Office Building looked all that different. Nor did it outside, except for the presence of more Council Guards everywhere.

79

For all of Dekkard's misgivings and concerns, the remainder of Quindi spooled out routinely, although there was a light late-summer rain that lasted from mid-afternoon until sometime past midnight, and the trip to the Trinitarian chapel for evening services was quiet. Because of services, the only ones who practiced with the knives, well after dinner, were Dekkard and Ysella. After that, Dekkard wrote a letter to Naralta, a letter that admitted to his sister that he was well aware of how incredible Avraal was and telling Naralta how he appreciated the advice of a slightly older woman.

When he went to bed, he slept soundly, but woke at his normal workday time. While he washed and shaved, he only put on a plain gray shirt and security-gray trousers that needed washing to go down to breakfast. He was the first down, except for Hyelda, and he immediately picked up the newssheet. There was nothing about the Council or the New Meritorists, but there was a large blank white space in the middle of the page, suggesting that something had been removed. *Security likely told the newssheet that they'd better not mention being censored. So they didn't print a single word about it.*

Dekkard smiled wryly. That smile faded when a story on the back of the front page caught his attention. As he read, his jaw dropped.

Three of the six Justicers of the High Justiciary announced late on Quindi that they received a petition containing a sworn and sealed deposition dealing with specified legal "irregularities" involving coal leasing procedures as practiced by the Ministry of Public Resources and petitioning for certain legal remedies. A direct petition may be forwarded from a regional justicer and, if accepted by half of the High Justicers, must be heard by the full High Justiciary in open court. Such petitions take priority, and the petition title and petitioner must be published in at least four major newssheets.

"In the matter of leasing public resources and properly recording such, a petition to the High Justiciary of the Imperium of Guldor." Petitioner is one Eduard Graffyn, an individual of legal standing in the matter of the petition. The initial hearing date is established as Duadi, 32 Summerend 1266, before the High Justiciary at the Fourth Bell of morning. So it be ordered.

Dekkard had a very good idea who the legalist behind the petition had to be and possibly even who the regional justicer might be.

"You're looking a bit stunned," said Ysella as she entered the staff room, wearing, surprisingly, a long cotton robe. Seeing his inquiring look, she added, "I thought it would be easier this way, but you had the same idea. You'll have to tell me what you're wearing so that I can pick the right ensemble."

"I'm more than a little stunned. Nothing on the front

page, but you'll find the small story on the bottom of the second page . . . rather interesting." He shook his head, then handed the newssheet to her.

As he looked at Avraal reading, just in a robe, he was aware of how striking she was. *Why just a robe? She's never come to breakfast in a robe before.* He quickly looked down for a moment.

When Ysella finished reading the story and scanning the rest of *Gestirn*, she looked thoughtful, but not nearly so surprised as he had felt.

"That's an incredibly clever legal maneuver. No matter what happens, they've reopened the Kraffeist Affair in a way that will be difficult to muzzle, because, if they do, it will be clear just how corrupt the Commercers are, and if they don't try to damp it down, at the least they'll come off as inept and sloppy." She smiled. "What do you plan to wear today? Possibly the rich blue barong?"

Dekkard laughed softly. "I'd thought that or the green one."

"I like the blue best on you."

"Then I'll wear that one."

Ysella seated herself, took a sip of café, then said, "I don't have any problems throwing your blades."

"Then you can get a set like mine . . . but I'd like you to try others just in case there's one that works even better for you."

"Are yours that different from most others?"

"The design is a bit cleaner, and they're heavier." After a moment, he added, "Have you heard any more from Emrelda?"

"No . . . but there's no reason I would. Why?"

"I was thinking about Markell. Except for a handful of people, it's like he didn't exist."

Ysella frowned. "Except for Emrelda and Halaard Engaard . . . he didn't."

"What about his family? Did he have any besides his parents?"

Ysella shook her head.

"You once said that Emrelda and Markell had a wide range of acquaintances . . ."

"Acquaintances, not friends. She said that the engineering profession was almost as reserved as Landor families. She's always said it's easier to talk to patrollers."

"So that, in some ways, that project was a perfect target for Siincleer Shipbuilding . . . or their engineering subsidiary."

"It was."

"I'm sorry." Dekkard didn't know what else to say.

"I think we'd better finish eating and go shopping." She offered a brief smile.

By a third before third bell, in the morning air that was slightly damper than usual, but also a touch cooler, Dekkard and Ysella were walking down Altarama toward Imperial Boulevard, since it was virtually impossible to hail a steamhack in East Quarter. As she'd indicated, Ysella was in a matching blue outfit, but with trousers, a thin jacket, a small blue purse, and a nearly totally transparent blue headscarf.

Dekkard occasionally glanced back, just to make sure no one was shadowing them closely. They were early enough in the day that the sidewalks bordering the boulevard weren't that crowded, and it only took a few minutes to hail a steamhack.

"Garlaand's Blades," said Dekkard. "Regency Way, a block south of the omnibus main terminal."

"Yes, sir."

"We can even take an omnibus to Emrelda's," Dekkard said to Ysella. "I'd forgotten that one line goes down Imperial to Camelia Avenue, and then east past Imperial University all the way to Erslaan . . . or we could still . . ."

"Let's see what we have to carry."

In less than a sixth the steamhack pulled up in front of a three story brick building set on Regency Way, a side street one block west of Imperial Boulevard, roughly midway between Altarama and the Imperial Palace. A

small black and gray sign over the door read HARCEL
GARLAAND: FINE BLADES.

"Two marks, sir."

Dekkard gave the driver three, then opened the door
and held it as Ysella got out. They walked toward the
store. The modest display window held far more than
knives, with axes, adzes, swords of various types, ma-
chetes, cane knives, and even a gladius in a gilded scabbard.

"That's quite an array of blades," observed Ysella.

"It is, but most of Garlaand's trade is in knives."
Dekkard opened the shop door and gestured for her to
enter, then followed her inside.

"We haven't seen you in a while, Sr. Dekkard," offered the wiry gray-haired man standing beside the
glass-fronted case that held various knives.

"That's because your knives hold up, Harcel. Even
under trying conditions."

"You've used them . . . in security matters?"

"A few times. There have been situations where they
were useful." Dekkard smiled politely. "But we're here
because my partner here has been working with knives
for a time now, and is ready for her own."

Garlaand offered a puzzled frown.

"Call it a broadening of skills. There are some empaths who handle weapons."

That brought a smile to the shop owner's face. "She's
good with yours?"

"She is, but I thought it might be best to see if anything else suited her better."

"If you don't mind . . . might I see your hand?" asked
Garlaand.

Ysella extended her hand.

"Is the weight of Sr. Dekkard's blades any problem?"

"No. I like the weight."

"I think you might do a little better with a blade of
the same weight that's just a bit longer . . . but we'll
have to see." Garlaand motioned to the archway behind

the display case. "We'll have you try several back in the practice area."

More than a third of a bell passed before Ysella settled on the knives, six in all, identical, but three for practice, and two to carry, with a spare, as well as a sheath for two knives. She immediately adjusted the sheath under the jacket, then eased the knives in. The practice knives went in a leather carrying case, along with the spare and the sheath that Dekkard had promised Nellara.

As Ysella handed over the mark notes to pay for them, including some from Dekkard for Nellara's sheath, Garlaand said, "You've been practicing how long? A couple of months?"

"More like a month," admitted Ysella.

The shopkeeper smiled wryly and looked to Dekkard. "I wouldn't get her riled up, sir."

"Even before she started practicing, I knew that."

"They're mostly for backup," said Ysella.

Or against other isolates or strong empaths. Dekkard didn't say that.

Garlaand just nodded, then said, "Enjoy the rest of the day."

"We intend to." Dekkard smiled.

Once they were outside on the sidewalk, he asked, "Steamhack or omnibus?"

"The omnibus is almost as fast, and I told Emrelda not to expect us until after fourth bell."

The two walked the block to the omnibus terminal, where they only had to wait a sixth to board the omnibus running the Erslaan route. They took a seat in the lower level near the rear, because that was usually less crowded, although that didn't matter, because it was early enough that only about two handfuls of riders boarded before the driver turned onto Camelia Avenue.

As the omnibus was about halfway around the gentle curve following the first block from Imperial Boulevard, the driver started to slow, then came to a complete stop. Almost instantly, a crowd, mostly of students, surrounded the front of the omnibus and began to push at it.

"We need to get off. Now," said Dekkard. "They're going to try to overturn it to block the avenue." Even with his first words, he was moving toward the rear emergency exit.

Ysella followed right behind him.

As soon as he opened the door, more students appeared.

His personal truncheon in hand, Dekkard dropped to the pavement and struck the nearest attacking man across the thigh, then turned toward a second, who froze for a moment, then backed away.

"To your left!" snapped Ysella.

Dekkard turned and barely managed to block a staff being half thrust and half swung, but then ducked under the staff and thrust his truncheon right under the center of the falling man's rib cage before darting to one side and felling a second man carrying an ancient sword with a blow to the knee just before he looked like he was about to swing the bar-like blade at Ysella.

"This way! Run!"

From somewhere nearer to the university, Dekkard heard shots as the two sprinted in the general direction of Imperial Boulevard. In moments, Dekkard realized no one was following them. He stopped and looked back. In the middle of the curve, he saw a handful of signs.

ENROLLMENT BY MERIT!
MERIT! NOT BIRTH!
MERIT! NOT MARKS!

The crowd was still working on tipping the omnibus. Beyond them, Dekkard saw figures in security blue moving toward the crowd. Then, as the omnibus turned on its side, Dekkard could make out the bright red shoulder patches, framed in a golden triangle. *Special*

Tactical Forces. Even as he recognized them, shots filled the morning, and the rioters began to fall.

"Steffan . . ."

"You're right. Hurry, but don't run. They're likely to shoot at people running."

The two walked swiftly to the north sidewalk. Dekkard kept looking back.

"No one's following us," Ysella said. "Not at the moment."

As he holstered his personal truncheon, Dekkard heard the steam scream of Security steamers moving toward the university from the east and south.

Both of them were breathing hard when they reached Imperial Boulevard, where they slowed their walk, moving north on the east side until they could hail a steamhack.

"We need to go to the Hillside area, Florinda Way off Jacquez on the north side of Camelia," said Ysella. "You'll have to take the long way. There's a demonstration at Imperial University."

"That's what the whistle screamers are for?"

"It is."

"I'll have to go halfway to the Palace to make sure we're not close."

"That's fine," said Dekkard.

Dekkard was still sweating when the steamhack pulled up on Florinda Way in front of Emrelda's house, but he immediately reached for his wallet.

"I'll take care of it," said Ysella in a voice that brooked no argument.

Dekkard did hold the door for her when she got out of the steamer, then closed it. Neither spoke as they started up the walk. They hadn't quite reached the front door when it opened, and Emrelda stepped out.

"You didn't have to take a steamhack . . ." Emrelda stopped and surveyed her sister, who looked as composed as ever, at least in Dekkard's eyes, and then at Dekkard, who doubted he looked that unruffled, and back to the leather knife case her sister carried. "What happened?"

"A riot at the university," replied Dekkard. "How about a drink while we tell you about it?"

"And a few other matters," added Ysella.

"Knowing you two, I'm sure there are." Emrelda smiled wryly, stepped back, and held the door while they entered, closing and bolting it behind them.

Less than a sixth later, the three settled into the wicker chairs around the low table, and Ysella looked to Dekkard. "You start with what's happened this week." To emphasize that she wasn't going to interrupt, she lifted her wineglass and sipped the Silverhills white.

It didn't take Dekkard long to summarize what had happened in the Council over the past five days, including the infiltration of the Council messaging system, and to describe what had happened at the demonstration that morning.

"No wonder you two looked a little out of sorts. That violent a demonstration here in Machtarn . . ." Emrelda shook her head, then frowned. "Were there regular patrollers there? There was no mention of special duties yesterday."

"All I saw were Special Tactical Forces," replied Dekkard. "The red-and-gold triangle patches."

"That's not good. Most of the patrollers dislike the STF types. They're worse than Security agents. The station captain thinks they never should have been created. Just like the agents, they're not allowed in the Patrollers Benevolent Society."

"They're not?" asked Dekkard.

Emrelda shook her head. "There's nothing benevolent about either of them. The Benevolent Society isn't a guild. Members choose who can belong."

Before Emrelda could add anything more, Ysella immediately said, "Do you have the name of the area Security chief you mentioned? Obreduur's contacts are digging up information on a Commercer public prosecutor in Siincleer. There are reports that he's closed cases for lack of evidence when he was the one who was responsible for its disappearance."

"You think that it might be tied to Markell and Halaard's deaths?"

"We don't know," said Dekkard, "but Obreduur's contacts are looking, and any information would be helpful." He took a small swallow of his Kuhrs. For some reason, his throat seemed particularly dry.

"His name was Karell Troyan. That's all I know . . . except that he's like most Security patrollers. They think that the agents, especially the Special Tactical Forces, aren't much better than brigands and thugs with red patches and guns. The patrollers in Siincleer have an even lower opinion. You're sure that there were Tacticals at the demonstration?"

"We saw two with the gold-and-red patches," replied Ysella. "Steffan told you that. They opened fire on the demonstrators."

"The gory details will be in broadsheets within days," added Dekkard. "I doubt anything detailed will be in *Gestirn*."

"Will that affect you?" Ysella asked Emrelda.

"I'll be given overtime. That will help."

Help? With what? Then Dekkard realized that, with Markell vanished and likely dead, and with Halaard Engaard dead, whatever income Emrelda had would be what she alone earned, and keeping a house the size of hers even without any debt couldn't be inexpensive. "Can we help?" Those words came out even without thinking.

Both Emrelda and Ysella looked at him.

"I don't need help now," replied Emrelda. "Markell got a bonus about a month before . . . everything happened. It's in a joint account. Since he's officially . . . still alive . . ." She swallowed.

"I'm sorry," said Dekkard gently. "I didn't mean . . ."

Emrelda looked to Dekkard. "I know. You're thoughtful and kind." She cleared her throat. "We've been very prudent. Everything's paid for. I can live here—carefully—on what I make. At least for quite some time."

"Have you heard anything from Cliven?" asked Ysella. "Recently?"

"He wrote me, saying I was welcome to come home any time. I wrote him back. I thanked him for his kindness, but told him I intended to remain here until matters became clearer. He wrote back earlier this week that he thought he understood, but that if I changed my mind, I'd always be welcome." Emrelda offered a hard wry smile. "There's no way I'd go back even if I were destitute. Not now, anyway."

Ysella nodded.

Dekkard understood what wasn't said.

"What does all this turmoil mean for you two?" asked Emrelda. "Besides more attempts on your councilor's life?"

"There might be new elections if matters get nasty enough," said Ysella. "They'd have to get very nasty for the Craft Party to win enough seats and to gain enough Landor support to form a government. I think there will be elections, but that the Commercers and Landors will cobble together enough seats to keep power." She looked to Dekkard.

"Avraal's right," he said, "unless the New Meritorists and others can show just how corrupt the Commercers have become. If that's the case, the Imperador will have to call for elections." Dekkard frowned. "That could turn even nastier, because if the Commercers lost control, they'd do their best to sabotage anything a Craft premier did, and the New Meritorists wouldn't help because they want to tear up the Great Charter."

Emrelda nodded, then said, "Since we can't do anything about any of that this afternoon, why don't the three of us fix some refreshments and enjoy them." She turned to Dekkard. "Do you have any familiarity with cooking or a kitchen, Steffan?"

Dekkard grinned. "My mother and sister wouldn't have had it otherwise. That said, I'm better at slicing or chopping or cleaning up."

"Good." Emrelda stood up. "We're having a butternut

squash soup, with a very large salad that will take a fair amount of washing, slicing, and chopping of the produce I got early this morning. The dessert is done. It's a lemon chiffon cake."

Dekkard rose and followed the sisters inside and into the kitchen.

80

Light conversation and good refreshments, including an excellent lemon chiffon cake, lager, and wine, filled the remainder of Findi morning and Findi afternoon, along with some cleaning up of dishes.

Just after the fourth bell of the afternoon, Emrelda announced, "It's time to take you both back. Just to be safe, we'll take a very much longer route that avoids Imperial University, the Council Hall, and the Palace."

"That's for the best," said Ysella.

Dekkard agreed, although he suspected that demonstrators might have avoided the Palace and its grounds, even if he had no logical basis for that conclusion.

On the circuitous route back to East Quarter, sitting in the rear seat by himself, Dekkard kept an eye out for Security forces, wondering if he'd ever find out how many people died in the university demonstration.

Emrelda stopped the teal Gresynt in front of the Obreduurs' pedestrian gate, then said, "I'll let you know what my schedule is. I might have to work next Findi."

"With everything that's going on," replied Ysella, "who knows what we'll be doing, but I'll message you."

Then Dekkard and Ysella got out of the steamer and watched as Emrelda made a U-turn and headed back toward Imperial Boulevard before they walked through the gate and up the drive.

Ysella stopped at the covered portico that led to

the side entrance of the house and turned to Dekkard. "Asking if we could help, Steffan . . . that was sweet." She paused, then added, "I liked that you said 'we.'"

"That's what I felt. I wasn't thinking. She's your sister . . ."

She reached out and placed a finger on his lips. "You don't have to explain."

He removed her finger gently. "I thought I should."

"You said what you felt. Emrelda was touched. So was I."

Dekkard stood there, just looking at her, taking in her grace and solidity, and wishing he had some way to convey all that he felt . . . or that she could sense all his feelings. *That's what comes of your being an isolate and her being an empath.*

Abruptly, she smiled. "Thank you for the day . . . and the knives." She lifted the leather case slightly.

"You bought them," he said softly. "I just wanted to make sure you had the right ones."

"I'll need to practice drawing and throwing."

"Getting the feel for that won't take you long."

"Not with your help. And I'll give the sheath to Nellara and tell her it's from you." She turned toward the steps up to the side entrance to the house, almost reluctantly, it seemed to Dekkard.

As he followed her up the few steps, Dekkard asked, "What do you think Ulrich will do?"

"Blame the New Meritorists and minimize the casualties."

"What about the petition about the Kraffeist Affair?"

"He'll find a way to minimize its effect. He won't even mention it if no one else does."

"As usual. But I wouldn't be surprised if Councilor Bassaana asks a few questions."

"He might not recognize her on the floor. Or he might say he won't answer questions until he has more information."

When they reached the foot of the staircase, Avraal

stopped and turned to Dekkard. "Except for the demonstration, I enjoyed the day. I haven't enjoyed Findis as much in years."

Dekkard swallowed, then said, "I haven't ever enjoyed them this much. You . . . make them special."

"So do you." She leaned back, set the leather case on the second step, then eased almost against Dekkard before she reached up with both hands, and drew his head down to where her lips met his.

Dekkard's arms, seemingly without volition, embraced her firmly, but gently.

After a long and gentle kiss, Avraal eased back slightly, as her arms went around him, and she looked up.

"You don't know . . ." murmured Dekkard. "I've looked at you . . . not knowing . . ."

"You know now," she replied with a mischievous smile.

"It has to be . . . only the beginning. You need to be courted . . . more."

The smile faded slightly. "Oh?"

"You can't sense me."

Her smile brightened. "Not as an empath, no. But I've worked with you closely for two years. You're honest in everything you do. Mostly. When you're not, it's painfully obvious."

"It's uncomfortable for me," Dekkard admitted. "But I can be noncommittal without lying."

"You're very good at that," Avraal agreed.

"How long have you known . . . that I . . ."

"Since the Findi you agreed to visit Emrelda."

"I never wanted to impose . . ."

"I know." Then she kissed him again.

When she eased her lips from him, she said quietly, "We can't do more. Not now. Not for a while."

It was Dekkard's turn to say, "I know. You're truly a Ritten, and anything more wouldn't . . ." He couldn't come up with the right words . . . or any words.

"Forget about the Ritten part," she replied in a warm

tone. "We have to get through the next weeks without any more entanglements, but it will be easier this way."

Dekkard frowned.

"Because you needed to know that I love you, and you needed to realize that you love me."

Dekkard kissed her a third time, longingly. This time, he was the one to ease away. "Knowing . . . and not . . . is going to be . . . difficult."

"For both of us."

Dekkard found her words reassuring, though he couldn't have said why.

She reached up and touched his cheek. "I'll see you in the morning."

He smiled. "I remember the first time you did that."

Avraal smiled in return. "So do I." Then she turned, picked up the leather case, and headed up the steps.

Dekkard stood there, thinking, especially about the adage of never getting involved with one's security partner. *And the fact that husbands and wives can't ever be paired in security duties.* He didn't even want to think about them not being partners . . . or not being together.

He took a long deep breath and made his way up the steps to his room, which was going to be warm . . . and somehow very empty.

81

Former Minister in Kraffeist Scandal Dies

Former Minister of Public Resources Jhared Kraffeist died suddenly last night from a fall at his home in the fashionable East Quarter of Machtarn. From all reports, Kraffeist tripped at the top of a formal marble staircase and suffered a fatal head injury. He was heading down to the main level to rejoin his wife in the sitting room when the accident occurred . . .

Minister Kraffeist served as Minister of Public Resources at the pleasure of former Premier Johan Grieg. After Premier Grieg's resignation was requested by the Imperador, following the revelations about the improper leasing of the Eshbruk Naval Coal Reserve to a subsidiary of Eastern Ironway, Premier Grieg's successor, Oskaar Ulrich, requested Minister Kraffeist's resignation. Throughout the entire investigation of the leasing scandal, Kraffeist maintained he did nothing knowingly improper . . .

Much of the supporting documentation disappeared prior to the Council investigation . . . few remaining documents show that a standard initial payment was made to the Public Lands account of the Imperial Treasury, and that a M20,000 commission was paid to Kharhan Associates. The only record of any entity known as Kharhan Associates was an account listed at the Machtarn branch of the Imperial Banque of Guldor, an account almost immediately closed with the proceeds of the commission withdrawn in cash and paid to one Amash Kharhan. There is no record of such an individual, according to the Ministry of Security.

Almost immediately after the terms of the lease became public, Eastern Ironway's Director of Logistics, Eduard Graffyn, vanished. Despite an intensive search by the Ministry of Security, no traces of Graffyn or his movements were uncovered. Then, this past Quindi, a legal petition was referred to the High Justiciary containing a sworn and sealed deposition dealing with specified legal "irregularities" involving coal leasing procedures as practiced by the Ministry of Public Resources and petitioning for certain legal remedies. The petitioner is stated to be Eduard Graffyn. The initial hearing date will be tomorrow before the High Justiciary at the fourth bell of morning.

Minister Kraffeist is survived by his wife . . .

Gestirn, 31 Summerend 1266

82

Although it was a while before Dekkard got to sleep, he slept well, but woke early, thoughts about Avraal mixing with concerns about the violence of the demonstration and speculations about the "return" of Eduard Graffyn, otherwise known as Sr. Muller. He washed and dressed quickly, but early as he was, he was definitely surprised to see Avraal already at the table, sipping her café.

She offered him a warm smile. "Good morning." Then the smile faded, and she gestured to the morning edition of *Gestirn*. "You need to read the front-page stories."

Since he always read the newssheet, Dekkard had an uneasy feeling. "That bad?"

"Just read them."

Dekkard read about Kraffeist's death, then said, "That wasn't an accident, not right after Graffyn reappeared. And neither the Premier nor the Imperador had anything to say."

"Why would they?" Her tone was sardonic. "It was just an unfortunate accident."

"How do you think they did it?"

"Frog poison along with an empblast of dizziness or something like it. Someone in the house likely removed the dart . . . That's just a guess." She offered a wry smile. "Keep reading."

Dekkard did. The second front-page story was about the riot at Imperial University, where an "as-yet-unknown number of Security patrollers and demonstrators died." Security Minister Wyath declared that "anyone creating civil disorder and refusing to disperse peacefully risks being shot . . . law-abiding citizens of Guldor should not have their lives endangered by political extremists."

Dekkard quickly riffled through the rest of the

newssheet but saw nothing else that seemed important. He set it back on the side table, poured his café, and sat down across from Avraal. "Good morning, lovely lady."

"Thank you."

Dekkard thought she might have blushed. "I did have an extraordinary afternoon and early evening. Thank you."

"Only when we're alone . . . for now," she said quietly. "Rhosali will be down in minutes."

He nodded. "The demonstration story doesn't mention the New Meritorists or Premier Ulrich. It also doesn't mention Special Tactical Forces."

"Would you expect anything else?"

Dekkard offered a brief sardonic laugh. "There will be more broadsheets with the gory details . . . and they'll be across all Guldor by the end of the week."

"Ulrich will use the demonstration as a justification for even more funding for Security." Avraal paused. "Do you think something will also happen to Graffyn?"

"Not today. As I understand the process, today is only to verify his identity and standing and for the justicers to rule on whether all parts of the petition are admissible."

"How long can the government drag out the hearings?"

Dekkard shrugged. "I don't know. Ingrella could tell us. So could Ivann or Svard. But my gut feeling is that it's a priority procedure that the High Court will rule on fairly quickly."

"Do you two ever talk about anything but the Council and laws?" asked Rhosali as she walked into the staff room.

"We were talking about the demonstration at the university," said Dekkard. "We wondered how many people got shot. The newssheet only said there were numerous fatalities."

"There were a lot of screamers just before noon yesterday."

"The students were protesting that untalented Commercer boys were being given preference over talented worker or artisan students."

Rhosali snorted. "That's a good way to get shot. Commercers don't like anyone questioning their privileges." She took her café and sat beside Avraal. "Just like they don't much care for paying decent wages. The councilor doesn't have marks the way the rich Commercers do, but he and the Ritten pay Hyelda and me more than most pay their maids and cooks."

Dekkard knew that, but was surprised to hear Rhosali say it.

Before any of the three could say more, Hyelda appeared in the archway. "The councilor wants to leave a third earlier than usual."

"Thank you," replied Dekkard, adding to Avraal, "Time to eat and not talk." Then he quickly started in on his croissants.

A sixth later, he was headed to the garage, and he had the Gresynt waiting when Obreduur and Avraal came out of the house.

Once in the steamer, even before Dekkard started down the drive, Obreduur said, "Avraal told me that you two saw part of the demonstration at the university."

"We barely escaped from an omnibus that the demonstrators overturned," said Dekkard, easing the Gresynt forward. "After that, patrollers and Special Tactical Forces took on the rioters. The Tacticals started shooting people. They didn't look concerned about who they shot."

"I can't say I expected a riot at the university. Not so soon, at least."

"Even after the Premier announced that he was restricting the enrollment of anyone who wasn't a Commercer or the child of professionals? And after the administration expelled students involved in the earlier protests, but only students who weren't Commercers? It wasn't stated quite that way, but that's how it turned out."

"Why do you think it happened now, Steffan?"

"Because classes start in two weeks. I'd guess that some students found out that their enrollment had been canceled. I'd also wager that the New Meritorists stirred things up."

Obreduur was silent for several moments, then said, "I'm going to need both of you ready most of the time for the next week or two."

"That bad, sir?" asked Dekkard.

"It just might be. There were protests at all the universities . . . except the Military Institute."

Even Dekkard hadn't expected multiple university demonstrations, but he could see why there wouldn't have been one at the Institute.

"Now . . . I need to write a few more messages."

In short . . . please be quiet.

No one said a word for the remainder of the drive. Council Guards were clearly present outside the Council Office Building and the covered parking, seemingly checking everyone's identity. Once he parked the Gresynt, had his passcard checked twice, and entered the building, Dekkard made a quick detour to post his letter to Naralta, then hurried upstairs.

The stack of letters and petitions on his desk was slightly larger than on any day the week before. As he settled in, he wondered, briefly, if even more people would write because of the university demonstrations. Then he shook his head. The number of letters about the Summerend demonstrations had been relatively few. Why would there be more letters about demonstrations by dissatisfied students? Yet more and more people were getting involved with the demonstrations. *Are they not writing because they don't think the Council will do anything?*

For the moment, and so long as he was an aide to a minority councilor, Dekkard couldn't do any more than he was doing. So he picked up the first letter and began to read. It was a complaint about the government setting waterway lock rates too high.

About a bell later, Obreduur stepped out of his personal office and motioned. "Steffan, if you'd join me."

Dekkard immediately rose, relieved that the councilor sounded—and looked—calm, and entered the office, closing the door.

Obreduur stood beside the desk. "We just got a reply to our request that Treasury Minister Munchyn look into the practice of tariff agents assessing imported art at low rates." He handed the single sheet to Dekkard. "Read it, and then we'll talk."

Dekkard took the letter and began to read. He concentrated on the words.

. . . based on the information provided and the possible impact on both the Imperial Treasury and on corporacions with large volumes of imported goods, the Treasury Minister has begun a thorough review on tariff assessment procedures. Given the technicalities involved and the potential scope of goods that might be involved, such a review may take several months . . .

The rest of the letter was politely perfunctory. It was signed by Johann Smythers, Assistant Minister for Taxation and Tariffs.

Dekkard shook his head and handed the letter back to Obreduur. "Munchyn isn't about to do anything . . . or not any sooner than he has to."

"What do you suggest we tell the Artisans Guild?"

"It doesn't sound like it would hurt for them to file that grievance petition against the Imperial Tariff Commission."

"The guild could also petition the Justiciary to require completion of the study by a date certain," said Obreduur, "but the petition should suggest that, due to the financial repercussions to all involved and the loss of revenue to the Treasury, that date certain should not be later than the first of Fallend."

"Would it hurt to recommend both?" asked Dekkard.

"It can't hurt. It probably won't help. Write a careful

response to Raoul Carlione quoting Smythers's letter, and recommending that the guild file both petitions so that the Ministry of the Treasury is well aware of the problem and the potential costs to the government. Once you've written it, give it to Ivann for review, and then type it up for my signature."

"Yes, sir." Dekkard paused, then said, "Would there be any downside to getting this to the newssheets?"

"If I signed a letter that quoted the assistant minister . . . the downside might not be too bad. I already intended to have Carlos make the suggestion to Raoul. Make sure that the quote is long enough and verbatim." Obreduur handed the Treasury letter back to Dekkard. "I'll be leaving for the councilors' dining room for a meeting at a third after fifth bell. If you'd tell Avraal."

Dekkard left the office, closed the door, and then stopped in front of Avraal's desk. "He's leaving for the councilors' dining room at a third after fifth bell."

She nodded, then gestured at the letter he held.

"A letter from one of Munchyn's assistant ministers. They intend to study the art-tariff mess into oblivion, so that Transoceanic's front organizations can continue to bleed independent artisans. I have to draft the response to the Artisans Guild."

"You only have to draft it," she pointed out.

"I know. He has to sign it and take the blame that he can't do more." *And more pressure if the letter or quotes end up in the newssheets.*

"Some staffers never quite feel that."

"Some councilors don't, either," added Karola tartly. "Unlike ours."

Dekkard couldn't help but smile, if briefly, at Karola's retort.

Dekkard finished the draft response to Carlione and carried in to Macri. "This is about the tariff problem with the Artisans Guild."

"I thought Svard was working with you on that . . ."

"There's no legal issue in the response. It's the political slant, and he wanted you to review it."

Macri nodded and took the draft.

"Any word about that supplemental disguised as a re-allocation?" asked Dekkard.

Macri smiled sardonically. "I figured out what they did, but it's perfectly legal."

"But if the legislation states that Guldoran—"

"It doesn't. It allocates the funding to the Minister of Transportation for purposes of funding urgent iron-way repairs and maintenance. In effect, he can give the funding to whatever ironway he wants. Unless we can get proof . . ."

Dekkard could see that, but . . . "We could still say that the Commercers are avoiding Council scrutiny and that there's no oversight, and that it's a stratagem to avoid complying with the requirements of the Great Charter."

Macri shook his head. "The bill reallocates unspent funds previously authorized. Oversight doesn't apply. I did some quick research. They've been padding funding of ministries who don't spend it all, even when they need it. They relinquish those funds back to the Trea-sury, and they go into the reallocation account."

"Which turns into a Commercer preference fund," finished Dekkard.

"Exactly. But it's complicated enough, with enough legal justification, that it would be politically difficult to get people enraged about it—unlike the Kraffeist Affair."

Dekkard could see that. "You'll explain that to Ob-reduur?"

"That's what I was working on."

"Then I'll let you get on with it. Thank you."

"Steffan . . . your instincts were right."

As he walked back to his desk, Dekkard realized that he should have figured out that such a preferential sub-sidy couldn't have been that easy to expose . . . or shut down.

Over the next two bells, he managed to draft replies to most of the routine correspondence, and, as he had suspected, there were only two letters about the New Meritorist Summerend demonstrations. Of course, it was too early to receive letters about the university demonstrations, but he still doubted there would be many.

Shortly after fifth bell, Obreduur stepped out of the inner office, and Dekkard and Avraal joined him. Dekkard checked his truncheon and gladius, although he'd never actually used it against an attacker, and he didn't know a security isolate who had. Still . . . he could, if it happened to be necessary.

The three encountered only a few handfuls of people in the main corridor and staircase of the Council Office Building and only a single councilor crossing the garden square, too far away to recognize. There were a great many more Council Guards in the Council Hall corridor, but only a few others. And half of them seemed to be messengers.

Avraal murmured, "So far as I can sense, they're all real messengers."

When they reached the dining room, Obreduur said, "Go have a leisurely bite to eat. I'll go straight to the floor from the dining room. The session on supplemental funding will last between two and three bells, and I want you both near when it ends. So don't go back to the office. When the chimes sound the end of the session, please be waiting."

"Yes, sir," both answered.

Obreduur smiled. "You couldn't possibly tell that you two work well together. I'll see you immediately after the session." Then he walked to the dining room entrance.

Dekkard didn't watch Obreduur, but everyone else nearby. Only when the councilor was out of sight did he look at Avraal. "Ready to eat? You barely ate any breakfast at all."

"You know I'm not a breakfast person."

"And you know that I eat that impossible quince paste with two croissants for breakfast." He grinned at her.

She shook her head, then said, "Food would be good."

Because it was so early there was no one ahead of them. Avraal decided on a chicken spinach enchilada with black beans and a side salad. Dekkard went for the mixed empanada plate, but added a small Imperial salad, reflecting that the nomenclature was a clear oxymoron.

As they left the cafeteria line, someone called out, "Avraal, Steffan, come join us."

Dekkard glanced at the hailer, only to discover that it was Laurenz Korriah, seated beside Shaundara Keppel.

"We'd love to." Avraal moved to the table and sat down across from Korriah.

Dekkard took the remaining seat, then had a swallow of his Kuhrs, absently deciding that he preferred Riverfall.

"Do you know what this meeting is about?" asked Korriah.

Dekkard managed not to ask "What meeting?" and answered, "I haven't the faintest idea. The councilor doesn't talk much about meetings with other councilors before he meets with them. Most times, not afterwards, either. What do you think it's about?"

"That beats me," replied Korriah. "He did mention something about a petition before the High Justiciary."

"You haven't heard?" asked Dekkard. "It was in *Gestirn* this morning." He took a bite of the salad.

"I don't read it much. All the stories are half Commercer puff pieces, and everything's presented out of context."

"Do you remember Eduard Graffyn—"

"The missing logistics director for Eastern Ironway?" interrupted Keppel.

"The same one. He's apparently reappeared and petitioned the High Court for remedies to certain leasing practices of the Ministry of Public Resources."

Korriah gave a low whistle. "No wonder the Commercers offed Kraffeist. I knew it had to be them, not that anyone could pin it on them, but I couldn't figure out why it happened now."

"He sent a sealed deposition with the petition—"

"This was in *Gestirn*?" interjected Keppel.

"A paragraph in the story about Kraffeist this morning and a small article in small print the other day," answered Dekkard, managing a bite of a pork empanada with verde sauce. He was definitely hungry.

"That figures." Korriah snorted. "Ulrich is going to want to shut that down. I'll wager your boss is getting together the Landors and Crafters on the Public Resources Committee . . . or some of them."

"That could be," said Avraal, "but some members of the Transportation Committee also weren't happy about being shut out by Ulrich."

Korriah smiled broadly. "This could be very interesting."

"If something doesn't happen to Director Graffyn," said Keppel.

"It doesn't matter," said Korriah cheerfully. "If something happens to Graffyn, the Craft and Landor justicers on the High Court will make that deposition public. If it gets bad enough, after all the riots, the Imperador just might have to ask Ulrich to resign and call elections."

"If the Imperador does that too quickly," suggested Avraal, "he'll be seen as allowing the Commercers to cover it all up."

"But if he doesn't do something . . . ?" countered Keppel.

"He'll be seen as weak and as the Commercers' marionette," said Korriah, "which he is."

"What do you think he should do?" asked Dekkard.

"Me? I'm just a security aide. What do I know?"

"After you get through with the disclaimers," replied Dekkard cheerfully, "I'd like to hear your thoughts."

Korriah offered a booming laugh.

Dekkard waited, using the moments to finish eating another empanada.

Finally, Korriah said, "I'd dismiss Ulrich and ask the Landors and Crafters to form a coalition government."

"A coalition when neither party has a plurality?" asked Ysella. "That's never been done."

"There's a first time for anything," replied Korriah. "Letting the New Meritorists get away with destroying fifteen regional Security offices was a first time, too. Not a good one. Security needs to get tough with the Meritorists, not students."

Dekkard nodded slightly, then took another swallow of Kuhrs. He doubted that "getting tough" with anyone would do more than buy time and enrage more people . . . and that was hardly a trade-off that led to solving problems, although he suspected Korriah might feel that way.

For the next third or so, he let the older Security isolate do most of the talking, noting that no one added much to what had been said, although he knew Avraal certainly could have.

After he and Avraal left the cafeteria, he asked her, "What did you get from that?"

"The Landors wouldn't do things that much differently from the Commercers, and they'd be more inept in doing it. Laurenz is more capable than half their councilors, but he'll never be more than a security aide if he stays with the Landors."

Because the waiting area was crowded, neither he nor Avraal said more than pleasantries while they waited for the Council session to end.

Surprisingly, within moments of the chimes signifying the end of the session, Obreduur was one of the first councilors to leave the Council floor, and he was alone.

"How did the meeting and the session go, sir?" asked Dekkard.

"The meeting went as expected, which was a relief, and the Council session on supplemental funding was . . . interesting."

Neither Dekkard nor Avraal said more as they walked toward the doors leading into the garden square.

Once no one was that close, Obreduur said, "The meeting was a discussion on the Kraffeist Affair. The session was a debate on the supplemental funding levels, especially on the amount allocated to Security. Most of the Landor councilors and all of the Craft councilors insisted on reducing that amount. While she didn't speak on the total funding level, Councilor Bassaana asked if the proposed funding included marks to replace the tonnes of dunnite paid for by the Navy but diverted by the New Meritorists."

"She said that?"

"She did, and Ulrich refused to answer the question. He just talked around it. Bassaana didn't object. She just wanted that information out in the public, and Ulrich clearly didn't. He didn't contradict her, which was smart, because that would have made an even more interesting newssheet story."

"Do you think the Imperador will do anything?"

"Not in the next day or so. He'll wait to see if things calm down. Ulrich definitely wants that as well." Obreduur glanced in Dekkard's direction. "You don't think they will, do you?"

"No, sir. I think the New Meritorists will try to keep people stirred up. What do you think?"

"I'm afraid you're right. I also worry that too much unrest will play into the Commercers' hands. Most people who aren't hurting in one way or another just want things to go on as they used to. The question is how many people are really hurting, how many feel they're hurting, and how many people who aren't laborers and poor sympathize with them."

More than you think and less than enough to force new elections. Dekkard didn't say anything as they walked past the fountain, concentrating. As they neared the Council Office Building, he finally said, "Is there any way to make Security a concern? I mean, they keep shooting women in the back and students, but they can't even keep their own buildings safe."

"That's a good point, Steffan."

"Except that there's no way you can get that message out that bluntly? But what if you asked during the debate how cost-effective it would be to retain Minister Wyath, given that, under his tenure, sixteen Security buildings were destroyed. What assurance does the Council have that the same thing won't happen again after appropriating millions of marks for rebuilding?"

"By the time the rebuilding is finished, one way or another, he won't be Security Minister, but I understand that wouldn't be the point of the question."

"If you ask it, and then see if that could get *Gestirn* to comment that several councilors have questioned Wyath's effectiveness . . . and later bring up the tariff issue . . . that the Treasury Minister seems unwilling to take steps to stem the loss of tariff funds . . ."

Obreduur laughed. "Those are all good points, Steffan, but perhaps a bit obscure to most people and most voters."

"Shooting women in the back isn't obscure," said Avraal. "Perhaps you could ask during the debate what fiscal purpose shooting women in the back served."

Obreduur shook his head. "I'd love to have a few junior councilors with the nerve that you two have. I'll see what can be done . . . feasibly and under the circumstances."

Dekkard had the definite feeling he'd pushed a bit too hard, but Obreduur had asked.

Once they entered the Council Office Building, no one spoke.

As soon as Obreduur entered the office anteroom, Roostof appeared and thrust a brown paper at Obreduur. "It's a broadsheet on the Imperial University riot. It claims that Special Tactical Forces shot over three hundred people and killed a hundred and forty-one, not counting those who were critically wounded and might die. They're everywhere, even in the Council Office Building."

"They can't be everywhere," said Obreduur sardonically. "If the New Meritorists had that kind of resources, there would be more and different kinds of unrest with more participants. They're targeting the Council, the capital, and the larger cities to create that impression with the Council and the Imperador." He paused momentarily. "But if the Premier doesn't handle this correctly, they just might gain a lot more supporters."

"Premier Ulrich isn't looking that good right now," offered Roostof.

"He's still Premier, and Wyath and the Security Ministry want to shoot every New Meritorist on sight."

"And the Council gave them that authority," said Avraal calmly.

"Barely," Obreduur pointed out. "Not a single Craft councilor supported the measure, and neither did eight Landors." After a slight pause, he added, "Let's all think about what we can do . . . that will be effective. I'm open to ideas. Just let me know." Then he entered the inner office.

Dekkard waited until Roostof returned to the legalists' office before he followed Avraal to her desk, where he asked quietly, "Did I push too hard?"

"Not any harder than I did. Remember, if there are new elections, he'll need some Landors. He can't afford to speak too stridently if he wants to have any hope of getting them."

"Was that why you mentioned shooting women in the back?"

"Of course. Noble Landors would never countenance shooting women in the back."

Dekkard tried not to wince at the quiet acid in her voice. "He might use that."

"We'll see."

Dekkard nodded.

Avraal offered a faint smile and added quietly, "You did what you could, Steffan. We'll talk later." Then she sat down and looked at the letters on her desk.

Dekkard walked to his desk and did the same.

83

On Duadi, Dekkard reached the breakfast room only moments before Avraal. He offered her the newssheet.

"Not before café. You can tell me."

Dekkard stood by the side table and read, while she poured her café and sat down. There were two articles of interest in *Gestirn*. The first was about the debate on the supplemental funding legislation, which included Councilor Bassaana's question, followed by the statement that neither the Premier nor the Security Ministry had revealed the New Meritorists had used military dunnite to destroy regional Security buildings.

Dekkard frowned. Bassaana had asked a similar question in the Council the previous week, but none of the newssheets had mentioned it. He couldn't believe that they'd overlooked it, and that meant that they'd chosen not to mention it . . . or that Security had censored it.

Why didn't they censor it this time? Or did Gestirn *slip it in after Security read the newssheet?* He paused. *Or was that allowed in there to give Ulrich some public support for blaming everything on Wyath?*

The second article was at the bottom of the sixth page, and it was very short.

> . . . the High Justiciary has informed this newssheet that it will hold today the initial hearing on a petition by Eduard Graffyn requesting a change in the procedures for granting coal leases on the lands of the Imperium on the grounds that the current procedures are insufficient to prevent misuse, as demonstrated in the instance of the Kraffeist Affair by the material in the deposition submitted to the High Justiciary. Because former Minister Kraffeist died of a fall at his home on Findi, the Court will be unable to summon him for testimony and may request other witnesses, as necessary.

Dekkard nodded slowly. Because the High Justiciary did have the final ruling on whether any restriction on publication of information exceeded the limits of the Great Charter, *Gestirn* would face severe sanctions for not printing the article as written, and if the newssheet didn't print it at all, the editors and owners could end up before the Justiciary. Also, the High Justicers had essentially stated that they had documented testimony about what had happened, which had to make Ulrich uneasy, even if he hadn't been premier at the time.

Dekkard handed the newssheet to Avraal. "I can't summarize. Page one and the bottom of page six." He probably could have summarized, but he wanted to see her reaction.

She accepted the newssheet with a slightly annoyed expression. That vanished as she read the front page, but her lips offered a faintly amused smile as she finished the second article. She handed the newssheet back and said, "I hate to admit that you were right. Ingrella must have something on some of the Landor or Commercer High Justicers, or one of them doesn't like someone."

"It might be both," said Dekkard, setting the newssheet back on the side table and pouring his café. He added croissant and quince paste to his plate and sat down across from her.

"It also looks like Ulrich is setting Wyath up to be dismissed for incompetence."

"Or someone at *Gestirn* is taking a great risk," he replied.

"Do you think anyone would?"

"It's possible that Security's censorship has gone beyond regulating accuracy, and someone at the newssheet could be trying to circumvent that." At Avraal's skeptical expression, he added, "It could happen."

"I'd still wager on Ulrich throwing Wyath into the winterheights."

"That's possible." Dekkard split his first croissant and added the quince paste.

They exchanged pleasantries as they ate, or rather as

Dekkard ate, and Avraal drank two mugs of café, and then both left the staff room, returning their plates and mugs to the kitchen.

When Obreduur entered the Gresynt with Ysella, he said nothing, and neither did Dekkard, who waited until he had the steamer headed north on Imperial Boulevard.

"Sir . . ." asked Dekkard very deferentially, mindful of how much he'd pressed Obreduur the day before, "what do you make of the stories in *Gestirn* this morning?"

"I wasn't surprised at all by the fact that *Gestirn* tried to bury the story on the Graffyn petition where the fewest people possible would read it. The Premier won't be at all happy. On the other hand, I was very surprised that the front-page story ran at all. I suspect that there will be repercussions, and that they won't be trivial."

"What do you think will happen?" asked Ysella.

"If Ulrich and Wyath are smart about it . . . nothing. There are times when it's best not to react, but I don't think they'll be able to resist the urge to do something." After a brief pause, Obreduur added, "Don't ask me what that might be. I'd just be guessing."

"Thank you," said Dekkard, unwilling to press further.

The profusion of Council Guards outside the Council Office Building remained, and Dekkard again had to go through the Security gauntlet to get inside the building and make his way to the office.

As soon as he entered, Karola said, "He wants to see you."

Dekkard's first thought was to worry that he'd done something wrong, but Obreduur just smiled and gestured to a chair, waiting until Dekkard was seated.

"I just received a message from Jens Seigryn. Johan Lamarr has decided, if elections are called in the next year, that he will run for councilor." Obreduur paused, as if waiting.

"I was much more impressed with him than with Haasan Decaro," Dekkard said, "and I would have been even if I hadn't learned what a bastard Decaro is."

"Decaro isn't always a bastard," replied Obreduur, "just when things don't go his way. That's an even bigger problem in politics, because too often matters don't go as we'd prefer."

Dekkard had seen that. He smiled wryly.

"Johan has let Jens know that he'd appreciate any background information he could use to present himself at the district party convention that will select the candidate in the next election. You have a knack for expressing issues in concise political terms . . ."

Sometimes far too directly for polite discussion among councilors, but suited to election campaigning? Dekkard kept his wry smile to himself.

". . . so I thought that you could summarize the issues involved in the art tariffs, since that technique, if not challenged, could be applied by the Commercers to other craft-produced goods."

"Such as watches?"

Obreduur nodded. "Also, and Ivann briefed me on this, you could generalize what the Commercers are doing with the reallocation bill to point out its use as a way to funnel funds to favored corporacions without oversight or public knowledge . . ." For the next sixth of a bell, the councilor pointed out other issues that Dekkard could write up for Lamarr. He concluded the brief meeting by saying, "Handle this first. I'd like to dispatch something this afternoon."

"Yes, sir."

Dekkard returned to his desk and set aside the more routine correspondence to work on the support papers for the Crafters guildmeister, glad to be of assistance, especially given the alternative of Decaro. He still wondered why Decaro had once tried to remove Obreduur.

He'd made a fair amount of progress when Obreduur stepped out of the inner office just a sixth before noon.

"You can escort me to the dining room. Feel free to get something to eat before you return to the office, but be back at the councilors' entrance no later than a third before third bell."

Dekkard and Avraal escorted Obreduur to the dining room, ate quickly at the staff cafeteria, and were back at their desks a good third before first bell, where Dekkard went back to work on drafting the short briefing papers. He actually finished all but one of the drafts just before he and Avraal had to return to the Council Hall to wait for Obreduur.

As they hurried from the office, she said, "You've been especially busy."

"Drafting briefing papers for Johan Lamarr. He's decided to stand for election, if there's one in the next year."

"Good . . . and there will be. I don't see how the Imperador can let Ulrich continue. Since it's an unspoken custom that a party only gets one change of leadership, if he feels he has to ask Ulrich for his resignation, he should call for elections."

"Do you think he will?" asked Dekkard.

"I'd like to think so, but since there's been nothing like this in years, who really knows?"

"Not since the Silent Revolution."

"Women will play a larger part in the next election."

Thinking of Ingrella and Gretna Haarl . . . and Avraal, Dekkard nodded, even as he wondered how much the difference might be.

The two reached the councilors' entrance a little earlier than necessary, but had to stand to the side because all the seats on the benches in the staff waiting area were taken.

Ysella studied those waiting, then murmured, "Nothing out of the usual."

"Good . . . and thank you."

Obreduur wasn't the first off the floor, but he was far from the last, and he joined them immediately. As was his habit, he said nothing until they were out of the Council Hall and walking through the garden square.

"We considered the reallocation bill this afternoon." He followed those words with an amused smile.

"I assume it passed," said Dekkard.

"It did, after the Council agreed to an amendment to the ironway section. Based on what you and Ivann found out, he drafted language that stipulates that no more than half the funds reallocated can be given to one ironway without a subsequent vote by the Council. It was adopted unanimously. Even Ulrich didn't seem displeased, and Councilor Bassaana thanked me. I told her you had been the one to discover what had been buried in the bill."

"I just found out about the supplemental. Ivann discovered how they did it."

"As in most political accomplishments, even minor ones, it takes a number of people to make it work. Some politicians craft the illusion that they're solely responsible for a law or good times, but that kind of illusion is always self-serving, and it's usually destructive over the years."

"I wouldn't have thought of an amendment like that," Dekkard admitted.

"Now you'll know to look for those possibilities," returned Obreduur.

When the three returned to the office, Dekkard finished the last draft briefing paper for Lamarr and took it to Margrit for her to type up, then went back to his desk to draft more responses.

Somehow, Obreduur dealt with everything, including making small revisions to the briefing papers for Lamarr quickly enough that Margrit typed them up in final form and got them posted, and that Dekkard was dispatched to get the Gresynt by a third past fourth bell.

He was just nearing the doors to the Council Office Building on his way to the covered parking when he saw Jaime Minz angling toward him. *This isn't going to be good.* Despite his initial reaction, Dekkard managed a pleasant smile. "Good afternoon."

"The same to you, Steffan." Minz moved so that he stood between Dekkard and the doors. "It looks like a warm afternoon, doesn't it?"

"Warm enough."

"I heard that you ran into some difficulties in Oersynt at the Summerend Festival . . . and that you, shall we say, cut through them."

"We weren't the only ones, according to the newssheets."

"That's true, but your boss survived because you and Avraal are among the best."

"I'm sure there are other teams as good." Dekkard knew Minz hadn't encountered him by chance, especially since he'd left the office later than usual, and later than most staffers.

"Not many. Like I said, you're among the best, but even the best can't always cut their way out, not in uncertain times. So far, that's allowed your boss to do what he does best. He's been extremely effective in increasing the power of the Crafters. He's amazing. One of a kind, you might say. Between him and Haarsfel . . . they've marginalized the Landors. But then, most of the Landors don't really know what they're doing. There's also the fact that there's really only the two of them. If anything happened to either of them . . ." Minz shrugged. "Continuing success in politics requires more than a dynamic duo."

"It seems to me that your boss is quite dynamic, especially with illusions."

"That's because his illusions reflect the hard underlying reality. Sometimes, in fact, those illusions are reality."

"I really have to admire you, Jaime. You're so adroit with pleasantries and casual observations."

"That's the way it is when you understand power, Steffan. Play the game right, like crowns, and you could be here a long time."

"I don't know that I'll ever be as good at games and illusions as you are, Jaime. I'm more comfortable with facts."

"In politics, sometimes facts are illusions. You have to know when that's so."

"I appreciate your advice and information."

"Glad to be of service, Steffan." With another warm and cheerful smile, Minz turned and headed in the direction of the main central staircase.

Dekkard was especially watchful and alert as he made his way to the Gresynt, and he spent a few extra minutes inspecting the steamer before he got in and lit it off. As soon as he had picked up Obreduur and Avraal, and he was on Council Avenue heading for Imperial Boulevard, he said, "Sir . . . you should know that Jaime Minz was waiting in the west entryway for me when I went to get the steamer. He had quite a bit to say . . ." Dekkard went on to relate the conversation as close to word-for-word as he could recall.

"What did you feel he meant to convey from what he said?" asked Obreduur, his voice seeming genuinely curious.

"It seemed to be a veiled threat to Avraal and me as well as to you. He seemed to be hinting that the Craft Party can't take too many more Landor seats . . . and that Ulrich won't be happy if you target Commercer seats . . . but he never mentioned anyone except you and Councilor Haarsfel . . . well, and Avraal and me."

"He's right. We can only win two more from the Landors, before they're down to sixteen, the minimum they're guaranteed by the Great Charter. What else?"

"He let me know that my time using throwing knives was about up."

"He wants you to think that, and you're going to have to be even more careful. With your skill, there will still be times when they'll be useful."

Dekkard would have liked to hope that he wouldn't have to use them again, but he had the feeling that was unlikely, at least in the near future.

After getting everyone back to the house, Dekkard checked both steamers thoroughly.

Just as he was finishing, Avraal entered the garage. "You're taking longer this afternoon."

"I thought a little more care might be useful. I checked it in the covered parking, too."

"I'm going to start carrying the knives all the time, the way you do," Avraal said quietly. "You're not to tell anyone, not even Obreduur. And you'll help me improve drawing and throwing. Starting tonight."

"Because of what Minz said?"

"That's only part of it. In Oersynt, there were two assassins. What if there are two again . . . or three?"

"We might have to worry more about them carrying pistols . . . or using military rifles from a distance."

"Not if they use untraceable intermediaries," she replied. "That seems to be a methodology common to both Commercers and New Meritorists. Besides, it can't hurt."

Only if you miss. He didn't voice the thought, since she probably wouldn't. He decided to change the subject. "What do you think about Johan Lamarr's decision . . . and Decaro?"

"Decaro won't be happy . . . and he's the kind that's dangerous."

"If there are elections . . ."

"When there are elections," she corrected him gently.

". . . the Craft Party District Convention will have to decide between the two of them."

"Such a choice will delight Gretna Haarl," replied Avraal dryly.

"Do you think she's that influential?"

"She might be. I had the feeling that she has much more backing in the Textile Millworkers Guild than Maatsuyt thinks, and in several others as well."

"Who would she back . . . among those two?"

"Lamarr . . . I'd guess. She doesn't care for either, but Lamarr is polite to her. She asked Jens Seigryn why the party couldn't pick a woman."

"You didn't mention this before. What did he say?"

"Something about Gaarlak not being ready for a woman councilor."

Dekkard winced, thinking about how Haarl would have reacted.

"You're right. She snapped back something to the effect that Gaarlak would never be ready if everyone kept saying that it wasn't time."

"They're both right," Dekkard replied. "Women need more visibility, and making her an assistant guildmeister was a first step. So was Ingrella's victory in getting women the same status and pay as male supervisors." He paused. "What do you think?"

"I don't like it, but after visiting Gaarlak, you're probably right." She motioned to the half-open door into the hall. "I need to wash up some. I feel grimy."

"You look wonderful."

"I feel grimy . . . and you have some specks of soot or grease on your forehead."

Dekkard smiled wryly and followed her out of the garage.

84

When Dekkard came down for breakfast on Tridi morning, he immediately noticed there was no edition of *Gestirn* on the side table.

"Hyelda . . . wasn't there an edition of *Gestirn* this morning?"

"No. The newsboy left a note. He said Security had shut down the newssheet."

"They shut it down?" Even though Dekkard had thought it might be possible, that Security had in fact done so still surprised him.

"That's what the newsboy said. That's all I know."

"Are you that surprised?" asked Avraal as she entered

the room. "We both thought yesterday's articles were unusual." She took a mug and poured her café, then sat down.

Dekkard followed her example, then looked across the table at her, seemingly unruffled in her security grays. "I was hoping there was a way out of this mess without more violence."

"Shutting down a newssheet," said Hyelda from where she appeared in the archway to the kitchen, "isn't killing people."

"No," agreed Dekkard. "What's interesting is that *Gestirn* could report on how many students and demonstrators Security killed or wounded, but when the newssheet reports what a councilor says about Security's incompetence or incompetence in the Ministry of Public Resources, it gets shut down."

"You think there's more there?" asked Hyelda.

Avraal laughed softly but ironically.

Hyelda shook her head and returned to the kitchen.

Dekkard took two croissants, then looked mock-mournfully at the tomato jelly, before adding some to his platter.

"You know," said Avraal gently, "most people won't make the connection you did. They probably should, but they won't. Either they don't really care, or they're stupid. The Great Charter limited freedom of the press because a totally free press always becomes a tool of the wealthy and powerful, but a regulated press is only accurate and effective so long as the government isn't perpetually dominated by one party."

"What you're saying is that someone always controls the press."

"That's right. The question is how much government can and should control it."

Dekkard snorted. "That's true of everything."

"Exactly. Too much government control, and you have tyranny. Too little, and you end up with plutocracy, which isn't much different from tyranny if you're poor or working in a manufactory."

Dekkard put dollops of tomato jelly on his croissants, and began to eat them slowly, interspersed with café.

He was still thinking about the *Gestirn* shutdown and what Avraal had said well after breakfast and even when she and Obreduur got into the Gresynt.

Almost immediately, Obreduur said, "I got an unsigned note in a sealed envelope from the newsboy this morning."

"Hyelda mentioned that," said Ysella.

"It said that the night editor was run down by a steam lorry last night when he left work. But all the fingers of his right hand were broken and there was almost no blood on his body despite severe injuries."

"So not only is *Gestirn* shut down by Security," said Dekkard, "but someone killed the night editor, presumably for printing material that Security decided was to be deleted or changed."

"That's a fair assumption, if not provable. Ingrella's going to send a message from her office to Carlos Baartol. He may be able to find out more."

"Is Ritten Obreduur at liberty to say what happened at the hearing yesterday?" asked Ysella.

"The only information that she had last night was that the High Justiciary met in chambers after the public hearing, which took less than a bell and was only procedural."

"What could they do?" asked Dekkard.

"They can deny the Graffyn petition. They can grant it. With either denial or granting the remedy, they can reveal what's in the deposition or not. Ingrella said that there's another option, but it requires the unanimous vote of all six justicers. She said she preferred not to tell me that option because, if even a hint of it surfaced, its effectiveness might be weakened or lost. I did not press her. I have no idea what it might be, but I suspect it must be something embedded in a precedent unused in centuries, but still valid."

Dekkard glanced sideways at Avraal. She gave the smallest nod. But then, with Avraal in the steamer,

Obreduur would not have lied. He just wouldn't have mentioned the option.

That's an indirect way of asking if either of us knows. "I have no idea, sir, but I'm definitely not a legal scholar."

"I don't know, either," said Ysella.

"Then we'll just have to see what the High Justiciary does . . . if anything." Obreduur's voice carried a slight hint of both frustration and resignation.

Dekkard wondered why Ingrella did not want to tell her husband, but that suggested that the two did not see eye-to-eye on the matter . . . and that Ritten Obreduur was a quietly powerful personage in her own right. He also had the feeling that the Commercers were the only ones doing anything, and that everyone else was just maneuvering meaninglessly . . . or at least uselessly. He kept that thought to himself and concentrated on his driving.

When Dekkard pulled up at the entrance to the Council Office Building, there were even more Council Guards visible, particularly around the entrance doors. "Sir, has there been a threat against the Council?"

"I don't know of any, but the Premier hasn't been particularly timely in informing the Craft Party lately."

Avraal stepped out quickly, then said, "I don't sense anything right now."

Obreduur hurried out of the steamer and said, "Be careful, Steffan." Then he closed the door.

Dekkard was exceedingly wary in driving to the covered parking, although he had to show his passcard at the gate to the covered parking, then after he got out of the Gresynt when he parked, and a third time to enter the Council Office Building.

"Has there been any word about the additional guards?" Dekkard asked Karola as soon as he entered the office. "Or why *Gestirn* was shut down by Security?"

"If there is, we haven't been informed," she replied.

Dekkard settled himself behind his desk and looked down at the small pile of letters.

Without his asking, Karola said, "Not all the mail is

here. They're checking all packages and anything suspicious. We got a notice that we'll have an afternoon mail delivery because of the delay."

Ulrich must be really worried, but what did he expect when he ordered Security to shoot anyone who even looks like a New Meritorist? And when they've proved they can get inside Security and into the Council Hall?

Avraal looked up from her desk and said, "Ulrich announced they'll finish dealing with the supplemental appropriation today. The councilor wants to leave for the dining room at a third past fifth bell."

Dekkard nodded, picked up the first letter, and began to read. Another complaint about the failure of the Council to deal with the New Meritorists, and from the phrase "worthless scum," he had the feeling it was either from a Commercer or someone who read the *Tribune* or the *Herald*—its equivalent in Oersynt.

By the time the councilor stepped out of his office, Dekkard had turned over all his draft responses to Margrit and was trying to write a logical set of steps for the Council to deal with the New Meritorists—not that Obreduur had even hinted at something like that. He slipped the notes he'd made into the side drawer and immediately stood.

"The same as yesterday," Obreduur said, as he led the way out of the office.

As the three neared the top of the staircase, Dekkard saw a pair of Council Guards, one posted at each side of the staircase, and another pair at the bottom of the steps. The two at the top looked closely at the three, but said nothing. Dekkard noticed that one looked quite a bit longer at Avraal, which both amused and annoyed him. The guards at the bottom seemed more concerned with those going up.

When they stepped out of the building into the garden courtyard, Dekkard saw more guards posted around the fountain. *Ulrich must have brought in every guard and has them working double time.* Another thought occurred to him. *With all those guards, it's more likely that, if the New Meritorists were to strike somewhere, it won't be here.* But Dekkard had no idea where it might be.

The Treasury Ministry might be a possibility, given that government ran on marks, but so did Machtarn Harbor; or perhaps key sections of the ironways, because trade fueled the wallets of the Commercers. The ironways might even be better, because Dekkard doubted Security watched that much, and Guldoran and the other ironways were very cost-conscious. The Palace and its grounds were a possibility, but that wouldn't actually have much of a real effect, and most of the New Meritorist attacks had resulted in physical and financial damage.

Inside the Council Hall, there might have been a few more guards, but Dekkard didn't see much difference. Once they saw Obreduur to the dining room, they headed for the cafeteria, where they were quickly served, given that almost no staffers were there. After a third or so, more staffers appeared, but none who approached.

"Almost everyone's wary," she said quietly. "They're waiting for something to happen."

"It won't be today. Tomorrow or Findi . . . or later. If the New Meritorists are going to do something, they'll do it when or where it's not expected."

"That's true."

The two lingered longer in the staff cafeteria than they usually did, but finally made their way to the staff waiting area. Unexpectedly, the chimes signifying adjournment rang at just a few minutes past second bell, and Obreduur was among the first to leave the floor and enter the main corridor. Dekkard and Ysella immediately met him and escorted him toward the courtyard.

"What happened?" Dekkard asked, but only after the three were in the square.

"The supplemental passed, mostly as proposed. Several minor amendments passed by unanimous consent. One didn't, and required a vote. As chairman of the Transportation Committee, Councilor Maastach offered an amendment to add funds to the Ministry of Transportation budget."

"Because you cut what Guldoran Ironway got under the reallocation bill?"

"He didn't say, but Saandaar Vonauer immediately supported it."

"Since he's the Landor floor leader," replied Dekkard, "that's not surprising. I wonder what Ulrich promised him." *To keep his head, possibly?* Except Ulrich would never have been that direct.

"It didn't matter. The same number of councilors as those who supported the ironway amendment voted to defeat Maastach's proposed amendment. He seemed surprised that it turned out that way." Obreduur smiled.

"That was all?"

The councilor nodded, then added, "Just after Ulrich adjourned for the day, he was handed a sheet by the record clerk. Whatever it was, he didn't like it, because he hurried back to his floor office."

Roostof was waiting for the three in the outer office. So was everyone else. Roostof held what appeared to be another broadsheet, which he immediately extended to Obreduur. "Word is that they printed thousands of these and that they're everywhere."

After Obreduur finished reading it, he laid it on Karola's desk faceup. He just motioned to it and stepped back. He didn't say a word.

Dekkard read the heading of the broadsheet and the bolded heads below.

THE GREAT COVER-UP

No Newssheets?
Editor Murdered, Hand Mangled, for Printing Facts?
The Commercers Can't Stand the Truth.
Commercers Cover Up Corruption, Murders, and Lies.
DON'T LET THEM! DEMAND THE TRUTH!

After everyone had read the broadsheet, since no one else said anything, but just looked at each other,

Dekkard said, "That's the first time they've mentioned a political party."

"It might be because they realize they don't have enough followers for a revolution," replied Obreduur. "By targeting the Commerce Party, it puts pressure on the Imperador not to give in to what he and the Commercers see as the mob. It also makes the Commercers more determined not to give in. That means that Ulrich and Security will crack down harder. That could turn more people against Security and the Commercers."

"Can't Ulrich see that?" asked Dekkard.

"I said it *could*. It also will turn people against the New Meritorists. Which people get more upset after the next round of suppression and killings will decide what happens."

"Do you think they'll do that?" asked Anna worriedly.

"I'm afraid it's more likely than not," replied Obreduur.

"Is there anything we can do?" pressed Dekkard.

"The Council, as it presently exists, won't oppose the Premier. The Imperador can only request the Premier resign or call for elections. I'm not about to guess at what he will do or when he might. I would suggest staying a good distance from any demonstrations." Obreduur picked up the broadsheet and handed it to Karola. "Add that to the file."

Then he turned and entered his office.

"Everyone, back to work," said Macri quietly.

Dekkard walked back to his desk and sat down, then looked at the new stack of letters, obviously from the additional mail delivery. He opened the first one.

85

The remainder of Tridi afternoon, the evening, and the night were quiet. Even knife-throwing practice was subdued, perhaps because Nellara was getting more consistent with her releases, and her knives were sticking deeper into the target, and those modest achievements meant there were fewer impatient sighs.

Dekkard slept adequately and woke abruptly on Furdi morning, although he couldn't have said why. As soon as he was on his feet, he began to worry about what might happen over the next few days, but he forced himself to concentrate on preparing for the day. Before that long he was headed down to breakfast. He did smile at the thought that Avraal would join him before long—if she wasn't already in the staff room.

Besides Hyelda, he was the first, and he looked to the side table. The newssheet set there was smaller than *Gestirn,* and when Dekkard picked it up he got faint smudges of ink on his fingers. He looked at the masthead—*The Machtarn Tribune.*

"Still no *Gestirn,* Hyelda?" he called into the kitchen.

"Won't be for a while, the newsboy said. The Ritten said to get the other one until *Gestirn* comes back."

"Thank you." While he was certainly not supportive of the political and economic views that pervaded every page of the *Tribune,* he supposed any newssheet was better than none.

He began to read.

Security Ministry Works to Restore Order

Over the past week, all across Guldor, hardworking Security agents have arrested and incarcerated over a thousand individuals belonging to the New Meritorists, the group behind the violent protests that have rocked all the major cities, particularly Machtarn. While Special Tactical Forces put down the disturbance earlier this week at Imperial University, many temporarily eluded government forces. "These so-called New Meritorists are nothing more than political terrorists, murderers, and thugs bent on destroying all we hold dear," declared Security Minister Lukkyn Wyath. "We will root out every last one of them, however long it takes."

One of the key leads in finding such terrorists is a book entitled *MANIFESTO OF THE NEW MERITORISTS.* Anyone who knows of someone possessing this volume is encouraged to report them to a Security agent, but not to a civic patroller. Civic patrollers are tasked with maintaining law in their localities, while Security agents deal with crimes against the Imperium . . .

Being arrested and incarcerated for merely having a book? Dekkard winced as he lowered the newssheet. *But you were the one who suggested that to Minz.* Even so, he hadn't expected that Security would arrest and incarcerate anyone who merely had the book.

The other front-page story was about the passage of the supplemental-funding bill, quoting Premier Ulrich as saying, "It's a good funding measure despite some Craft amendments that will make improving the ironways more difficult and cumbersome." The story also highlighted the need for significant funding to rebuild Security buildings damaged or destroyed by the New Meritorists. It did not mention where the dunnite had come from, Dekkard noticed. He scanned the rest of the newssheet and replaced it on the table, then poured his café and took his croissants and some tomato jelly before sitting down.

He didn't start eating, but just sipped his café, listening for the sound of Avraal's boots on the tiles of the back hall floor. When she stepped into the staff room in her grays he looked up and said, "I've always admired that even in security grays you look incredibly stylish."

For just an instant, she looked surprised. At least, Dekkard thought she did. Then she smiled warmly. "You know . . . I've always thought the same of you . . . but I never dared say it."

That stunned Dekkard, so much so that he didn't know what to say.

"I also love that about you, when you look surprised at a compliment, because I've never liked people who just accept compliments as their due, or ignore them."

There's so much I love about you. But he only said, "I can't tell you how much I appreciate both the compliment and what else you said."

Avraal walked around the table, stopped just behind his chair, bent down, and kissed him lightly on the cheek. Then she straightened. "I still need my café. The newssheet is the *Tribune,* isn't it?"

Dekkard managed to reply without too much of a delay. "It is."

"What's in it? I hate reading it." Avraal poured her café and seated herself across from Dekkard.

"A story about how Wyath is arresting and incarcerating anyone found reading the New Meritorist manifesto and one where Ulrich said the supplemental was good legislation despite the Craft amendment that will hamper improving ironway maintenance."

"That shouldn't surprise you."

"It didn't. How did you sleep last night?"

"I slept well, although I did have a dream about trying to throw a knife and not being able to draw it fast enough."

"You've only been at this for a month or so. You're doing remarkably well. Much better than I did at first."

Avraal smiled. "It could be that I've had a better instructor."

"Well . . . at least one far more interested in your success."

Before Avraal could reply, Rhosali hurried into the staff room. "What sort of success?"

"Knife-throwing," replied Avraal.

Rhosali shook her head. "All you two talk about is work . . . and that's all you do."

"We're just driven, boring security aides," replied Dekkard mournfully.

"Pfui!" replied the maid. "You're not boring. Anyone who protects the councilor and has to kill people isn't boring."

"You see right through us," said Dekkard.

Rhosali looked at Avraal. "What happened to him this morning?"

"He read the *Tribune*."

"Still no *Gestirn*?"

"There's no word on how long Security will keep it shut down."

"There are times when I almost agree with those Meritorists," replied Rhosali.

"Do you think many people feel that way?"

"About Security . . . the agents and the STF . . . lots of folks do." The maid put a croissant on her plate. "Lots of folks."

After that, the conversation died away, and before all that long, Dekkard drove the Gresynt out of the garage and down to the portico, where he waited for Avraal and Obreduur.

After driving onto Altarama, he waited for several blocks before asking, "Did you read the story in the *Tribune* about arresting people because of what books they had in their houses?"

"Unfortunately," replied Obreduur. "I thought even Wyath wouldn't go that far, but he's using some of the authorizations in the emergency legislation dealing with the New Meritorists in rather . . . creative ways. Ingrella's already working on that, but fixing ill-thought law through the Justiciary takes forever. Now . . . if you'll excuse me . . ."

"Yes, sir." Dekkard could tell that Obreduur was again writing something.

As the Gresynt neared Council Avenue, Dekkard could see, several blocks ahead, that the Square of Heroes was filled with people, certainly hundreds if not even thousands. *Another New Meritorist demonstration?*

Dekkard didn't see any signs, and the New Meritorists had always carried them to demonstrations, but he couldn't look for very long as he turned onto Council Avenue. "Sir, there appears to be a demonstration at the Square of Heroes."

"The idiots will get shot," said Obreduur. "Ulrich and Wyath are looking for a way to show that they're in control."

When Dekkard pulled up in front of the Council Office Building, the number of guards appeared to be the same as it had been for the last week, and, after he dropped off Avraal and the councilor, he again had to offer his passcard to guards three times before he got into the building and took the back stairs. What also hadn't changed was that letters and petitions were waiting.

"The Council won't be in session today," Avraal said.

"Convenient for Ulrich. That way no councilor can ask embarrassing questions."

"We might also get through the letters and petitions on our desks."

Dekkard looked down at the stack before him. "If nothing else happens. But with that demonstration in front of the Palace, I wouldn't wager on it."

"Word won't get to us until midafternoon," predicted Karola.

Dekkard didn't argue, and that was for the best, because he spent almost all of his time in the morning and early afternoon writing out draft responses. He did notice that there were a few more messengers in the office.

That changed just before second bell, right after another messenger delivered something to Karola and she carried it in to Obreduur. Within minutes, she returned and went to the door of the side office. "The councilor wants a word with everyone."

In moments, Raynaad, Roostof, Macri, Anna, and

Margrit were all in the anteroom, just as Obreduur stepped out of his office.

"As most of you know, there was a demonstration this morning outside the Palace grounds. The number of demonstrators isn't known exactly, but appears to have been between three and five thousand. They refused to disperse, according to Security Minister Wyath. So he called in the Special Tactical Forces. When the demonstrators still refused to disperse, the STF opened fire. Casualties among the protestors number in the hundreds. The Premier will address the Council about this at fifth bell tomorrow morning." Obreduur paused, then added, "I suggest all of you be very careful in where you go in the next few days."

"The STFs shot people because they wouldn't leave?" asked Raynaad.

"I don't know any more than I told you," replied Obreduur. "I'll let you know when I do."

And that won't be soon. Dekkard kept that thought to himself as he studied the others, noting that while most looked concerned, Roostof appeared grimly resigned, and Margrit looked appalled.

Obreduur inclined his head, then motioned for Karola to join him as he reentered his private office. Everyone else returned to their desks, except for Dekkard and Avraal, who had never left theirs.

"He's worried, isn't he?" asked Dekkard.

"He is. Wouldn't you be?"

Dekkard nodded. "So am I, but the only thing I can do is finish drafting letters so that I'm ready if he needs something." Obreduur would; Dekkard just didn't know what it might be . . . or when.

Although Dekkard looked up every time a messenger appeared, Obreduur didn't ask for anything for the rest of the workday, except for Dekkard to get the Gresynt.

The councilor was silent and thoughtful, not reading or writing the entire time, and Dekkard couldn't remember when that had last occurred. After leaving Avraal and Obreduur at the portico, Dekkard forced himself to go over both Gresynts methodically. Ingrella's steamer was almost as warm as the councilor's, suggesting that she'd just returned as well.

When Dekkard finished wiping down the Gresynts and turned to leave the garage, he looked up to find Avraal standing just inside the door. "I'm sorry. I didn't hear you."

"That's all right. I've only been here a few minutes. I need you to read something." She held up what looked to be a note.

"Something from Emrelda?"

"It just arrived. It's more than something."

Dekkard heard the concern in her voice and took two quick steps to join her. She handed him the note, but retained the messenger envelope. Dekkard immediately read the note.

Avraal—

You should know this. I'm on extended duty at the station because of the demonstrations at the Palace. I won't be back at the house until late evening, if then.

The Patrollers Benevolent Society of Machtarn has learned that none of the demonstrators in front of the Palace this morning were armed. Because several members of the PBSM also discovered that the Special Tactical Forces planted weapons among the bodies, the PBSM just informed the Minister of Security, the Premier, and the Imperador, in writing, that if Security agents or Special Tactical Forces continue to shoot civilians, all patrollers will feel free to use their weapons to protect those civilians, even if it causes casualties among the STF and agents.

I'll do the same, if I have to.

The signature was Emrelda's.

Dekkard read it twice, just to make sure he'd read it correctly. "I almost don't believe it . . . except she said more than once that the regular patrollers hate the agents and the STF."

"She's said that for several years. You come with me."
She motioned to Dekkard, then turned and made her
way to the study, where both Ingrella and the councilor
sat. They both looked up in surprise.

"From your expression, you have something of import," said Obreduur.

Avraal handed him the note.

Obreduur read it, then handed it to Ingrella. When
she finished, she returned it to Avraal, then nodded to
her husband.

Obreduur cleared his throat. "If indeed that happens,
it may be what it takes to force the Imperador to request
Ulrich's immediate resignation as premier and to call
for new elections. If he doesn't, there will be even more
blood on the streets . . ."

"He'll need to request the Craft Party to recommend
a temporary premier as well," said Ingrella. "Otherwise,
nothing will change."

"The Craft Party, because it has the next most seats?"
asked Dekkard. "Can he do that?"

"He can," replied Ingrella in the voice of legal authority. "It's only happened three times since Laureous the
Great, but the precedent is there."

"I'm not exactly holding my breath," said Obreduur
dryly.

"Other circumstances may affect the Imperador's decision as well," said Ingrella.

Obreduur raised his eyebrows.

"Axel," said Ingrella, with a hint of exasperation,
"we've done what we can. Now all we can do is wait."
She looked to Avraal and Dekkard. "If I'm not mistaken,
tomorrow will be a day of great rhetoric and public
gnashing of teeth. Depending on what the Imperador
does, Findi could either be a time of stunned quiet or
fighting in the streets. Either way, you two need to
spend time together. Enjoy dinner, and try not to talk too
much about what you can't control."

Obreduur smiled wryly. "When she talks that way . . .
it's a good time to listen."

Avraal reached out and took Dekkard's hand. "It's time for us to leave and do what she suggested." She paused, then added, "But we're still having throwing practice after dinner."

"I'll tell Nellara and Gustoff," said Ingrella with a smile.

"Thank you."

"It will keep them from worrying, and it will reinforce the point that you can't just sit around and wait when you don't know what's about to happen. It's much better to do something constructive," declared Ingrella cheerfully.

Once Dekkard and Avraal were away from the study, she added, "We're going to talk."

Dekkard grinned amiably. "That's spending time together."

Avraal gave the smallest of headshakes as she led the way out to the covered portico. There, she stopped.

"Where do you want to begin?" Dekkard asked deferentially.

"I don't know. Anything could happen, but . . . Ingrella is so calm. I don't see how she can be. Maybe the worst is over."

Dekkard shook his head. "Even if the Imperador does request Ulrich's resignation as premier and from the Council, and calls for elections, that doesn't mean that everything's solved. If the new elections don't shift power from the Commercers and Landors, everything will be right where it is . . . if not worse, because the Commercers will believe that it wasn't their positions as a party that caused the problems, but the incompetence of Grieg and Ulrich. They may tone things down for a bit, but the New Meritorists aren't going away, and there will be more and more violence before long."

"We have a chance. I know we do."

"We do," agreed Dekkard, "but winning itself won't change anything. Even if the Craft Party wins the most seats, even if we win thirty seats . . . it's still going to be a mess. The New Meritorists aren't going away just because we won. Something will have to be done about Security agents and the STF . . . and about tax and tariff laws. I doubt if we really have enough experienced people to head all the ministries, either, although Ingrella probably can help enormously just because of who she knows. Also, even if they're not in the majority, the Commercers will oppose everything that will make Guldor a better place for more people than just the well-off. They'll use their private operatives wherever they can. You think we've had problems now . . ." He shook his head.

Avraal smiled sadly. "You're right, but we have to try."

"We are trying, remember?"

She stepped forward and put her arms around him.

86

On Quindi morning, Dekkard woke early, washed and dressed quickly, and hurried down to see what had been reported in *The Machtarn Tribune*.

Palace Guards, Security Forces Attacked

Early Furdi morning, thousands of ill-clad and obstreperous demonstrators filled the Square of Heroes across from the Imperial Palace. Shouting incoherent slogans and platitudes, workers who abandoned their workplace and other indigents demonstrated in support of overthrowing the Great Charter and instituting mob rule and personality politics. They then mocked and reviled the outnumbered Palace Guards, who were vainly trying to maintain order . . .

The protestors, demonstrating against the government's efforts to find and incarcerate the New Meritorist criminals responsible for destroying more than fifteen Security buildings across Guldor, refused repeated requests to disperse. After those refusals, the demonstrators, some with firearms, attempted to attack the Palace Guards, who had been reinforced by several detachments of the Security Special Tactical Forces. The STF was forced to open fire to protect the Palace Guards and the Palace. Despite the attempts at moderation by the Palace Guards and STF, the demonstrators managed to inflict wounds or otherwise injure thirty-one guards and STF security agents. None appeared to be serious.

None of them serious? Dekkard frowned. All the demonstrations previously set up by the New Meritorists had resulted in casualties and fatalities to guards and patrollers. Then he recalled Emrelda's note . . . and the fact she'd said that the demonstrators had been unarmed. And he'd seen no signs or placards. Had the demonstration been a stratagem to sacrifice people, if unwittingly, to show the brutality of Security, and, secondarily, of the Commercer-dominated government? He continued reading.

Casualty figures for the demonstrators remain speculative because many who were injured fled. More than three hundred died in the Square . . .

The Premier and the Imperador are scheduled to meet this morning to discuss the demonstration and other recent events . . .

Dekkard shook his head as he finished the article, then paused when he heard Avraal's boots on the back stairs, although he barely heard her steps, given how light on her feet she was. He waited until she'd almost finished her first mug of café before he handed the newssheet to Avraal.

She took it without a word.

He poured his café and put two croissants on his plate, along with the tomato jelly he wished were quince paste or even guava jelly, then sat down and took a sip of café. At first he thought the café was a touch more bitter than usual, but it didn't seem that way after a second sip. *Your imagination . . . because of the article?*

Avraal finished reading the newssheet and carefully replaced it on the side table. Then she took several more sips of café. She ignored the croissants. Finally, she said, "There's not a word about the regular patrollers refusing to back Security."

"I noticed that. Would the newssheets know that? According to Emrelda, the society only wrote the Minister of Security, the Premier, and the Imperador. None of them would want it made public that the STF detachment planted weapons."

"The *Tribune* might know that. I wouldn't put it past them not to print those details," replied Avraal.

"We'll just have to see if we can find out more once we get to the office."

"From what Ingrella said last night, we're not going to find out much of anything today." Avraal took a healthy swallow of café. She did not reach for a croissant.

"What do you think will come out of the meeting between the Imperador and Ulrich?" asked Dekkard.

"Who knows," she replied tiredly. "The Imperador still might back Ulrich, the way things have been going."

"You're worried. More than a little."

"The future of Guldor just might depend on what the Imperador does, and I'm not sure I trust him to do the right thing."

"He did ask for Grieg's resignation."

"That was just a cover-up."

"People weren't getting shot right in front of the Palace then," Dekkard pointed out. "Also, if there's a revolution or if Ulrich remains in power, either way, it's bad for the Imperador. In the first case, the New Meritorists would do away with him. In the second, he'd become even less important."

"That doesn't mean he'll do the right thing."

Dekkard understood that. "I don't know that there's much we can do."

"I'm not sure there's much anyone can do . . . except the Imperador. That's why I'm worried." Avraal forced a smile. "I'm spoiling your breakfast. Go eat your croissants. You'll need them the way things are looking."

Dekkard smiled back. "I'll do my best, even with tomato jelly."

She shook her head, then smiled again, if only briefly.

Dekkard slowly ate his croissants, then finished his café. "I'm going to get ready."

"I'll be there shortly."

After Dekkard took his plate and mug to the kitchen, when he left the staff room, he stepped to one side as Rhosali approached.

"You're up early. What happened?"

"Besides yesterday's massacre of unarmed people at Heroes Square? Or that the *Tribune* didn't mention that they were unarmed? Not too much."

"What will happen now?" asked Rhosali.

Dekkard shrugged. "We don't know. We don't even know when we'll find out. It's like everything's stopped until the Premier and Imperador meet."

"Won't there be more demonstrations?"

"I'd be surprised if there were one today. There hasn't been the killing of so many protestors in decades, if not longer. I'm guessing there's a bit of shock. But that will only last a little while."

"Last Findi, my uncle said things could get worse."

"He's right. They could. They could also get better, but that will take time, and people are impatient."

Rhosali frowned, then said, "Uncle said that, too." Then she added, "You look like you're in a hurry. I'd better not keep you." With that she stepped past Dekkard and into the staff room.

Dekkard finished getting ready, and then lit off the Gresynt, waited for a bit, and eased it down the drive to the portico, where he waited almost a third of a bell for Obreduur and Avraal.

The drive to the Council Office Building was quiet, with no signs of protestors near the Square of Heroes, the Palace, or the Council, although, after dropping Obreduur and Avraal off, Dekkard did have to go through three checks of his passcard before he was inside the building. He didn't see anyone he knew well in the corridors, either.

The stack of letters and petitions waiting on his desk was about the same, which meant he'd likely be able to finish his draft responses by noon.

He'd been working on responses for a little more than a bell when Obreduur came out of this inner office. "Craft Floor Leader Haarsfel has called a closed caucus of all the Craft Party councilors at fifth bell in the Waterways Committee Chamber. I'll need both of you to escort me there and wait."

"Do you know what it's about, sir?" asked Dekkard.

"Haarsfel didn't say. I imagine it's to discuss the current situation, and the options open to the Craft Party, if there are any, given what was in the note I read last night. I'd like to leave at a third before the bell." Obreduur stepped back into his office and closed the door.

By the time Dekkard and Avraal left their desks to escort Obreduur to the Waterways Committee Chamber, Dekkard judged he was more than two-thirds of the way through the letters, there being no petitions in the stack.

When they passed the floor entrance and neared the committee chamber, Dekkard saw Councilor Hasheem standing near the door, talking to Councilor Zerlyon. Near them, but not close enough to overhear, were Erleen Orlov, who still clearly didn't have a partner, and Zerlyon's two security aides, Chavyona Leiugan and Tullyt Kamryn.

Obreduur moved to join the other two councilors, while Dekkard and Avraal moved toward the three aides.

"We ought to move back a bit," suggested Avraal.

"Since you two are here," said Leiugan with a light tone, "do you think the rest of us could leave?"

"If you want to hand over your pay for the day, Chavyona," returned Dekkard dryly.

Kamryn and Orlov both grinned.

"How do you put up with him?" teased Leiugan.

"She doesn't," countered Dekkard. "I just do whatever she tells me."

All five aides stopped talking as three more Craft councilors neared—Haarsfel, Mardosh, and Safaell.

Obreduur turned. "Avraal, Steffan . . . if you'd check the chamber. If there are clerks inside, have them leave."

Avraal led the way, but slowed as she neared the chamber door. "There are two inside. I don't sense anything unusual."

Dekkard moved ahead, opening the door and stepping inside the committee room set up in the same way as all the large committee rooms, with a long desk on a raised dais extending almost the width of the chamber and places for up to nine councilors.

The two clerks at the rear corner desks looked up.

"It's time for the Craft Party caucus," Dekkard said. "You'll have to leave until it's over."

"This is our office," protested one.

"Not for the next bell or so," said Dekkard cheerfully.

Avraal must have projected something, Dekkard felt, because the older clerk stood and said, "If we must. It's most irregular."

"Now, please," said Dekkard firmly.

In moments, the two clerks were out, and Dekkard and Ysella moved to just outside the double doors. "The committee chamber is empty, sir."

"Thank you," replied Obreduur, moving toward the pair. "Since Floor Leader Haarsfel has no security aides, I'm going to have to ask you two to guard the door. Once everyone is here, you're not to allow anyone to enter, until either Councilor Haarsfel or I tell you otherwise. I'll stay here with you until it's time to start."

Perhaps two minutes before fifth bell, Councilor Waarfel arrived, the last of the twenty-three Craft councilors. Obreduur followed Waarfel into the committee room, closing the door as he did.

Dekkard glanced to the far side of the corridor where more than thirty Craft security aides stood or milled around. He couldn't help smiling slightly. They were the far greater deterrent to interruption. He and Avraal were largely symbolic. "Those two clerks were rather annoyed." His eyes scanned the main corridor. "They must not be asked to leave very often."

"Almost never. Haarsfel doesn't believe in caucusing except when it's absolutely necessary, and usually he can use the main Council chamber."

"If he can't now," said Dekkard, "then the Commerce Party must be using it, and that means something happened at Ulrich's meeting with the Imperador."

"Don't get your hopes up," said Avraal dryly. "It could be that the Imperador just called for a replacement of Ulrich without elections. Despite what you said last night, I wouldn't put it past Ulrich to have weaseled that out of Laureous."

"If that's the case, Machtarn is going to be a very unsettled city for some time," predicted Dekkard.

In the quiet that followed, Dekkard tried to discern what might be going on in the committee chamber, but the doors and walls were thick enough and well-insulated enough that he could hear nothing. "Can you sense anything?"

"Through those doors? Hardly."

Each minute that passed felt like a sixth or third to Dekkard, even as he wondered what had happened between the Imperador and the Premier . . . and how that would spool out for the Craft Party, the Council, and, indeed, all of Guldor. *And how the New Meritorists will respond to whatever has happened . . . and will occur.*

Surprisingly to Dekkard, little more than a third of a bell had passed when one of the doors eased open slightly and Obreduur stood there. "Most of the councilors will be leaving. Open the doors and step just inside and wait there."

Much as Dekkard wanted to ask what had happened, he didn't, especially given the seriousness in Obreduur's voice. Instead, he and Avraal did exactly as ordered.

Dekkard watched as two or three small groups of councilors briefly formed and then began to disperse. He studied each councilor who passed as he or she left. From what he could see, none of them appeared depressed, although several definitely appeared worried. Finally, the chamber was empty, except for Haarsfel and Obreduur, who then walked to where Dekkard and Avraal waited.

"Avraal . . . Steffan . . . you two will be accompanying us to the Palace of the Imperador. He officially requested Ulrich's resignation as premier and from the Council. He also dissolved the Council, called for new elections, and requested that the Craft Party choose an interim premier."

"Your councilor is the choice of the Craft Party," added Haarsfel. "It's only temporary, unless we can win more seats and allies in the election."

"When is the election?" asked Dekkard.

"The Imperador sets the dates, within the limits of the Great Charter," replied Obreduur. "No less than two weeks, no more than four, and always on a Findi. He chose two weeks from tomorrow."

"He's hoping that will minimize Commercer losses," added Haarsfel.

While he managed not to blurt anything incoherent, Dekkard found himself having trouble grasping the fact that Obreduur was Premier, even just temporary acting Premier.

"I'll fill you both in on the details later. They're very interesting." A certain wry humor infused Obreduur's words.

"Very interesting indeed," added Haarsfel. "We need to go to the east entrance to the Council Hall. We'll be taking one of the Council limousines to the Palace."

"What about the Security Ministry?" asked Avraal.

"Once accepted by the Imperador, even an acting premier can ask for resignations," declared Haarsfel.

"Any appointments as heads of ministries are only temporary, however, until the next government takes office. It's not usually even worth doing. We need to get moving." He looked to Avraal. "You two lead the way."

Dekkard let Avraal set the pace, which was a fast but not rushed walk, while she concentrated on sensing and he looked ahead for anyone who appeared out of place. He didn't like the fact that Wyath remained Security Minister for the present, and he hoped that they could get to the Palace before Wyath found out.

As Haarsfel had promised, a limousine—a black Gresynt with the Council insignia on the front hood—was waiting at the east entrance to the Council Hall. A Council Guard stood beside the steamer and opened the middle and rear doors as the four approached, then seated himself in front beside the driver once Dekkard, Avraal, and the two councilors were seated.

Dekkard glanced to Avraal as the limousine turned onto Council Avenue.

"Nothing out of the ordinary . . . yet," she said in a low voice.

Dekkard almost smiled at the incongruity of her words, although she had been referring to security matters. Going to the Palace in a Council limousine, possibly with the first Craft premier of Guldor in centuries, was certainly out of the ordinary.

In the rear seat, Haarsfel cleared his throat, then said, "You two will stay with us when we enter the Palace until the moment when we're ushered in to see the Imperador. You will wait there until we return."

"Thank you for making that clear to Avraal and Steffan," said Obreduur quickly.

The driver turned the limousine onto Imperial Boulevard, heading north, then three blocks later turned right onto the south side of the Square of Heroes. As the driver made his way around the square toward the formal entrance to the Palace of the Imperador opposite the middle of the square on the north side, Dekkard looked closely. The Square of Heroes was empty, the oval of white marble pillars that surrounded the statue of Laureous the Great on his charger somehow looking lonely in the hazy midday sunlight. Then Dekkard saw almost a score of men and women and two small steam lorries—and a handful of Palace Guards. It took him a moment to figure out that they were cleaning up the square—especially the bloodstains—after the previous day's carnage.

Only a day ago? That in itself seemed surreal, that just the day before Special Tactical Forces had been shooting unarmed protestors right in front of the Palace and now no one was there but a cleaning crew.

The driver slowed as he turned in to the entrance drive to the Palace, coming to a complete stop just before the shimmering golden gates—polished brass, Dekkard knew—which stood open, but were guarded by four Palace Guards in their red-and-gold uniforms.

"The Premier-select to see the Imperador at His Excellency's request," announced the driver.

"He's expected. Use the east portico entrance."

"Thank you." The driver eased the limousine through the open gates and up the white stone drive that stretched more than a third of a mille before it reached the Palace proper, a three-level structure of pale golden marble that stretched some three hundred yards end to end. Small oval gardens surrounded by elaborate topiary hedges took up about half the space of the slope, the rest being a meticulously groomed lawn with stone paths and carefully groomed low trees, their size controlled so as not to diminish the visual impact of the Palace as seen from the city. The east wing of the Palace was where the Imperador conducted Imperial business, while the center portico was the entry for Imperial functions, and the west portico was used for personal and familial purposes. A few minutes later, the limousine glided to a stop under the east portico, where a Palace Guard stepped forward and opened the limousine doors. After the four exited the steamer, a naval lieutenant who looked barely older than Dekkard stepped forward.

"Councilors, the Imperador is expecting you. If you'd come with me."

This time, Avraal and Dekkard trailed Haarsfel and Obreduur as they went through the polished bronze doors and into a broad entry hall floored in white marble edged with green marble shot with golden lines. The walls were lined with paintings, which, at a glance, depicted scenes from the history of the Imperium of Gold. One picture portrayed a naval battle involving warships under full sail. Dekkard suspected it was from the Great Trade War of 988. Another depicted the capitulation of Jaykarh, which had occurred far earlier.

As he and Avraal followed the lieutenant and the councilors along the hall, Dekkard turned his concentration to those few in that part of the Palace—a woman carrying a leather case turning in to a smaller side hall, an older man standing in an alcove talking to a Navy captain, and two men with a ladder working on a bronze wall lamp.

The lieutenant turned right along an equally broad corridor, walked some fifteen yards, then stopped short of a door with a single, if large and muscular, Palace Guard beside it. "The Premier-select to see His Excellency."

"One moment, please." The guard stepped inside the door and shut it, only to reappear almost instantly. "Councilors, you may enter."

As the door opened and the two councilors began to enter, Dekkard saw Avraal concentrating, not that it would have been that noticeable to most people. After the door closed, she gave the smallest nod to Dekkard and the two moved to the side, next to the lieutenant.

"Don't know as you could have done anything anyway," said the guard quietly.

Nothing except kill a few people, and that would be too late. Dekkard just nodded.

The four waited for more than a sixth, but less than a third, before the door opened and Haarsfel stepped out, followed by Obreduur. Both had very sober expressions on their faces.

"Yes," said Obreduur to the unasked question, "I'm now the very temporary Premier, for almost exactly two weeks. After that . . . we'll have to see."

"Congratulations, sir," said the lieutenant, gesturing back the way they had come.

"Thank you," replied Obreduur.

No one spoke until they reached the limousine, still waiting in the shade of the portico. Then the lieutenant said, "The best of fortune to you, Premier."

"We'll all need it, Lieutenant. I do appreciate your words."

Once the four were in the limousine, the driver eased the steamer out of the shade into the sun and headed back down the drive. The cleaning crews were still working hard at scrubbing the stones of the Square of Heroes, and none of the workers even glanced in the direction of the passing limousine.

Finally, Haarsfel said to Obreduur, "The Premier's floor office is now yours to use."

"I'd rather not use it more than necessary, but we do have to ask for two immediate resignations."

Haarsfel's eyebrows rose. "I understand one."

"Treasury. Munchyn's been instructing tariff assessors to undervalue imports that compete with products made here in Guldor. That's not exactly good for Imperial revenues. Their deputies should be able to handle their ministries for two weeks, especially if I send a letter to each explaining the Imperador's concerns for his people."

They'll handle it better than did either Wyath or Munchyn. But that could have been just hope on Dekkard's part, since he knew nothing of either deputy minister.

"How do you know Munchyn instructed them?" asked Haarsfel.

"Because when I inquired about it and pointed out what was happening, he had an underminister write back a stalling letter saying the matter needed to be studied. When a councilor points out that tariff assessors are essentially breaking the law and costing the Treasury marks . . . and the response is that more study is needed, something's wrong. Either the junior appointees are doing this on their own, which I doubt, or Munchyn's in on it." Obreduur paused, then added, "There's been far too much of that sort of thing going on."

"If the elections go well, we might be able to do something about it."

"First we have to win, Guilhohn," Obreduur said quietly.

And persuade enough Landors and Commercers to support him. And Dekkard wondered if that that might not be even more difficult.

In a few more minutes, the limousine came to a stop outside the east entrance to the Council Hall, where Dekkard and Avraal immediately got out and checked the entrance area before Dekkard opened the rear door. But there was no one outside the doors except for the Council Guards, who appeared no more and no less interested than they usually did, although they didn't ask for passcards, possibly because they recognized Haarsfel.

Once inside the Council Hall, Avraal asked, "Where are we going?"

"To the floor office. I need to get the proper stationery to send out those two letters and to notify the lieutenant-at-arms that he'll need to send two of his messengers to two ministries this afternoon. Then we'll go to the regular office to prepare them for dispatch."

"I'll walk with you," said Haarsfel. "I'm certain that Hansaal will be waiting there to see what happened, hoping that he has a chance to be premier, even for two weeks."

Just as Haarsfel had predicted, waiting just outside the floor office of the Premier was Hansaal Volkaar, the

Commerce Party floor leader. "So you're the acting Premier now, Axel?"

"For two weeks and a day or two. Then we'll see."

"You're going to move in here this moment? Not wasting any time, are you?"

"No. I'm not moving in at all," declared Obreduur. "I am going to pick up some stationery and the seals necessary to handle the requirements of a temporary premier, as well as several suggestions from the Imperador. But I'll be operating out of my own office. The elections will decide who moves into the floor office."

"Noble of you."

"I'm not trying to be noble or ignoble, just practical."

"This is just a brief aberration, Axel. Nothing more."

"What's happened is definitely an aberration, Hansaal, except it's been anything but brief. After the elections, whatever happens, I hope we can return to the original practices of the Great Charter. I'd look forward to that." Obreduur smiled warmly.

Volkaar frowned. "They were too idealistic to last. That's why they didn't."

"That's where we're a little different. I'd like to see if we can make that idealism work again. But we can talk about that later."

Volkaar offered an amused smile. "There won't be any need for that, I'm sure."

Then he turned and walked away.

In less than a sixth after he entered the floor office of the Premier, Obreduur had what he needed. "I'll carry it all. If anyone should attack, you both need your hands free."

The walk back to the Council Office Building was uninterrupted, but when the three reached the top of the staircase and walked toward the office, the door to the office of each of the Craft councilors between the center stairs and Obreduur's office was open, and a staffer would ask, most politely, "Is it really true?" Or words to that effect.

Obreduur's response was largely the same. "That the

Imperador accepted me as acting premier? Yes, it is. For two weeks, and then we'll see what the election brings."

All the rest of Obreduur's staff stood waiting around Karola's desk.

Before anyone could ask, Obreduur smiled, then said, "Yes. Temporary or acting premier until the election results are known. All of you are going to be very, very busy. Now . . . I need just a moment with Avraal and Steffan to discuss security arrangements. Then everyone can join us."

Obreduur led the way into the inner office. Dekkard came last and closed the door.

"Security arrangements?" asked Avraal sardonically.

"That's not all, but they're simple. You two, both of you, will need to be with me everywhere outside of this office or the house, at least until the elections. Also, I can't ask for Wyath's and Munchyn's resignations by letter. I'll have to invite them here, and you'll need to screen them and whoever comes with them this afternoon. That's it. Now . . . any questions I can answer quickly?"

"Can you tell us what the Imperador said?" asked Dekkard.

"If it stays between you two . . . and Ingrella."

"It absolutely will," replied Dekkard.

"He said that he had no choice because of what was in the petition sent to him by the High Justiciary and because the STF had been caught planting weapons on dead unarmed protestors."

"He didn't mention the patrollers being against the STF?" asked Dekkard.

Obreduur smiled faintly. "He didn't, and it wouldn't have been wise for me to say anything about it. I have no doubt that he mentioned it to Ulrich and didn't like what Ulrich said. I doubt he would have even considered asking for a Craft selection for premier otherwise."

"Was there anything else," prompted Avraal.

"He also said that if whoever wins the election cannot

improve the situation, he won't hesitate to call another election."

"You can interpret that at least two ways," said Avraal sardonically.

Obreduur shook his head. "Just one. He wants the unrest stopped, and he wants it done quickly and effectively. The problem is that whatever is quick won't be effective in the long run, and whatever is effective in the long run won't be quick."

"What if you show improvement?" asked Avraal.

"That *might* buy time."

"What about showing him some of the long-standing problems created by the Commercers?" asked Dekkard.

"That might give us a little more time. But we have to win the election, or all of that doesn't matter in the slightest. Now . . . you'd better open the door."

Dekkard did, and for the next sixth Obreduur explained what had happened, then eased everyone out by saying, "I need to write two letters immediately so that I can get them dispatched."

Dekkard forced himself to concentrate on dealing with the letters on his desk that seemed a great deal more mundane. *Except they aren't mundane to the writers.* With that thought, concentration became a bit easier.

In less than half a bell, Obreduur dispatched the two letters by special messenger and then retreated into his office. Within another third, he handed a number of handwritten notes to Karola for dispatch to other councilors. Another third passed, and more notes went out.

Just about the time that Dekkard finished the last of his drafts and returned to his desk after giving them to Margrit, the office door opened, and a Council Guard stepped inside. "Security Minister Wyath to see the Premier."

Both Dekkard and Avraal stood.

The man who followed the guard was thin, from his long face to his polished black shoes, his hair gray, with watery blue eyes somehow magnified by the lenses of his wire-rimmed glasses. His suit was security blue, his shirt white, his cravat a plain rich blue. Wyath walked straight toward the door to the inner office without speaking. A second Council Guard stepped into the office, and the two stood flanking the door.

Dekkard glanced to Avraal, who nodded. At her nod, Karola opened the inner door and announced, "Security Minister Wyath, sir."

"Have him come in."

Wyath entered the office silently, and Karola closed the door.

Dekkard and Avraal moved and took positions on each side of the door.

Dekkard could hear voices, if barely. After less than five minutes, the voices stopped, and the office door opened. Wyath stepped out and walked to the outer door, where one of the Council Guards opened it, and the three left the office without a word.

Since Wyath had left the door to Obreduur's personal office open, Dekkard took the liberty of looking in.

Obreduur stood by the half-open window, then turned. "You and Avraal can come in. Close the door."

Dekkard motioned for Avraal to enter, then followed and shut the door.

"He had a letter of resignation in hand. He didn't say much, except that he knew the Imperador and the government needed someone to blame. He also said that anyone who followed him wouldn't have the option of doing much differently from what he'd done."

That didn't surprise Dekkard.

"What I could feel, besides a certain disgust," said Avraal, "is that he's the kind who can't see anything but what he believes is so, even when there's evidence to the contrary."

"At times, we're all like that, I think," replied Obreduur. "That's why it's vital to have those around you whom you trust but who don't think the way you do. I didn't realize that until I married Ingrella. Too many politicians don't, and the more power you have, the easier it is to shut out what you don't want to hear."

"Do you think Munchyn will be the same?"

Obreduur smiled wryly. "I have no idea, because I've never met with him. We'll see."

"Thank you, sir," said Avraal. "We'll leave you to deal with everything."

"I do have a few more notes to write, and a letter to the acting Minister of Security directing him not to have STF forces fire on anyone unless they're attacked with firearms or unless he's secured permission from me."

The two left, and Dekkard closed the door quietly and returned to his desk, taking out the notes he'd been working on in trying to lay out a set of steps to deal with the New Meritorists. *A little optimistic, aren't you?* Except that he didn't see anyone thinking about it, and it was better than just sitting at his desk.

Just before third bell, and well after Karola had dispatched more notes and at least one letter, another Council Guard opened the office door and announced, "Treasury Minister Munchyn to see the Premier."

Unlike Wyath, Munchyn looked more like a rotund chipmunk who barely came to Dekkard's nose, except that his eyes were small and a cold icy green. Like Wyath, he ignored the staffers in the outer office and walked straight to the door Karola had opened for him as she announced his arrival.

Dekkard and Avraal once more positioned themselves outside the door.

"He's mean," she murmured. "And angry."

"Do we need to—"

"Not yet."

Then abruptly, she opened the door and stepped inside.

Dekkard followed, truncheon in hand, moving past Avraal, toward Munchyn, who had frozen for an instant, slamming the truncheon down across the minister's wrist. Something that looked like a wooden pistol dropped to the floor.

Munchyn started to reach for something else, but he doubled over as Dekkard brought the truncheon up into his celiac plexus.

Two of the Council Guards burst into the room.

"He tried to kill the Premier," said Avraal calmly. "There's a wooden dart sling on the floor in front of the desk."

Obreduur looked totally aghast.

"You . . . can't . . . make . . . me . . ." gasped Munchyn, his hand fumbling something toward his face, as one of the Council Guards straightened him up.

"No!" snapped Dekkard, but he couldn't reach Munchyn with hand or truncheon as the guard pulled the Treasury Minister back and upright.

Munchyn jabbed the short needle-like miniature blade into the side of his own neck. In moments, he was convulsing.

"Frog poison," declared one of the guards.

"Take him to the infirmary and have the Council doctor make sure. I'll need a report."

"Yes, sir." The younger guard looked stunned. "Sir . . . the Treasury Minister . . . we never thought . . ."

"Neither did any of us," replied Obreduur.

Two thirds later, after the guards had carted off Munchyn's body, and the Guard Captain had apologized at least several times, and posted two guards outside the office in the corridor, the entire staff stood inside the inner office, while Obreduur related what had happened, ending with ". . . without Steffan and Avraal you all would be mourning my untimely heart attack . . . or, given them, possibly my murder by a Treasury Minister distraught by being removed from his position."

"There haven't even been elections," said Macri. "Why would he try to kill you now?"

"They must have figured this would be the one chance where I wouldn't be heavily guarded."

"That means," said Dekkard, "the Commercers, or

some of them, think the Craft Party has a good chance of winning the elections. Otherwise, they wouldn't bother."

"It also means that you two"—Obreduur looked to Dekkard and Avraal, standing side by side—"are going to have to be even closer to me until the elections. If we win, the risk won't be quite as great. Then the Commercers will shift to trying to sabotage whatever plans we have." He paused, smiled sardonically, and added, "I don't know about any of you, but I've had enough excitement for the day. It's time to go home."

87

Despite the excitement in the office earlier, Obreduur decided that the family would still attend services at the East Quarter Trinitarian Chapel on Quindi evening. Whether that was to offer thanks or an attempt to maintain a family routine, Dekkard had no idea. Either way, neither he nor Avraal sensed anything wrong before and during the service, and the return to the house went smoothly, as did dinner.

After eating, Dekkard and Avraal retreated to the portico.

"With things so unsettled, I don't know that we can go to Emrelda's tomorrow," said Dekkard. "She'd have to come here to see you."

"To see us," corrected Avraal. "But she has the same problem. She sent a note saying that she'll have to work tomorrow and it's noon to second night bell."

"Did she say why?"

"Only that the demonstrations had disrupted every station in Machtarn. Can you imagine that?" she added sarcastically.

"You didn't sense anything unusual about Wyath, then?"

"I didn't say that. He was mostly disgusted that he had to submit his resignation to an acting premier, I suspect particularly to an acting Craft premier."

"Obreduur said he couldn't ask for his resignation by a letter."

"He had to know what a letter effectively ordering his presence meant," Avraal pointed out. "He had the letter of resignation ready. That was just to get it over with as soon as possible."

"Do you think he knew what Munchyn would try?"

"I doubt it. I couldn't feel enough beyond Munchyn's anger to sense much more, but Munchyn was prepared."

"So he had to be aware Obreduur was looking into the tariff underassessment problem, and there had to have been enough evidence that he couldn't get rid of it or claim he wasn't involved. That also means that what Carlos Baartol discovered circumstantially is more than circumstantial, and that some large corporacions and their subsidiaries are involved. Still . . . to try to murder even an acting premier?"

"There has to be more there," concluded Avraal.

"What exactly did you project to slow Munchyn?"

"Slobbery dog-like affection, followed by ice. Hate would have bounced right off him, and I had the feeling that nausea might have as well. He's the type who lives with self-loathing all the time . . . or lived with it."

"There's a certain benefit to being an isolate," Dekkard said. "I don't know how you live amid a swirl of feelings."

"I don't, Steffan," she replied gently. "I can block all but the strongest emotions without much trouble. I can't do it when I'm on duty, though, not when I have to be able to sense purpose, anger, or hate from as far away as possible."

"Can all empaths do that?"

"No. Most lower-grade empies can't. That's why most people think empaths feel everything. But less sensitive empies don't need to because they don't sense as deeply."

"How do you feel about being with an isolate whose feelings you can't ever sense?"

Avraal laughed softly. "I love it, just as . . ." She hesitated. ". . . just as I love you."

"I love you. I hope you, somehow, can feel that."

She smiled. "I know that. In Oersynt, at the Fairwind, you weren't protecting Obreduur so much as me. I could see that."

"Don't tell him," Dekkard said dryly, feeling both chagrinned that he was so transparent and relieved that she understood.

"I'm sure he already knows that. That's another reason why I decided to carry throwing knives. We *have* to keep him safe."

I still have to keep you both safe. But all Dekkard said was, "I know."

"Just hold me for a bit. We have a long two weeks ahead."

That was something Dekkard already knew, but he was more than willing to comply with her request. *More than willing.*

88

Findi morning Dekkard woke at his normal weekday time, even though there was no reason to. He washed and shaved, but donned older clothes for breakfast and made his way downstairs to an empty staff room. To his surprise, there was a copy of *Gestirn* on the side table. He began to read.

The lines across the top and just below the masthead stated that *Gestirn* was resuming printing after the interim Premier had lifted the restrictions imposed by the former Minister of Security, who had resigned at the request of the acting Premier. The first article was short.

Early yesterday morning, Imperador Laureous requested the resignation of Oskaar Ulrich, both as Premier and as a Councilor of the Sixty-Six, and called for new elections to take place on Findi, 12 Fallfirst 1266. No reason was given. The Imperador also requested that the Craft Party present a candidate as acting Premier, since with the resignation of former Premier Ulrich and an unfilled Commerce seat in the Council, the Craft Party presently holds the plurality of seats. That candidate, Axel Obreduur, Councilor from Oersynt District, was accepted by the Imperador.

So the Imperador didn't have to break precedent. Stretch it, perhaps, but not break it. That both amused and troubled Dekkard. He also noticed that there was no mention of the role played by either Ingrella's inspired petition to the High Justiciary or by the implied threat by the Patrollers Benevolent Society of Machtarn. He turned to the second and longer story.

Treasury Minister Attempts Murder of Premier, Then Suicides

When Treasury Minister Isomer Munchyn was summoned to meet acting Premier Obreduur, it was a foregone conclusion that Munchyn would be asked for his resignation. What no one expected was that Munchyn would draw a wooden frog-poison gun and attempt to assassinate the acting Premier, an attempt foiled at literally the last moment by Councilor Obreduur's security aides and by Council Guards. Then Munchyn, while being pulled away from the Premier, stabbed himself in the neck with a tiny poisoned blade. He died before a doctor could be summoned.

While the Premier has not spoken about the attempt, sources in the Treasury Ministry revealed that, as Councilor, Obreduur had requested that Munchyn look into reports of special tariff treatment of imports by subsidiaries of large Guldoran corporacions . . .

The acting Treasury Minister had no comment except that he would be looking into the matter . . .

Dekkard was about to replace the newssheet on the side table when Avraal stepped into the staff room. Instead he dropped it on the corner of the dining table, stepped forward, and hugged her, murmuring, "It's so good to see you."

She returned the embrace, then eased out of his arms. "We still have to get through the next two weeks. Only brief embraces in public." Then she smiled. "But it's good to see you weren't swept away by my attire."

Dekkard realized that she still wore a robe. He almost said that he wasn't interested in the robe, but then realized that that might have been taken as pure lust. *Not that there's not lust; it's just not all lust.* "You look good in anything."

"So do you."

"Thank you. I'm not sure I believe it, but thank you." Dekkard stepped back. "Just sit down. I'll get you your café . . . and you can read what *Gestirn* had to say about what happened yesterday." He picked up the newssheet and handed it to her, then poured her a mug of café and set it before her. Only then did he get his own café and plates for both of them before sitting down across from her.

She finished the newssheet and placed it on the table. Then she took a sip of café, then another.

Dekkard took several sips of café and waited. Finally, he took his croissants and some of the guava jelly that had replaced the tomato jelly.

Finally, Avraal set down her mug and smiled. "You're patient. Thank you."

"I'm not patient. I understand you don't want to talk until you've had some café."

"That's fair enough. I'm glad the stories are accurate. I doubt that Hansaal Volkaar is as happy with them.

They might cost them a seat or two. I'm glad they reported that Council Guards were present."

"I have my doubts. Still . . . I think the stories might help get some Landor councilors to support Obreduur . . . if we win a few more seats."

"Not openly."

"That's the beauty of the Great Charter. It does allow councilors to vote their conscience without sacrificing everything. Of course, the New Meritorists would claim that a councilor's vote should always be personally public, which, in time, would destroy councilors' rights to oppose their party without losing everything."

Hyelda appeared in the kitchen archway. "The councilor asked me to tell you he'll need you in your security grays by third bell. He's expecting visitors." Hyelda paused. "You think I should call him 'Premier' now?"

"Just call him 'sir,'" suggested Dekkard. "At least until he becomes premier for real . . . if that happens. But I'd wager he'll be more comfortable with 'sir' here in the house."

Avraal nodded.

By a third after the second bell of morning, just after Hyelda and Rhosali had left for their usual day off, Dekkard and Avraal were in their security grays waiting in the staff room when Obreduur appeared. "You might as well join me in the study."

The two rose and followed Obreduur to the study, where he gestured for them to sit.

"We're going to have to cram a great deal into the next few days, because, with the elections coming up on such short notice, we . . . that is, you two and I, will be leaving for Oersynt this Duadi on the Night Express. You'll be wearing security grays during the day, with your long truncheon, but not the gladius, and gray suits for evening engagements, of which there will be one every night. So pack accordingly."

"Just you, not Ingrella?" asked Dekkard, wishing he hadn't when Avraal rolled her eyes.

"Ingrella would help some, but she has legalist commitments here, as well as dealing with Nellara and Gustoff. People won't care too much if she's not there. They will if I'm not."

"Is there anything special we need to do?" asked Avraal.

"Keeping all of us safe will be special enough," replied Obreduur wryly.

Dekkard could see that was all Obreduur wanted to say. So he asked, "Can you tell us who this morning's visitors will be?"

"Haarsfel, Hasheem, Mardosh, and Zerlyon, although Harleona will be spending time after the meeting with Ingrella."

That told Dekkard that Obreduur was setting the groundwork for committee priorities just in case he did have the opportunity to lead the Council of Sixty-Six and form a government.

The councilor's eyes held a twinkle as he said, "That's right, Steffan. We won't have much time after the elections. So, in the event we do gain control of the Council, we need to be ready to act, with legislative proposals that will address some of the worker and New Meritorist concerns without playing into the hands of the Commercers . . . and we need to know what junior Commercer councilors would like that we can support as well as anything that the Commercers might push that's got problems that aren't obvious."

"What about the Navy and Security and keeping order?" asked Avraal.

"With the regular patrollers opposed to Security agents and the STF, I've already sent instructions that STF detachments aren't to be used except in case of heavily armed demonstrators. I very much like Steffan's idea of splitting Security into two parts . . . but I'd prefer transferring the STF to the Army. We'll have to move more carefully with the Navy to make certain that it's not being used for corporacion purposes, but the marshals there won't be in the slightest displeased with

Ulrich's removal, not after the way he pinned much of the blame on them when the Navy never knew where the coal was even coming from."

"What about Munchyn?" asked Dekkard.

"I have to wonder if Munchyn was paid, indirectly, of course, to have the tariff inspectors undervalue those imports," said Obreduur. "I've asked Carlos to look into Munchyn's financial position to see if his bank accounts are larger than they should be or if he'd bought property he couldn't afford. There may not be anything, but there has to be something. Otherwise . . . I can't see why he'd try assassination and then suicide."

"Unless someone had a hold over him," suggested Avraal.

"You couldn't tell anything like that, could you?"

"Not unless whoever it was happened to be in the same room as Munchyn."

Obreduur nodded slowly. "I had that feeling, but it was worth asking."

At that moment, the sound of the heavy bronze knocker echoed from the front door, and Dekkard and Avraal immediately rose.

"Have the councilors come to the study, but you and any security aides should remain in the front sitting room, not the staff room."

Which places us between the front door and the study, rather than out of the way. "Yes, sir," replied Dekkard.

Both Dekkard and Avraal hurried into the front hall.

"One man," said Avraal.

Dekkard opened the door to see Councilor Hasheem, without Erleen Orlov. "Come in, Councilor. He's expecting you."

Within minutes, Guilhohn Haarsfel arrived, also without a security aide, but from what Dekkard had discerned, he hadn't had one in years, and Dekkard had to wonder why the Craft floor leader didn't have to worry. *Or is he one of those what-will-be-will-be fatalistic personalities?*

On the other hand Harleona Zerlyon, who followed

Haarsfel, was accompanied by both Chavyona Leiugan and Tullyt Kamryn, while Councilor Mardosh brought Stavros Rhennus. Once the five councilors were gathered in Obreduur's study, all the security aides took seats in the sitting room.

"I never thought I'd see a Craft premier," said Rhennus, "even an acting one."

"If the elections go right, he might be more than acting," suggested Kamryn.

"That has to be what they're planning for." Leiugan looked to Avraal. "How likely is it?"

Avraal didn't answer immediately, but finally said, "I don't know. I do know that in the last election, we gained enough seats to have only two less than the Commercers. If we get three more and they hold what they have, we'd have twenty-six seats to their twenty-five seats, but that makes fifty-one, and since the Landor Party can't have less than sixteen, the party with the higher plurality gets the advantage. So that would leave us with twenty-six and the Commercers with twenty-four."

"But it could go the other way, couldn't it?" asked Rhennus.

"It could," said Dekkard, "but it all depends on which districts each party takes. If we win current Commercer seats, or the Landors do, then we'll have a plurality. It gets chancier if we pick up Landor seats and not Commercer seats."

"Frig . . ." muttered Kamryn. "Never thought we'd need help from the Landors."

"We'll need help from them anyway, even if we take Commerce seats," Avraal pointed out. "Even if we pick up six seats—that's the maximum we can hold, and that many is unlikely—we'd still need four councilors from other parties to support us, and very few Commercers are going to want to support a Craft premier. We have slightly more in common with Landors, at least right now, than with Commercers."

"Even if we win thirty seats, won't the Landors stick with the Commercers?" asked Rhennus.

"They very well could," admitted Avraal, "but the Commercers have opposed freight rate regulations, and there's evidence that the ironways and barge consortiums are giving lower rates to industrial goods than to produce and agricultural goods. And the Commercers almost pushed through the elimination of the swampgrass tariff, which would have hurt the Landors in the southwest . . ."

"What you're saying is that the Landor councilors could go either way," said Leiugan, "for the first time?"

"There's also the possibility that a few Commercer councilors might quietly support Obreduur," added Dekkard, "because they've been ignored or actually hurt by their own party."

Kamryn shook his head. "All of that means that we don't know, and we won't know, even after the election."

"Not until the new Council meets," said Avraal.

"What will happen to you two," asked Leiugan, "that is, if your boss becomes the real premier?"

Dekkard and Avraal exchanged glances. He nodded to her.

"We haven't even talked about it. As you must know from *Gestirn* this morning . . . we've been occupied just keeping him safe."

"How did you two manage that?" asked Leiugan.

"We were close enough, and Avraal sensed what was about to happen," said Dekkard, "but she could tell you better than I . . ."

"I warned Steffan. He moved faster than I've ever seen anyone move . . ."

As Avraal finished describing what had happened, Dekkard repressed a shudder. It had been *so* close. *Too close. How often can you keep doing that?* He decided not to think about it, especially since there was little he could do about the situation. *Except to keep practicing and to stay alert . . . possibly for almost every moment over the next two weeks.*

From there the conversation drifted into an almost desultory ramble on the New Meritorists and what effect they might have on the election, if any, and speculations on why Ulrich and Wyath had ordered or allowed the mass shooting at the Square of Heroes.

As the room became quiet, Dekkard realized he needed to send a quick letter off to his parents and Naralta. Telling them he'd be in Oersynt, but with the caution that he didn't know how much free time he might have, given the need to assure Obreduur's security.

A good third before the fifth bell of morning the study door opened. Hasheem, Haarsfel, and Mardosh, along with Rhennus, left immediately while Obreduur, Ingrella, and Zerlyon went back into the study and closed the door.

"They're planning what to do in the Justiciary Committee, one way or another," said Dekkard.

"The councilor thinks it's very possible we could get a Craft government," replied Leiugan.

"Did she say why?"

"I asked her. She just said one word—'Women.' That was all."

Dekkard noted Kamryn's amused expression and asked, "You don't think so?"

"I wouldn't say no, but I think it's unlikely."

"So was the Silent Revolution," said Dekkard dryly. "But it still happened. For that matter, the New Meritorists shouldn't have been able to destroy fifteen regional Security headquarters, but that happened as well. When you look back, you can see how they both happened, but people didn't look in the right places. Women are taking over more and more positions in the stronger guilds and they're strengthening guilds that were once weaker."

"I don't see that," Kamryn replied.

"As Steffan pointed out," said Avraal, "it all depends on where you look. We'll see if he and your councilor are right on election day . . . and after."

"We'll see." Kamryn's tone was doubtful.

The three presumably meeting on the Justiciary Committee finished at a third past noon, and Councilor

Zerlyon and her two aides were on their way in a sixth after that.

Once the front door shut behind them, Obreduur turned to Dekkard. "If you'd ready the large Gresynt, Steffan, you can drive all of us, including Nellara and Gustoff, to Don Miguel. All of us, but especially you two, deserve a good meal."

Dekkard was more than happy to oblige.

89

On Unadi morning the only story in *Gestirn* dealing directly with politics or government was an article on Obreduur, reporting on his rise from river stevedore to guild steward to assistant guildmeister to guildmeister, and from there to district guild coordinator and his appointment to the Council upon the death of his predecessor in an unfortunate "domestic incident."

Dekkard smiled sardonically at the circumlocution of Lewes's murder by his wife.

Obreduur also moved up the morning departure time so that the three of them would be in the office half before the second bell. That didn't surprise Dekkard, and he wondered how many other changes might be coming. *But then, the election might not change anything that much, not if the Commercers and Landors stick together.*

Dekkard did wait until Avraal had time with her café before he asked, "How do you feel about going to Oersynt? When I asked you last night, you said you wanted to think about it."

She pursed her lips for an instant. "I worry. In a way, it doesn't matter where he is. If the Commercers want to strike at him, they'll try. He's worried, too. You notice he didn't hesitate to say we were going with him. And he's going alone, without family."

"That makes sense, either way," Dekkard pointed out.

Avraal just looked at him.

"You're right," he admitted, "but it would make sense either way."

"I think we should bring spare knives."

"I'd already thought of that."

"And pack every cravat you have."

He smiled. "You told me that last night."

She smiled in return. "I wanted to make sure you remembered."

After that, they ate quickly because they knew they had less time, even though Dekkard had gotten up earlier, but he actually had the Gresynt under the portico soon enough that he waited several minutes for Obreduur and Avraal.

Once everyone was settled and Dekkard turned onto Altarama, before Obreduur could get too involved in papers or writing, Dekkard asked, "Is there anything else different today that we should be aware of?"

Obreduur laughed softly. "Not that I know. Remember, this is also a first time for me."

"Yes, sir, but you've been around much longer."

"That's true enough, but the Commercer premiers have never been exactly informative about everything."

Dekkard understood that, and didn't ask any more questions on the drive to the Council Office Building, where he dropped off Obreduur and Avraal.

He was still stopped three times before entering the building, but the last Council Guard was more respectful.

"I'm sorry to have had to stop you, sir, but there have been too many incidents this year. I hope your councilor can put things on the right rails before long."

"So do I . . . and thank you."

Dekkard was feeling almost cheerful as he posted the letter to his parents and then made his way up the staff staircase to the second level, but just after he came out of the door, he saw someone walking toward him. His hand moved toward his truncheon before he recognized Caarsten Thaarn, the isolate security aide of Councilor Waarfel.

"Steffan!"

"Caarsten, I haven't seen you in a while." Except for glimpses of Thaarn, it had been months since they'd actually exchanged words. "How are you and Alympiana doing? Have you had to deal with those New Meritorists?"

"In Aloor? You have to be jesting. There are more shells of houses than occupied dwellings. If it weren't for the tin mines . . . and they're playing out . . ." Thaarn shrugged.

Dekkard had known that Aloor had become a backwater after Laureous the Great had taken it, but he hadn't realized that it was still that impoverished. "Count yourself fortunate. At least you didn't have to deal with exploding buildings and assassins." He paused just slightly, then said, "How are things going otherwise?"

"Well enough . . . but . . . well . . . Alympiana and I have been thinking."

"Oh . . . ?"

"Well . . . if the Craft Party picks up a seat or two . . . any new councilor might need security aides . . . you understand?"

Dekkard definitely understood, especially given Waarfel's reputation. "I don't know as anyone will contact me about that, or even Councilor Obreduur, but if it does come up, I'll do what I can for the two of you." Dekkard still had trouble thinking and speaking of Obreduur as premier. *And since he's not calling himself that* . . . "You want to stay as a team, I take it?"

"Absolutely."

"I'll see what I can do," Dekkard repeated.

"Thank you, Steffan." Thaarn offered a grateful smile before hurrying away, in a swift walk that suggested he didn't want to stay away from his office long.

In turn, Dekkard walked quickly to his own office, where the small pile of letters and petitions on his desk was about the same size as the one he'd gotten on Quindi. He picked up the first letter and began to read.

As he made his way through the correspondence and drafted replies, he absently noted that there were definitely more messengers, and that they were quietly but noticeably more deferential to Karola. If Obreduur didn't remain as premier, that would change again, of course.

At a third after fifth bell, Obreduur came out of the inner office. "We're going to the dining room. I'll be meeting several councilors there. It's likely to take a little over a bell. That will allow you time to eat."

Once the three were out in the main corridor, Obreduur said, "I have some interesting news, but I'll wait until we're outside in the garden courtyard."

Interesting news? Dekkard was definitely curious, but he and Avraal just waited until they were in the shade of the roofed portico joining the two buildings.

"Jens Seigryn sent a heliogram. The Craft Party Committee for the Gaarlak district met late yesterday and chose Johan Lamarr as the official party candidate for councilor."

"Isn't that what you wanted?" asked Dekkard.

"It's what I hoped for, but it's the committee's decision. Jens said the debate was acrimonious and that Haasan Decaro got almost violent when the vote for Lamarr was announced."

"That won't change anything, will it?" asked Avraal.

"It could if Haasan persuades the Machineworkers to vote for another party's candidate, or not to vote."

"Who did the Landor Party pick?"

"Someone I've never heard of, a Willem Macaarth. Jens says he's a self-important nonentity, but he'll still likely pick up most of the Landor votes."

"And the Commerce candidate?" pressed Dekkard.

"The younger son of the presidente of the Banque of Gaarlak, one Elvann Wheiter. He was likely to have been the bigger threat, especially if the local Craft Party had decided on Decaro instead of Johan Lamarr, but Lamarr's respected by many local business interests."

"It sounds like they picked well. You might get another Craft councilor," said Avraal.

"You can't tell until the votes are counted," said Obreduur dryly.

After a moment of silence, Dekkard spoke. "Sir . . . I had an interesting encounter this morning . . ." He went on to relate the brief conversation with Caarsten Thaarn.

Obreduur nodded when Dekkard finished, then said, "I can understand their interest. How good are they at security? Do you have any idea?"

"I don't," confessed Dekkard. "No one's hinted at anything even remotely suggesting a lack of competence. So it's likely that they're decent. Beyond that . . ." He shrugged.

"I've run across Alympiana a few times," added Avraal. "She's a strong natural empath, but I get the feeling that her training wasn't as strict as it could be. She's certainly stronger than most security empaths, and that counts for a great deal."

"Hmmm . . . you're saying they're better than average, but not outstanding."

"That's likely," agreed Avraal. "But they've worked together for almost six years, and that means they'll be better at first for a new councilor than even an excellent isolate and an outstanding empath who've never worked together before."

"I'll keep that in mind." Obreduur looked to Dekkard. "What did you promise him?"

"Only that I'd do what I could."

"That's fair. Thank you."

As they approached the heavy bronze doors to the Council Hall, Dekkard took in the Council Guards and the two staffers standing in the shade of one side of the portico, but neither looked or shifted position as Obreduur walked past and entered the building. The three reached the dining room without incident.

Dekkard and Avraal watched until Obreduur was inside, and then made their way to the staff cafeteria. There, he opted for beef empanadas, while she chose a chicken salad of sorts. They'd barely seated themselves when a stocky woman Dekkard didn't recognize approached the table.

"Avraal . . . I haven't seen you in *ages*," offered the older dark-haired woman.

"Sometimes, it happens that way." Avraal half turned. "Steffan, meet Kenalee Foerstah. She's a legalist for Councilor Guldurs Freenk. Kenalee, this is Steffan Dekkard."

"The other half of the heroic pair. I'm pleased to meet you. And congratulations on your councilor becoming Premier."

"It could also be rather temporary," replied Avraal.

"Possibly not," said Foerstah. "You know Guldurs has to stand down, and it's likely that the Craft Party will pick up that district . . ."

Dekkard listened as Foerstah made a thinly veiled appeal for help in getting a new position.

"Keep in touch," said Avraal, when Foerstah had finished. "After the election, we'll both know more about where things stand."

"Thank you. I appreciate it." Foerstah looked to Dekkard. "It was good to meet you, Steffan."

"And I, you." Dekkard smiled warmly.

Once Foerstah was out of earshot, Dekkard asked quietly, "How good a legalist is she?"

"She has to be fairly good." Avraal shook her head sadly. "She and Caarsten Thaarn won't be the last who come looking for a special siding to a job."

Dekkard had to agree. Then he took a brief swallow of his Kuhrs and several bites of his empanada before asking, "Who do you think Obreduur's meeting with?"

"The better question might be who he isn't meeting with. No matter which party forms the government, he'll have more power . . . and more problems."

Dekkard finished eating his empanadas; then he sipped

the last of the Kuhrs while Avraal methodically demolished exactly half her chicken salad . . . and stopped.

"That's more than enough," she declared. "We should head back to the dining room. He might be early. We also might hear more there." She stood.

So did Dekkard.

When they reached the corridor across from the dining room entrance, Dekkard saw Laurenz Korriah and Shaundara Keppel waiting, separate from a larger group of security aides. "You suggested listening. Should we see what Laurenz and Shaundara have to say?"

"Why not?" she agreed with a smile.

As they neared the two, Dekkard said cheerfully, "Laurenz . . . waiting for the boss?"

"The same as you are, Steffan." Korriah laughed, softly for him, which meant that it could be heard for yards, if not farther.

"You were right about the Imperador calling new elections quickly," said Dekkard. "I thought he'd wait longer."

"I thought it would be even sooner, but when Ulrich shut down *Gestirn* after planting guns on those protestors, even the Imperador couldn't ignore that. Having the STF shoot unarmed people . . . and then plant weapons on women and kids? How stupid was that?"

"Definitely up there in stupidity," added Keppel.

"What's your boss going to do after he becomes Premier for real?"

"First, his party has to win the election," Dekkard pointed out.

"The Craft Party is going to win the most seats," Korriah declared. "Your boss already has enough councilors' votes to be Premier. Whether he stays Premier depends on what he intends to do."

"He knows that," interjected Avraal quietly but firmly.

"Knowing and doing are separate things," said Korriah.

"You're right," said Avraal, smiling. "And, there are

different ways to get things done. One way or another, you'll see what he can do."

"Laurenz," said Keppel quickly. "He hired them. How effective have they been?"

Korriah laughed once more, then shook his head. "Never thought of it that way. You two have stopped . . . what . . . three assassinations?"

"More than enough," said Dekkard.

"And then there was that incident in the covered parking . . . Guard Captain Trujillo told me about it."

Keppel frowned. Avraal lifted her eyebrows.

"Some lowlifes were wearing guard uniforms and breaking into steamers. They attacked Steffan. It didn't work out the way they thought." Korriah inclined his head to Avraal. "You're right. You and your boss like to do things quietly. Sometimes that's better. Sometimes, it's not."

Dekkard grinned. "So we can call on you when quiet doesn't work?"

Korriah grinned. "You can certainly ask."

The four stopped talking as a group of councilors emerged from the dining room. They were all Commercers, including Marryat Osmond, Vhiola Sandegarde, Charls Maastach, and Gerard Schmidtz, three of whom had been committee chairs in the just-dissolved Council, and none of them appeared especially happy, so much so that Dekkard murmured to Avraal, "Are they as unhappy as they look?"

"More worried than unhappy," she said quietly.

Once the Commercer councilors and their waiting aides departed, Korriah shook his head. "Sorry bunch. Marks don't always buy what you think."

"Sometimes," added Avraal, "when people are bought with marks, they don't stay bought."

"More often than not," said Keppel.

It was almost two thirds past the first afternoon bell when several Landor councilors left the dining room, most with thoughtful expressions. The ones Dekkard recognized were Kharl Navione and Breffyn Haastar.

"We'll see you later," said Korriah, just before he and Keppel moved in behind Navione and Haastar.

"Until later," replied Dekkard.

Several minutes passed before Avraal spoke. "The way Laurenz described the incident in the covered parking . . ."

"It didn't happen that way. The guard captain was the one who questioned me personally. That theft story was a way to cover up what really happened. There's also the possibility that Korriah is lying, but he's not the type, and he's not stupid. That means Trujillo either decided to cover it up or was told to. I'd wager the latter."

"That's a wager I won't take." She stopped talking and motioned toward Obreduur, who had just stepped out of the dining room . . . alone.

The two immediately joined him.

"Did you have a good meal?" asked Obreduur.

"A fair meal," replied Avraal, "and another position seeker . . ." She went on to explain.

When she finished, as the three stepped out of the Council Hall and under the covered portico heading toward the Council Office Building, Obreduur said, "I'll ask Ingrella to make a few discreet inquiries. If she's what she seems to be . . . well . . . we'll see."

"We also had an interesting conversation with Councilor Navione's security aides," said Dekkard. "I got the feeling their councilor just might have been meeting with you, but that wasn't what was most interesting. You recall when I was attacked in the covered parking, I'm sure. Well, the good Guard Captain Trujillo told Laurenz Korriah that I'd been attacked by a pair of thieves intent on rummaging through steamers . . ."

"That's suspicious, but not something we can address now."

"I didn't think so, but I thought you should know."

Obreduur took a long slow breath, but kept walking. He finally said, "There are far, far too many reports and hints of untoward behavior involving the Council and the ministries. It might take years . . ." He shook his head, then smiled. "But then, that's one of the functions of staff . . . and even other councilors."

"If you get to be Premier," said Dekkard.

"First, I have to get reelected," Obreduur pointed out.

"Is anyone running against you?" asked Dekkard.

"I'd heard that Vandenburg was thinking about it, but I haven't heard who the Landor candidate will be. Most likely, the Commerce candidate will be Villem Draforre, the vice-presidente of the Rio Mal Banque. He's hinted earlier that he might run, and he'll never be presidente of the banque. He doesn't lack marks or confidence."

"Does he have a chance?" asked Dekkard.

"Every candidate has a chance until all the votes are counted. That's why any good politician never takes anything for granted."

"But you'll still worry about all the problems ahead," Dekkard replied.

"True, but for the moment there isn't much we can do. Almost all the Council has either already left for their districts or will be leaving tomorrow. Those few who can't stand for reelection are packing up." Obreduur cleared his throat. "Don't worry about letters or petitions for the rest of the day. The mail will drop off, and Macri and the others can handle it while you're gone. What you both need to do is summarize my positions on the issues that people will ask about. No more than two sentences. You won't have time for much more, but some of those who can't ask me might ask you, and you can't say you don't know."

Once the three returned to the office, Dekkard sat down and began to write . . . and think. He only had a few pages written when he had to leave to get the Gresynt, and he was still thinking even after he'd driven home, garaged the Gresynt, and was wiping down both steamers.

Avraal was waiting in the back hall when he left the garage.

"You didn't say anything on the way home," she said.

"I was thinking. So much of what we do doesn't reduce to a few sentences. How do you explain food prices are higher in Machtarn because the ironways charge more per decem for grain and produce because they take up more space per decem than do manufactured goods, and that's why so much produce goes by barge, which is slower and more food gets spoiled."

She looked at him and said, with a smile, "I think you just did."

"They were long sentences."

They both laughed.

90

On Duadi morning, upon rising, Dekkard looked at the almost completely packed traveling case, the arrangement of clothing with which he'd spent entirely too much time the night before, then proceeded with preparing for the day. He was in the staff room before either Avraal or Rhosali, and he immediately picked up the copy of *Gestirn*. The first-page main story was about a late-summer spoutstorm that wreaked havoc on houses south of the center of Point Larmat. The other story was about the various councilors who'd had to stand down.

Dekkard kept reading. On the third page he saw an interesting story header—NAVY CONSTRUCTION COSTS SOAR—and decided to read further.

. . . the largest percentage increase in the budget of the Imperial Navy for the past five years has been in construction of naval facilities . . . set of figures buried in budget submissions to the Council of Sixty-Six show the cost per square yard almost doubled over the period . . . interviews with professional engineers revealed that Navy construction projects have gone predominantly to Siincleer Shipbuilding or its subsidiaries or Haasan Design . . . smaller corporacions competing with these two behemoths who successfully won bids have subsequently suffered tragedies, unexplained fires, disappearance of key personnel, even problematic deaths of key senior personnel . . . most recent was the case of Engaard Engineering . . .

. . . the upshot of these events is a lack of competition and markedly higher costs to the Imperial Treasury, as well far higher revenues and profits for both Siincleer Shipbuilding and Haasan Design . . .

Dekkard frowned as he replaced the newssheet on the side table. The story didn't actually accuse anyone, but the implications were certainly there. He couldn't help but believe that Obreduur and Carlos Baartol had something to do with it, although not a single politician or political party was mentioned.

After Avraal arrived, Dekkard waited until she'd had her first mug of café before having her read the story. Then he waited.

"It's true, but they'll keep on doing it."

"For a little while," replied Dekkard. "I think the story is a setup . . . or the first shot of a salvo, and I'd wager Obreduur wanted it published before the elections."

"So, if we gain control, he can point out that he's only following the lead provided by *Gestirn* before he became premier?"

"He could then hold hearings and bring up everything, and it would illustrate another aspect of Commercer corruption."

"If . . . if the Craft Party wins enough seats and gains enough other councilors as allies."

"The beauty of it is that the story accuses no one, and if Haasan or Siincleer object loudly, it will just bring more attention to the problem."

"I'm not about to hold my breath," declared Avraal. "Neither will Emrelda."

"I wouldn't advise it," replied Dekkard with a sardonic smile.

Avraal mock-glared at him, then smiled back.

Because they needed to leave early, they both ate quickly and then left the staff room.

Dekkard barely had the Gresynt under the portico before Obreduur and Avraal arrived. Both were careful to stay under the roof because of the steady warm rain that had been falling since sometime before dawn.

Since Obreduur started arranging papers in the rear seat almost as soon as Dekkard started down the drive, Dekkard immediately asked, "Did you read that story in *Gestirn* about Navy construction costs?"

"I did. *Gestirn* was cautious. I understand there was more to it than that. Someone came up with extensive documentation. I wouldn't be surprised if a more solid version doesn't appear in newssheets in Siincleer, Point Larmat, and possibly Uldwyrk."

"Do you think the Council will be able to get ahold of that documentation?" At that thought, Dekkard thought of Markell's package, still in Obreduur's safe . . . where it would have to remain for some time.

"Most certainly . . . when the time is right. Now . . ."

"Yes, sir." Dekkard turned his full attention to driving, especially since he knew that, with the rain, traffic on Imperial Boulevard would be slower and trickier.

When he dropped Obreduur and Avraal off at the entrance to the Council Office Building, Dekkard saw there was less traffic and even a smaller number of Council Guards in their yellow waterproofs, then realized that was because most of the councilors and some staff had already departed to begin campaigning. After he parked the Gresynt, he dashed across the street, but still had to stop, if under the entry roof, to have his passcard checked before entering the building.

Inside, as Dekkard made his way to the staff staircase and then headed up to the second level, he noted that there might have been slightly fewer staffers in the corridors, but not many, given that most staff didn't campaign. He had just stepped out of the staircase and into the upper corridor when he saw an all-too-familiar burly figure moving toward him—Jaime Minz.

"Good morning, Jaime. What inspiring insights do you have on this delightful rainy morning?"

"No great spiritual insights, Steffan. It's good to see that you're still here, and that your boss is enjoying his brief tenure as acting premier."

"I don't know anyone who would call being premier, even acting premier, enjoyable. What are you doing these days?"

"I'll be on the staff roll until the election, and then I'll be taking a position as an assistant director of security for Northwest Industrial Chemical."

"Oh . . . after what Councilor Bassaana said on the floor, I can see where they might need some help in improving their security procedures dealing with dunnite."

"Now, Steffan . . . aren't you assuming a bit much?"

"Not too much. The Navy requires three manifests for everything and has sentries everywhere. But then, they're easier to blame. We've all seen that. I'm sure you'll fit right in with Northwest." Dekkard smiled. "If I don't see you any time soon, I do wish you well."

Minz smiled pleasantly in return. "Oh . . . you'll be seeing me around. I'll still be in Machtarn, but do give my best to Avraal." Then he turned and walked briskly down the corridor.

Dekkard smiled wryly. *People like that always land on their feet . . . until they don't.*

Once in the office, Dekkard looked at his desk and was shocked to discover no letters or petitions on it.

Avraal smiled at him. "There isn't much, and Felix, Svard, and Ivann can handle it. We're supposed to keep working on sentences and phrases to describe what the councilor stands for . . . and, if we think of anything new that he could say, to write it up and give it to him before fifth bell, when we escort him to his meeting in the dining room."

Dekkard didn't quite groan. Letters and petitions were definitely much easier.

The next three bells emphasized that point. Dekkard could use specific acts to show a wider concern, as in the tariff-assessment problem where the councilor was working for Guldoran artisans against cheaper and lower-quality imports. Or where he'd worked out a way for woodcrafters not to work with wood that damaged their health. On the other hand, by amending the reallocation bill, Obreduur had kept Guldoran Ironway from getting almost all of the additional rail-maintenance funding, but how did that help various crafters or working people? And getting better Sanitation job descriptions approved for Machtarn wasn't going to mean much to workers in Oersynt, even if the principles could be adopted elsewhere.

By a third before fifth bell, Dekkard had what he'd written up ready for the councilor and was more than glad for a break.

Obreduur came out of the inner office, took the papers from the two, and handed them to Karola. "If you'd have them typed up and put them on my desk."

"Yes, sir."

Dekkard concentrated on being alert, especially once they were walking—with almost no one else around—under the roofed portico to the Council Hall, since he still recalled a rainy evening in spring. But nothing happened, and after Obreduur left them, he and Avraal went to the cafeteria, which was almost empty. They both had milanesia, fowl for Avraal, veal for Dekkard, Kuhrs for both, and after paying they took a wall table for four.

"Jaime Minz had a few words to say to me this morning . . ." Dekkard quickly related what transpired, and the fact that he hadn't had the chance to tell Obreduur, then took a long swallow of his Kuhrs.

"That sounds like he's been hired to be an influencer here in Machtarn. Besides telling Obreduur, if you see Amelya Detauran, you might pass that on. Councilor

Bassaana might like to know that, given that she has a large minority interest in Northwest."

"If I do, I will." Dekkard took a bite of the veal milanesia, then asked cheerfully, "Are you ready for a long ironway trip?"

"About as ready as you are," she replied dryly.

As instructed, Dekkard and Avraal were walking down the corridor toward the dining room entrance just before first bell. Dekkard noticed that Micah Eljaan and Malcolm Maarkham stood a little ways away talking with three other security aides, but since the five were so engrossed, Dekkard stopped well short of joining, them as did Avraal.

"No other aides around," said Dekkard quietly.

"Most councilors have already left."

No one at all emerged until a third after the bell when Councilor Charls Maastach and another councilor walked out casually, with no security aides waiting.

Then Dekkard remembered that Maastach had been required to step down.

After several minutes, another three councilors came out. Dekkard immediately recognized Saarh, but not the other two. He was about to ask Avraal about them when Obreduur appeared and joined them.

"Did you have a good meeting?" asked Dekkard politely.

Obreduur offered a humorous smile. "I won't find that out until after elections, and that's if we're successful. Right now, we need to get back to the office. The Night Express leaves at fourth bell."

For Dekkard, Avraal, and the councilor the next two bells were a rush, but by a third before fourth bell they were on board the Night Express to Oersynt.

Although each had a separate compartment, given that sharing sleeping quarters would have been politically inexpedient, as well as cramped, Dekkard and Avraal were sitting in her compartment as the express pulled out of Imperial Station at precisely fourth bell.

"Did you bring any novels to read?" asked Avraal.

"I didn't think about it. We haven't been exactly un-occupied. Did you?"

She shook her head, then added with the hint of a mischievous smile, "I'm just glad I won't have to compete with *The Scarlet Daughter*."

Dekkard laughed, then leaned over and kissed her cheek, well aware that the compartment door was open.

91

Dekkard slept only moderately well on the Night Express, partly because he was aware that Avraal was only a compartment away. He knew that didn't make any sense. For two years, she'd been sleeping in the room adjacent to his, and that had never affected him. *Except for most of that time you didn't realize you were in love with her.*

He awoke early, washed up as best he could, and shaved at the tiny sink, trying to be careful that he didn't cut himself . . . and was successful, at least as far as he could see. Once dressed, he wrestled the fold-down bed back into place, and then opened his compartment door.

Less than a sixth later Avraal's door opened, and she asked, "Could I join you?"

As she closed her compartment door, he could see her bed was down. That didn't surprise him, since he'd had to use some force to replace his bed.

"We'll wait for Obreduur to get breakfast," she said. "It might be safe enough, but . . ."

Dekkard nodded. "How did you sleep?"

"Well enough, but the light seeped in."

"That's right. You're on the east side of the carriage. We should have switched compartments."

Avraal frowned.

"I tend to wake up early anyway. You don't . . . or

not as early," he added quickly. "You could have slept a little later, anyway."

At that moment, Obreduur peered in. "Good! Shall we go have breakfast?"

Breakfast in the dining carriage was mixed. The café was good, almost excellent, and there was even quince paste for the croissants, but the croissants were stale and a touch soggy. Dekkard ate them anyway, if with a slight excess of quince paste.

Slightly before fourth bell of the morning, the express crossed the Rio Mal, under a greenish-gray sky and light rain, and came to a stop in the Guldoran Ironway station in Oersynt.

Dekkard gathered together the baggage for the porters. Outside the station, Jareld Herrardo was waiting, fortunately under an overhanging roof for loading, with a dark blue Gresynt, either the same steamer as the one he'd used to transport them weeks earlier or one identical to it. He seemed to force a smile as he called out, "Welcome to Oersynt . . . again!"

Dekkard and Herrardo got the luggage loaded fairly quickly, and Herrardo said, "We got word last night that Villem Draforre is the Commerce candidate, and that the Landors picked Edmundo Wustoff. All we know about him is that he's the younger son of one of the largest landholders between Oersynt and Malek."

"We'll just have to see, but I'm inclined to believe Draforre is the greater danger," replied Obreduur. "Can I see the schedule?"

Herrardo handed sheets to each, then said, "The first visit is at first bell—that's at the wholesale produce center. I didn't want to schedule too closely. Guldoran's had some delays lately because of rain damage to one of the lines between here and Gaarlak. But that will give you a chance to clean up at the hotel and get something to eat."

"If we're ready earlier," said Obreduur, "we can visit some of the shops near the hotel."

Herrardo handed the councilor a heliogram envelope. "You need to read this."

Obreduur took the envelope and settled himself in the rear seat.

Herrardo had barely left the station when Obreduur cleared his throat, then said, "Jens Seigryn sent a heliogram this morning from Gaarlak. Johan Lamarr was killed last night in a fire and explosion at the family clock- and watchmaking business. The explosion was apparently triggered by a barrel of solvents that was either leaking or improperly stored, if not both. He'll keep us informed of what happens next."

"That wasn't an accident," said Dekkard.

"Why do you think that?" asked Obreduur evenly.

"The man I met in Gaarlak was on top of details. He was precise and knowledgeable, and Lamarr timepieces are known for their precision. People like that don't make careless mistakes, and they seldom hire careless people."

"From what I sensed of Lamarr," added Avraal, "I'd agree with Steffan."

"So would I," said Obreduur, "but if the local patrollers can't come up with any evidence that leads to someone, then the cause of death will remain as an accidental death."

"Does that mean that Haasan Decaro will replace Lamarr as the Craft Party candidate?" asked Dekkard, strongly suspecting that he already knew the answer.

"Unless there's evidence to link Haasan to the explosion . . . and there won't be," replied Obreduur. "Haasan's always been good at hiding his tracks, and he's been even better at making sure that anyone who knows anything won't speak up. There's also enough support among some of the rank-and-file patrollers for him that unless the evidence is overwhelming, Security isn't about to charge him. Then, there's also the feeling among some guild members that Lamarr's been successful enough that he's part Commercer. That's another reason why the District Convention vote was so contentious."

"And why you were asked to go to Gaarlak?" asked Dekkard.

"Certainly part of it."

"So what can you do now?" asked Dekkard.

"That's up to the district Craft Party, and they'll have to come to an agreement," said Obreduur. "It will be Haasan Decaro, regardless of the suspicion about Lamarr's death, because Decaro is the only candidate right now who can get enough votes to take that seat from the Landors." He paused. "In the meantime, we have more than a little campaigning to do."

A sixth later, Dekkard arrived at his room at the Hotel Cosmopolitano. Unlike the previous visits to Oersynt, this time Obreduur had only a single room, flanked on each side by Dekkard's and Avraal's rooms. Dekkard quickly washed up and then brushed off his grays.

Then he waited out in the corridor for Avraal, and the two of them waited a few minutes for Obreduur before the three headed down to the restaurant, where they ate. Dekkard opted for grilled chicken in flatbread, with Riverfall lager, Avraal for an Imperial salad, and Obreduur for the house onion soup topped with cheese.

By a third after fifth bell, the three were walking west on Copper Avenue, where they stopped at a small stationery store next to the hotel.

"Only two people there," said Avraal.

Dekkard opened the door, while Obreduur and Avraal entered, then followed them inside. The store was slightly less than four yards wide, and perhaps four to the rear wall of the front room, with a door to whatever lay behind on the right side of the back wall. An open-fronted glass case two yards long and waist high displayed papers in various sizes, tints, and shades.

"I'll be with you in a moment, sir," said the woman behind the counter, apparently ringing up a sale on the large bronze mechanical cash register.

"There's no hurry," Obreduur replied cheerfully.

The customer, an older woman stylishly dressed in an off-white linen suit, finished paying, then stepped away from the counter, before pausing to look at a display of letter openers.

Dekkard suspected she was curious and wanted to know who or why the well-dressed man accompanied by two security aides happened to be in the shop.

Obreduur stepped up to the counter. "I'm not a customer, at least not at the moment. I'm Axel Obreduur . . ."

"Your name is familiar, sir, but I can't say from where . . ."

"I'm the councilor of the Sixty-Six from Oersynt, and just wanted to remind you to vote in the election a week from Findi."

The shopkeeper offered an amused smile. "You'd prefer I'd vote for you, I take it?"

Obreduur smiled in return. "I'd certainly appreciate it, and it might even be in your interests, since I'm running, as I have before, as the Craft Party candidate. Our interests do tend to favor smaller shops over the interests of large corporacions. Might I ask what you feel is the matter that most needs the attention of the Council?"

"Stopping those New Meritorists. You'd think Guldor was Atacama the way they're acting."

"We do have problems," replied Obreduur, "but destroying the longest-lasting and most successful government in the world isn't the way to fix them."

She looked at him more intently. "You're the councilor. What do you think the biggest problem is?"

"That the Commerce Party has held power for too long and become corrupted. Every week there's another story about abuse of power."

"Like the Kraffeist Affair?"

"That's just one."

"How would you and the Craft Party be any better?"

"We'd have to prove we're better, because people who haven't voted for us are skeptical. We're also the ones who've made small changes for the better even though we're not in power."

Behind Obreduur, the door opened.

The shopkeeper glanced to the door, then said, "I'll have to think about it."

Obreduur stepped back. "Please remember to vote. I'd like your vote, but do vote."

As the clerk moved to deal with the customer who had just entered, the older woman who had waited took a step toward Obreduur and said, "You're the young councilor they tried to kill two weeks back, aren't you? That's why you have security with you, isn't it?"

"I'd have to say yes to both questions."

The older woman nodded. "I'll vote for anyone those Meritorists want to kill."

"If you can encourage your friends and family to vote, I'd very much appreciate it."

"I'll see what I can do." She gestured toward the door. "Go ahead. You have people to meet. I'm in no hurry."

"Thank you," said Obreduur warmly.

When the three were outside walking toward the next shop, which sported the name Darisha's, and which appeared to feature women's wear, Dekkard murmured to Avraal, "Usually, you can at least warm up . . ."

"She was strong-minded enough almost to be an isolate."

"I wondered."

Inside Darisha's, two young women in deep purple dresses trimmed in white looked up as Obreduur entered. Then one stepped forward and said, "Might I help you, sir?"

"You can, but not by selling me anything. My name is Axel Obreduur, and I'm the incumbent Craft councilor. I'd like to know your thoughts about what's important to you about government . . . and, if possible, persuade you to vote for me in the election a week from Findi."

"There's an election a week from Findi?" asked the first shopgirl.

"The Imperador announced it last week," said the second. "Where were you?" She turned to Obreduur. "Can you get us better pay, sir?"

"The best we've been able to do is to get women paid as much for the same job as men."

"That won't help much here. The owner doesn't hire shopboys."

"You're really a councilor?" asked the first shopgirl.

"I am."

"What's it like? Have you ever met the Imperador? What's he like?"

"We spend a lot of time trying to help people and working out how to spend government funds in the way that will do the most good. I only met the Imperador briefly. He was very pleasant, but concentrated on the matter at hand."

"Is he tall?"

"I'm about the same height as he is."

"Would you like to buy a dress for someone?" asked the first shopgirl.

"I'd never buy my wife a dress if she weren't here, but thank you. You've been very kind, and I hope you'll both vote in the election."

Obreduur led the way from the shop.

The third stop was at a bookstore. An older man stood behind the counter and looked curiously at Obreduur as he entered, then shook his head in what might have been disbelief, before saying, "You aren't Councilor Obreduur, are you?"

"I'm afraid I am." Obreduur smiled wryly.

"My brother talks about you all the time. You're the acting Premier now, aren't you?"

"Just until the election, and that's why I'm here."

"Don't worry, sir. We'll both vote for you, and so will our wives. Our cousin's a woodcrafter for Guldoran Ironway. He told us about how you stopped them from using yellow cedar. Just like all corporacions. It's all about marks . . ."

Some minutes later Obreduur gracefully extracted

himself from the bookstore, and the three turned and walked back toward the hotel to meet Herrardo.

"I'd hoped to stop in a few more shops," Obreduur said. "It's been a while since I've actually walked the streets here, but the first two stops might help."

Dekkard could see that. The man in the bookstore would have voted for Obreduur anyway, while the most of the others hadn't even known who he was.

The blue Gresynt was waiting at the hotel.

"Out gathering some more voters?" asked Herrardo as the three entered the steamer.

"Trying," replied Obreduur cheerfully. "We can always use more votes."

Herrardo swung the steamer onto Copper Avenue, then turned south on Second Street in the direction of the ironway station. In minutes, the Gresynt approached the Wholesale Produce Center of Oersynt, an oversized square building that filled an entire block, albeit a small block, less than three blocks from the ironway station. Herrardo slowed the steamer short of the loading docks and turned in to a parking space marked FOR OFFICIAL BUSINESS.

Obreduur was definitely an official, but Dekkard doubted that campaigning came under the definition of official business. He also doubted that anyone would raise the issue.

The four got out, with Herrardo leading the way up a set of steps constructed of heavy timbers and grayed by years of soot, beside the last loading dock, to a door, which he opened. At the end of a short hallway was another door, which led to an enormous hall, a good twenty yards wide, and close to seventy long.

"This hall is for the smaller growers," said Herrardo, clearly talking to Dekkard and Avraal. "The center hall is for the larger growers, and the far hall is for flowers. You'll have to keep moving if you want to meet everyone you can in this hall in the four bells before you need to go back to the hotel and change for dinner."

Obreduur walked to the nearest stall, almost empty, except for a few bushels of potatoes.

The single man there turned. "Not much left, sir."

"I'm not here for the potatoes," replied Obreduur. "I came late because I didn't want to get in the way of customers. I'm Councilor Axel Obreduur." He paused for an instant to see if the grower showed any sign of recognition, then went on. "I'm running for reelection in the election a week from Findi. I'd like to know what you'd like or need from government, and also to ask if you'd consider voting for me."

The grower shook his head. "The only thing I want from government is not to increase my taxes and to keep the rivers from flooding my lands."

"Are you near the Mal or the Azulete?"

"South bank of the Mal, ten milles east of the iron-way bridge."

"So you're concerned about the Eshhaart levee?"

For the first time, Dekkard could see that the grower looked interested.

"Who wouldn't be? It's nearly fifty years old."

"You've got yellow norths there. They usually don't grow in bottomland. Or am I missing something?"

Dekkard took a quick look at what was in the nearest bushel basket. They just looked like potatoes to him.

The grower grinned. "Those are from the hillside terraces. I sold off all the Chuiven whites first thing this morning. How'd you know that?"

"I started out as a stevedore in Whulte years ago. I saw a lot of potatoes . . ."

"What did you say your name was?"

"Obreduur . . . Axel Obreduur."

"I'll think about it, Councilor. If you'll excuse me . . ."

"You need to take care of things. I appreciate your talking to me."

Obreduur moved away past a now-empty stall to a smaller one, in which mushrooms were displayed, in far smaller baskets. Dekkard recognized the giant browns, and the stringy orientals, and the white button mushrooms, but not the light brown stringy ones.

"You a restaurateur looking for the best for your tables? I've got the very best," said the wiry man in brown trousers and shirt.

"They look superb," replied Obreduur. "I wish I were shopping for a restaurant. For this variety and quality, you must spend a long time at it."

"The family's been at it some forty years . . ." The man paused. "What's your interest?"

"In a way . . . keeping you and your family in business. I'm Axel Obreduur—"

"The councilor . . . the one who's the acting Premier?"

"That's right."

"What are you doing here in the produce market?"

Obreduur grinned. "Trying to ask you to vote for me in the upcoming election. The one a week from Findi."

"You're really him?" The man's eyes strayed to Dekkard, then lingered on Avraal, before he looked back to Obreduur. "You must be. They're security, aren't they?"

"Unhappily, they're necessary."

"Why did you come here? You're not a Landor."

"No . . . but I started out as a stevedore, and I know more than I'd like to about working hard. I try to meet people I haven't met before. That's why I'm here."

"I never thought . . ."

Obreduur smiled again, quietly. "Councilors are people, too. Some worked with their hands, some worked as legalists, or a teachers, or machinists . . . or for corporacions. You need to see us, and we need to see you. That's why I'm here . . . and, of course, to try to get you to consider voting for me."

"It's good to meet you, sir . . . but I'll have to think about it."

"That's all I can expect, but whatever you decide . . . please vote."

Obreduur moved to the next stall . . .

Dekkard could tell that it was going to be a long afternoon . . . and that, incidentally, he would learn bits and pieces of information he'd never heard before.

In fact, it did take almost four bells for Obreduur to walk through just the hall serving the smaller growers. He talked at least briefly to everyone at the more than sixty stalls that he visited . . . well over a hundred people, by Dekkard's count, since there were often more people than a single grower at many of the stalls.

Dekkard was more than glad to sit down in the Gresynt for the ride back to the Hotel Cosmopolitano.

"Did you learn anything this afternoon?" asked Obreduur cheerfully.

"I knew that campaigning was hard work," replied Dekkard, "but I learned more about produce than I ever thought I would." He turned to look at Avraal. "I imagine you knew some of that."

"Some. You have to remember that I grew up on one holding, and we just visited the equivalent of more than fifty."

"When we get back to the hotel," Obreduur said, "you'll have a little less than a bell to change before we leave for Fangio's."

"Yes, sir. Who might be at the dinner?" Dekkard knew where Fangio's was, because he'd heard, on and off growing up, of the restaurant as expensive and prestigious, but the itinerary hadn't mentioned the attendees by name, just that it was a campaign dinner for local business owners and their spouses, presumably, Dekkard surmised, for businesses larger than shops and smaller than corporacions who had donated to the Craft Party, very generously, since contributions to candidates were absolutely forbidden.

"Herrardo?" asked Obreduur.

"Offhand, I can't remember the entire guest list but it's only ten couples, plus you, Avraal, Steffan, and me. I know Leon Frazeer, Heinrich Sommes, Alfredo Andolini, Maercel DeHines, Marshal Austen, Lucien Garcia, and Gloriana Saffel are coming, all with their spouses. I should remember the other three . . ."

Just as Herrardo pulled up in the entry circle of the hotel, he said, "Elizabetta Higgbee, Quentin Harrowes, and Sammis Lerron, also with spouses, except Harrowes. His fiancée will be with him."

"Fiancée?" asked Obreduur.

"His wife died suddenly in Springfirst. She'd been ill for years, tubercular degeneration."

He certainly didn't waste any time. Dekkard raised his eyebrows and looked at Avraal, who returned his unasked question with a cynical smile.

"I'll see you here at a third before sixth bell," said Herrardo as the three exited the Gresynt.

Once they were inside the hotel and headed up to their rooms, Dekkard asked, "The dinner's for the larger contributors to the party?"

"For some of the largest contributors, especially Leon Frazeer and Quentin Harrowes. Gloriana Saffel's also important, because she owns the largest clerical training and employment service in Oersynt. Her trainees provide clerical services for the local party. Some of the greatest support isn't always marks." Obreduur stopped before his door. "We'll meet here just before we go down to meet Herrardo."

Dekkard made sure Avraal was in her room before entering his, then getting himself ready with one of the clean gray suits, a white shirt, and the black cravat Avraal had given him. He did choose the personal truncheon, as well as his knives.

He was the first back out in the corridor, followed by Avraal, who wore a gray suit as well, except with trousers rather than a skirt, clearly emphasizing she was there for security. Obreduur wore a black suit, with the red cravat commonly worn by councilors.

At almost precisely a third before sixth bell, Herrardo, attired in a fashion similar to Obreduur, except his cravat was a deep green, drove the Gresynt away from the Hotel Cosmopolitano. The drive to Fangio's was short, only about half the distance between the hotel and Geddes Square. When they arrived, Herrardo turned the Gresynt over to the restaurant's parking valet, and entered the building with Obreduur, followed by Avraal and Dekkard.

The maître d'hôtel immediately appeared, in deep blue livery with pale blue piping. "The private dining room is ready, Councilor, Sr. Herrardo." He led them down a side corridor parallel to the front of the building, then stepped through the open double doors.

While Herrardo and Obreduur talked with him, Dekkard and Avraal studied the chamber, since they would be screening those who attended as they entered and were greeted by Herrardo.

The left side of the chamber was arranged as for a reception, with sideboards and servers, while the right side was arranged with tables set up in a U shape. Dekkard judged that there were four long tables forming the U, two forming the base, in the middle of which Obreduur would be seated, and one for each side of the U, doubtless with Dekkard at the end of one side and Avraal at the end of the other.

To Dekkard's eye, the décor was slightly overaccented old Imperial, with dark wood paneling and pale blue hangings trimmed with gold. The linens on the U-shaped tables were also pale blue, and the table napkins of a golden linen. Dekkard decided that those invited must have been *very* generous contributors to the party.

After a few minutes, the maître d'hôtel departed, and Herrardo joined Dekkard and Avraal at the doors while Obreduur went to one of the sideboards and obtained a beaker of lager, most likely Riverfall.

Dekkard could understand that. Once the guests arrived, he'd have little time to drink, at least until dinner was served, and even then he wouldn't eat or drink that much.

Before that long, a couple entered Fangio's and immediately turned toward the private dining room. The raven-haired woman looked to be ten years younger than the slightly paunchy and graying man.

"Lucien Garcia and his wife Somera," murmured Herrardo, who waited for the two to reach the doors before saying, "Lucien, Somera, we're so glad you could come this evening."

"Somera wasn't about to turn down a dinner here when you're paying, Jareld."

Somera smiled and said, "We both know he's the one who thinks that way."

"We're just glad you're both here. This evening, the councilor has two of his aides here, Avraal Ysella, who handles land and women's issues, and Steffan Dekkard, who deals with artisan matters and tariffs."

"And both clearly deal with security," replied Sr. Garcia.

"Only when necessary," said Avraal, "and that's very unlikely this evening."

"We're glad to hear it," replied Lucien Garcia. "Oh . . . there's the councilor. We should go talk to him before he's surrounded."

"Indeed," agreed Somera pleasantly before continuing with her husband.

Dekkard was very well aware that Somera Garcia's eyes had lingered on him far more than for casual interest. He glanced to Avraal and raised his eyebrows, nodding slightly in the direction of the Garcias.

Avraal remained perfectly calm as she said quietly, "Just passing casual lust. That's all."

Beside her, Herrardo smothered a laugh, momentarily turning his head away from the next two approaching couples. Then, after regaining his composure, he said, "Sammis and Adelye Lerron, then Heinrich and Berthe Sommes."

After those two couples entered, Herrardo said quietly, "Gloriana Saffel and Titus Steffans. They're married. She kept her name because of the business."

Business? Then Dekkard recalled that she trained and placed clericals. As she neared, he found himself surprised, because he'd expected either a large or flamboyant personage, but she wore a tailored black silk jacket, with matching trousers, and an off-white silk blouse. Titus Steffans had a thin black brush mustache and wore a dark green suit with a silver shirt and a silk cravat that matched the color of his suit.

After the introductions, Gloriana looked to Avril, then Dekkard, before saying, "I wondered who was good enough to save him. Thank you both. I hope we'll have a chance to talk." She smiled pleasantly, then headed directly toward Obreduur. Her husband followed, a half step behind.

For the next sixth, couples appeared and then entered the chamber.

At almost half past sixth bell, Herrardo said quietly, "Everyone is here except Quentin Harrowes." He glanced toward the restaurant entrance and added, "I take that back. Here comes Quentin with Mellorie Maaske."

Dekkard studied the pair as they approached. Harrowes was a big man, handsome and taller than Dekkard, and just slightly broader, but with only a hint of extra weight, thick silver hair, and an easy smile that he flashed at Herrardo. Mellorie Maaske reminded Dekkard of a vole, small and alert, with brown hair, brown eyes, and faultless pale brown skin. She had to be at least twenty years younger than Harrowes, but when she glanced sideways at him, her expression was close to that of pure adoration.

Once the couple entered and headed toward Obreduur, Herrardo closed the double doors and smiled wryly. "Time to mix and mingle."

Avraal glanced at Dekkard. "We'll compare notes later."

He nodded. "It should be interesting." As he made his way toward one of the sideboards, he just hoped it wasn't too interesting. After obtaining a beaker of Riverfall, he took several steps away from the sideboard and then took a healthy swallow.

"I heard that you're very highly rated in martial arts," said a sultry voice to his right.

Dekkard didn't have to turn to know who it had to be, but he smiled as he moved to face Somera Garcia. With her was another woman, and it took him an instant to recall that she was Andrea Andolini. "That was years ago, and the real world doesn't care much about academic prowess or scholastic athletics . . . as I'm sure both of you ladies know."

"I'm very sure that such prowess has proved . . . useful," replied Somera.

"That, and having a very good partner," said Dekkard. "I'm afraid you have me at a disadvantage. All I know about either of you are your names, and that you're presumably from the Oersynt area, and that the Council thinks highly of you."

"Or of the contributions made by my husband," suggested Somera, who then nodded toward Andrea Andolini, "and those made from your inheritance by your husband."

"Actually, I had to . . . persuade him to contribute. He's still aspiring to be a Landor." Andrea smiled pleasantly. "You're a bit too handsome and muscular to be one of the councilor's river rats. Where did you come from?"

"An artisan background here in Oersynt. My father's a decorative-plaster artisan, and my mother's a portraitist."

"And she's very good," interjected another voice, which belonged to a plain-faced woman with a smile that radiated warmth. "She did my niece's portrait last year." She glanced at the thin man who had just joined her. "Even Maercel thought it was excellent, and he doesn't even like art."

With the name Maercel, Dekkard made the connection—Maercel and Norah DeHines. "I'll have to tell her . . . when I get a chance."

"You and your partner have been rather busy, from what I've read in the newssheets," said Maercel DeHines.

"That's true, but most of our time is spent working in his office helping people one way or another."

"Jareld mentioned you've been involved in tariffs. Can you explain?"

"The Artisans Guild in Machtarn discovered that tariff inspectors were misassessing tariffs on imported art and art objects . . ." Dekkard went on to explain, and as he did Somera Garcia and Andrea Andolini drifted off, while Gloriana Saffel moved closer.

"That explains a lot," said Maercel DeHines.

"About more than tariffs, as well," added Gloriana Saffel. "You and your partner do a great deal more than security, obviously."

"There's no point in our sitting around when he's in the office," replied Dekkard.

"That makes sense," replied the clericals magnate, "but most people don't think anything out as much as they should. Axel does, and he's either found people who can think as well . . . or taught you."

"A little of both, I'd say," replied Dekkard. "And I suspect you do your best to train your people to handle more than the merely clerical, and that's why you've been successful."

Gloriana glanced to Maercel. "Doesn't that tell you why Axel's been successful?"

"There are lots of reasons why he's been successful." Maercel nodded to Dekkard. "A pleasure meeting you." Then he took his wife's arm and guided her away.

Gloriana shook her head. "Maercel's a bit too much old Imperial."

"You mean . . . he wishes the Silent Revolution hadn't happened?"

She smiled. "I like you. You must have sisters or a strong mother."

"Both. I also have a strong security partner, and I listen to her."

"That's been one of Axel's greatest achievements."

For a moment, Dekkard didn't follow. Then he said, "You mean listening to Ingrella?"

"And others, because of her . . . it's why this election could be different. But we'll just have to see."

Different because he's listened to women? "Different in what way?"

"If it is, you'll see . . . and from what you've said, you'll understand. If not, then I'll have been wrong . . . and I do so detest it when that occurs. Please . . . do tell me about your sister and mother."

Given the quiet iron in her voice, Dekkard smiled, and said, "My sister is four years older . . ." then went on.

When he finished, Gloriana nodded. "They did well by you. I imagine we'll be hearing more about you in the years ahead." She smiled pleasantly, then bustled off.

Dekkard was still wondering what that was all about when he was joined by Quentin Harrowes and his fiancée.

"Mellorie wondered how you ended up working for Axel," said Harrowes.

"I could say that it's because my family settled here before I was born, but after the Institute I took another year of security training—"

"You're an Institute graduate and just doing security?"

"Not just. I'm also an assistant economic specialist."

"Ah . . . that makes much more sense . . ."

Another third of a bell passed before a series of chimes rang and Herrardo called out for everyone to take their places at the U-shaped table, as designated by their place cards.

Dekkard sat at the end of one of short tables, flanked on the left by Elizabetta Higgbee and on the right by Adelye Lerron, neither of whom he had spoken with except when they entered the chamber, but before he could even say a word to either, Obreduur stood and waited for the murmurs to die down.

"I've been told that I need to say a few words," began the councilor. "So I'll begin with the two most important words this evening. Thank you. The Craft Party has a chance—right now it's only a chance, but it's a solid good chance—to form the next government of Guldor. We wouldn't have that chance without the help of every person in this room. Over the past ten years, you've been behind us, and it's made a difference. Who would have thought that we'd ever have the plurality in the Council? Even without controlling the government we've been able to make a difference, and that's because of you. So . . . again . . . thank you . . . and that's as short as I can make it. Now . . . enjoy the food, drink, and the company."

With that, he smiled again and sat down.

"For a politician," said Adelye Lerron, "he certainly never talks that much about himself. Not in public, anyway." She looked to Dekkard. "Is he that different in private?"

"Not really. Sometimes, he'll give detailed explanations, and he also asks questions. They're never stupid questions." Dekkard paused while a server refilled his beaker.

The two women saw their wineglasses refilled, and Elizabetta, a petite middle-aged woman with a somehow commanding presence and iron-gray hair, asked, "You're closer to this than we are. How do you think the election will come out?"

"I think the Craft Party will win the plurality of seats. Whether that will allow the councilor to form a government depends on things I don't know."

"You sound somewhat like him."

"He's taught me to be careful in expressing opinions where I don't have the facts to back them up." *Even if you do just that far too often.*

"Facts are useful, but are just as often misused, usually in support of power," replied Elizabetta. "That's why many women mistrust them."

"Why do you say that?" asked Dekkard.

"Because she's the dean of Women's Studies at the university," said Adelye Lerron, "and she built that college from almost nothing."

Dekkard nodded, trying to make the connection. "Do you think men misuse facts more than women?"

"Women can't afford to be wrong about facts," said Elizabetta almost primly. "Especially in dealing with men. Even if they're correct, they're treated with skepticism. That allows men to beat down everyone with facts, true and false. Besides, you can lie most effectively with facts."

"I've seen that more than a few times." Dekkard smiled, feeling like his face was forming into a permanent pleasant smile.

Although Dekkard did little but make pleasant conversation for the remainder of the dinner, he felt absolutely exhausted when he settled into the Gresynt for the ride back to the Hotel Cosmopolitano. That didn't stop him from being alert when he got out of the steamer at the hotel, and especially when he and Avraal escorted Obreduur to his chamber.

"We need to talk," said Avraal. "Your room."

Dekkard smiled. "Why always my room?"

"Just a preference of mine . . . and it's nice to be in a man's room that's neat."

Dekkard didn't argue, just led the way to his room, opened the door, and gestured for her to enter. Since there was a side chair and a small armchair, he motioned for her to take the armchair.

As soon as she sat down, she asked, "Gloriana Saffel . . . what did she say to you?"

"Just that Obreduur thought things through and seemed to hire people who did, or that he managed to teach them that. She also made a comment about how this election might be different. I asked her why she thought that. She avoided answering that by insisting that I tell her about my sister and mother. Then she said they'd done well by me and that she'd be hearing about me in the years to come . . . and she left, just like that. Did she talk to you?"

Avraal frowned slightly, then offered an amused

smile. "She did. She asked about you, especially if you respected women."

"What did you tell her?" Dekkard asked, not knowing if he'd like the answer.

"I told her the truth . . . that, while you're definitely your own man and can be stubborn, sometimes you respect them too much. She looked at me and told me that I'd better take care of that. And then she left. Did you see where she was seated?"

"At the part of the table you might call the head table, but not next to Obreduur."

"Exactly."

"Meaning that she's very important in some way."

"Much more, but it's more than that her clericals probably gather information for her. There's something else there."

"We should ask Obreduur."

"I did. He just said that we'd see how important she is. You sat next to Elizabetta Higgbee. Did you learn anything about her?"

"She's the dean of Women's Studies at Oersynt University, and I got the feeling she comes from wealth and has been using it to expand her college . . . and possibly for other causes. She thinks men misuse facts more than women."

"Do you agree with her?"

"I hadn't thought about it that way, but when she made that point, I had to agree . . . mostly. I think powerful women may do it as well, but since there aren't as many of them, men are usually the ones who predominate in factual lying."

"Factual lying . . . that's a good way of putting it."

"Did you find out anything else interesting?" asked Dekkard.

"Not that much. All the men, from what I could hear and feel, are pretty much what they seem to be, some a little more, some a little less. What about you?"

"Only that one of them, Norah . . . DeHines . . . had a niece who had her portrait painted by my mother . . .

and she said that the portrait was excellent. Gloriana Saffel told me that Norah's husband was too old Imperial . . . meaning—"

". . . that women should have stayed in the bedroom, nursery, and kitchen."

Dekkard nodded.

Avraal stood. "We need to get some sleep."

Dekkard stood as well, but he moved forward and put his arms around her.

She embraced him warmly for a long moment, followed the hug with a brief kiss, then stepped back. "Right now . . . we don't need any more complications."

I'd love some complications. "I understand." *I don't have to like it, but I understand.* He turned and walked her out of his chamber and to her door, watching until she was safely inside before heading back to his own room.

92

On Furdi morning, Dekkard hurried down to the lobby and picked up a copy of *The Oersynt Press*, reading through it as he climbed the stairs and while he stood waiting for Avraal and Obreduur. Most of the news was local, and there was an article on page one below the fold about Obreduur's return and about how he'd be splitting time between Oersynt and Malek.

Dekkard was more than glad that he'd written his family, although, in looking at the schedule, he doubted that he'd have any time to see them. He was still thinking about that when Avraal left her room.

She glanced at the newssheet he still held.

"There's not much there about politics except a short story about Obreduur being here to campaign." He offered her the newssheet.

She shook her head, and Dekkard didn't press.

Moments later, Obreduur appeared and led the way down to the hotel restaurant. Neither Obreduur nor Ysella said anything as they first sipped their café, except to order. Respecting their need for the café to take effect, Dekkard didn't say anything either, beyond ordering.

Finally, Obreduur said, "The dinner went as well as it could have."

"Something that had to be done, but which won't gain votes?" asked Dekkard.

"Not in this election, but you need to let people know you value and appreciate them. Any event that provides good food and drink and lets them be heard usually can't hurt. Herrardo will be joining us shortly. We'll see if he has anything to say that we might have missed."

Dekkard took a sip of café and hoped it wouldn't be too long before his croissants and orange juice arrived.

"Did either of you discover anything?" Obreduur took another sip of café and waited.

"Only things about people that you know," Dekkard finally replied. "The fact that Elizabetta Higgbee is a dean at Oersynt University . . . and I assume that Gloriana Saffel uses her contacts with her former clerical trainees to gather useful information . . . among other things."

"She's proved very helpful . . . and not just to me." Obreduur smiled. "She's also trained some of the party volunteers." He looked up. "Here comes Jareld, and he looks concerned." He gestured to the empty chair across the table from him.

Before sitting down, Herrardo handed a heliogram envelope to Obreduur.

Obreduur took the message out, read it, and then replaced it in the envelope and handed it across the table to Herrardo. "The Gaarlak Craft Party chose Haasan Decaro as the replacement candidate for Council." He paused, then added, "By acclamation."

"So that's it?" asked Dekkard.

"He's the Craft candidate. Obviously, the party

doesn't want any more squabbles and wants to win the election." He smiled wryly. "Better our bastard than a Commercer bastard. Jens will keep us informed and take care of anything that needs to be done there."

"Do you think he can win?" asked Avraal. "Especially with the opposition of many of the textile workers?"

Obreduur shrugged. "Right now, he's the only one who has a chance. There are those who'd make far better councilors, but that doesn't matter if they can't get elected. That's where idealists like the New Meritorists get it wrong. A popular and principled idealist can do nothing without the votes, and you can't defeat an unprincipled party like what the Commercers have become just with ideals. It takes votes."

"But what if all a party elects are popular and unprincipled candidates?" asked Dekkard.

"You have the Commercers. We can afford a few lessthan-perfect candidates. Occasionally, we can even replace them with someone better. We'll be all right as long as we only have a few bastards. Popularity is always a temptation, something that the New Meritorists have yet to realize."

"They've been awfully quiet," said Herrardo. "Do you think they'll disrupt the elections?"

"Who can tell?" replied Obreduur. "I'm guessing that the Imperador's immediate demand for Ulrich's resignation and his call for new elections caught them off guard, and they're regrouping. If the next government is still Commercer, I suspect the demonstrations will get worse. They certainly won't go away, even if we're the government."

Dekkard had one unanswered question. "Speaking of problems, what about Gretna Haarl? She didn't care for Lamarr, but she was really opposed to Decaro."

"The message didn't say, but someone must have gotten to her," said Herrardo, "because Decaro couldn't have been acclaimed over her opposition. Maybe Jens or someone pointed out the downside of not having any councilor . . . or made some agreement."

Dekkard wondered if the price had been making Haarl the guildmeister of the Textile Millworkers. He couldn't imagine her changing her vote for anything less.

"Doubtless there were promises made," said Obreduur dryly. "There always are. Some are real, and some are illusory. Sometimes the ones we think are real turn out to be illusory, and what we thought was an illusion turns out to be real. That happens in politics more than you think." He took a deep breath. "In the meantime, we need to get ready. We'll be going house to house north of Iron Avenue and west of Fifth Boulevard. In that area, most of the wives stay home. Those who don't have nursemaids or nannies, and many of them can vote. Then, after second bell, we'll be going to the Sanitation depot, and we'll meet with the lorry crews as they come off the lorries. Late afternoon, I'll be speaking to the Tulip Hills Garden Club, and tonight, we'll be at a meeting of the Ironway Maintenance Guild."

"The councilor will be the first candidate appearing," said Herrardo.

"That meeting is not an evening engagement," Obreduur added, looking at Ysella. "Both of you stay in security grays."

"The hall's not in the best of locations," added Herrardo.

In less than a sixth, the four were back in the Gresynt heading west on Copper Avenue, then north on Fifth Boulevard. The mechanics for visiting houses were the same as what Obreduur had done before—a clever introduction, an inquiry about concerns, some follow-on that personalized the matter for the person—usually a woman—with whom he was talking, and a quiet request to vote, hopefully for Obreduur. After less than a bell, Dekkard realized why Herrardo had chosen that neighborhood—prosperous, but not wealthy, where women would be home and where they wouldn't feel threatened by a knock on the door, and where they'd feel slightly flattered by a distinguished-looking councilor asking for their thoughts and their vote.

Even so, by the time it was a third before second bell, Dekkard's feet were sore, and he was slightly hoarse, because often Obreduur asked him or Ysella to do the introduction, doubtless to save Obreduur's voice.

Meeting the Sanitation lorry crews was just a variation on the same general approach, except Dekkard and Avraal were more involved, often answering questions addressed to them. Dekkard was surprised to learn that a number of the lorry drivers were women, usually muscular women, but women, and Obreduur often let Avraal take the lead with them.

From the Sanitation lorry depot, Herrardo drove them to the Tulip Hills Trinitarian Chapel, northwest of Syntaar Field, where the Tulip Hills Garden Club met in a large classroom, most likely used for scripture classes.

Obreduur surprised Dekkard when, in his talk to the club members, largely older people and mostly women, he observed in passing that tulip petals could be substituted for onions in some recipes, although, as a former stevedore, he found tulips too elegant to eat. Almost everyone smiled at that.

After Obreduur finished talking and answering questions as he mingled with the group, the four then stopped at a small bistro two blocks from Syntaar Field and ate, before Herrardo again took the wheel and drove them to a dingy oblong building adjoining the main ironway rails that headed north to Oost and then to Kathaar. The paint on the stucco walls might once have been white, but had become a dismal gray from the deposit of years of locomotive soot that no amount of paint could totally cover or washing could remove.

Inside wasn't much better, although the hall was well-swept and as clean as it could have been. There were battered wooden benches that might have held a hundred, although the ironway workers standing around and talking quietly looked to number somewhat less.

A lean and angular man in worn brown canvas trousers and a long-sleeved brown shirt immediately walked toward the four. "Councilor Obreduur, Jose Rikkard.

I'm glad you're here. Sr. Draforre informed us at the last moment that, due to a family illness, he wouldn't be able to make it. He must have had a better offer," Rikkard finished sarcastically.

"I'm happy to be here."

"Councilor . . ." Rikkard looked slightly uncomfortable. "You know my men . . . they're not much for speeches and the like."

"That's fine with me," replied Obreduur. "What if I make a very short statement, and then just let them ask me what they want. My statement will be brief, I promise you."

"That sounds good to me." Rikkard sounded relieved.

"Shall we start?"

"Oh . . . of course." Rikkard walked to the low platform and stepped up, followed by Obreduur. Then he gestured to the benches and waited until everyone was seated. "Councilor Obreduur will make a very short statement. After that he'll answer any questions anyone has."

"Thank you." Obreduur inclined his head to Rikkard. "I am glad to be here. As some of you know I've been councilor for several years, and I've worked as hard as possible to make changes that benefit working people. I've also done my best to stop laws and regulations that hurt you. I'll also be honest. Until we can get a Craft government, that is all I—or any Craft councilor—will be able to do. Even though I'm acting Premier at the moment, that's an empty title because the Council has been dissolved. That means there's no way to make better new laws or get rid of bad older laws until after the election. I'm here to ask for your vote in the upcoming election because I believe I can and will do more for you than either a Landor or a Commerce councilor will ever do." He paused. "I said I'd be short. Now, what are your questions . . . or what you want to tell me?"

For a moment, there was silence.

Rikkard broke the silence. "He did say he'd be short.

Allard, you were talking earlier this evening. You want to tell the councilor about it?"

A stocky and bearded young man stood. "You worked with your hands. Have you forgotten what it was like?"

"I haven't. I haven't forgotten loading leaking barrels of pickles and smelling like cheap vinegar and rotten cucumbers from the ones that broke. Or the fingers that got broken and didn't heal right. Or the two toes I lost when a loader was careless . . . and I know I'm fortunate because I know too many who didn't live to be my age—not that I'm even that old . . . and I didn't have to deal with locomotives or runaway rail carriages or freight cars." Obreduur paused just momentarily. "But that's not the real question. The real question is what I can do to make your lives better. How can I make sure that more of the marks you make for the ironway come back to you and don't go to men who've never worked and struggled with machines where a careless move can kill you?

"The answer is that I've done what I can. I kept the ironway woodcrafters from having to work with poisonous yellow cedar. I've amended legislation to keep government funds going to maintenance and not corporacion coffers . . . but that's not enough. We need a Craft government, not a Commerce government, and we need your help. If you vote for me, that will help. If you can, write friends or family who live in other districts. Beg, plead, persuade . . . tell them to vote Craft . . ." He looked straight at the bearded man and added, "You can't tell that I feel strongly, can you?"

Allard offered a shy grin. "Not at all, sir."

Another man stood up. "It seems to me that the law doesn't work fair. A working man down on his luck maybe pinches a split of rotwine and ends up working the roads on a chain, could be for a month or more, with the patrollers watching him every moment for years to come, and that's if he even gets another spot of work. Some corporacion whiteshirt uses legal cheatery to steal public coal and sell it marked-up to the Navy for millions of marks . . . and what does he get? He gets a fine, maybe loses his position, and the corporacion pays the fine—less than the profits they made. That isn't justice to me."

"It isn't to me, either. Right now, as I told you, I can't fix everything, but some of you might recall that I fired the Treasury minister. You know why? Because he was telling tariff agents to cut the import tariffs on foreign goods so that the corporacions could import cheap stuff and make it hard for small crafters to sell good work made here in Guldor. If there's something wrong, let me know. I can't try to fix things if I don't know what's broken."

After that the questions and comments came faster.

". . . law says that crosstie shops have to be vented, but they keep shutting the windows. Breathing all those creosote fumes, that'll shorten a man's life . . . if doesn't kill him first . . ."

". . . not requiring the new air brake systems on coal haulers . . . claim the law only applies to passenger expresses and regular freight haulers . . ."

". . . track walkers buy their own kerosene lanterns . . . company lanterns don't work . . ."

All in all, Obreduur spent more than a bell answering questions and responding to comments.

Dekkard watched the workers, but didn't see signs of anger, although several of the men asking questions sounded frustrated with Guldoran Ironway, and that Dekkard could understand from his own limited contact with Director Deron.

Finally, Rikkard stepped up on the platform. "We're beginning to repeat the questions, and the councilor's been talking a lot longer than we said we needed. I think we ought to give him a hand."

The applause, while not wildly enthusiastic, was definitely more than perfunctory, Dekkard thought.

Rikkard accompanied the four back outside to the Gresynt, then said to Obreduur before the councilor could enter the steamer, "Thank you. Some of the older men know about you, but the younger fellows didn't understand that you've been there." He paused. "Do you think there's a chance you might be premier and we'll get a government that looks out for working folks?"

"The elections will tell that," replied Obreduur. "I'm hopeful, but we'll just have to see."

Dekkard felt better once Herrardo had the steamer headed back toward the Hotel Cosmopolitano, although he really couldn't say why he'd been worried at the meeting.

Because the Commercers might understand that Obreduur could become premier and might try something?

He shook his head. He just couldn't say.

After they got out of the Gresynt at the hotel, Obreduur turned to Dekkard. "The last time we were here, you only had a few bells with your family, and this time doesn't look much better. However, I've looked at the schedule, and I'd like to invite them to an early supper here at the hotel on Findi evening. We don't have anything after the long afternoon meeting until the next morning."

"That's very kind of you, sir. I think they'd like to meet you." Dekkard also understood that Obreduur was worried enough that he didn't want to be without security. *Or he promised Ingrella that he wouldn't be.*

"You'll like them," added Avraal.

"With that observation," replied Obreduur, "how could I not?"

93

On Quindi morning, Dekkard was up early, writing and sending off a message to his family, paying extra for the hotel message service. After that, he and Avraal escorted Obreduur to a breakfast meeting of the Oersynt

Civic Association, a group of small business owners and corporacion midlevel managers ostensibly formed a decade or so earlier to improve the central city area of Oersynt. Even after the bell and a half spent there, including half a bell exchanging pleasantries, Dekkard wasn't certain what the association did with its funds.

As they sat in the dark blue Gresynt while Herrardo headed east on Copper Avenue, driving them toward the neighborhood where they would spend several bells in door-to-door canvassing, and while Obreduur read through a stack of messages that had arrived that morning Dekkard leaned closer to Avraal and asked, "How did they like what he said?"

"What do you think?"

"I couldn't tell," he replied quietly.

"Neither could I," she said. "I didn't sense any anger. There was some interest, and the two women and the one man with small shops were pleased. The others were mildly interested or bored, as if they already knew what he'd say."

They probably did. It still bothered him. How could they not see what the Commercers were doing? *Or don't they care so long as they benefit?* Most likely the latter, given what he'd seen of most business types.

A sixth of a bell later, Herrardo pulled up in the parking area of a Trinitarian chapel. Dekkard didn't see the chapel's name, but he looked at the name on the street sign, which at first he thought read PLEASANTRY WAY but upon a second look realized was PLEASANT WAY.

All the pleasantries are getting to you. He studied the houses across from the chapel. The neighborhood appeared remarkably similar to the Fifth Boulevard area through which Dekkard had trudged on Furdi. That also made sense, given that it was a workday.

Three bells later, after knocking on the doors of some fifty dwellings and talking to roughly thirty married women and ten older couples, and on some fifteen doors where no one answered, Dekkard and the others returned to the Gresynt, and Herrardo drove them to a luncheon meeting of the Oersynt Outing Club, which took place in a large function room of the not-quite-sprawling Hornbeak Bistro.

As soon as Obreduur entered the function room, a short not-quite-rotund man who reminded Dekkard of a spectacled owl appeared.

"Welcome, Councilor! I'm Pietyr Domanov, the club secretary. We're so glad to see you. Miriam will be thrilled. She just has to meet you."

Dekkard followed closely, as did Avraal, while Domanov guided Obreduur to a tall and extraordinarily thin woman with brilliant silver hair. She reminded Dekkard of a crane or perhaps a fish heron.

"Councilor . . . we're so pleased to have you. We only wish it had been possible for your wife to come. We're so indebted to her for the legal efforts that forced the Ministry of Public Resources to enforce the Water Dumping Act. Already, we're seeing a return of the birds along the stretches of the Rio Mal north of Malek . . ."

Obreduur smiled and nodded when she finished, then said, "I'm glad to be here. I do wish Ingrella had been able to come, but she's rather busy helping others such as the Outing Club . . ."

Despite Obreduur's warmth and grace, Dekkard suspected he would have preferred that Ingrella be there. Before long, someone rang a bell, and Miriam escorted the councilor to the head table, where after several brief announcements, she said, "We're so happy to welcome Councilor Obreduur, and we've persuaded him to say just a few words." She seated herself.

Obreduur rose. "As you know, I'm just grateful to be the husband of the noted legalist who has spent much of her life fighting for improvements in the legal status of women and of our public lands. I won't speak too much of her achievements, notable as they are, because you all know them. I know a bit more about other aspects of public resources, such as the lamentable Kraffeist scandal, where the Commerce-appointed Minister of Public Resources signed away coal rights on land reserved for naval use, lands that were supposed to be reserved, not exploited when an ironway didn't plan far enough ahead ... Foresight, on the other hand, is exactly what all of you here are known for ..."

In just a few minutes, Obreduur concluded. "Since I wasn't invited here to give a campaign speech ... all I'll say is when you vote a week from tomorrow, I hope you'll support the candidate who exhibits the foresight for which all of you are known. Thank you very much."

The spinach and veal milanesia with the mixed greens that Dekkard and the others were served was actually quite tasty ... and Dekkard was more than a little hungry.

As they left the Hornbeak Bistro, Dekkard realized, belatedly, that most of the doors on which they'd knocked and more than half of the meetings were with people who he would have thought more likely to vote Landor or Commerce.

But then, with years of guild and craft experience, where he has less support is among those likely to vote Landor or Commerce. And it wasn't as though Obreduur ignored his base.

The next stop after the Hornbeak Bistro was Geddes Square, where they arrived to see Arturo Degarcion putting up the Obreduur banner that he had also set up weeks earlier before the webball game at Syntaar Field. Even more surprising was that almost a dozen people had gathered even before Obreduur reached the banner.

The first to speak to Obreduur was a woman with a child, both unusually fair-skinned, suggesting an Atacaman background. "Councilor, sir ... I was born here, but the voting clerk says I can't vote ..."

"If you were born here, you should be able to vote. Sometimes, it's more complicated than it should be. Can you remember a name and an address?"

"Yes, sir."

"The name is Adariana Galoor. The address is 499 Fifth Boulevard. She is a legalist with the local guild coordinating office. Tell her I sent you, and see her this afternoon or tomorrow. She can help you."

"Thank you, sir."

A white-haired woman, well-dressed in a lavender linen suit and matching headscarf, walked up to Obreduur and immediately spoke. "Did you know that this summer there was a Meritorist demonstration right here in the square . . . and that Security agents brought in soldiers to break it up? What do you think of that, Councilor?"

"I heard about the demonstration. There were others at the same time in other cities across Guldor. I'm very much opposed to the use of violence, but . . . unfortunately, so long as the Commercers control government and refuse to address real problems, demonstrations will continue."

"Then the demonstrators should be gaoled . . . or shot if they attack lawful authorities."

"They have been," said Obreduur, "and that has led to more demonstrations."

"It's absolutely disgraceful. Don't they have any manners? Any sense of decency?"

Dekkard wondered why Avraal hadn't been able to calm the woman, unless . . . He turned and mouthed, "Isolate?"

In return, she nodded.

Dekkard stepped forward slightly. "My mother was very upset by the demonstrations. Could you tell me what they were all about?" He used his body to guide her away from Obreduur.

"They had signs. I wasn't about to read them. Why would I read trash like that? People like that are up to no good."

"I don't imagine you'd agree with what they said, but if you want the councilor to oppose them, it's very helpful for him to know why you oppose them."

"Young man, I know what I know."

"I'm sure that you do. What exactly do you want the councilor to do?"

"He needs to stop such outrages."

"That's exactly what he's working on." *If not in the way you'd like them stopped.*

"Why didn't he say so?"

"He would have. Because my mother didn't see the demonstrations, I wanted to hear what you saw." *Also true, if misleading.*

"Well, she didn't miss anything. Such ruffians. Absolute vagabonds." She paused. "He is going to do something about them, I hope."

"He definitely is."

"Good." Then she turned and walked away.

Dekkard eased back nearer to Obreduur.

Three bells later, after a steady stream of people to see Obreduur, Arturo folded up the banner, and everyone got back into the Gresynt. Herrardo turned the steamer back toward the hotel.

"Exactly who will be at the public-health-care gathering tonight?" asked Dekkard, not caring too much whether Herrardo or Obreduur answered.

"Physicians, nurses, and aides who work in the three public hospitals in Oersynt," replied Herrardo.

Dekkard didn't know all that much about public hospitals, only that, from what he'd heard, he didn't want to be in any hospital, especially a public one.

"Your security grays will be better for tonight," added Obreduur.

Once the four got back to the hotel, they ate a moderately quick and early dinner in the hotel restaurant, which left Dekkard and Avraal about two-thirds of a bell to freshen up.

When Dekkard entered his room he found a message envelope in the inside door drop. He immediately opened it, although he suspected it was from someone in his family.

Steffan—

It's so thoughtful of the Councilor to invite us to dinner, and at the Hotel Cosmopolitano. We debated on

*not imposing on his schedule, but decided he wouldn't
make the invitation if he didn't mean it. So the three of
us will be there at fifth bell. I'm really looking forward
to it . . . and to talking more with Avraal.*

The signature was that of Naralta, of course.

Dekkard smiled, then laid the message on the narrow
desk and went to wash up.

A little over a third later, he left his room and waited
in the corridor for Avraal, who appeared in minutes.

"Naralta accepted the invitation for dinner tomorrow," Dekkard said evenly. "She's really looking forward to talking with you."

"I'm sure I'll enjoy talking with her."

At that moment, Obreduur emerged from his room,
and Dekkard passed on the acceptance to him.

"Excellent. That will provide a respite from campaigning." He paused, then asked, "How are you finding it?"

"Interesting, but tiring."

"Interesting in what respect?" Obreduur gestured
toward the staircase down to the lobby, then started
walking.

"The difference in the people you meet."

"That's one very good aspect of campaigning. It re-
minds me of that diversity . . . and Oersynt's not nearly
so diverse as Hasheem's district, for example."

"You spend some of that time campaigning and
meeting people who are less likely to vote for you. Is
that . . . ?" Dekkard left the question hanging because
he'd been about to ask if spending time with those
people was wise.

"No . . . some would say it's not wise. But for me, it's
necessary. I still represent them, and they need to know
that I take them seriously. That's one of the reasons why
Gaarlak and a few other districts are likely to go Craft
in this election. The incumbent councilors, even those
stepping down like Emilio Raathan, have taken their
own natural base for granted and not bothered to

cultivate a presence among those more likely to vote for other parties."

Dekkard frowned. "Doesn't that verge on the personality politics advocated by the New Meritorists?"

"There's a difference. I'm letting them know who I am and asking for their vote. I'm not tying my name to particular votes or government programs or projects . . . only to what I've accomplished." He smiled wryly. "At least, I try to keep my words along those lines."

Dekkard was still thinking that over as Herrardo drove them to the public-health-care meeting.

Central Public Hospital was a long two-story, faded red brick building more than ten blocks south of the hotel and only a few blocks from the wholesale produce building and the ironway station, an area filled with four- and five-story tenement buildings, all of which doubtless only had cold running water, if that, and adjacent to the garment district.

Herrardo parked the Gresynt in one of the two vacant spaces with a sign that read FOR OFFICIAL BUSINESS. As he got out and shut the steamer door, he said, "This isn't the best part of Oersynt," which Dekkard already knew, "but around the hospital's pretty safe, because there's almost no one with any marks here, except the physicians, and those who work here don't have that much. The gathering is in the meeting room, which is adjacent to the chapel."

Once inside the hospital Dekkard could immediately smell, if faintly, the eucalyptus scent of disinfectants, along with a bitter odor that he could not identify.

Herrardo led the way to the center of the building, then turned right. That corridor ended at a set of double doors with heavy copper handles.

Before Herrardo could open the doors, someone did from the inside, and a woman in pale blue trousers and coat—the colors of a nurse or physician—spoke. "Good. You're right on time. Please come in. I'm Dr. Pheryna Bornikova." She turned and led the way into a chamber lit solely by a handful of wall lamps. More than a score of others, all in hospital coats and trousers, stood in the middle of an open space in front of wooden folding chairs that had been set in a rough arc.

Dr. Bornikova turned. "Do you have a prepared statement or speech, Councilor?"

Obreduur smiled wryly. "I could give one, but I'd really rather hear what all of you have to say about what the Council has done, or not done, for hospitals. I'm also open to suggestions, with the understanding that I'm only one of sixty-six. I do know that the funds you receive from the Council are inadequate."

"Inadequate?" responded a man who didn't look that much older than Dekkard. "That's like saying a starving child is a bit hungry. We can barely come up with one meal a day for the charity patients, and most of that is paid for by the Trinitarian Relief Fund. We're patching broken windows with paper tape."

An older woman, a nurse, Dekkard thought, said, "We often have to do minor surgery with minimal anesthesia, or sometimes none at all because we're always in danger of running out of chloroform."

"We're also short of carbolic acid for sterilizing instruments and scalpels . . ."

"There's never enough soap to clean bed linens and everything else . . ."

Through it all, Obreduur mostly listened. Finally, when it was obvious that the hospital personnel had said all they could or wanted to say, he said, "Thank you. You've been very clear on what you need and why you need it."

"Can you give us your word that you'll get us the marks and supplies we need?" pressed a short man in blood-splattered blues.

"That depends on the results of the election. I've always pushed for more funding for public hospitals. I'll continue to do so. If the Craft Party wins the election and can form a government, you'll get more. Will it be enough? Not immediately. Far too many needs have been ignored by the current government for too many years. If the Commercers remain in control, I don't see things changing."

"Then why are you here?"

"Because I'm hopeful. Also because I hope you'll persuade friends and family in other districts to vote Craft. And, most important . . . because, if we do win, I have to know what you need."

Dr. Bornikova stepped forward. "The councilor has listened, and he's been forthright. We can't ask for more right now." She smiled coolly. "If you win, we'll definitely be asking for more."

"That's only fair," Obreduur replied warmly. "Thank you. I do appreciate the opportunity to hear the problems you've had to face."

Bornikova walked to the doors with them, then looked to Obreduur. "I will say that you're the only one who had the courtesy to respond to our request. Thank you for that."

"The way your people talked and questioned was as important as what they said. I just wish more councilors could have heard them. I'll do my best to convey not only the needs, but the urgency of those needs."

"We'll be watching."

"It won't happen immediately," Obreduur replied. "And it will be a struggle."

"Isn't everything? Good evening, Councilor." Bornikova opened one door.

As the four walked down the antiseptic-scented hallway from the meeting room on their way out of the hospital, hearing occasional cries and moaning, Dekkard couldn't help thinking about the anger and desperation he'd heard voiced by professionals seemingly always short of the resources they needed to help people.

By the time Dekkard returned to the Hotel Cosmopolitano, all he wanted to do was to collapse and get some sleep. From looking at Avraal, he suspected she felt the same.

94

Both Dekkard and Avraal could sleep later on Findi morning because there was no early-morning meeting. Obreduur had told them the night before that he had arranged to have breakfast sent up to his room and that he'd meet them at a third before fifth bell. Dekkard did sleep later, but only until a little after first bell. He took his time washing and dressing, then sat in his room wondering if Avraal was awake and if he dared knock on her door. He worried some about Obreduur, but when he heard a cart he looked out and watched, but the server never entered Obreduur's room, because the councilor pulled the cart in himself and closed the door.

A third passed, and then there was a gentle rap at his door. He walked to the door, and opened it, ready for anything or anyone—but not for the hug that Avraal gave him.

"You didn't even lurk around my door," she said cheerfully.

"I'm not much of a lurker." Or at least he hadn't been after the dressing-down Naralta had given him when he'd been ten.

"Let's have breakfast."

"Breakfast? Not just café?"

"It's late enough that I'm hungry."

Wonder of wonders. "So am I." Dekkard stepped out of his room and closed the door. As they headed down to the lobby, he said, "There's something I'd like to know."

"Oh?"

"When we were in Gaarlak, Obreduur wasn't exactly pleased with Haasan Decaro. He was trying to get several others to consider running for councilor in the next election. He was pleased that Johan Lamarr decided to run. Then Lamarr dies in a fire that most likely was set up by Decaro, and Obreduur almost shrugs when the

Gaarlak Craft Party settles on Decaro as the replacement candidate. Somehow . . . there's something else going on."

"I can tell you that Obreduur was very upset when he read that heliogram."

"Then why didn't he do something? Or is it that the Craft Party needs to win that seat and Decaro is the only remaining candidate who can?"

"We don't know that, but he believed what he was saying. He was also angry about it."

"He also said that the Gaarlak Craft Party had to make the choice, but Ulrich appointed Aashtaan's replacement . . ."

"That was after Aashtaan was elected, not before," Avraal pointed out. "The district party chooses candidates. The national political leader has the final say on replacing an elected councilor who dies or resigns, but usually listens to the district party."

When they entered the restaurant, Dekkard said, "Two, please."

In moments, they were seated at a wall table. Dekkard ordered his croissants, along with fried ham slices. Avraal ordered a fruit plate and one croissant.

After taking several sips of his café, Dekkard asked, "What did you think about the hospital meeting? Were they as frustrated and angry as I thought they were?"

"Dr. Bornikova was cold and resigned, with some anger. The younger people were angrier."

"That suggests that the older ones are used to doing without adequate resources and don't think things will get better."

"The hospitals have never been a high priority for the Commercers. Most Commercers go to private clinics. So do well-off crafters and tradespeople."

Dekkard already knew that, but he hadn't realized how comparatively few marks went to the public hospitals. "Do you think more people will want to talk to the councilor before the webball game?"

"We'll just have to see. I'd guess there would be a

few more with the election only a week away." Avraal offered a mischievous smile. "I'm much more interested in dinner and seeing how your family interacts with the councilor."

"I wonder about that, too."

"You're not worried?"

"They'll be polite, but I don't see them being excessively deferential. At least not my mother or Naralta." Dekkard grinned. "Besides, you're the one descended from royalty, and that didn't affect her."

"You didn't tell her that, did you?" Avraal looked appalled, then made a disgusted face. "You didn't even find that out until after I met them." After a pause, she added, "You can look so earnest and straightforward, but . . ." She shook her head.

"Just like you can look so stylish and proper . . . and fall in love with throwing knives."

They both laughed.

After breakfast, they returned to their respective rooms to finish getting ready for the day. Before long, both were waiting in the corridor. Obreduur joined them, and at a third before fifth bell, the three entered the dark blue Gresynt. Herrardo drove them to Syntaar Field, where Arturo Degarcion was already setting up the banner, and almost fifteen people were waiting for the councilor. Only a few even glanced at Dekkard. More than a few eyed Avraal.

Some of the questions that Dekkard overheard were familiar:

". . . what are you going to do about those radical Meritorists?"

". . . do about how the ironways overcharge crafters and growers?"

"What are you going to do for the working man?"

"You're not going to increase taxes on small shops, are you? It's hard enough for us to make ends meet without more taxes . . ."

And some of the questions weren't so familiar.

"Are you one of those fellows in Machtarn who

thinks politics is some sort of game, like webball or plaques?"

"Do you really think you can get my vote by showing up a few times a year?"

"Did you ever meet my great-aunt Winona? Thought you must have, the way she talked about you. Died last year . . . just wondered . . ."

"Can you tell me there's any real difference between any of you fellows?"

When they left the field a little over a bell later, Dekkard realized he'd never even asked or thought about who the Oersynt team happened to be playing.

From Syntaar Field, Herrardo turned the Gresynt onto Third Boulevard toward the Oersynt Guildhall for the afternoon reception or get-together for members of all guilds in Oersynt. Admission was free, but limited to the first five hundred guild members who signed up.

Slightly less than a sixth later, Herrardo eased the Gresynt into the "official business" section of the parking area behind the three-story yellow brick building. As before, he led them toward the rear kitchen entrance, guarded by a single Security patroller, obviously picking up a few extra marks. There were several more in front, Dekkard suspected.

"Good day, Councilor," offered the patroller.

"The same to you," replied Obreduur.

"Did you get enough to eat?" asked Herrardo.

"That I did." The patroller smiled as the four entered the building.

Unlike the previous function held there for Obreduur, this time there were no tables for seated dining, but tables with finger foods set at intervals throughout the hall and sideboards along the walls, with servers at each to dispense lager, wine, or what looked to be a red punch.

As the four left the kitchen and stepped into the hall proper, a round-faced and balding older man stepped forward, accompanied by a woman.

It took a moment for Dekkard to recognize Leon

Foerrster, the Craft Party chairman for the Oersynt district, and Ryanna Wreaslaan, the guild liaison.

"I'm glad to see you looking so healthy, Axel," said Foerrster heartily.

"There haven't been any more . . . difficulties, have there?" asked Wreaslaan.

"Not so far," replied Obreduur. "A few people who've voiced dissatisfaction with the Council and politicians, but that's to be expected."

"These days, what else can you expect?" said Foerrster. "You'd think that they'd get the idea that the Commercers have been in control for decades, and that they're the problem."

"Only a small percentage of the people really understand politics. The rest only think they do . . . or don't care."

"We thought we'd let people in and let them get drinks and something to eat before you speak. There's a small platform on the north wall."

"It's about time to open the doors. Are you ready for the onslaught?"

"The sooner the better."

Foerrster raised a hand and several men and women moved to the double doors and pulled them open. While men and women surged into the hall, Obreduur moved back and stood in front of the small platform. Avraal and Dekkard flanked him, if roughly half a pace back.

For several minutes, no one seemed even to notice the councilor. Then a dark-haired man in a black barong walked quickly toward Obreduur. Dekkard looked to Avraal.

"He's excited, but happy," she said quietly.

"Councilor Obreduur, I just wanted to thank you." The man stopped and smiled broadly, then added, "I'm Jalaan Kahn, craftmeister of the woodcrafters at Guldoran Ironway. I don't know how you persuaded those mark-loving bastards to switch from yellow cedar to cherry, but we're all grateful you did. Even the corporacion is pleased the way the paneling and trim are turning out on the newest carriages. Not that they'll say much."

"I'm glad it worked out. It took a little doing."

"Whatever it took, we're grateful. The crafters at Eastern Ironway aren't so fortunate."

"They're still working with yellow cedar?"

"They are . . . poor bastards. Eastern squeezes marks even more than Guldoran." Kahn offered an embarrassed smile. "I don't really have much else to say—"

"I'm sure you do," said Obreduur. "Are there other crafters in your family?"

Kahn smiled. "Just one. That's my daughter. She started in the shop as an apprentice last year. She's got the touch. A bit hard for her at first, but the older hands came round." He looked to Avraal, then back to Obreduur. "She's younger than your aide. Thank you again, sir."

Kahn hurried off.

Another man, older, in a worn blue suit approached Obreduur shyly. "Sir, I just wanted to meet you."

"I'm glad to meet you. Might I ask your name? And what your guild is?"

"Jacquet Deblanc. I'm a wheel lathe operator at the locomotive works."

"That takes skill and then some," replied Obreduur. "Much more skill than I ever had as a stevedore. You must have been at it for some time."

"Almost twenty years, sir. It's better now than when I started. It could be even better."

"Is there anything I could do?"

"I don't think so. I just wanted to meet you."

The next person to address Obreduur was an older woman. "Good day, Councilor. Will your wife be here?"

"I'm afraid not. Legalists don't get campaign breaks. Is there anything I could tell her?"

"Not really . . . well . . . except we'd like her to think about making the mills here in Oersynt pay women the same as men."

"Which mills, might I ask?"

"All the Rio Mal mills, sir."

"I'll let her know that."

For the next third Obreduur talked to another seven or eight people. Then a series of chimes rang out, and Leon Foerrster climbed up on the low platform, where he waited for the crowd to quiet down.

"Some of you are here for the food and drink, and some of you are here to meet Councilor Obreduur. For those of you lost in the back, he's going to stand up here and say a few words. Just a few, he insisted, because he's not here to give a speech, but to meet all of you." Foerrster gestured.

Obreduur stepped onto the small platform and surveyed the room, drawing out the silence before saying, "I'm here for two reasons. First . . . to meet all of you. Second . . . to remind you to vote Craft Party in next week's election. We have a chance to change government with this election. Don't you all think it's time for a change? That change is overdue? That more marks should go to those who actually make and transport the products of Guldor? That workplaces should be safer? And that Guldoran workers shouldn't lose jobs because Guldoran corporacions build manufactories in Noldar and enslave susceptibles to make cheap goods to sell here?

"It's one thing to compete against skilled workers in other lands; it's another to have to compete against slave labor. We don't allow cheap sussie labor in Guldor, and you shouldn't lose jobs to it so that Commercers can have record profits." Obreduur paused. "I said I'd be short. Vote Craft. That's all I'll say from up here. But do come and talk to me!" With that, he stepped down from the platform.

As he resumed his place, he said quietly, "It's not that simple. It never is."

For the next three bells, Obreduur talked with close to two hundred people, until Foerrster had the chimes rung. Even so, more than another third passed before Herrardo led the way back to the Gresynt.

"How do you think it went?" asked Dekkard.

"To the right!" snapped Avraal.

Dekkard turned to see a man charge around the corner of the building, then stop and start to raise what appeared to be a long-barreled revolver. Dekkard's first knife was in the man's shoulder before the attacker could aim the revolver. A second knife hit just under his ribs.

The man struggled to lift the weapon, but by then Dekkard had reached him and slammed the revolver out of his hand with his truncheon. The man—who couldn't have been much older than Dekkard—looked stunned, then started to reach for the knives.

"Don't!" ordered Dekkard. "Unless you want to bleed out right here." *He might anyway.*

A series of screeching whistle blasts filled the air as the patroller who had been posted by the kitchen door hurried toward them.

"Who sent you?" demanded Dekkard.

"Wouldn't you like to know?" The man's uninjured hand went to his mouth, and he quickly bit down and then swallowed.

"Which Commercer?" asked Dekkard.

The patroller stopped, looking at the attacker, then to Obreduur.

"He tried to shoot me. They stopped him. He just swallowed something."

The attacker shuddered, then began to convulse.

Dekkard winced.

In minutes more patrollers arrived. They listened to the patroller who'd been there, then briefly questioned Obreduur, Avraal, and Dekkard.

After the questioning, the oldest patroller searched the body. "He wasn't carrying any identification, just spare cartridges in one pocket."

Dekkard hadn't expected otherwise.

Then the patroller recovered the two knives from the body. He was frowning as he stood. "These two knives are different."

"That's right," said Avraal. "The longer and narrower blade is mine."

The patroller handed her the narrower blade. She bent and wiped it clean on the dead man's pale green barong, before replacing it in its sheath.

Dekkard did the same after he received his blade.

The three exchanged glances. Then the oldest one looked to Obreduur, questioningly.

"They're both security aides. There's nothing that prohibits an empath security aide from being armed or using weapons."

"But . . . she's an empath . . ."

"The attacker knew the councilor would have an empath protecting him. That was one reason I took up working with throwing knives. It's more dangerous for a single isolate to deal with an attacker carrying firearms."

The older patroller shook his head. "There's nothing else we need any of you for. Just be careful, Councilor."

"We've been trying to be careful." Obreduur smiled wryly. "It's hard, though, when people keep trying to kill you."

Once the four were in the Gresynt heading back toward the hotel, Avraal said, "I didn't want to complicate matters, but the attacker was a susceptible. He'd been emotionally directed to kill the councilor and not get caught. He was so focused on the councilor that I didn't catch that until he chewed that suicide pill."

"Can that be done?" asked Herrardo.

"It can," replied Avraal. "It takes a strong and focused empath and a very sensitive sussie. Even so, controlling another's actions isn't always successful, but this was set up so that I wouldn't have a chance to realize the situation until it was too late."

"Who do you think was behind this?" asked Herrardo.

"Someone with Commercer ties," replied Obreduur.

"Except this assassin carried a revolver," said Dekkard.

"All the other attackers carried semi-automatic pistols. Even the New Meritorists used semi-automatic pistols. But that could be a diversion or just to make it simpler for the sussie."

"That's not exactly reassuring, Steffan, although I must say that this has been the most exciting month in many years." Obreduur's soft laugh was sardonic. Then he said, "I think it's best we don't mention the fact that the attacker was a susceptible . . . for a number of reasons." After a moment, he added, "It also appears that you made a very wise choice to take up knives, Avraal."

"It helped that I've had an excellent instructor."

For all that had occurred, Herrardo eased the Gresynt to a stop in front of the doors of the Hotel Cosmopolitano at only a third past fourth bell.

"Third bell tomorrow morning?" asked Herrardo, turning in his seat to address Obreduur.

"Third bell," acknowledged the councilor.

"There's no one near that feels dangerous," said Avraal as she followed Dekkard from the steamer, but she led the way into the hotel lobby, followed by Obreduur, and then Dekkard.

Dekkard's family sat on a bench near the restaurant entrance. When Dekkard saw them, he asked, "Do you want to go up to your room first, sir?"

Obreduur shook his head. "That's your family ahead on the bench? Introduce me, and we'll have dinner."

Dekkard moved forward and guided Obreduur and Avraal to where Raymon, Liliana, and Naralta now stood. "Mother, this is Councilor Axel Obreduur. Councilor, my mother Liliana, my father Raymon, and my sister Naralta."

"Steffan is proud of you," Obreduur said immediately, "but he doesn't say much about you. In fact, he seldom talks about himself, either, and only if asked."

"He's always been like that." Naralta's eyes smiled as she added, "That might be because, as the children of artisans, we were always told that the work conveyed more about you than anything you could say."

"It still does, daughter," replied Liliana, an amused tone in her voice. "Art also lasts longer than the spoken word."

"Why don't we get settled for dinner," said Obreduur, "and then we can continue the conversation, and we can explain why we were delayed." With a smile, he turned and led the way into the restaurant, where the six were ushered to a corner table, a table, Dekkard noted, with more space around it than the others nearby.

While the restaurant was less than half full, if that, due to the very early time for dinner, several diners did look at the group curiously as they were seated.

Obreduur looked to Dekkard. "Would you like to explain?"

Since that wasn't really a question, Dekkard said, "Apparently, there are people who worry that the councilor might not just be the acting premier, but might actually become the premier of the next Council . . ." From that preface, he explained what had happened after the afternoon reception.

"That's three attempts on you," said Naralta to Obreduur, "if I've counted correctly."

"It's definitely unprecedented," replied Obreduur, "and I wouldn't be here without Steffan and Avraal. Together, they're quite an impressive team. Having said that, I'd like to hear more about the three of you, since Steffan tends to be protective." He smiled, adding, "Not that I'm not extraordinarily glad that he is."

"We're artisans," replied Liliana. "We're fortunate that people like our work and are willing to pay for it."

"You're more than an everyday artisan," replied Obreduur. "According to my sources, you're one of the finest portraitists in Oersynt, if not in all Guldor."

Naralta smiled, a smile of pleasure and amusement, Dekkard thought. Even his father smiled, if more quietly.

"Your sources must have wanted to curry favor with you," replied Liliana dryly.

Obreduur laughed. "You sound like my wife." He

looked up as the server approached. "We should order drinks, or this poor man will stand around politely until we do. I'll have a Riverfall . . ."

In the end, the men ordered the Riverfall lager, and the women the Northcoast white.

"You left Argental so that you could pursue your art unfettered," Obreduur said once the server had left.

"You might say that," replied Liliana.

"I can't believe Argental would let such talent go," said Obreduur. "How did you manage it?"

"With great difficulty. We succeeded, and that is what matters."

"You were shot at, weren't you?" interjected Dekkard.

Liliana offered a puzzled expression to Dekkard.

"You wrote me that you never forgot the sound of shots."

Liliana offered a smile both chagrinned and amused. "You're like your father. You forget nothing. Yes, the border guards shot at us. They wouldn't have even seen us, if the blizzard hadn't stopped so quickly."

Escaping through a silverstorm while under fire . . . Dekkard was still taking in what his mother had said when Obreduur spoke.

"You went through a silverstorm and survived? That's . . ." Obreduur appeared at a loss for words.

"We were young. Raymon prepared carefully. He almost lost some of his toes it was so cold."

Raymon just nodded. Naralta appeared as surprised as Dekkard felt.

After another moment of silence, Obreduur said, "I think it's time to order."

When the server came to him, Dekkard ordered lemon veal with risotto and green beans.

After the server left, Obreduur turned to Raymon. "You haven't said much. I'm curious. Is what you do with decorative plaster here in Oersynt that different from in Argental?"

"Different? The technique is the same. Everything else is better. I don't have architectural inspectors declaring that what I do is too artistic. Or not functional enough. I don't have customers trying to pay me less by threatening to go to the inspectors. I can accept or reject a project. And the winter is much shorter and warmer."

Before Obreduur could speak, Liliana asked, "Will there be others who try to kill you?"

"I have no idea. But then, three months ago, I had no idea that anyone wanted to kill me. I knew that the Commercers didn't want the Imperador to call for elections. I knew that they've been trying to cover up crimes and improper behavior, and I knew that the former premier often had security agents observing me. Those were some of the reasons why I've maintained a full-time security team and why I was so anxious to hire Steffan. As young as he is, for a security aide, that is, he's among the best. So is Avraal."

"She's likely the best security empath of all those working for the Council," added Dekkard quickly.

"I'd agree," replied Obreduur.

"Will things get better after the election?" asked Naralta.

"Not immediately. If we win a clear plurality, and if we can form a government, then, in time, I believe we can improve life for working people, crafters, and artisans. The Commercers won't be totally happy at first, because they'll lose certain unfair advantages. In the long run, they'll be happy too. That's because they're happier when people buy more, and poor people can't buy as much. Prosperous people can. So by making more people prosperous . . ."

"But that will take time . . . and during that time, there might be more attempts on your life," pressed Naralta.

"That's possible."

"But it's less likely if he becomes premier," added Avraal, "because he'll be more visible, and the popular reaction to an attempt on his life would be severe, especially by the New Meritorists, particularly if it's tied to Commercer sources."

"So the hard part will be getting through the next week or so?" asked Liliana.

"Probably," said Obreduur.

"Did you ever foresee Steffan working for a councilor?" asked Avraal.

"No," replied Raymon. "We only hoped he wouldn't become a naval officer. I thought commercial security was a possibility." He smiled. "Lila said that would be a waste of his talent and determination. She was right. As usual."

"Why did you think that?" Avraal asked Liliana.

"It was just a feeling. Even when Steffan was working for his father, he insisted on doing things as well as he could. Sometimes . . . it was painful."

"For all of us," replied Dekkard wryly. "Especially when I tried to duplicate a plaster casting of a full ornate old Imperial crown molding. That was almost a disaster."

"I can't believe anything you did was a disaster," said Avraal.

"It wasn't," replied Raymon. "It was almost perfect."

"It just took me four attempts and three days to do what my father could do in two bells," said Dekkard. "And it wasn't near as good. Barely acceptable, if that."

"A little better than that," corrected Raymon.

"And you should have heard his language." Naralta's smile was one of amused recollection. "For all three days."

"As I recall," said Dekkard, "it was shortly after that when Mother suggested I take the competitive exams for the Institute."

"Sometimes, events like that work for the better," said Obreduur. "I wasn't really strong enough to be a stevedore. Breaking my fingers didn't get that across, but when a loader dropped a barrel of pickles on my boot because I wasn't moving fast enough . . . and I lost two toes and almost died from the infection . . . that was when I decided to go to trade school. I figured even working as a clerk was better than what I'd been doing . . . and one thing led to another . . ."

From that moment on, the conversation revolved around family anecdotes, as well as a few more from Obreduur's life.

Before Dekkard knew it, the dinner, and dessert, was over, and the first bell of evening had long since chimed.

"We shouldn't keep you any longer," Obreduur said warmly. "I'm so glad that I had the chance to meet you three." He grinned and added as he stood from the table, "And that you instilled patience and determination in Steffan."

"You were so kind to ask us for dinner," replied Liliana. "I can see why Steffan appreciates working for you."

"I appreciate his working for me, and especially saving my life. So does my wife."

The six left the restaurant and walked out into the hotel lobby. There Naralta hugged her brother and said quietly, "Just be careful . . . and don't lose her."

"I intend to be careful on both counts."

"You'd better." Then she stepped back.

Dekkard just watched as Naralta and his parents crossed the lobby. Once they were out of sight, he turned.

"You and your entire family are quite remarkable," said Obreduur quietly. "I suspected that, but they certainly confirmed it."

"I knew it had been difficult, but they never would talk about it."

"They didn't want sympathy," said Obreduur. "They wanted recognition based on their art."

Dekkard could understand that. *But why now? Because you're old enough to understand and appreciate that?*

"If you don't mind," said Obreduur, "I need to work on some messages to send out first thing in the morning."

"Yes, sir."

Dekkard was still thinking over dinner as he and

Avraal escorted Obreduur up the steps to the second level.

Once they had Obreduur safely in his chamber Dekkard walked Avraal the few yards to her doorway. "Do you want to talk? It's not that late."

"Not tonight. I need to think over some things."

"Do you want to talk it out with me?"

She shook her head, then reached up and took his head in her hands, drawing him down to her, then kissed him, a long, gentle, yet passionate expression. When she released him, she said quietly, "You're even more remarkable than your parents. Anyone less couldn't have survived, let alone triumphed."

Dekkard leaned forward and kissed her, in much the same way as she had him. Then, after looking into her eyes, he said, "You're even more remarkable."

She smiled, an expression both warm and amused. "We both may be remarkable, but we both need to think and to sleep." The last word was gently emphasized.

95

On Unadi morning, Dekkard and Avraal didn't have a chance to talk privately because Obreduur woke them early to go to a last-minute breakfast meeting of the Ironway Servitors Guild, after which Herrardo drove them to Central Square. After setting up the banner near the fountain and statue of Laureous the Great, Dekkard surveyed the square. While the fallen masonry from the explosion of the regional Security headquarters had been removed from Victory Avenue and the surrounding buildings and sidewalks, no apparent effort was evident either to rebuild, repair, or demolish the structure.

Most likely the acting Minister of Security is waiting for the election results and a new Minister of Security.

Then Dekkard shook his head, realizing that not enough time had passed even to work out engineering plans.

As the morning passed, and Dekkard began to sweat in the steamy air that was far more summer-like than fall-like, Obreduur stood under his banner and talked to everyone he could—and that was a considerable number because, once word got out to the shops around the square, many working in the area came to question him, or just to pay their respects. Several porters and two doormen from the Fairwind Hotel also talked to Obreduur, if briefly. One even asked Obreduur not to talk badly about the hotel because of the assassin dressed like a doorman.

"I wouldn't think of it," the councilor replied. "That wasn't your fault or the hotel's. Assassins don't care who else gets hurt."

After about three bells, Obreduur had Avraal and Dekkard take down the banner, and Herrardo drove the three from Central Square to the cloth market, where Obreduur spent another three bells going from stall to stall, the same way as he had in the produce market.

From the questions Obreduur asked, Dekkard could tell that he was familiar with fabrics as well, but one interaction surprised him.

Obreduur looked at a bolt of deep blue cloth, nodded, and asked the vendor, "Hemp cloth?"

"The very best. Much softer than cotton or linen. It lasts twice as long."

Dekkard frowned. He knew that hemp was used for rope and canvas . . . but fine cloth?

"It requires steam processing," Obreduur explained to Dekkard, "but the results are worth it. Not that I have many garments made of it."

"You should, honored Councilor."

"I should, but Craft councilors seldom have the funds for such fabrics. But thank you, and please consider voting for the Craft Party on Findi."

Along the way Dekkard also discovered that cotton

naturally came in at least four colors, tan, red, green, and brown, none of which was a surprise to Avraal or Obreduur.

The four left the fabric market at a third before fourth bell, and Herrardo drove south almost to the Rio Azulete, where, at about a sixth before fourth bell, he eased the Gresynt to a halt on the street outside the parking area and next to the omnibus stop for Ferrum Steamer Works. "I'll be on the side street over there. It's not a good idea to ask for votes from Ferrum workers with a Gresynt nearby. They'll assume the worst."

Dekkard could see that, but had to admit that he wouldn't have thought of that difficulty.

Dekkard and Avraal took out the banner and the poles and set it up against the outside wall of the long roofed shelter for those waiting for omnibuses, of which two stood empty, waiting for the shift change, having presumably just delivered workers for the evening shift.

Even before they had the banner completely in place, a man approached, grizzled and limping, although Dekkard doubted he was more than fifteen years older than Dekkard himself.

"You really the councilor? You don't look like a crafter."

Obreduur held up his left hand, turning it so that the other could see the two permanently bent and scarred fingers. "I got those as a river stevedore. I hope you don't mind if I don't take off my boot to show you the toes I don't have."

"That all?"

"That's when I went back to school and decided I could help working people more by trying to get them better working conditions."

"You been successful?"

"Sometimes . . . and sometimes not."

The grizzled man laughed and spat to the side. "Leastwise, you admit you sometimes fail."

"We all fail at times. What we do after that is what matters."

"Some of us don't get that many chances."

"Some of my family didn't, either."

The man nodded. "Best of luck." He walked past the councilor toward the manufactory.

Within moments of the steam whistle blowing at fourth bell, workers began to stream out of the works. The older men tended to walk toward the parking area, filled with Ferrums of various colors; the younger workers, mostly men, and some women, walked to the omnibus stop.

Most of the first workers coming toward the waiting omnibuses barely looked at the councilor or his aides and rushed to board. All they wanted, clearly, was to leave the works as soon as possible. After the first omnibus filled and departed and as the second one began to fill, several workers stopped and looked at the banner and the councilor.

"Are you really Councilor Obreduur?" asked an older woman, her voice dubious.

"For better or worse."

". . . told you so," murmured the slightly younger woman beside her.

"Why are you here?"

"There's an election on Findi. I'm here to ask you to vote, preferably for me, since I am the Craft Party candidate."

"You don't need to ask. I'd never vote for either the landed pigs or the mark-stuffed-shirts."

"I appreciate that. And could I ask you to persuade your friends and family to vote as well?"

"You look pretty well-off," said the younger woman.

"I started as a river stevedore, then went to school, got a little education, eventually became a guild steward, and then a guildmeister . . ."

"You're the one," said the older woman, "the one the Commercers tried to kill." She turned to the younger woman. "Remember? Two, three weeks back, at Summerend?"

"And you're really here?"

"I am. This election is very important—"

"We know. We'll vote," declared the older woman as she and her companion hurried toward the next arriving omnibus.

After that, the conversations tended to be much shorter, but in the next two-thirds of a bell Obreduur talked to at least thirty more workers, and more than that listened while he spoke. Then, the sidewalks were bare.

Once Obreduur entered the steamer, he said to Herrardo, "Time for our last meeting of the day."

Dekkard frowned. "Sir . . . this was the last one on the list." In fact, the Ferrum works was the last event on the schedule before they left for Malek the first thing on Duadi morning.

"It was indeed," replied Obreduur. "But there's one more. It was best that it not be listed. I don't mind people finding out afterward, but not before the fact. We're going to the meeting place of the Working Women Guild of Oersynt."

Even Herrardo looked surprised. "Sir . . ."

"I promised Ritten Obreduur. She arranged it. You wouldn't want me to break that promise, would you, Jareld?"

Herrardo shook his head. "Not if you promised her. Where are we going?"

"It's just off Fifteenth Boulevard on the Rio Mal Road. It's in the old Trinitarian chapel there. You might recall . . ."

"Oh . . . the one where the Oersynt Civic Association protested to the district councilors that the transfer to the guild was an unseemly use of a formerly sacred space?"

"I believe they claimed it would profane the space," replied Obreduur dryly. "That's it."

As Herrardo pulled away from the omnibus stop, Dekkard felt like shaking his head at the reaction of the Oersynt Civic Association, but did not. *Women who work in brothels or the streets need all the help they can get.* "Do they have a legalist?"

"A very junior and inexperienced one, although she's very bright, according to Ingrella. Why do you ask?"

"I've been thinking that, if we win, and you form a government, we ought to try to pass a law that allows all women working the streets or in unlicensed sex establishments the right to be represented by the guild."

"How would you justify it?"

"They're far likelier to adhere to the guild's guidelines and health practices, as well as to know their legal rights and responsibilities."

"Some wouldn't want to pay guild dues."

"Then they don't get guild services." Dekkard paused, then added, "But if they call on a guild legalist, they have to agree to pay dues for the subsequent year."

"They still might not," Obreduur pointed out, "even if they received legal representation."

"Does it matter, so long as the law has that requirement?" asked Dekkard dryly.

Abruptly, Obreduur laughed. "I see your point."

Avraal looked sideways at Dekkard and smiled.

The meeting hall of the Working Women Guild was indeed a worn yellow brick building that had the configuration of a Trinitarian chapel, but the property was neat, if largely bare of vegetation except for some ancient maples and meshgrass that covered most of the grounds. It was roughly twenty blocks, as the raven flew, southeast of the Hotel Cosmopolitano, and was surrounded largely by small shops and occasional tenements. The parking area was modest, but while it could have accommodated twenty steamers, there were only three others there when Herrardo came to a stop in a spot marked by a metal sign with the barely decipherable word VISITOR painted upon it.

"You're sure this is the place, sir?" asked Herrardo.

"We may be a little early, but it is the place. Most of the women in the guild wouldn't be able to afford steamers. We might as well go in."

Dekkard immediately got out and opened the rear

door. Then all four walked to the doors of the former chapel.

The woman who greeted them looked younger than Dekkard, at least to him, and wore a cream linen suit with her wavy brown hair drawn back. "We're glad you could make it, Councilor. I'm Tarisha Vereen, the guild legalist."

"I'm pleased to meet you, Legalist Vereen," replied Obreduur. "My wife has spoken highly of you."

"I can't say enough of her, sir. I'm very glad that you're here. We're ready any time you are. Some others may join us." She gestured toward the area that had once been a sanctuary.

More than thirty women waited in the ancient pews, some sitting alone, others in groups of two or three. Avraal and Dekkard stood just below the low dais that was the only remaining hint of the sanctuary's previous function, while Obreduur and Vereen stood in the middle of the dais.

"Councilor Axel Obreduur is here to talk to us about the election . . . and to answer any questions you may have." Vereen turned to Obreduur. "Councilor . . ."

"Thank you." Obreduur paused, then began. "I do wish that my wife, who has worked on legal issues affecting working women, particularly women like you, could have been here. That wasn't possible. I'm here to urge all of you who can vote to do so in the forthcoming election. Next Findi, to be exact. I'd also like you to consider voting for the Craft Party, and to urge anyone you can influence to vote Craft. This isn't just about me, although I would prefer to be reelected. It's about what's in your own best interest. Some of you may recall that just before the last election some five years ago, the Commercer councilor from Ondeliew tried to pass a law that would have classed women who worked in the brothels or massage parlors as part-time workers, which would have meant you would have lost the right to vote, as well as certain other legal protections. Fortunately, with the advice and help of my wife and the

Guilds' Advisory Committee, a strong enough effort defeated that Commercer councilor. The Commerce Party does not and never will favor your best interests. I won't belabor the point, except to again ask you to vote . . . and vote Craft. Now . . . if you have any questions . . ."

"What else, if anything, has the Craft Party done for us?" The extremely fair skin of the older woman who spoke suggested she'd come from a very much less than affluent background.

"Without control of the government, what we can do with laws has been limited. Craft legalists, however, have been successful in litigation forcing corporacions and businesses to pay women the same wages as men when they do the same job and to require that their job titles be identical. These legalists have also been successful in assuring that working women retain their rights to vote and to hold property independently . . ." After several more examples, Obreduur finished by saying, ". . . while we have accomplished this, doing so through lawsuits requires a laborious effort. A Craft government offers the possibility of using the law to clearly require compliance . . ."

"Offers the possibility?" The questioner's tone was bitterly ironic.

"That all depends on how many seats we pick up . . . and that is up to you and voters all across Guldor."

"What about the service tax on brothels and massage parlors? No other small business has an additional special tax levied on it."

"Part of that tax is to pay for health inspections," replied Obreduur. "I doubt that a majority of any Council would repeal that tax, but I'd be willing to investigate the use of revenues from the tax to see if they're being used as required . . ."

The questions only lasted another third before the young legalist stepped forward. "Thank you, Councilor, for your straightforward and candid answers."

A scattering of applause followed her words.

Most of the women left without a word.

Two, however, did move toward Obreduur.

The younger one simply said, "Thank you. I didn't know about that councilor from Ondeliew." Then, she turned and left before Obreduur could reply.

The second was the woman who had asked the first question. "Are you really as good as you come across?"

"I did my best. My wife would have been able to address the issues more personally. All I can say is that, in the areas that most affect you, I'm strongly guided by my wife's recommendations, and she's spent more than twenty years fighting to make things better for women."

"Fair enough." With that, the older woman also turned and left.

Once the meeting room was empty, Vereen said, "They won't say much, but what you said, and how you said it, seemed to reach most of them. I certainly appreciated it."

"Thank you again," said Obreduur.

None of the four said much as they walked back to the dark blue Gresynt.

Dekkard could see how the women at the meeting could be skeptical of almost any man. *But, skeptical as they might be, neither the Landor Party nor the Commerce Party will ever do anything for them.* Yet he still wondered if they saw it that way. *Or are you just rationalizing?*

96

Obreduur, Avraal, and Dekkard were at the Guldoran Ironway station in Oersynt well before the first morning bell on Duadi in order to catch the Veerlyn Express, which left precisely at the first morning bell. As they had before, the three sat in the parlor carriage, where Obreduur had two seats to himself, one of which held a case full of various papers, and Avraal and Dekkard had the seats facing him.

The carriage was less than half full, and held a mixture of travelers, almost all men, but given that both Avraal and Dekkard were in security grays, no one directly approached them.

While Avraal was sensing and feeling out those in the compartment, Dekkard did overhear one murmured comment:

". . . wonder who he is, with two security types . . . doesn't look all that impressive . . ."

Obreduur wasn't theatre-idol handsome, but he was moderately good-looking, and he definitely projected warmth when he was talking or meeting with people, but Dekkard had to admit that, at the moment, the councilor looked more like a harried corporacion director than the Premier of Guldor.

Dekkard turned to Avraal. "Do you sense anyone to worry about in the carriage?"

"Not that I can tell. It's also a little unlikely that anyone would try here . . . but you never know." She looked down at the schedule for the day.

"It doesn't look that much different from what he's been doing all along," said Dekkard, "except there aren't any fundraising dinners."

"There's no point to them right now. Votes are what count."

"You don't think he's in any danger of losing, do you?"

"He's often said that a politician is always in danger of losing until the last vote is counted and he's definitely won."

"Is that why Decaro will likely win in Gaarlak . . . because Councilor Raathan hasn't put much effort in keeping in touch with people?"

"That . . . and all that Obreduur—and you—did there during the Summerend recess."

"Me? I just gave a few short statements about the importance of the Craft Party."

"Exactly. That's more than Raathan has done in years. What Obreduur did with you was to show that the Craft Party has both experience and talented young men, and that both care for working people. That's something that neither Decaro nor Lamarr could do. Lamarr understood that. I doubt that Decaro does. He'll end up as out of touch as Raathan was, except sooner, and we could lose that seat whenever there's another election."

"Doesn't anyone understand that? Surely Jens Seigryn does."

"I'm sure he does, but he's only a coordinator and liaison. Gretna Haarl does, and that may make a difference when she becomes guildmeister."

"You think she will?"

"Sooner or later. Most of the Textile Millworkers are women, and she's been active in pushing for their rights. Maatsuyt doesn't have her energy."

"I thought you found her abrasive."

"She definitely can be that, but people forgive a lot when that abrasiveness helps them."

"I can see that." Still, Dekkard wondered.

"I hope you don't mind, Steffan, but I think you should try to get a little nap. The next few days are going to be long . . . and this morning was early."

"What about you?"

"We both don't have to stay awake, and I can sense something sooner than you can."

"Are you sure?"

"I'm sure."

Following Avraal's suggestion, Dekkard leaned back and closed his eyes. He wasn't certain he slept, but he dozed, and was awakened by a gentle kiss on his cheek and the words, "We're almost at Malek."

Dekkard shook his head, trying to become alert. Then he smiled and said, "I could get very used to being awakened like that."

"Then I'd better not do it very often. I wouldn't want you to take it for granted."

"I don't think I'll ever take you for granted."

"Promises, promises." But her words were said teasingly.

"Thank you for letting me sleep. I was more tired than I thought."

"You can return the favor, sooner or later."

"I will."

As the express slowed to a crawl and then stopped, Dekkard immediately studied the station platform. It was almost empty, and the other travelers in the carriage were preoccupied with making their own preparations to disembark. Was that because almost no one, and certainly none of the newssheets, could conceive of a Craft premier? If Obreduur did become premier, would the comparative lack of attention change? Dekkard couldn't help but wonder.

By the time the three left the station proper, Ingrella's cousin Tybor was waiting in the loading area with a dark blue Gresynt.

Once he loaded the luggage, Dekkard asked Tybor, "Is that the same one as last time?"

"Of course. I told them that the councilor didn't use it for the entire time he'd leased it before. They wouldn't give it for nothing, but they agreed on half-price. I thought that was fair."

"More than fair," said Obreduur from the rear seat. "They were paid for nine days we didn't use, and they gave us five days at half-price. I'm glad you asked. It probably wouldn't have been the best idea for me to do that in person. Not right now, anyway."

"Where to?" asked Tybor.

"Back to the house. We'll leave our cases there, and pick up the banner from the garage. Then Steffan can drive us all back to your house and drop you off. After that, we'll be heading for the old market square."

"You sure you don't need me?"

"Getting the steamer for us and taking it back on Findi is a great help, and I don't think you'd enjoy all the appearances we'll be making."

"I don't see how you do it. Then, I don't see how Ingrella does what she does, either." With that, Tybor guided the Gresynt away from the old station.

Dekkard smiled wryly at Tybor's comments. He and Avraal had reviewed the schedule for the time in Malek—four to six appearances a day for the next four days, with each two-to-three-bell block of time either greeting people in halls or squares or markets or going door to door counting as a single "appearance," definitely meant that the next four days would be crowded indeed.

And that's understating it.

97

Duadi's schedule was every bit as crowded as Dekkard suspected, beginning with two bells of going through the old market square of Malek and stopping at every booth and stall, followed by another door-to-door canvass of an area in northwest Malek, prosperous enough that most of the women were home and happy to talk to Obreduur. After that came a visit to Lacemakers Lane, and then another shift-change meeting with workers from the old flour and furniture mills, where Dekkard set up the banner in the space between the two mills, which Dekkard recalled from the earlier visit to the Women's Clerical Guild Summerend Social, held in the assembly hall nearby. Then came an early dinner at Lucynda's, after which Obreduur met with everyone who worked at the restaurant. The last stop for the evening was at the Duadi Evening Club, a social group for older people.

Tridi, Furdi, and Quindi followed the same general pattern, beginning even earlier in the day, and not ending until well after the second night bell.

On Findi—election day—Dekkard and Avraal were

at the breakfast table before Obreduur, sipping café and waiting for their eggs Malek, those tasty cooked eggs enclosed by a thin sweet cinnamon pastry crust glazed with honey. After Avraal had finished most of her first mug of café, Dekkard said, "It feels almost unnatural to know that we don't have a day filled with seeing people we don't know—"

"Quite a few of whom he remembers," interjected Avraal.

"—and may never see again," finished Dekkard. "Or at least for another year or election."

"You never know who you will or won't see again, Steffan," said Obreduur as he entered the breakfast room and sat down. "Or under what circumstances."

"You make an effort to meet people you don't know," said Dekkard.

"*Some* people I don't know. You can't neglect those who support you to gain new supporters, but you can't just rely on past supporters, either. Like everything in politics, it's a balancing act." Obreduur took a long swallow of café.

"You said you were going to vote around third bell this morning. Are we coming back to the house after that?"

"No. Put your bags in the steamer. We'll swing by Tybor's house around fifth bell and pick him up. Then you'll drive us to the station. We're on the noon local back to Oersynt, and that will take a good three bells."

"Where are you voting?"

"The meeting hall of the East Lake Trinitarian Chapel."

Elgara appeared with a platter of eggs Malek. "I thought you should have something special on election day, sir."

Obreduur smiled broadly. "Your eggs Malek make any morning special, Elgara."

"That's kind of you, sir."

"You're the one showing the kindness," returned Obreduur.

"To all of us," added Dekkard.

Delicious as the eggs Malek were, all too soon break-fast was over, and Dekkard hurried up to the small bedroom, finished getting ready for the long day, and completed packing his case. Then he carried it down and put it in the leased steamer, adding Avraal's case, and then Obreduur's.

Dekkard followed Obreduur's directions to the Trini-tarian meeting hall. Then he and Avraal accompanied the councilor to one of the voting registrars, where Ob-reduur obtained a ballot, which he carried to a curtained voting booth, marked the ballot, folded it in half, and left the booth and deposited it in the locked ballot box.

"Now all you have to do is wait, Councilor," said one of the registrars cheerfully.

"And wait some more," replied Obreduur. "Have you had many people so far?"

"According to the count, a good thirty more than we had by this time last election. That's what I remember, anyway. A few more folks that I know, but never saw vote before."

"I hope they remember my name," replied Obreduur. "That's if they like what I've done."

Two of the three registrars smiled.

Dekkard would have wagered that the non-smiling one was the Commercer registrar.

After several minutes more of casual conversation, in between voters signing and certifying their presence and obtaining ballots, Obreduur said, "Much as I enjoy talking with you, I see more people coming, and it's time for us to leave."

Obreduur led the way out of the meeting hall, then stopped to greet an older couple. "Maervyn . . . Gla-dora . . . I'm glad to see you here early."

"We always vote early, Axel. You know that," replied the woman.

"That's why I'm glad to see you."

"I imagine you'll check a few of the voting halls," said

Maervyn in a deep and rasping voice, "before you go to Oersynt?"

"A few, anyway, just to see the turnout."

"Don't let us keep you," rumbled Maervyn.

"You're not keeping me. I don't see you two often enough."

"We need you more in Machtarn than here, Axel," said Gladora. "Especially if you become premier."

"That's up to the voters . . . and at least a few other councilors."

"Hope there are a few less idiots voting today," grumbled Maervyn, "and more who understand that the Commercers haven't done right by the working men."

"And women," added Gladora. "Now . . . on your way, Axel. We're perfectly fine."

"I can see that. Until later." Obreduur offered a warm smile.

Dekkard was amused to note that Obreduur still stopped to talk to two other couples and one older woman before they reached the steamer.

Then for the next two bells, Avraal and Dekkard accompanied him into ten more voting halls before he directed Dekkard to head back to pick up Tybor.

Before Dekkard reached Tybor's house, he asked, "What did you learn from the visits?"

"You heard everything that they said. What do you think, Steffan?"

"More people are voting earlier. Since it's not raining and doesn't look like rain, I'd say that means they're worried. But Commercers could be worried that Crafters will control the Council, just as Crafters are worried that another Commercer Council would hurt them."

"I saw the same thing, but if you'd looked at the faces of the Commercer registrars, they didn't look happy. Avraal . . . could you tell anything?"

"The Commercer registrars were anything but happy. The Landor registrars were resigned, and the Craft registrars were hopeful."

"That suggests we did well in Malek, and probably in Oersynt, although we'll know more when we reach the Guildhall there. Whether that's happening elsewhere in Guldor, it's far too soon to tell."

Even before Dekkard came to a full stop in front of the house, Tybor was hurrying out and down the walk to the Gresynt. He opened the middle door and sat in the middle row. "How does it look, Axel?"

"Moderately favorable here in Malek, but it's still early. Elsewhere . . . who can tell?"

Dekkard eased the steamer away from the house, heading south toward the river and the ironway station. In less than a third, he had turned the Gresynt back over to Tybor, and gotten a porter to wheel the cases onto the parlor carriage of the local, a definite step down from the various expresses, although Dekkard had the feeling that the faded and worn elegance of the carriage suggested it had once been an express parlor carriage. Less than a third of the seats were taken, hardly surprising, since it was close to midday, a Findi, and election day as well.

According to the schedule, after Obreduur reached Oersynt, Herrardo would meet them, take Obreduur, guarded by Avraal and Dekkard, on a tour of key voting halls, followed by a stop at the Oersynt Guildhall, where Obreduur would meet with Craft Party officials before leaving for the ironway station, where the three of them would take the Machtarn Night Express, arriving in Machtarn between fifth bell and noon on Unadi.

As he sat beside Avraal, while they studied two late-arriving passengers—two graying women—just before the carriage doors closed, Dekkard murmured, "I think we're going to be two very tired security aides by this time tomorrow, and tomorrow afternoon will be long."

"Very long . . . but longer if it looks like the Craft Party gets a definite plurality."

"Much, much longer, if that happens," said Obreduur, seated across from them. "If that occurs, I imagine that Hansaal Volkaar and Saandaar Vonauer will confer to see if they can form a coalition government. Those discussions will take a day or two before they fail."

"You're that sure we'll win?" asked Dekkard.

Obreduur shook his head. "I'm not sure of that at all. Not yet. But *if* we get close to thirty seats, they'll have great difficulty agreeing on terms, and enough Landors will balk at the conditions demanded by Volkaar and the Commercers. So . . . in the end—that is, if we get close to thirty seats—we'll be offered the chance to form a government with the expectation that we'll fail after a few weeks."

"What are the chances of failure actually happening?" asked Dekkard.

"I have no idea," replied Obreduur. "There hasn't been a Craft government in over two hundred years, and that one only lasted a year and a half. I'd like to think we could do better, but speculating on that makes no sense unless we get the necessary seats, until the Commercers and Landors fail to agree, and until and unless we're given the opportunity to form the government."

"You make it sound rather improbable," replied Dekkard.

"That's because it is. It's not impossible, and the odds are in our favor, but whether the Commercers will allow us into power, for even a brief time, remains to be seen. I'm thinking that they won't make enough concessions to the Landors to form a coalition government, but they might. If they do . . . then events will get very, very interesting. But it's all speculation until the votes are all counted. In the meantime, I'm going to try to take a nap." With that he leaned back and closed his eyes.

Obreduur had to be tired to say that, because Dekkard had never heard those words before and the councilor seemed to work endless bells.

Dekkard turned to Avraal. "This time, it's your turn to get some rest."

She smiled. "I won't argue."

In moments, both the councilor and Avraal seemed to be asleep.

For the next three bells, Dekkard kept watch, although none of the other occupants of the parlor carriage seemed in the slightest interested in the councilor, while the local made two stops on its way to Oersynt. Dekkard had the feeling that Obreduur was guardedly optimistic, but worried that something unforeseen might occur.

Even before the local slowed to a stop at the Guldoran Ironway station in Oersynt, Avraal and Obreduur were awake, although neither spoke.

As before, Herrardo was waiting, if with a different Gresynt, this one a dark gray. "More people are voting, from what we've heard. We can stop at perhaps three voting halls before you meet with Chairman Foerrster and the others at the Guildhall. You'll have to be back here by a third past fifth bell to catch the Night Express."

"I'm in your hands, Jareld," replied Obreduur.

"Yes, sir." Herrardo accelerated away from the station.

Over the next bell, Obreduur visited four halls where voting was taking place, after which Herrardo took the four to the Oersynt Guildhall.

As Dekkard and Avraal flanked Obreduur on his way through the front doors, Dekkard realized, belatedly, that it was the first time that he'd entered from the front, and not from the kitchen. Obreduur's destination wasn't the main hall, but a smaller conference room, where Leon Foerrster and Karlena Koerr were seated with small stacks of paper in front of them and where a messenger hurried out just after the councilor entered.

"How does it look?" asked Obreduur.

"The early indications are good," replied Koerr. "We're seeing even more guild members voting than in the last election. There are a few more Commercers voting as well, but you had a very healthy margin in the last election. It's looking good."

"Have you heard anything about Gaarlak?"

"We just got a heliogram from Jens," said Foerrster. "He thinks not as many Landors are voting, but more

Commercers are. Usually, the Commercers come in third there, but it's a cause for concern."

"What about Chuive? Devoule was killed in the Summerend New Meritorist demonstration, and the Commercers were never that strong there."

"Too early to even have an indication."

"You can't do any more here, Axel," said Foerrster. "You might as well head for the station. If we do well, you'll have more than enough to handle in Machtarn." Then he looked to Dekkard and then Avraal. "Keep him safe. He's the only Craft councilor capable of forming and holding together a government."

"You're overstating, Leon," replied Obreduur gently.

"I don't think so. Not this time. Why do you think they've sent so many assassins after you?"

"I'm not the only one."

Foerrster offered an amused smile. "No, but you're the only one where they kept trying. You might be safer now, since you're more visible as the acting Premier. Also, with the elections in progress, they might prefer to form a coalition and keep you out that way, but I wouldn't count on it. It wouldn't hurt to be a little early to the ironway. Just be careful."

"We will," replied Obreduur.

Avraal led the way back to the front doors.

Herrardo was waiting within yards of the entrance and in minutes had the steamer headed back to the ironway station.

Although Avraal was especially careful while Dekkard arranged for a porter to wheel their cases to the Machtarn Night Express, neither of them discerned any signs of possible attackers. In fact, it appeared that the express wasn't even fully booked, possibly because there were fewer reasons for influencers and corporacion directors or officials to go to the capital when nothing would be decided until after the elections.

Once the express headed out of the station and across the Rio Mal bridge, the three went to the dining carriage and had a leisurely dinner. Even before they sat down,

Obreduur did say, "No talk about elections or politics tonight."

"How about history?" asked Dekkard.

"If it's history that took place before 1200, fine," answered Obreduur.

"Do you think any of the political parties anticipated the Silent Revolution?"

"No. Ingrella's studied that period. She believes that it took almost ten years to plan and set up. The history books treat it as if it all took place in a year or so, but nearly thirty councilors died over two and a half years, including a premier and a premier-select. Some fifteen wives of councilors also died, mostly at the hands of their husbands. It's the most hidden conspiracy in the history of the Imperium. To this day, no one knows for certain most of those involved, although many believe Princess Ilspieth had a role in it." Obreduur waited until the server had delivered two Riverfall lagers and a Silverhills white for Avraal before continuing. "That, paradoxically, may be why very few women even attempted to run for Council in the decade following the Suffrage Amendment to the Great Charter."

"That makes sense," replied Avraal. "Any women eager to seek office immediately would have been viewed with suspicion. Then . . . they still are."

Dekkard took a swallow of his lager, deciding he might as well enjoy the conversation and the dinner.

98

Despite the narrow compartment bunk, Dekkard was tired enough to sleep well, at least until the morning light seeped into his compartment. So he shaved and washed up as well as he could in the tiny sink, and then dressed in a relatively clean set of security grays. Then, after converting his bunk back into a couch, he opened his compartment door and waited for Avraal, wondering just how the election had turned out.

Roughly two-thirds of a bell passed before Avraal emerged from her compartment. "Good morning, early riser."

"Good morning. How did you sleep?"

"Fairly well . . . until I started dreaming about the election. The dream turned into a nightmare because the Commercers repealed the Suffrage Amendment, claiming that women were no better than susceptibles, and we lost six seats, and the Commercers had thirty." She shook her head. "I suppose the sussie part was because of that susceptible assassin. I feel sorry for him, and I'd like to rip out the mind of whoever set him up."

"It's the sort of thing that Commercers like Minz would think up," said Dekkard. "I don't see the New Meritorists doing it."

"Neither do I."

"But . . . your dream was also telling you how important women are to the Craft Party."

"They're important to all working families. Wasn't that true in your family?"

Dekkard nodded. "Marks were tight until Mother established herself as a portraitist." After a pause, he asked, "Is that as true in Landor families?"

"Not in the same way. I did notice that families where the woman took a greater role in managing the lands tended to be better run and more prosperous. Not always, but usually."

"What's your feeling about the election—despite your nightmare?"

"I do feel we picked up at least a seat or two and that we'll have the greatest number of Council seats. Whether that will be enough seats for a working majority . . . I have no idea."

"My feeling exactly," said Obreduur from where he stood in the compartment door. "Let's go have breakfast . . . and no more talk about elections. Two bells from now . . . we'll have a much better idea."

At breakfast, no one said too much at first, not until Avraal started on her second mug of café, when she said, "I've been thinking . . . even if you can't form a government . . . can you at least press for a Council investigation of what happened to Markell . . . and the way the big engineering firms are operating? They have to be costing the government millions of marks."

"I can try," replied Obreduur. "Volkaar might find that useful as a way of demonstrating the Commerce Party isn't beholden to engineering corporacions. Even if we do form a government, that would still be the best way to start investigating corporacion misfeasance . . ."

The three lingered over café for almost two bells, generally avoiding government and politics, and touching on more personal topics, such as Nellara's increasing self-confidence and whether it was natural maturation or whether her increasing proficiency in knife-throwing might have helped.

As they rose to leave the dining carriage, Obreduur turned to Dekkard. "By the way, there will be a Council limousine waiting to take us to the Council Office Building. I arranged that before we left. We'll use it to return to the house late this afternoon, and then we'll return to our normal routine tomorrow morning. I thought that might be a bit more secure."

"A great deal more secure." *And it will allow us to focus our full attention on security.*

For the last bell of the journey, Dekkard found himself looking out the compartment window and wondering just what they'd discover when they reached Machtarn.

The express came to a halt at the station platform at a sixth past the fifth bell of the morning. Obreduur held back until the passengers most in a hurry in their carriage had gotten off, and then Dekkard got off with the cases and summoned a porter.

But when Obreduur and Avraal stepped out of the carriage, two men in worn white linen suits immediately hurried across the platform toward the councilor. "Premier Obreduur! Premier Obreduur! We're from *Gestirn* and the *Tribune.* Could we have a statement, sir?"

At those cries, several of the remaining disembarking passengers turned to look at Obreduur with various expressions, ranging from curiosity to surprise. Dekkard didn't see any looks of disgust or disdain, but that was simply a matter of chance. "I think that means your days of relative obscurity are over, sir," he said quietly.

"We'll see." Obreduur looked to Avraal.

"They feel like they're newsies," she said.

Dekkard still moved forward, ready to act.

The two men, one apparently younger than Dekkard, slowed as they took in the two security aides, then stopped short of the three.

"We'd just like a few words, sir," said the older man, his hair slightly graying. "I'm Thom Carares from *Gestirn,* and this is Domenick Mychaels. He's from the *Tribune.*"

Avraal nodded slightly to Obreduur. Dekkard kept surveying the platform, but it was emptying quickly.

"Together?" asked Obreduur.

"I didn't know enough to find you," said the younger man. "I prevailed on Sr. Carares to let me trail along with him."

"I'd be happy to offer some words, but since I haven't seen the election results, I can't say much."

"It appears, from the early returns, that the Craft Party has at least twenty-eight seats, and might gain one or two more. What do you have to say about that?"

"If it turns out that way after all the results are in, I'd have to say that it represents years of hard work by a great number of dedicated people."

"Do you think the failure of the Commerce Party to deal with the New Meritorists influenced the election?" asked Carares.

"Usually, a number of factors affect elections. The New Meritorists gained much of their support from people who felt left out by Commercer acts and policies. The previous government failed to understand that, and just made the situation worse by shooting demonstrators."

"Do you plan to continue as premier?" asked Carares.

Obreduur laughed softly. "That's not my choice. It also depends on all the other councilors. Even if the Craft Party gains thirty seats, unless we get four more, the Imperador may offer the Commerce Party the first chance to form a coalition government. One way or another it will still be up to the councilors as to whom they select as their candidate for premier. If I happen to be that person, I'll be very honored."

"But you're the one who masterminded it all," declared Mychaels.

"I'm only one of several people who've worked to achieve these election results."

"Are you considering your wife for the position of Minister of the Justiciary?" asked Mychaels, almost impatiently.

"That's not possible. Even if it were, she informed me that she would not have considered any ministerial appointment."

"Then who will you consider?"

"The most qualified candidates, of course." Obreduur laughed gently once again. "I'll be happy to answer questions with more specifics at the proper time, if indeed I'm the one who ends up with that responsibility."

"It's been reported that you've been the target of several assassins. Is that true?" pressed Mychaels.

"It is."

"Do you know why?"

"That would only be a guess on my part. The assassins all either were killed or killed themselves, and there was no evidence found to lead elsewhere. As both your newssheets have reported, I'm far from the only councilor who has been the target of assassins."

"You're one of the few who's survived, sir," pointed out Carares.

"I'm fortunate to have two very good security aides."

"When will you know if you'll be Guldor's next premier?"

"It won't be before Quindi, when the new Council convenes. Depending on the Council votes, it could be Quindi . . . or it could take several days. Your judgment is as good as mine."

"If you become premier, what will your priorities be?"

"I'll be happy to answer that if and when I'm premier. Thank you both for your courtesy." Obreduur inclined his head, then began to walk toward the station.

Avraal and Dekkard flanked him, with the porter and the baggage cart following.

"That's only the beginning," observed Obreduur. "When I don't give them what they want, they'll ask you or others. I'd prefer that you reply by saying, 'It would be best if the councilor answered that.'"

"Except, if you become premier," said Dekkard, "it would be best if the Premier answered that."

"You're optimistic, Steffan."

"I'm not that optimistic, sir. Everything's a bit of a mess. I wouldn't be surprised if you're asked to be premier so that you have to handle the problems. I suspect that the Commercers believe you can't, and that they'll be back in power in a year . . . or less."

Obreduur's laugh was slightly bitter. "You just might be right. Then what?"

"We figure out a way to solve the problems, and it will be years before the Commercers have a chance at regaining power."

"*That* might be considered unrealistically optimistic," returned Obreduur dryly.

As they left the station proper, Dekkard immediately spotted the black Gresynt limousine with the Council insignia on the hood—and with an armed Council Guard standing beside it.

Perhaps twenty people stopped, stood, and watched as Obreduur and his small entourage approached the limousine. Dekkard studied the small crowd, then looked to Avraal.

"Nothing suspicious," she replied. "Mostly curious."

"Premier!" The guard saluted.

"At ease," replied Obreduur, "and thank you."

"My pleasure, sir."

Despite Avraal's words, Dekkard was breathing much more easily once the Council limousine was on Imperial Boulevard headed to the Council Hall.

He said quietly to Avraal, "I worry about all those people gathering around him. That won't stop if he becomes premier."

"Most of them won't be a problem, not with small crowds, like the one at the ironway station."

Meaning that we might need help if there are large crowds.

True to form, in the back of the limousine, Obreduur was writing. Messages, Dekkard thought.

Before that long, the limousine pulled up in front of the Council Hall's east entrance, where the three got out, leaving their luggage with the long steamer, and entered the Hall.

"We'll go straight to the Council Office Building," said Obreduur. "I need to know more before I do anything, and that's where the messages I need to see will be."

The corridors in both the Council Hall and the Council Office Building were eerily quiet, but that was scarcely surprising, since most councilors were in their districts, and with the Council dissolved, what staffers could do was limited, and the majority of councilors tended to allow staff more time off in the days before the election and on the day afterward.

Duadi would be another matter, and by Quindi, when the new Council was sworn in, the corridors would be back to their usual state.

The moment Dekkard opened the office door for Obreduur, Karola called out, "He's here!"

Almost immediately, everyone in the side office surged into the anteroom.

"Congratulations, sir!" declared Macri. "Or should we say, congratulations, Premier?"

"Hold off on the premier title," said Obreduur. "Even if the Council votes for me, the Imperador has to confer it, but I appreciate everything that all of you have done over the last few years. It wouldn't have been possible otherwise. Now . . . give me a few minutes to go through all the messages and heliograms, and I'll tell all of you what I know."

As Obreduur closed the door to his inner office, Macri looked at Avraal and Dekkard and asked, "Were there more attacks on him?"

"One more," said Avraal. "In Oersynt. Likely someone hired indirectly by the Commercers. Steffan questioned him, but he swallowed a suicide capsule, and I couldn't sense any reaction."

"Why do they hate him so much?" asked Margrit.

"They don't," said Macri. "They fear he'll succeed, and they've done too many illegal things that will come to light if he becomes premier. I wouldn't be surprised if a great number of documents, all across Machtarn, are being burned today. There will likely be suspicious gaps in the records of many corporacions . . . and likely in some ministries as well."

"At the very least," added Roostof, "he's made the corporacions more cautious. That will continue for a time, even if he doesn't become premier."

"That's not enough," declared Raynaad. "He has to be premier if there's going to be any real change."

"He'll be premier," predicted Macri, "but all any of you are to say is exactly what he said, that the Council will decide. Is that clear?"

Everyone nodded, although Raynaad did so slowly.

Dekkard sat down at his desk and looked at the empty surface, one of the very few times when he'd arrived and found no letters or petitions awaiting him. He felt like he should be doing something while he waited.

Before long, Obreduur opened the inner office door. "Everyone, come in. Leave the door open just in case we get messengers." Then he walked back into the office and stood in front of the desk, waiting until everyone was gathered.

"First . . . I did win reelection, with the widest margin so far. The latest message from the Craft Party headquarters states that we have definitely won twenty-nine seats in the next Council, and we might win one more. The Commercers have nineteen seats, and the Landors have seventeen seats. There's one undecided seat. Also, apparently our trip to Gaarlak in Summerend did some good. I received a separate message from Jens Seigryn that Haasan Decaro did win that seat over Elvann Wheiter, with the Landor candidate coming in third. There was a difference of less than two thousand votes between Decaro and Wheiter."

"You said that would happen," commented Macri.

"I thought it likely." Obreduur smiled wryly. "Now . . . we have to see what the Council will do when it convenes on Quindi. It's going to be strange to be the one convening the Council. It's been something like two hundred years since there was a Craft premier, even an acting one, convening the Council." He paused. "In the meantime, I'd like to meet with each of you, individually, for a few minutes, beginning with Ivann."

As Dekkard filed out of the inner office with the others, he couldn't help but wonder exactly what Obreduur would have to say to him. He watched as Macri left, with a vaguely pleased expression, then Roostof, Raynaad, and Avraal. Avraal had a slightly amused expression as she said, "You're next."

Dekkard entered the inner office, closed the door, and sat down in the middle chair. "Sir?"

"You know, Steffan, I'm still amazed at how unfailingly polite you are. Yet, at the same time . . . I don't quite know what to say to you. Without you, I wouldn't be here."

"Sir . . . it took both of us."

"I understand that. You and Avraal are a team, and together you're outstanding. But I worry about you."

Dekkard frowned. "Me, sir?"

"You're far too perceptive and intelligent to spend the rest of your life as a security aide, or even as a legalist."

"You want me to go elsewhere, sir?"

"By the Three, not at all! I just want you to understand that, if the time comes when you feel constricted . . . or bored . . . I'll support and help you in any way I can to allow you to move on to whatever you feel will fulfill you."

"Sir . . . you've paid me well, and in the past year, you've widened my understanding and knowledge. I like doing what I do here. Somehow . . . it feels . . . right."

"You're very good at it, too. In time . . . perhaps not even in the too distant future . . . you might want to think about a career on the political side. Have you thought about that?"

"I can't say I have, sir. I've just been trying to learn everything I can."

"I've noticed. That's an admirable trait. Try not to lose it. It will serve you well, in anything you do."

"Sir . . . what about Avraal? She's incredibly intelligent, perceptive, and works hard, too."

Obreduur smiled broadly. "I've already told her almost exactly what I've told you. She could have an outstanding political career also . . . except she'd be limited to staff positions, or a senior position in the guilds or a corporacion. She's an outstanding empath, but . . ."

She could never be a councilor . . . just because she's an empath. "That's . . . so wrong . . . in a way. I mean, I understand the reason, but . . ."

"We can't make everything right, or even better, all at once, Steffan. You've seen that already."

"I know, but it's more obvious when it's someone you know." *And love.*

"I understand that. Believe me, I do."

"Oh . . . that Ritten Obreduur can't be a minister if you're premier . . . and she's the most qualified in Guldor?"

"Exactly."

"That's wrong, too."

Obreduur shook his head. "It's not wrong. Other- wise, we'd already have whole families of Commercers leeching off the government. It's just unfortunate. Her advice and counsel will be invaluable." Obreduur did not speak for several moments, then said, "You've ben- efitted from Avraal's advice and counsel. It appears that way to me . . . or am I mistaken?"

"No, sir. I listen carefully to her."

"That's excellent . . . I hope . . . I hope you continue."

Dekkard wondered what Obreduur might have said and had not. "You will let us continue as a team?"

"I'd never think of breaking you two apart. You're so good together, and I think you each benefit from the other. If I am selected as premier and accepted by the Imperador, I'll also be able to pay you both a bit more."

"You've been generous, sir."

Obreduur laughed softly. "Given how many times you two have saved me, you're worth far more than I could ever pay." Again, Obreduur paused. "Is there any- thing else I haven't covered or you'd like to know?"

"I'll think of questions as soon as I leave, but I don't have any right now."

"You can always ask me, Steffan."

"Thank you." Since Obreduur remained seated, Dekkard asked, "Is there anything else?"

"That's all for now," replied Obreduur warmly. "If you'd have Karola come in next?"

"Yes, sir." Dekkard rose and left the inner office, say- ing as he paused by Karola's desk, "You're next."

"Thank you, Steffan."

Dekkard returned to his desk, thinking about the number of Obreduur's almost awkward pauses in his talk with Dekkard, all of them somehow connected with Avraal, enough so that it was clear Obreduur knew that the two had a bond that was far more than professional.

But you can't get married and keep working together. Nor can you become intimate and have it discovered and keep working together. Was that what he didn't want to bring up? But he also as much as said you'd both be idiots if you let go of each other.

Dekkard took a deep breath. *We've kept putting off dealing fully with what we feel . . . but how much longer can we keep doing that?*

For the next two bells, Dekkard's thoughts seemed to go in circles, and he was more than ready when Obreduur left the inner office and said, "I'm leaving. Everyone go home. You'll have more than enough work ahead."

As soon as they left the office, Dekkard concentrated on just one thing—and that was Obreduur's security. That wasn't difficult, since the corridors and the garden courtyard were even more deserted than they had been earlier.

On the ride back to the Obreduurs' house in the Council limousine, once Obreduur settled into working on various papers, and wrote messages, Dekkard looked at Avraal. "Somehow, this is all so surreal. I really never thought . . ."

"That he'd actually have a chance of becoming premier?"

"I thought he would eventually . . . just not so soon."

"Sometimes, you have to take the chance when the opportunity presents itself . . . or you may not see it again."

That also applies to you. After a slight hesitation, Dekkard said, "That's becoming obvious." *Painfully obvious.* "We need to talk."

"We do," she replied gently.

Once the limousine delivered the three, Dekkard carried his case and Obreduur's into the house, then took his own upstairs, dropping it on the bed, and immediately leaving his chamber, only to nearly collide with Avraal in the narrow hallway.

He started to reach for her.

"Not here," she murmured, "and not yet. We need to talk, remember?"

"Where?"

"The garage. It's even more private . . . for conversation." She smiled almost mischievously. "Besides, you need to check the steamers. I'll come with you."

Dekkard led the way to the garage, where he did check and fill both Gresynts with water and kerosene, as well as wipe down Ingrella's steamer. Then he turned to Avraal.

"You said we needed to talk," she said. "I'm listening."

"Even before you made that comment about losing the opportunity, I was thinking about that. I love you, and I love working with you . . . and I really don't want to lose either."

"Neither do I." She moved closer, then touched his cheek gently, before putting her arms around him, and pressing her lips and entire body against him.

Finally, after some time passed—Dekkard wasn't sure he knew how much . . . and didn't care—Avraal eased away from him, but still held his hands. "You needed to know that. You also need to know that I want exactly what you want. Do you feel that?"

Dekkard had to swallow before he could answer. "I do."

"We need to be patient for just a few more days. We need to get Obreduur in place as premier, and without any allegations or rumors about improper behavior by his security aides. Then . . . we can decide what to do."

"Will you marry me? I've never really asked."

She kissed him again, gently, but longingly. "You've already asked in every way but words. Yes. I will, but we need to go about it in a way where we can do the best we can for both of us."

"I never thought otherwise. How long . . . do you think?"

"A week at least, likely two. It might have to be longer."

Dekkard winced.

"I know. I feel the same way." Her words felt as though they had cut through his heart. "It's taken a while . . . we can make it."

If she can make it ... so can you. "Then we'd better get ready for dinner, before someone gets the wrong idea."

She laughed. "They already know what we have in mind, but I chose the garage because no one would dare to say that we'd be that improper here. They might think it ..."

"Do you want to try?" Dekkard offered the words teasingly.

"Don't tempt me." Letting go of one hand, and grasping his other more firmly, she led him toward the side door out of the garage.

99

On Duadi morning, Dekkard was the first one downstairs, although he knew it wouldn't be long before Avraal joined him. He immediately picked up Hyelda's copy of *Gestirn* to see what the newssheet had printed, if anything. The headline on the front-page story read: POSSIBLE PREMIER AWAITS COUNCIL. The story was largely accurate, but Dekkard had to wonder what might have appeared in *The Machtarn Tribune*. The other lead story confirmed the final allocation of Council seats by party: twenty-nine Craft, twenty Commerce, and seventeen Landor.

He had barely seated himself when Avraal appeared, but he immediately stood and poured her café.

"Thank you." Avraal smiled warmly and sat down. "Was the newssheet story accurate?" She took a sip of café.

"It was, and the other story said we only got twenty-nine seats." Dekkard reseated himself.

"Only?"

"I could hope for more. It would make matters easier for Obreduur."

"A nine-seat margin should be sufficient, unless the Landors decide to capitulate totally."

"I can't see Navione doing that, but some of the others . . ." Dekkard shrugged.

"Vonauer won't go to the Commercers. He can get a better deal from Obreduur. He should be able to hold most of the Landors."

Rhosali hurried into the staff room. "Is he really going to be premier?"

"It's possible, even likely," said Dekkard, "but nothing's certain until the Council votes on Quindi." He took two croissants and two slices of quince paste.

Avraal looked at the quince paste and shook her head.

Dekkard just grinned. Then he asked, "Have you heard anything from Emrelda?"

"Before we left, I said I'd send a message when we returned. I did, but she likely didn't get it until late yesterday because she was working. So I imagine I'll hear from her later today. I still worry about her."

"So do I."

Avraal looked at Dekkard quizzically.

"She's your sister. When bad things happen to her, it affects you. Besides, she's a good person who didn't deserve what happened."

"No . . . she didn't . . . and neither did Markell."

"All we can do now is support her, and, in the new Council, try to put a stop to that sort of Commercer abuse."

"That won't be enough."

Nothing would be enough, not for Markell. But Dekkard knew that Avraal knew that, and there was no point in saying it.

Breakfast was uneventful, and before that long Dekkard was driving Avraal and Obreduur down Alta-rama toward Imperial Boulevard.

Obreduur said almost nothing on the rest of the drive to the Council Office Building until Dekkard began to slow as he approached the building entry. "Just so you two know, I'll be having a meeting in the dining room at noon, and I'm expecting Jerrohm Kaas this morning. He's one of Carlos's legalists."

For a moment, Dekkard frowned, then realized that Obreduur was still worried about possible attackers and wanted them to know about Kaas. "Anyone else today, sir?"

"If there is, I'll have Karola let you know."

After letting Obreduur and Avraal off at the entrance, and then parking the Gresynt, Dekkard made his way to the office, and was only stopped once to show his passcard—and then given an apology.

"I'd rather have you be careful," replied Dekkard, "than not and allow someone who shouldn't be there into the building."

"Thank you, sir."

The familiar stack of letters and petitions was awaiting him on his desk, and he had the feeling that those stacks would be growing—at least if Obreduur became premier. With a slightly ironic smile, he picked up the first one and began to read.

Slightly after fourth bell, a Council Guard escorted a thin-faced blond man in a dark brown suit into the office and announced, "Sr. Jerrohm Kaas."

Dekkard immediately studied the legalist, knowing that he'd be seeing more of Kaas in the days ahead.

Karola looked up and smiled. "Legalist Kaas is expected." Then she stood and escorted Kaas into the inner office.

The Council Guard sat down on the bench just inside the door, and Kaas spent more than a bell with Obreduur before emerging, looking at none of the councilor's staffers as he left, again accompanied by the guard.

When Obreduur emerged from the inner office at a third before noon, Dekkard had finished drafting his replies to all the correspondence that had been left for him. From a glance at Avraal's desk, she had as well.

Neither Dekkard nor Avraal said anything as they escorted Obreduur until they were comparatively alone crossing the courtyard garden on the way to the Council Hall, when Dekkard said, "Might we ask about this meeting?"

"It's with Haarsfel and Saandaar Vonauer. One way or another, it won't be terribly long. I appreciate it if you're waiting in the corridor by first bell."

"We'll be there," said Avraal.

After making certain that Obreduur was safely inside the councilors' dining room, Avraal and Dekkard walked quickly to the staff cafeteria, less than a third full, with at least a few faces that looked totally unfamiliar, possibly staff members of councilors newly elected, although Dekkard certainly couldn't have sworn to it.

Almost out of habit, Dekkard had beef empanadas and rice, while Avraal had an Imperial salad. They'd been seated for only a few moments before Laurenz Korriah and Shaundara Keppel appeared.

"Could we join you?" asked Keppel.

"Of course," replied Avraal.

"Thank you." Korriah's eyes remained on Avraal. "You knew this was coming, didn't you?"

"He's not premier yet," replied Avraal. "He might be or he might not be. That depends on what the Landor councilors decide . . . and possibly even a few Commercers."

Korriah laughed. "You can demur all you want. It's almost a foregone conclusion he'll stay premier."

"Why do you think so?" asked Dekkard, emphasizing the "you" just slightly.

"First, because too many Landor councilors are tired of getting screwed by Ulrich and Volkaar. Second, because some Commerce councilors likely are, too, even if they'll never admit it, even privately. Third, because your boss always keeps his word." Korriah laughed again. "Part of that's because he doesn't promise a lot, but he delivers what he promises. Fourth, it's the only way the Imperador can keep things from getting much worse. And, even when your boss becomes premier, things will get worse before they get better."

Dekkard had to agree with Korriah's points, especially the last one. But he grinned and asked Korriah, "So why are you here right now?"

"So that I can tell you two in the future what my boss needs or would like and there won't be any fingerprints. Seibryg's a very traditional city, but we need stronger protection for workers, or we're going to have a lot more trouble with the New Meritorists."

"Especially women," added Keppel almost sharply, "but he can't say so publicly."

"The Landors there wish there had never been a Silent Revolution?" asked Avraal.

"Not quite, but almost," replied Keppel. "The Commercers are even worse. They're still angry about the Susceptible Protection Act."

"That was passed thirty years ago," said Dekkard.

"To the Commercers in Seibryg, that was yesterday," said Keppel sardonically.

Dekkard managed not to wince, instead saying, "We'll do what we can. It would be helpful for everyone, you understand, if he's not blindsided."

Korriah nodded. "That sort of shit doesn't help anyone." Then he grinned and looked at Avraal. "You're carrying knives now, like Steffan. How's that working?"

"Well enough that she stopped another would-be assassin in Oersynt," said Dekkard.

"You couldn't?" said Korriah, looking at Dekkard.

"I'm not massively impressive like you, Laurenz. He was mentally unbalanced, without identification, carrying a long-barreled revolver, and a pocketful of cartridges and little more. He didn't get off a single shot."

"It took both our knives," added Avraal.

Korriah looked at Keppel.

"No, Laurenz," she replied, deadpan. "You're massively impressive."

Korriah burst into laughter, shaking his head at the same time. Finally, he just looked from Dekkard to Avraal and back to Dekkard. "And you two look like such nice people."

"We are," replied Dekkard. "We just don't like people trying to kill our boss. How was your veal?"

"Three's curse if I remember." Korriah shook his head, then grinned once more. "I really did think you were a nice guy, Steffan."

"We're all disillusioned, Laurenz," said Keppel. "I once thought the same of you." She couldn't quite conceal her smile.

"Sometimes, Shaundara, your tongue is sharper than their knives."

"Only sometimes?" she riposted.

Dekkard looked down at his empty plate. He didn't recall even eating. "Duty is about to call. We'll need leave in a few minutes. Do you mind if I pass on the request you didn't make because there shouldn't be any fingerprints? In words only, of course."

"That was the point," said Korriah, with another grin.

This time Dekkard was the one to shake his head.

Within another sixth, Dekkard and Avraal were walking along the main corridor.

"That was interesting," he observed. "Most likely, it won't be the last."

"It may be one of the more enjoyable interactions of that sort," replied Avraal.

Dekkard suspected that was also likely.

They only had to wait a few minutes for Obreduur to emerge from the dining room.

"Back to the office, sir?"

Obreduur nodded, his thoughts clearly elsewhere.

Dekkard waited until they were crossing the garden courtyard before he quickly related the interaction with Korriah and Keppel.

"Thank you. That's useful . . . and good to know. I suspected something of the sort, but Kharl has always been pleasantly formal, and I imagine it will remain that way on the surface. Just remain open without committing to anything except conveying such indirect messages."

As soon as the three reached the office, Karola handed Obreduur a sealed heliograph message. "It's urgent."

Obreduur took the envelope, opened it, and extracted the single sheet. His face stiffened slightly as he read. Then he said to Dekkard and Avraal, "We need to talk."

Dekkard followed Obreduur and Avraal into the inner office, closing the door.

Obreduur walked to his desk, then turned and said slowly, "That heliogram was from Jens Seigryn."

"What happened?" asked Avraal.

"Haasan Decaro died of heart failure this morning. Apparently, he was putting on a pair of brand-new boots."

Dekkard stiffened, then murmured, "Boots . . . Curse of the Three."

Obreduur nodded. "No one will ever be able to prove it . . . and fewer will want to."

That was confirmation enough for Dekkard about who Obreduur thought was immediately responsible. Indirectly responsible was another question, and Dekkard had a fair idea that it had to be one of two people, if not both. *And that raises other questions.*

"Now what?" he asked quietly. "The local Craft Party has to come up with a replacement?"

"Not exactly," replied Obreduur. "Since Decaro was elected, the district Craft Party makes a recommendation to the political head of the party in the Council."

"Is that you or Haarsfel right now?" asked Avraal.

"That all depends. Since Decaro was elected as a member of the incoming Council, his replacement can't be approved or rejected until the new Council is sworn in. If the Council votes me in as premier, the approval or rejection is my choice. If we can't form a government, and Commercers and Landors do, then Haarsfel is effectively the head of the Craft Party in the Council, and the choice is his."

"Does that mean that until the seat is filled," asked Dekkard, "the Craft Party has only twenty-eight votes instead of twenty-nine? Could that affect your ability to form a government?"

"At this point, it's one of several factors that could make matters difficult."

"When is the Gaarlak Craft Party committee meeting?" said Dekkard.

"Tonight. If they can't come up with a candidate tonight, they'll meet again tomorrow afternoon. After all the fighting over the nominee the first time, it could take days, but most likely not weeks. Then, again, I could be surprised."

Dekkard had the feeling that the heliogram had indeed surprised Obreduur, but that Decaro's death itself hadn't. And that meant . . . *What? That something hasn't gone as planned?*

He decided to ask something he'd wondered for a long time. "Now that Decaro's dead, can you tell us why he wanted to kill you?"

"Because, when I was regional coordinator for the guilds, I discovered that he'd been taking marks from guild members, shaking them down on the quiet. He'd just replaced the previous guildmeister, who'd actually written cheques to his mistress and his own banque account. According to Ingrella, I couldn't prove what Haasan was doing, not before the Justiciary. So I told him if it continued . . . I'd bring it up with the Advisory Committee, unless he cleaned up the guild. At that point, all the Council wanted was for the corruption to stop and everything to remain quiet."

"And?" asked Avraal quietly.

"Haasan agreed . . . and, from what I could determine the shakedowns stopped. Then . . . a year later . . . if I'd picked up those boots, I'd have been shot. Again . . . no proof . . . and by then Haasan had actually cleaned up the guild, and the Council wasn't about to remove him . . . and I ended up as councilor. We remained at a polite arm's length from then on." Obreduur shrugged. "Not exactly an ideal situation, but with me no longer working for the Advisory Committee, I wasn't a threat to him."

"Then why did the Craft Party want you to go to Gaarlak?" asked Avraal.

"To raise interest in the Craft Party, and, if I could, to persuade Haasan not to run. Quietly, of course."

"Was the assassin at the Ritter's Inn his doing?" asked Dekkard.

"Most likely, but I have no way of proving that."

For a moment, Dekkard didn't know exactly what to say. "It was right after the reception where you had me speak."

"Obviously, he took your failure to endorse him . . . rather personally," said Avraal.

"He knew I wouldn't. That had to have been planned earlier." Obreduur straightened. "There's not much we can do at this point, either about Haasan or what the Council decides. If you two are caught up on correspondence, you might write down, in case I am selected as premier, what you think are the most important priorities for the new Council . . . and why."

"Yes, sir."

"On your way out, would you tell Ivann that I need to see him. He needs to know about Haasan's death as well."

"Yes, sir."

After they left the inner office and Dekkard had relayed Obreduur's request to Macri, he walked back toward his desk, stopping beside Avraal when she gestured.

"You know . . ." murmured Avraal.

"Later . . ."

She nodded.

For the rest of the day, Dekkard struggled, not so much with priorities, but with their order and the reasons for that order. Clearly, in his mind, one of the most important issues was how to reassure the working people and the shopkeepers that the new government would be more concerned with their needs—but how best to address and express that concern was definitely going to be difficult.

In the end, it was after dinner before Dekkard and Avraal met under the portico.

"It was the bootmaker, wasn't it?" asked Avraal.

"That . . . or she was set up to take the fall if someone looked deeply." Dekkard paused. "The thing is . . . Obreduur was surprised by the heliogram, but not so much by Decaro's death. That's what I saw, anyway."

"That's what I sensed as well. He wasn't so much surprised at Decaro's death as when or how it happened."

"Maybe Decaro just made too many enemies. Obreduur's statement that no one was going to look deeply into it suggests that." After a moment, Dekkard added, "After the district party chose Decaro as Lamarr's replacement, Obreduur said something to the effect that Jens Seigryn would have to deal with it."

"You think . . . ?"

"It's certainly possible, but it's looking to me like they'd planned something, and someone else beat them to it . . . and that has Obreduur worried."

"Maybe it really was the bootmaker," suggested Avraal. "She might have been afraid of the power Decaro would have as councilor . . . and she knew that Decaro had already planned the earlier attempt to kill Obreduur. We'll have to keep all that in mind . . . but I don't know that we'll ever find out."

Dekkard just nodded, then asked, "I saw you got a message. I assume it was from Emrelda. How is she?"

"She's doing as well as she can. She has Findi off this week and invited us to spend the day."

"I'd like that . . . but if you wanted time with her without me . . ."

Avraal smiled. "You're sweet, but we're going together. You might have to spend a bell reading on the veranda, but that wouldn't be an ordeal, I'm sure."

Not in the slightest!

100

For Dekkard and Avraal, Tridi was much the same as Duadi had been, although the corridors of the Council Office Building were now returning to a semblance of what Dekkard thought of as normal, except they were also crowded with the handcarts removing the personal property and effects of councilors who had been defeated and those who had retired or been forced to stand down. In addition, some returning senior councilors opted to move to what they perceived as better offices among those of departing councilors. Obreduur could have chosen to move to another office, but had decided against it, since most of the vacated offices were on the lower level amid those of largely Commercer councilors, and since none of those available were any larger than his present spaces.

Dekkard suspected that Obreduur also didn't want to deal with the hassles of moving an office while thinking about and trying to research possible ministerial appointees ... although Dekkard knew that Ingrella had to be deeply involved.

Even by the end of the day on Tridi, Obreduur had received no word from the Gaarlak District Craft Party, and only a heliogram from Jens Seigryn that discussion was apparently heated, especially since Gretna Haarl had appeared before the leadership as the new guildmeister of the Textile Millworkers and opposed several proposed replacements, particularly the former guildmeister. According to Obreduur, Seigryn was going to try to suggest a compromise candidate in hopes of breaking the bargejam.

There was more speculation in the Furdi-morning edition of *Gestirn* about whether enough Landor and/ or unhappy Commercer councilors would break with their leadership and vote for a Craft premier as well as another small article on how the likely Craft candidate, the acting Premier, was keeping a low profile.

Even so, when Dekkard finished parking the Gresynt and walked into the Council Office Building that morning, he wasn't totally surprised to see Amelya Detauran heading directly toward him.

"Congratulations to you and Avraal . . . and your councilor."

"Thank you, but at best, congratulations might be a little premature."

"Would you mind if I walked up with you?"

"Not at all." While it was clear that Detauran wanted something, Dekkard was curious to know what that might be.

The two entered the staff staircase, which seemed empty of others at that moment.

"From what Kaliara has been able to piece together, you and Avraal have stopped three or four assassination attempts on your boss. Is that accurate? Or have there been more?"

"There have been some that weren't reported, but I'd have to deny saying so."

"I thought so, and I told Kaliara that it was my guess that there had been more. She's very upset about that. There have been several attempts on her as well. Do you know if Premier Obreduur will address the excesses of Security?"

"He's looked into those problems, and he has some ideas. I think it's fair to say that he'll do something that will directly address those abuses, but I can't say what or how swiftly."

Detauran did not say more until they left the staircase on the second level. Then she stopped next to the wall and looked directly at Dekkard.

He waited.

"Kaliara doesn't want another Commercer premier. At least not for some years. She can't and won't say anything. But she wants that message conveyed."

"I can do that."

Detauran nodded. "Now . . . a personal question. Are you going to let Avraal slip through your fumbling fingers?"

That question did surprise Dekkard. For a moment, he just stood there. Finally, he said, "No. I've promised. Somehow."

"Kaliara might be able to help there, too. She knows a lot of senior corporacion types. If you need to, keep it in mind." Then she smiled. "I'll see you two around."

Then she turned and strode off.

Dekkard was still puzzling it all over when he walked into the office and asked Karola, "Is anyone with him?"

She shook her head.

"I need a moment."

Karola just gestured to the inner office.

Dekkard opened the door and walked in, closing the door quietly but firmly.

Obreduur was standing by the partly open window, taking in the slight early-fall breeze. "You look like you have some news."

"I do." Dekkard went on to relate what Amelya Detauran had conveyed about Councilor Bassaana.

"Do you trust the information?"

"I trust the source. She's always been accurate and truthful before. She also speaks in a way that suggests she's closer to her councilor than are many security isolates. And she's mentioned her councilor's dissatisfaction with the Commerce leadership before. That suggests to me that she's telling the truth about the attempts on her councilor."

"That's very interesting. We'll see how the vote comes out. If several Commercer votes show up, then that will also give me a stronger position in dealing with Security." Obreduur frowned, then said, "You've seen more of what goes on with a councilor's job and life than most staffers ever do, simply because I've required more security than most. Honestly now, what do you think?"

"I think you're doing a difficult job, trying to do the

best for everyone when almost no one is looking for what's right, but wanting what they want."

"Don't you find that depressing? Especially when campaigning?"

"Not that depressing, sir. People are what they are. Even the best government can't be perfect." Dekkard smiled wryly. "I might be a little more depressed if I were actually a councilor, but that's one of the really good aspects of the Great Charter. Most people can't focus their unhappiness on their councilor, only on the party. But they can express their frustrations, and they can ask for change. Of course, it's a two-edged blade, because a councilor who's weak or incompetent isn't directly held accountable, but if his party . . . or her party . . . doesn't deal with such a councilor, they risk losing the seat. Isn't that what you've used in gaining seats for the Craft Party?"

"I'd like to think so." Obreduur laughed softly, then asked, "What about campaigning? What do you think of that?"

"It's work. Some nights, my feet hurt. It's also necessary, it seems to me. I learned a lot just by listening."

"That's usually the case," Obreduur said dryly. He paused, then said, "Thank you. I appreciate the information."

Dekkard inclined his head, turned, and headed back to his desk to struggle with the document on priorities for the new Council.

101

Quindi morning, both Dekkard and Avraal were up early, because Obreduur had informed them the night before that they needed to leave almost a bell earlier. He'd also informed them that they needed to wear their dressier gray suits, rather than security grays, because the results of the vote for premier might be almost unprecedented and of possible historical significance. Of course, that meant that he wouldn't be wearing his gladius, but that was no loss, given that he'd never actually used it, not in over two years.

Dekkard was glad the vote was on Quindi because his two gray suits hadn't come back from the cleaners until Furdi afternoon, and when he'd mentioned that to Obreduur, the councilor had just smiled and said, "Steffan, it might be wise to expand your dress wardrobe with your coming increase in pay."

"I agree," Avraal had said.

Facing such unanimity, Dekkard had replied, "Once I'm paid."

As he dressed, he looked at the gray suit, of far better quality than he'd ever purchased before, and one that he wouldn't have purchased without Avraal's encouragement, and the gray cravat that Avraal had given him. Two years before, he'd never considered that he'd be part of one of the greatest political changes in centuries. He hadn't been totally convinced that it would actually happen until Furdi morning, when Amelya Detauran had drawn him aside and delivered her message.

Once dressed, except for the coat, he made his way downstairs, where he immediately picked up *Gestirn*. The lead-story headline was direct enough: HISTORIC VOTE POSSIBLE. He quickly read the story, but there was nothing new in it, and he replaced the newssheet on the side table. Then, hearing Avraal's steps on the back staircase, he poured her café and then his own, but did not sit down.

He couldn't help but smile when she entered the staff room in the tailored and stylish gray suit, if with trousers rather than a skirt. "I just poured your café."

"Perhaps I should dress this way every morning."

"It might not be practical, but I wouldn't mind." Dekkard waited for her to sit before seating himself. "It could be a very special day, but we'll have to be very careful. We wouldn't want anyone to spoil it."

"You two look like theatre idols," said Rhosali as she stepped into the staff room.

"No. Steffan does. I'm just presentable."

"You look gorgeous," Dekkard protested.

"You're not exactly objective."

"And you are?" he asked wryly.

"We need to eat," said Avraal. "It's going to be a long day."

Dekkard had to agree. He served Avraal a croissant and took two for himself, along with two slices of the quince paste.

Avraal did finally eat most of the croissant, but only after two mugs of café.

Then they left the staff room to finish getting ready. Dekkard tried to be especially careful of his gray suit in readying the Gresynt, but he had it under the portico before anyone else was there.

He was momentarily surprised to see Ingrella walking beside her husband, with Avraal behind the couple, but realized immediately that Ingrella definitely needed to be present in the reserved section of the gallery when the vote took place. The councilor wore a dark blue suit with the bright red cravat, but he still carried the case that was stuffed with papers and messages. Ingrella wore a tailored suit of the same dark blue, with a nearly transparent silver headscarf.

Once everyone was in the Gresynt, Dekkard eased the steamer down the drive, but at the end, rather than turn right onto Altarama, Dekkard turned left, announcing, "I'm taking a different route this morning."

Obreduur didn't even look up from his papers.

Ingrella said, "That's not a bad idea."

The detour added a few minutes to the trip, since Dekkard didn't get onto Imperial Boulevard until he was a good five blocks north of his usual entry point. Intent as both Dekkard and Avraal were, neither discerned anything presenting a threat or danger.

When Dekkard turned onto Council Avenue, Obreduur looked up from his papers and said, "Take us to the east entrance of the Council Hall. Avraal will escort us in, and Ingrella will wait in the spousal lounge. Then you can park as usual. Avraal and I will walk to the office."

Dekkard frowned, but then Avraal escorted Obreduur into the Council Office Building every morning. *Except this isn't every morning.*

"We'll be fine," Avraal murmured. "I am carrying knives."

Dekkard followed Obreduur's directions, but he did get out of the Gresynt and walk to the east entrance doors before returning to the steamer and driving back to the covered parking. Several Council Guards studied him, but apparently they all seemed to recognize him. *You've been walking past them for two years largely unrecognized and in a matter of days now they know who you are.* That thought bemused him, but didn't distract him as he made his way up the staff staircase.

Karola looked bewildered when he stepped into the office.

For the first time ever, he realized he was actually in the office before Obreduur and Avraal. "Ritten Obreduur came with us this morning. They escorted her to the lounge and are walking through the courtyard back here."

"Oh . . . of course. I knew she was coming, but the councilor didn't mention the details." After a moment, Karola added, "No, there isn't anything for you to draft."

Less than a sixth later, Avraal and Obreduur entered the office, and Karola handed Obreduur several messages, some of which were clearly in heliogram envelopes.

"Thank you." Obreduur nodded and then closed the door.

Dekkard turned to Avraal. "There wasn't any trouble, was there?"

"No. He had to stop by the premier's office to deal with a few official matters. They didn't take that long.

We'll have to escort him back there before fifth bell so he can deal with some more last-moment arrangements."

Abruptly, the inner office door opened and Obreduur stood there. "Steffan . . . if you'd come in. There are some details I need to go over with you." Obreduur had an expression on his face that Dekkard couldn't read as he turned and walked into the inner office.

Dekkard looked to Avraal.

"He's disturbed, but not angry, and a little amused, in a strange way. You'd better go in."

Dekkard followed Obreduur, closing the door.

Obreduur sat down behind the desk and gestured to the middle chair. "This may take a few minutes."

"Have I done something wrong, sir?" Dekkard had the feeling something was different, but what, he couldn't tell.

"By the Three, no. You've done more than anyone could have hoped . . . but . . . it is going to be a little awkward."

"Awkward?"

"This might explain it better." Obreduur leaned forward and handed Dekkard a heliogram envelope.

Dekkard took it.

"You need to take it out and read it."

Dekkard extracted the single sheet and read.

After long and careful deliberation, the Craft Party of the District of Gaarlak recommends one Steffan Delos Dekkard as the replacement for the deceased Haasan Hyel Decaro as the Councilor for the District of Gaarlak . . .

There was more but Dekkard read those words again. They didn't change.

"This isn't some sort of jest, sir, is it?" Dekkard asked.

Obreduur's voice was both somehow pleased and sad. "No, it's not. I also have heliograms from Jens Seigryn and Yorik Haansel, confirming it. After almost three days of bitter and acrimonious debate, Gretna

Haarl offered you as the only compromise candidate that the Textile Millworkers would accept. I have always thought that, in time, you would make an excellent councilor. I had never planned on it happening this soon. That's why I have very mixed feelings. Your instincts are good. You're incredibly intelligent, and you learn quickly, but . . ."

". . . there's a great deal I don't know and need to learn."

Obreduur nodded.

Dekkard's next words were instinctive. "I'd be better with Avraal."

"You can't fraternize with staffers. Anyone's staffer. You know that." For all the evenness of Dekkard's words, the councilor was smiling.

"But I can marry her . . ."

Obreduur stood and walked to the office door. He opened it and said, "Avraal, you're needed here."

After Avraal entered the office, Obreduur stepped out, closing the door.

Avraal looked at the closed door, then at Dekkard, who stood, and asked, in a tone between puzzled and slightly cross, "Can you explain?"

Dekkard shook his head. "I'll try." He handed her the heliogram. "You need to read it first."

She read it. Then she read it again. "It's not a terrible joke, is it?"

"Obreduur says that it's not. He said he'd hoped that I'd be a councilor someday. I don't think even he expected this. I think they'd planned for someone else." He looked at her. "I didn't want it like this. But, without you, I'll make too many mistakes. Yet . . . I don't want you thinking that's why . . ."

She stepped forward and put her finger on his lips. "I know that. I've always known that, and the answer to the question you asked earlier is still the same. Yes . . . and yes."

"But . . . there are so many things . . ."

"Steffan . . . what did I say—"

"I understand. This may be the only chance. It's just so sudden."

"Together . . . we can do it." She leaned forward and kissed him.

After gathering himself together, Dekkard walked to the door and opened it.

Obreduur looked at the two and walked back into the inner office. "And?"

"You're gaining a councilor and losing a security aide. We can still—"

The acting Premier shook his head. "Only until the moment you're sworn in later this afternoon. Don't worry. I've seen the way you two look at each other, and I earlier asked Carlos if I could hire Isobel Irlende temporarily if you two married. He agreed. She'll learn things valuable to him, and she's almost as good as you are, Avraal, as an empath, and she's better than decent with weapons."

"Then . . . why . . . ?" offered Dekkard.

"She usually makes far more than the Council can pay. Allowing her to work for me for a bit is also a favor. I'll be sending Carlos a message shortly for her to come to the office this afternoon. I may need a little unofficial protection back from the floor after the session is over."

The next two bells both dragged and flew by, and before Dekkard knew it, he and Avraal were escorting Obreduur to the premier's floor office.

They stood in the area just inside the door to the main corridor of the Council Hall, just waiting and watching as Obreduur signed and sealed various papers.

At a sixth before noon, Obreduur turned to Dekkard. "Just wait here, Steffan. I'll send the lieutenant-at-arms for you when the time comes."

One of the clerks looked up with a puzzled expression.

"This is Councilor-select Dekkard for the Gaarlak district. The district party insisted. You saw all the papers."

"Yes, sir. We just didn't know . . ."

"It's unusual . . . but not unprecedented." Obreduur smiled. "And the other security aide is his fiancée. It's already been an interesting day."

Dekkard turned to Avraal and murmured, "Let's hope it doesn't get any more interesting."

When Obreduur left the office through the door that led to the Council floor, one of the clerks motioned to a small shuttered window beside that door. "Just open the shutters. You can't see much besides the desk of the presiding councilor, but you can hear most of what goes on. That's so we can see when we need to go out for anything the Premier or the presiding councilor needs."

"Thank you."

"You'll be out there soon enough."

Dekkard and Avraal moved to the window, where he eased the shutters open. All he could see was the dais dominated by the narrow desk of whoever was presiding and the front row of the councilors' desks, where four councilors stood. The two he recognized were the Craft floor leader, Guilhohn Haarsfel, and Obreduur. The other two might have been Vonauer and Volkaar.

Dekkard could hear murmurings and bits of conversation, both from the gallery above and from the floor as the chamber filled, but none of the conversations were clear to him.

Then the chimes struck the six bells of noon, followed by a single echoing deep chime that seemed to reverberate through Dekkard—as he expected it had been designed to do.

An individual wearing the green and black dress uniform of the Council Guards strode to the middle of the dais, directly before the desk behind which Obreduur now stood, and struck the floor with the gold and black ceremonial staff. Then he declared in a deep voice, "The Council is now in session," after which he pivoted and marched off the dais and down the steps on the side away from Dekkard.

After a long moment of silence, Obreduur declared,

"The first order of this council and of this session is the swearing in of the duly elected members of the Council of Sixty-Six. All councilors now present stand to be sworn."

Dekkard saw the councilors in the front row stand behind their desks, as well as heard the shuffling and rising of the others.

Obreduur read the oath of office, phrase by phrase, as the new and reelected councilors repeated each phrase.

"I solemnly swear that as a Councilor of the Sixty-Six, I will uphold the Great Charter and all of its provisions, in both letter and spirit, that I will by word and deed defend those provisions, and that I undertake my sacred duties and responsibilities of my own free will, without reservation or hesitation."

"The Council now stands ready to conduct its necessary business," declared Obreduur.

After those words, Guilhohn Haarsfel, as the Craft Party floor leader, stepped forward and cleared his throat. "The Craft leadership has proposed the name of the acting Premier, Axel Laurent Obreduur, as its premier-designate. The vote is for or against the candidate. All councilors have a third in which to register their vote and deposit a plaque."

As Haarsfel finished speaking, Obreduur gestured, and the deep gong chimed once.

Dekkard watched as each councilor walked to his or her party's plaque box and picked up two of the colored tiles, one signifying yes, one no, then walked to the double box set on the front of the dais, where one tile went into the ballot slot and the other into the null slot.

As he kept watching, he found that his mouth and lips were getting dry. He looked to Avraal. "How do you feel?"

"Nervous, unsettled. The whole chamber feels unsettled."

Dekkard wished he could have voted, but the procedures were what they were.

Finally, the deep chime rang again.

"The vote is closed," declared Obreduur. "Floor leaders, do your duty."

The three floor leaders watched as each voting tile was removed from the ballot box and placed in one of two columns in the counting tray. Each column was also separated by party. Then the clerk wrote the vote totals on the tally sheet, and each of the three floor leaders signed the sheet. As the floor leader of the party with the greatest number of councilors, Haarsfel carried the tally sheet as he stepped onto the dais.

"Those councilors approving Councilor Axel Obreduur as the Council's selection as premier of this council—twenty-eight Craft councilors, eight Landor councilors, and five Commerce councilors, for a total of forty-three. The Council has elected Axel Obreduur as premier."

A modest wave of applause immediately issued from the councilors and from the gallery.

"He did it. He actually did it," said one of the clerks behind Dekkard and Avraal.

Haarsfel was smiling broadly as he gestured to Obreduur. "Acting Premier and Premier-select Obreduur."

"Thank you. All of you. As is precedent, I will not offer my address to the Council until I am officially accepted, and, if accepted, I will address the entire Council at the opening of the session on Unadi. There is one other item, however. As some of you may know, the councilor-elect from the Gaarlak district died of heart failure earlier this week. The decision on his successor was made entirely by the district Craft Party. After a lengthy and protracted debate, they recommended Steffan Delos Dekkard as the replacement councilor for the Gaarlak district. Some of you may know Councilor-select Dekkard, and his selection was as much of a surprise to me as it was to him. Lieutenant-at-Arms, please escort the councilor-select to the floor."

The same uniformed figure who had opened the Council session walked to the door from the Premier's floor office and opened it. Avraal squeezed Dekkard's hand, then released it, as he followed the lieutenant-at-arms to the center of the floor, and then turned to face Obreduur.

Moments later, he found himself repeating the words of the Councilors' Oath that he had heard earlier.

"You are now confirmed as councilor, and to carry out your duties," intoned Obreduur, adding after a pause, "There being no other pending matters before the Council, the Council stands adjourned until noon, Unadi, the nineteenth day of Fallfirst."

The deep gong chimed again.

Obreduur was smiling as he descended from the dais. "You're a councilor, but I'm going to have to impose on you and your fiancée for an additional duty. I have to present myself to the Imperador."

"It would be our pleasure."

At that moment, Councilor Hasheem appeared. "Congratulations, Axel, or should I say Premier?"

"Not yet, and I'm still Axel, except when I'm presiding or it's some most formal affair."

Hasheem turned to Dekkard. "It's somehow fitting that one of those who saved a councilor is now a councilor himself. I might be a little prejudiced, since I was the one you two saved."

"I'm just glad we were able to," replied Dekkard.

In moments, the chamber was at least half empty, those remaining seemingly largely Craft councilors, one of whom was the Craft floor leader, who moved toward Dekkard. "Welcome to the Council, Steffan. It's good to have you here, although I'm a bit puzzled as to how Axel managed it."

"He didn't, sir. Apparently, several influential guild members I met earlier this year were behind it. Premier Obreduur was correct in saying that he was as stunned as I was."

"You're going to have to work to keep that seat, you know. Really work."

"That struck me immediately, sir."

"Guilhohn," interjected Obreduur, "I've been informed that the Imperador is waiting, and I'm going to have to borrow Steffan for one of his last security duties."

"You really didn't know?"

Obreduur shook his head. "I really didn't. I'd thought they'd select some longer-standing party leaders. Steffan's recommendation came right out of the green."

Haarsfel offered an amused smile. "Enjoy yourself with the Imperador."

As Dekkard reentered the Premier's floor office, following Obreduur, one of the clerks appeared and handed Dekkard a bronze oblong. "There's your passcard, Councilor, and here's your lapel pin."

Dekkard took both, feeling slightly overwhelmed.

Avraal extracted the pin from his hand and immediately put it in place on his gray jacket, then murmured, "We're still security, for now. Something could still happen."

Her words weren't quite cold water, but they did ground him, and he moved beside her as they followed Obreduur out of the floor office and toward the east doors of the Council Hall.

As had been the case before, a black Gresynt limousine with the Council insignia on the front hood was waiting at the east entrance. A Council Guard stood beside the steamer and opened the middle and rear doors as the three approached. The guard seated himself in front beside the driver, once Dekkard, Avraal, and Obreduur were in place.

In a way, Dekkard was glad that Haarsfel had been with them the first time they had gone to the Palace. *Otherwise, it would be even more overwhelming.*

From Council Avenue, the driver turned north onto Imperial Boulevard, then circled around the Square of Heroes. Unlike the last time, there were people in the square, mostly close to the oval of white marble pillars surrounding the statue of Laureous the Great. The driver turned in to the entrance drive to the Palace,

stopping just before the shimmering golden gates—
where stood four Palace Guards in their red-and-gold
uniforms.

"The Premier-select to see the Imperador," announced
the driver.

"He's expected. Use the east portico entrance."

"Thank you." The driver eased the limousine through
the open gates and up the long white stone drive to a
pale golden marble edifice that dominated the low rise
overlooking the city to the south. Dekkard still mar-
veled at the gardens with their elaborate topiary hedges,
hedges edged with gold and rose fall flowers, beyond
which was the meticulously groomed lawn with white
stone paths.

When the limousine came to a halt under the east
portico a Palace Guard stepped forward and opened the
limousine doors. After the three exited the steamer, an
older naval lieutenant, possibly one who had come up
through the ranks, stepped forward.

"Premier, the Imperador is expecting you. If you'd
come with me."

Dekkard found it interesting that the officer simply
referred to Obreduur as Premier.

Avraal and Dekkard trailed Obreduur through the
polished bronze doors and into the entry hall with its
white marble floor edged with gold-lined green marble.
As he and Avraal followed the lieutenant and Obreduur
along the hall, Dekkard noticed immediately that there
were quite a few more servitors watching them than had
been the case the last time.

*Because a Craft premier is so unusual? Or for some
other reason?*

With that thought, Dekkard redoubled his concentration, looking for any sign of the out-of-the-ordinary.

The lieutenant turned right along another broad corridor, then stopped short of a door with a single, if large
and muscular, Palace Guard beside it. "The Premier-
select to see His Excellency."

"One moment, please." The guard stepped inside the

door and shut it, only to reappear almost instantly. "Premier, you may enter."

Dekkard and Avraal waited for little more than a sixth before Obreduur stepped out, with an expression that was somber, but possibly contained a hint of amusement. "The Imperador accepted my right to form a government."

"Congratulations, Premier," said the lieutenant, with more than token warmth in his voice.

"Thank you, Lieutenant. I appreciate it," replied Obreduur.

No one spoke until they reached the east entrance, where the limousine, and its guard and driver, waited in the shade of the portico. Then the lieutenant said, "The best of fortune to you, Premier." Then he looked closely at Dekkard. "That's a councilor's pin."

"He was just sworn in," said Avraal, "but he has to finish his duties for the Premier."

"That's very encouraging, Councilor," said the lieutenant quietly. "My best to you."

"Thank you."

As they walked toward the Council limousine, Avraal looked to Dekkard and said, "Emrelda will never believe it."

"What won't she believe?"

"Any of it."

"She will," Dekkard said with a smile, "when you tell her she has to help plan a wedding."

And when she sees us together.